John Harman's absorbing thriller about a gigantic and ingenious fraud is peopled with men and women whose love of money drives them on to outrageous crimes. From the discreet Swiss bankers to the ruthless Mafia bosses, from the bloody guerrillas to the high-ranking men of the English professional classes, greed is the theme and blood is the price.

Money For Nothing

John Harman

HEADLINE

First published in 1988
by HEADLINE BOOK PUBLISHING PLC

First published in paperback in 1989
by HEADLINE BOOK PUBLISHING PLC

ISBN 0-7472-3123 0

Printed and bound in Great Britain by
Collins, Glasgow

HEADLINE BOOK PUBLISHING PLC
Headline House
79 Great Titchfield Street
London W1P 7FN

FOR ABIGAIL
and for my children
JASON, SARAH and BEN

Book I

Chapter One

The man's face was as grey as the crumpled suit he wore. He sat perfectly still on the red leather bench, his eyes fixed unwaveringly on the robed figure of the judge. His hands gripped the guard rail to his front, its shiny brass dull and smeared from the sweat of his palms.

From where he was seated on the front bench, Edward Addingham watched the man as half his mind recorded the slow, ponderous tones of the judge's summing up. Mentally he was registering each of Lord Justice Ireland's legal points; the same points he himself had made in his summary for the prosecution. His Lordship was merely giving the nails that Addingham had hammered into the man's coffin the final tap of legal approval.

It had been a long trial, almost three weeks, and at first it had been a contest of wills between barrister and defendant. In the beginning Alan Swindon had stood up well to Addingham's attacks; in the early days he had been contemptuous of the tall gaunt figure with the bird-like features and flapping black gown. But Addingham had mastered his case, had known it in detail. He knew exactly what Swindon had done and how he had done it. So, within the vast piles of papers on the desk before him, he had known which documents were vital, which figures to doubt, which contracts to question. And as he had cross-examined the witnesses, subtly leading them to agree to facts he already knew were true, he had sensed Swindon's rising anxiety. When, finally, he had come to cross-examine

3

Swindon, he had seen the fear in his eyes. Swindon had
believed that no one could understand his business as well
as he, yet Addingham did. Impossibly, he had come to
know the how, the where and the what; the why had never
interested him. The black-gowned barrister with his
scrawny neck and hooked nose had become a vulture in
whose eyes Swindon had seen the cold, flat stare of the professional predator. Slowly he had crumbled. He had
admitted nothing but he had begun to bluster and contra-
dict himself and then, finally, he had lied. And Edward
Addingham QC had smiled calmly to himself as he sifted
the piles of documents and knew he had won.

Swindon was a big man, tall and heavy. In the first few
days he had dressed immaculately. Now he seemed smaller
and thinner; he had worn the same suit for a week.

Addingham crossed his extended legs; the black Oxfords
gleamed dully, the sharp crease of the pinstripes puckering
where his ankles crossed. He leaned back, his hands deep in
his pockets, his wig tipped over his forehead. The polished
red leather of the bench creaked as he shifted position. The
Junior Council for the defence looked across and smiled
faintly. Addingham inclined his head. It was difficult not to
fidget, the bench was uncomfortable and although it was
early April, within the Royal Courts of Justice the air was
hot and dry. Beyond the Junior, Addingham could see the
scowling profile of the QC for the defence.

Addingham had first been briefed on the case in the
autumn of 1960, more than two and a half years previously.
The instructing solicitors had arranged a conference with
their client, Sir Nicholas Jeffries, the chairman of one of
the city's largest life assurance companies. Jeffries had
arrived at Addingham's chambers in the Inner Temple late
one November afternoon. The two men already had a
nodding acquaintance; they moved in the same circles, were
members of the same clubs. Sir Nicholas was accompanied
by Oliver Blackmore, a senior partner in the firm of

solicitors. Addingham's clerk had shown them into the large, book-lined room. After Blackmore had made the formal introduction and they had seated themselves, Addingham had begun.

'I've read the papers,' he said. 'You have an excellent case. However, I think you are wrong to think of bringing a criminal prosecution.'

Sir Nicholas's eyes narrowed. 'That man is guilty of fraud.' His tone was hard and sharp.

'Maybe so, but I must tell you that in a criminal case the onus of proof is considerable. We would have to prove fraud beyond all reasonable doubt.'

'There is no doubt.' Sir Nicholas's usually florid face turned deep red and his eyes glittered with malevolence. It was well known that when Sir Nicholas Jeffries became angry, senior directors in City firms quailed and thought of their pensions. Addingham, though, remained unperturbed.

'Sir Nicholas, I appreciate your feelings,' he said smoothly. 'Perhaps it would be better if you could give me some more information.'

Sir Nicholas struggled to regain his composure and when, after a few seconds, he finally spoke, his voice was as measured as if he were addressing his board of directors.

'As you know, the financial institutions in the City are broadening their investment policies. For years we have put our money into safe investments, gilt-edged securities, blue-chip companies and so on. Now, we are investing considerable sums in new areas. We've invested quite heavily in some of these new property companies. Frankly, the returns they show are remarkable and of course most of the young men running them are the right sort of people. They know the City and how we do things.' Sir Nicholas paused for a few moments. 'But we are also anxious to be seen helping new industries,' he continued, 'technological expansion and so on. Hence we were introduced to

Swindon's company by a merchant bank.' He went on to explain how his company had invested substantially in Swindon's company.

'It's a booming business,' he continued, 'in aircraft electronics. Swindon built it up from nothing. The man comes from nowhere, left the RAF at the end of the war as a flight sergeant or something, but he does understand the business. We were very pleased with the investment, the return on capital was good, growth prospects excellent. We had a thirty per cent shareholding in the company and I saw no reason why we should not increase it. Swindon took some persuasion, but eventually we became majority shareholders with ninety per cent of the company. Naturally, we kept Swindon on as managing director with a very well-paid contract. The business continued to do well and so we agreed that it should buy two other companies.' He stopped.

'Please continue.' Addingham was encouraging.

'Then things changed, the company began to make serious losses. We had a man on their board, of course, but we are a financial institution – we understand money, we don't understand business. It transpired subsequently that we had paid well over the odds for the two companies. Both of them had old assets which needed to be replaced and neither had any real potential to expand. What's more, Swindon, hiding behind nominees, was the majority shareholder in both of them. We had been deliberately misled. Of course, when we found this out, we raised it at an extraordinary general meeting. The man had the effrontery to offer to buy back our share in his company for next to nothing. He actually laughed.'

The memory of Swindon's laughter rankled Sir Nicholas's corporate soul. His voice was raised as he continued. 'The man is a crook, he ought to be in prison. One way or another he has taken over a million pounds of our money. All we have to show for it is a company on the verge of bankruptcy. I suppose one should expect this kind of thing if one employs barrow boys – but we ought to protect ourselves from his type. We do have a code of morality in the City, you know; that man doesn't know the meaning of the word. Frankly, Mr Addingham, I cannot understand your reluctance to prosecute.'

Addingham nodded briefly. 'Sir Nicholas, not only do I understand your feelings, but I also endorse your sentiments. However, the fact remains that, although what Swindon has done is probably fraudulent, it would be difficult to prove. I, as you know, Sir Nicholas, am a specialist in company law. I am not a criminal lawyer. Criminal work is petty, the people with whom one is forced to associate, on both sides of the law, are sordid and incredibly stupid. I do not relish the prospect of building an intelligent and conclusive case merely to cast it before twelve jurors who are little better than imbeciles. Frankly, Sir Nicholas, that is what could happen if we pursue a criminal prosecution. We will have a jury composed of working-class idiots and women. They would not even begin to understand my case and would probably find Swindon not guilty. That would be disastrous. It would turn the City, its institutions and, speaking perfectly bluntly, Sir Nicholas, you most of all, into a laughing stock.'

Sir Nicholas remained quiet for a few seconds. The thought of the City's ridicule made his blood run cold. His voice, when he finally spoke, was subdued. 'I see what you mean. What then is the alternative?'

The question pleased Addingham. The case was to be fought his way. Apart from the considerations he had already mentioned to Jeffries, there was also the matter of his fee. Fighting the case through the civil rather than the criminal courts would be far more lucrative for Edward Addingham. He sat back in his chair and explained.

'There is in the law the phenomenon known as civil death. It is rarely invoked nowadays, but it is, as you might gather, the destruction of an individual through the civil law. Excommunication in medieval times is an example of civil death. It is the loss of legal personality and of all possessions. What I propose is the equivalent for our friend Swindon. If we conduct this case correctly we can ensure that the only job he will ever have again is as a rat catcher. We can, by way of both damages and costs, bankrupt him absolutely.'

Addingham watched the effect of his words on his visitor. Sir Nicholas's hands began to shake and his face took on a patina of sweat. Addingham was torn between faint amusement and vague disgust at the old man's lust. 'Of course,' he continued, 'there is the possibility of a subsequent criminal prosecution. As you know, much of company law carries criminal penalties and I think it highly likely that after pronouncing judgement, the judge may recommend criminal proceedings. We may, ultimately, render Swindon unemployable, bankrupt and in custody. We could also,' he continued, 'expect to recover your money.'

Sir Nicholas rose to his feet. 'That is of lesser importance. It is essential that we protect ourselves from spivs. I don't care how long it takes or what it costs, so long as we win.'

And won they had. Swindon's manipulations and deceptions had been more complicated than they had first thought, but Addingham had doggedly followed his tortuous trail and finally cornered him. The law of big business was his territory and he knew it better than anybody. Now he sat languorously on the front bench of a courtroom in the High Courts of Justice watching the destruction of his quarry. He had no personal feeling about the man.

Sir Nicholas Jeffries' hatred, however, had not sustained him. It may have perversely contributed to his destruction, for he had died, painfully but swiftly, of cancer a year previously. His successor had decided that the case should be continued.

There was a movement behind Addingham, the creaking of a bench, and Oliver Blackmore's dark and heavy profile slid into view, close to the barrister's right shoulder.

'Gone well, then?' He kept his face to the front, his eyes, like Swindon's, on Lord Justice Ireland. It was a statement that required no response. Blackmore had worked closely with Addingham on the case over the past two years and it was as much due to him that they were on the winning side.

'My God, it's hot in here,' Blackmore said in a low tone. 'How the hell does he stand it?' He nodded towards the old man in his red robes seated at the raised bench.

'High temperatures are necessary to keep our judges alive,' whispered Addingham. 'Ten degrees cooler in here would destroy half the judiciary.'

They sat listening to the judge, Blackmore leaning forward on the bench behind Addingham. He was a big man, over six feet and heavy, but his size was not due to excesses of the flesh; his was the bulk of power and the careful good living of money. He was just over forty and full of vigour, with long dark hair, blue eyes and a ruddy complexion, all testimony to his Scottish ancestry. He had been elected a Member of Parliament in his late thirties and was considered to have a spectacular political future. His work rate was tremendous; he was tireless both in his parliamentary duties and in his legal practice. Addingham, who considered himself to be brilliant, acknowledged that Blackmore had an intellect almost as great as his own.

'Damages?' queried Blackmore in a hoarse whisper.

'I estimate they'll be over a million pounds,' replied Addingham. They both stared at the ruined man sitting across the courtroom. In addition to damages, Swindon would have to find at least a hundred thousand pounds for the costs of the case. Early in the proceedings Blackmore had engaged the services of an investigator who had meticulously checked and itemised all Swindon's assets. The investigator had cost a great deal of money; the information he wanted was held by people who, because they were bound by the terms of their employment not to reveal such information, required sizeable sums of money to divulge their secrets. The investigator's work had ensured that Swindon could neither transfer his assets abroad nor give them to his wife; he was, in Blackmore's words, to be caught 'with the goods still on him'. In paying for the costs of the case, Swindon would also be paying for the privilege of having himself investigated.

They listened intently as the judge continued his summing up. 'There are in this case,' he pronounced, 'certain aspects which appear to be a matter of criminal rather than civil law, not least of which is perjury by the defendant. Lying under oath is a serious matter and cannot be tolerated. Businessmen must realise that any financial manipulations undertaken by their companies which breach the law are just as criminal as any other form of theft. It is the duty of the courts to stamp down hard on this sort of thing.' He looked directly at Addingham and Blackmore, both of whom nodded sagely at his words.

'I am therefore instructing that papers relating to this case should be prepared and sent to the Director of Public Prosecutions, who may decide that criminal proceedings should be instituted.' He paused and settled himself more firmly on his chair before continuing. 'In view of the seriousness of this case, and the losses which an honourable institution has suffered, I award them damages of one million, four hundred and fifty thousand pounds. Costs of the case to be borne by the defendant.'

Sir Nicholas Jeffries' posthumous victory was complete. Swindon was destroyed. There was a subdued movement within the dark panelled courtroom as reporters on the press bench rose and made for the doors, bowing to the judge as they half ran to find a phone. The case had attracted considerable attention in the financial press; the size of the damages would make headlines.

Everyone in the courtroom rose and nodded in obeisance as the judge shuffled off the raised platform. Blackmore moved down to stand next to Edward Addingham. 'Pompous old bastard.' His eyes followed the little figure as it disappeared through an oak door behind the bench.

'It's rather encouraging to be commended for a well-presented case,' Addingham responded dryly.

'Unnecessary,' Blackmore replied flatly. 'We knew we would win.'

Addingham felt piqued. 'They may appeal.'

Blackmore looked past his colleague to where Swindon stood in a huddled group with his solicitor and barristers. Addingham turned and followed his gaze. The defeated man lacked any animation, his eyes were glazed and lifeless, his mouth hung open. He looked like a sick dog, dying on its feet.

'I think not,' said Blackmore, staring at the group. 'There's no fight left there and, what's more, no money!' He turned abruptly to Addingham. 'I must go.'

'I have arranged for our friend to meet us in my chambers at eight o'clock,' said Addingham. 'He will come to your offices first.'

'Good,' replied Blackmore. 'Until then.' He turned and walked swiftly towards the double doors at the back of the courtroom. He moved easily for a large man, threading his way quickly through the groups of bewigged barristers and sober-suited solicitors. Addingham noticed that he didn't even glance in the direction of Swindon and his group of legal advisers.

The defence barrister walked across the courtroom to congratulate him as Addingham began to gather up his papers. Around him, knots of men talked, the noise of their amiable chatter floating upwards in the warm atmosphere. He was as at home in the heat and the smell of the court, the wood-lined walls, the leather benches and dusty papers, as a weasel in a warren full of rabbits.

As he bundled the last of his papers together and handed them to his clerk he thought of the coming meeting in his chambers. If it had been a good day, then it promised to be an even better evening, for in the company of Oliver Blackmore he intended to hold the first in a series of highly confidential meetings with some of his closest business associates. At these meetings Addingham, Blackmore and the others would conspire to create a highly complicated yet extremely profitable commercial venture, which, within a short period of time, with a minimum outlay of capital and with absolutely no risk, would realise a return of millions.

Edward Addingham, with a little help from his friends, was about to commit fraud on a multi-million-pound scale.

The Royal Courts of Justice stand at the eastern end of the Strand, within a few yards of Temple Bar, Fleet Street and the City of London. Built in the last quarter of the nineteenth century, their spired turrets, perpendicular columns and Gothic arches appear like some great medieval castle abandoned in the traffic. They are an accurate reflection of the English legal system, for while from the outside they have all the impressive architectural solemnity of high Victorian Gothic, inside they are a maze of stairways, corridors and chambers. Like the law, the only people who know their way around the place are the lawyers.

Addingham disrobed in a small chamber next to the courtroom and climbed a narrow stairway. He was carrying a dark blue cloth bag, which contained his gown and wig. He strode down the great central hall of the courts, his heels clicking on the mosaic floor as he passed beneath the soaring, rib-vaulted roof and the massive paintings of past judges, incarcerated in gilt frames hanging high on the stone walls. He reached the great Gothic arch, the main entrance to the law courts, and stood beneath it, grateful to be breathing at least partly fresh air. It was late afternoon; the light outside was soft and grey and the slight breeze carried a faint vibration of coming spring. The coldest winter in fifteen years had only just, at the beginning of April 1963, released its bitter grip.

The traffic in the Strand was building up as commuters sought to avoid the rush hour. Addingham descended the broad, shallow steps and crossed the road to Twinings. The man behind the counter noticed that the well-known Queen's Counsel, normally aloof and distant, seemed excited. There were two red spots on his usually sallow cheeks; his eyes were bright and he was almost friendly.

With the blended teas nestling next to the horsehair wig in his bag, Addingham walked eastwards along the Strand, turned into Inner Temple Lane and headed towards his chambers in Crown Office Row.

The premises of Warminger, Poister, and Blackmore were situated on the northern side of Lincoln's Inn Fields, within easy walking distance of the law courts and the four Inns of Court. Oliver Blackmore had a large office on the third floor, at the front of the building, allowing him a view over the green square of the Fields to the Royal College of Surgeons on its southern edge.

Night had fallen, the lights from the other side of the Fields shone through the branches of the trees in the darkened square. Blackmore's visitor arrived just after seven thirty and was shown up to his office.

'Oliver, my dear chap. How nice to see you again. Not too late, am I?'

Ashley Brighton was, in Blackmore's opinion, unusual for a senior accountant. What distinguished him was not the fact that he was a crook; Blackmore supposed a considerable number of accountants were, to a greater or lesser extent. It was Brighton's extrovert personality which set him apart from the rest of his profession, and which Blackmore liked. Generally he found accountants to be dull and grey men, as boring as goldfish. 'Let me get you a drink,' he said.

Brighton moved to the great sash window behind Oliver's desk and looked out over the darkened square. He was in his late forties, short and plump, and what little hair he had was white. He was dressed in a flamboyant and expensive style.

In his early days as a chartered accountant, Ashley Brighton had taken over a small firm of accountants in the provinces, added his own name to those of the other partners and expanded the practice, opening offices in major cities. In the early fifties he had been approached by an old and illustrious accountancy firm in the City which needed an infusion of new blood in order to survive. To the outside world it had appeared to be Brighton's firm which was taken over; in reality it was Ashley Brighton who had been the boa constrictor and Glynnis and James the tethered lamb. Brighton had swallowed them whole, but had kept their name. He had ruthlessly expanded the amalgamated practice, ensuring that as the corporations grew in size and power, his firm did likewise. He had become the senior partner in one of the country's largest accountancy practices.

Blackmore handed him his drink. 'Cheers,' he said. 'Addingham expects us about eight.'

'Good.' The portly accountant turned from the window. 'I hear you've won the Swindon case.'

'News travels fast.'

'All over the City, old man.'

They finished their drinks and Blackmore put on his overcoat. They left the offices and headed towards Addingham's chambers, their footsteps echoing on the pavements of the poorly lit Inner Temple. They reached the staircase leading to the chambers and climbed the stairs to the first floor. A heavy wooden door opened into a hallway lined on both sides from floor to ceiling with thick law books. An old woman was on her knees washing the dark brown linoleum. She looked up as they entered.

'Mind my floor!' she screeched.

Blackmore ignored her, walking across the wet surface to

a door set in the wall of books. He knocked and opened the door. Brighton grimaced an apology to the cleaner and followed Blackmore across the newly washed floor. Muttering to herself, the old woman went back to her task.

Addingham was sitting at a massive oak table which served as his desk. The table top was inlaid with dull green leather and edged with fading gilt. It was piled high with papers and legal briefs bound by narrow pink ribbon. He rose and came round the table to shake Brighton's hand.

'Please,' he said, 'let me take your coat. Sit down. Would you like a drink? Oliver, I know, likes whisky in the evening, or I have an excellent sherry if you prefer.'

Brighton elected for a whisky, which he noticed was the same brand of fine malt that Blackmore had offered him. They seated themselves, Blackmore and Brighton on a Chesterfield, Addingham in an armchair opposite. It was a large square room with leaded windows and dark green velvet curtains which had been left undrawn. The walls were covered, like the hallway, with shelves of law books, and an expensive carpet covered the floorboards in front of Addingham's desk. Two table lamps at each end of the Chesterfield and a large reading lamp on the desk radiated a warm yellow light. They talked for a few minutes about the City's reaction to the events of that afternoon.

'Shall we get down to business?' asked Blackmore.

Brighton glanced sharply at the door; Addingham intercepted his glance. 'Relax, my dear Ashley,' he said, 'the crone is as deaf as a post.'

The accountant pulled some papers from his briefcase and handed copies to the others. 'Papers one to four,' he said in a brisk professional tone, 'are the audited figures of Thornbury Engineering Limited. They show a company experiencing some difficulties in maintaining its trading position, with a considerable reduction in its annual profits but still, in the end, having an underlying strength and on the whole remaining a reasonably healthy business. Papers five to eight show the true position, which is that within a few months the company will be insolvent.'

The room was quiet as the three men studied the figures before them.

'Why do the officially audited figures not show the company's true position?' asked Addingham.

'Because my firm are the auditors and I choose that they shouldn't,' Brighton replied.

'I appreciate that,' Addingham's voice was faintly acid. 'But how are you able to hide the true picture?'

'I take it you are not really interested in the technicalities,' replied Brighton, 'so I will explain in general terms.' He paused. 'By the way, is there any more of this excellent whisky?'

Addingham rose to replenish the glasses. Blackmore took a half-corona from a cigar case and lit it.

'I knew Joseph Thornbury as a boy,' continued Brighton. 'We were at Rugby together. His grandfather started the business, and Thornbury Engineering was, before the first war, one of the largest manufacturers of boilers and heating appliances in the country. I doubt if there is anyone of our age who doesn't at least know the name.'

Addingham crossed the room and handed Brighton his drink.

'But like so many others, the company didn't diversify. It continued making coal-burning boilers even after the last war and when oil became cheaper and plentiful it suffered. Industry wanted oil-burners but Joseph Thornbury thought oil would run out or become expensive so he didn't change. About five years ago, he saw the light and started switching production to oil-burning boilers. I think they might have survived; things were beginning to look up – when Joseph had a stroke. Now he's a vegetable in a nursing home, paralysed, can't talk, can't do anything.'

He stopped and took a large sip of whisky; the others studied the bottoms of their glasses.

'His son, Richard, took over the business. Useless. Not interested, sees himself as some sort of playboy. The whole business has been held together by Thornbury's financial director – who is on his last legs – and by me.'

'What's the son like?' queried Addingham.

'Weak, greedy, and immoral, but not stupid. Would do anything to get his hands on more money. He's not interested in maintaining the company or in regenerating it. He has no compunction about seeing hundreds of men put out of work so long as he can indulge himself.'

'The law does not require him to be concerned with his workers, only with his shareholders,' remarked Blackmore. 'Is he a major shareholder?'

'Yes, he has about thirty-five per cent, and his mother and sister have sufficient to ensure that between them the family has control. The rest of the shares are owned by the financial institutions and by Smithson-Perez who are their bankers.'

'Why don't they realise how sick the company is?' asked Addingham.

Brighton reflected before he replied. 'Institutional shareholders are really only interested in the value of their shares. Thornbury's shares haven't grown in value, but neither have they slumped, so although the shareholders are disappointed, they're not panicking. Thornbury Engineering is nationally known, on paper it's worth millions. People do not expect nationally known companies to collapse. However, the main reason is that accounting is often a matter of postponing things. In Thornbury's case, everything it appears to own is mortgaged, all its factories, machines, vehicles, even the family home. All the assets are old and need replacing urgently but they cannot be replaced because all the money the company does manage to make goes in paying the interest on their debts. It's a downward spiral.'

'How long do we have?' asked Blackmore in a quiet voice.

'Nine months at the outside. Next January we will start to audit the figures for this year and it will not be possible to disguise the company's situation any longer.'

'Nine months may not be sufficient,' said Addingham sharply. 'Can't you cover up the situation for longer?'

'Short of obvious and detectable malpractice, no.'

Blackmore raised his eyebrows, Brighton caught his glance. 'It's being caught that worries me, Oliver.' He looked across at Addingham. 'I've got away with it because Millburn, their old finance director, is past it. He prepared their accounts according to instructions I passed verbally through Richard Thornbury. Those accounts have hidden how much is owed and to whom; so lenders do not know of the existence of other lenders. My firm merely audits the books, we are not required to seek out misleading accounting. When the inevitable enquiry into Thornbury's affairs occurs, their accountants will be severely censored, whereas my firm will merely receive a mild rebuke.'

Addingham was not to be put off. 'Surely you can extend it for a few more months?'

The accountant sighed wearily. 'Edward, I cannot. Millburn retires at the end of this month. A new man will soon begin to see the accounts are in a mess and that the company is in trouble. We can keep the new man busy on other things for a while, but not for long.'

Blackmore leaned forward and spoke directly to Addingham. 'We can't ask Ashley to compromise himself. There's no point to our plans if we cannot maintain our professional integrity after this is all over.' He turned to Brighton. 'Can the company survive long enough for our purposes?'

'I can ensure that it does,' he replied.

'Very well then,' Addingham capitulated. 'We have nine months.'

18

There was silence for a few seconds. Wisps of smoke from Blackmore's cigar hung in the yellow glow of the lamps like clouds of cirrus. The room was warm, the atmosphere charged. They stared at each other, a common pulse beating at their temples. It was the moment of final commitment. From here, there would be no going back. It was Blackmore who finally squeezed the trigger and sent the enterprise on the long spiral down the barrel. He stood up quickly and the others started in surprise.

'How soon can you arrange a meeting with Richard Thornbury?' he asked.

They parted in Fleet Street, Brighton to travel north, Addingham and Blackmore to share a taxi to Westminster. They sat silently, side by side, staring at the bright lights of the shops and theatres. After a while Blackmore turned to his companion. 'The man who replaces Thornbury's accountant.'

'What about him?'

'It's important we choose the right man.' There was something in the way Blackmore spoke, his tongue the tip of submerged malice. He was staring at the back of the driver's head as the cab accelerated along Whitehall. 'I think the plan is perfect, Edward. Nevertheless, we are talking about a great deal of money and even if no one personally suffers, certain people will feel a sense of loss.'

Addingham was feeling tired. 'I can't see what you're driving at.'

'When this business is finished, a lot of people will be baying for blood. A large amount of money will have disappeared, so somebody will be expected to suffer. We need a sacrifice, someone to appease the furies, otherwise the authorities may start to pursue enquiries. That might be a nuisance.' He looked directly at Addingham. 'Someone to throw to the wolves.'

'Put them off the scent?'

'More than that, Edward. Give them a taste of blood. Satisfy their indignation. That sort of thing.'

'It's a pity their old accountant is retiring. He would have been perfect,' said Addingham.

'A great pity. What we must do now is find the right replacement. A high calibre scapegoat.'

'Can we find one in time?'

'I would have thought so. It never ceases to amaze me how many fools and sheep we have in the professions.'

Addingham grunted.

'By the way,' Blackmore went on, 'we are having some people in for drinks, a few people in the Party. Why don't you join us? Joanna would be pleased to see you.'

'Thank you, no.' Addingham let his head drop back onto his seat. 'I would be poor company. Give Joanna my regards.' Addingham felt drained and empty. The adrenaline which had been pumping through his system all day had curdled and turned sour. He was peevish. He could see no reason why he should add his lustre as a victorious Queen's Counsel to a gathering of politicians, merely to enhance Blackmore's career. Blackmore was not above using him but he was damned if he would allow the solicitor to bathe in his reflected glory.

His mind continued in the same fretful fashion as the cab pulled up outside Blackmore's London house in Lord North Street.

'Are you sure you won't come in?'

'No, I'm very tired.' He managed a wan smile. 'Thank you all the same.'

Blackmore got out of the taxi. All the house lights were on and from within came a gentle hubbub. He turned to Addingham. 'I shall be in touch.' The taxi drove off; before it had turned the corner of the short street, Addingham was regretting his decision not to join the party. His large apartment in Knightsbridge would be cold and empty, it was too late for dinner at his club and his housekeeper would not have left him anything to eat.

'Where now, sir?' asked the driver.

'Basil Street,' Addingham replied wearily and slumped back into his seat.

At about the same time that Addingham was arriving at his empty apartment and Blackmore was having his second drink, Alan Swindon was checking into an expensive hotel near Hyde Park Corner. He was already drunk, but inside his case was an unopened bottle of whisky. He lay on top of the big bed in the luxurious room, drinking steadily. Finally, he got up and telephoned his home. He spoke gently and as steadily as he could to his wife and daughters. He did not say much about the outcome of the trial but instead talked about the future, of holidays and of being together. One of his daughters cried, she wanted him to come home. He promised to see them all early the next day and rang off. He lay back on the bed, took another drink and then swallowed the entire contents of a bottle of sleeping pills.

The venomous spectre of Sir Nicholas Jeffries filled the room and pervaded his poisoned brain. It watched as Swindon obligingly carried Addingham's promise of civil death to its literal conclusion. Swindon was a man who had lusted after a system that had despised him, yet perversely he was making his exit in a manner the system would approve. It was not because he was bankrupt that he was orphaning his children, or because he had been found to be dishonest. It was because he had failed and because of the hatred of men whose approval he had sought. Men who had destroyed his hope, who had turned his bright future into a worthless past. Men who had left him nothing to live for.

It was dark and raining heavily as Addingham hurried into Simpson's in the Strand. He stood in the doorway and shook the rain from his umbrella before walking into the restaurant's reception and depositing his wet coat and umbrella. Ashley Brighton was waiting in the upstairs bar, seated in a deep armchair near the windows, watching the rain bouncing off the car roofs.

'What would you like to drink?' he enquired.

'Sherry, dry, thank you.'

Addingham stretched his long body in an armchair while Brighton ordered the drinks. 'Where is Thornbury?'

'I'm afraid he's never punctual,' replied Brighton, smiling at the irritated Addingham.

It was less than a week since their meeting in Crown Office Row. Brighton had learned that Richard Thornbury was in France and after some difficulty had contacted him. Thornbury had agreed to have dinner with Brighton and Addingham on his first evening back in London. Brighton had met him earlier in the day and had given him a fair notion of the subject to be discussed. A waiter brought Addingham's drink. He was sipping it slowly when Brighton rose from his seat to greet a young man who had entered the bar.

'Richard, my dear fellow. How good of you to come. What can I get you?' Ashley Brighton was at his most effusive.

Addingham shook the newcomer's hand as Brighton made the introductions. Richard Thornbury was in his twenties, a tall, good-looking young man with a finely-boned face and deep brown eyes. His hair, which was long and dark, hung over his right eye; throughout the evening he kept flicking it back either with his hand or with a sudden jerk of his head. It was an oddly feminine gesture and about the only feature of Thornbury's personality that Addingham found attractive.

Brighton ordered more drinks. 'Tell me, what have you been doing in France?'

Thornbury launched into a long story about negotiations to buy a large and expensive yacht. It was an amusing story and soon Brighton was chuckling heartily. Addingham smiled at appropriate moments and took stock of Thornbury. Undeniably, the young man had looks, style, and was an accomplished raconteur; Addingham could see why he needed money. Without it he would be like a sailor without the sea.

After another round of drinks, they went downstairs to eat. The restaurant was less than half full and they chose a secluded booth and ordered. The conversation was bland and genial. Thornbury dominated, Brighton cheerily kept things going while Addingham said very little. Thornbury noticed that the barrister picked at his food and hardly touched the Mouton Rothschild '49 which both he and Brighton were drinking steadily. He also noticed that Addingham had a habit of smacking his lips together, making a sound like a small child eating ice cream.

After dessert the conversation turned to business and the shaky condition of Thornbury Engineering.

'I have been explaining to Edward and the rest of our friends the current state of Thornbury Engineering,' Brighton told him.

'Really? What is the current state, by the way?'

'Come now, Richard, you know how bad things are. We are able to hide the real facts only by using unrealistic accounting practices.'

Thornbury laughed. 'When you're in trouble, the only realistic accounting practice is to count the number of dorsal fins you can see in the water. Sharks and accountants both have the ability to smell blood.'

Addingham leaned across the table. 'If your creditors smell trouble, they will put the bite on you quicker than you can blink.'

Thornbury was taken aback at his aggression.

'You have three choices, Richard,' said Brighton smoothly. 'Work extremely hard and pull the company out of trouble, go down with it, or use the company to make yourself a great deal of money.'

'How much money?'

'Over two million pounds,' said Addingham.

Thornbury sat perfectly still, staring at the barrister. 'That's just my share?'

'Absolutely,' said Brighton.

The young man took a sip of wine; a few drops spilled, blood red, onto the white linen of the table cloth. He put his glass down carefully. 'If that's my share,' he said, 'then the total must be one hell of a lot more. Enough to make the proceeds of a bank robbery look like a raid on a piggy bank. That means it's bent. It has to be criminal.'

Brighton coughed. 'Come now, Richard,' he said. 'There is no need –'

Addingham interrupted him, staring fixedly at the young man. 'Does that bother you?'

Thornbury stared back, then flicked the hair out of his right eye. 'In itself, not at all. But I don't relish being caught, which is, I understand, an occupational hazard of criminals.'

Addingham continued to stare. Finally he spoke. 'Mr Thornbury, crime is an ugly word. Like cancer. And like cancer it is uglier when it is known to exist. If it remains undetected then it can be said not to exist. The perfect crime is a contradiction in terms; if a crime is known then it cannot be perfect. There will always be some policeman snooping around trying to solve it. What we are about to embark upon is not a crime, it is a highly entrepreneurial business venture.'

Thornbury let out a loud, sharp laugh. Some nearby diners looked across, Brighton jumped and Addingham reddened in anger. Brighton could see how much the barrister despised this pretty young man with the insolent tongue. But the years of self-control, the training never to lose sight of his objective, held him together, forcing him to stay cool and controlled. Addingham breathed deeply and said, 'There are, involved in this enterprise, five of the most professional businessmen in the country. The project is involved and extremely complicated. What we are about to do has never been done before, at least not to anyone's knowledge. A lot of careful thought has gone into it, it will take a long time to execute and it will be perfect. No one is going to detect it. We have the intelligence, the brains and the know-how. Those ignorant fools in the Fraud Squad, or anyone else for that matter, cannot outwit us. It's people like us that they turn to for free advice.'

Brighton grunted in agreement. Thornbury stared at both of them. Finally, he shrugged his shoulders. 'I don't have a great deal of choice, do I? Hard work is not my scene and as for going down with the company, well, if I wanted to do that kind of thing I would have joined the Royal Navy. I certainly don't intend to end up like that poor bastard who killed himself the other day, so I'll go along with you. What am I supposed to do?'

'For now,' said Addingham, 'nothing. We have a great deal of preparatory work to do. A company will soon be formed, in Panama, in which you will be a shareholder. Your shareholding will be through a Liechtenstein trust which will act as nominee for you and the rest of us. Your interest in the Panamanian company will therefore be anonymous. You will be expected to put up working capital of three thousand pounds.'

Thornbury nodded.

'This company will acquire the ownership of a large piece of land on an island in the Caribbean. We will also establish a bank in the Caribbean which will borrow –'

'You mean we shall own a bank?' interjected Thornbury.

'Don't be silly, Richard,' said Brighton. 'Anyone can form a bank out there for little more than you've got in your pocket right now.'

'The bank is essential to our plans,' Addingham continued. 'As Ashley says, it is not at all difficult to register a bank, nor does it require capital.'

'So where do I fit in?' asked Thornbury.

'Your company will eventually purchase the land for the sum of fifty million dollars.'

Thornbury flicked the hair out of his eyes. The room was filling up as the theatre crowd came in for supper. It was noisy and warm in the expensive restaurant and the claret was making his head muzzy. So was this strange and disturbing man who talked of fortunes and Caribbean land.

'That's more than fifteen million pounds. Thornbury Engineering couldn't raise fifteen hundred.' He looked at the other two. 'How in hell can a bank which on your own admission can get started for the cost of a stamp find that kind of money? And for land in the Caribbean? Thornbury Engineering needs land in the Caribbean like I need a dose of the clap. And yet, somehow, out of all this I am supposed to emerge with over two million pounds. How?'

Addingham stared at him. 'Do you really care?'

The young man flushed. 'No, frankly I don't give a shit. I can see you would prefer me not to ask all you grown-ups irritating questions. But supposing I end up with egg on my face. How do I know that I will get my share of this pot of gold? I ought to be told some of the details.'

'You will be told what you need to know and no more. The people involved with us in this enterprise are men of integrity, men who can be trusted absolutely. I can assure you that your interests will be protected and that you will receive your share in full. There can be no suggestion of double dealing if we are to succeed. But we must be discreet.'

Thornbury sat quietly, toying with his empty coffee cup. 'Very well,' he said finally, 'I have found, Mr Addingham, that discretion is the better part of cowardice and I am a confirmed coward. If you are concerned that I might shoot my mouth off, don't be. I have absolutely no interest in the details of your clever little caper except for my share of the goodies. And,' he added, 'the freedom to enjoy them. You need me, Mr Addingham, or more accurately you need my company, and I need you. You are the only person so far this week to have offered me two million pounds. So I guess I'll have to trust you and the others. Insofar as this exercise is concerned, I will do exactly as you require, including keeping my mouth shut.'

Brighton fidgeted and his cherubic face wore a look of concern as the two men stared at each other across the table.

Addingham broke the silence. 'I think we understand each other.'

Richard Thornbury put his napkin on the table and made ready to leave. 'Never this side of hell will we do that, Mr Addingham. But we have, as they say, reached an accommodation which will suffice. And now I must go. I have a date. With a married lady as a matter of fact.' He laughed and stood up. 'Discretion prevents me from saying more, you understand.' He held out his hand to Addingham. 'Thank you for supper. No doubt I shall be hearing from you.'

Addingham stood up. 'There is one more thing. Your accountant, when does he leave?'

Thornbury shrugged and looked enquiringly at Brighton. 'A couple of weeks.'

'His replacement. We must find the right man to replace him. It's very important,' said Addingham.

'I'm sure it is, but Ashley will find a good man. Nothing to do with me.'

'I don't want a good man.' Addingham was intense.

Thornbury raised his eyebrows. 'Well, there aren't many good men left, are there?'

Addingham ignored the remark. 'We want the right man. We will find him but you must appoint him. It's important.'

'Whatever you say. And now I really must go. Goodbye.'

Thornbury kept the look of distaste off his face as he shook the barrister's cold, limp hand. 'Goodbye, Ashley.' He turned and walked away.

Addingham sat down.

'What do you think? Will he do?' Brighton asked.

'Yes, he will do,' said Addingham, staring at the littered table. 'If he does as he's told and keeps quiet.'

'Yes, I think he will,' said Brighton. 'He is tougher than he appears.'

Addingham looked up. 'Never confuse a glib tongue with strength of character, Ashley. Our friend is weak and greedy but we are his only chance for the soft life. That gives us a hold over him. At least for now. Afterwards, it may be different.'

'He'll be all right,' Brighton retorted. 'He's not a bad fellow really.'

'That man,' said Addingham, 'is a perfect example of what comes of giving the wrong sort of people the right sort of education.'

Chapter Two

Henry Dundonald smoothly slid the Jaguar alongside the kerb and switched off the engine. It was a beautiful April morning, the tall Georgian houses in Lord North Street were washed in pale sunshine and the plane trees in Smith Square had a fuzzy halo of new green leaves. The church clock in the square at the end of the street showed a little before noon as Dundonald got out of the car.

Even at his most jaundiced, Edward Addingham could not have accused Henry Dundonald of being the wrong sort of person. He was, in fact, very much the right sort of person, with the right education, the right address and, particularly, the right ancestors. He was, on his mother's side, a scion of the great merchant banking fraternity of Smithson-Perez; his father's people had owned vast tracts of land in the north of England since the Reformation.

The young Dundonald had been sent to Eton, whence he had emerged to join his father's old and traditional regiment of foot. He had served in the army for ten years, then resigned his commission to go into his mother's family business. He had been with Smithson-Perez for more than eight years and never tired of telling new acquaintances that he had 'started at the bottom', which meant it had taken him three months to become a director. In fact, he had proved to be an astute merchant banker, hard and tough, quick to spot an opportunity and, if necessary, take a risk. He had developed along the way the most important of a banker's assets, a network of personal contacts which fed him constantly with useful information.

He rang the doorbell of the house and stood with his hands clasped behind his back, surveying the street as if it were a parade ground. He was a tall man, with thinning blond hair brushed straight back. His eyes were blue, his nose long and straight and he had a clipped blond moustache. He was wearing a soft brown trilby, which he removed as the housekeeper opened the door. 'Henry Dundonald to see Oliver Blackmore,' he announced.

Through the vestibule was a large reception lounge. At the far end, facing Dundonald, was a wooden staircase which ascended to a half-landing and then turned back and up to the floors above. To the left of the staircase was a stairwell leading down to the kitchens and dining room. On its right was a large pair of panelled wooden doors which were closed. Dundonald made himself comfortable on a dull green leather Chesterfield beneath the front window.

'Henry, how delightful to see you again.' He looked up. Joanna Blackmore was gliding down the staircase, looking, as she always did, elegant and beautiful. Joanna was accomplished in the art of entrances: even with an audience of one she managed to stage her entry to the best effect. With her arms outstretched she moved gracefully towards Dundonald, kissed him lightly on his cheek and held him at arm's length.

'You look wonderful,' she said appraisingly. He felt himself colouring. Joanna, along with most women, embarrassed him. 'How is Anne? And the children?'

He replied that his family was well. She let him go and walked to a drinks cupboard. The doorbell rang.

'That will be Jeffrey. Could you let him in?'

He opened the front door. On the doorstep stood the Right Honourable Jeffrey Frimley-Kimpton, MP. 'Hello, old boy,' he said. 'What are you, the bouncer?' He laughed as he stepped past Dundonald through the lobby and into the room.

Jeffrey Frimley-Kimpton was one of Dundonald's most useful contacts. His position and personality allowed him access to some of the most powerful people in the government and in business; his knowledge of what was happening or about to happen was invaluable to Dundonald, to the bank and to a large number of other people. He owned and managed a successful public relations company, which allowed him access to even more information. Frimley-Kimpton was essentially a broker of information. What he knew had a price, which the people who needed to know were willing to pay. He was sometimes paid off in money but more often he was rewarded with directorships or inside information about which shares to buy to make a quick killing; often he was paid in kind, expensive gifts for himself and his family – trips abroad, new cars, crates of good wine. Nothing that Frimley-Kimpton knew could be called classified information; what he knew was of a more intimate nature: who was sleeping with whom, who was in favour, who was out, which contracts were about to be awarded and to whom. It was a mixture of gossip and hard commercial information, essential in helping to piece together what was really happening in Whitehall and the City. He would have been intrigued to learn that his titbits of gossip, distilled through various sources, were considered high-grade intelligence by at least three East European espionage agencies as well as the French Secret Service and the CIA.

Frimley-Kimpton was also a well-established Member of Parliament. He had no pretensions to high office: his membership of the House of Commons was as necessary to his trade as union membership to a boilermaker. He was seldom against anything and was in favour only of those issues which would prove popular with his constituents and had a good chance of being won. On most issues he sat on the fence, so much so that among the more committed members of the House he was called 'Splits' Kimpton.

'Jeffrey, darling.' Joanna advanced and kissed him on his cheek. Frimley-Kimpton was not a man to be embarrassed by Joanna or any other woman, he was coming to the end of his third marriage and he had a string of women all over town. Usually, when he wasn't making money, he was making love. He was medium height and heavy about the body, but he had a vitality and an air of polished authority that attracted women. Although he was in his mid-forties he still had a full head of hair, greying at the temples. His eyes were deep brown and he had a mobile, sensuous mouth. He held Joanna's hands and kissed her. She was, in her stiletto heels, as tall as he. Dundonald was quietly amused to notice that it was Joanna's turn to be embarrassed.

She released herself. 'What would you like to drink?'

Both men asked for gin and tonic and the three sat with their drinks, talking of children and their schools.

The double doors of panelled redwood were suddenly thrown open and Oliver Blackmore strode into the room.

Dramatic entrances, thought Henry Dundonald, are a feature of this family.

'Sorry,' said Blackmore gruffly, 'I have to present a paper to the Joint Parliamentary Committee this afternoon. Had to finish it.'

Frimley-Kimpton smiled to himself indulgently. Oliver Blackmore was a career politician with his eyes set on powerful places. It was necessary for him to impress Parliamentary committees.

'Shall we talk in here?'

He led the way back into his study. It was a small room, panelled in walnut. Blackmore sat at an antique desk, the other two sat in deep leather armchairs opposite him. Behind them, the wall was lined with books. To their left the windows and a glass-panelled door looked out onto a small tiled patio, which served as a garden to the house. The patio was surrounded on all three sides by a high wall, painted white and profusely draped with ivy and honeysuckle which grew from elegant earth-filled urns. In the sunlight it was a pretty scene, like a small corner in a Renaissance garden, somehow odd when viewed from such a traditionally English room.

Joanna supplied more drinks. 'Oliver,' she said, 'I'm having lunch with Margaret in Dover Street. What are you going to do?'

'I'll eat at the House,' he replied.

She bade them farewell and closed the doors behind her. Blackmore got straight down to business, telling them of the meetings with Ashley Brighton and dinner with Richard Thornbury.

'Addingham says we shall never have a better opportunity. Thornbury is as good as we can expect and he will keep his mouth shut. The problem is time, we don't have as long as we thought.'

'I can fly to Liechtenstein whenever you wish,' said Dundonald, 'and Max Gonzales is ready in Panama.'

'What about the money?' asked Frimley-Kimpton.

'You must have three thousand pounds in cash by a week today, to be taken personally to Addingham's flat in Basil Street. He is the only one of us who isn't encumbered,' he waved his arm towards the closed doors, 'by wives, children, and the like.'

'That's fifteen thousand pounds,' said Dundonald.

'Twenty-one thousand,' Blackmore corrected. 'Thornbury has to put up his share and John Portalier has already given his share to Edward Addingham.'

'What then?' asked Frimley-Kimpton.

'We have to get the money to Switzerland somehow.'

'I thought we were going to buy stamps,' said Dundonald.

'As I said, we don't have the time. It could take weeks to

find the right stamps. Then we have to find a Swiss dealer who is willing to purchase them and for the right price. I know it's foolproof but it takes too long.'

'You're not suggesting the bloody stuff goes out in a suitcase, are you?' asked Jeffrey Frimley-Kimpton.

'Yes I am.'

'Carried by whom?'

'By you.'

'You're mad. It's too dangerous.'

'Not for a Member of Parliament, it isn't.' Blackmore was calm as he addressed himself directly to his fellow politician. 'You yourself admitted that MPs never get stopped coming in. Who would ever think to stop one going out?'

'But if I was, that would be the end, wouldn't it? I don't intend to see my career crashing around my ears at Heathrow airport. Get yourself another boy. Or better still, do it yourself, Oliver. You're a Member, too.'

Blackmore sighed and glanced at Dundonald. It took them fifteen minutes to persuade Frimley-Kimpton that the risk of carrying twenty-one thousand pounds out of Britain in a suitcase was, for him, minimal, especially when compared with the ultimate prize. Blackmore thought it best not to tell him the penalties he would face if he were stopped.

After the Second World War, the pound, which for so long had been the reserve currency of the world, second only to gold, was weak. The dollar was the new currency of international trade. To maintain its strength, the pound had to be protected. In 1947 the Exchange Control Act was passed. This prevented anyone taking sterling outside Britain without the permission of the Bank of England. Even holiday-makers were allowed only a limited amount of money to take abroad. Companies and individuals who sought to buy foreign property, stocks and shares or any foreign assets, had to pay a high price, a premium, which sometimes was almost double the original price. As the premium was calculated in dollars it became known as the 'dollar premium'. The Exchange Control Act was hard law, it had teeth and it could bite; even minor infringements were met with heavy fines. To contravene the Act was a crime. A number of people went to prison, some for long periods, for breaking the law on exchange controls. What Oliver Blackmore was proposing to Frimley-Kimpton carried a prison sentence of up to seven years.

'If you can attach yourself to some official mission travelling to Switzerland you will be absolutely safe,' said Blackmore.

'Very well,' said Frimley-Kimpton with reluctance, 'I'll see if there is one. If there isn't . . .'

'If there isn't, you'll have to invent one,' Blackmore told him sharply. 'Now, let's get on. We must have numbered accounts in a Swiss bank. Henry, that's your department.'

'Simple,' said Dundonald. 'It would be best if I flew out to Zurich at the same time as Jeffrey and picked up the money there. I can arrange the accounts and all the other details.'

'Shall we travel together?' queried Frimley-Kimpton.

'No,' said Dundonald. 'I shall be on a separate flight but we ought to be in the same hotel.'

Blackmore got up from behind the desk and left the study. He reappeared with a bottle of gin, bottles of tonic and a bowl of ice on a silver tray.

'Help yourselves,' he said, 'bloody housekeeper has gone out.'

It was stuffy in the room. Blackmore opened the door leading to the walled garden. For the next hour the three men carefully worked out the details of the trip to Zurich and the method whereby Frimley-Kimpton could smuggle out the money. Finally Blackmore announced, 'I think we've got everything under control.'

'There is one more thing, old boy,' said Dundonald, 'and it's important. The point of taking out cash is to ensure that we don't leave a trail of paper, no copies of bank transfers, cancelled cheques, statements and so on, which could be followed up in the unlikely event that someone got onto us.'

'Yes, we know all that,' said Frimley-Kimpton.

'Obviously, we will keep records and official documents to a minimum,' Dundonald went on, 'but nevertheless, we are bound to have some. What's more, internally, among ourselves, there will be quite a lot of paper. You yourself, Oliver, said that Ashley Brighton gave you and Addingham copies of Thornbury's accounts. That means there are at least three sets of sensitive documents loose already. We won't get a receipt for our money when we take it to Addingham's apartment but no doubt we shall have records of who has put up money, numbers of bank accounts and so on. The further we go into this the more paper and records there will have to be.'

'I don't see what you're getting at,' said Frimley-Kimpton.

'I think I do,' said Blackmore quietly.

Dundonald continued, 'We are, to all intents and purposes, a company. We shall be in business for nearly a year and we expect to make a vast profit. We need a company secretary, someone to hold the pieces together.'

'We can do that between ourselves,' said Frimley-Kimpton.

'I don't think we can. Don't you see, it's the old army principal, one person has to be responsible for supply, one person for communication, one person for keeping the records, otherwise it will be a total cock-up. We need a record of our expenses, we need a fund of money for day-to-day operations. After my trip to set things up, someone will have to visit Zurich from time to time to check up. And who is going to correspond with Liechtenstein and Panama and everywhere else?'

'Are you suggesting one of us does the job?' asked Blackmore.

'Who?' asked Dundonald. 'All of us have businesses to

attend to. It's going to look highly suspicious if we have files in the office that even our personal secretaries cannot see. And we can't leave them lying around at home.'

'What about Addingham?' asked Frimley-Kimpton.

'Definitely not,' replied Blackmore. 'Edward is brilliant but he wouldn't be any good at that job. Henry is right, we must be removed from the minutiae. We need a company secretary. If we don't have one, we may lose control of the details, and we might just make a mistake which would destroy us.'

They sat quietly for a few moments until Blackmore broke the silence. 'We won't solve it sitting here,' he said. 'For the moment we will ask Ashley to take on the job, while we look around.'

The three left the house together and parted on the pavement next to Dundonald's car. Blackmore and Frimley-Kimpton crossed Smith Square and turned left onto Millbank, walking slowly towards the Houses of Parliament. The constable on the gate recognised them both and saluted. Frimley-Kimpton gave him a cheery wave and even the big, normally dour Blackmore managed to smile. The constable attributed their good spirits to the end of a hard winter and the fine spring day.

Henry Dundonald drove to the Army and Navy Stores, where he purchased two expensive suitcases. They were identical, both strong with good locks. He bought a third case, similar but larger, and equally strong. Before leaving he made sure that one of the smaller suitcases fitted snugly inside it. He threw them all into the boot of his Jaguar.

Blackmore phoned Addingham and Brighton that evening from the House of Commons. Speaking cautiously he told them briefly of the meeting earlier in the day, and told Addingham to expect everyone at his flat in a week's time.

During the following seven days all of them raised three thousand in cash. Richard Thornbury borrowed the money from his mother, the other five were more subtle.

Addingham sold a fairly good painting to a dealer who paid cash; Dundonald brought his money in from abroad, 'piggy-backing' it onto a large transfer of bank funds. The other three cashed cheques on various bank accounts and sold shares. No one drew attention to himself by withdrawing a large amount of cash in one lump sum.

During that week Jeffrey Frimley-Kimpton's antics in manufacturing a safe passage to Switzerland caused wry amusement among his fellow conspirators. The day after the meeting he held a press conference at which he accused the major banks in the EEC of conspiring with the Swiss to undermine the value of the British pound. The financial press gave his accusations little space and even less credibility, but certain sections of the press, paranoic about the European Community, gave his statements great attention. He didn't have a shred of proof that what he said was true, but it was impossible for the banks to disprove it, so most of them ignored him. In the following days Frimley-Kimpton claimed to have substantial evidence. The newspapers which had taken up the story made an even greater clatter while serious financial observers came to the conclusion that the politician was becoming an unmitigated pain. No one could see what he had to gain, it was not one of his usual hobby horses, certain to win in the popularity stakes. The European banks continued to ignore him but the Swiss, sensitive as always about their banking system, reacted predictably. The senior representatives of the Swiss banks in London called at the Mayfair offices of Frimley-Kimpton's public relations consultancy. The MP was adamant, no one could convince him that the banks were not conspiring. 'It would take,' he told them, 'the chief executive of the Swiss Banking Federation to convince me otherwise.' Within twenty-four hours he had received an official invitation from the Swiss Banking Federation to fly to Zurich. He told them he would 'consider it'.

*   *   *

Frimley-Kimpton arrived at Addingham's apartment in Knightsbridge at a little after seven, just as the light was fading. The mansion block in Basil Street was classically Edwardian, built of brick the colour of tangerine and complete with pale Portland stone architraves. The wide entrance hall had a marbled floor of black and white squares and a broad staircase with a massive polished banister of dull red wood. In the middle of the stairwell a wrought-iron lift shaft ascended to the floors above.

The lift cage crashed and rattled its way to the top floor. The others had already arrived, gathered in the drawing room which was large and rectangular with two bay windows looking out towards the park. The room was furnished with solid, expensive furniture and a deep red carpet. The walls were hung with a number of original French and Italian oil paintings. Addingham had opened a few bottles of claret and was serving Blackmore and Dundonald who were standing at the windows, talking quietly and watching the gathering dusk. Brighton sat at a polished wood bureau, counting a large bundle of ten-pound notes. Frimley-Kimpton was appalled at the size of the pile of money as he deposited a briefcase at Brighton's side.

'Rather a large bundle, isn't it?' he said.

Brighton nodded but said nothing as his plump fingers with their bright, manicured nails riffled quickly through the notes. Frimley-Kimpton joined Blackmore and Dundonald, and watched unhappily as Brighton extracted the money from his briefcase and added it to the bundle. Addingham handed him a glass of wine.

'You've been receiving some remarkable publicity in the last few days,' he said.

Frimley-Kimpton turned to his host. 'As a matter of fact the Swiss called me today. They want me to go across to see some of their chief men whenever I want. When,' he asked Dundonald, 'will it suit you?'

'Today's Thursday,' replied the banker. 'If you can

arrange to fly Tuesday evening and stay at the Baur au Lac in Zurich that would suit me admirably. It's important to be in the same hotel. I can complete everything within a day or two at the most.'

'I'll phone them tomorrow,' said Frimley-Kimpton. 'I'm sure Tuesday will be acceptable; they're anxious to talk. As a matter of fact, I've received a few letters from business-men about these European bankers. Do you know, I rather think that there is some truth in the matter; these damn Continentals are conspiring to do us down.'

Dundonald shrugged. 'Of course they are. The point is, we do the same, so do the Americans and the Arabs and the South Africans. Everybody does it. If I were you I would let it drop after next week. Your name has come up a few times in the last few days, you're not too popular with the British banks, you know. Everyone thinks you're rocking the boat. I think you've done well fixing the invitation but after next week I'd let it drop.'

'It's a good political issue, all the same,' mused Frimley-Kimpton. 'I've had a number of people –'

'You'd best drop it,' growled Blackmore. 'The only sup-port you'll get is from the hysterics on both fringes, the people who hate capitalism or those who hate Europe. You'll get no support anywhere else. There's been some comment in the House already. Europe's a sensitive issue, what with the government's application for membership of the Community. Stick to the unimportant stuff, Jeffrey, more hospitals, preserving the countryside, that kind of nonsense. Stay with this one and you'll have a hard time from above. Drop it next week and the big boys will think you are a fine co-operative fellow.'

Frimley-Kimpton was sufficiently well-acquainted with the warp and weave of political life to understand the mes-sage. 'Very well, I'll play it up until Tuesday and then let it slide. Reluctantly,' he added.

'I think it's important that none of us receives too much

publicity in the next few months,' observed Addingham dryly.

'This is a marvellous room, old boy.' Frimley-Kimpton was anxious to change the subject.

'Do you think so?' The barrister was visibly pleased. 'Let me show you some of the paintings.'

He took Frimley-Kimpton and Dundonald on a tour of the apartment. The barrister possessed a good collection of Renaissance paintings which he was delighted to show off. When the three returned, Brighton was standing with Blackmore near the window of the darkening room. Addingham fussed around, switching on the lamps and refilling the empty wine glasses.

'This is excellent,' said Brighton holding up his wine glass. 'Who are your people, Edward?'

'Corney and Barrow – very reliable.'

'Is it all there?' asked Dundonald, inclining his head towards the pile of notes on the bureau.

'Exactly right,' replied Brighton. 'Twenty-one thousand in twenties, tens and fives. I have a breakdown of the numbers.'

'I don't think we need that right now, I think perhaps we ought to get it put away.' Dundonald left the room and returned a few seconds later with the three suitcases he had bought seven days earlier. He had spent an hour scraping and scuffing the largest in order to disguise its newness and had stuck on it some travel labels, taken from his own luggage.

Brighton placed the bundles of notes, bound with broad elastic bands, into one of the smaller cases. They fitted with about an inch to spare.

'We need to pack it tighter,' said Dundonald.

Addingham found some copies of *Country Life* and *The Tatler*, which Brighton put on top of the money until the suitcase was tightly packed. Dundonald locked the case and placed it snugly inside its larger brother which he also locked.

Frimley-Kimpton eyed it without enthusiasm. 'My God, it's heavy,' he said, testing the weight.

Each of them in turn lifted the suitcase. They concluded that, although heavy, it was not extraordinarily so and was unlikely to be considered unusual by baggage handlers.

All of them stood staring at the suitcase. Within it was the embryo of their fortune, and to Frimley-Kimpton had fallen the midwife's role of delivering it through a hostile atmosphere to safety in a Swiss vault.

'More wine?' Addingham broke the silence.

The group moved away from the case towards the fireplace as he refilled their glasses. Blackmore leaned an elbow on the marble mantelpiece and stared impassively at the painting hanging on the wall above.

'I suppose,' said Brighton, 'we ought to drink a toast. Gentlemen, to the safe journey of Jeffrey Frimley-Kimpton and to the complete success of our enterprise.'

Solemnly they sipped their wine.

Dundonald gave Frimley-Kimpton the third, empty, suitcase. 'Put your clothes and things you need in here. I'll pick it up on my way to the airport and take it out as mine. We can swap cases in Zurich.'

'By the way,' said Brighton, 'I've been thinking about who we should ask to join us as company secretary, to handle the detail. I believe I know the right man.'

Addingham was immediately on his guard. 'Who?'

'His name is Simon Woodberry. He's a solicitor, read Law at Oxford. That's where I met him. He practised for a few years in London, then his people died. Left him quite well-placed; a few thousand acres in Oxfordshire. He married rather well, his wife's people are actually pretty wealthy. The upshot is that he settled in Oxfordshire and now only practises sufficient law to keep his hand in. He does some legal work for a few well-heeled landowners and racehorse owners in the West Country and for one or two business firms in the Midlands. He has a small office and just a couple of clerks. There are no other partners.'

'Does he shoot?' asked Dundonald.

'Yes, he's very keen. Why?'

'I know him. Damn good shot. I've shot with him in Perthshire a couple of times. First-class fellow. He would be absolutely right.'

'Wife's name is Felicity?' asked Blackmore.

'Yes. Do you know her?'

'Joanna does. I've met them at dinner parties.' Blackmore ruminated for a few seconds. 'I think he would be excellent for what we have in mind.' He glanced at Addingham who looked agitated. 'I can recommend him, Edward.'

'I'm sure you can,' snapped Addingham, 'but with the greatest respect, Oliver, supposing you're wrong? Have you considered what is at risk? The consequences? I've worked hard on this scheme. I do not intend to see it jeopardised.'

Blackmore's voice when he spoke was slow and powerful, yet it had a soothing quality. 'Edward,' he said, 'all of us appreciate how hard you have worked on this project. Of course we know it was your idea originally. However, you invited us to join because you considered that together we could make an effective team. We each have something to contribute. Simon Woodberry is known to three of us and we all know that personal knowledge is always the best way of ensuring that one gets the right person for the job. Woodberry appears absolutely right, no partners to ask awkward questions, far enough removed from any of us. Most important, he is the right kind of person.' He paused and then said, 'I suggest that we make some further enquiries about him. Discreetly,' he emphasised. 'If what we know about him is confirmed, then I recommend that we ask Ashley to approach him.'

'Supposing he says no?' Addingham continued to be nagged by insecurity.

Henry Dundonald let out a sigh of exasperation. He knew Addingham was reputed to be brilliant and that his brilliance allowed him a certain paranoia but the man was twitching like a frightened horse. As far as Dundonald was concerned, anyone who could shoot as well as Woodberry had to be as sound as a bell.

Blackmore gave Dundonald a frown of annoyance. 'Edward,' his voice continued to massage Addingham's nervousness, 'if Woodberry is any sort of a businessman he won't say no. What reason would he have to turn us down? We all know the risk is minimal while the potential is enormous. He'd be a fool to say no. A man like him is not going to be concerned with the ethics of the enterprise; he's a solicitor, for God's sake, his concern is with the letter of the law. No, I think we must turn our attention to what we offer him as a reward. Should we pay him a fee or make him a partner?'

Blackmore had neatly turned Addingham's attention to the terms of Woodberry's association with the group. They spent the next few minutes discussing the role of their company secretary. They agreed that as his risk would be equal to theirs, he should be made a full partner and have an equal share of the proceeds.

Dundonald emptied the last of the wine into their glasses. The five partners stood easily and in a relaxed mood around the beautiful fireplace, their Savile Row suits and handmade shoes fitting them as perfectly and naturally as their money and status suited their lives. The power and influence they exuded suffused the rich room's atmosphere as distinctly as their cologne and as tangibly as the swathes of cigar smoke which hung in the still, warm air. All of them were in their prime, all in the ascendant in careers which would bring them even greater wealth and power. For them there were few qualms and no doubts.

Frimley-Kimpton and Brighton shared the lift down to the street. The two men had known each other for some years.

'Oliver Blackmore was pretty adamant that you should

drop your campaign against the banks,' observed Brighton.

Frimley-Kimpton gave the portly accountant an appraising look. 'In politics, old boy, it's a godsend if you can know for certain the outcome of a situation. Oliver knows that the Party Whips want me to stop making trouble. He will speak to them next week and tell them that he has persuaded me to drop the whole issue. The result will be that when I let the matter drop, Oliver will be considered by the big boys in the House to be a bloody decent chap.' He laughed good-naturedly.

Brighton smiled. 'You politicians, so devious. You never miss a chance to cash in on events.'

'There's nothing personal in it. It's just that Oliver is too much of a politician to miss an opportunity like this. He emerges with his reputation enhanced, and the whole thing won't have done me any harm either. There is nothing wrong in stirring things up now and again so long as one drops it as soon as one is told. It makes the prefects think one is a co-operative fellow, which,' he laughed, 'I am.'

They had reached the street. 'Addingham wouldn't approve of Oliver's antics,' said Brighton.

'I suggest we don't tell him. He may be brilliant but he does tend to get emotional about things. He wouldn't understand.'

'He is brilliant,' agreed Brighton. 'When he first told me about the idea I thought he was mad. But the more I listened and the more I thought about it, the more I realised what a marvellous scheme it is. Connecting a worthless strip of land on Pinta Leone with Thornbury Engineering is pretty clever.'

'Addingham does have friends on the island,' said Frimley-Kimpton knowingly. 'You must admit that helps.'

'It's always useful to have friends in the right place, old man,' Brighton replied. 'Can I give you a lift? My car is just round the corner.'

'Thank you, no, I'll grab a cab. I'm expected for supper by nine thirty.'

Brighton had the impression that Frimley-Kimpton was anxious to get away. Probably off to 'supper' with one of the nubile young women with whom he was frequently seen, Brighton thought.

'Good luck on the Swiss trip,' he said.

They parted, Brighton to dinner with his wife in Hampstead, and Jeffrey Frimley-Kimpton to the warm, moist thighs and hip-churning energy of a girl whose name he couldn't remember.

Chapter Three

The island of Pinta Leone lies in the Caribbean, east by south-east of Nassau and the Grand Bahama and about 250 miles due north of Haiti. Shaped like an elongated diamond, it is about 150 miles long and, at its broadest, 40 miles wide. The island is dominated by a mountain range which runs its entire length like a spine, starting in the south-western corner as a group of small hills, green and thick with vegetation. In the north the mountains rise to a height of more than 10,000 feet and spread across the entire width of the island, forming an impenetrable mass of crags and cliffs, punctuated by deep valleys of snake-infested jungle.

The island was first sighted in 1498 by Christopher Columbus on his third voyage of discovery in the service of the King and Queen of Spain. Columbus sailed past the northern tip of the island and noted in his log that the island was mountainous and uninviting. It wasn't until 1553 that the island was circumnavigated by Sebastian de Ocampo who discovered that, in contrast to the north, its southern and middle parts appeared lush and benevolent. Furthermore, on the south-west coast was a great bay which formed a perfect natural harbour. It was named Nuvo Grado.

The man allotted the task of settling the island was the first mate on one of de Ocampo's ships, a small, barrel-chested Maltese by the name of Leone Obispo. The island was officially named Santa Isabella, but it was little Leone who was king there and the captains of the great ships that called at the island marked it Pinta Leone on their charts. And when their ships were captured by the French or the English, then the name spread to their charts too.

The island of Pinta Leone became a jewel of the Spanish empire, its Vice-Regency a position to be prized and intrigued over at the Spanish court. The great galleons from Mexico and South America lay at peace in the safety of the great harbour, their cargoes of gold and silver safe from the English and French privateers; the fortress of Nuvo Grado was believed invincible. Then in 1694 the French took it and held it for over a hundred years.

The British had cast envious eyes on Pinta Leone and its great harbour for almost three hundred years. They finally possessed it without firing a shot. Over a polished table in Vienna in 1815 the island was ceded to Britain by France as part of the price of Napoleon's defeat. The British believed they had gained the brightest ruby in the Caribbean, but instead they found a dying ember. The silver and tin mines were worked out; the soil, tilled unceasingly for so long, was yielding less and less.

As the island declined, so too did the great family Portalier. Some said that the Portaliers were bastard descendants of Leone himself, others that it was the island's priest, Francisco Coranado, who, in a rare moment of human weakness, had started the line. Under the Spanish the ancient family had owned great tracts of land and many mines. With the coming of the French they had adopted the name of Portalier. It was an adroit move; the family increased in importance until finally they became the power behind the French rule. The English, anxious to maintain the status quo, used the Portaliers to advise them on how best to govern their new possession. As the island's importance declined so the Portalier dynasty was given an increasing role in its government. For the Portaliers, governing Pinta Leone required little effort; they were as old as the island itself, it was in their blood, their bones were in its soil. As travel became easier, so the excesses in which successive generations of the family had indulged at home took on an international character. From about the 1870s the Portaliers of Pinta Leone were good copy for newspapers. The men, virtual rulers of an exotic Caribbean island, were to be seen at Biarritz or Baden, or taking the waters at Evian, always in the company of beautiful women. Their sons went to Eton and Cambridge before themselves joining in the public displays of wealth and carefree living.

But the playgrounds of Europe were expensive; so too were the Parisian whores and Italian boys. Each generation sold or mortgaged what it owned in order to indulge itself. By the middle of the twentieth century the Portalier family, like the island, was broke; beneath the Caribbean sun of Pinta Leone and behind the sophisticated charm of the Portaliers there prevailed nothing but increasing poverty and the premonition that a long and bloody history was closing in.

Following the departure of his guests, Edward Addingham sat in his drawing room, slowly sipping the last of the wine. His thoughts were turned to the past, to his first meeting with Johnny Portalier, a meeting which in the tortuous fashion of things was the beginning of his scheme.

It had been at Cambridge. Portalier, who was a year ahead of Addingham, had already achieved considerable notoriety. They met at a college party. John Portalier was tall and lean, with shining black hair, deep brown eyes and skin the colour of polished copper. He was clever, he had a quick mind and a cynical humour. He appeared rich, with a wisdom in the ways of the world which went far beyond his twenty years. Addingham had never met anybody who impressed him so much. John Portalier sensed the attraction Addingham felt for him, and used it. Addingham was a tall gangling youth, gaunt and acned, his hair already thinning, and he twitched and fidgeted constantly. He took refuge in his mind and hid his self-consciousness behind a cold, articulate logic and a barbed and cutting tongue. He had no friends; except John Portalier.

Portalier appreciated Addingham's brilliance or, more accurately, its potential; he knew that whatever his friend became, he would reach the very top, and Addingham was set on the law. To have a friend destined to become an eminent officer of the court was, in Portalier's view, highly desirable. One never knew, he calculated, how things might turn out but he was pretty sure that at some time in his life he would need the services of a sympathetic and influential lawyer. He had already been expelled from Eton. So for the first and only time in his life Edward Addingham was used. Portalier befriended him, as he might have done a dog, and taught him the ways of the world and the meaning of sensation. The ugly youth loved him for it. In time Portalier even came to like Addingham, though he found his friend's brilliance, like charity, much more admirable at a distance.

In the early summer of 1938, Johnny invited Addingham to travel with him to his home on Pinta Leone. 'It looks as though we shall all be at each other's throats again soon, Edward old boy, and it may be your only opportunity to see my jolly old homeland. Come out with me, why don't you, though I'm afraid I'm a bit short of cash at present, so you'll have to find your own fare.'

Addingham was flattered by the invitation and managed somehow to scrape together the money for his journey. His father had been a civil servant and although when he died his mother was not left badly off, there was little cash to spare for trips to the Caribbean.

Addingham found that he did not much care for Pinta Leone. It was appallingly hot and his fair skin came out in blotches. The island smelled, and the inhabitants, who appeared to sit around and do nothing all day, smelled even worse. And there was a strange disreputable air about

Johnny's family. They lived in a large colonial-style mansion built in the hills behind Nuvo Grado, which had, even to Addingham's uninitiated eyes, seen better days. Johnny's father was very dark and grossly fat; he sat around the house in a dirty shirt smoking cigarettes which had a strange, pungent odour. His classical education at Eton and Cambridge appeared to have availed him nothing, he smelled as badly as the rest of the inhabitants. Johnny's sisters quietly laughed together in corners and looked at the young Edward with knowing eyes. Johnny's mother kept to her room with a bottle of white rum for company. The family was attended by four or five young women, all of whom, Addingham noticed, affected an attitude of casual intimacy towards Johnny which seemed to border on insolence.

One night Addingham was awakened by the noise of a furious row coming from one of the great rooms below. He could not make out the words but managed to distinguish Johnny's voice and that of his father. The next morning, when he and Johnny set off on a tour of the island, Portalier was curt and sullen; he drove the big, open-topped Bentley at breakneck speed along the rough roads. After an hour or so of reckless driving, he slowed down and began to point out places of interest on their route. The road, he told his friend, had originally been built by the Spanish and circuited the whole island. Further on near the island's northern tip they would be driving high into the mountains.

They stopped for lunch at a fishing village well north along the island's eastern shore. After their meal Johnny's spirits rose and he became more his charming and effusive self. But as they travelled north the road grew steadily worse and Johnny's good spirits evaporated; although he was no longer sullen, he was quiet and pensive. Addingham had never known him to be so distant. To their left, no further than a mile, the mountains sprang up, towering directly out of the rocky soil. To their right, running for mile after mile parallel to the road, was a low mangrove swamp. Beyond the swamp about two miles away was the faint shimmering line of the sea.

Suddenly Johnny stopped the car. He glowered at the landscape and lit a cigarette. Addingham remained silent. After a while Johnny turned towards him. 'Cast your eyes over my inheritance, Edward. Everything you can see, all the land from the mountains,' he jerked his head at the grey walls of rock to their left, 'to the sea.' He stretched his arm over the door of the car and flicked his cigarette into the swamp. 'From that last village, two miles back, right up to Arrowhead Point. All of it, for fifteen miles, belongs to me. Isn't that impressive? The only trouble is that the whole fucking lot isn't worth a bucket of seagull shit. A few thousand acres of swamp and desiccated rock. Worthless. My father's legacy to his son.'

'I thought your family owned a lot of land on the island,' Addingham said in surprise.

'A few years ago, anything on this island worth owning was owned by my family. Now there's nothing left but this.' He looked over the landscape. 'Most of the island is owned by the Americans, the big fruit companies. They are the masters now. Not the Portaliers. Last night my father told me that the house is mortgaged up to the hilt and over. You see, my father has some rather expensive habits. Very soon the banks will foreclose and that will mean goodbye to the house.'

Addingham had never seen his friend so dejected. He felt completely inadequate in the face of his depression.

'We're broke,' Johnny continued. 'There's no more Cambridge for me.' He saw the look of anguish on Addingham's face. 'Don't worry, Edward, I'm coming back for a few weeks. I need to leave Cambridge with some sort of honour. But after that,' he shrugged, 'all I've got is the prospect of showing tourists round the island. Can you see me in a peaked cap?'

'You can do more than that, Johnny, you're clever enough. You can do anything.'

'Perhaps I could, old boy, but there are two problems. Firstly, I don't have your penchant for hard work, life seems to have too many distractions. Even more important, I'm the wrong colour. Oh, I know I have the right accent and all the other attributes of the English gentleman, but I'm not English and I'm not a gentleman. I'm a rich nigger who is really quite amusing. Take away the money and what's left? A poor black bastard with a smart mouth.'

Addingham was appalled. 'Johnny, you mustn't talk like that. I'll help you.'

Portalier looked at him and smiled. 'I know you would if you could, old boy, but I don't need help. What I need is money, lots of it. All I own in the world is out there. My father has tried to sell it, and people just laughed. Who wants a few miles of swamp and rock? I'm glad there's a war coming,' he continued, 'in a war there are always unusual opportunities for someone like me.'

'They don't have mercenaries these days,' replied Addingham dully.

Portalier laughed. 'I wasn't thinking of actually fighting. Not my line.' He stared at Addingham for a few seconds, then smiled, his old, entrancing smile. 'I'd be grateful if you could keep what I've said to yourself, old boy. I'd like to maintain the image for a while longer if I can.'

'Of course I will,' Addingham told him, relieved that his friend's depression seemed to be lifting.

Portalier started the car and they followed the road further north, driving between the mountains and the swamp. Eventually they turned west and began their ascent into the mountains. The road was no more than a track, weaving and bending as it climbed up and over the mountain passes. Sometimes the walls of rock came almost to the edge of the track, then without warning they would be driving through thick, dark jungle. Once they ran over a snake wriggling across the track.

The jungle began to thin out and soon they were through to the coast. The track was still high above sea level, and from their vantage point Addingham could see stretching away to both left and right a broad beach, its pale, golden sands washed by the deep blue sea and bordered by a wide strip of lush green vegetation which, as they continued their descent, turned out to be banana groves.

'My God. Magnificent!' exclaimed Addingham. 'What a pity you don't own this beach. People would pay to come here.'

'My grandfather did own it,' said Johnny flatly. 'But he sold it. The old man conned an American company into buying the whole strip on this side of the island.'

'Conned?'

'Absolutely. He told them it would make a marvellous development for rich holiday-makers. What the old man didn't tell them is that the wind hereabouts comes predominantly from the south-east; the rain clouds are blown over the mountains and deposit everything they have along this stretch of coast. It has one of the highest rainfalls in the whole of the Caribbean. It rains on average every other day.'

'It's beautiful when it isn't raining,' said Addingham.

'That's how the old boy got away with it. When the Yanks found out, they were wild. But they had the last laugh; they sold the whole lot to one of the American fruit companies. The weather is ideal for tropical fruit.'

'If your grandfather hadn't sold it, you could have been making money out of all this.'

Johnny laughed as he negotiated the big car round the curves of the descending track. 'I don't suppose I would, old man. I expect I would be looking for some mug to buy it, just like he did. I can understand perfectly why they sold everything; it's just bloody hard when you're last in line.'

The sun was falling into the sea as the car reached sea level and they turned south onto the good road. They drove fast through the beautiful landscape towards Nuvo Grado.

Addingham went to bed early, the heat and long drive had tired him. He awoke about midnight, the house was quiet and dark. He needed the bathroom and padded along the corridor. He noticed that the door of Johnny's bedroom was ajar and that the light was on. From inside the room came the quiet creaking of a bed. Silently he pushed the door open. Kneeling at the side of the bed, her back to the door, was one of the young serving girls. She was naked. Streams of perspiration flowed down her copper back, over her rounded hips and into the moist, dark fissure between her buttocks and thighs. Spreadeagled and naked on the bed before her was another of the serving women, her hips raised and her legs spread wide. The young girl's face was buried in the glistening clump of hair at the base of the woman's heaving belly. Addingham could hear the soft sucking noises as the girl's lips and tongue nibbled and probed the wet, exposed orifices before her. The woman on the bed was pushing herself down upon the face beneath her while she, in turn, sucked frantically at the full and rigid penis above her. For kneeling on the bed, his legs spread wide and his body leaning forward, was Johnny, panting like a dog, his penis moving deep and rhythmically within the woman's mouth.

The hand of God flashed out of the night and smacked Edward Addingham on the face. It snatched at his heart, crumpled it like a dried leaf and threw it across the expanse of emptiness which had opened inside him.

The woman beneath Johnny moved her hands up to his buttocks and gently caressed them; slowly she pushed them apart and inserted a finger deep within him. Johnny fell further forward onto his hands, moaning and jerking violently as he climaxed, pushing himself further into the woman's throat. He threw his head back and opened his eyes. For a few moments he stared directly at Addingham standing immobile in the darkened and half-open doorway, then his eyes rolled up into his head as the ecstasy took him. The woman beneath him began to gargle noisily as her climax came. She grabbed at the kneeling girl's hair and twisting it cruelly pulled the face even tighter into her crotch, thrusting and rubbing. The girl squealed at the pain as the woman continued to suck noisily on the hard muscle in her mouth. Finally, she let out a low gurgling moan.

The noise shook Addingham out of his daze. He staggered to the bathroom and vomited, again and again, until there was no more. He remained there, locked in for hours, leaning against the wall and trembling violently, until at last he was able to creep back to his room to spend the rest of the night weeping bitter tears.

He never knew whether Johnny had seen him. If he had, he gave no sign of it. He was, in the last few days of Addingham's visit, his usual smiling, cynical self. When it was time to leave, he saw his friend safely aboard the boat for Europe.

'Bon voyage, old boy,' he said. 'I'll see you in the autumn.'

Standing at the stern of the boat as it sailed slowly out of the placid, golden harbour, Addingham noticed how quickly the figure of John Portalier faded into the background of Nuvo Grado.

Work eased the bitterness and confusion that memories brought. Addingham had learned in one awful lesson that he had not the capacity to enjoy his body as he had seen them enjoy theirs. He felt deprived and deeply resentful so he applied his bright and bitter mind to the study of the law and found in that his consolation.

Johnny arrived at Cambridge at the beginning of term. True to his word, he staged his departure from the university in a way which was, for him, an honourable exit. He was sent down after being found in bed in a local hotel with two women, who just happened to be the wife and daughter of his history professor. He left under what his contemporaries called a cloud, but no Portalier had ever been expelled from any institution, club or hotel under a cloud, their exits had always been accomplished with great style and under the brightest lights available. Johnny went out in a blaze of glory. No one, with the exception of Edward Addingham, had any inkling that the money had run out; everyone believed that Portalier was off to paint the world a bright and blazing red.

The following year, Addingham took a double first; within weeks of coming down from Cambridge the war broke out and he was drafted into military intelligence. His duties took him to America and the Middle East, and although he would have preferred to be practising law, he found the work interesting. He heard nothing of John Portalier and supposed that he was sitting it out in some safe, neutral haven.

The war ended and Addingham began to practise at the Bar. The first years were hard but slowly his name became known. He concentrated on commercial law; he won a few cases that he should have lost and his reputation grew.

In 1947 Pinta Leone became, for the first time in four hundred years, virtually self-governing. The British had no time for poorer colonies; the island became a protectorate. In the years immediately following the war, Johnny's name appeared frequently in the gossip columns of the world's press. Photographs and reports of parties in the south of France and in smart ski resorts regularly included Johnny Portalier. It was an expensive life style and Addingham occasionally wondered where Johnny was getting the money; somehow, the poverty that in 1938 seemed inevitable had been averted.

Addingham took silk in 1956 and shortly afterwards won a highly publicised case. A few weeks later he received a phone call in his chambers from Portalier. Johnny was staying with friends at Ascot and he suggested they dine in London. They dined at Le Coq d'Or in Stratton Street. Johnny was as charming and as cynically amusing as ever. They swapped stories of the war. Johnny, as Addingham suspected, had sat it out in Mexico where he had married a lady of considerable wealth. They had separated a few years later. Portalier was very amusing about his life and Addingham chuckled heartily at his stories. As the evening progressed, so Addingham became more relaxed. His experiences in the war and his successes at the Bar had made him as wise about the world and its ways as Portalier. Even Johnny's looks were fading, he smoked and drank incessantly and Addingham could see that dissipation was beginning to corrode him at the edges.

Over the following years, they dined together at infrequent intervals. Addingham's reputation for acid law grew, while Johnny continued his jet-set existence. Each time they met, Edward noted the deterioration in his friend's appearance. Johnny became fat, his once lustrous skin took on the texture of parchment, the whites of his eyes became yellow and the pupils unnaturally dilated. Addingham was sure he was taking drugs. It was clear that the hereditary disease of the Portaliers was breeding in the body of John Portalier, the last of the line. Pleasure was destroying him. Johnny would suck anything in, blow anything out, contort his body to any new depravity for the sake of sensation. Every pulse within him was permanently pushed to full throttle, every sensory channel within his body had its controls locked wide open. Sensation was shaking John Portalier's system to pieces.

They were dining together at a new restaurant in Beauchamp Place. It was a perfect June evening in 1962. The skyline of London was changing as the new towers of concrete and glass rose from the bomb sites. Plastic and television were changing the face of the land; there was scandal in the air, prosperity in the streets and the future was as bright and guaranteed as stainless steel.

Johnny had been recounting stories of his wife. 'You ought to marry, Edward,' he said.

'I don't think so,' replied Addingham. 'What do I need a wife for? All I need is a good cook, a housekeeper, and the occasional whore. All of those services are of a temporary nature. It's illogical to enter into a permanent contract to secure them.'

Johnny chuckled. 'I agree. Women are far better as casual labour than as fixed overheads. But what I meant was, a wife would be good for your career.'

'A wife would be bad for my career. She would want children.'

'Not all women want children, Edward. Find one who doesn't. One day you'll be a judge and judges ought to be married. It gives them an air of maturity, the public wants to think that they suffer too. Of course you must make the right choice; as long as it is a good commercial arrangement, it will last.'

'Why don't you remarry?' asked Addingham.

'I would if I could, but I think I've let myself go to seed too long. To be frank, it would be useful to marry some old hag who's stinking rich, God knows I know enough of them. But I doubt if they'd have me. Pity, as I'm afraid there are signs that my old money tree may be dying.'

'Really?' Addingham endeavoured to keep the interest out of his voice. Johnny had never before given the slightest hint of how he came by his evident wealth.

'Afraid so. All the bloody wog politicians at home on the island have got ideas above their station. They want a socialist government, for God's sake. It's this Cuban business. It's given every thick nigger in the Caribbean ideas of equality. The Americans should have stepped in there a lot bloody quicker.'

'They may still do so,' said Addingham.

'Too late now,' replied Portalier. 'The fact is that some

tinpot politicos on Pinta Leone want a new set-up. They want to nationalise everything, the land, the banks – and they're just the moderates. We've got communist guerrillas in the mountains.'

'Is that serious?'

Johnny shrugged. 'There have always been bandits in the mountains, runaway slaves and the like. God knows how they ever lived there. But they were never a serious problem. These bloody people, though, they're organised and they've got modern weapons. Someone is providing the money. They've already shot up a few farms and a couple of police convoys. And they've got plenty of sympathisers in Nuvo Grado who tell them what's going on.'

'We've sent troops out, haven't we?' asked Addingham.

Johnny laughed. 'A battalion of the Dorset Light Infantry came out four weeks ago. So far all they've done is to improve the economy by spending their money on beer and whores.'

'What has all this got to do with your earning a living?'

Portalier sipped his brandy thoughtfully and lit another cigarette. 'When I was in Mexico during the war, I met some Americans who needed a representative down there. They were exporting government army surplus and importing pharmaceuticals.'

It was unlike Johnny to be so esoteric. 'You mean drugs and gun running,' Addingham said dryly.

Johnny shrugged. 'I needed the money, old boy.' He reached across the table for the bottle of Courvoisier and poured himself another large glass. He took a gulp of the brandy; a few drops spilled onto his shirt front which was straining across his belly. 'I carried on working for them even after I was married. The money was bloody good and the work was exciting. Then when the war ended I persuaded my wife that we ought to spend some money and see something of the world, or what was left of it. I told my American friends that I was off for a little trip and they accepted it quite happily. I had done a bloody good job for them and I think they appreciated it. The bottom had anyway dropped out of the arms business, so we shook hands all round and off I went. We had a good time for a few years and then the cow began to whine about the money not lasting for ever. She got very mean and stingy towards the end. It's ironic,' he reflected, 'when I first met her she had a wide open cheque book and the tightest little cunt you could wish for. When it finished it was just the opposite, she was as tight as a miser's arse with the loot but her pussy was the size of Fingle's fucking cave.'

Addingham wrinkled his nose slightly at Portalier's words and began quietly to smack his lips together.

'The bitch was fucking them by battalions. One afternoon I walked into our hotel bedroom in Paris to find her sandwiched between two hairy young bellboys. They were banging her so hard from both sides it's a wonder she wasn't paste. Anyway, one advantage of a classical education, old boy, is that it teaches one a certain amount of *savoir faire*. I waited in the drawing room next door until Batman and Robin had finished trying to meet head-on somewhere in the middle of her plumbing, walked in and smacked the slut in the teeth. It wasn't the first time I'd caught her at it but it was certainly going to be the last. After all, one doesn't mind that kind of thing if one has sufficient funds to buy some fun of one's own, but being cuckolded in poverty is definitely not on. I put her name onto a couple of large cheques, emptied our joint account and went back home. My father was dead, the house had gone, and I had no money. I'll tell you, old boy, the prospects looked grim. And then, straight off the plane came salvation.'

'Plane?' queried Addingham.

'Of course, you wouldn't know. They built an airstrip during the war, now we have regular flights to Jamaica and Florida. Anyway, a very serious attorney from Miami flew out to see me, totally unannounced. He said that he represented a business organisation in Florida which had heard about me from some of their colleagues in Texas.' He paused. 'You know, I think it's laughable that the only people that have ever given me a good report, so to speak, are a bunch of Italian gangsters.' He drained his glass and reached for the bottle.

Addingham stared hard at his friend. 'Do you mean you're in with the Mafia?'

'Not a term they like, old boy.' Johnny poured himself another brandy. 'Too emotive, visions of tommy guns and dead bodies in the spaghetti. Out of date. These people are highly organised businessmen. They may choose to ignore the law sometimes but they are also adept at using it – when it suits them, of course. This character from Miami knew more about company law in Pinta Leone than I knew existed.'

'Company law? Do you have any?' Addingham smiled slightly.

'Exactly, old boy. Exactly.' Johnny lit another cigarette.

'What do you mean, exactly?'

'This fellow said I was in a unique position to help them and that they would pay me very well for my trouble. I'd said yes before he'd finished asking.'

'Pretty impetuous.'

'Not really. I'd worked with them before. And I was broke. And they're not the kind of people to whom one says no. This chap said they wanted me to form a bank. I damn near peed my pants. I thought he said rob a bank.'

'Form a bank?' Addingham was incredulous.

'Easily done. You see, when your government ditched us they were in such a hurry that they didn't pay much attention to our company law. The laws governing companies, banks, trust funds and so on in Pinta Leone are rudimentary. Not that they're used that much anyway. Companies have to make their books balance and have them audited occasionally and that's about it. There are no reporting requirements at all. The same is true for banks; so long as our Minister of Finance approves, anyone can start one.'

'It doesn't sound an attractive centre of commerce to me.'

Johnny leaned across the table. 'That's because you're a pompous old bastard making lots of money out of complicated law. The Caribbean is becoming one of the most attractive commercial centres of the world. All the big multinationals are moving in, the insurance companies, the banks, the property companies. It's all about tax avoidance. None of the islands have sophisticated banking laws, some of them have special tax treaties with the United States, all of them have the minimum requirements for financial reporting. It's open house.'

'Not for legitimate organisations. They have certain requirements to meet.'

'Don't be naive, old boy, you know as well as I do that the difference between the multinationals and my friends is that much.' Johnny held his thumb and forefinger close together. 'The big companies may have shareholders and government contracts to worry about but they break the rules when it suits them. The point is that they are not breaking any rules in the Caribbean because there are none. It's all legitimate.'

Addingham frowned. 'Why would your friends in the Mafia have a legitimate interest in avoiding tax? They make their money illegitimately.'

Johnny nodded. 'I know, but ever since Al Capone was imprisoned for tax evasion they've been concerned about what to do with their money. Imagine it. There they are, making millions out of drugs and prostitution and all such lovely service industries but they can't declare the money. The authorities would want to know where it came from. They can't spend it, not even a tenth of it. There would be a posse of agents from the US Internal Revenue Service knocking on the penthouse door, asking how they could afford to live in such style. So what can they do?'

Addingham disliked being asked childish questions 'Invest it somehow,' he replied.

'Exactly.' Johnny lit another cigarette, drawing the smoke down into his lungs with gusto. 'In legitimate businesses, old boy. Some of it goes into trust funds and the like, but most of it is invested in straight businesses which have cash coming in, race tracks, laundries, garages, cinemas, anywhere it's difficult to prove how much money comes in. They push the illegal money through the straight business as income, takings at the door.'

'That means they pay tax on the profits,' observed Addingham.

Portalier shrugged. 'These people have teams of lawyers, sharp as whips, figuring out ways of avoiding tax and bending the law.'

'So where do you fit in?'

'I'm the laundry man.'

'The what?'

'The bank is the laundry and I'm president of the bank. We wash the money.'

Addingham stared at Johnny.

'It's dirty money, Edward. Money from crime is dirty. If it's to be used for legitimate purposes it has to be laundered.'

Addingham could not shake the mental image of thousands of dollars spinning round in a washing tub.

'This fellow from Miami explained that a bank in Pinta Leone could take cash, hold it for a while and then deposit it in banks in Switzerland, Liechtenstein or Panama. The point is that because of our banking laws, or lack of them, we don't have to tell anyone where the money comes from or where it goes to. Up until then the chaps in Miami had been taking suitcases full of dollars out of the country and depositing them in Swiss bank accounts. The authorities were getting wise to it, and although Swiss bankers are pretty used to characters coming in off the streets with suitcases full of cash, even they were perturbed at getting a million dollars a week wrapped in newspaper.'

'A million a week from women and drugs? My God!' Addingham was shocked.

'You know the Americans, old boy, if they're not stuffing, they're puffing. Usually the money comes in by sea, we move it by inter-bank transfer to accounts in Switzerland. Official bank couriers and all that. The money ultimately ends up in Liechtenstein or Panamanian trust funds which then lend to my friends. All perfectly legal. We are a well-established bank. I've been president for five years.' Johnny extracted a business card from his wallet and gave it to Addingham. Engraved in gold copperplate, it read: 'John Portalier – President – The First Bank of Pinta Leone.'

'Impressive,' murmured Addingham looking at the enormous, perspiring figure seated opposite him. 'And now it's all about to finish?'

Portalier nodded. 'The clouds are on the horizon. If these left-wing cretins get their way they will nationalise the banks, tighten up Customs. If there's a socialist regime, my friends will pull out, there are plenty of other places they can go.' He emptied the last of the brandy into his glass, raised it in silent salute and drained it in one noisy gulp. He wiped his mouth on his napkin. 'It would be nice if the money could last as long as I do. This stuff,' he indicated the brandy bottle, 'is beginning to affect me. Had a bit of an attack a few months ago, got a glimpse of the old grim reaper.' His face took on a lugubrious expression.

Addingham was in no mood to bear with Johnny's maudlin thoughts. He changed the subject. 'Did you ever sell that strip of land in the north?'

Portalier took a few seconds to focus on the question. 'What? Oh that, no. I still own it. I showed it to some of my

American friends, they laughed like hyenas. They said nobody could make money out of that. They said it was the shittiest piece of real estate they had ever seen.'

It was a casual question and an off-hand answer. There was no reason why the strip of land should have stayed in Addingham's mind when Johnny's revelations had given him so much to ponder. But it did. Like a cuckoo's egg.

Johnny paid the bill. It was almost midnight; outside, the night air was still and cool. The racket of the day had given way to the pulsing hum of London's night. They shook hands and Addingham saw Johnny into a cab. He walked the few yards to his flat, deep in thought.

In the following months the barrister made an intense study of the laws and tax treaties of the Caribbean. The knowledge was extremely valuable; he was able to advise clients about far more sophisticated methods of avoiding tax or investing money in the offshore financial centres. Addingham was always punctilious in observing the law, and his schemes became renowned for their ability to use the letter of the law to break its spirit.

And then one day, months after his meeting with Portalier, the cuckoo's egg hatched. It came in a flash, the whole plan, perfect in all its details. He was sitting in court, listening to a witness giving evidence. One second his mind was quiet and easy, the next, the plan had flipped up in his brain, like a schematic drawing flashed onto a screen. It took him some seconds to grasp what it was that had so suddenly pushed every other thought out of his head. When finally he understood, he reached for a notebook and began scribbling furiously while the witness blithely continued his evidence in a monotone, and the opposing barristers wondered what the witness had said to precipitate Addingham's sudden activity. The plan's details were already fading, blurring at the edges. Addingham's subconscious had done its work, it would take his conscious mind days to crystallise the details as definitely as they had been for those few short moments. But he recorded enough to know that the cuckoo had laid a golden egg.

The scheme became an obsession. Addingham wrote out every detail in his diminutive spidery handwriting; he analysed and examined it from every possible angle. He sat for hours in his flat, his lips smacking together noisily, thinking of what could go wrong. There was nothing, it was perfect. Its weakness was in the people he would need. People were weak, they made mistakes, they tarnished everything. It was people who corrupted the law. The law was perfect, like his plan. A mind like his could make the law bend to his will but people were obstinate, they didn't bend. He thought hard about the people. Brighton was his first choice. Ashley Brighton, he knew, sailed close to the law, but he was clever: outside a small band of cognoscenti no one knew. Ashley was good with people, he could manipulate them and with his help Addingham would find the others. But first and most important, he needed Johnny, for without him there would be no plan. He wrote to Portalier asking to see him as quickly as he could arrange a trip to London. He fumed as each day passed without word; it was three weeks before he received a reply. Johnny was in Switzerland at a clinic near Cortina and expected to be in London within a few days.

When they met, Addingham saw some improvement in Portalier's appearance. He had been drying out, he was at least twenty pounds lighter, and he was making an effort to limit his drinking. He arrived at Addingham's flat at just after eight o'clock. It was a bitterly cold night in early February 1963; the country was gripped in the worst winter for years. A high wind and scudding showers of snow battered and rattled the windows of the drawing room. Addingham's housekeeper had laid a fire which filled the room with mellow heat. Portalier declined the offer of whisky and accepted a glass of claret. He and Addingham seated themselves in two wing chairs set opposite each other across the crackling fire. The lights were subdued and the room was filled with dancing shadows.

Addingham came straight to the point. 'That land of yours,' he said, 'in the north, I'm interested in it.'

Johnny raised his eyebrows in surprise. 'Really? That's interesting.'

'What do you mean?' asked Addingham.

'Nothing, go on.'

'Prime land with good beaches suitable for hotel and holiday development in the Caribbean is selling for seventeen hundred and fifty dollars an acre; you own forty-five square miles of land, which is approximately twenty-nine thousand acres. I propose that we should sell that land and make fifty million dollars.'

Inside Portalier the laughter began to churn. He had come all the way to dreary, ice-bound England to hear Addingham tell him a fairy story. He looked at the barrister across the fire's glow. Addingham was sitting absolutely still, his fingers steepled, the tips touching just beneath the point of his chin. Above them, in the shadows, Portalier could see the sharp points of his eyes staring intently at him. For an instant he felt a pang of ancient fear. The urge to laugh died. 'You're serious?' he said quietly.

'Deadly serious. Not only can it be done but it can be done in such a way that no one will ever connect it with us.'

'How?'

He listened as the barrister explained in his precise tones how the gigantic fraud was to be perpetrated. There was no emotion in Addingham's voice, no rhetoric, no rushes of enthusiasm papering over gaps in the logic. He explained simply yet graphically each step of the scheme, the kind of people he would need, the roles each of them would fulfil. He talked for over an hour with the firelight flickering on the walls around him, and by the end Portalier knew that it could be done, that he could be exceedingly rich. When

Addingham finished, it was quiet in the room, they could hear the affluent ticking of the grandfather clock in the hall.

'Well? What do you think?'

Portalier was twisting the stem of his glass between his finger and thumb. He stood up. 'May I help myself?' He walked across the room to the decanter, poured himself a glass of claret and returned to his seat. 'Frankly, old boy,' he said when he was seated, 'I think it's brilliant. By the way, this is very good.' He held up his glass.

'I'm glad you think so.' Addingham's voice was quietly pleased.

Johnny raised his glass in salute to his host. 'Unbelievable. A fortune from a strip of worthless land sold to a bankrupt company. All with the help of a phoney bank and the Miami Mafia. Marvellous. Money for nothing. Absolutely bloody fantastic.'

'It's not so unusual really,' Addingham told him. 'Most business is based on making things appear worth more than they are. One day a company's shares are worth millions, the next day they are wiped out. What happened to the millions? It's not what things are worth, it's what people will pay.'

Johnny nodded. 'Greed makes the world go round, old boy. Thank God.' They discussed in detail the immediate moves that had to be made. Addingham made sure that Johnny understood exactly what was needed of him in the forthcoming weeks. He also got his friend to write him a cheque for three thousand pounds sterling.

It was past eleven o'clock before they finished. The wind had died and it was snowing. Addingham had arranged for Johnny to stay at an hotel in Basil Street. He helped him on with his overcoat and opened the door of the flat. They walked out onto the darkened landing and stood by the cage waiting for the lift to crank and clatter its way up. Johnny was due to fly to New York the following day and from there to Miami.

'It's a pity you can't call direct,' said Addingham, 'but

keep in close touch, write or send telegrams, and be careful what you say.'

They shook hands as the lift arrived. Johnny stepped inside and turned to face Addingham, his hand hovering over the button. 'You know, Edward,' he said with a faint smile, 'when we were at Cambridge, one of the reasons I valued your friendship was the belief that one day I would get into some kind of trouble with the law and you would help me get out of it. It never occurred to me that it would be you who would propose that I break the law. Don't you find that strange?' He didn't wait for a reply. The gates of the gilded cage crashed shut and Johnny, still staring at Addingham, descended into the gloom.

Chapter Four

Jeffrey Frimley-Kimpton's departure for Switzerland was marked by a minor blaze of publicity and the popping of flashbulbs. His office had called the airline on the morning of his flight and made the point, none too subtly, that his trip was of 'national importance' and as a Member of Parliament he expected personal attention. His secretary also called the newspapers; the financial editors had little interest in Frimley-Kimpton or his travels, but they advised their reporters who covered the airport to look out for him. There was always the chance of a good picture or a usable quote. He arrived at Heathrow in the late afternoon. It was raining slightly. The chauffeur of a hired Daimler was behind Frimley-Kimpton, carrying the heavy suitcase. They were both sweating as they approached the check-in desk, though for different reasons. A young man dressed in the uniform of the airline was standing close to the desk.

'Mr Frimley-Kimpton?'

Frimley-Kimpton was startled by the question. 'Yes.'

'Good afternoon, sir,' said the young man, 'we were expecting you.'

'Oh really,' he replied vacantly. The vapour from the churning fear in his stomach was affecting his brain. He handed his tickets to the pretty blonde girl behind the desk. The girl smiled at him, blue eyes and white, even teeth. Her smile began to clear his head like warm sun on morning mist. 'Good.' His voice was more definite.

'I think we can dispense with all these formalities, sir,'

said the young man. He reached across the high counter and plucked the tickets from the girl's hand. The smile switched off.

There was a loud crash. It was the sound of a heavy suitcase dropping onto a hard floor. Frimley-Kimpton froze. He pictured the case burst open and thousands of five-pound notes swirling across the terminal like leaves. He looked round slowly. The case was intact, unceremoniously deposited by the scowling chauffeur. The airline official raised a hand and snapped his fingers, a burly baggage porter emerged from nowhere and picked it up. The Honourable Member watched closely; there was no look of surprise on the man's face at its weight, he held it easily in his large hand. It swung in his grip and banged against the chauffeur's leg. The porter watched impassively as the driver rubbed his bruised shin.

'That case has some rather important papers in it,' said Frimley-Kimpton to the young man.

'Don't worry, sir, it will be perfectly safe. Now, if you would like to follow me.' He set off, followed by the porter. Frimley-Kimpton looked over his shoulder.

'Thank you, Alfred,' he said imperiously, 'that will be all.'

The chauffeur, whose name was Eric, watched him disappear into the throng. Not even a sodding tip, he thought, and limped away. Outside, a young policeman was taking the number of his car.

Frimley-Kimpton, walking behind the porter, kept his eyes riveted on his case. Suddenly, he was accosted by a group of men who surrounded him completely. Over their shoulders he could see his case disappearing towards the passport control desk.

'Mr Frimley-Kimpton, could you give us a statement of what you hope to achieve by this visit?' The photographers' cameras flashed. The suitcase had come to rest at the feet of the passport officer who was eyeing it suspiciously.

Frimley-Kimpton was divided between a compulsion to protect the suitcase and a reflex response, whenever the press were around, to give them a good story. His brain switched to automatic as he repeated the statement he had made to the papers a few days earlier. To the reporters, this was dull news. Preoccupied as he was, Frimley-Kimpton did not immediately sense their lack of interest but after a few desultory questions he realised that they were merely going through the motions. 'Gentlemen,' he said, 'I'm sorry, that's all I have time for. Thank you.' The group of newsmen ambled off towards the bar like a herd of heavy buffalo making for the waterhole.

Frimley-Kimpton turned towards the officials standing at passport control, and glanced down. The case was gone. His stomach boiled up as he felt his sphincter snap shut. Somehow he walked towards the men, a sickly smile on his face.

'That's all right, sir,' said the passport officer, 'go straight through.'

He started in the same direction as the other passengers; the young man was saying something.

'What?' he asked.

'If we go this way, sir, we can avoid the crowds.' They retraced their steps and, turning into a deserted corridor, descended a flight of stairs and emerged onto the wet tarmac. A car was parked nearby.

'Here we are,' said the young man. There was no sign of the suitcase or of the airline porter. They got into the car which immediately drove off. It drew up beneath the wings of an airplane, the young man opened the door and Frimley-Kimpton got out. He found himself at the bottom of the aircraft steps; a stewardess, smiling expectantly, stood at the top.

'Well, goodbye, sir,' said the young man, 'have a pleasant trip.'

The Member of Parliament mumbled and limply

extended his sweaty hand. The young man grasped it firmly and Jeffrey Frimley-Kimpton's party lost a vote. He ascended the steps, oblivious of the drizzling rain, his legs shaking. The plane was empty, the crew were making the last-minute checks before the passengers would be crammed into buses like cattle and driven out to the aircraft. The stewardess smiled sweetly and settled him into a seat in the first-class cabin. He stared dazedly for some seconds at a faintly familiar object which was securely strapped to the rear partition of the stewardess's little pantry. It was the suitcase. He leapt up and tested the catches. It was still locked. It was as heavy and secure as when he had last seen it. He slumped into his seat, the fear evaporating from his system. He took out his cigarette case and with a hand still trembling lit a cigarette.

'I'm sorry, Mr Frimley-Kimpton. I'm afraid you can't smoke until we are airborne. Can I fix you a drink instead?'

Frimley-Kimpton looked up at the pretty smiling stewardess. His face was only inches from her loins.

'I'd like a very large brandy,' he replied.

A white Mercedes was waiting on the tarmac as the plane touched down at Zurich airport. While the rest of the passengers were asked to keep their seats, Frimley-Kimpton was allowed down the steps to the waiting car, his suitcase carried by a steward. Another young man, dressed in a dark business suit, was waiting by the car.

'Mr Frimley-Kimpton,' he said in heavily accented English, 'I am with the Swiss Banking Federation. May we drive you to your hotel?'

'By all means,' he replied, 'very kind.' He was in an expansive mood, created by a combination of relief and brandy.

The driver took the suitcase from the steward and placed it carefully in the boot of the car. They drove round the airport ringroad and out through a checkpoint manned by armed police who saluted as they whisked past. It was evident that guests of the Swiss Banking Federation were not bothered by the inconveniences of passport and Customs checks. Nor was their luggage.

Night was falling as they sped south-east towards the city. The young man switched on a reading light located over the rear seat and handed his guest a single sheet of typed paper. It was a schedule of meetings arranged for the following two days. Frimley-Kimpton was going to be busy, he calculated that it would take all his consummate skill in bullshit to see him through. He was heartened, however, to see that his hosts had arranged a number of cocktail receptions; as both a politician and a public relations man, Frimley-Kimpton was an expert in flannel, which, he had found, was always much better when thoroughly soaked in gin.

The bellboy deposited the suitcase on the rack in his room in the Hotel Baur au Lac in Zurich's Talstrasse. Frimley-Kimpton phoned room service and ordered a bottle of brandy. He felt clammy after his flight and so he showered, though as his clothes were in Dundonald's suitcase he was forced to put back on his damp shirt and creased trousers.

Just after nine o'clock he heard a sharp, military rap on the door. Dundonald strode into the room as if it were a barracks and deposited the third suitcase on the bed. 'All your things are in there, old boy.' He walked over to the large case of money and picked it up. 'No trouble?'

'None, it went like clockwork,' said Frimley-Kimpton smoothly, his terror at the airport conveniently forgotten. 'Did you have a good flight?' Dundonald had flown out earlier in the afternoon.

'No, chaotic as usual. Place was mobbed with bloody tourists. Completely disorganised scrum.'

'Why don't we have dinner?' suggested Frimley-Kimpton. 'In the restaurant.'

'Not a good idea, old boy, can't leave this.' Dundonald

tapped the suitcase. 'Come up to my suite, we can eat there. I'll trot along with the case, you come up when you're ready.' He marched out of the room carrying the suitcase. Frimley-Kimpton changed his clothes and helped himself to another brandy before joining his old acquaintance for dinner.

At precisely ten thirty the following morning Dundonald arrived at the discreet entrance to a large building in a side street off the Neiderdorfstrasse in the centre of Zurich. Although unimposing, the building was the headquarters of one of the most powerful and prosperous banks in Switzerland. Dundonald pushed open the heavy swing doors and walked into a large banking hall where some customers were quietly conducting their business. A dark-suited attendant approached and spoke to the tall Englishman in German.

Dundonald shook his head in annoyance. 'Henry Dundonald to see Dr Stekenmuller,' he said brusquely.

'Ah yes, please follow.' The attendant walked ahead and Dundonald, carrying the smaller suitcase, followed close behind. The previous night he and Frimley-Kimpton had unlocked the cases and extracted the magazines which had been used as packing in the smaller case. Even so, the merchant banker found twenty-one thousand pounds a substantial weight. They entered a small lift of polished steel and ascended. Opposite the lift on the fourth floor was a reception desk, standing next to which was a middle-aged lady.

'Mr Dundonald, good morning. I am Herr Dr Stekenmuller's secretary. Please follow me.' Her English was perfect. She spoke to the porter in rapid German who bowed slightly and re-entered the lift. They walked along a corridor hung with a number of oil paintings in rich gilt frames. The carpet was light cream with a pile inches deep. They passed through the secretary's office and into the office of Herr Dr Franz Stekenmuller, the bank's chief executive.

One entire wall of the large room was a window, covered in cream lace curtains which matched the colour of the carpet.

The other walls were lined in light brown hessian, also hung with a number of paintings. Stekenmuller's massive desk was placed before the window but he led Dundonald to a round conference table in a corner of the room.

When the Swiss banker had received Dundonald's telephone call the previous week he had been happy to rearrange his schedule in order to meet the Englishman. Any director of the great English merchant bank, Smithson-Perez, was important. Stekenmuller had spent some time checking on Dundonald; he had looked him up in the bankers' *Who's Who* and discreetly asked around his international circle of banking friends. Everything he had learned had increased his curiosity as to why the English banker should wish to see him, especially as Dundonald had emphasised the need for privacy as a condition of their meeting. The director's curiosity was not diminished by the fact that the tall, fair Englishman who entered his office was carrying a suitcase. His face, however, remained impassive as they shook hands; he was, after all, a Swiss banker. The secretary brought in a tray bearing a pot of coffee, two cups and a small selection of patisserie. She closed the door silently as she left. Dundonald came straight to the point. 'Herr Dr Stekenmuller,' he said, 'I am here in a private capacity.'

The Swiss banker understood immediately. Under Swiss law the banker-client relationship was sacred and privileged; for the banker to reveal anything about a client's affairs would be a criminal offence, punishable by imprisonment.

'I understand,' he said wisely in his excellent English.

Dundonald continued: 'I represent a group of businessmen who wish to operate a joint account in this bank. The account will be numbered and private. Inside this suitcase is twenty-one thousand pounds sterling which I wish to have checked and converted into dollars at today's rate of exchange. I should add that I am using your bank to transact this business because to use my own bank might involve me in a conflict of interests. I think it's important we bankers maintain our professional integrity, don't you?'

'Of course,' replied Stekenmuller.

He picked up the phone and spoke rapidly in German. Within seconds the door opened and a young man entered. The Swiss banker nodded at the suitcase by the side of his guest's chair, the man picked it up and left quietly. Stekenmuller took a gold pen from an inside pocket. 'I take it,' he said, 'the account is to be operational, you are not using it for investment?'

Dundonald spent the next thirty minutes detailing how the account was to be used and Stekenmuller made occasional notes. Both of them were experienced in the ways of international money management; there was little need for questions. Stekenmuller's curiosity was satisfied. He was unperturbed that the man opposite him had broken the law of his land by smuggling money out of the country and that whatever enterprise was intended, tax would never be paid. There were many men of high estate and public office who had similarly broken the law of England. Many of them had secret accounts in his bank. He was happy to do business with all of them, though sometimes he smiled quietly when he read in his newspaper their speeches, some denouncing capitalism, others advocating patriotism. He considered that the English had developed hypocrisy into a fine art; it had become their strongest characteristic, permeating their politics.

The young man re-entered the room, deposited Dundonald's empty suitcase by his chair and handed the banker an expensive leather folder before leaving. Stekenmuller checked the folder's contents. It contained a bank statement showing the number of the account, its operative code name and the amount deposited, which was fifty-nine thousand dollars. It also contained a number of other papers. He passed the folder to Dundonald who likewise checked its contents. 'Yes, that seems perfectly in order,' he said.

'The code must be used in all communication,' said Stekenmuller. 'All bank statements and other material will be kept here until we receive your instructions. I assume you will keep a separate check on the movement of funds.'

Dundonald nodded.

'I have also made the arrangements you required. That is where you are to go.' He passed Dundonald a sheet of paper. 'Herr Schellenberg expects you this afternoon. You understand that it was necessary for me to tell him who you are?'

Dundonald nodded again.

'Herr Schellenberg will not see anyone unless they are highly recommended,' the banker continued. 'I think you need have no fear that he knows your identity. His security is excellent.' Stekenmuller smiled dryly and then glanced out of the enormous window of the room. 'You have a lovely day, the drive should not take you more than two hours.'

They stood up. 'Thank you, Herr Dr Stekenmuller. I am grateful for your time. I, or one of my colleagues, will be in touch from time to time. Goodbye.'

They shook hands. The secretary accompanied Dundonald back along the opulent corridor and down to the modest entrance of the great bank.

He walked to his hotel through the busy centre of Zurich in the bright sunshine, swinging the empty suitcase. Back in his suite he packed his few clothes into his suitcase, locked it and fitted it snugly into its larger brother. After signing his bill he walked across the elegant foyer to the hotel entrance. Waiting for him, gleaming in the sunshine, was a hired car which his secretary had arranged the previous week. Dundonald signed the papers handed to him by an attractive young woman.

'I'll leave it at the airport tomorrow about noon,' he told

her as he got in and adjusted the driving seat to his long legs.

He drove across the Stauftacher-Quaii and turned east. Quickly he left the city behind and the rolling green hills gave way to dark grey mountains. On his left was the Zurichsee, the long narrow lake which runs south and east from the city. Across the stretch of water the mountains rose sharp and massive, their reflection shimmering in the blue water. The road dipped and twisted along the southern shore of the lake and he made easy progress through the broad valley. A few miles to his right he could see the huge bulk of the Glarner Alps, the patches of snow on their peaks glistening in the bright sun.

After a couple of hours the road swung left, heading north; he followed this for a few miles and then, turning right, crossed a bridge over the Rhine and entered the principality of Liechtenstein. He parked his car in the town square of Vaduz, the capital. Behind the square, hundreds of feet up a vertical rock face, stood the great castle of Franz Josef II. The castle, jutting precariously from the sheer mountainside, dominated the square and the tiny capital, imparting an air of opera to the sunny afternoon scene. But Dundonald knew that the country had more to offer than a picture-postcard scene of peasants dancing and singing in an alpine Ruritania. He was acutely aware that the peculiar combination of Liechtenstein's commercial law, its rules of trusts and trustees, and the privacy of investors made the country a haven for all those who needed to conduct international business away from the gaze of the authorities.

Dundonald consulted the paper in the leather folder that Stekenmuller had given him. He walked across the square and found the address he sought. On a board outside the house in gold lettering were written the names of the anonymous trust companies represented by the office within.

The building was a high narrow house with the upper floors jutting out over the street. Instead of the usual wooden front door, the building had a door of heavy polished steel. Dundonald rang the bell. The voice box at the side squawked in German. 'I am here to see Herr Schellenberg,' he said. 'I have come from Herr Dr Stekenmuller.'

'Enter,' said the box and the heavy steel door swung smoothly open. He walked down a carpeted passage as the door clicked shut behind him. Halfway down the passage was another door of thick and faintly green-tinged glass. Dundonald guessed it was bulletproof. On the other side of the door, through the glass, he could see a very large man who was unlike any solicitor's clerk he had ever seen before. The man pressed a button in the wall and the glass door swung silently open. Dundonald stepped through. Close up the big man looked even more ominous. He was three or four inches taller than the Englishman, with broad shoulders and narrow waist. He had close-cropped hair and was scarred about the eyes. It was fairly obvious that the bulge beneath his left armpit was a holstered gun. Ex-military, thought Dundonald, German army, paratrooper maybe. Just old enough to have seen action in the last couple of years of the war. As tough and deadly as a nickel-plated bullet.

'You have Herr Dr Stekenmuller's note,' the man said in guttural English. It wasn't a question, more a statement.

God help me if I don't, thought Dundonald, as he fished it out of the leather folder the Swiss banker had given him.

The man glanced at it quickly. 'Ja,' he nodded. 'You have a briefcase?'

'No.'

'So, excuse please.' The big man's hands flashed over Dundonald's body, from the nape of his neck to his ankles. Dundonald had undergone body searches in the army but in 1963 it was not a common experience even for international travellers. The man had frisked him before he had time to protest.

'So, it is well.' The man's lips parted but the smile was as warm as an arctic blizzard. He was as unlike the men with whom Dundonald had soldiered as a hawk from sparrows. If they had men like these, how in hell did we ever win? thought the banker as the tall man led him up a flight of stairs.

Like his associate in Zurich, Herr Schellenberg surrounded himself with the good things in life. The furniture in the building was solid and expensive, the walls liberally bedecked with paintings. Dundonald had no artistic appreciation but like all good bankers he could smell money. At least two of the Picassos were originals.

The room into which the armed clerk showed Dundonald was opulently furnished with heavy mid-nineteenth-century furniture. The floor was covered in a vast Chinese carpet, the walls panelled in wood, with subdued lights fitted beneath pelmets. The view from the windows looked out over the square and beyond it to the meadows by the river.

The man who crossed the room to greet him was a surprise to Dundonald. He was short and slim, with dark hair and rimless glasses. Most surprising, he was young, at most in his early thirties. Dundonald found it disconcerting to conduct such important business with someone who was younger than himself. The fact that he stood at least six inches taller than the Liechtenstein lawyer also unsettled him; he was like an aristocratic Afghan hound confronted by a small terrier. However, Schellenberg had been highly recommended by Stekenmuller and it was evident to Dundonald that the young man took security very seriously.

'Close the door, Otto.' The English was perfect. The heavy panelled door closed. On his way through the building Dundonald had been conscious of the noise of typewriters clacking, telephones ringing. With the closing of the door all noise ceased instantly.

'Shall we sit here?' Schellenberg smiled and led the way to some low leather chairs set round a coffee table.

'Now,' he said, 'what can I do for you?'

'I represent a group of businessmen. We have an account in the bank of Herr Dr Stekenmuller. We wish to form a trust company in Liechtenstein which will administer our account and business affairs. The trustees will be Dr Stekenmuller and yourself. That is, if you are agreeable?'

The little lawyer shrugged. 'We shall see, please continue.'

'There will be seven, perhaps eight, beneficiaries of the trust to be administered by you and Dr Stekenmuller. They are, or will be, joint owners of the Swiss account. Instructions on the formation of the trust will come from the bank. You will be required to send monies to a company in Panama which will be involved in real estate development. Communications will come direct to the trust from Panama and will be passed on to the bank. Later on, monies will be transmitted from Panama to you here, and you will pass them to the account in Switzerland. The currency will be, in all cases, United States dollars. We expect the exercise to be very profitable.'

The Liechtenstein lawyer raised his eyebrows in surprise. The Englishman had outlined the classic international trust fund. All its business would be conducted in simple but effective codes. It would be able, by virtue of the three 'locked doors', Panama, Liechtenstein and Switzerland, to evade close inspection by anybody. Any investigative authority would be up against the perfectly legal secrecy laws of all three countries. It was a system operated by multinational corporations in order to evade tax or syphon off funds for the purpose of bribery; it was used by the Mafia and by the political parties of the Western world to raise or hide money, and by the despots of Africa and the Middle East to hide the fortunes they had embezzled out of their countries. It was used by the regimes of Eastern

Europe, and by the intelligence services of the world as a secret source of funds to pay for espionage and assassinations.

Herr Schellenberg was surprised that Dundonald knew so much about the system and how it worked. Most English bankers were not so well informed, and the number of people who knew about international tax avoidance and the use of offshore financial centres was anyway very limited. Those who knew did not broadcast their knowledge; it was not in the best interests of the organisations or people operating the system to give it undue attention. Although Herr Schellenberg himself always acted entirely within the law of Liechtenstein, those who used him were rarely acting within the law of their own countries. Another limiting factor was that those who used the Liechtenstein lawyer and his Swiss and Panamanian colleagues were already rich. His services and the international system of which he was a part was designed to preserve and enhance, hide or redirect existing wealth. Schellenberg was in the business of making the rich richer. After all, he reasoned, it was not he who had invented greed, he merely provided the means by which his clients could satisfy their needs. It was an extenuation echoed internationally by bankers and lawyers, pimps and pushers, and by all the successful procurers in all the professions that served the whores of Mammon.

The lawyer's eyes behind his spectacles were calm as he considered the tall, fair Englishman across the coffee table. 'I have decided,' he said, 'that I would be honoured to institute a trust on your behalf and serve as your trustee with Herr Dr Stekenmuller.'

'I'm very glad to hear it, Herr Schellenberg. I'm sure you will both be excellent trustees. Naturally, you will take your initial fees out of the account in Zurich. If our enterprise is as successful as we anticipate, then the trust will wish to make an *ex gratia* payment to the trustees.'

The Liechtenstein lawyer nodded in satisfaction. For the

following hour the two men quietly discussed the details of the trust and the instructions it would be required to follow. Schellenberg made notes in his neat, precise handwriting, copying details from the papers given to Dundonald by Stekenmuller; at no time did Dundonald commit anything to paper.

It was almost four o'clock before they finished their discussions. Dundonald stood up, towering over the little lawyer, who gathered up his notes from the coffee table and placed them carefully in a manilla file on his desk. 'Everything will be done as you require,' he said. 'I expect to hear shortly.'

The door opened and a secretary stood waiting to show Dundonald out. The two men shook hands, Dundonald followed the girl out of the office, past the paintings and the offices full of sounds of business, past the tough German who bowed briefly, and out into the sunshine of Vaduz.

Suddenly he realised he was hungry, he hadn't eaten since breakfast. He had coffee and pastries seated outside a café in the square and then drove slowly south, out of Vaduz, looking for an hotel. He found one to his liking high in the mountains between Vaduz and Triesen.

After checking into his room he showered and went down for an early dinner. He dined on the terrace of the hotel. From where he sat he had a magnificent view of the great wide valley of the Rhine curving gently away to the south, flat and green between the towering blue-grey bulwarks of the mountains. Here the Rhine was a young river, as straight and narrow as a canal; it cut through the middle of the valley like a glistening ribbon of steel, bending with the curve of the valley away in the distance.

He enjoyed a delicious plate of veal washed down by the local white wine. From the terrace he could see the mountains of Italy, Switzerland, Austria and, far to the north, Germany. As a merchant banker Dundonald appreciated the importance of being at the centre of events; of being in the middle of everything that was happening. On that beautiful May evening he felt a particular satisfaction, dining in the heart of Europe, content in the knowledge of a day's work well done and happy at the prospect of shortly becoming a very rich man. He considered the heart-lifting view of the valley. Its beauty passed him by completely although the thought did occur to him that the terrace would have made a marvellous gun emplacement: with a battery of artillery he reckoned he could have dominated the entire valley.

Jeffrey Frimley-Kimpton returned to London in a happier and more contented frame of mind than when he had left. His two days in Zurich had been a succession of meetings and cocktail parties with members of the banking community. He had listened politely as they explained why they manipulated Europe's currencies. They had listened politely as he explained why the pound needed special help. Neither side really cared what the other had to say but as long as the gin kept coming it was easy enough to stand, glass in hand, and appear interested. Everyone made the best of it as the flashbulbs popped. On the last afternoon of his visit Frimley-Kimpton had been scheduled to meet the president of the Swiss Banking Federation. He had no idea what he could say, how he could fill the hour allotted for their meeting. He was shown into an enormous room, in the centre of which was a dark mahogany table polished to the appearance of glass and capable of seating at least fifty people. He and his host sat at one end of the great table, diminutive figures beneath the paintings of former presidents.

The head of the Banking Federation was a small man with a brown puckered face and white hair. He looked like a gnome. He too wondered how he would fill the hour allotted to the meeting. For two days he had racked his brains trying to guess why Frimley-Kimpton was creating all the fuss. He knew the man was a politician and an opportunist, but he failed to see what the Englishman expected to gain. They talked for some time of the need for greater understanding.

'Frankly, Mr President,' Frimley-Kimpton said casually, 'I think your problem is one of image. If people understood the Swiss banking community more, if you had better public relations, then these problems wouldn't arise.'

The president's eyes gleamed in understanding. So that was it, Frimley-Kimpton had created all the noise and publicity just to obtain the Swiss banks as clients of his public relations business. One had to admire the man's nerve. Well, so be it, he thought, if that's what it takes to keep him quiet then it will be blackmail well spent.

Thus it was that Frimley-Kimpton relaxed in his first-class airline seat, sipping a brandy and soda, content with the world. In his pocket was a document which appointed his company the public relations consultants of the Swiss Banking Federation. The contract was for three years with an annual payment by the Federation of a very large fee. The offer by the little president had come as a complete surprise to Frimley-Kimpton and it was only afterwards that he had realised that, for once, the Swiss had been caught out by their own deviousness. They had thought that all along he had been after their lucrative account for his public relations company.

As the plane started its descent into Heathrow, Frimley-Kimpton felt the peculiar satisfaction of a man who had successfully broken the law and put into motion a chain of events which would ultimately make him very rich. He also felt the surprised delight of someone who had accidentally managed to make a large sum of money on the side, out of a totally unforeseen opportunity.

The thought of something on the side turned his mind to a young woman who lived off Sloane Square who was the proud possessor of a wonderfully formed body and a highly imaginative mind. He resolved to call on her and decided that the little chauffeur, whatever his name was, could drive him there and wait outside the flat for a few hours before driving him home. Do him good, he thought, the damn fellow was bloody surly.

Ashley Brighton manoeuvred the big Bentley past the noisy roadworks and the shouting labourers. It was a bright, sunny Saturday morning; he was dressed in a tweed jacket and a pair of cavalry twill trousers, and having spent an hour working in his office in the City, he was now heading west towards Gloucestershire and the home of Simon Woodberry.

The first part of the journey was tedious. The Bayswater Road was crowded and the A40 round the White City was in a state of chaos as the roadworks for the new fly-over slowed traffic to a crawl. But as London was left behind, the traffic thinned out and the car cruised rapidly past the Art-Deco factories on the Western Avenue, heading for the Chilterns. Brighton drove slowly through Gerrards Cross and Beaconsfield which were busy with Saturday shoppers, before beginning the gentle climb into the heart of the green rolling hills, past West Wycombe and the long hump of Bledlow Ridge. Soon the Bentley was swishing down between the chalk escarpments of the Chilterns' western edge, towards the outskirts of the city of Oxford. Brighton had made good time. He swung north off the Oxford ring road and drove through the small town of Woodstock, skirting the grounds of the great palace of Blenheim, bathed in bright sunshine. A few miles further north he turned left and headed west, into the heart of the Cotswolds.

Brighton was on his way to enlist the services of Simon Woodberry. As they had agreed, all the partners had made discreet enquiries about Woodberry. Everything they had learned supported the belief that he was the right man for the job. Addingham, though, had continued to be nervous. He had phoned Brighton several times. 'I don't like it,' he had rasped into the accountant's ear. 'He wasn't part of the plan, what do we need him for? We can manage perfectly well between ourselves. I don't like bringing in a newcomer. It's dangerous.'

'But we do need him,' Brighton had placated. 'Dundonald got back from Zurich last week and he says there is a lot of work to be done at this end. He's got a number of papers from the bank which are locked in his desk. He will be very relieved to get them out of the house. Edward, we need someone to handle the details.'

'Very well,' the barrister had finally snapped, 'I don't like it, but you're the one who's supposed to be a good judge of people.' His voice was full of scorn.

Brighton was indeed a good judge of character; that was why he had first been sought out by Addingham. Brighton had always had a fascination for figures but he had also developed an interest in the people who made them. He had learned early that the talent to manipulate both figures and people was a rare combination; most accountants he knew rarely raised their heads above the balance sheets and were as sensitive as lead. His perception had brought him to the forefront of his profession: so sure was he in his judgement that for years he had padded along the law's fine line as sure and easy as a fat cat who could count.

He had been surprised to receive Addingham's phone call three months previously, inviting him to dine at his club. The two men had known each other slightly for years but their acquaintance had never gone beyond business.

There had been no preliminaries. Addingham was awkward with small talk. They had sat in a corner of the large dining room and the barrister had immediately launched into a detailed description of his scheme. Addingham was as unemotional as he had been at the meeting in his flat with John Portalier just three days earlier. Brighton had listened quietly, his head bowed, spooning up the hot Brown Windsor soup and eating a slightly stale roll. He had not been even mildly surprised that the renowned Queen's Counsel seated opposite him was advocating a series of serious criminal acts. In Brighton's view, the barrister was proposing a highly attractive business venture, one which would make him even more wealthy. The fact that the enterprise would transgress some tedious and stupid rules was irrelevant, the rules were made to be kept only by the tedious and the stupid. Who better to manipulate the figures than those who balanced them? Who better to break the law than those who made it? It was all perfectly logical. He was halfway through the roast pork before Addingham finished.

'Well?' asked the barrister.

'It will work, undoubtedly.'

'I know it will work,' Addingham said impatiently, 'but who else do I need apart from yourself? And can you find the right company to buy the land?'

Brighton's eyes shone with repressed humour as he considered the tall figure across the table. 'The first one is easy. Most of the people I know would dearly love to be involved in this. However, only one or two will be absolutely right. I would like to think about it, if you don't mind. As for the company, well, that's a different proposition. What makes it more difficult is that it has to be on the verge of insolvency.'

'It's absolutely essential.'

'I don't quite see why.'

'If you were a drug addict who died from an overdose, nobody would be surprised. It would only confirm everybody's predictions. So, if you are a company which is badly managed and you buy a parcel of useless land and thereby become insolvent, then everyone's attention would be directed towards the insolvency, not the land transaction. That would be, after all, the last mistake in a long line of blunders.'

'It's like kicking a man when he's down,' said Brighton casually.

Addingham frowned. 'It's nothing like that at all. You'd be amazed at how much litigation is undertaken because of personal vendetta. If a chairman gets his feathers ruffled, he goes to law. If we sell this land to a healthy company, when the real facts emerge the directors will move heaven and earth to find out how they got caught and who they can sue. It would be even worse if the company crashed solely because of our scheme. We need to find a company with incompetent directors, one which is practically bust.'

Brighton nodded in understanding. 'It might be better if the directors were crooked. The easiest people to cheat are cheats.'

'Exactly,' agreed Addingham. 'Sooner or later the fact that the land is useless will emerge, but with the right company, when the truth comes to light we can close down all our activities and destroy every trace of what led up to the sale of land. There will be no trail to follow; the creditors will blame everything on the directors for incompetence.'

'Very well,' said Brighton. 'It may take some time.'

'Be as quick as you can,' said Addingham. 'And the people – you know what needs to be done, and who we need to do it.'

They had parted on the steps of Addingham's club. The weather was freezing. Sheets of black ice were riveted to the road and St James's was deserted. Addingham hailed a cab which slithered away in the direction of Knightsbridge. Brighton made his way cautiously on foot towards his club where he had arranged to stay the night, a solitary little figure shuffling over the dark shining ice in the gusting winds of Pall Mall. Unlike Addingham, he had no illusions about what constituted kicking a man when he was down. He was going to find a company which was just about flat on its back and then he, Addingham and some others were not only going to kick it, they were going to crush it completely and utterly, under the useless weight of twenty-eight thousand acres of swamp and rock.

Brighton had started his recruitment campaign immediately. He had made a short list of the companies which might be suitable. One was Thornbury Engineering. The more he had thought of it, the more it had become obvious that Thornbury's was ideal. Joe Thornbury was never going to get out of hospital. Richard Thornbury was pliable and the rest of the board counted for nothing. For the past year Brighton had been holding the company together in order to sell his substantial shareholding at a good price.

Considering Thornbury had led Brighton to think of Smithson-Perez and Henry Dundonald. He was perfect, he knew something about Thornbury and he had good contacts in South America. Brighton had phoned Addingham. 'We need a money man. Not only is Henry an excellent banker, his connections in South America are extensive. He can set up the Swiss account and find us the right lawyer in Panama. He also happens to be connected with a company which might be what we are looking for.'

'Which is?' enquired Addingham.

'I'd rather not say at this stage if you don't mind. I need to make some more enquiries.' Brighton did not intend to tell the barrister about Thornbury until he had disposed of the last of his shares. They agreed that Brighton should broach the matter with Dundonald. He called the banker, whom he had known for some years, and invited himself to lunch. They ate in one of the smaller ante-rooms of the bank, which were reserved for signings and intimate lunches. Brighton explained the plan to Dundonald, pausing only when a white-gloved waiter discreetly entered to serve them or refill their wine glasses. When Brighton finished the banker leaned back in his chair and eyed his guest speculatively.

'I take it you want me to join?'

'Yes.'

'As an equal partner?'

'Of course.'

'I shall be expected to do a considerable amount of running around and organising.'

'I know, but all shares will be equal,' said Brighton evenly.

Dundonald stared at a portrait of his maternal grandfather on the far wall. 'Very well,' he said after a few seconds, 'I'm happy to join. Actually,' he leaned forward, 'it's a bloody good idea.'

The waiter, in his black tails, sidled in. He poured two liberal glasses of port and left the decanter on the table. They both accepted a cigar, which he clipped. 'Look here,' said Dundonald, when the waiter had gone, 'I know someone has to be left holding the baby but I don't want any friends of mine to be caught.'

'Of course not,' Brighton replied. 'I think you'll find that there will be a queue of people wanting to get on the bandwagon, you can take your pick.'

'You think so?'

'I share Addingham's opinion,' Brighton continued. 'These property developers are nowhere near as talented as they think. They are immature and greedy, and one day there is going to be an almighty crash. You'll find no shortage of young bucks eager to lend the money.' He laughed quietly. 'If you play your cards right, old boy, the bank can make some money as well. You could come out of this thing smelling of roses.'

'That thought had not escaped me,' murmured the banker.

A few days later Brighton had taken Dundonald to meet Addingham in a luncheon club just off Chancery Lane, where they discussed the part the banker would play in the scheme. Addingham had been delighted with Brighton's choice, though his next recommendation did not please the barrister nearly as much.

'But why do we need him? The man is as artful as a monkey. He sleeps with half the women in London. What possible use can he be to us?'

'I've known Frimley-Kimpton for years. He isn't as devious as you believe, and he can keep his mouth shut. He's extremely well-connected. As an MP he gets around a lot. Anything that we wanted he could get, anybody we wished to influence, Jeffrey could do it. He's more powerful than people realise. If things were to go wrong he might be vital, he could get to the right people and persuade them to take the pressure off.'

It was a good argument. If things went wrong, Frimley-Kimpton knew enough about the private lives of powerful people possibly to forestall any prosecution of the conspirators. Of course the knowledge of what they had done would become known and their careers would be ruined, but the Honourable Member might be able to prevent criminal prosecution and publicity in the newspapers.

Brighton and Dundonald had met Frimley-Kimpton in the bar of the House of Commons. Dundonald had explained the plan while Brighton had listened and looked on; he had seen the hard gleam appear in Frimley-Kimpton's eyes and knew instantly that he would be a willing partner. Afterwards, as they were leaving the bar, Oliver Blackmore had walked past them. The three nodded briefly to the bulky solicitor.

'You know Blackmore then?' asked the elated Frimley-Kimpton. The others replied that they knew him slightly. 'You know he's working with Addingham on the Swindon case. Apparently it's very important, it comes to trial in the next few days. If they win it will do them both a lot of good.'

They had taken their leave of Frimley-Kimpton, promising to contact him shortly. In the taxi on his way home, Brighton had begun to think about Blackmore. A couple of days later he phoned Addingham.

'Blackmore?' said the barrister in surprise. 'I've never thought about it. Certainly he's the most competent man I've met in a long time. But why do we need him?'

'He completes the team, Edward. With him we have a management structure. You are the ideas man, the creative element, I'm the people man, and figures of course, Henry is the money man, the banker, Jeffrey is the one who can influence people and provide the public relations, smooth things out. But we need a general manager, someone who can communicate with all of us, someone who can take hard decisions if necessary. I hear Blackmore is very tough.'

Addingham saw the sense of it. Blackmore was as hard as granite. He would be the bedrock of the enterprise, he could hold the others together if the going got tough.

'I think you ought to raise it with him,' Brighton continued, 'you know him best.'

He did, the next day. They had been working in Addingham's chambers for a couple of hours, making the final preparations for the trial of Alan Swindon. When they had finished, Addingham suggested a drink. As he sat on the Chesterfield, Blackmore noticed that the barrister was edgy. Addingham seated himself at the other end of the large sofa and straightaway launched into his plan. The pale blue eyes beneath the heavy brows remained fixed on Addingham as the details were unfolded.

'And that's it?' asked Blackmore.

'All of it.' Addingham looked at his companion enquiringly.

Blackmore stood up abruptly and drained his whisky glass. The sudden, swift movement startled Addingham. He strode to Addingham's desk, deposited his glass, retrieved his heavy black overcoat from the back of a chair and picked up his bulging briefcase.

'I'm due at the House in fifteen minutes,' he announced. His bulky body towered over the seated barrister. 'Call

Brighton and tell him we want a shortlist of companies by Friday. If I know Brighton, he has probably found what we are looking for already. Tell him we must have a meeting in two weeks' time, at which we will identify and discuss the company we need to use. There's no point in hanging around, we had better get on with it.' He opened the door of Addingham's room. 'Thanks for the drink, I'll see you in court.' The door crashed shut behind him.

Brighton smiled to himself as he recalled Addingham's phone call. He had sensed Blackmore's impatience behind the barrister's request for the name of the company. Blackmore was a wise choice. He was not an ordinary type of solicitor. Blackmore was quite prepared to tell a famous Queen's Counsel what to do. None of them was ordinary, Brighton mused as he drove through the market square of Stow-on-the-Wold. That's why they were together, involved in this enterprise. It was not an undertaking for ordinary men.

About ten miles north-west of Stow, Brighton turned off the road and drove through a large, ornamental gateway onto a gravel drive which led to Woodberry's rambling seventeenth-century manor house. The parkland through which he drove was scattered with trees and great rhododendron bushes. The branches of the horse chestnuts lining the drive were heavy with red and white flowers standing straight like candles. He rounded a curve in the drive and came in sight of the beautiful house. He stopped opposite the front porch and got out. From somewhere off to the right he could hear the sound of children's voices; he walked along the front of the house towards the sound, his footsteps crunching on the gravel. The manor house had two storeys and a profusion of square leaded windows. Strands of wistaria, deep blue against the pale grey stone, clung to the walls. In front of him, at the far edge of the front drive, was a low balustrade of Portland stone, beyond which a beautiful lawn fell away in a gentle slope, levelling off into a broad green carpet which swept round the side and rear of the house. Playing croquet on the lawn were four children; seated nearby, a man was reading a copy of *The Times*. One of the children noticed Brighton standing beyond the low balustrade and spoke to the man.

'Brighton, my dear chap.' Woodberry stood up. 'Forgive me, I didn't hear you arrive.' He padded across the lawn and up the slope to his visitor as the children, leaning on their croquet mallets, eyed the newcomer. Simon Woodberry was in his early forties. He had a wide, weatherbeaten face and thick dark hair flecked with grey. He was slightly under average height although taller than his visitor. He shook Brighton warmly by the hand; it was the hardened handshake of a man who spent most of his time riding and shooting and very little seated behind a desk.

'It's good to see you, let's have a drink.' He led the way through a pair of French windows into an oak-beamed drawing room. He poured two large gins and tonic which they took outside and drank sitting on a wooden bench, watching the children continue their game.

Felicity Woodberry joined them. She was taller than her husband and, like his, her face was weatherbeaten. She was wearing riding breeches which served to emphasise her broadly spread rump, the result not only of bearing children, but of her passion for horse riding. Felicity liked to chatter; they sat with their faces turned towards the sun, talking of old friends and old times, until lunch was served. The children came indoors and were introduced to Brighton before they were hustled away by a maid to eat in the kitchen. The three adults ate in the dining room. After lunch Woodberry suggested a walk over the estate. He led Brighton down a long passage to the gun room, where he found a pair of Wellingtons which came somewhere near to fitting his guest's small feet.

Woodberry took a double-barrelled Purdy from the glass

gun cabinet. 'Would you like a gun?' he asked. 'We might see a few rabbits.'

Brighton declined. Woodberry took a handful of cartridges from a drawer, broke the gun and led the way outside through a side door. They crossed the lawn and took a path which climbed gently up a small ridge at the rear of the house. From the top they could see a series of rolling meadows and cultivated fields, broken up by grey stone walls. A mile to their left was a smooth steep hill, a clump of oaks standing on its summit.

'That's Shearing Hill,' said Woodberry. They started walking at a gentle pace towards the hill. As they walked, Brighton introduced the purpose of his visit. He told Woodberry of the phone call he had received from Addingham and the dinner at his club. He began to describe the scheme in great detail. He took his time, matching the tempo of his delivery to their gentle pace. A rabbit scampered out of the edge of a field but was gone before Woodberry had time to lock the shotgun. They stopped at a gate set in a stone wall from which a path led upwards to the clump of oaks on the hill-top. Woodberry leaned an elbow on the gate and listened quietly as Brighton continued with his explanation.

'I see,' he said when Brighton had finished. He said no more but unchained the gate and pushed it open. They walked slowly up the hill in silence, Woodberry deep in thought, his hands in his jacket pockets, the broken gun under his arm. Brighton was grateful for the silence, his breath came in short fighting rasps as he plodded up the steep slope. They reached the top and he sank exhausted onto a fallen log at the edge of a small copse. It was shady and cool and after a few minutes he took out a cigarette. Woodberry was standing with one foot on the log, slowly filling his pipe. He jerked his chin towards the north-west.

'The Malverns,' he said.

Brighton could see the purple and blue hills on the distant

horizon. For a few minutes they smoked in silence, contemplating the view.

'Two million pounds, you say.'

'More,' Brighton replied.

Woodberry turned and surveyed his property. The manor house nestled in a dip in the Wolds, with the park, dotted with lindens and horse chestnuts, spreading out before it; the fields and meadows were traversed by grey stone walls and there were sheep in the pastures beyond the road. After a while he sat down on the log next to Brighton. He took his pipe from his mouth and began prodding the tobacco in the bowl. He looked at his companion.

'It's illegal though, isn't it? I mean, what you and the others are proposing to do, have already done, it's criminal?'

'Oh come on, old boy,' Brighton said gently. 'It's a commercial proposition. Robbing banks is criminal, hitting an old lady over the head with a brick and stealing her handbag is criminal. Everything else is just business.'

'You think so?'

'Of course, don't you? Look, we need you. You complete the team. We need a company secretary and you are exactly right for the job.'

'There are plenty of others who would be equally good,' said Woodberry.

'But we know you, and you know us, or some of us.' Brighton followed his companion's gaze over the countryside. 'You can own a lot more of this with two million pounds.'

Woodberry glanced at him sharply. The accountant had read his thoughts easily. He went back to tampering with his pipe. Finally he looked at Brighton and his broad face broke into a grin.

'Why not?' he said. 'It's foolproof, as far as I can see, and if you're involved then it has to be pretty safe.'

He stood up slowly, locked the shotgun and fired at the

rooks which were sitting on the highest branches of the oaks. Two of them fell to the ground, one still flickering its wings; Woodberry picked it up and snapped its neck. As they walked down the hill and over the rest of the estate, Brighton answered his friend's questions about the details of the scheme and the part he would be expected to play. Back at the house they went into the study and continued their conversation over large whiskies.

Felicity broke them up at about six o'clock. 'Come on, you two,' she commanded, 'you can't talk business all night. I want some company.' They moved into the drawing room and sat chattering easily. It was after eight when Brighton finally left.

'I'll phone you at the beginning of the week,' he said to Woodberry who was leaning against the Bentley, his face framed in the open window. 'We shall meet shortly and I'll introduce you to the others.'

Brighton drove south, turning east onto the A40 at Burford. It had been a good day. Simon Woodberry was a valuable addition to the group; Addingham's fears were groundless.

Although the soles of his feet were burning from the rubbing they had undergone inside the borrowed Wellingtons, Brighton felt a sense of physical wellbeing. The sunshine of the day was gone and the evening sky had turned a shiny, metallic grey. As he drove towards London and home, Brighton noticed that the vivid yellow of the fields of rape was reflected in the sky like the glow of a giant buttercup beneath the grey chin of dusk.

Chapter Five

Johnny Portalier turned up the collar of his coat and emerged from the entrance to Addingham's mansion block. Flurries of snow whirled and jigged in the light of the street lamps as he hurried to his hotel. Retrieving his key from reception, he walked upstairs to the residents' lounge. It was warm and well lit; he sank into a chintz-covered armchair, lit a cigarette and ordered coffee and a small brandy. The Swiss doctors had warned him off hard liquor but tonight was special. Johnny was a shipwreck who had caught sight of the lifeboat and jubilation burned inside him like the lights of land. The journey to blizzard beleaguered Britain had been worth it; now he felt that everything might come right.

New York was as cold as London, the airport at La Guardia was battered by showers of snow. Johnny phoned Miami from his room at the Plaza and the following afternoon a sleek black Cadillac, gleaming in the warm sunshine, was at Miami airport to whisk him eastwards to Miami Beach.

The Bermuda Bay Hotel was a giant block of white concrete, similar to the other prefabricated towers which, surrounded by blue swimming pools, dotted the sun-soaked strip of beach for miles. The hotel belonged to Victor Maggiore who owned and controlled a great number of properties and business enterprises in Florida. Victor was one of the most powerful of the organisation's elder statesmen and, as befitted the status of a Mafia chieftain, he lived in fortified splendour in the hotel's enormous penthouse.

A private elevator shot Johnny and his driver up to the penthouse. A beautiful young woman greeted him and fixed him a drink, which he sipped slowly as he waited in the reception lounge. After a few minutes the door to the study opened and Victor appeared. 'Johnny,' he said, 'how are you? It's great to see you. Gee, you're looking great. Just look at this guy, doesn't he look good?' He was at his most effusive, which meant he had no time to talk. He was an elderly man of medium height, dark and heavy, and slightly stooped. His hard brown eyes were bright as he grabbed Johnny's hand and steered him into a corner of the room. 'Look,' he said quietly. 'It's great to see you. We'll talk real soon. Right now I've got some guys in from Texas.' He jerked his head in the direction of the open study door. 'It's important business. Why don't you go to your room, freshen up, rest, and we'll get together real soon, eh? I'll send someone down, OK?'

Johnny smiled sweetly and said he understood. Whatever business preoccupied Maggiore, it was obviously important, the penthouse was full of silent, unsmiling bodyguards. What Johnny had to say could wait, at least for a while.

He was showering in his room when she arrived. She must have had a pass key, for suddenly she was leaning against the open door of the bathroom. 'Hi,' she said. 'I'm Vicky.' She was no more than sixteen, with freckles on her nose and long flaxen hair. She was wearing white tennis shorts and her legs were long and tanned. She was staring at the naked Portalier. Suddenly she smiled at him, shrugged off her blouse, wriggled out of her shorts, and stepped into the shower. Her naked body was full and firm against Portalier's skin. Her slim, quick hands soaped his body, working the lather over his back and belly and then around his loins. His body jerked into life. She caressed him slowly as she washed the soap away and then gently took his stiffened member into her mouth. The hot water streamed down his back, and the cubicle was filled with steam. The girl's head, level with his belly, moved rhythmically, her long nails delicately teasing his scrotum and her soft mouth sucking long and lovingly on his penis. She was kneeling before him on one knee, her wet hair hanging over her shoulders in braids of pale yellow, her tanned body glistening under the streams of water. The steam and the surging in his belly made him fight for breath. With one hand he steadied himself against the tiled wall of the shower, while with the other he held the girl's head, urging her on in her work. He came in a rush, and in a series of growling, subdued grunts. Then, as the hot burning liquid pumped from between his legs, the pain came. A vice of breathless agony began to crush the walls of his chest as his left arm turned numb. He staggered and fell, sliding down the shower wall onto the girl. His eyes were bulging with the agony, his mouth opening and closing like a fish's. The girl struggled out from beneath him. Her blue eyes opened wide in horror when she saw his ashen face.

'Oh God,' she whispered. 'Oh Jesus, I gotta get out of here.'

Portalier weakly caught her leg. 'Help me,' he croaked, his breath coming in short rasps. 'Pills. The dresser.' The pain across his chest was agonising.

The girl kicked out at him and he let go. She turned and scampered out of the shower on all fours, her slim buttocks disappearing out of sight. Slowly, he crawled out after her; by the time he reached the bathroom door she had gone. He inched across the bedroom floor and after an eternity reached the box of tablets. He swallowed two of them and leant his back against the bed, panting. Gradually, the pain subsided. He eased himself onto the bed and after a while he fell asleep. The ringing of the telephone woke him; it was one of Maggiore's aides. Johnny sat up carefully, he was shaking and his legs felt weak but the pain had eased and his breathing was steadier. For a long time he sat on the edge of the bed, waiting for the shakes to subside. It was his second serious attack; the girl had almost sucked the life out of him. He'd have to take things easily, he thought, if he was going to get through the next few months.

He returned to the still running shower, then dressed slowly and rode the elevator to the penthouse. Victor was waiting in the study. The curtains were undrawn, the glass sliding doors open to the night air and the roof garden. Below them glittered Miami Beach, the rear lights of the cars making red, staccato patterns along the straight lines of the strip. Out in the blackness of the ocean, ships' lights flickered like diamonds on midnight cloth. The balmy night was filled with the scent of flowers and the sea. Victor was seated on a long sofa; Johnny took an armchair opposite. Various aides of Victor's were clearing the room and rearranging the furniture. One man was carrying a large white placard on which was drawn a street plan; lines had been drawn from a square in the middle of a road to locations around it. The plan meant nothing to Johnny. The man spoke in rapid Italian to Victor, who then turned to his guest.

'Johnny, we went on so long, you know how it is. Jeez, you look great. Europe was good, eh?' He leaned forward conspiratorially and touched Portalier's knee. The backs of his hands were freckled with dark-brown liver spots. 'How was the one I sent you? Good, eh?'

The memory of the seizure made Johnny feel sick. He smiled through gritted teeth. 'Absolutely marvellous, Victor.' He hoped his voice held sufficient enthusiasm.

Maggiore nodded and leaned back. 'OK Johnny, what's on your mind, what can I do for you?'

Portalier took a deep breath. 'Victor, I want to set up another bank on Pinta Leone.'

'Why? What's wrong with the one we got already?' The old man looked cautious.

'Nothing, but I want to sell some land and I need a bank to help me do it. I can't use First National for obvious reasons so I need a new one. Anyway, another bank on the island would be very useful to you.' Johnny was following word for word the story Addingham had told him to tell; Maggiore's responses were exactly as the barrister had predicted.

'How?' The question was tinged with suspicion.

'Because then you can justify the amount of money First National is moving to Switzerland. I know that right now no one is asking questions, but if the authorities ever changed the rules, First National would be in the clear.'

Maggiore's brows were furrowed as Johnny continued. 'If First National lends money to my new bank it can charge very high interest. The interest my bank pays will be the money First National moves to Switzerland. So First National will appear to earn its money legitimately.'

'So what do you get out of all this?'

It was as if Addingham had written the script. 'Victor, I am president of First National so I am as keen as you to protect our interests. However, on my own account I shall have a bank which will have considerable funds.' He waited for Maggiore's reaction.

'Johnny, you're a good guy and we've been together a lot of years but I don't know about lending you millions of dollars for a land deal. I'd have to think about it.'

Johnny looked concerned. 'Victor, I haven't explained myself properly. You don't actually lend any money at all. It's all on paper. First National appears to loan my bank say two hundred million. We appear to pay interest on the loan and First National appears to earn its money legitimately. There's no money involved at all.'

Victor leaned back and looked at his visitor speculatively. After a few moments he nodded. It was a good idea, it moved the bank one step further away from the immediate gaze of the authorities. 'OK, Johnny,' he said softly.

'It's a good idea. What the hell, it's just a few loan documents, we can get it organised pretty quick, no problem.'

'Victor, that's marvellous.' Portalier's voice held just the right tone of satisfaction. 'There is something else. I've thought of an idea I think you might quite like.' Johnny was leading into the second act of the play. 'In order to handle the sale of my land, I need to form a company in Panama. Naturally, it will have no assets,' he shrugged, 'but I want it to appear established.'

Maggiore smiled. 'Who the hell is going to trade with a two-bit company in Panama?'

'Quite,' Johnny agreed. 'On the other hand, if the company was worth a few million it would be quite a different matter. Plenty of people would be willing to do business, lend money, provide guarantees and so on.'

'So OK, find a few million and you'll have yourself a good business.' The old man continued to smile.

Portalier leaned forward towards him. 'I don't need to do that, Victor. I've got a way of making a company that was formed for two hundred dollars yesterday, appear worth ten million today.'

The smile vanished from Maggiore's face. 'How?'

'By pumping up the assets,' said Johnny coolly. 'Firstly, I can have the date of formation backdated, any pliable lawyer or accountant can arrange that.'

'Yea, yea, but how are you going to get the money?'

'In America, bond and share certificates are not registered in a central registry, which means that possession is usually sufficient proof of ownership. Just like money. And like money, the only way to know that the possessor is not the owner is to have a note of the serial numbers of stolen share certificates.'

'So?'

'Some people in this organisation make a living by selling stolen or forged stock certificates. What you call "bad paper". At any one time you probably have millions of dollars' worth of valueless and illegal stock certificates somewhere around. What I propose is to borrow those certificates and have my company's books inspected by a firm of accountants. The books will have been so arranged that the company will seem to have traded very profitably and to have amassed the certificates we appear to own. The ones borrowed from you.'

Maggiore was staring at Johnny, a look of concentration on his face. His usually agile mind was numbed. It was too simple, nothing that simple could work. 'It won't work,' he grunted.

Johnny was amused to see the conflicting emotions cross the old man's face. 'Why not?'

'The accountants will pick it up.'

Johnny smiled. 'Come on, Victor. Accountants have the mentality of children at a circus, they are beguiled by things being balanced. The company's books will show we own a few million in shares and bonds, we open the safe and,' he paused, 'there they are. They will be perfectly satisfied.'

'But they'll report details of the stock certificates.'

'Only for a report which they give to the company. And which is confidential.'

He waited for the significance of his suggestion to sink in. It didn't take long. Maggiore knew a good thing when he heard it; Portalier's scheme opened the doors to fraud on a massive scale. The Mafia boss could form countless companies, recycling in every case the same portfolio of stolen and forged shares. Those companies could then borrow large sums against the non-existent assets, and having borrowed, disappear completely. 'It might work.' He did not wish to appear over eager.

'Why don't we try it out, Victor? If you send a man down to Panama when I'm ready he need only be there for a couple of days, maybe only for a few hours. What have we got to lose? If it works, you might be able to do the same thing here.' Johnny smiled. He knew Victor had already seen the possibilities, the avarice in the old man's eyes glittered like ice.

'OK, Johnny. We'll give it a try. It seems like maybe a good idea. If you can work it in Panama, we'll try it someplace else.'

They talked for another few minutes about the details of the scheme and the new bank in Pinta Leone. Johnny stood up to leave. They shook hands and Victor grasped Portalier's arm warmly as they walked to the door.

'Good seeing you, Johnny, and great to hear your ideas. Stay in touch. I'll get things moving this end.'

Johnny felt his heart racing as he returned to his room. He had been performing for two hours, remembering his lines and playing to his audience. It was amazing how well it had gone and uncanny how accurate Addingham's prediction had been. He took two more of his pills and lay on the bed, fully dressed. He dozed fitfully but he made no attempt to turn off any of the room lights. He was frightened that if the darkness came it might last for ever.

The lights in Victor Maggiore's bedroom also burned all night. The old man lay between the silk sheets staring at the ceiling. The meeting he had held in the afternoon had been one of great significance. It was the most important assignment his organisation had ever been given and, if properly executed, would change the history of the world. Yet it was his conversation with John Portalier which concerned him most. Portalier he knew was a jackal. It was true that he had been educated among those with a better pedigree, but he remained a jackal nevertheless. And it was because he was a jackal that Maggiore employed him, and, within certain limits, relied on him. But now, something was wrong. Portalier had come up with two brilliant schemes; schemes which would greatly enrich Maggiore and his organisation. Yet Portalier wanted nothing for his idea, merely the chance of trying it out. The plan to inflate companies' assets by using stolen bonds could reap millions, yet the jackal had asked for nothing; no percentage, no piece of the action. That worried the old man. He guessed that someone was behind Portalier; the fat black man wasn't clever enough to think up those ideas by himself. And, he asked himself, what did Portalier stand to gain from his land deal? The only land that Portalier owned was a worthless strip of swamp in the north of the island. No one could sell that. There were other things too. Portalier had lost weight yet looked ill; he hadn't had a drink all evening and when asked about the girl he had looked sick. It was all wrong, and Maggiore, the Mafioso chief, had only survived numerous attempts on his life and liberty because he had a refined instinct which told him when things were wrong.

As the sun rose out of the sea and the eastern sky turned bright pink, Maggiore decided to go along with Johnny's plans at least for the time being. But he also decided to have a close watch kept on John Portalier and to have enquiries made concerning his recent activities in Europe.

They met at Blackmore's. They had agreed that Woodberry should be introduced formally to the partnership, and all of them except Addingham were anxious that he should take over his role as quickly as possible. Addingham was still fretful about bringing in a stranger and, unlike the others who were thankful to pass over incriminating documents, hated the idea of handing over his papers. Blackmore had spoken forcibly to him. 'We're agreed, Edward, and that's that. It's safer if Simon Woodberry has everything. Suppose something happened to you? If your papers fell into the wrong hands it would be mighty awkward for the rest of us.'

Reluctantly Addingham had agreed.

They decided to meet at midday; Blackmore was very busy, it was impossible for him to get away from the House of Commons in the evenings. The others had been happy to travel to his home in Lord North Street. It was a warm day in early June, the sky was bright and hazy with the heat and the streets were full of the colour of girls' dresses.

Seated on the window-seat of the first-floor drawing room, Jeffrey Frimley-Kimpton was idly watching two girls with bare legs and bright blouses stretched tightly over their breasts saunter along the warm pavements. He was nursing a large gin and tonic. He had been introduced to Woodberry and like everyone else had been impressed. The man looked like a gentleman farmer but he had a lawyer's mind and it was evident that he understood the finer details of the plan.

The others were standing in the middle of the large rectangular room, talking. They were waiting for Henry Dundonald to arrive. Halfway along the left-hand wall was a stairwell descending to the ground floor. Large double doors divided the room from a small office which was directly above the study on the ground floor. Oliver Blackmore's secretary, a tall good-looking red-head who wore expensive jewellery, usually worked in the office though on that particular morning she was working in Blackmore's office in the House of Commons. Joanna Blackmore had decorated and furnished the drawing room with immaculate taste; every item of furniture and every painting fitted perfectly; it was a room in which the famous and powerful were frequently entertained.

A phone rang and Blackmore disappeared into the small office. He emerged a few moments later. 'That was Henry,' he said. 'I'm afraid he's going to be late.'

Addingham was clearly annoyed. Dundonald was due to report on his trip to Switzerland. 'Why?' he asked peevishly.

'He had to attend a signing. A large loan apparently. I'm sure he won't be too long.' He turned to Woodberry. 'Another drink?' Blackmore took his glass and moved away to a drinks cabinet.

Woodberry turned to Addingham. 'Pleasant room.'

'One or two reasonable paintings,' the barrister replied haughtily.

Standing a few feet away, Ashley Brighton was quietly amused by the sight of the thin, pale-faced barrister stooping slightly to conduct an icily polite conversation with the solidly-built landowner whose weatherbeaten face came only to the level of the barrister's scrawny neck. Brighton thought it unlikely that his friend would recognise Addingham's coldness for what it was. Woodberry was not a man sensitive to atmosphere. Brighton moved closer as Oliver Blackmore returned with Woodberry's drink. To Addingham he said, 'You will be interested to know that Simon thinks he knows the right man to replace Thornbury's accountant.'

'With respect, I'm not sure you could know what kind of man we require.' Addingham was aloof.

'I think I know precisely,' replied Woodberry in an even tone.

Brighton caught the glance that Addingham shot Blackmore. 'Tell us then,' said Blackmore.

'His name is George Stansgate. I knew him at school. Complete idiot. Man's a fat pompous buffoon, can't ride, can't shoot, can't do anything as far as I can see. He was a captain in the pay corps during the war.' He said it with derision; like the others, Woodberry had had a good war. 'My wife knew his wife before they married. After he got married he went out to Africa. Tried a few things and failed at them although he did manage to qualify as an accountant out there. A few years ago he came back and tried to set up his own firm. He hasn't made a go of it, so for the past couple of years he's been touching everyone he knows, including me, for a job.'

Brighton noticed that throughout Woodberry's description, Addingham had been staring directly at Blackmore. He watched the bulky solicitor raise his eyebrows and nod, almost imperceptibly.

'I must admit that from your description he sounds interesting,' Addingham conceded coldly.

'I'm glad you think so, Edward,' said Brighton. 'Richard Thornbury and I have arranged to interview him next week.'

'Excellent,' said Blackmore.

'But you will keep us informed, you won't make a decision without talking to me first?' Addingham was anxious.

'Of course not.' Brighton was conscious that Addingham was beginning to accept Woodberry and it seemed to be an appropriate moment for him to say: 'Perhaps we could pass our files to Simon now, while we are waiting for Dundonald to arrive.' A pained expression crossed Addingham's face. He glanced angrily at Brighton. Woodberry looked expectant. The barrister took a manilla file stuffed with papers and documents from his briefcase. The papers were covered in his thin spidery handwriting, all the notes and plans he had made since the scheme had first struck him. He handed the file to Woodberry with the same expression that the generals wore at the surrender of Singapore.

'I sincerely trust you won't fall off your horse and let these get into the wrong hands,' he said.

Woodberry laughed loudly at the notion of either possibility. 'These papers will be kept where no one will find them. Ever.' He glanced through the file. It contained a number of legal documents. 'What are these?' he asked.

Addingham took them from him. 'Portalier's rights to the title of his land,' he said. The others gathered round. Addingham selected a document. It was entitled 'A Grant of Land by His Gracious Majesty King Louis XVI. To the Family Portalier'. 'This,' he announced as if he were in court, 'is a copy of the original French title deed which was held by Portalier. This,' he held up another document, 'is a copy of an affidavit signed by one of the most respected translation agencies in America that it is a true copy and translation.' The partners peered closely at the first document. In the second paragraph it read: 'A grant of land on the north-east shore of Pinta Leone, which shall be one league inland and five leagues long, from Pinta de Fletche to the village of Cabella.'

'How long is a league?' asked Frimley-Kimpton who had joined the group from his seat by the window.

'Three miles,' replied Woodberry.

'Forty-five square miles,' said Brighton. 'That's an awful lot of acres, isn't it?'

'Six hundred and forty in a square mile,' said Woodberry promptly, 'so that is . . .' He took a slim, gold pencil and a small notebook from his breast pocket and made some calculations. 'Twenty-eight thousand, eight hundred acres.'

'Quite right,' murmured Addingham.

'You say that development land out there sells for seventeen hundred and fifty dollars an acre?' Blackmore asked Addingham.

'That would be,' Woodberry continued his calculations, 'over fifty million dollars.' He frowned at the figures in his notebook.

'At today's rate of exchange,' Addingham took up the conversation, 'that's exactly eighteen million pounds.'

Even after expenses, after paying the lawyers in Liechtenstein and Panama, they each stood to make well over two million pounds. The room was quiet as they contemplated their fortunes. They heard the front doorbell and the housekeeper ascend from the basement kitchen to admit Henry Dundonald.

'Sorry I'm late,' he said as he reached the top of the stairs and walked into the room. Blackmore poured a drink as Brighton took him to meet Simon Woodberry. 'You know each other, of course,' he said as they shook hands.

'Last year, Rannoch Moor,' said Dundonald. 'Glad to have you with us. I have a number of papers you should have.' He took a folder out of the slim pigskin attaché case he was carrying. 'They mainly refer to my trip to Liechtenstein.'

'I think you ought to bring us up to date on your meeting there,' said Addingham.

'Of course,' Dundonald replied, 'but before I do I must tell you that it's unlikely that I can go to Panama in the next few weeks.' He took a glass from Blackmore. 'Thank you.'

'For God's sake, why not?' Addingham's reaction was instant. 'This really is too bad. You can't decide not to go, just like that. We have a plan, Henry, you must stick to it.' Two bright spots of colour had appeared on his cheekbones.

Dundonald was offended by the barrister's tone; his neck stiffened and the colour rushed to his slightly protruding ears. 'I really cannot allow you to adopt that tone with me. I am not a young subaltern up before the CO. I am a director of the bank and I have certain obligations.'

'Nevertheless –'

'Perhaps,' Ashley Brighton the peacemaker interrupted, 'we could ask Henry what has happened to change the plan.'

'The loan we signed this morning is for a chemical plant in Saudi Arabia and is one of the largest we have ever negotiated. I shall have to spend some time in Saudi, starting next week.'

'You could fit in a couple of days in Panama, between trips,' stated Addingham.

'They happen to be on opposite sides of the globe, old boy. If I was seen there, questions might be asked. I am rather well known in my profession, you know. It's quite possible I would be seen. It's all very well going to Switzerland. I'm a banker, I go there often and men like Stekenmuller and Schellenberg are,' he paused, 'European. Utterly reliable. It may be different in Panama.'

Blackmore interrupted. 'The lawyer there, what's his name?'

'Max Gonzales.'

'Are you saying he isn't reliable?'

'He's reputed to be very reliable. Associate banks of Smithson-Perez all over South American have used him for transactions that needed to be handled . . . delicately. However, I don't want to be seen in Panama when I should be in Saudi. It might draw attention to all of us. Also, I don't want Gonzales to know who I am and my connection with the bank. All he knows so far is that someone in England has been recommended to him. I telexed him a couple of weeks ago using a code name, asking if he would be prepared to do some work for a trust company in Liechtenstein. He replied saying he would. I propose that Simon goes in my place.'

'With respect to Woodberry, I hardly think he's qualified,' said Addingham.

'Why not?' responded Dundonald. 'He can handle it as well as I can. It would only take a couple of hours for me to brief him. There's nothing terribly complicated in what Gonzales has to do.'

They debated the matter for a few minutes and finally Addingham's objections began to fade. Aside from the fact that it was not part of his original plan, he could think of no other reason why Woodberry should not go to Panama in place of Dundonald. 'Very well,' he said finally. 'Perhaps you can make arrangements to fly out as soon as possible, after you've been briefed. Now,' he turned to Dundonald, 'perhaps Henry will bring us up to date on his trip to Switzerland. Before he begins though, I think we ought to congratulate Jeffrey on successfully getting the money out to Zurich.'

There was a subdued chorus of 'Hear hear' and 'Well done'. Frimley-Kimpton smiled benignly at the quiet applause. It was an appropriate moment for Blackmore to replenish their drinks; only Addingham shook his head in refusal.

Dundonald quickly and lucidly described the details and outcome of his meetings with the banker in Zurich and the lawyer in Liechtenstein. The others listened attentively.

'Very well,' said Addingham when he had finished, 'I think we are up to date on the current position. Certainly, things are beginning to happen and there will be a lot to do in the next few weeks. I suggest we talk to each other frequently and I will convene the next meeting when appropriate. I'm delighted that everything has gone so smoothly.'

'Actually,' responded Dundonald, 'I did have one problem.' The attention of everyone was instantly riveted on him.

'What?' Blackmore's voice was sharp.

'It was at the lawyer's, Schellenberg. He asked me for the names of other beneficial trustees. I must admit I hadn't expected to be asked for names, I was absolutely tonguetied. I didn't know what to say.'

'You didn't give him our names?' Brighton was incredulous.

'Don't be bloody silly, of course not. I just didn't know what to say. Then the most bizarre notion came to me.' The room was silent, the others staring at him expectantly. 'At school I had to learn the names of all the Archbishops of Canterbury. Well, sitting there in front of that sharp little lawyer, some of the names came back to me. So . . .' he crossed the room to his attaché case and extracted a sheet of paper, 'I gave him the names of a few of our archbishops. Here they are.'

All the others except Blackmore burst into loud barks of laughter.

'I've assigned each of us a name, including Thornbury and Portalier,' he continued, 'I assumed you would be joining us, Simon,' he smiled at Woodberry, 'so I've assigned you a name also. Of course Schellenberg knows my real identity. That's unavoidable. But nevertheless, for the purposes of this enterprise I've called myself Mr Dunstan.' He glanced up and caught sight of Oliver

116

Blackmore's glowering face. 'Something wrong?'

'I have no desire to be known by the name of any English bishop,' Blackmore stated coldly.

'Pardon?'

'My family have been Presbyterian for generations,' he said emphatically. 'We were Covenanters from the beginning. My ancestors fought bloody wars to prevent your cursed bishops telling us what to do and how to worship. I did not join this partnership to be given the name of an English bishop.'

Everyone laughed. It was a typical example of Blackmore's humour, yet Brighton sensed that, unbelievably, he meant it; that the prize of over two million pounds was slightly sullied by the fact that to get it, Oliver Blackmore would have to adopt the pseudonym Mr Lanfranc, a long dead Anglican archbishop.

Woodberry looked at the list to find his alias. 'I suggest I call myself Boniface in Panama.'

'Good idea,' said Addingham.

'In fact,' continued Woodberry, 'as our little company needs a name, could I suggest that we call it the Archbishop's Enterprise?'

Everyone, except Blackmore who continued to look petulant, thought it was an excellent idea; even Addingham conceded that it was a good sugggestion.

Dundonald offered to buy Woodberry lunch at Lockets and brief him on the trip to Panama. They set off in bright sunshine to walk the few hundred yards to the restaurant with Woodberry keeping a tight grip on the bulging briefcase he carried.

As they walked, Dundonald apologised for Addingham. 'He's a bit high-handed at times,' he said. 'He resents you slightly because you weren't orignally part of his plan. He can be rather emotional, I'm afraid.'

'Not at all,' Woodberry responded. 'He reminds me of a

horse I once had, highly strung.' He paused. 'Had to have it put down in the end.'

They both laughed.

George Rupert Stansgate sat watching the beads of water slide diagonally across the glass as the rain spattered against the windows of the train. Outside, the countryside around Berkhamsted swayed past, the greens and browns merging into the grey clouds of the warm June day. The train was due to arrive at Euston in under thirty minutes, yet sitting comfortably in his seat, Stansgate had the bemused feeling that he had arrived already. His mind had not fully come to terms with the events of the day; he felt that he was in the middle of a dream and was terrified that at any moment he would awake to find himself back in the nightmare that his life had become.

He was sitting in the first-class compartment of the train. There was no way he personally could have afforded such luxury; Thornbury Engineering had paid for his journey, as they had also paid for his marvellous lunch. But, most important of all, they had offered him a job, a wonderful job, which up until that day he wouldn't have believed was possible for him. He was, as of two o'clock that afternoon, group financial director of Thornbury Engineering.

It had been a long and gruelling interview. The accountant Brighton and young Richard Thornbury had asked him a lot of questions about his past achievements and career. He had done his best to gloss over what he knew had been the failures; but so much of his life had been a succession of dreary defeats, he had not thought that he had performed well. After a while, Brighton had left the interview to make a phone call. After he returned he offered Stansgate the position. Stansgate had been taken by surprise; he had considered, for a moment, asking for time to think it over, giving the impression that he had other offers. But the position, with its salary and fringe benefits, was so overwhelmingly attractive he had blurted out his acceptance immediately. He had noticed Richard Thornbury's grin; the young man was obviously delighted that he was joining the company.

If only, thought Stansgate, his father had not deserted his mother, perhaps he might have become as rich and well-established as Richard Thornbury. As it was, his mother had scraped and saved and spent every penny of her small inheritance to send her son to a good school. Her sacrifices had been to little avail; Stansgate did not do as well as his contemporaries, even though both he and his mother always considered him to be at least as good as any of them. Somehow, things always conspired to work against him. He had not even had a good war.

He married in the late forties and took his new wife off to Northern Rhodesia where he found a job as the manager of a tea plantation. He soon learned that the white man's burden was a pain in the arse, and that school had not educated him to lead those who were not prepared to follow. His wife bore him two children; the eldest, a girl, he doted on, the younger one was a limp and sickly boy. He decided that he needed a professional qualification and chose accountancy; after years of study, he finally qualified. By that time the winds of change were beginning to blow and they were wafting a nasty smell of blood and independence under his nose. His marriage was breaking down, he suspected his wife was sleeping with other men, and so he decided to return to England with his family. They rented a house in Pinner. He had intended to start his own accountancy practice but things were difficult. As he was not a very good accountant, all he could manage were the accounts of local shopkeepers. Money was short, he had no real friends, and his clients found him superior and pedantic. He drank excessively, a legacy of Africa, he was overweight and overbearing, and he was pretty sure his wife was having another affair.

He couldn't understand why his life had never run smoothly, why it always shuddered and stalled and threatened to seize up completely. Finally, he decided to contact old acquaintances, friends of his wife, people from school and the army, people he hadn't seen for years, in the hope of finding a decent job. Then, just three weeks previously, he had received a phone call from Simon Woodberry, a man he scarcely knew, and now the nightmare had dissolved into the dream of all his years.

He shifted his bulk into a more comfortable position within the seat. His belief in the system had been vindicated, his mother's sacrifices had, in the end, been worthwhile. Being part of the network, being an old boy, having connections, had proved their advantages. There was no doubt in his mind that the phone call he had received from Woodberry was the most important of his whole career, it would change the direction of his life. He owed his good fortune to Woodberry and he resolved that as soon as he got home he would call him to express his thanks.

The plane lifted off the runway and climbed into the indigo sky. Max Gonzales watched with narrowed eyes as it became a glinting sliver of distant steel against the setting sun. The man who called himself Boniface was on his way home to England, leaving the Panamanian lawyer with a full set of instructions and a lot of unanswered questions.

Boniface was not what Gonzales had expected. He had spent two days at Gonzales' offices instructing him, in his clipped English accent, on the part that he would play in the enterprise. Like Stekenmuller and Schellenberg, Gonzales had been impressed. It was a good scheme, it used the law of business to full effect, and it would realise an enormous profit out of which Gonzales would earn a huge fee. The lawyer smiled as he turned to leave the departure lounge. Most of what Boniface required of him was illegal, but, like his counterparts in Europe, the men whom he would never meet, he treated the law as the whore out of whom he made his expensive living. It could always be abused if the money was good enough.

By the time he reached the car park, night had fallen and a warm breeze was waving the palms. Boniface had promised that the funds to launch the enterprise would be transferred from Liechtenstein within a few days. In the meantime there was much for the lawyer to do; his most important task he meant to carry out immediately. Gonzales was about to drive to the hotel where the man Boniface had stayed, to induce the desk clerk, by payment of a sufficiently large bribe, to reveal the true identity and address of his new client. Not for nothing was Gonzales one of Panama's smartest lawyers: he was a man who knew the power of knowledge and the value of insurance.

The enterprise was gaining momentum. Like a bullet spinning down a rifle barrel, the money was flashed through the international financial wires at high velocity. Upon his return to England, Woodberry called Addingham and subsequently sent a coded telex to Schellenberg in Liechtenstein, who in turn issued instructions to Stekenmuller's bank which, within twelve hours, had triggered the transfer of thirty thousand dollars to a newly opened bank account in Panama City.

Max Gonzales soon found the company he needed; trading in commodities and real estate and formed in the 1940s, it had been dormant for the past three years. Gonzales bought the company, which amounted to no more than the lease on a suite of offices, some furniture and effects, and the name, Caicos and Caribbean Company Incorporated, for less than six thousand dollars. The purchase price of Caicos and Caribbean, as well as the initial fees for Gonzales, were agreed via telex by Schellenburg who received his authority from the man calling himself Boniface, who telephoned him every Tuesday and Friday morning.

Gonzales was an expert in the fabrication of fairytale accounts. He began immediately to rewrite the recent history of the company. By amending official documents and redrafting balance sheets, monthly statements and accounts, he quickly made it appear that the Caicos and Caribbean Company had been purchased by a Liechtenstein trust more than two years previously, since when it had traded very profitably in stocks and shares. Within ten days the company appeared to have a profit of fifteen million dollars, and credits and cash to the value of half a million dollars deposited at the Bank of Nuvo Grado.

Max Gonzales telexed his unknown master in Liechtenstein that the company's accounts were 'now in order', which message was passed on to Boniface. Upon hearing the news, Simon Woodberry told Schellenberg to send a telegram to Mr Thomas Cranmer c/o The Main Post Office, Pinta Leone. It was time for John Portalier to go to Panama.

Portalier was glad to receive the order to start moving. Time had been passing slowly. For a while after his meeting with Victor Maggiore he had been busy establishing the new bank. The island's Minister of Finance had agreed to its formation after Johnny told him that he would be appointed chairman and that he would receive a substantial payment out of the profits. It had taken two weeks and cost one hundred dollars to incorporate the bank in accordance with the sparse laws of Pinta Leone; the brass plaque discreetly advertising the bank's presence just off Nuvo Grado's main thoroughfare had cost three times as much. It was the bank's most expensive asset and it made the Bank of Nuvo Grado truly unique, the only hundred dollar bank with a three hundred dollar shingle in the world.

Victor Maggiore, true to his word, had instructed his attorneys to draw up a series of loan documents. The manuscripts, impressive and couched in the solemn wording of financial law, testified and affirmed that the Bank of

122

Nuvo Grado had guarantees, loans and lines of credit from the First National Bank of Pinta Leone to the value of one hundred and eighty million dollars. Victor had also identified what 'bad paper' – stolen or forged stock certificates – was currently available within his organisation. While the papers were being prepared, Johnny had flown to New Orleans with the original land deed granted to his ancestors and taken it to an old and reputable firm which specialised in the translation of historical documents. After they had done their work he had insisted that an affidavit be sworn that their translation was accurate.

After despatching copies of the papers to Addingham, Johnny had flown home to find the bank established and nothing else to do. He had occupied one day of waiting by travelling north to see, for the final time, the land of swamp and rock that was the last Portalier possession on Pinta Leone. He spent the day talking to an eccentric American who had been living and working in the barren surroundings for almost a year. Since then, he had spent his time in enforced idleness; so it was with a sense of relief and growing excitement that he boarded the plane which would take him to Miami and thence to Panama.

He spent three days in the offices of the Caicos and Caribbean Company Inc. He gave Gonzales a list of stolen stock certificates which Maggiore would make available, when the time came, and handed over the original deed to his land. For an instant, as he watched Gonzales place it carefully in the office safe, he felt a taste of the bitter end; the Portaliers and their land were finally separated. Gonzales explained how the company's books would be arranged to show that the land had been purchased from Portalier for the sum of ten million dollars, payment comprising mainly US stock certificates. Portalier liked Gonzales, he formed the impression that the lawyer was directing the highly efficient operation with flair; he was, as Johnny had expected, a clever Latin American lawyer whose smiling face hid a mind that figured all the angles.

Portalier flew back to Pinta Leone in company with Gonzales. The day after they arrived, Gonzales travelled north to survey Johnny's recent estate as well as the beach on the other side of the island which would serve as its 'alter ego'. The next day he settled down with his sharpened pencils in the newly rented offices of the Bank of Nuvo Gardo and proceeded to fabricate a set of accounts which would synchronise with the concocted activities of the Caicos and Caribbean Company. He also found time to write a glowing report describing the most magnificent beach in the Caribbean which, along with the photographs he had taken, would form the basis of an attractive sales brochure.

At the end of the week Gonzales flew home, his work completed. He had done a good job: under the anonymous control of the partnership in England, he had conjured out of a few thousand dollars and a mass of accounts a corporation and a bank whose combined assets totalled almost two hundred million dollars, and which owned what appeared to be one of the most valuable pieces of real estate in the Caribbean.

It was impossible to tell that the corporations were built on phantom collateral, that the assets were imaginary and that at the first sign of investigation they would evaporate absolutely. They appeared as substantial and well-founded as any of the world's great corporations, solely because the paperwork, the company's books and accounts, made them appear so. It was unnecessary for the corporation to have substance, it was only necessary for it to appear as if it did. They were ready.

Chapter Six

The ringing of the telephone shattered the peace of the darkened room. Addingham awoke with a start. It was almost three thirty, he had been asleep less than two hours. He leaned across the bed, fumbling for the phone.

'Edward?' The voice was distant and familiar.

'Who is this?'

'John. John Portalier. Can you hear me?'

Addingham felt as if his head was filled with fur. He groped for the bedside light and switched it on. 'Where are you? What do you want?'

'Edward, I'm in New York.' Portalier sounded as if he were pleading.

'For God's sake, do you know what time it is? What the hell are you doing in New York?'

Portalier ignored the angry question. 'Edward, something has come up, we can't go through with it.'

The brain cleared instantly. 'What are you talking about? What do you mean?' Addingham's voice could have cut glass.

Three thousand miles away he heard John Portalier draw a deep breath. 'There's been some trouble in the mountains, the guerrillas have shot up a police patrol. The socialists say it's the government's fault . . .'

Addingham could have screamed; he closed his eyes in an effort to control himself as the remote, slightly disconnected voice kept coming at him.

'. . . the President has agreed to hold elections at the end of next month. Edward, there's no way the socialists won't win and as soon as they're elected they'll nationalise the land and the banks and everything else they can lay their hands on.'

Ice was creeping down Addingham's spine. It was shocking news, an event for which he was not prepared. His mind was striving to clutch at any straw which would prop up his collapsing plan. 'The end of next month. Maybe we could still do it. We could move everything forward . . .' Even as he said it, he knew it was impossible. It was dangerous and stupid to think things could be rushed. He could hear the resignation in Portalier's voice.

'No, we can't, Edward. In ten days' time the President is going to announce the election. After that the world will know what the socialists intend to do. They want to cut all ties with Britain, nationalise everything, grant amnesty to the bandits in the hills. It'll be another bloody Cuba; nobody will touch the place. I'll have to get out, and I'll have to tell my friends to do the same. They'll have no more use for me and I can't stay here, I've had it.'

The gall in Addingham's soul made his eyes sting with tears. The thought of his brainchild being cast onto the midden of what might have been was unbearable, and on top of that John Portalier was feeling sorry for himself. 'For Christ's sake, you said that the socialists hadn't a chance of winning an election for years.' His voice was bitter with reproach.

The distant tones of resignation continued. 'So I was wrong. The guerrillas have been active and the lefties have made political capital out of it. Anyway, Edward, it was a good idea, bloody shame it didn't come off.'

'No, wait,' Addingham shouted down the phone. 'Where are you staying?'

'At the Plaza.'

'Give me the number.' Addingham wrote it down. 'We're not beaten yet,' he continued, 'we have ten days, we'll think of something. Now look, I'm going to talk to some people at this end. Right now. So don't go away, don't leave your room until you hear from me. I'll call you sometime in the morning, I mean the morning over here. Don't go away.'

Johnny rang off. Addingham sat on the edge of his bed staring into space, trying to think of a solution to the problem that the politics of Pinta Leone had created. The silence of the large flat was disturbed by the quiet sound of his lips smacking together. After an hour he dialled Oliver Blackmore's number. Blackmore was irritated at being woken until he caught the desperation in Addingham's voice.

'What the hell, I'm awake now,' he growled.

For Addingham there was reassurance in the deep timbre of his voice, it was reliable and solid, like mahogany. He heard Joanna's sleepy enquiry in the background. 'Go to sleep,' he heard the gentle order. 'It's a client, urgent business. Go on,' Blackmore said into the phone.

Addingham finished telling him the news.

'I see.' Blackmore was unemotional. 'Very well, I shall think about it. I'll call you before nine o'clock this morning and tell you what ideas I have. If any,' he added soberly. The phone went dead.

For what was left of that night, Addingham paced the rooms of his flat while Oliver Blackmore sat on a sofa in the first-floor drawing room of the house in Lord North Street, sipping whisky and scheming.

Blackmore's call came at eight thirty. 'I can't talk on the phone, meet me at the Hyde Park for breakfast, fifteen minutes.'

The dining room of the hotel was crowded with businessmen doing deals over breakfast. They took a table by the windows looking out towards the park and the riders on Rotten Row. Blackmore ordered porridge followed by bacon and eggs, Addingham asked for coffee.

'I have an idea which might work,' announced Blackmore. 'It's all down to your friend Portalier; if he can play his part we can do what's necessary here.'

As he outlined his plan, Addingham realised how right Ashley Brighton had been to recommend the burly solicitor. Blackmore had the natural politician's ability to come to terms quickly with new realities. His plan was crude but simple, it had a good chance of being successful and, most important, there was no way in which any of them could be implicated.

Addingham left Blackmore eating toast and marmalade at the hotel and caught a cab back to his flat to phone New York. He knew that explanations over the phone were risky but he had no alternative.

Although it was four thirty in the morning in New York, Johnny was awake and sober. But he was less than enthusiastic about what he was being asked to do. Addingham was forced to be insistent. 'You yourself told me that everyone else on the island knows what they're going to do before they do it themselves, and you know who can get the information to the people up country. I cannot see how you could possibly be linked to it.'

'It may not work, all the same,' Portalier said unhappily.

'I'm aware it may not work, but can you think of a better alternative?' Addingham asked angrily. The night's mood of desperation had been replaced by one of resolve. 'It's up to you to make it work. You can do it, Johnny.' He tried to sound encouraging. 'Just think of what's at stake.'

The thought of the two-million pound prize was uppermost in Johnny's mind as he made the long return trip from New York to Pinta Leone. Immediately on his return he went to one of the town's better hotels which served as a mess for the officers of the Dorset Light Infantry. The officers were pleased to see him, he was a frequent and popular visitor. Johnny was neither surly nor obsequious, he was educated, witty and very amusing, 'the best coon on the island'.

He emerged five hours later apparently the worse for drink, having left his drinking companions, a major and two captains, sprawled in armchairs dead drunk. They had enjoyed a marvellous evening, Johnny had been extremely entertaining and they had all drunk an enormous quantity of gin. In fact the amount of alcohol the officers had consumed was surpassed only by the amount of military information they had divulged in their confidential gin-thickened undertones. Not that they would remember, the booze had cauterised their brains, all they would retain the next morning would be thick heads and hazy memories of a bloody good night.

The following afternoon Portalier visited a brothel. It was not an establishment he normally frequented, its speciality was serving the needs of British Army officers. The bordello's madam was honoured by his visit. He told her he had been recommended by some of his officer friends to ask for a certain girl. She was brought down for his inspection. He had to admit she was attractive, she was about twenty with white even teeth and skin like polished ebony. What made her even more attractive was the fact that she was the half-sister of one of the most militant of the guerrillas hiding in the mountains to the north. The girl had joined the world's oldest profession in order to learn. She had learned to turn the trick, for while the sunburned, hearty men pumped her body full of England, she pumped their minds empty of secrets. Johnny booked her for the whole afternoon. She took him up to her room.

'Gently,' he softly admonished her when they were lying on the bed, 'gently. I am not one of your white pups who come as soon as they are inside you. Let us drink and take our time and I will teach you some things.'

They sat naked on the bed drinking red wine, which made Johnny talkative. 'I have no love for the English,' he told her, 'they are like all the others who have raped our island. Now, they will have even more blood.' He saw her eyelids flicker with interest.

'How will they have more blood?' she asked nonchalantly.

Johnny drained his glass before continuing. 'In two days a small group of soldiers will go on patrol into the mountains. Their generals want action, something to show the people at home, so the soldiers have orders to kill every man, woman and child they find. Of course,' he added, 'they will rape and mutilate the women first. If they cannot find anyone in the mountains, they will attack one of the villages in the foothills, kill everyone and blame it on the rebels.'

The girl's eyes widened in horror.

'I know,' said Johnny, 'it is terrible but the men in the mountains always avoid the troops, they are frightened of them. They do not know that the British soldiers are only boys who have never seen bloodshed and who would run away if they even saw a bandit.'

'How do you know all this?' asked the girl moving closer to him.

'I know many of the British officers. They told me. It was they who told me about you.' He smiled at her. 'They said you were very good and they were right. They told me much about their plans last night, when they were drunk, but of course they are secret so I may not tell you any more.'

The girl nodded in understanding and moved her hand between Johnny's legs. Her interest was as aroused as the throbbing organ she gently caressed.

It will not take much to make this one come, she thought, nor to coax the knowledge from him. 'But when will the British do this awful thing?' she asked as she gently teased the tip of his penis.

First Lieutenant Adrian Danby-Crown watched critically as the drivers manoeuvred the big Bedfords into position. It was an hour after dawn. The lieutenant and his men had driven in convoy through the night from Nuvo Grado; somewhere in the darkness the trucks had turned off the good road which led north and had plunged for miles along the narrow track until, just as dawn was breaking, they had reached their destination, a large clearing surrounded by jungle four thousand feet up in the northern mountains. The men had boiled tea and breakfasted on their rations as the light had grown stronger. Now, as the trucks were being parked in positions of maximum concealment, the lieutenant and his men were making ready to go on patrol.

The lieutenant's voice cracked out across the clearing: 'Sergeant Powis.' The sergeant doubled across and halted smartly in front of the tall, young officer.

'Sergeant, I shall take the platoon with me. You will remain here with the rest of the men and the drivers.' For a moment a scowl passed across the sergeant's broad face, then he snapped to attention and saluted.

Danby-Crown watched him double away, shouting at the men as he went. In the lieutenant's opinion, Powis was a damn good sergeant, it was unusual for him to scowl at an order. Probably, he thought, he's as bored as I am.

He turned to survey the steeply rising jungle beyond the clearing. This was the fourth patrol he had led since coming to the Godforsaken island. The previous three excursions had been a total waste of time; he and his men had crashed and stumbled about in the jungle for hours on end only to emerge dog-tired and soaked in sweat, having seen nothing and accomplished nothing. The lieutenant expelled a weary sigh. He wanted action. The Danby-Crowns were an army family, every male member for the past eleven generations had been an officer in a regiment of the line and all of them had seen action. The sharp blue eyes which that morning surveyed the jungle had watched in their misty past Napoleon's Old Guard storm the hill at Hougourmont; within the lieutenant's aquiline nostrils lingered the pungent smell of the guns at Salamanca. The thin red line ran in his blood; the regiment was his soul and action was his birthright. Real action, he reflected as he turned back to the clearing to watch the men's final preparations, not charging around in the jungle, chasing after bandits he was convinced didn't exist. He hated it, he felt like a Boy Scout not a soldier, and if Sergeant Powis felt like that too, well, he for one could understand it.

Sergeant Powis could not have described how he felt that morning except that he was uneasy. It was the way he had felt in Malaya and Korea just before he went into action. It didn't make sense, there was no prospect of action in this place. Nevertheless, things weren't right. The uneasy feelings had started as the patrol motored north in the night and had grown with each passing hour. They were even stronger now the lieutenant had told him he was to stay behind. The sergeant liked the lieutenant; in common with most regular soldiers, he preferred his officers to be gentlemen, and normally he would have been grateful that he was to be spared a hot, sweaty day, hacking his way through the jungle. But he wasn't. In fact he had been tempted, when the lieutenant had ordered him to remain behind, to argue, to request that he go too. But there was no point in that, he had no reason to question the order. Just his inexplicable sense of foreboding.

'Bloody Nora,' he muttered to himself as he marched across the clearing. 'Better get a grip, getting frightened in my old age. Corporal Walker!' he bellowed. The corporal ran across to him.

'Sarge?'

'Get those idle buggers moving, Corporal. Bloody Nora, what a shower. And Corporal, you keep a sharp eye open up there.' He saw a smirk appear on the corporal's face. He thinks I'm getting to be an old woman too, thought Powis. He leaned forward until his face was only inches from the corporal's. 'Something wrong with your face, laddie?' he growled. 'You watch yourself or I'll have your stripes.'

Within minutes the men were ready, their packs on and their weapons checked. They set off, one man two hundred yards ahead of the main column which, led by the lieutenant, disappeared in single file into the jungle.

The platoon followed a narrow track, climbing steeply up into the heart of the thick vegetation. After an hour the path levelled off and within a few hundred yards widened into a small clearing. They were halfway across the clearing when from somewhere ahead and out of sight came a high-pitched scream. It stopped as abruptly as it had begun. Without a word of command every man in the platoon stopped dead, staring ahead at the place in the dark of the trees from where the blood-chilling cry had come. It was in that instant, when the platoon was frozen in its tracks, that without warning the jungle on either side erupted into murderous rifle fire. At the sound of the first shot every bird within three hundred yards rose into the air, screeching with fright. In a second the clearing had become a cauldron of noisy terror and sudden death. Danby-Crown turned to his men; already three of them had gone down under the hail of bullets. He yelled at them to take cover though in truth there was no cover for any of them to take; the lieutenant and his men were in the centre of the perfect killing ground, as exposed and vulnerable as sheep in a slaughter house.

The lieutenant turned to his front. From the edge of the clearing a group of men had emerged. They were dressed in jungle camouflage and carrying machetes. Danby-Crown could see the sweat glistening on their black faces as they began running towards him. He fumbled for the holstered revolver at his side as a young infantryman fell at his feet, blood pouring from a gaping hole in his throat, his arms flapping and his heels drumming the ground in a screaming tantrum of death. First Lieutenant Adrian Danby-Crown had got his wish, the last few seconds of his young life were filled with action. He fired at the nearest of the fast-running guerrillas who flipped over sideways, his machete spinning away into the jungle; he fired twice at the next man but missed. The guerrilla was upon him before he could fire again. The raised machete, gleaming in the dappled sun, arced downwards and sliced into the side of his neck with tremendous force, cutting through the jugular vein, the mastoid muscles and the windpipe as if they were butter. The lieutenant's head, held to his body by a few strands of muscle, lolled to the side as his knees buckled and the martial blood, pumping up from the severed jugular, burst into the air like a fountain and spattered the leaves with its rich, red pedigree.

Sergeant Powis, sitting in the shade of a truck, heard the popping of distant gunfire. He remained perfectly still for some seconds, listening as the faint fusillade continued, then leapt to his feet. The distant firing continued for another minute and then it stopped. He listened intently, but there was no more, only the ceaseless noise of the jungle birds. He shouted at the radio man to contact the platoon as he issued a stream of orders to the few men under his command. Within minutes the drivers had immobilised the trucks and were digging rifle pits at strategic points in the clearing, and the rest of the small squad was ready to move out.

William Powis was forty, twice the age of the men he commanded. He was a short, powerful man, built, as they said in Hunslett where he came from, like a brick shithouse. He led the six young soldiers at a heart-cracking pace up into the jungle. Sergeant Powis was an old hand, he knew the sound of an ambush when he heard it and he knew that jungle ambushes did not have survivors. His was not a mission of rescue, it was the hope of vengeance that spurred him on.

They reached the open ground in less than forty minutes. From a distance they could hear voices so they circled the clearing cautiously and came in from the north. The six young soldiers who charged into the clearing that day had two great advantages, they had surprise and Sergeant William Powis. The man they loved and feared was at their head as they came screaming out of the jungle, bayonets fixed, firing from the hip. There were about thirty guerrillas bunched up in a group, totally unprepared for a sudden counter-attack. They stared as two of their number fell, then turned and ran – except one of them. He stood his ground waving his machete until a burst from Powis's Sterling blew the man's chest to bloody fragments. Three more were caught by bullets before the group made the safety of the jungle and disappeared.

Powis and his men stopped at the centre of the clearing, their chests heaving, the adrenaline pumping through their systems. They looked around. It took them some moments to register what exactly it was they were looking at. The bodies of their comrades had been butchered; the clearing was strewn with bloody limbs and entrails of men who two hours before had been eating breakfast. Whether they had been dead or alive when their heads, arms, legs and privates had been hacked off and their stomachs ripped open no one could know. Corporal Walker retained his stripes but both his legs had gone and his eyes had been gouged out. The head of First Lieutenant Adrian Danby-Crown was stuck on a pole, it was impossible to identify his body, it had been hacked to bits. It was a sickening sight. Sergeant Powis had seen it before in Malaya and Borneo, but it was not a scene to which any man could become used. He fought hard to resist the rising tide of vomit within him.

'Bloody Nora,' he said, closing his eyes.

The young soldiers who had charged the clearing with Powis had neither seen nor ever imagined such things before. Two of them slumped to the ground, their weapons discarded, weeping like children. Others were steadily being sick. Powis watched numbly as one young soldier, tears streaming down his face, began woodenly smashing the face of a fallen guerrilla with his rifle butt.

Slowly, Powis the soldier took repossession of Powis the man. He ordered the men to one end of the clearing, swearing and shouting and kicking them until finally he had them disciplined and alert once more. He sent two of them back down to the trucks with orders to radio HQ. He and the others dug in, creating a small defensive fire base. He was sure that the guerrillas would not return but the work gave the young soldiers something to do and it was necessary for them to protect the pathetic remains of their comrades.

For many hours the sergeant and his men stayed dug in at the edge of the clearing. The jungle around them had become deathly quiet, the incessant noise of the birds had eased; the men heard nothing except the rustlings in the undergrowth as nameless creatures of the jungle crawled towards the congealing blood and raw red meat of what once were men. As the afternoon sun grew hotter, the faint sickly smell of putrefying flesh came to them.

The relief column arrived just after six; Powis and the others had spent all day guarding the butchered bodies of their comrades. It was a day none of them would ever forget; it would disturb their nights for months to come. As they set off back down the trail, the airwaves crackled with the first news of the disaster.

News of the massacre was greeted with horror in Britain. The popular newspapers carried banner headlines screaming of atrocity and brutal slaughter, though as most of their readers had never heard of Pinta Leone, all of them took space to explain why British troops were stationed on the island. The army, out of deference to next of kin, tried to play down the butchery but the papers got wind of it anyway and most of the grisly details were spilled across their pages. Questions were asked in the House of Commons; among the many members who had something to say on the subject were Oliver Blackmore and Jeffrey Frimley-Kimpton, both of whom made impassioned speeches to the House advocating a strong reaction to the massacre. An emergency session of the Defence Chiefs of Staff was convened and within three days a spearhead battalion of Marine commandos was enplaning at RAF Brize Norton, on its way to reinforce the troops already on the island. The President of Pinta Leone flew to London for urgent talks, and returned home a day later: martial law was to be declared, there would be a curfew in Nuvo Grado; the incipient fires of rebellion were to be smothered by the khaki blanket of the British Army. The President also announced that the elections would be postponed until further notice.

A senior civil servant from the Foreign Office flew to Washington to explain the movement of troops to the island. Since Cuba, the Caribbean had been judged a sensitive area by the Americans. The senior official in the State Department with whom he met was grateful for the explanation, though privately he considered the movement of a few hundred British soldiers to a tinpot island pretty small time, especially when compared to the American build-up of men and materials in Vietnam. Now that, in his opinion, was really something.

Some of the partners were almost as horrified as the public at the news of the massacre. Henry Dundonald sought out Blackmore in a quiet corner of his club. 'I know we all agreed to it, Oliver,' he said in an undertone, 'but sixteen dead, butchered for God's sake, that's too much. It's bad when casualties get into double figures. There's bound to be a stink at the War Office.'

'That,' said Blackmore coldly, 'was the whole point. They were soldiers. They were paid. Every profession has its occupational hazards. Theirs is dying, even dying like that.'

Later that day, however, and in private to Addingham, he remarked: 'Your friend Portalier exceeded his brief. He was told to create an incident. Half a dozen dead would have been enough, not a whole bloody platoon chopped to bits.'

In the end, though, they all agreed that the scheme had worked far better than they could have hoped. Blackmore's predictions concerning the reaction of the British authorities to insurrection had proved entirely accurate, the government and army would maintain the status quo; there would be no change of government on the island for a long time to come. The partners knew the publicity would have no effect on their plans, the massacre would soon sink beneath the horizon of public interest. The scandals surrounding the recent resignation of the Minister of War were eclipsing all other items of news. Sure enough, within a week, pictures of white-bodied squaddies gambolling on a beach near Nuvo Grado were flashed onto the nation's television screens; after that, the name of Pinta Leone disappeared from the news.

Forgetting was not so easy for the wives and mothers of the fallen men. As the army chaplains knocked on the doors of the houses in Salford and Sunderland and all the other places, they were assailed and perplexed by the recurring question: why? There was no answer, either for them or for the mother of First Lieutenant Adrian Danby-Crown. She too could not reconcile the loss of her lovely, clean-limbed boy to any reason why. At the memorial service which they held for him in the Shropshire village church, she stood tall and erect with her mind locked on thoughts of England and her face set rigid against the tears. They carved his name with pride on the family memorial where it joined the names of his fathers and uncles; ancestors whose bodies, like his, lay in distant corners of the world and whose lives, like his, had been laid down for a reason that they never understood and for a cause which was not their own.

'I was hoping I might have a word.' George Stansgate hovered in the doorway of Richard Thornbury's office with a look of expectancy.

Thornbury looked up from his copy of *The Times*.

'George,' he announced heartily. 'Yes, of course. Come in, old boy. Sit down.' Stansgate eased his bulk into a chair across the desk from Thornbury. 'Well now,' enquired the young man, 'tell me, how are you settling in here? Actually,' he continued without waiting for an answer, 'something has just come up which I wanted to talk to you about.'

It was as well that Thornbury had not waited for an answer as Stansgate would have found one difficult. He had been in the job less than a month and was delighted with his new status. He was staying at the best hotel in town, eating and drinking on his expense account, while at the weekends he and his family toured Warwickshire in the new company car, seeking to buy a house which would suitably reflect his new position in society. Life was good, though the job was strangely puzzling. The company's accounts were very complicated and far beyond his ability. Somehow they seemed to hide more than they revealed; it was taking him a long time to understand them. Thornbury's factory was, even to his inexperienced eyes, working at half-pace, the long corridor of offices on the floor above the red-brick Victorian factory were silent and musty, peopled by old men who had worked for Thornbury Engineering for years. They were polite to Stansgate but uninterested. It was as if nothing had happened since Joseph Thornbury collapsed at his desk two years previously, as if the company which bore his name remained in a state of shock. Stansgate had seen Richard Thornbury only once since he had come to work for the company. On the day he started, Thornbury had shown him his office and then left him to get on with it. There was no doubt, Stansgate thought, that young Thornbury adopted a very casual attitude to the management of the family firm, though this morning he appeared quite animated.

'Our bankers have sent us this.' Thornbury passed a colourful brochure across the desk: it was an expensive production, six pages of thick, glossy art paper liberally decorated with colour pictures. It described in glowing terms a strip of development land along a shore of Pinta Leone. Much of the copy was devoted to describing the island as a paradise for holiday-makers. Title to the land, the brochure stated, was held by the Caribbean and Caicos Company Inc. of Panama City, which company was offering the land for sale.

Stansgate frowned. 'Isn't this the place where those chaps were murdered by terrorists?'

Thornbury waved his hand, dismissing the objection. 'Oh, that's all forgotten,' he said airily. 'I expect the people out there are keen to get some investment in the place now – stability, that kind of thing.'

'Are you suggesting we follow this up?' Stansgate was confused.

'I think we should, don't you?'

'Actually I was hoping to talk to you about these figures.' Stansgate placed a bundle of files on the desk. He looked across at Thornbury, a frown over his fleshy features. 'I'm not sure whether the company is as healthy as these figures suggest. It may not be the right time for trying something new. After all, we don't know about property development and I don't think we have the money for an investment of this nature.'

Thornbury leaned back in his seat. 'Oh, come on, George, one can always get hold of money. The banks are falling over themselves to lend. Smithson-Perez will probably lend us what we need, they gave us the notion in the first place.'

'But an investment of this size might seriously jeopardise the company; we would be massively over-extended.'

Thornbury leaned forward with a warm smile. 'Look, you are the finance director, why don't you jump on a plane and go and talk to these chappies, Caribbean and whatever, in Panama? If they appear substantial, then pop over and see the land. If it's any good then we can consider it. What have we got to lose? If we go ahead we would do the company a lot of good, the news would definitely improve our share price. And think,' Thornbury's smile broadened, 'if we invest, you can spend most of the winter in the sun.'

Stansgate stared at the young man. 'You mean you want me to go over there?'

'Can't do anything unless you see what we're buying, old boy.'

'When?' The fat man was bewildered.

'What's wrong with now? You can be on an airplane tomorrow. Spend a few days looking around, talking to the right people, entertain them, you know, make an impression. Draw whatever money you need from the company cashier.'

Thirty hours later George Stansgate, seated in a first-class cabin high above the Atlantic, sipped his gin and tonic and gazed at the clouds slipping by. The life which he had spent years trying to kick-start had suddenly, in the past month, roared into being and turned into a high-octane, six-cylinder existence. It was exhilarating, as different from the past as light from dark, and yet Stansgate was conscious that, as ever, he was barely in control. What once he could not start, he now wondered whether he could stop. Events were carrying him along with the same inevitable momentum as the aircraft in which he sat.

The plane touched down in the midday heat of Panama and by the time he had walked to the reception building, Stansgate was soaked in sweat. He was worried that Mr Gonzales, who had so promptly replied to his telex the previous day and who had promised to meet him at the airport, would not recognise him, and was therefore relieved when a swarthy, middle-aged man made an unerring march across the airport lounge and shook him warmly by the hand. 'You must be Mr Stansgate,' he said, smiling broadly.

Stansgate was even more gratified when he found that the

Caribbean and Caicos Company had booked him into one of the best rooms at the El Continental and that waiting in his room was a magnum of champagne glistening in a bucket of ice.

Throughout the two days he spent in the city he was continually impressed. Gonzales was a charming and genial host; it was obvious to Stansgate that he was both an astute businessman and the director of a highly successful company. The lawyer allowed Stansgate a cursory examination of his company's books. 'Of course,' he said, 'if Thornbury Engineering expresses a deeper interest in the property then we would allow you a closer inspection of our affairs.'

Stansgate nodded wisely; even from the brief examination, he could see that the company was extremely profitable, much more so than Thornbury's. Not that he intended to admit it to his host. He considered it important to keep up appearances in front of foreigners.

Gonzales showed him the original deed to the Portalier estates. The faded yellow paper, implanted with the great red seal of Louis XVI and covered in fine French copperplate script, had been framed and put under glass. Stansgate read the translation and noted the affidavit.

On the second evening in Panama he dined with Gonzales at one of the city's best restaurants. Towards the evening's end, Gonzales confided his plans. 'Mr Portalier, from whom we purchased the land, will be meeting us and giving us a tour of the property. He is president of the Bank of Nuvo Grado, one of Pinta Leone's most important banks. The bank could be very useful to you if you purchase the land, I recommend you study it closely.

'We hope,' he continued, 'to sell the land to a large European company which will develop the area with taste and discernment. We have circulated two thousand brochures similar to the one you received to major companies and financial institutions in Europe. We don't want to sell to the Americans, they own most of the island already. However, it really does depend on who can meet our price. We couldn't contemplate selling for less than fifty million dollars. After all,' he continued smoothly as Stansgate started in surprise, 'we have fifteen miles of the best coastline in the Caribbean. Developed by the right people it could become the most famous coast in the world, more renowed than Miami Beach or the Côte d'Azur. The company which develops that coastline will become internationally famous, and its directors,' he paused and shrugged his shoulders, 'they will be very rich and powerful men.'

Stansgate stared at the man seated across the table, and within his hazy brain grew the images of ambition.

'I hope,' continued Gonzales, 'that it will be a company such as yours, solid, British, as reliable as Rolls-Royce, which will buy our land.'

Stansgate smiled weakly.

The following day they flew to Pinta Leone. The Dakota came in from the west, sweeping low over the sparkling sea and the great harbour of Nuvo Grado before bouncing to a halt on the runway of the airport a few miles east of the city. The rough landing did nothing to improve Stansgate's disposition; he was suffering from an overwhelming hangover and had endured the agonising flight slumped in his seat, expecting at any moment to erupt with vomit. The blinding Caribbean sun only served to increase the hammering in his head as he weaved his way slowly across the tarmac towards the reception area. He waited wretchedly as the Customs official stamped his passport while Gonzales, who appeared to be in perfect health and totally oblivious to Stansgate's condition, kept up an amiable conversation. After they cleared Customs Gonzales led his companion outside to where a tall man was leaning against the side of a large, American car. The man and the car seemed to form a complete entity, they were both big, black and highly polished.

'Mr Portalier,' greeted Gonzales, 'so nice to see you

again. May I introduce you to Mr Stansgate, the financial director of Thornbury Engineering in England.'

Stansgate shook hands with Portalier who beamed a welcoming smile. 'Delighted to meet you. It's good of you to come so far to visit our little island. I hope that your journey will prove to be worthwhile.' He turned slightly towards Gonzales. 'Now, may I suggest a drink?'

Before either of them could reply, Portalier signalled to a young man dressed in a chauffeur's uniform who leapt from the car and, smiling deferentially, deposited their luggage in the trunk.

Portalier's suggestion of a drink had set fresh waves of nausea awash in Stansgate's stomach; reluctantly he accompanied the others to the airport lounge. Portalier ordered white rum which Stansgate found soon settled his stomach and elevated his mood back to the euphoria of the past two days.

The chauffeur drove slowly westwards towards Nuvo Grado as Portalier, sitting with his visitors on the roomy rear seat of the Buick, delivered a short lecture on the history and economy of the island. Stansgate was surprised to discover that Nuvo Grado was a busy city; its wide, tree-lined streets were heavy with traffic and thronged with brightly dressed pedestrians and groups of off-duty soldiers dressed in olive green fatigues who looked thoroughly bored.

The car turned off the main avenue into a side street and stopped opposite a tall and narrow white building. The large rectangular windows set high up on the building's face were covered by grilles of dark iron; next to the heavy wooden doors was a brass plaque etched with the copper-plate script: 'The Bank of Nuvo Grado, established by decree of the Ministry of Finance, Pinta Leone'. As the chauffeur helped him ease his bulk out of the car, Stansgate's attention was caught by the plaque. It gave the building an aura of quiet dignity; he could tell immediately that this was an institution that did not broadcast its riches, that here success was achieved by discretion and acknowledged with restraint. It all seemed somehow very English.

Inside the bank was a large room with high ceilings and a tiled floor. The light from the windows filtered down through wooden screens as long-bladed fans smoothly disturbed the air; it was cool and subdued after the heat and clamour of mid-afternoon Nuvo Grado. Portalier led the way past a number of clerks working at their desks into an office which was furnished in Spanish style, with a massive oak desk and a number of bright rugs covering the mosaic floor. He crossed to a drinks cabinet in a corner as his guests seated themselves in comfortable armchairs. Over drinks Portalier outlined their plans. They would, he said, be visiting the coastline in the next day or two but that evening he intended to show them some of Nuvo Grado's night life.

'It might surprise you to find that we do have some rather, eh, sophisticated entertainment,' he said knowingly. In the morning Stansgate could inspect the bank's books. 'Just so you may be satisfied that we have some financial muscle,' Portalier said with a smile. Afterwards he planned to take Stansgate to the hotel which served as the mess for the officers stationed on the island.

'I'm sure that you will be interested in their opinions about the island,' he said. 'I know that they will be interested to know that your company may invest here.' Portalier stopped, the smile dropping from his face as he stared intently at Stansgate. 'I must ask you, however, for complete discretion as to the exact nature of your interest. It would be absolutely disastrous if word got out that the land was available. You understand?'

Stansgate nodded vigorously and said that he did, though in fact he didn't, not quite, not if two thousand detailed brochures had been circulated. Nor could he understand why he needed to inspect the bank's accounts. But Portalier was obviously serious, and Stansgate was happy not to reason why.

After more drinks the chauffeur drove the sweating Englishman to his hotel. After he had freshened up, Portalier and Gonzales collected him for dinner. They dined at a restaurant overlooking the harbour and watched the colours of the great stones of the castle and harbour walls turn from golden yellow through ancient purple to the midnight blue of tropical night. They left the restaurant late and drove to a house on the outskirts of the city wherein a young woman with a magnificent body set to work on Stansgate, making the rolls of corpulent flesh flap with ecstasy as she deftly milked the last drops from the little white worm hanging beneath his massive belly.

The following morning, Billy Jamaica, the chauffeur, drove him to the bank where his two companions were waiting. After a few welcoming words, Portalier delegated the task of explaining the bank's business to Gonzales, who took Stansgate on a rapid survey of the ledgers. It was difficult to keep up; the heat and the alcohol as well as the draining effects of the previous night were taking their toll. Even so, Stansgate quickly formed the impression that the Bank of Nuvo Grado, like the Caicos and Caribbean Company, was an extremely profitable institution.

After Gonzales had finished, and Stansgate had lied that he understood the accounts perfectly, they left the bank and walked slowly through the sunshine of the busy city until they arrived at a large and rather dilapidated hotel. The officers of the Dorset Light Infantry were delighted to welcome John Portalier and his two friends; Stansgate was the first Englishman they had seen for some weeks and he was quickly made the guest of honour. They stayed for lunch and remained until late afternoon, drinking.

'What brings you to the island?' enquired a major.

'My company is thinking of investing here,' Stansgate replied. 'I've come to survey the place.'

'On a recce, eh?' responded the major. 'Bloody good idea, this place could do with more British involvement. It could make a marvellous holiday resort. Not like those awful places in the Med where the yobs and the other ranks go. I mean a good sort of place. There's everything here, you know. So what's your interest then?'

Stansgate was cautious. 'Actually, it's something in the holiday line of country but I can't say too much at this stage, I'm afraid.'

'Of course, of course, quite understand, old boy.' The major was embarrassed. An orderly appeared with a tray of drinks as Stansgate continued.

'What concerns me is the trouble you've had here, you know, that business a few weeks ago. No point in investing if the natives are restless or they all want to go communist or something.'

The major's face darkened. He shook his head slowly and stared at the floor. 'Can't understand that business. Totally out of character. I've served in Africa and the East. The wogs here are the friendliest I've come across. The bandits were laughable, all they'd done was shoot up a few policemen and farmers. They were going to have elections, you know, their party was set to win . . .' His voice trailed away. 'Then Danby-Crown and his blokes got the chop. You know what the bastards did?'

Stansgate nodded.

'Disappeared now, of course.' The major was talking in a low tone, almost to himself. 'Not a sign of them. The Marines are out in the mountains but not a trace. We'll have them though, sooner or later we'll have those bastards.' He stopped for a few moments and looked up. 'It's out of character. There's only a few of them, that's certain. Most of the people here just aren't interested in politics, too bloody lazy.' He took a long drink from his tumbler. 'Don't worry, old boy, the wogs here are all right. There's no chance of any lefty government getting in, not while we're here. Not while we've got the place like that.' He extended a tightly clenched fist.

Portalier's car arrived at about five and returned Stansgate to his hotel. The others called for him later and they drove out to a restaurant on the outskirts of the city. After the meal and a few bottles of wine they returned to the house of the previous night where Stansgate was again reduced to squeaks of ecstasy as the harlots practised their skills.

The following day was spent sightseeing in Nuvo Grado. Stansgate was faintly puzzled that no mention had been made of their intended visit to the coastline. Unknown to him, it was pouring with rain in the north although it was a perfect day for sightseeing in the city and drinking in the pavement cafés. But when the next day came and went, dissipated like those gone before, he became perturbed. He raised the subject at dinner that evening.

'Why of course,' Portalier exclaimed, 'we really must do something about it. Perhaps tomorrow. I'll see if arrangements can be made.'

To Stansgate it seemed as if the others had forgotten the purpose of his visit, as if they were more concerned with his pleasure. It appeared that they really liked him and he made no protest. He was enjoying a sweet and heady existence and he had no mind to end it sooner than need be. Here, in a place where mañana was considered urgent and pleasure the only imperative, the fat Englishman was content to let events take their course.

The phone in his bedroom rang early the following morning and Stansgate's brain, muzzy from the previous night, took some seconds to realise that the caller was John Portalier announcing that their trip to the north had been arranged and that the car would call for him in an hour.

As they were leaving the city, Portalier unfolded a map of the island and pointed to their destination. He passed it across to Stansgate and watched impassively as the Englishman ringed the long strip of land with his fountain pen. The map showed a number of roads leading out of the city, some straight into the mountains, others skirting to the east or west. It became evident, as the rolling green hills on their left gradually grew into mountains, that they were taking the direct route along the island's eastern seaboard. The main road led directly north, skirted the mountains at the top of the island, and then turned south, running down the western edge to terminate back in Nuvo Grado. The car made swift progress on the metalled road. It was a warm day and Stansgate was glad that Billy Jamaica had brought a few bottles of champagne packed in ice. He and Gonzales laughed heartily as their host popped a cork through the open window at a peasant leading a donkey loaded with produce.

The champagne, combined with the heat and the somnolent rhythm of the car, made Stansgate drowsy; slowly his eyes closed and his head sank into the cradle of his multiple chins. He awoke with a start. He had no idea how long he had dozed but what had disturbed him was a change in the rhythm of the car. He blinked at the bright sunlight and stared out of the car's open windows. They were speeding up a narrow mountain road, the powerful car surging into the bends as Jamaica expertly worked through the gears. 'Where are we?' he asked.

'Ah, you are awake.' Gonzales smiled benevolently and poured him a glass of champagne.

'We thought we'd take a diversion into the mountains, old boy,' said Portalier unfolding the map. 'We'll come out just here where you'll get a much better view of the entire coastline.' He pointed to a spot on the map.

With the map spread across his knees and a glass of champagne in his hand, Stansgate tried to follow the route but after a few minutes he abandoned the attempt. The map showed a fine tracery of narrow mountain roads, it was impossible to tell along which of them they were travelling.

He leaned back in his seat and watched the rapid changes of the passing scenery as walls of grey rock, inches from the car, were replaced by wide valleys filled with thick jungle.

They travelled for about another hour and then, suddenly, they were at the top of a steep road which twisted and turned down a shoulder of the mountain. At the foot of the descent was a broad ribbon of green trees beyond which, about three miles' distant, was a strip of golden sand and the blue Caribbean. It was about noon, the light from the sun directly above them made the whitecaps glitter like diamonds. The scene stretched as far as Stansgate could see in both directions; its beauty took his breath away. 'My God,' he exclaimed, 'it's magnificent.'

Portalier looked at him. 'Strange,' he mused, 'the last time I came this way was more than twenty years ago. I brought a friend who was with me at Cambridge. It seems like yesterday.'

'Twenty years is a long time,' agreed Gonzales. 'To a man of forty it is the difference between youth and old age.'

Stansgate had no interest in the philosophical turn of the conversation; he had seen paradise and believed he could buy it.

Portalier noticed his excitement. 'I think you'll agree it was worth the diversion,' he said.

'Absolutely.' Stansgate took out his pen and on the map marked the spot which Portalier had previously indicated and where he believed they had just emerged from the mountains.

The car tore down the mountainside and levelled off on the straight stretch of road which led from the mountains to the sea. Stansgate noticed that the trees seemed to be cultivated.

'Small fruit farmers,' said Gonzales in answer to his query. 'They lease the land. No problem, you could push them off any time you wanted. They have no rights.'

They reached the broad highway running between the

beach and the groves of fruit trees. 'Turn left, Billy,' ordered Portalier. They drove slowly along the golden beach for a few minutes until they came to a village.

'This is Pinta de Fletche,' said Portalier.

Stansgate consulted the map. The name Pinta de Fletche was marked but there was no indication of any village, just the promontory which formed the northern tip of the island and which on the map appeared far sharper and more jagged than the gentle jutting peninsula that he could see. He showed Portalier.

He shrugged his shoulders. 'We don't have ordnance survey here, old boy. This part of the world needs to be brought up to date, which of course is why you're here.' He smiled benignly.

They drove slowly past the village. It stank of rotting fish and Stansgate declined the invitation to walk around it.

'The village marks the end of the beach in this direction,' said Gonzales. 'If we drive further on, beyond the headline, you'll find that the coastline begins to turn south.'

'Yes, I see,' said Stansgate studying the map. 'So that means we're here.' He marked the location. 'And that direction is south-east?' He pointed down the road behind them.

'Absolutely right,' said Portalier. 'Now we shall go back to the other end of the beach. If you look at the mileage indicator, old boy, you can see how far it is. Turn the car round, Billy.'

'By the way,' asked Stansgate as Jamaica swung the car round to face the opposite direction, 'do you have a compass?'

'Of course,' Portalier responded promptly.

The chauffeur stopped the car and passed across a square rosewood box inside which was a ship's compass. They got out and moved away from the car. Stansgate spread out the map as Portalier set the compass on a small rock. It showed north pointing out to sea, the direction in which they were facing read south-east, and to the south was the grey bulk of the mountains. Stansgate checked the map; the directions corresponded. As he looked up he caught both Portalier and Gonzales watching him closely.

'I just thought I'd check,' he said lamely. 'Merely for interest.'

'Of course, old boy.' Portalier's brown face broke into a beaming smile.

The accountant endeavoured to hide his embarrassment. He looked down at the compass in its box. 'This is beautiful,' he said, picking it up.

Portalier gently took it from him and closed the lid. 'Isn't it,' he replied. 'It was a present to my grandfather from a captain in the Royal Navy.' They sauntered back to where Billy Jamaica was leaning against the Buick.

The car moved off smoothly and for the next few minutes they drove at a leisurely pace alongside the golden beach. Portalier and Gonzales kept up a running commentary on places of interest as they drove, pointing out where it would be possible to build hotels and villas and marinas. Stansgate could see that every inch of the strip had potential.

'We've had a survey done,' Gonzales said. 'It's all rock underneath, no problem for building; you could build sky scrapers here if you wanted.' After they had travelled for half an hour the road began to bend away from the beach. Jamaica stopped the car.

'That's it, old boy,' said Portalier. 'Well, what do you think?'

'It's marvellous,' responded Stansgate, unable to disguise his enthusiasm. 'The problem will be to convince my company.'

'I'm sure you'll do that,' said Gonzales.

'A toast then,' said Portalier, opening another bottle of champagne. 'To Thornbury and the right decision.' The trio laughed noisily as the car moved off again.

Within minutes the road had moved in close under the

shadow of the mountains, leaving the sea about three miles away to their left. The land between was desolate, rocky and sparsely covered with stunted trees. From the fast-moving car, Stansgate could just make out that the land formed a sharp promontory around which he could see the spray from waves crashing on rocks. As they sped south it changed its nature and gradually became a dark and ominous mangrove swamp which stretched away to the shore-line and bordered the road for mile after mile.

'Christ, what a difference,' commented Stansgate. 'One would scarcely think it was the same island, let alone the same coastline.'

It took them almost two hours to return to Nuvo Grado, much longer than Stansgate would have thought possible. He said as much to Portalier as they were driving past the shanties on the city's edge.

Portalier smiled. 'The English have a poor sense of distance.' His tone was patronising. 'This is a large island. Before they built the new highway the journey north took much longer.'

Stansgate was not prepared to dispute why their return had taken so long, his head was aching and he felt slightly sick from the effects of drinking champagne in a car at high speed.

'However,' Portalier continued, 'whoever develops the coast should consider constructing an airport, one capable of taking planes from America and Europe.'

'An airport?' Stansgate was incredulous.

'Of course,' said Gonzales. 'It would enhance the development enormously. I expect the government here would provide some financial help.' Portalier nodded in agreement.

'Even so, it's a bit much, isn't it?'

'Not for the right people.' Portalier was offhand. 'Whoever we sell to must be prepared to think big.'

Gonzales' tone was equally cold. 'If that's beyond

Thornbury's ability, well,' he shrugged, 'there are others who will be prepared to develop the place properly.'

Stansgate had forgotten the possibility of competitors. The thought that someone else could have what he had come to consider his, could live the life that he had lately led, sickened him.

It was a thought that constantly recurred on his long flight home two days later. He had enjoyed a final night with his two friends and then taken his leave the next morning, standing in the bright sunshine at the airport. As they had shaken hands both men had impressed upon him the need for speed; they had implied that others were coming to see the land and although they personally liked him, the sale of the beach would be on the basis of first come, first served.

As the aircraft flew steadily east into the rising sun, Stansgate's euphoria drained away. He was exhausted, his system was saturated with alcohol and he was coming down to earth.

It was raining when they landed at Heathrow, there was a strike and he had to wait more than an hour for his baggage. The cab ride through West London and the train journey to Pinner was depressing, for although the weather cleared, the pale sun of Pinner was still only an anaemic counterfeit of the great burnished orb of Pinta Leone.

Back with his family he discovered that his sickly son was ill yet again. He was pleased to see his daughter and told her all about the island and something of what he had done there but his wife was showing all the signs of having enjoyed his absence and was resentful at his return. It was a bleak homecoming, especially after the warmth and sensual pleasure of the past few days.

Richard Thornbury, however, was eager to see him. Stansgate was summoned to his office as soon as he arrived at the factory and made to recount the details of his trip and his opinions of Portalier, Gonzales, their organisations, and the land they had to sell.

Stansgate was fulsome in his praise of all of them, especially the land, and his spirits were lifted as he saw that Thornbury was enthusiastically taking it all in. He was even more heartened when Thornbury asked him to prepare a detailed report and description of his trip and the land, though he was surprised when the young man returned his first draft suggesting a large number of amendments and additions.

'Detail, old boy, detail,' he said. 'Exact location of the land, where the airport could be sited. Where we could build the hotels. Draw a plan of the beach, include their surveyors' assessment, all of that.'

It took three attempts by Stansgate to produce the fifteen pages of typescript which satisfied Thornbury and which finally constituted, along with the original publicity material and a local surveyors' report, a very impressive document.

'It's not what you say to people like Smithson-Perez, it's how you say it,' commented Thornbury as he attached to the report a covering letter. The letter, which gave Stansgate the credit for the report and for investigating the potential investment, was more proof that Thornbury was seriously interested in buying the beach on Pinta Leone.

Stansgate was elated. Secretly he had assumed that the sudden desire to invest in the Caribbean had been a passing fancy and that the requirement to borrow fifty million dollars and the need to construct hotels and all the other amenities of a modern holiday resort would have cooled the young man's ardour. But none of it had deterred Thornbury, and he had appreciated the need for quick action. The young man was, when he wanted to be, extremely efficient. He was also, the fat accountant found to his surprise, very considerate.

'Look,' he said after the thick envelope had been despatched to Henry Dundonald at Smithson-Perez, 'you must be very tired. Why don't you take the rest of the week off. You deserve it.'

Stansgate was grateful for the offer. He was desperately tired. He spent the next few days at home with his family, all the while praying that the merchant bank would agree to loan Thornbury eighteen million pounds.

On the second day of his absence Richard Thornbury booked a flight to Geneva. There, he opened an account at a respectable Swiss bank before flying back to London where the following day he opened another account at a bank in Piccadilly. The ticket for the flight to Geneva and both the bank accounts were registered in the name of George Rupert Stansgate.

Chapter Seven

There were a dozen of them seated round the long table of the dining room. The waiters had served the summer pudding and were hovering, ready to bring in the coffee and liqueurs. Outside, through the high windows of the bank, the sun was emerging after a morning of showers.

The room was noisy with conversation; earlier there had been talk of the scandals which in that summer of 1963 were frightening the mighty; everyone present had connections with the powerful people who were deeply implicated in the notorious events daily paraded in the pages of the newspapers.

There was a lull in the chatter. Henry Dundonald leaned across the table to address his chairman. 'I've had a proposal from Thornbury Engineering,' he said loudly. The noble lord was not deaf, but Dundonald wanted everyone to hear what he had to say. 'They've found a stretch of land in the Caribbean which they say could be developed into a first-class holiday resort.'

'Really?' replied the chairman. 'Any good, do you think?'

'It's a good proposal,' Dundonald responded.

'How much do they want to borrow?'

'About eighteen million.'

'Lot of money,' observed someone further down the table.

'It's a lot of land, apparently. About fifteen miles of good beach,' said Dundonald.

157

'Will we do it, do you think?' enquired the chairman.

Everyone's attention was on Dundonald as he leaned back in his seat. 'I think not,' he replied slowly. 'It's a beguiling proposition but really we're committed in the Middle East. I don't think we should stretch ourselves too broadly. There will be problems with exchange controls and I'm not altogether too sure about overseas property development. It's a dangerous game.' Out of the corner of his eye he caught some of the younger directors grimacing at his cautious attitude. 'I think we should let it go,' he said.

The chairman nodded in agreement and was turning to the man on his left when Dundonald continued.

'We could take a brokerage fee if we introduce the scheme to a property developer; someone who knows the business.'

'Excellent idea.' The chairman raised his voice. 'If anyone knows someone who may be interested, please see Henry Dundonald.' It was an invitation to anyone present to make some easy money both for himself and for the bank which would take, as an introductory fee, one per cent of any loan negotiated between Thornbury and the property company. The man who successfully introduced the scheme to a developer would be included in a share of the profits and would be invited to become a well-paid non-executive director of the property company. It was through such inside dealings, through its network of contacts and favours, that the City and its daylight citizens flourished.

The phone in Henry Dundonald's office rang the following morning. It was his secretary announcing that a Mr Eastcote wished to speak to him. The voice on the other end of the line was smooth, yet insistent. Nigel Eastcote was one of the new breed of property developers, public school and pushy; he affected the English aggressive style. He was twenty-six and a millionaire many times over.

'Hello,' he said, 'this is Nigel Eastcote. Look, I hope you don't mind me ringing you out of the blue like this but

actually Ian Silver suggested I call you. I understand you
have an option on a land deal in the Caribbean. Could we
talk about it? Perhaps over lunch?'

'No, I don't think so, thank you. I'm happy to talk, but
not over lunch.' Dundonald was deliberate. 'I suggest we
meet in my office. I would prefer to keep things fairly
formal.'

'Of course. Absolutely. I understand,' Eastcote
responded immediately. Ian Silver, one of the directors
who had been present at the previous day's lunch, was a
close friend and had told him that Dundonald was pedantic
in matters relating to the bank.

'Could you come here at about ten o'clock tomorrow
morning? We could talk then.'

'I'll be there,' Eastcote replied. 'Goodbye.' The phone
went dead.

Eastcote's Rolls-Royce drew up outside the columned
entrance of the bank at two minutes to ten the following
morning. He was about medium height, good-looking with
light brown hair and pale blue eyes. He was remarkably
photogenic; and that, combined with his money and glittering life style, made him beloved of the newspapers.
Dundonald considered him ostentatious and something of
a spiv. After the young man had been ushered into
Dundonald's office and the two men had talked over coffee
about mutual acquaintances, the banker took out a brown
manilla file.

'This is the proposal I received from Thornbury Engineering,' he said. 'It is the only copy and is, of course,
confidential. I shall allow you to read it now in my presence. Should you indicate an interest in principle, I shall
write to Thornbury so stating. You will have forty-eight
hours in which to open preliminary discussions with them.
Should you not contact them within that time I shall expect
the return of this document. I would ask you not to have

any copies of it made. Should your negotiations with Thornbury go well, then the bank, as honest broker in the transaction, will expect the payment of one per cent of any final loan.'

He passed the file to Eastcote, stood up, turned to the tall windows and with his hands clasped firmly behind his back watched the construction workers on the new buildings going up along London Wall.

Eastcote stared at the long straight back of the banker. Christ, he thought, this fellow thinks he's still in the army. Pompous prick. This had better be good. He turned his attention to the documents. It was. At the end of ten minutes' reading he was impressed. He coughed faintly and Dundonald swivelled round. 'I should tell you,' he said as Dundonald sat down at his desk, 'that I am interested in principle. Very interested. Can I ask you why you and Smithson-Perez do not wish to pursue the proposal?'

'Certainly,' responded Dundonald. 'Currently we have numerous proposals under consideration; most of our investment is in European commercial development or Middle East construction. Therefore I do not consider this proposal as attractive as many of the others we are considering.'

'I understand,' said Eastcote in a serious tone. Inwardly he was buoyant. He calculated that if the investment was only half as attractive as the report suggested it would still be a wonderful coup. Such a holiday resort would make him internationally famous; Thornbury Engineering, as far as he could see, would cause him no problems. He would lend them the money and then, once they were heavily mortgaged to him, he would contrive to take them over and strip out their most valuable assets. Part of Eastcote's well-concealed delight also centred on the opportunity to snatch a highly profitable undertaking from under the superior nose of the stiff and punctilious Dundonald whom he considered to be hidebound by the unwritten self-regulating rules of the City's institutions. The young Eastcote represented a new generation of financial manipulators who had come to despise the City's institutional practices and to break them without compunction; they were financial gunslingers who always played to win, unconventional and spectacularly successful.

Eastcote's own investment and property company was worth, on paper, more than ten million pounds; a fortune he had conjured out of nothing in less than five years. The rest of the City looked upon him and his kind with a mixture of admiration and disdain. Eastcote for his part was constantly eager for opportunities to humiliate the likes of Henry Dundonald and Smithson-Perez by creating successes out of projects which they had been too cautious to consider. He was in a marvellous mood as he bounded down the few steps of the bank's entrance, the proposal under his arm, and climbed into the back of the waiting Rolls.

From the windows of the second floor, Dundonald watched him go. There was not a trace of emotion on the banker's face, not a sign that he was pleased he had successfully accomplished his part in the great deception. He was merely reflecting on how much he disliked young men who dressed in mohair suits, sought the attention of the newspapers and who allowed themselves to be chauffeured everywhere in Rolls-Royce motor cars.

George Stansgate slowly climbed the staircase leading to the musty corridor of offices on the first floor of Thornbury's factory. It was almost nine thirty and the start of another day working through the perplexing and mysterious accounts of the company. It had been a week since his return from the short holiday he had taken at Richard Thornbury's insistence; a week in which the details of his journey to Pinta Leone had flickered in his brain and a yearning had grown like a canyon within him.

At the top of the stairs he was surprised to see Thornbury; he had not seen him since the day they had posted the proposal to Smithson-Perez.

'Ah, I'm glad you're here,' Thornbury clapped him lightly on the shoulder. 'Can you come into my office?' He closed the door behind them. 'Look,' he said, 'I've heard from Smithson-Perez. They've turned us down, I'm afraid.'

The emptiness inside Stansgate engulfed him; the disappointment was like a blow which rocked him on his heels. Thornbury smiled at his reaction. 'No need to take it quite so hard, old boy,' he laughed. 'In fact, things may have worked out for the best. The bank has passed on the proposal to a developer. Here, read the letter.'

Stansgate took the sheet of expensive cartridge paper and endeavoured to focus his mind on the short, simple sentences beneath the embossed crest of the bank. He got the sense of it on the second reading and his flattened hopes rose again.

'But why isn't the bank interested?' he enquired. 'You said they sent us the brochure in the first place.'

Thornbury looked surprised. 'Did I? Well, you know banks, old boy. Anyway, the point is that Nigel Eastcote is one of the best property developers around; in the end he's a much better bet than the bank.'

'If he's interested,' responded Stansgate in a dull tone. 'He's only got a couple of days to contact us.'

'He already has.' Thornbury laughed. 'He's coming up today to talk. Actually, his sister was at school with mine.'

The Rolls-Royce slid into Thornbury's yard just after twelve o'clock. Thornbury went down to greet Eastcote at the little cubicle with the sliding window which was the company's reception and accompanied him to his office where they were joined by Stansgate.

After the introductions, Thornbury opened the cocktail cabinet. 'Not much, I'm afraid,' he said. 'Gin or whisky, that's about all. Don't use this place very often.'

Eastcote had whisky, the others gin. They sat down on the hard, upright chairs. Thornbury and Eastcote had a number of friends in common and much of their conversation excluded Stansgate who found it difficult to follow their formalised slang. After about half an hour, Thornbury suggested lunch. Eastcote insisted that they take the Rolls; they drove south towards Worcester to a large hotel with a good restaurant. Over lunch the conversation turned to the reason for Eastcote's visit.

'I must congratulate you on an excellent proposal,' he said to Thornbury.

'Nothing to do with me,' Richard Thornbury replied with a smile. 'Entirely the work of George, my financial director here.'

'Really?' Eastcote was surprised as he looked at Stansgate whom he had written off as an overweight and pompous accountant. 'It's very good. Could you tell me more, do you think?'

For the following twenty minutes, Stansgate talked about the island and the investment. He endeavoured to keep his voice neutral and to appear impersonal but his enthusiasm for the idea became apparent almost immediately. Eastcote was particularly interested in the financial state of the Caicos and Caribbean Company and the Bank of Nuvo Grado. 'Don't know much about banks in that part of the world,' he said, 'but it could be useful.'

'Especially for transferring money,' acknowledged Thornbury.

'Ah yes, the money,' said Eastcote. 'Well, I can quite see why you need me for that but, frankly, I don't see why I need you.'

'What do you mean?' Stansgate enquired.

'What he means,' said Thornbury, smiling broadly, 'is what is to stop him negotiating directly with our friends in Pinta Leone – you know, cutting us out of the deal.'

Stansgate was shocked. 'You can't do that, it isn't ethical.'

Eastcote laughed, a short sharp bark. 'Ethical? I had lessons in ethics at school. Never understood them. Not that it matters, I haven't come across them since.'

Thornbury chuckled loudly. Stansgate was perplexed by his attitude; he was making no attempt to protect the position of his own company; in fact, he seemed more in sympathy with Eastcote and his hints at double-crossing them.

'I believe the people in Pinta Leone understand the meaning of ethics,' Stansgate stated. 'Thornbury Engineering have first option on that land and I'm convinced they'll honour that.'

'Don't be too sure,' said Eastcote. 'In these things it's first come, first served.'

Stansgate remembered that Portalier and Gonzales had said the same thing. He felt the victim of a conspiracy, struggling alone without help.

'They'll be prepared to wait,' he responded, 'while we raise the money.'

'You'll have to be quick,' said Eastcote, 'they won't wait long. Smithson-Perez have already said no.'

'There are other banks,' Stansgate said haughtily. 'Anyway, I don't suppose that even you have that kind of money in your account. You'll have to raise the money as well.'

'I would imagine that I'm a lot better than Thornbury Engineering at doing that, if you don't mind me saying so.'

'Exactly, old boy, that's why you're here, isn't it?' Thornbury leaned across the table. He was smiling. 'You'll borrow the eighteen million and pay interest at a couple of per cent over bank rate. But you'll make us pay interest at four or five per cent over bank rate. You'll make money on the deal even before you start. Thornbury'll mortgage the land to you so in the event of our default, you'll own it. Either way, you'll have an exclusive contract to develop the whole bloody beach. We both know that by using

Thornbury you can eliminate all risk while making even more money.'

'Well, that's quite true,' acknowledged Eastcote, 'if, of course, you agree to such an arrangement.'

'We both know that we will,' Thornbury said quietly. For a few seconds they were silent as each of them considered the tacit agreement they had joined. Once again Stansgate was surprised by Richard Thornbury's commercial acumen, his ability cynically to perceive the motives behind Eastcote's presence. Thornbury had demonstrated the same perception when they had drawn up the report for the bank; it was almost as if he was prepared, as if he knew in advance what to say in order to get what he wanted. In this case, what he appeared to want was an agreement which would be completely to Eastcote's advantage. Thornbury Engineering would carry all the risk in the hope of making a massive profit when the land was developed.

'Jolly good,' said Eastcote breezily. 'I'll get my solicitors to talk to your people and we'll have some draft heads of agreement drawn up. In the meantime, I suppose I ought to go and see the promised land.'

'The sooner the better,' said Thornbury. 'We've agreed they won't wait long.'

Eastcote smiled.

'We ought to go next week if you can arrange it,' stated Stansgate.

The smile on Eastcote's face was replaced by a look of puzzlement. 'We?'

'Of course, old boy,' Richard Thornbury interjected. 'You really ought to go with George, he's the link between us and the people over there. After all, we are partners.' He raised his glass as he emphasised his last remark.

Eastcote did his best to keep the look of distaste off his face as he comtemplated at least seven days and twenty thousand miles in the company of the fat accountant. He reached into his inside pocket for his diary.

One of the most profitable elements in Victor Maggiore's large and illegal organisation was the stealing and forging of stock certificates, and the most efficient salesman of 'bad paper' was Joe Collioure. Joe was a 'paper hanger' and proud of it. He looked the part, tall and elegantly dressed with hair greying at the temples and gold-rimmed spectacles. He had passed millions of dollars' worth of useless bonds and share certificates onto unsuspecting people and organisations. But the mission in which Joe was currently engaged and about which he had been briefed personally by Victor was a new and puzzling departure from his more usual methods of operation. In the case beneath his seat were two separate bundles of stock certificates and bearer bonds. Each collection had a face value of millions of dollars, or would have had were it not for the fact that all of them were either forged or stolen. Joe's assignment was to hand over one of the fake portfolios to a man in Panama City who would keep it for no more than twenty-four hours. Subsequently he was to fly to an island that he had never heard of, somewhere in the Caribbean, where he was to repeat the process. With the return of the second collection he would receive fifteen thousand dollars in cash as payment for the service he had provided.

Joe was astute enough to know that the certificates were part of some great fraud, a guess endorsed by Victor who had told him to learn as much as possible about the use to which his bad paper would be put, and to pay particular attention to the people involved and their places of business. Joe smiled to himself. Maggiore had apparently discovered the potential to be realised not only from selling bad paper, but from renting it. It was like Hertz hiring out stolen cars. The thought made him chuckle quietly. He eased himself into a more comfortable position in his seat as the Dakota's engines droned southwards. He felt drowsy and closed his eyes to doze while, unnoticed, four rows ahead the only two Englishmen on the midday flight from Miami to Panama City sat awkwardly in each other's company, fervently wishing for the end of their long journey from London.

George Stansgate could not define precisely what it was that was so different about his second trip to Panama. Max Gonzales had met him and Eastcote at the airport and driven them to the El Continental where awaiting them were the luxurious bedrooms and ice-cold champagne he had come to expect. Perhaps, thought Stansgate, it was Eastcote who made the difference. The man was a business machine, constantly figuring the angles. On the journey he had talked loudly of nothing but his successes, of the men and the companies he had made or broken. After hours of exposure to this unrelenting aggression, Stansgate felt battered.

He also sensed a subtle change in the demeanour of Max Gonzales who seemed more deferential than before, content to allow him to do most of the talking. Stansgate was flattered, if a little puzzled. He required some help to explain a few of the accounts to Eastcote, but the property developer quickly grasped the financial complexities of the Caicos and Caribbean Company, which he named C3, and by the second day needed little guidance. He was greatly impressed when Gonzales extracted from the safe the French deed to the land on Pinta Leone. 'It would look marvellous on an office wall,' he said.

While he was admiring the copperplate script, Gonzales gently pulled Stansgate aside and said, 'I think you should show our friend some of the assets.' He indicated the open safe which was filled with bonds and stock certificates. Stansgate called Eastcote across as he took a handful of the certificates out of the safe. Each one of them was to the value of a hundred thousand dollars, issued by the largest of the American corporations.

Eastcote stared in amazement. 'My God!' he exclaimed. 'How much have you got in there?'

'According to the accounts,' replied Gonzales picking up a ledger, 'almost fifteen million dollars' worth.'

'And you keep it all in that safe?'

'Normally no.' Gonzales smiled. 'We hold them in a bank deposit, but I thought you would wish to see them. After all, figures in the accounts only really mean something if you can see what they represent.'

Eastcote nodded vaguely in agreement as he sorted through the certificates.

'I have a complete breakdown if you require it,' said Gonzales.

'I don't think we need that right now,' replied Eastcote. 'So,' he looked up, 'you purchased the land on Pinta Leone from the Bank of Nuvo Grado for six million dollars, half cash and the other half in negotiable bonds. And now you want fifty million?'

Gonzales shrugged. 'Wait until you see it,' he said. 'We are merely charging what the market will pay. The land originally belonged to the family of Mr Portalier who is now president of the bank. He holds power of attorney to act for this company in any sale transaction.' He paused and then said slowly, 'Of course, we would be happy to sell the land through the bank if that would help ease any problems with the British exchange controls.'

Eastcote knew that it would. In common with many other property developers, he had set up a 'secondary bank', an institution which had a licence to lend and borrow money. It had originally been established merely to service his own property deals but in the heady days of the early 1960s, Eastcote's bank had taken on an identity of its own; now it was handling business worth millions of pounds, all related to complicated property transactions.

Eastcote knew that if his own 'bank' loaned the eighteen million pound purchase price of the land to the Bank of Nuvo Grado, the Bank of England could probably be persuaded that the transaction was an inter-bank loan, which meant there would be no dollar premium.

To Stansgate's surprise, Gonzales told him over dinner on the eve of their departure that he would not be flying to the island with them. 'You know all there is to know, you don't need me,' he said. Again, Stansgate was puzzled by Gonzales's reticence, his wish to keep his dealings with Eastcote at arm's length. Stansgate's main concern on the flight across the Caribbean, though, was whether he could adequately explain the Bank of Nuvo Grado's finances on his own.

When the Buick that had met them at the airport dropped them off outside the bank's offices in Nuvo Grado, Eastcote was surprised by their quiet and refined exterior. 'Some money about here, old boy. I can smell it.' He nudged Stansgate and nodded at the brass plaque.

John Portalier was waiting for them in his office. He was as charming and hospitable as always, and it soon became clear that Eastcote, despite the fact that he had come prepared to treat him as an adversary, liked him. After their second round of drinks, Portalier invited his visitors to begin their inspection of the bank's accounts.

'Stansgate here knows our books pretty well,' he said. 'Perhaps he can explain the basics and I'll fill in the details when necessary.'

For the second time in forty-eight hours, Stansgate found himself stumbling through unfamiliar accounts. Portalier listened amiably to the obese accountant's faltering explanations while Eastcote sifted impatiently through the figures, occasionally barking out a question which, usually, Portalier had to answer. It took a day to complete the inspection of the accounts; it was in the afternoon that Portalier revealed the bank's assets, the stock and share certificates left with him by Joe Collioure earlier that morning. He took the bundles out of his safe and deposited them in piles on the mahogany desk in his office.

Eastcote checked a figure. 'According to this, you should have twenty million dollars worth of these bonds,' he said. Stansgate looked flustered as John Portalier smoothly agreed. Eastcote picked up a pile of the certificates and inspected them. 'You know,' he said, 'Caicos and Caribbean have a few million dollars' worth of these things too.'

'Of course,' Portalier replied. 'Most major organisations in this part of the world hold US negotiable bonds. The Caribbean is a business community which believes in real money.'

Eastcote nodded. 'So I see. You also have over one hundred million dollars in loans from the First National Bank of Pinta Leone.'

Portalier smiled. 'We are very fortunate. The bank was founded by North American business interests and both they and we are looking for good investments.'

'One of which is C3 in Panama,' observed Eastcote. 'Your accounts seem tied in with theirs.'

'Of course,' Portalier said again. 'Mr Gonzales runs a very profitable organisation. We are glad to be so closely associated with him. But we are very cautious about the organisations in whom we invest. After all, we are a bank.'

Eastcote nodded wisely, but later in his hotel room he was more elated. 'Don't you see,' he said to Stansgate, 'they are the same business. A trading company in Panama funded by an offshore bank, both of them simply awash with money. It's perfect. If I can play it right, then once I've bought the land, I can get these people to fund the whole development. All I have to do is raise eighteen million pounds and buy that bloody beach.'

'We,' interceded Stansgate.

'Yes, of course,' Eastcote laughed. 'We. Don't worry, old boy, I won't double-cross Thornbury, there's no point.

This deal is so perfect, it's not true. If the beach is as good as you say, then we're made for life.'

They dined without Portalier who had earlier apologised that he would be unable to join them. He called Stansgate early the following morning. 'The car will be round in half an hour,' he announced. 'I hope Eastcote appreciates the land as much as you.'

'Aren't you coming with us?'

'Can't, I'm afraid,' said Portalier, 'but don't worry, everything is laid on.'

A smiling Billy Jamaica arrived at the hotel with the Buick stocked with cold champagne and a hamper of food. Stansgate apologised to Eastcote for Portalier's absence, though in his desire to see the land he hardly seemed to notice. They followed the same route that Stansgate had taken just a few weeks before, driving along the highway on the eastern edge of the island before turning off into the mountains. This time they encountered an army patrol, which stopped them.

'Hello, where are you two off to?' enquired the young lieutenant in charge.

Stansgate remembered Portalier's earlier words of warning. 'Oh, just touring,' he replied nonchalantly. 'We are interested in investment on the island.'

Eastcote offered the young lieutenant a glass of champagne.

'No bandits about then?' he asked.

'Absolutely none,' replied the lieutenant, gratefully sipping the champagne. 'Gone to ground permanently I think.' He finished his drink and handed the glass back through the open car window. 'Enjoy your visit.'

Billy Jamaica seemed anxious to make up for lost time; he drove the car at a furious pace along the narrow mountain roads.

'Slow down,' ordered Eastcote. 'I'm spilling my bloody champagne.'

Suddenly they were out of the mountains, at the top of the steep descent which led to the beach. Beyond the strip of golden sand, the sun glinted on the blue Caribbean.

'Well, what do you think of it?' asked Stansgate proudly. He was amused to see Eastcote's reaction, which exactly mirrored his own when he had first caught sight of the beach.

'Fantastic,' murmured Eastcote. 'Fantastic.'

For the next few hours they toured the area, driving up and down the coast road. Stansgate pointed out the areas for development that he had included in his report and Eastcote marked them on the map. They stopped for lunch and as they sat on the beach, watching the ocean whisper up onto the sand, Billy served them the contents of the hamper. The few local inhabitants they saw ignored them. Billy brought the ship's compass from the car and handed it to Stansgate, who said: 'I've already confirmed the location but I think you ought to do the same.'

Together they checked the map against the compass whose reading confirmed that they were on the north-east of the island on the stretch of coastline marked on the map by Stansgate.

It was in the middle of the afternoon, on their last drive along the beach, that the only mishap of the day occurred. The car suddenly swerved and came to a stop. Billy got out to investigate. 'Puncture,' he said. 'Won't take long.'

Neither of his passengers was at all perturbed; they were both full of champagne and the wellbeing of men who expected to make a fortune out of paradise. In fact it took the scowling and agitated chauffeur more than two hours to replace the wheel. By then the sun was beginning to dip into the sea and shadows were lengthening along the beach.

They roared south along the highway towards Pinta Leone. The sun set and the sky turned the colour of Brighton rock. Night fell. Eastcote was full of plans; hotels and marinas and a great international airport were soon constructed within his imagination.

They met Portalier the following day at the bank. East-cote at first seemed inclined to haggle. 'It is an excellent piece of property,' he said, 'but you are asking a very high price.'

Portalier scowled. 'Mr Eastcote, this is the Bank of Nuvo Grado, not a stall in the bazaar. The bank and I are acting on behalf of the Caicos and Caribbean in this matter and neither they nor I are prepared to haggle. We are asking a fair price for the property and George will tell you that there are other interested parties who are prepared to pay what we are asking.'

Stansgate could only nod in agreement as Eastcote looked at him in surprise.

He turned back to Portalier. 'Very well,' he said, 'we shall meet your price.'

Portalier's face registered neither surprise nor pleasure. His expression remained fixed. 'Any purchaser would be expected to do that. More important is the question of when?'

'When?' queried Eastcote.

'Absolutely,' said Portalier. 'In this part of the world we conclude our agreements swiftly. When would you anticipate completion of the deal?'

Eastcote looked surprised. It was the first time that Stansgate had seen the young man lose his haughty demeanour. 'Well,' he was hesitant, 'I suppose when all the papers are drawn up and the formalities completed. However long that takes.'

'If your City law firms can be persuaded to work at a slightly faster pace than usual, it could all be completed inside a month.' Portalier turned to Stansgate. 'Don't you agree, George? I presume,' he continued without waiting for an answer, 'that Thornbury Engineering are still the principals in the arrangement?'

Stansgate said they were.

'Then,' Portalier's face broke into a smile, 'I suggest we

get down to business.' It took them two hours to work out the method whereby the British exchange control regulations could be avoided and eighteen million pounds exported to Panama without incurring the payment of another six million in dollar premium.

They agreed that Eastcote's property company would lend Thornbury Engineering eighteen million pounds. Thornbury would immediately deposit the money in Eastcote's secondary bank which would then convert the sum to fifty million dollars and lend it to the Bank of Nuvo Grado which in turn would pay the purchase price of the land direct to C3 on Thornbury's behalf. With the help of understanding lawyers and accountants the transaction would be viewed by the authorities as a genuine inter-bank loan and would escape the dollar premium. Eastcote and Stansgate also agreed that Thornbury Engineering and Eastcote's property company would together set up a separate company which would hold the deeds to the land and develop the entire coastline.

'It will take all the assets that Thornbury Engineering's got to fund our share in the new company,' said Stansgate gloomily.

'For God's sake,' Eastcote barked, 'sell it completely and put everything into this. Why make boilers in Bromsgrove when you can make cash in the Caribbean?' The three men laughed and Portalier opened another bottle of champagne to celebrate their agreement. They toasted each other and their success before Eastcote and Stansgate departed for the airport and England where the lawyers would construct the long and tedious documents which would mean for each of them the fulfilment of their avaricious dreams.

By the time that the plane bearing Eastcote and Stansgate had arrived at Heathrow Airport, a telex from Mr Thomas Cranmer in Panama City addressed to Mr Boniface had been collected from an accommodation address in

Paddington and its coded contents communicated to Addingham, Blackmore and the rest.

'Our friend says it's going well,' Woodberry told them. 'Everything's on schedule. We should have completion in a month.' The partners were pleased to receive the news and would have been even more pleased had they known the eagerness with which Nigel Eastcote was rushing to clinch what he called the deal of a lifetime.

It took him, on the first day of his return, just two hours and fifteen phone calls to raise eighteen million pounds. By five o'clock that afternoon, the managers of four pension funds, two insurance companies and a number of secondary banks had agreed to commit the total purchase price of the land to Eastcote. In return they were promised an attractive rate of interest on their loans and invited to form part of the consortium which would develop the lucrative piece of real estate. All the men who had committed sums of money down the telephone knew Eastcote well and admired his infallible Midas touch.

In the days that followed, letters and contracts flowed out of Eastcote's plush offices in Curzon Street. Loan documents were drawn up, contracts negotiated and amended while a stream of telexes ran between London, Panama and Pinta Leone. The lawyers who in Eastcote's absence had been arranging the loans between his property company and Thornbury Engineering were requested also to negotiate the formation of a new, joint company.

Eastcote had brought back with him a set of the published accounts of the Bank of Nuvo Grado. Armed with these he, his lawyers and accountants went to see a man at the Bank of England who finally agreed that the loan by Eastcote to the bank was legitimate and that there would be no dollar premium to pay.

After four weeks of intense activity the deal was ready for completion. The documents which showed the money moving from Eastcote to Thornbury Engineering and back again had been completed; the outside loans, at an interest rate of two per cent over bank rate, had been finalised with Eastcote's bankers, and the Thornbury loan at four and a half per cent over bank rate had been agreed, though not without some protest from George Stansgate.

John Portalier flew in from Pinta Leone. The Caicos and Caribbean Company had given him power of attorney to sign all the papers relating to the sale. At a short meeting on a warm morning in early August, he, Eastcote, Stansgate and Richard Thornbury met in the Curzon Street offices to finalise the great sale. Portalier handed Eastcote the framed land deed as well as the deed of sale from C3 and the documents acknowledging the loan. In return, Eastcote gave him a banker's draft made out on the Bank of America for fifty million four hundred thousand dollars.

The four men shook hands before Eastcote's secretary came into the office with some glasses and a bottle of champagne in a bucket of ice. After they had celebrated the deal's successful completion, Eastcote hung the framed land deed on the wall above his desk. He had been right, the ancient document with its copperplate script and great red seal did indeed look impressive on his office wall. Portalier viewed it with an impassive stare; the tinge of remorse he had once suffered at seeing the last of the family land had gone. He was glad to see the end to title deeds and contracts; his share of the fifty million dollars nestling in his pocket was what interested him.

Although Thornbury Engineering, as the prime borrowers, had rights to title of the land, Eastcote, as the lender, had insisted that he retain not only the title deed but all the other legal documents, a fact remarked upon by Stansgate afterwards as he shared a cab with Richard Thornbury.

'Why not?' Thornbury said, smiling broadly. 'It's Eastcote's money, although,' he added reflectively, 'it isn't, is it?' He laughed. 'It's probably a lot of poor bastards' savings for their pathetic pensions. Anyway, it doesn't really matter, the joint company will eventually hold all the documents. By the way,' he looked at Stansgate, 'Eastcote's agreed that you should be managing director of the new property company. Not sure what we're going to call it yet though.'

Stansgate was elated, though faintly surprised that Eastcote had agreed to his new appointment. The news drove out the remaining fears and queries he held about the enterprise, for somewhere in the back of his mind had been a worm of crawling doubt. In all the high-powered manoeuvrings, the sleek and clever negotiations, the high stakes and expensive offices, he could not comprehend the role of Thornbury Engineering; he couldn't see what they stood to gain from an investment which bled them white and would not give them a return for years.

Richard Thornbury's explanation that the deal would improve the company's share price wasn't sufficient. It seemed to Stansgate that Thornbury had the greatest risk and the least possibility of gain. But as the taxi swung round Hyde Park Corner, and George Stansgate gazed at the tourists lying on the summer grass of Green Park, the worm of doubt was drowned in the tide of rising ambition.

That afternoon, John Portalier hired a car and drove to Upham where Addingham, who was in recess from the courts, had a weekend cottage. Addingham's daily lady served them drinks as they sat in the sunshine of the large, but untidy garden. Portalier passed the banker's draft to Addingham and watched with faint amusement as the barrister examined it carefully, smacking his lips together.

'You know, Edward,' said Portalier, 'when you first told me about your scheme, I wondered whether it would work; certainly I thought the game was up when I called you from New York. And now here we are, and it's all over.'

'Not quite.' Addingham's bird-like features broke into a frosty smile as he returned the draft to Portalier. 'That money has to be put through Panama and Switzerland and our people in both places have to be paid off.'

Portalier flew out the next day to New York and from there to Panama. Accompanied by Max Gonzales, he spent a busy morning at one of the largest banks in the city arranging for the fifty million to be credited to the account of the Caicos and Caribbean Company. He then set about arranging for the transfer of the money from Panama to Switzerland. Watched by Max Gonzales, he sent a coded message under his alias of Cranmer to Schellenberg in Liechtenstein. That afternoon, the Panamanian bank's telex machines chattered into life and within minutes their coded and secure instructions had transferred fifty million dollars from Panama to the account of an anonymous trust fund in Liechtenstein. Later that afternoon the money was transferred from Liechtenstein to a numbered bank account in Switzerland, and a coded telegram was despatched to Mr Boniface in England requesting instructions.

Woodberry picked up the telegram from the Paddington accommodation address the following day and set about telephoning his partners, all of whom were, at the height of summer, out of London. Addingham was in Hampshire, Dundonald was in Scotland awaiting the start of the grouse season. Ashley Brighton was at his holiday home in St Cyprien and both Blackmore and Frimley-Kimpton were somewhere in northern Italy. Richard Thornbury was dividing his time between London and Southampton making ready to go sailing in the Mediterranean.

By early evening Woodberry had finished his task. He had informed all of them that the partnership had made more than fifty million dollars and each of them was individually richer by almost two and a quarter million pounds.

That night as they slept, a dozen men forcibly stopped a train in Bedfordshire and robbed it of more than two and a half million pounds in used bank notes. It was, so the newspapers said, the biggest robbery in the history of British crime.

Addingham in later conversations with his colleagues at the Bar was scathing of the great train robbery. 'Any fool can rob a train,' he said. 'Those people are mindless idiots, nothing but gangsters. They're bound to get caught and for what? A paltry couple of million that they'll never spend.'

His eminent friends were unanimous in their agreement; like him, they were seriously worried that the country was suffering a crisis in morality and a breakdown in law and order.

In the weeks that followed, both Gonzales and Portalier were instructed to close down their respective organisations. The three accessories, Gonzales in Panama, Stekenmuller in Switzerland and the lawyer Schellenberg in Liechtenstein were variously propitiated. Gonzales, for his part, was paid one million dollars, the money being deposited in his numbered account in Switzerland; the two Europeans were each paid half a million dollars in recognition of their work as trustees. The remaining money, forty-eight million dollars, was divided into eight and deposited in the numbered accounts which bore the strange and ancient names of long dead archbishops.

It was during that time, when the summer season was at its height, that the name Thornbury Engineering began to appear with increasing frequency in the financial press. Word of the purchase of a vast tract of beautiful real estate on the island of Pinta Leone, the scene of a savage massacre of British troops only months earlier, was leaked to the papers. Nigel Eastcote and Richard Thornbury were interviewed frequently by the financial press. Thornbury in particular revelled in the attention he was receiving from the media.

Details of the purchase were described in the press and a few people who knew the island were puzzled by the newspaper's description of the beach's location. One woman wrote to Eastcote directly, saying that the paper had mis-printed the location, the beach was in fact on the north-west of the island, not the north-east. Eastcote threw the letter away, he had no time for cranks. But it was the middle of summer and very few people seriously read the financial press; what few copies of the papers finally fetched up in Pinta Leone weren't read at all.

The news did, however, have a startling effect upon Thornbury's share price; within three weeks it doubled. This seemed just another example of Nigel Eastcote's brilliant astuteness; any enterprise which was connected with his name seemed naturally to grow richer.

The upward surge of the company's shares was greatly helped by the individual efforts of all the partners who, separately and unknown to each other, had bought substantial blocks of shares in Thornbury at their lowest price and had, through their individual influence, created a swelling rumour of the fortune to be made through investment in the company. The directors of Smithson-Perez which had for many years been a major shareholder in Thornbury Engineering were delighted to see what had long been a dead and low-yielding investment begin to show a profitable return. They were therefore greatly surprised when in the middle of September, after four weeks of a continuing upward spiral in Thornbury's share price, they received an internal memorandum from Henry Dundonald advising the bank to sell its shares.

'But why?' expostulated the bank's chairman at a board meeting the following day. 'For the first time in more than ten years the shares are worth having.'

'Exactly,' retorted Dundonald. 'If we sell now, we will show a profit.'

'But we'll lose all the future profits after they develop the land,' said the chairman. Most of the others present nodded in agreement.

'Don't forget they are tied up with Nigel Eastcote now.'

It was the voice of Ian Silver sitting near the far end of the long boardroom table.

'That's one of the things that concerns me,' Dundonald said flatly.

'What do you mean?' asked Silver.

Dundonald stared down the table at him. 'I know that Eastcote has friends here and I know that the man who told him about the Caribbean proposal will probably have been well rewarded.'

The younger man reddened slightly.

'Don't misunderstand me,' Dundonald continued, 'none of us has anything against that. It's only decent that profitable information should be rewarded. The bank itself has done well; we've been paid over a hundred thousand pounds for introducing Eastcote to Thornbury.'

'So why sell?' questioned the chairman.

'Because I don't think Nigel Eastcote is as clever as he thinks he is.' Dundonald's voice was unemotional. 'I don't think any of these property developers are, even with their big developments and secondary banks. I don't think they really understand money. Sooner or later they'll get it wrong, then it will be us who has to bale them out.'

'What makes you think that Eastcote has got it wrong?' asked Silver. 'He's just purchased the best piece of estate property in the Caribbean.'

'But will he have the money to develop it?' responded Dundonald. 'None of the money raised to purchase the land was his own, it's all borrowed, and Thornbury Engineering haven't any money, they're borrowing from Eastcote. As for Richard Thornbury, he couldn't manage a booze-up in a brewery. There's no money and no management. I say sell out now while we have the chance.'

In the end the board agreed that the bank should sell their shares. Eastcote, when told of the decision by Ian Silver, was livid.

'Bloody typical,' he fumed. 'Dundonald is just a boring

banker, about as adventurous as my old grannie. You've got to be quick and devious in this business. Anyway, I'll buy the shares myself, it will be the bank's loss.'

When the bank's block of Thornbury Engineering shares were put onto the market, Eastcote was ready to snap them up. The movement of so many shares depressed their price for a few days, until it became known that it was Eastcote himself who had bought them, then the price reached new heights. To many people in the investment community, the bank's decision to sell when there was so much growth left in the shares came as something of a surprise.

Frimley-Kimpton said as much to Oliver Blackmore when they met one morning in the House of Commons. 'Dundonald is protecting the interests of his bank,' commented Blackmore. 'It's been six weeks. It can't be long now before the truth comes out.'

'I bought a fair number of shares some time ago. Should I sell now, do you think?' asked Frimley-Kimpton.

'I would,' said Blackmore. 'I've just sold mine.'

'You bought some too?' asked Frimley-Kimpton in surprise.

'I imagine all of us have,' said Blackmore. 'There's no harm in making a bit of extra capital. After all, we're the only people with the real inside information, aren't we? But now's the time to sell. I'd tell the others to sell too. Eastcote's a fool but it can't be long before even he begins to smell a rat.'

Nigel Eastcote got his first scent of the rat in a hotel in Virginia Water the following Sunday. He was returning to London from the New Forest, where he and his girlfriend Camilla Billingham had been staying with friends for the weekend. It was on a long straight stretch of the A30 that the Silver Cloud developed an alarming wobble. He pulled into the side. One of the rear tyres was flat.

'Shit,' he expostulated. 'We'll have to call the RAC.'

Despite the delay he was in a buoyant mood, it was a fine evening and just a few hundred yards ahead stood a large hotel.

'What time is it?' he asked Camilla.

She looked at her watch. 'Quarter past eight.'

'Let's walk up to the hotel. We can sit in the bar until the fellow has fixed it.'

They set off, walking at the side of the road with streams of Sunday traffic racing past. The sun was dipping below the line of fir trees on their left. 'You know,' said Eastcote, raising his voice against the roar of the passing cars, 'the last time I had a puncture was on Pinta Leone. It took ages to fix and by the time the fellow had finished, the sun was going down over the sea and the whole sky, right to the horizon, looked as if it was on fire.' He nodded in the direction of the trees where the sun's rays were seeping like blood through the dark mass of the conifer forest.

They arrived at the hotel. Eastcote bought two large pink gins and settled Camilla comfortably in the lounge bar before going off to find a phone. It was a busy night and he was told he would have to wait.

They had just finished their second round of drinks when Camilla, who had been staring vacantly out of the window at the gathering dusk, turned to Eastcote. 'Nigel, didn't you say that your famous beach was on the north-east of the island?'

'Not famous yet, darling,' he laughed, 'but it will be soon.'

'But is it on the north-east?'

'Yes, why?'

'Then how could you have seen the sun setting over the sea?'

Eastcote felt icy prickles at the nape of his neck. A frisson of fear scurried down his back. He stared at her for some moments, a blank expression on his face.

'I don't really know,' he said weakly, 'there must be

some explanation. I hadn't thought of it before.' He continued to stare at her pretty, doll-like face, eyebrows raised in enquiry. It was a good question and he wasn't sure if he was going to like the answer. Geography had not been one of his best subjects at school, but even he knew that the sun did not set in the east.

The following day, Eastcote telexed Max Gonzales requesting him to confirm that the details on the maps were accurate and that the beach really was on the east coast of the island. As he did so he recalled a letter from some crank telling him that the newspaper had misprinted the beach's location.

There was no reply to his telex and the fear inside grew a little stronger. He sent a telex to Portalier: a reply came back the following day which said that Portalier was away, travelling in Europe, he would not be back for some weeks. He telephoned Richard Thornbury in Bromsgrove, only to be told that the young man had just gone away, sailing off the south coast of France and they weren't sure when he was coming back. He was transferred to George Stansgate's extension.

'Look,' he said as soon as Stansgate came on the line, 'that bloody beach is on the east coast, isn't it?'

It took Stansgate some moments to work out who owned the loud and angry voice at the other end of the line. 'Oh, it's you,' he said. 'Yes, of course.'

'Then how is it that we saw the sun going down over the sea?'

Stansgate's slow mind pondered this for a few seconds. 'Did we?'

'Yes, we did,' said Eastcote, trying hard not to shout and failing.

'Um, maybe we were on the curve of the bay.'

'There aren't any bloody bays.'

'I'm not sure what you're driving at.'

'Jesus Christ,' exploded Eastcote. 'How do I know that what I saw is what I bought?'

'Well, of course it is,' said Stansgate. 'It must be.'

'Why must it be? Anyway, I'm going out, just to make sure. I've telexed Gonzales and Portalier. Neither of them have come back to me. It's all wrong, something smells.'

'Perhaps I should come with you,' said Stansgate.

'Why? It's not your bloody money. You stay here and tell that fucking playboy Thornbury that I want to talk to him as soon as he gets back.' Eastcote slammed the phone down.

Stansgate was shaken. He couldn't understand Eastcote's angry outburst. It was obvious, at least to him, that the land they had seen was the land they had purchased. He thought back. Had the sun been setting into the sea? According to the compass it couldn't have been. If only he hadn't drunk so much champagne.

Eastcote arrived in Panama three days later. It was there that his forebodings were crystallised into a lump of fear in the pit of his stomach, for the offices of the Caicos and Caribbean Company had disappeared. The suite that they had occupied was empty, the plaque outside the office had gone and there was no trace of the company. Eastcote spent two days in the city trying to track down Gonzales. All the lawyers of that name to whom he spoke turned out to be eminently respectable and working for reputable firms. One of them told him that there was a Max Gonzales in Panama, a lawyer who worked for himself and specialised in company law, but he didn't know where he was or what he was currently doing. Eastcote contacted the authorities to enquire about the Caicos and Caribbean Company. There was very little they could do to help him. They were not required by law to supply information to foreigners but they did tell him that the company had gone into voluntary liquidation four weeks before, apparently owing millions of dollars to a bank on the island of Pinta Leone. They were not prepared to tell him the name. They didn't need to, Eastcote knew. He made a fuss but the officials couldn't understand why. As far as they could see, he had his land and C3 had the purchase price of the land. So what was the problem? He said he wished to issue a complaint but was firmly told that he had no grounds for complaint against C3. The only people who had the right to complain was the bank and nothing had been heard from them.

He caught the next flight to Pinta Leone and took a taxi from the airport to the narrow street in which the bank was situated. He was relieved to see its plaque still in position outside, but inside it was silent and deserted. The fans were still, the air was hot and fetid and all the furniture had gone. Eastcote made enquiries at the island's Ministry of Finance, which, the plaque so proudly announced, had issued the bank's charter. The ministry was located in a small office overlooking the harbour. It was staffed by one young man who, so he told Eastcote, was studying to be a lawyer. He was very helpful. Yes, he said, the bank had only been founded for a few months but no, there was absolutely no suggestion of malpractice. The bank had gone into voluntary liquidation. It had been owed millions of dollars by a company in Panama City which had liquidated itself. The only other foreign bank on the island, the First National of Pinta Leone, had then called in all its loans. So, the Bank of Nuvo Grado had ceased trading, having settled any debts that were outstanding. No, they hadn't, Eastcote told him viciously, the bank owed him, or more accurately his bank, fifty million dollars.

The young man smiled pleasantly. He didn't know anything about that. It wasn't contained in the information his ministry had been given. Eastcote fumed. Ask the other bank, he ordered, the First National.

The young man shook his head. There was no legal requirement for the banks on the island to reveal anything and he told Eastcote that the people at the First National were very secretive. All except Mr Portalier, of course, who was very pleasant and helpful. He was from one of the oldest families on the island. He was president of the First National.

Eastcote leapt upon the last bit of information like a dog onto a rabbit. Surely that wasn't right. Portalier had been president of the Bank of Nuvo Grado; how was it he was also president of the First National Bank of Pinta Leone?

There was nothing to stop a man being president of two banks if he wanted, the young man told him; perhaps Eastcote should talk to Portalier when he returned from Europe.

Eastcote told the man he couldn't wait that long. He intended to go immediately to the First National and enquire of them what had happened to his money. The young man frowned and shrugged his shoulders. He doubted if they would tell him anything.

He was right. Eastcote found their premises in a side street not far from the harbour, but unlike the Bank of Nuvo Grado they did not boast an affluent exterior. The plaque on the outside was made of wood, its script bleached illegible by the sun. The building itself was dilapidated. The First National comprised two rooms, a small outer office, and a slightly larger inner room in which a massive safe covered the whole of one wall. It also contained, Eastcote noticed, a camp bed which he thought was a strange piece of furniture for a bank.

The young man in the outer office was pleasant although not very helpful. He couldn't really tell Eastcote anything. Then a large, swarthy and very tough-looking man emerged from the back room. Eastcote again enquired about Portalier and the bank. 'I need to know what happened to them,' he said. 'I know that you were their prime lender. In fact, they appeared to have loans from you for a considerable amount, so you must know what has happened.'

The large man gave him a hard look. 'Fuck off,' he said.

Eastcote was completely taken aback. 'What?'

'Fuck off.'

In his time Eastcote had exchanged a lot of hard words with bankers but never until then had he been told to leave the premises in such an uncompromising manner. He became angry.

'Look here,' he said, 'you can't talk to me like that. I demand to know what has happened.'

The swarthy man leaned forward until his face was inches from Eastcote's. He had an American accent. 'We don't know anything. We don't know nothing about any other bank. Mr Portalier ain't here, so you can go piss up a rope. And don't come round again. If you do, I'll cut your cock off and shove it up your nose.'

Eastcote stared blankly into the man's face and felt his penis shrivel as he contemplated the threat. He had an uncontrollable urge to sneeze. He emerged into the bright sunlight a defeated man. He knew, then, that he had been conned.

The following morning, after a sleepless night in his hotel, he hired a taxi. The cab driver gave him a puzzled look when he pointed to the area on the coast which had been ringed on the map by Stansgate. This time they didn't go through the mountains. They carried straight along the highway until, finally, they reached their destination.

The driver slowed the cab to walking pace.

'Is this it?' queried Eastcote incredulously. About a mile to his left was the wall of the mountains, sheer, grey and forbidding. The land that lay between it and the road was pitted and strewn with great rocks. On his right stretched the swamps, disappearing into the distant line of the sea. They stank of decay. 'Is it all like this?' asked Eastcote.

The taxi driver shrugged. 'All the way to the north. Miles of it, just like this.'

'No one lives here?'

'Fer-de-lance.' The man's eyeballs rolled in his head.

'What?'

'Snakes, very dangerous.'

Eastcote had an abiding horror of snakes. He wound up his window. They drove on at a slow speed and the depressing scenery unrolled for mile after mile. Eastcote studied the map that Stansgate had given him, turning it first one way and then the other, trying to discover the route that he had taken before. He stared out of the window, mournfully contemplating the desolate scenery sliding past the car.

After about half an hour, they rounded a bend. A caravan with an American jeep alongside it was parked on the left of the road. Sitting on a stool outside the caravan, a man was rolling a cigarette. He was old and grizzled with a grey, ragged beard. Around him on the rocky ground were surveying instruments and gauges. Eastcote ordered the taxi driver to stop and got out.

'Morning,' he said in an unhappy voice. The man turned his weather-beaten face up towards him. His eyes were hard and suspicious. He continued to roll his cigarette.

'Do you know this part of the country well?' asked Eastcote.

'Should do,' the old man drawled. 'Been living here long enough. Why?'

'I'm surprised to see this.' Eastcote indicated their surroundings. 'The last time I came to this part of the world, I went through the mountains and came out on a wonderful beach, miles of sand and fruit plantations.'

'That's on the north-west coast,' said the old man.

'I thought it was on the north-east.'

'Nope. You won't find any pretty beaches on this side of the island.'

Eastcote's heart sank. 'The north-west, you say. Who owns that?'

'Fruit companies,' said the old man. 'They lease the land to the locals. Good country for it, it rains a lot.'

'Rains?'

'Sure, all the time.'

'Still,' said Eastcote almost to himself as he turned away, 'it's a bloody sight better than this.'

'Depends on what you're looking for,' said the old man and lit his cigarette.

Eastcote walked slowly back to the cab and slumped into the back seat. The driver set off at the same slow pace through the desolate landscape. They reached the northern tip of the island where the road ran beneath the prow of the mountains. They followed the road as it turned towards the south-west. Gradually, the scenery improved and soon Eastcote saw familiar territory. They were travelling south along the golden beach he thought he had bought. He gloomily surveyed the spot where he and Stansgate had eaten their lunch believing they had purchased paradise. As his thoughts sank even lower the clouds opened and torrential rain swept the landscape. He nodded to the driver who accelerated southwards towards Nuvo Grado.

That night he got very drunk but by the following morning his depression had been replaced by blind fury. He visited the island's police headquarters and filed a complaint against Portalier. The police were very polite and wrote down everything he said but he could see they did not take him seriously.

He did the same in Panama City, filing a complaint against Gonzales and his company, C3. Again, everything was written down but there the police asked for proof of his allegations and it was then he realised that proof was going to be very difficult. All the documents in his Mayfair offices proved that he had loaned Thornbury Engineering eighteen million pounds to purchase a fifteen-mile stretch of beach on the north-east of the island. The sombre and desolate tract of land he had just visited. Although his famous beach was not what he had been led to believe it was, it would be a difficult task proving that he had been misled.

During the flight to England, it occurred to him that both the fat accountant, Stansgate, and his employer Richard

Thornbury might also have played a part in defrauding him.

He phoned Richard Thornbury from the airport as soon as his plane landed. Thornbury was still away sailing off the south coast of France so he spoke to Stansgate. 'We've been had,' he snarled, 'conned, or at least I have. Only, it isn't my bloody money, is it? In the end it'll be down to Thornbury. That beach you showed me isn't the one we bought. We've just paid eighteen million pounds for forty-five square miles of crap. You'd better have a bloody good explanation, and so had pretty boy Thornbury when he gets back.' He slammed the phone down.

What he didn't know and what the stunned and confused Stansgate didn't know was that Richard Thornbury wasn't coming back. Ever.

Chapter Eight

The partners' fears about Richard Thornbury had emerged during the summer when he was receiving the attention and flattery of the financial press. Each interview he gave expanded and exaggerated the role that his company had played, and would play, in the development of the beach. Much of what he said was not reported, but two newspapers quoted him as saying that the deal was a great coup by Thornbury Engineering who had been developing and working on the project for many months before the merger with Nigel Eastcote.

Addingham phoned Ashley Brighton. 'He's not supposed to say that,' he said angrily. 'Frankly, I'm beginning to wonder if he's the right man for us.'

'A bit late now to wonder that, old boy,' Brighton replied. 'The deed is done, and anyway, I don't think we would have done everything so quickly without him. But I must admit he does like the sound of his own voice.'

Addingham expressed his fears to Oliver Blackmore. 'Even Ashley admits that he talks too much. He likes the limelight, he's attracting unnecessary attention. I'm going to have strong words with that young man.'

Blackmore grunted. 'No. Wait. Find out from Brighton when he's next in London and where he's staying. Let me see if I can do anything.'

Thornbury was sitting in the 007 bar in the Hilton. He'd come to London on family business and had met Brighton earlier. They'd had a blazing row. Brighton complained bitterly about the publicity that he seemed actively to be seeking. Thornbury replied he could handle it perfectly. He also told Brighton that in October, when he returned from sailing in the Mediterranean, he intended to withdraw a large chunk of the money which lay in the Swiss bank account under his assumed name. He intended, he said, to puchase and refit a large, ocean-going yacht. Brighton was aghast. All the partners had agreed they would not, once the money had been deposited, start spending amounts which would call attention to themselves. The fact that big spending might prompt questions as to the source of the money had been impressed upon Thornbury from the outset.

'People are going to ask questions,' said Brighton angrily.

'Nonsense,' replied Thornbury. 'None of my friends gives a shit where the money comes from. So long as it keeps coming.'

'Never mind your friends. What about the tax authorities? Supposing they ask?'

'I'll tell them the business is doing well.'

'But it isn't. You're borrowing money to buy the land. You couldn't justify the purchase of a rowing boat through the business.'

'I don't give a damn for the tax man,' snapped Thornbury. 'I'll spend my money as and when I please.'

Sitting in the darkened 007 bar, Thornbury smiled to himself as he remembered Ashley Brighton's anguished expression. Gradually he became aware of a large, heavy man sitting on the stool next to him who before long engaged him in conversation. Thornbury enjoyed the encounter, primarily because he did most of the talking. Finally the man took his leave. 'Goodbye,' he said. 'I've enjoyed our chat. I hope we meet again.' They shook hands and he left, moving rapidly across the room.

* * *

Oliver Blackmore phoned Addingham at his flat in Basil Street. 'I think you'd better come across,' he said. 'We need to talk. Joanna is out for the evening. Can you be here in twenty minutes?'

Addingham arrived at the house in Lord North Street in an anxious mood ten minutes later. Blackmore led him up to the first-floor drawing room and settled him down on the Chesterfield. He poured his guest a large malt whisky before seating himself opposite. Dusk had fallen and the side lights in the room bathed it in a wan yellow glow. Blackmore leaned forward towards Dundonald.

'I have just spent an interesting hour talking to Richard Thornbury at a bar in the Hilton.' A look of consternation passed across Addingham's face. 'It's all right,' Blackmore assured him. 'I was just a casual stranger, he had no idea who I was, but I got him to talk a lot. I'll tell you now, Edward, that young man is our Achilles heel. He said enough tonight to convince me that under pressure he would tell everything he knows. We have to get rid of him.'

Addingham's head jerked back as if his face had been slapped. 'What do you mean?'

'I think you know what I mean.'

'You're talking about murder.'

Blackmore shrugged. 'It would be better if he had an accident. Either way, I'm talking of putting him beyond the reach of anybody who might want to ask questions.'

'We could persuade him to go away,' said Addingham.

Blackmore shook his head. 'It wouldn't work, Edward. Sooner or later the money would run out and he would come back. He likes the limelight. Dead, we're guaranteed his silence. Alive, he's a threat.'

Addingham had paled; he began to smack his lips together.

'Another drink?' Blackmore rose and moved across to the decanter of whisky. He poured his friend a liberal measure.

'How?' asked the barrister, taking the drink Blackmore handed him. 'You're not suggesting that we do it?'

'Of course not.' Blackmore seated himself in the armchair. 'In fact, I suggest we don't even tell the others. They don't need to know. Dundonald wouldn't care but Woodberry might and Brighton and Frimley-Kimpton would probably quibble.'

'Most people quibble at murder,' murmured Addingham.

'I doubt if your friend Portalier does. He has friends who run a successful business murdering people.' He raised his eyebrows.

A look of understanding crossed Addingham's face. 'The Mafia?'

'Exactly so.'

Addingham thought for a few seconds. 'How?' he repeated.

'Our young friend leaves near the end of September for a month's sailing. He has a boat called the *Suzi Wake*, moored in Monte Carlo harbour. I think it would be preferable if he disappeared while he was out of the country. A lot less fuss, if you follow me.'

Addingham nodded.

'It's merely a question of briefing Portalier. He can get his friends to undertake the work. I suggest you contact Portalier immediately and fly to New York for a meeting.'

'Fly to New York?'

'Well, it's hardly something you can discuss on the phone, is it? The courts aren't sitting, you've got time. Get over to New York and brief him as quickly as you can. Take a photograph of Thornbury with you. I think we ought to allow twenty-five thousand dollars. That should cover it adequately.'

'Bit steep, isn't it?'

'Cheap at twice the price, Edward, if it guarantees our security. We can have the money telegraphed from

Switzerland through London to any bank in Miami specified by Portalier's friends. That will keep it anonymous. Just tell Woodberry it's for expenses in the US, extra payments for the hire of those forged bonds, something like that.'

Addingham sat quietly for a few seconds, quietly smacking his lips. Finally he said, 'Do you think all this is really necessary? It seems so final somehow.'

Blackmore stood up. 'There are sixteen dead already,' he said. 'What difference will one more make? Another one?' He lifted Addingham's empty glass.

The barrister nodded.

Addingham telexed Portalier and two days later flew to New York. They met in his room in the Plaza Hotel. Portalier listened silently as Addingham explained what was necessary and gave his friend the photograph of Richard Thornbury. Portalier stared at it for a few seconds.

'Are you sure you know what you're doing?' he said.

'Absolutely,' Addingham replied. 'Are you sure your friends can handle it?'

Portalier let out a short sharp laugh. 'It's their business, Edward. The fact that they have to do it in Europe makes no difference. These are professional people. It'll be done.'

Portalier flew to Miami the following day and sought an interview with Victor Maggiore. 'Some business friends of mine in Europe,' he said, 'have a problem which would be solved should this man,' he passed across the photograph of Richard Thornbury, 'be moved out of the way. He will be, shortly, sailing in the Mediterranean. His base is Monaco. My friends are prepared to pay fifteen thousand dollars for successful completion of the contract.'

Victor nodded wisely. 'I see. There will be expenses.'

Portalier nodded. 'Another five thousand?'

Victor screwed up his face. 'Let us say ten thousand.'

'Twenty-five thousand?'

Victor shrugged. 'For that money you have a guarantee.'

'Very well,' said Portalier. 'I'm sure they will agree. Half the money will be passed through London to whatever bank you choose in the next twenty-four hours. The rest upon completion.'

'Fine,' said Victor rising slowly. 'Johnny, it's good to see you. I would ask you to stop over for a few days but life is busy. You know how it is.'

Portalier smiled and said he understood. He was relieved that he did not have to endure Victor's hospitality. All that summer his health had been gradually improving; a few days in Miami with Victor's constant supply of booze and teenage whores would undo what progress he had made. He was glad to get on a flight back to Pinta Leone.

Victor Maggiore was intrigued. He had learned much from his 'paper hanger', Joe Collioure, about John Portalier's scheme and he was keen to know more. He knew it was something big and he guessed that the man on whom the contract was to be taken out was part of the plot. Victor had hoped that he would learn more about Johnny's scheme but he had not been lying when he told Portalier that he was busy. Victor and his closest henchmen were working on the final details of another, far more important assassination. The price of that contract, for the elimination of just one man, had been four million dollars and until it was completed he would have no time to pursue his interest in the plans of John Portalier.

The two men who stepped off the Paris flight at Nice airport were scarcely noticeable among the crowds. They both looked like natives of Provence, they had black hair and dark eyes and were deeply tanned although a closer inspection of their casual summer clothes would have shown them to be American. They didn't appear well off; they took the crowded bus which ran east along the rocky coast road from Nice to the principality of Monaco, but once there they checked into the Metropolitan which was expensive, a favourite of the rich tourists who liked to enjoy the hot September sun of Monte Carlo.

The town was full of young men who had come to gamble and to pick up the young and beautiful girls who spent their days sunbathing topless on the decks of the fabulous yachts in the harbour. These two seemed no exception; immediately after they had checked into the hotel they set off for the crowded marina to admire the yachts and the women who decorated them. One boat particularly took their interest, the *Suzi Wake*, registered in Southampton. They spent a long time looking at her, which to a casual observer would have seemed strange, for she was not, by the standards of the other boats gently rocking in the water around her, a remarkable craft, nor did she have pretty girls sunbathing on her decks. But Monte Carlo was busy and there were no casual observers showing any interest in the actions of two young men dawdling along the harbour.

It was late in the afternoon before there was any sign of life on the *Suzi Wake*. Five attractive girls and three young men emerged onto the deck, sauntered down the short gangplank and made their way laughing and talking noisily up the steep and narrow streets towards the Casino. The two young men quietly followed. The happy group made their way to the Boulingrins, the large square outside the Casino, where they sat at a pavement café drinking white wine and soda water. The two men sat on a bench under one of the palm trees. At that time in the afternoon the Boulingrins was full of young men staring at the long tanned legs of the pretty girls in their mini skirts, but unlike the others, the two men did not pay eager and animated attention to the passing women. They were perfectly still, their attention riveted on the group across the square. And any casual observer would have shuddered to see their eyes, for they were black and deadly; the shining eyes of mambas.

After a while one of the girls left the group and wandered along the Rue de Grimaldi looking at the dress shops. One of the men followed her at a discreet distance. She was a beautiful child, not yet twenty, tall and shapely with long blonde hair. She had a generous spirit, prepared to give her time, attention and body to any man who could amuse her, and she found the tall American who accidentally bumped into her outside one of the shops attractive; his eyes were dark and sexy and after a few minutes of happy banter outside the shop she readily accepted his invitation to go for coffee. She was English, she told him, and she was staying on a boat owned by her friend Richard Thornbury. She loved Monte Carlo, the people were so friendly and it was such fun. Every night she and her friends went to a discotheque which was, she explained, a new idea; instead of dancing to a band, everyone danced to rock and roll records. They danced there every night until the early hours of the morning. She and her friends weren't staying in Monte Carlo for much longer; in a few days, she said, they were sailing to Corsica to spend a couple of weeks on the island. Then he said he had to go, which she thought was a shame. Perhaps, she said, they might meet at the discotheque. He smiled sweetly and said that he hoped so. He sauntered back and rejoined his companion, and together they returned to their hotel.

That evening they made a call from a phone box to San Remo across the border in Italy. The following morning they hired a car and drove to Menton where they met a man who had just driven a truck loaded with fruit and vegetables across the border. They followed the truck in their car as it drove up into the hills behind Menton. It stopped at a deserted spot and the driver got out and retrieved two suitcases hidden beneath the produce in the back of his truck. The three men exchanged a few words in Italian before the truck driver climbed into his cab and headed back towards the border and San Remo. The two young men transferred the suitcases into the boot of their car and drove carefully back to Monte Carlo.

That afternoon they went shopping. They bought eight shiny, galvanised buckets, a few lengths of steel rope and two bags of cement. Then they went in search of a boat to hire. It didn't need to be big, they said, or comfortable, but it had to be fast. They only wanted it for two or three days, no more. Eventually they found what they were looking for and while one of them went below to inspect the engines, the other one pulled out a wad of money and peeled off a number of notes to give to the man in the boat yard. They took the boat out into the blue Mediterranean for a trial. It was fast enough for their purposes. When they sailed back into harbour they moored as close as they could to the *Suzi Wake*.

In the evening they transferred the contents of the car to the boat and on its small deck began making their final preparations. One of the men emptied the contents of the cement bags into the buckets. He attached lengths of wire rope to each of the buckets and then poured sea water on top of the cement. He left the buckets on deck overnight. To any casual observer it would have seemed a strange ritual but there were no casual observers. There was just the sound of laughter and the clink of glasses in the night as the brightly lit boats bobbed gently on the shimmering reflections in the water.

The following day the man who had bumped into the beautiful girl met her accidentally as she was walking with her friends at the harbourside. He stopped to say hello. She was disappointed, she said, that she had not seen him at the discotheque. He said he was glad to see her still in Monaco, whereupon she replied that tomorrow they were setting off for Corsica and tonight was the last chance he would have to dance with her at the disco. He smiled gently and wished her a good trip. The girl still thought him attractive although this time she noticed that the man's eyes were constantly fixed on Richard Thornbury who was standing laughing and chatting with the rest of the group as they waited for her to rejoin them.

Later that night, as the sound of the discos wafted across the harbour, the two men stole aboard the *Suzi Wake* and slipped into her forward cabin. One of the men was carrying a suitcase out of which he took about twenty pounds of a grey plastic substance. He stuffed the plastic explosive into a small locker far forward in the cabin just above the bow of the yacht. He then extracted from an insulated container a simple radio receiver, attached by wires to two detonators. He stuck the detonators into the plastic and angled the radio receiver so that it would easily receive a radio signal from somewhere nearby. The men covered their handiwork with some old sail cloth they had found in the locker and then crept off the *Suzi Wake*, leaving no sign of their visit.

It was almost midday before Richard Thornbury and his crew were ready to set sail for Corsica. The yacht moved smoothly out of the harbour and set a course south-east. There were a number of boats dotted around in the sea and the crew did not notice a small craft about a mile astern which seemed set on the same course as themselves, but as the hot day wore on and they sailed further out into the Mediterranean so the sea became empty of other craft and by mid-afternoon the horizon was completely clear.

The small boat, which had kept its distance, began rapidly to overhaul the *Suzi Wake*, although as most of the crew were eating lunch in the forward cabin they didn't notice. One of the men on the deck of the small boat held a small radio transmitter wired up to the boat's batteries. As they drew abreast he flipped a switch on the transmitter. Immediately there came from deep within the *Suzi Wake* a loud thud. The yacht's bow jerked up out of the water and then fell back. She continued her course for a few seconds as if she had done no more than playfully leap a wave; then, as the tons of water came roaring through the great gaping hole in her bow, her own speed ploughed her into the sea. Anyone who had been in the forward cabin was smashed into boneless pulp against the bulkhead.

The two men standing on the boat deck a little way off watched impassively as the *Suzi Wake*'s back broke. The bow disappeared, the stern flipped up at an oblique angle and then she slid beneath the water and with a rush the sea closed over her. There was nothing left but bubbles and a few items of debris.

Suddenly a blonde head broke the surface. It was the girl the man had met in Monte Carlo. She was gasping for breath. The two men watched her wave weakly when she saw their boat. She began to strike out in their direction. They steered the boat slowly towards her until they were within a few yards.

'Please,' she gasped, 'help me.'

The man who the day before had spoken so kindly to her reached down and grasped her hands to pull her aboard. She was naked. Halfway up he flipped her over, so that her back and buttocks were arched over the broad, wooden handrail. Her legs kicked obscenely in the air. The man held her tightly draped backwards over the handrail as if she were on an altar. His companion stepped forward and with one downward arc viciously stabbed a thin-bladed knife into her heart. As he pulled it out, a thin spume of blood followed, spraying into the white-flecked waves. She squawked once, like a chicken. The man with the knife altered his position slightly and then swung the knife hard into the side of her neck. As he retrieved it she coughed and a great gob of blood erupted from her mouth; slowly it rolled down the valley of her breasts, over her firm brown belly and came to rest in the soft, glistening thatch of hair between her legs. She kicked feebly for a few seconds and then was still, her wide open eyes fixed unseeing in a dead reckoning on the empty horizon.

The man wiped the handle of the knife carefully and then threw it overboard while his companion maintained his hold on the girl's body. Then he tied one end of wire rope round the dead girl's bloody neck and tightened it hard. He threw the other end of the rope, attached to a bucket full of hardened cement, into the sea. The girl jerked away from the side of the boat as the weight dragged her under the water, out of sight.

The two men stayed around for an hour, watching the water carefully for signs of wreckage or survivors. One of them donned a snorkel and mask and swam round and underneath the boat while the other scrubbed its side clean of any telltale drops of blood. When they were finally satisfied that they had successfully accomplished what they had been sent to do they threw overboard the buckets of cement, the radio transmitter and any other incriminating evidence. Slowly they sailed away from the spot. In that time no other ship had come within sight.

When they got back into Monte Carlo late that evening, they moored the boat and told the man that they had to leave, and thanked him kindly for the hire. They stayed one more night at the Metropolitan and the following morning checked out. One man returned to Nice to take a flight to Paris and thence to America. The other crossed into Italy, caught a train to Rome and from there a flight back to the USA. Nobody noticed them go. Nobody had noticed them come.

It was a week before enquiries began to be made about the whereabouts of Richard Thornbury and his companions. By that time what little was left of them at the bottom of the Mediterranean could never have been identified even if it were found.

Nigel Eastcote knew that there was no way he could hide the news of his disastrous mistake for long. Some financial journalists had enquired about his plans for development but he had fobbed them off, waiting for the return of Richard Thornbury.

He telephoned Camilla Billingham and poured out his tale of woe. She was less than sympathetic. 'What do you mean you've bought the wrong land? You can't buy the wrong land, not when there's miles of it.'

'I'm telling you we've bought the wrong land,' he said gruffly.

'You can buy the wrong pair of shoes, you can even buy the wrong handbag but I don't see how you can buy the wrong land.' Camilla was beginning to find Nigel Eastcote tedious.

'Well, we have,' he retorted.

'Anyway,' she said just before she put the phone down on him, 'what do you mean, we?'

Eastcote went to see his lawyers and spent three hours with the senior partner. He explained in detail what had happened. 'What can we do?' he asked woefully.

'Not a great deal, I'm afraid,' said the eminent solicitor, peering at Eastcote over his spectacles. 'The contracts are all watertight which, as we drew them up, is no more than one would expect. You are the legal owner of fifteen miles of swamp in the Caribbean. The fact that you thought you'd bought something different is going to be difficult to prove.'

'But nobody in their right minds would build a holiday resort on a swamp.'

'I don't think we could use that as a defence,' said the lawyer.

'What?' Eastcote was bewildered.

'That you were mentally unstable at the time you purchased the land.'

Eastcote blinked. 'I wasn't.'

'Exactly,' said the lawyer.

'Defence against whom?' Eastcote was having trouble keeping up.

'Against all the people who loaned you money for this project. Not only will they want their money back, they are likely to sue you for negligence, if nothing else.'

'But those people are my friends, they trust me.'

'I doubt if they will any more, Mr Eastcote,' said the lawyer unhelpfully, 'nor would I count too much longer on their friendship. After all, the men who backed you have to report to boards of trustees. They themselves may have some explaining to do.'

'So what can we do?'

'Well, we can't sue C3 in Panama,' said the lawyer, leaning back and staring at the ceiling, 'they're in liquidation.'

'We can sue Gonzales.'

'I wouldn't recommend it.'

'He's a crook.'

'We don't know that. International litigation is both difficult and expensive, in places like Panama it's virtually impossible. And anyway, what could we prove against him? I fear we don't have a case.'

'What about Portalier and that bloody bank of his?'

'Definitely not.' The lawyer sat upright. 'We spent a long time at the Bank of England persuading them that the Bank of Nuvo Grado was a legitimate and well-founded institution. A few weeks later it has disappeared completely. This firm finds that a most embarrassing state of affairs, Mr Eastcote. It is quite possible that when the Bank of England gets to know of what's happened, it will require you to pay the dollar premium.'

'But I've been conned,' Eastcote cried. 'The land isn't worth the money I paid. It isn't worth anything.'

'As far as they're concerned, that is your look-out. They may force you to pay six million pounds and take criminal proceedings against you.'

Eastcote stared at the carpet. 'Oh Christ.'

'The fact is, Mr Eastcote,' said the lawyer coldly, 'the institutions that lent you the money will look for the recovery of their eighteen million pounds plus undoubtedly the interest owing, and the Bank of England may well want six million pounds in dollar premium. So you should think of recovering twenty-four million. The only people you can do that from is Thornbury Engineering. I recommend you initiate proceedings against them immediately.'

'Right,' said Eastcote. 'Right. When Richard Thornbury gets back from swanning around in the Mediterranean, he's going to walk into a blizzard of writs. He won't know what's hit him.'

'You haven't heard, then?'

'Heard what?'

'Thornbury's gone missing.'

'Gone what?' Eastcote jumped up. 'The bastard has disappeared with my money. He's run away. I'll kill him.'

'I don't think Mr Thornbury has run away. He and his sailing companions have disappeared in the Mediterranean. They're about ten days overdue. I'm afraid the worst is feared.'

Eastcote sat down again. 'That shit would do anything to get away from me!' he cried.

'You can look to Thornbury Engineering for the recovery of the eighteen million,' the lawyer said evenly. 'You have a legal claim against them. They are mortgaged to you for that amount. I also think that you can probably get them to pay the dollar premium. However, the fact remains, Mr Eastcote, that if what you tell me is accurate, then a fraud has been perpetrated in which Thornbury's accountant, Stansgate, seems implicated. I suggest you make a complaint to the Fraud Squad. You have evidence: maps that Stansgate gave you, a brochure of the island. I think it would help us considerably if we could show that you were the innocent victim of a fraud. A criminal case against Stansgate may also reveal hard evidence of accomplices. If it does, a case might be made against Gonzales or Portalier or some other persons.'

Eastcote decided to take his lawyer's sensible and extremely expensive advice and instructed him to start proceedings against Thornbury immediately. There were already rumours; he had received calls from a few journalists who had heard that all was not well. Camilla Billingham, who had more connections than a plumber, had spitefully been telling some of her financial friends that Eastcote had got it wrong. Thornbury Engineering shares had started to drop with the story of Richard Thornbury's disappearance and as each day went by and the hope of his return faded, so the shares lost more value. And then the story broke in the financial pages that Eastcote was sueing Thornbury Engineering and that the land in Pinta Leone was not the glowing garden of Eden that had been described. The reports also hinted at the possibility of criminal prosecutions. In a day the value of Thornbury's shares halved and within a week the bottom had dropped out of them completely.

For George Stansgate the story was a bombshell. He was continuously phoned by reporters requesting a statement but he had none to give. Ever since Eastcote's call from Heathrow, a numbing fear had been slowly growing inside him. He could not understand how they could have bought the wrong land, but he knew he'd paid little real attention to the purpose of his first visit to the island; he had been so full of booze, so beguiled by the women, and the feeling of power.

Eastcote had called him twice since his arrival back in England, demanding to know when Richard Thornbury was returning. Stansgate had no idea. He was as keen to see the return of Thornbury as Eastcote, for in his absence the company's elderly retainers who shuffled along the Victorian corridors looked to him for answers that he couldn't give. When they finally learned that Thornbury was missing, presumed dead, the old men had shaken their heads and retreated back into their offices, and the company had ground to a halt. Union representatives of the workers came to see Stansgate and demanded to know what was happening. The local bank phoned him, the company was up to the limit on its overdraft, there wasn't enough money to pay the next week's wages. Then came the news that Eastcote was sueing them. Writs were served on the company and on Stansgate personally, who, in the absence of anywhere else to turn in desperation, called Brighton.

The accountant was curt and to the point. 'You've gone to the wall,' he said. 'There's nothing to do but call in the Receiver and go into liquidation. You're bankrupt. There's not much I can do, I'm afraid.'

Stansgate had been made captain of a ship which from the outset was bound to sink. Now that he was in the water, he was being abandoned to the sharks.

Eastcote, too, was having problems. When Thornbury went into liquidation its largest creditors were the banks, who would have first choice of what little was left. The golden boy of high finance was suddenly the target of every hack journalist. One enterprising newspaper asked its Caribbean correspondent to fly to Pinta Leone. He sent back photographs of the beach on the north-west coast which Eastcote thought he'd bought and of the swamps which he actually owned. Scorn was heaped upon the property developer's head. Another paper printed a story that the Bank of England had been hoodwinked into letting Eastcote off payment of the dollar premium. The publicity was becoming embarrassing, not only to Eastcote but also to the financial authorities. Some important pension funds had backed Eastcote. What was bothering the authorities was that certain of them belonged to the trade unions. Public knowledge of the misappropriation of their money could have serious political repercussions.

A man from the Bank of England phoned a man at the Treasury. It was agreed that panic had to be averted; private enterprise had to be seen to work. And so it was arranged that the British taxpayer, through the Bank of England, would underwrite any losses incurred by Eastcote's mistake, which meant, in the final analysis, repaying the eighteen million pounds nestling out of reach in a Swiss bank vault beneath the streets of Zurich.

The accountants appointed by the Official Receiver to wind up Thornbury's affairs found that the company was in total financial ruin. They decided that it was necessary to cut out all inessential expense, so they sacked the entire workforce.

On the first Friday following the Receiver's appointment, the men found inside their weekly pay packets a terse note telling them that their services were no longer required and they had been made redundant with one week's money in lieu of notice. Many of them had worked for Thornbury's all their lives and as they shuffled past the factory's iron gates, they began to feel what the young men with the pressed suits and adding machines had told them they were – unnecessary.

George Stansgate fared marginally better. Because of his contract he was given a month's notice and because he was one of their own kind, the young men were more flexible with him. They said he could have time off to look for another job but they would be grateful if he came up from Pinner once or twice to answer questions and to help them go through the complicated accounts. Naturally they would pay his train fare, though it would only be second class. His company Rover they took back immediately and they asked him if he would mind settling his last expense account himself.

Stansgate stumbled out of the building into the pale sunshine of a late October Friday; he had been at Thornbury Engineering exactly sixteen weeks. They had been the climax of his existence and although he tried to hang onto his dignity he had the feeling that he had lost his chance and there wasn't to be another one.

MONEY FOR NOTHING

It was a long and tiring journey back to his rented house in Pinner, made longer by the time he spent drinking in the station bar. When he finally arrived home he found two policemen waiting for him. They wished to interview him, they said, in connection with the land deal on Pinta Leone. They were evasive about why, but they were persistent with their questions. Stansgate told them the whole story in the most dignified way he could manage, seated in the front room of his three-bedroomed semi. He was embarrassed; he was tired, perplexed and drunk. He tried to hide his fright and the humiliation of his redundancy behind a pompous and condescending façade. After he had told them the story, the detectives asked him to go over it again. There were a number of inconsistencies in his second version and the policemen swooped like hawks picking up mice. It was gone midnight before they stood up to leave. They were courteous and thanked him for his help but, they said, they would have to come back again to clear up some points. He watched them walk down the short garden path to their car, parked in the dark suburban street.

He turned out the lights and made to go to bed. At the top of the darkened staircase was a small pyjama-clad figure. It was his daughter, woken by the departure of the detectives. She was shivering, either with cold or with fear of the silent, darkened house. Stansgate held her, pulling the small shaking body close into his great bulk.

'It's all right, darling,' he whispered, seeking to calm her, though in fact it was he who was consoled by her closeness and warm sleepy smell.

He returned her to her room where he remained for some time, sitting on the edge of her bed listening to her breathing and staring into the dark, his mood as deep and black as the night.

Jeffrey Frimley-Kimpton bumped into Brighton on the steps of his club. It was lunch time. 'I'm meeting some people,' said Frimley- Kimpton, 'but they haven't turned up yet. Come and have a drink.' They seated themselves in a corner of the bar.

'I was sorry to read about Joseph Thornbury,' said Frimley-Kimpton. The last survivor of the Thornbury line had died in his sleep a few days previously. Although he could not have known about the demise of his company, the old man's condition had gone into decline at about the same time that the company, which had been his life, had gone into liquidation.

'Merciful release, I suppose,' said Brighton.

'No word of the young Thornbury?'

'None, I'm afraid,' replied Brighton. 'There's no hope now. It's been six weeks.'

They stared at each other in silence for a few seconds, each hoping that the other was not thinking what he was thinking about the publicity-seeking Thornbury.

'The company is in a complete mess,' said Brighton, adopting his professional voice. 'There's nothing left. It's all mortgaged to the hilt.'

'Does that reflect upon you as the auditors?' asked Frimley- Kimpton.

'Not really. The firm would have gone down anyway. It's been blamed on bad management and the company accountants, particularly our friend, Stansgate. I've been through his desk. He'd no idea what he was doing.'

'I hear he is under investigation.'

'Eastcote has made a complaint to the Fraud Squad. Of course it would be better if the whole thing died quietly. But whatever happens, we've taken precautions. Thornbury arranged it so that Stansgate would be implicated.'

'Excellent.' Frimley-Kimpton saw his visitors enter the bar. 'I must go. By the way,' he said standing up, 'I think we ought to have another meeting, final accounting and all that sort of thing. Perhaps a lunch. I'd quite like to start spending a little money. And we ought to decide what we are going to do with Thornbury's share. It's no good to him, is it?'

'I'll suggest it to the others,' said Ashley Brighton, making ready to leave.

He telephoned Addingham the following day.

'Good idea,' said Addingham. 'Get your friend Woodberry to prepare a final set of accounts. Tell him to arrange the venue and the date and tell him that John Portalier will join us for lunch.'

John Portalier was flying to England to play what he thought would be his final role in the great deception.

It would have surprised Eastcote, had he known, that both Portalier and Max Gonzales had been most helpful to the police in their enquiries. The detectives had written to the vacated offices of the Caicos and Caribbean Company and to their surprise had received a prompt reply from Gonzales who had furnished them with a full and complete statement.

Stansgate, he wrote, had known all about the land before he had flown to Panama though Gonzales had no idea how he could have known that it was for sale. However, Stansgate had expressed a keen desire to purchase it and was prepared to pay up to fifty million dollars. Gonzales had been surprised that he was prepared to pay so much for swamp and rock, but being a businessman he had accepted the offer. He and Portalier had taken Stansgate to see the area and far from being dissuaded, the man had seemed even more animated; he had, so Gonzales said, talked of filling in the swamps, and establishing holiday resorts. Gonzales also described Stansgate's subsequent visit with Eastcote, how he had taken charge and how he had insisted on taking Eastcote to Pinta Leone without Gonzales.

Almost everything in the statement contradicted what the detectives had been told by Stansgate. Then they heard from John Portalier. He wrote to say that he was flying to England on business and would be happy to give them a statement personally. Two detectives arrived at Portalier's hotel in Basil Street just after ten o'clock on a November morning. Portalier took them to a corner of the upstairs lounge, where the three men seated themselves in a close group in the chintz-covered armchairs. They remained together there for more than two hours.

Everything Portalier told the policemen corroborated Gonzales' statement. While the younger of the two detectives wrote feverishly, Portalier told them of the financial arrangements that he, Eastcote and Stansgate had made to buy the land. There was never any doubt, he told them, about the location of the beach; he and Gonzales had taken Stansgate to the north-east. If Stansgate had subsequently taken Eastcote to some other location in order to mislead him, then neither he nor Gonzales had been aware of it. He was emphatic; there was no possibility of confusion about the land. 'Of course,' he said, 'the arrangements they made to buy the beach were well within the law of Pinta Leone.' Whether they were acceptable to the British authorities was a matter the detectives should talk to Stansgate and Eastcote about. He told them that his bank, the Bank of Nuvo Grado, had ceased trading when the other bank on the island, the First National Bank of Pinta Leone, had called in its loans. Portalier had written to Stansgate informing him that the bank was closing purely as a matter of courtesy. Neither Nigel Eastcote nor Thornbury Engineering had any claim against the bank. Portalier told the detectives that the bank had merely acted as a channel for the transaction. C3 in Panama had the money, Thornbury Engineering had the land. It was a perfectly legal transaction.

The detectives returned to their offices in Scotland Yard. They had found much of what Portalier had told them confusing, for they were ordinary policemen who had been trained to catch more obvious thieves and to detect less subtle and ingenious crimes. They had no experience of international finance, offshore banks and complicated land deals. Indeed it was difficult for them to detect if a crime had been committed at all, and if it had, whether it was within their jurisdiction. The inspector assigned to the case turned to the professionals, the international lawyers and accountants, for help. One of those whose advice he sought was Edward Addingham, but the clerk in Addingham's chambers told him in no uncertain terms that his master was too busy to hand out free advice to the police. There were other qualified men, however, who did ponder what the inspector told them and who were unanimous in informing him that the whole affair was too complex for him to think of bringing any successful prosecution for fraud against Gonzales or Portalier, or their organisations. It was anyway unlikely that either man had committed any crime under British law. But, they told him, there was probably a good case against Stansgate for breaches of the Companies Act, the Protection of Depositors Act, the Exchange Control Act and the Prevention of Fraud Act. There was also a good case against Eastcote for currency offences.

It was ironic that Eastcote, who had first brought the police into the matter, should himself become the subject of investigation. The inspector would have relished the irony had not a young solicitor from the office of the Director of Public Prosecutions phoned to tell him to lay off. The DPP knew all about the case, the solicitor told him, and agreed absolutely with the advice that the inspector had received. However, the Director of Prosecutions would not be taking any action in Eastcote's case.

'But,' the inspector growled down the phone, 'Eastcote could be prosecuted for evasion of exchange controls.'

'Perhaps,' replied the solicitor, 'but it's a complicated case and there is no guarantee that we would win. And as you know, the DPP is really only interested in cases where we have a bloody good chance of winning. Anyway, there's plenty of evidence against the other fellow, Thornbury's accountant. As far as the DPP is concerned, the police can nail that one to the cross. Eastcote is involved with too many financial institutions, which are likely to panic if they think there's been any criminal activity. The authorities have their own methods of dealing with the likes of Eastcote. He will,' the solicitor assured the inspector, 'be severely dealt with by an institution with vastly greater powers than the police, Her Majesty's Treasury.'

Eastcote had already received, by special messenger from the Treasury, Letters of Direction, in answer to which he was expected to give every detail of his dealings on Pinta Leone. Again, he made the journey across London to his solicitors in the City. He was surprised to find that they too had received similar Letters of Direction. The senior partner was deeply disturbed. His firm had been very happy to represent Eastcote while his company was doing well; they had been able to charge him a lot of money for their help and advice. But now the golden boy was evidently slipping, his casual attitude to the law had implicated one of the City's most reputable legal practices, and it was time to drop him.

'It is extremely embarrassing for my firm, Mr Eastcote,' the senior partner said. 'We have never, in all our history, received anything like this.'

'Well, don't answer it,' said Eastcote offhandedly. 'I'm not going to answer mine.'

The solicitor leaned across his desk. 'Mr Eastcote, these Letters have been issued by the Lords Commissioners of Her Majesty's Treasury. This is not some paltry summons by a magistrate. The penalties for not answering are draconian.'

'But if I answer these, I'll be implicating myself. I don't have to do that. Not according to English law, I don't.'

'Yes, you do, Mr Eastcote,' said the solicitor flatly.

'They'll still have to prove I did anything,' retorted Eastcote.

'Quite the reverse. It will be up to you to prove you didn't. They don't have to prove anything. This is a Treasury investigation, Mr Eastcote. We're not talking about justice here. You're guilty unless you can prove otherwise.'

'You should have told me all this before,' said Eastcote bitterly.

'You should have stayed within the law.'

'I did. Well, most of the time I did. Look, the fact is, I've been defrauded of eighteen million pounds. What am I going to do about it? Not one of you buggers seems to care.' He was almost crying.

'Bad language doesn't help,' said the lawyer haughtily. 'I'm afraid, Mr Eastcote, that we can no longer represent you in this matter.'

Eastcote opened his mouth to expostulate, but the lawyer kept on speaking.

'By replying honestly to these Letters of Direction, we will be forced to implicate you further in this matter. After all, we acted upon your instructions, believing them to be honest. I'm afraid that as we will be forced to implicate you, we cannot continue to act for you. There would be a conflict of interest. I'm sure you can appreciate that. I must ask you to obtain advice from some other firm.'

So Eastcote was abandoned. He touted his predicament around the rest of the law firms in the first division of London's legal community, but word was out. All of them found various excuses not to take on his case. Finally, he found a small legal practice in Bayswater which was prepared to take him on, but only upon payment of a large retainer.

It had become obvious that, whatever happened, he would be required to pay the six-million-pound dollar premium. He was under siege from all sides, for the financial institutions which had loaned him the capital had taken out proceedings against him for repayment. No one paid any attention to the fact that he'd been defrauded.

The focus of interest was his personal predicament, for there were rumours that he was bust. The gossip in the City said that his property company was worthless, and that he was heading for bankruptcy. However hard he tried, Eastcote could not persuade anyone that he was the victim of a conspiracy that had cost him eighteen million pounds. It was like a conjuring trick. Nobody noticed the money had been spirited away, because all the spotlights were on the once glittering Eastcote being sawn in half financially.

The inspector at the Fraud Squad felt that he had been robbed too. Gonzales and Portalier were too distant and probably not guilty of any crime for which they could be prosecuted in England. He had been told to lay off Eastcote. There was only one person left through whom the inspector could justify his existence, George Stansgate. The inspector sent two detectives north to Bromsgrove to see if there was anything they could discover. In a drawer of Stansgate's desk they found what they were looking for. Beneath a pile of papers were stubs of an airline ticket indicating a flight to Zurich. There were two bank statements, one from a Swiss bank showing a deposit of five thousand in cash, and one from a bank in London showing three regular deposits of one thousand pounds. There was also the letter to which Portalier had referred in his statement; it was addressed to Stansgate and stated that the Bank of Pinta Leone was about to cease trading. Under another pile of papers was a draft copy of the surveyor's report which Eastcote had said Stansgate had given him. The detectives checked it against the typewriters in the building. It had been typed on the machine outside the accountant's office. There was also a receipt from a printing company in Wealdstone. The detectives visited the company, which was within a few miles of Stansgate's house. The owner told them that a man had visited the works a few months before and had asked for a glossy brochure to be printed about some island in the West Indies. He had only wanted half a dozen copies printed, which the owner thought was unusual; it had been an expensive job for so few copies. The owner couldn't remember what the man looked like; he thought he was big but that was all he could remember. He had paid cash and had called himself Stanstead or something like that.

One Friday, exactly three weeks after he had been made redundant, Stansgate was again visited by the police. They spent two hours in the front room of his house, questioning him about the payments into the London bank and the deposit of cash in Switzerland, about his role in Thornbury and about the printing of the brochure. Stansgate was unable to answer their questions; he had no idea what they were talking about. His pomp and bluster gave way to fright and bewilderment.

At seven o'clock that evening the detectives accompanied him to the local police station where he was formally charged. Stansgate stood heavy and erect in the bare and dirty detention room as one of the policemen cautioned him.

They marched him to the cells and told him he could apply for bail in the morning. They took away his tie, his braces and his shoe laces and left him. He cried, great racking sobs of anguish that shook his corpulent body. It was his nemesis. His world had collapsed.

He was not the only one to weep that night; millions more cried as the news came out of Dallas that a young man sitting in an open car had been caught in an assassin's cross-fire which had blown his brains all over his wife's pretty pink suit. Kennedy was dead, and for millions it was a black and bitter night.

Victor Maggiore was not one of those who wept. When the news came through to the luxurious penthouse on the strip, Victor poured himself a generous brandy and quietly smiled in the knowledge of a job well done.

Chapter Nine

Saturday dawned grey and chilly; a sense of doom seemed to fall with the early morning drizzle. The world was stunned by the news. The rain stopped, but the sky stayed grey and full of tears. Everywhere people felt that they had lost a part of themselves; they remained indoors and listened to the news. Foreboding crawled the streets. The air was like an indrawn breath – waiting.

Simon Woodberry noticed that London was deserted when he arrived at Paddington. He had caught an early train from Oxford so that he could oversee preparations for the partners' final meeting. The taxi driver who drove him to his club in Carlton Terrace chattered nervously. He thought it was the Cubans who had done it, he said, getting back at Kennedy for the Bay of Pigs. But maybe it was the Russians. Maybe they were launching their missiles now. He looked up at the grey and threatening skies as if expecting to see the missiles dropping upon Hyde Park. Woodberry listened with half an ear. He had been shocked by the news but nothing about the Americans or their way of life surprised him. He didn't understand them or their politics. Assassinating presidents seem to be part of the vulgar tradition of the United States.

He arrived at his club. Stanley, the doorman, looked solemn as he helped Woodberry off with his coat. He too talked of nothing but the assassination, which irritated Woodberry. There were other things happening in the world, he thought, besides the death of some brash and impetuous American. These people were acting as if Kennedy had been a personal friend. He spoke sharply to Stanley.

'You have the names of all my guests?'

'Yes, sir.'

'Send them up to the room as soon as they arrive,' he said, writing his name in the visitors book.

'Will you sign them in, sir?'

'Later,' replied Woodberry. 'Ask them to sign the visitors book as they come in. I'll sign for them when we've finished.'

'Very good, sir,' said Stanley and went back into his wooden cubbyhole beneath the staircase.

Woodberry had hired a luncheon room overlooking the Mall. In the middle of the room was a long polished table, one end of which had been set for seven. A waiter appeared through a door at the far end of the room, beside a small bar stocked with bottles. At Woodberry's request he assembled a gin and tonic.

Brighton was the first to arrive and after the waiter had handed him a drink the two friends stood looking out across the Mall to the park. They were both short men and the great Georgian windows towered above them. They talked briefly of the news but neither was willing to dwell on the depressing event half a world away. They had reason to be elated and their conversation quickly turned to the success of the enterprise. The next to arrive was Jeffrey Frimley-Kimpton, shortly followed by Dundonald, then Blackmore and finally Addingham in the company of John Portalier. The waiter served drinks as Addingham introduced Portalier to the others.

Addingham called the meeting to order and the partners seated themselves at the other end of the table from where the places for lunch had been laid. Addingham sat at the table's head with Portalier on his immediate right and Woodberry, as company secretary, on his left. Woodberry took from his slim pigskin attaché case a number of documents which he gave to his colleagues. They were drafted in his neat and precise handwriting, showing the income and expenditure of the Archbishop's Enterprise since its inception. Every item of expense was neatly recorded: the flights to Switzerland by Dundonald, Frimley-Kimpton and Thornbury, and to Panama by himself; the payments to the men who had served them; all expenses incurred by each of them, small or large, including twenty-five thousand dollars spent by Portalier in America. The total amounted to just under three-quarters of a million pounds. This had been subtracted from the sum of eighteen million pounds, the sterling equivalent of fifty million four hundred thousand dollars, to show a final net total of seventeen million two hundred and fifty thousand pounds. On another sheet were inscribed the names of eight archbishops and against each one was recorded one-eighth of the total. Every man in the room was richer by two million, one hundred and fifty-six thousand, two hundred and fifty pounds.

The group studied the figures in silence. At last Addingham looked up. 'Does anyone have any questions about the accounts?'

The others shook their heads. 'These look perfectly in order,' said Brighton.

'Very well,' said Addingham, 'we can take the accounts as accepted. Thank you.' He nodded briefly to Woodberry. He had become reconciled to the necessity of the country lawyer within the partnership, yet he had never come to like him. To Addingham, Woodberry would always be an outsider.

'Please continue,' he said.

Woodberry extracted from his case eight envelopes, each bearing the name of one of the partners. He distributed them, leaving on the table in front of him his own and that of Richard Thornbury. 'You will find in the envelope the number of your personal account in the Swiss bank as well as your ecclesiastical alias. You will also find instructions concerning how the accounts may be operated.'

They tore open the envelopes and read the contents. Each of them pocketed the slip of paper with the account number. 'Does anyone have any questions?' asked Dundonald.

'It all seems straightforward,' Oliver Blackmore observed.

'I have one,' said Henry Dundonald. 'Who else knows our account numbers?'

'What do you mean?' asked Addingham.

'Simply this,' replied Dundonald. 'All that I need in order to obtain money from this account is my pseudonym and my private account number. Who else knows my account number?'

All eyes were on Simon Woodberry who, when he replied, spoke slowly and deliberately. 'I obtained these account numbers from the bank,' he said, 'when the money was divided into eight equal shares. I listed one of the numbers alongside each of the names you so imaginatively invented for us. Then I wrote out the instructions you have before you and finally I destroyed the original list. You have my word that I no longer have any knowledge of your account numbers.'

'Well,' Addingham asked Dundonald, 'does that satisfy you?'

'Perfectly,' said Dundonald. 'If Simon Woodberry assures me that any list which once existed has been destroyed, then I am quite happy to accept it.'

'Good,' said Addingham.

'Chairman,' said Woodberry, formally addressing Addingham, 'speaking of destroying lists, can we have assurances that no one here now has any document or any other piece of evidence which relates to the enterprise?'

'Yes, of course,' responded Addingham. He peered round the table at his colleagues. All of them shook their heads.

'Absolutely nothing,' said Brighton. 'You have it all, Simon.'

'Thank you,' said Woodberry. 'Could I ask that at the end of this meeting you return to me all the papers I have given you – with the exception of your bank account number, of course.''

The others nodded in assent.

'I think, gentlemen,' said Addingham, 'that we may congratulate ourselves on the completion of a successful exercise. I must thank every one of you for the part that you have played in bringing it to a successful conclusion, but I think that special thanks should go to John Portalier.' There was a subdued chorus of 'Hear hear'. Portalier's brown face broke into a dignified smile and he inclined his head slightly.

'Chairman,' said Frimley-Kimpton. 'I have another question.'

'Yes?'

'What do we intend to do with Richard Thornbury's share? I think it's safe to assume that he isn't coming back.' There was silence round the table. Brighton noticed that Portalier shot a slightly amused and quizzical look at Addingham. The silence unsettled Frimley-Kimpton. He continued: 'Well, I don't mean to be grasping, but if the man's dead, the money's no good to him. Is it?'

'We are sure he's dead?' asked Woodberry.

'Beyond any reasonable doubt,' said Blackmore. 'Jeffrey's right. It's no use being unduly delicate about these things. If Thornbury is dead, there's no point in his money rotting in a Swiss bank.'

'The money belongs to his next of kin, his mother and his sisters,' said Addingham.

'You're not suggesting we give it to them?' Frimley-Kimpton asked.

'It's not ours to give,' said Addingham. 'It belongs to Thornbury's estate. However, it is obvious that if his family inherited the money there would be a lot of awkward questions from the authorities, who would attempt to trace its source. I don't think any of us wish to run that kind of risk.' Addingham paused. The room was filled with the silence of assent.

'I suggest,' he continued, 'that Thornbury's share is divided equally between all of us here. Does everyone agree?'

They nodded.

'Very well. Can you arrange that?' Addingham turned to Woodberry.

'Yes, I think so.' Woodberry frowned slightly as he thought through the process of transferring the money. 'I have Thornbury's account number here,' he touched the envelope in front of him. 'All I must do is sign for it myself, using his pseudonym. It shouldn't take long to transfer the money to your accounts. I shall phone all of you when it's been done.'

There was a pause and then Addingham said, 'Well, gentlemen, that's it. There's nothing left except to thank you all for your help and for your yeoman service. I am sure you will agree it was worthwhile. The past few months have had their difficulties but I am delighted that it has all turned out so successfully. Now, I believe we have time for a drink before lunch, for which we have to thank our secretary, Simon Woodberry.'

The group stood up. As the others wandered across to the small bar in the corner, Portalier remained talking to Ashley Brighton while Woodberry slowly worked his way round the table ensuring that he retrieved all the documents which he had issued a few minutes earlier. When he had finished he joined Portalier and Brighton.

'How long will it take before Thornbury's share of the money is released to the rest of us?' asked Portalier.

'I estimate a week, no longer. I only have to put Thornbury's alias on a few documents.'

'What was it, by the way?' asked Brighton.

'What?'

'Thornbury's alias.'

Woodberry consulted a piece of paper he was holding in his hand. 'Thomas Becket.'

Portalier let out a short bark of laughter. Both the others looked up at him in surprise. He was smiling. 'Excuse me,' he said and wandered off to join the others at the bar.

'Curious fellow,' said Woodberry dismissively.

'Yes,' said Brighton, 'but it's strange just the same that Richard Thornbury should have been given that name all those months ago. Perhaps they had always intended it.'

There was something in Brighton's tone which caused his friend to stare intently at him. 'What do you mean?'

'Nothing really,' he replied. 'It's just curious that Becket was the one murdered in the cathedral; you remember, "Who'll rid me of this troublesome priest?" I wonder if someone asked who'll rid me of this troublesome playboy?'

'You don't know that for sure, do you?' Woodberry's voice was a strained whisper.

'No, not for sure, but Thornbury's demise did stop a lot of us worrying. He was getting out of hand. And there's that interesting item in the accounts for expenses in the US.'

'But you're talking about murder.' Woodberry glanced in the direction of the group at the bar.

'No, I'm talking about suspicion,' said Brighton. 'I have a cynical disbelief in coincidence. Richard was becoming a liability. Then through a fortunate quirk of fate he drowns in the Med. Convenient. No more chance that he'll shoot his mouth off. Stone dead hath no fellow, Simon.'

'But it's murder,' said Woodberry again.

'Look, Simon, forget it. There are already sixteen men dead on Pinta Leone.'

'But we didn't mean that,' protested Woodberry. 'We only wanted a small incident. That wasn't our fault. This is different.'

'Not for them it isn't,' retorted Brighton. 'They're dead and Thornbury is dead. Maybe, just maybe, they all died for the same reason.'

Woodberry stared at him.

Brighton shrugged and smiled. 'What the hell, Simon, we don't know anything for sure. What we know is that we're a lot richer now than we were six months ago. Forget it.'

He patted his friend on the shoulder and walked across to join the others at the bar. Woodberry watched him for a few seconds and then slowly gathered up the rest of the papers. Then he summoned the head waiter to serve lunch. They arranged themselves at the luncheon end of the table in the same order as they had been seated for their earlier business.

The food, as Woodberry had promised, was excellent. They started with asparagus soup and went on to boeuf Wellington. The burgundy was perfect. Their conversation encompassed both the assassination and the notorious events of the summer. They discussed the government and how long it was now likely to remain in power. It was an agreeable experience, good food and wine shared by a group of friends gossiping about politics, money and power.

It was over brandy that Portalier dropped the bombshell. The others were listening to a story recounted by Jeffrey Frimley-Kimpton. Portalier turned to Addingham who seemed slightly nauseated by some of the more bizarre antics being described.

'By the way, Edward,' he said, 'my land may turn out to have been worth what Thornbury paid for it after all.'

'What do you mean?' queried Addingham, glad to be diverted from Frimley-Kimpton's scandal.

'An old oil prospector has been working on it for about a year. As a matter of fact, he asked my permission to survey the place a couple of months before we met in your flat.'

Addingham's mind went back to the bitter February

night. He recalled Portalier saying that it was 'interesting' when he had broached the subject of the land. 'An oil prospector?'

'The whole bloody place is oozing with the stuff.'

Addingham stared at him in disbelief.

'Can you imagine,' Portalier continued, 'another few months and I would have been able to sell it myself. All the money would have been mine.' He laughed a brief, humourless laugh. Addingham continued to stare at him until he became aware that all conversation round the table had ceased. Everyone had overheard Portalier's last remark and was staring at him.

'I'm not complaining,' Portalier went on, leaning back in his chair. 'This business has made me enough to keep me in my vices. I just think it's faintly ironic. They prospected for oil before the war without success and when this old fellow came along and asked to explore the land I thought he was mad. In fact,' he reflected, 'he probably is a bit mad. I've spent a few days with him, now and again. He lives in a caravan by the side of the road in the middle of nowhere. Anyway, he came to see me, drunk as a skunk. Said he'd finished prospecting and he was sure there was oil along that coastline. He reckons the land's worth about forty million.'

'Is he right, do you think?' asked Oliver Blackmore in his granite voice. 'I mean about the oil?'

'I would guess so,' replied Portalier. 'He's not the kind of chap to get it wrong. He said it's fine crude, whatever that is. He's off to tell some oil company in Houston about it. Of course the old boy doesn't know that I don't own the land any more.'

'But don't you see what this means?' Addingham blurted out.

Blackmore watched him appraisingly as the others started in surprise at the outburst.

'We can buy it all back,' he continued in an excited tone.

'We can reverse the process and double what we have made.'

There was no response. Blackmore was leaning far back in his seat, slowly blowing smoke from his corona at the ceiling. The others looked nonplussed.

'Who owns the land now?' asked Addingham to the group in general.

'Technically, it's one of Thornbury's assets,' said Brighton, 'but it is under the control of the Official Receiver.'

'If what Portalier says is right, Thornbury Engineering may survive after all,' said Dundonald. 'Eastcote may even get his money back.' Everyone chuckled.

'But why should he?' Addingham was agitated.

There was silence. At last Frimley-Kimpton said, 'I'm sorry, old boy, but I don't follow you.'

Addingham was clearly exasperated. He pushed his chair back from the table, rose to his feet and leaned forward until his hands were resting on the table among the litter of coffee cups. 'This partnership,' he began, 'has made a lot of money from the sale of a piece of land which we knew was valueless but which we were able to convince other people was worth fifty million dollars.' The room was quiet, from outside came the faint hissing of car tyres on the wet surface of the Mall. 'It was a classic exercise in marketing,' he continued. 'Corporations do the same thing all the time. It's the purest form of the capitalist process. In my view what we did was quite legitimate, no more questionable than printing a photograph of one hotel in Spain, knowing full well that the bloody tourists will be made to stay somewhere completely different. No worse than charging twenty times more than the actual cost of manufacturing a product because that is the price people are prepared to pay, the price the market will bear.'

The others nodded in assent.

'Eastcote was the market. He was prepared to pay the

asking price. In fact, he was happy to pay for what he thought he was getting. He wanted to buy status and power and more wealth, and we accommodated him, we sold him a dream, we sold him the sizzle not the sausage. Now somebody wants to buy the sausage because it turns out that it's full of fine crude.' He glanced at Portalier. 'Apart from the prospector and an oil company in America, we are the only people who know that. Why shouldn't we capitalise on what we know? If we don't, the people who will benefit will be Eastcote and Thornbury Engineering and the Official Receiver. Why should they benefit? What have they done to deserve it? It is we who made the market out of nothing. It is we who took the commercial risk. Eastcote took no risk. Like all his kind, he was dishonest, he thought he could cover himself so that there would be no risk. He was a fool and therefore he was easily fooled. It's a bad principle to allow fools to make money. We have new knowledge of the situation. It will be us, I suggest, who will be the fools if we don't use it to full advantage.'

'Are you suggesting that we buy back the land and sell it to the oil company?' asked Frimley-Kimpton.

'That's exactly what I'm suggesting. Eastcote believed that piece of property was valuable when we knew it wasn't. Now the situation is reversed; he believes it isn't and we know it is. The Official Receiver will be happy to sell it for next to nothing to anyone who is prepared to buy it. It shouldn't take us too long to work out how we may repurchase the land.'

Everyone looked at Portalier.

'Well, if you want, I suppose I could repurchase it,' he said nonchalantly.

'I think not,' said Blackmore from across the table.

'I agree,' Addingham said. 'It would be wrong for just one member of the partnership to own our only asset.'

Portalier smiled. 'You can rest assured that I won't try to double-cross you, Edward,' he said. 'Like everyone else,

I've done very well out of the partnership. I have no intention of trying to go it alone.'

'We have no intention of giving you the opportunity,' said Dundonald bleakly.

Portalier raised his eyebrows in mild surprise, and Addingham quickly took control of the conversation. 'There's no question of not trusting you, old boy,' he said. 'It would be wrong in this arrangement for one partner to share too much of the burden and, more to the point, we do not want to expose you unnecessarily. As it stands the authorities have no interest in you even though Eastcote is bleating that he has been conned out of fifty million dollars. At present, the authorities have a faint suspicion that a crime may have been committed but they have no inclination to pursue it. My guess is, they've given up. Any blood they want they intend to get out of Eastcote and, of course, from the accountant fellow at Thornbury. That would all change,' he said, looking at Portalier, 'if you repurchased the land for a fraction of what was paid for it. It would appear too slick, a lot of people would suddenly take an interest. No, we have to devise some means whereby the partnership can remain hidden while we find an agent to repurchase the land on our behalf for as little as possible. It shouldn't be too difficult but this is not the place to discuss the details. What I suggest,' he continued, his tone lightening, 'is that we have another glass of this truly excellent brandy. We should at least double our return from this enterprise.'

There was a murmur of approval and Woodberry rang for the head waiter.

About half an hour later they emerged into the street. Woodberry stood at the front doors of the club shaking hands with his guests as they left. Afterwards he put on his overcoat and was about to leave when Stanley the doorman asked: 'Will you sign for your guests now, sir?'

Woodberry signed with a flourish and added the occasion for the lunch, then followed his departed guests into the murky November afternoon.

Later on that same dismal Saturday, George Rupert Stansgate, having surrendered his passport, was released on bail from Harrow and Wealdstone police station. He stumbled down the steps of the station, bleary-eyed and smelling of prison cells. He waited twenty minutes for a bus to take him back to his home and his shocked wife and children. He trembled as he waited, it was cold and he had no overcoat. The people at the bus stop spoke in muted voices of the tragedy in Dallas. Stansgate, unaware of any tragedy except his own, stared fixedly ahead as if trying to see a way out of his nightmare.

At home his wife stared at him silently aghast, her eyes filled with a mixture of cold contempt and horror. For her their marriage had been nothing but a succession of disappointments, culminating in the ultimate humiliation; he had spent a night in jail. Whether Stansgate was guilty or not was immaterial, what mattered was that he had failed her. She was filled with the bitterness and gall of a woman who had married a failure and a fool and whose friends had not. There was no consolation for Stansgate in the arctic atmosphere of his wife's resentment, an act of kindness from her was as likely as sunflowers in Siberia.

He sought his daughter's company, hoping to find some solace in her innocent affection. But even she was distant for, young as she was, she could sense that this time the emnity in the air was permanent. Stansgate was quickly left alone to do what little he could to save himself.

Big Phil Fitzpatrick read the report carefully. It was a simple document, bound in a plain brown file. Except for three telephones, the file was the only item that occupied the great gleaming deck of teak which was his desk.

Everything about Phil was big: the office in which he sat was a vast arena of dark carpet and panelled walls; it was scattered with heavy leather armchairs and solid pieces of furniture. The hands which rested idly on either side of the report were big, though they were soft, with manicured nails, their backs dappled with brown liver spots; forty years before they had been rock hard and calloused from working on the oil rigs in the Gulf of Mexico.

Fitzpatrick had started out as a redneck in the Gulf and had worked his way up from the bottom of the barrel. In those early days as he clawed his way up he had frequently used his great fists to impose his will upon other men; but in the last ten years, since he had become president of Miranda Oil, it had been his sharp, wily brain which had enabled him to expand his empire. During the years that it had taken Fitzpatrick to get to the top, he had made a lot of enemies but it was one of the few friends that he still retained from the early days who had written the report lying on the desk.

He and Sammy Luff had started out in the oil business together. Luff had a nose for oil. He had found it where other men had believed it couldn't exist. He worked exclusively for Miranda Oil and he had never in all his assignments let the company down.

According to the document in front of Big Phil, written in an untidy but evidently educated style, Luff had first visited the island of Pinta Leone during the war and had thought then that the land held oil. He had only been able to return to the island in January 1963, when he had obtained the permission of the owner to prospect land on the northeast coast. For months, he had surveyed the whole area, testing and boring until finally he had become convinced that beneath the swamps was a vast reservoir of fine crude. And if Luff was sure, then Big Phil Fitzpatrick was sure as well.

He finished reading the report and then, slowly and carefully, read it again. When he had finished he walked to a safe in a corner of the room and deposited the file within it. He stood at the windows of his office, staring unseeingly at the changing skyline of Houston. Miranda had become Fitzpatrick's life, his obsession. The oil that Luff had found would be expensive to wrestle out of the ground, it would cost more, per barrel, to produce than it could be sold for. But Fitzpatrick was sure that one day the price of oil would change. Sooner or later, he figured, the Arabs would realise the value of the black gold they owned and would demand their price: then those oil companies who had reserves sitting in the ground would prosper. Fitzpatrick screwed up his face as his crafty mind figured the angles. The location of Luff's find concerned him. Since Kennedy's assassination just a couple of weeks previously the nerves of the nation had been jittery. The Johnson administration had not yet settled down and most people believed that the Cubans had been behind the killing. Central America and the Caribbean were in turmoil. It was possible that Sammy Luff had found a billion barrels of oil sitting in the middle of a powder keg.

But Phil Fitzpatrick had the necessary qualifications to be an oil company boss. Not only did he have strategic vision and the ruthless, single-minded drive essential to realise that vision but, as important, he had an extensive network of contacts at all levels, in all walks of life, including some who worked in very specialised and discreet departments within the government.

He returned to the safe, took out an address book and opened it. He lifted the handset of his private phone and dialled a Washington number. His call was answered almost immediately.

'Hello,' said a girl's voice.

'This is Phil Fitzpatrick. I'd like to speak with Haines Horowitz.' He waited a few seconds.

'Phil, how are you?' came a voice from fifteen hundred miles away.

'Good,' said Fitzpatrick simply. 'I've got something I'd like to talk over with you. I may have found something valuable. I need advice.'

The voice at the other end had a quality of guarded brightness. 'OK, great. Let's get together.'

'I can be in Washington next week,' said Fitzpatrick.

The voice hesitated. 'No, I don't think that's a good idea. This town is pretty twitchy since Dallas. A lot of people know you and know me. If it's confidential we should meet quietly in New York. Can you make that?'

'Sure,' said Fitzpatrick.

'Why don't we say a week tomorrow? My people have the use of an apartment downtown in Manhattan.' Horowitz gave him the address. Fitzpatrick wrote it down and rang off.

New York was cold. The Christmas decorations were up and Macy's was a blaze of light but somehow the city seemed sullen and depressed. The apartment was located in a well-preserved brownstone on the south side of Gramercy Park. The trees in the square were bare and skeletal, their branches made ghostly by the lights of the sidewalk. The building superintendent was a middle-aged man who seemed to be expecting Fitzpatrick. He opened the main door to his visitor and led him across a small ornate lobby. The building was about seventy years old and had been well preserved by its generations of affluent tenants. The small elevator in which the two men rode up to the fourth floor was panelled in polished rosewood and along its rear wall was a small bench of well-used red leather. They got out and the super rang the bell of one of the apartments. On its front door was a Christmas wreath of holly. A young man opened the door and took Fitzpatrick's overcoat.

Horowitz was waiting for him in the living room. He was a tall, thick-set man with black hair and a sallow skin. His eyes were black, covered by heavy, half-closed lids. He had an air of conspiracy, tinged with menace. He and Fitzpatrick had been acquainted for a number of years. They had a mutual regard based mainly on the appreciation of how useful each was to the other.

Horowitz held out his hand. 'Phil, good to see you.'

The two men shook hands and Horowitz put his arm round Fitzpatrick's big shoulders and steered him towards the well-stocked bar in the corner of the room.

'You look great,' he told Fitzpatrick. He kept his arm round Fitzpatrick's shoulders as they reached the bar and a young man appeared and prepared to serve them drinks.

'I keep in shape,' said Fitzpatrick, slapping his solid gut with an open palm.

Horowitz released him. 'What'll you have?'

'The usual,' responded Fitzpatrick.

The young man behind the bar had been well briefed, for he poured a large measure of Fitzpatrick's favourite bourbon into a tumbler filled with ice and then added a splash of branch water. Horowitz asked for an Irish whiskey. The young man finished and moved quietly away. There were within the apartment a number of similar young men, all apparently in their mid-twenties, tall and well-built, with close-cropped hair and intelligent eyes.

Horowitz led the way to a large comfortable sofa in the middle of the room. They sat down.

'OK, Phil,' he said. 'What's on your mind?'

Fitzpatrick took from an inside pocket a sheaf of folded paper and handed it to Horowitz. It was a copy, which he had made privately, of Sammy Luff's report. Horowitz took out a pair of horn-rimmed spectacles and began to read. Fitzpatrick sipped his drink slowly and watched him.

After a few minutes Horowitz looked up. 'This prospector, you think he's right?'

Fitzpatrick nodded slowly. 'You can bet your life. Of course I've sent a team down to check it out, but I've never known him wrong.'

Horowitz stared at him. 'Bully for you, Phil. This is a big find. I think I'll buy more stock in Miranda.' He smiled.

'Do it now,' said Fitzpatrick. 'The price is good. But what I want from you, Haines, is information. You're the guy who watches the Caribbean, you know what goes on there. What about this place Pinta Leone? They had trouble, didn't they? I don't want to develop a big oil field and then have a bunch of goons nationalise it.'

'Sure,' said Horowitz. 'I understand.'

One of the young men padded across the room. 'Sir? Can I fix you another drink?'

Before Fitzpatrick could reply the attendant had gently slid the tall tumbler out of his hand and was walking towards the bar. Fitzpatrick watched him for an instant and then turned his attention back to Horowitz. Unheard by the big oil man, another of the Ivy League men had appeared at the far end of the sofa and was bent over, whispering into his master's ear. Horowitz was staring at the carpet, listening intently.

'Right,' he said quietly, 'right. Sure, I remember. OK.' The young man finished, looked up, smiled at Fitzpatrick and then faded into the shadows of the room.

Fitzpatrick felt the heavy tumbler, filled with bourbon, being pressed into his hand.

'Look, Phil,' said Horowitz, 'most of this is pretty confidential. I'd be glad if you keep it just between us.'

'Sure,' said Fitzpatrick.

'By the way, do you mind if I keep this?' Horowitz held up the sheaf of papers.

'Go ahead,' replied Fitzpatrick. He had expected Horowitz would wish to keep the report, it was the trade he had to make to hear what he was about to be told; his secrets for Horowitz's.

'Basically,' said Horowitz, 'Pinta Leone is a one-horse island. The Brits have had it for the last hundred and fifty years and they still have some kind of connection. The island's economy is shot: there's some sugar and there's fruit which is owned by American companies. The British support the place financially but they've been trying to dump it for years. Of course, if they did then it would be

Uncle Sam who would have to pick up the bill so we aren't keen to let them do it. Nobody had any interest in the Goddamn place until this.' Horowitz inclined his head towards the papers lying on the sofa.

'But haven't the British got troops there?' asked Fitzpatrick.

'Yeah,' said Horowitz. 'That's the funny thing. The place has a tinpot Government, and there's been a revolutionary opposition up in the mountains for the last few years. One of our people is on the inside with the guerrillas.'

Fitzpatrick raised his eyebrows in surprise.

'Sure. We've got people in every revolutionary movement in the Caribbean and Central America,' Horowitz said blandly. 'We got it wrong about Cuba, Phil. We didn't reckon those guys meant anything and we hadn't penetrated their organisation, so when Castro took over we couldn't control it. We learned from the mistake. Now, we've got our people infiltrated everywhere. That way, we'll know what's going on. We can influence things.'

Fitzpatrick nodded. He understood the importance of influence. 'So what happened on Pinta Leone?'

Horowitz shook his head slowly. 'That's the funny thing, Phil. Pinta Leone had the dumbest bunch of freedom fighters in the history of the world. Christ, they couldn't have frightened your granny. Most of the time they were drunk. The Czechs smuggled in a crate full of arms, machine pistols, that kind of thing, and a couple of those jerks accidentally shot themselves. That was about all the action there was. Then one day they just went berserk.'

'Why?'

'I don't rightly know. There were about a hundred of them in total and they must have all gone nuts at the same time. Our man was in Russia when it happened.'

Fitzpatrick looked startled.

'He was in an NKVD training camp for insurgents out in the Urals. What the hell, Phil, the commies don't know who our agents are. A lot of our guys have gotten trained courtesy of the USSR. We've learned a lot. But when our guy finally came back he found that this bunch of goons had got wind of some British patrol which they had figured was coming up into the mountains to rape the women or something. So they'd gotten themselves shot full of drugs or booze, and set an ambush.' He paused. 'The funny thing is they knew where the Brits were going to be and it was a pretty good ambush because they wiped out the whole patrol. But it was pointless, especially as they butchered all those guys afterwards. All they succeeded in doing was to have a state of emergency declared and a whole battalion of British Marines looking for them. Once the booze wore off, and the dumb assholes realised what they'd done, most of them decided they didn't want to play revolutionaries any more and shipped out as quickly as they could. Now there's only about a dozen of them left. The thing is, we never got to the bottom of why they did it. Something provoked them.' He shrugged. 'Kind of curious. Anyway, Phil, you can forget about there being any trouble. What there is we know about. In fact, we can control it.'

'Good,' responded Fitzpatrick.

'Tell me, who else knows about this?'

'You and I, and Sammy Luff, the prospector.'

'Anyone else?' asked Horowitz.

Fitzpatrick looked contemplatively at the carpet. 'Yeah,' he said, 'could be. Sam likes to drink and if he drinks enough he talks. I figure the guy who owns the land might know.'

'No one else?'

'I wouldn't think so.'

'Good. Are you going to go for it?'

'Sure,' said Fitzpatrick, 'if the price is right.'

'Listen, Phil, whatever the price, it's got to be right.'

Fitzpatrick stared hard at him. 'Are you telling me how to run my business now?'

Horowitz smiled. 'This is Uncle Sam's business too, Phil.'

'How's that?' asked Fitzpatrick.

'If there is oil on that island, we want it to be owned by a good old-fashioned American corporation. We can fix the government to be pro American and that way we can keep out the Brits.'

'I thought they were supposed to be our friends. I thought you wanted them to stay on Pinta Leone.'

'Not if there's oil there we don't, that changes everything. The Caribbean is Uncle Sam's back yard, Phil. We don't want anyone else in our back yard. We've got the Cuban problem, we don't want any more problems. The British are a pain in the arse. They've got more toffee-nosed faggots giving our secrets to the Russians than a Harlem hooker's got crabs. The Europeans should stay in Europe. We've been picking up crap left by the French in Vietnam.' Horowitz picked up his glass. 'So, Phil, Uncle Sam would be mighty grateful if you secure that oil find as quickly as possible. If you've got any problems, let me know. You know how it is, you help us, we help you.'

Fitzpatrick nodded. He knew the system well enough. 'Sure,' he responded. He drained his glass as Horowitz stood up. The meeting was at an end. One of Horowitz's assistants appeared with his overcoat and helped him put it on. Horowitz walked with him to the apartment door and out into the lobby where they waited for the elevator. He was still carrying the report that Fitzpatrick had given him.

'By the way, Haines, most of that stuff is pretty confidential, I'd like it to stay between ourselves.' Fitzpatrick was mimicking Horowitz's earlier remark.

'Sure, Phil,' came the smiling reply. 'I'm not going to show it to Esso. After all, I'm a stockholder.'

The elevator arrived and the tough-looking super stepped out as Horowitz and Fitzpatrick shook hands.

'Keep in touch,' said Horowitz. 'Let me know if there are

any problems.' Fitzpatrick nodded and stepped into the elevator.

The Christmas celebrations came and went and the year slid fitfully beneath the surface. Many were glad to see it go, for it had marked the end of an innocence.

To Phil Fitzpatrick, Christmas was an unwarranted interruption of business. He had despatched one of his senior vice presidents to Pinta Leone with instructions to open negotiations with the owner of the land. The emissary returned to Houston on New Year's Eve and reported to Fitzpatrick.

'This guy's name is Portalier,' he announced, sitting across the vast desk from his boss. 'He's some kind of educated nigger, British. He talks like an English milord with a mouth full of marbles. The uppity bastard told me he didn't want to talk until after Christmas. He knows the land has oil in it, for Christ's sake. Sammy Luff must have told him.' The man shook his head ruefully at the thought of a world which allowed black men to be educated and oil prospectors to shoot their mouths off. 'He says he wants to talk to some other people.'

'Shit,' exploded Fitzpatrick. 'This is Sammy's fault, I ought to cut his liver out. Who's he talking to, Shell? British Petroleum?'

'He wouldn't say. He just said to come back at the end of January.'

Fitzpatrick raged inwardly; but years of practice and a few costly mistakes had taught him the value of patience. He had no alternative, so he waited.

As soon as the man from Miranda had left him, Portalier sent a telex to the accommodation address in Paddington. It was collected two days later by Woodberry who took a cab to Lord North Street where Addingham and Blackmore were waiting. The house was cold and empty, Blackmore's wife and children were in Norfolk for the holidays and the fire which the housekeeper had laid in the upstairs drawing room threw only a grudging warmth into the room. Woodberry laid the telex on a low onyx coffee table.

'Miranda?' queried Blackmore. 'I've never heard of them. Are they big enough?'

'Certainly,' responded Addingham, 'and eager enough, according to Portalier.'

'Yes, but is he right?' asked Woodberry. 'We have to take quite a risk on his judgement.'

'Of all of us,' Addingham replied flatly, 'I would say that John Portalier is the most competent at judging the extent of other men's greed. It would appear that Miranda Oil is very keen to acquire that land. When can you fly to Zurich?'

Woodberry pulled a wry face. 'Awkward,' he said. 'I've got a house full of guests and it's the middle of the hunting season.'

Blackmore scowled and Addingham smacked his lips together impatiently.

'I suppose,' Woodberry continued, 'I'll have to miss a day's hunting, won't I?'

He flew to Switzerland on the second day of the New Year, to the amazement of his wife and house guests, none of whom had ever known him put business before sport. He had telephoned Schellenberg in Liechtenstein and arranged to meet him at the Zurich bank in the offices of Dr Stekenmuller. The two men were waiting when he arrived.

'Good morning, gentlemen,' he said as he was shown into the office in which seven months previously Henry Dundonald had deposited twenty-one thousand pounds in cash.

'Mr Boniface,' greeted Stekenmuller. 'Allow me to introduce Herr Schellenberg.'

They shook hands.

'Please be seated.' The three men deposited themselves on a suite of low easy chairs.

'Perhaps, Mr Boniface,' said Stekenmuller seriously, 'you could tell me the number of your personal account at this bank.'

Woodberry reeled off the number, as well as the date the account was opened and the amount it contained.

'Good,' nodded Stekenmuller. 'Just a precaution, you understand.'

'Of course,' said Woodberry.

'We received instructions,' continued Stekenmuller, 'from Mr Thomas Becket, which were endorsed by both you and Mr Lanfranc, to close his account and to credit the other accounts in the partnership with equal amounts. This has been done, I have the statements.' He handed Woodberry a large envelope.

'Mr Becket decided to resign from the trust,' explained Woodberry, 'and therefore by agreement he paid back his share to the trust.' Woodberry placed the envelope in his attaché case. He turned towards the little lawyer, Schellenberg. 'Is the trust still in existence?'

Schellenberg frowned in concentration. 'Technically yes. Although we,' he gestured towards Stekenmuller, 'have been remunerated for our services, the trust has not, as yet, been disbanded.'

'Good,' responded Woodberry. 'We, my partners and I, wish you to revive the trust. We intend to repurchase the land on Pinta Leone.'

Schellenberg's face betrayed no emotion. 'From Thornbury Engineering?' he enquired.

'No,' Woodberry replied. 'Thornbury has gone into liquidation and is now in the hands of the Receiver. Are you acquainted with the role of the Official Receiver in Britain?'

'Yes, of course,' said Stekenmuller.

'Good, then you will know that the Receiver will be anxious to sell off any disposable assets which might help relieve Thornbury's burden of debt. The Receiver should be eager to sell that land.'

'I see,' said the banker. 'Have you any idea how much the trust will be expected to pay?'

'Between fifty cents and one dollar an acre; certainly no more than thirty thousand dollars.'

'It is a little less than the price paid,' observed Schellenberg dryly.

'That's all it's worth. The land is quite useless. Nothing but swamp and rocks.'

'Then why do you wish to purchase it?' asked Stekenmuller. Neither man thought it wise to enquire why Thornbury Engineering had paid fifty million dollars for it.

'Nature conservancy,' replied Woodberry. 'That stretch of land is the habitat of some of the rarest birds, reptiles and insects in the whole of the Carribean. I represent a group of men who are dedicated to the preservation of the environment. We wish the land to be purchased in order that it may be kept as a nature reserve.'

The two men stared at Woodberry. They knew it was a lie but it was sufficient explanation for their purposes. As professional men they were not expected to believe their client, only to represent his interests. They were happy not to know the truth for it relieved them of any moral responsibility; they could now claim with equanimity that theirs was a nature conservancy trust.

Schellenberg studied the man who called himself Boniface. He had the look of a person who might be close to nature, though not of one who was interested in preserving it. More a hunter or farmer, with his weatherbeaten face and toughened hands. Although physically different from the tall, blond and arrogant Englishman who had visited Stekenmuller in the spring of the previous year, this man had much the same demeanour. And like the other, he carried a symbol of a certain type of Englishman, a soft brown trilby.

'As it was you who managed the sale in the first place,' said Woodberry, 'you know the extent of the land and the land deeds, but under no circumstances are you to reveal that this trust supervised the original sale of the land by the Caicos and Caribbean Company, and of course my partners and I are to remain completely anonymous.'

The other two nodded their heads in agreement.

'We wish the purchase to be completed as quickly as possible, certainly by no later than the end of this month.'

Schellenberg and Stekenmuller looked surprised.

'I think you'll find they'll be prepared to sell quickly,' Woodberry concluded.

He was right. Schellenberg made an appointment to see the accountant who was acting as the liquidator and flew to London. The man was something of a naturalist himself and was interested in what flora and fauna the land contained. Schellenberg was coldly disdainful.

'I do not know anything about the land,' he said. 'My instructions are to negotiate with you for its purchase. My clients will offer you up to thirty thousand dollars or ten thousand pounds if you are prepared to sell immediately.'

The accountant was surprised. Of all the assets that Thornbury owned, the land should have been the most valuable but his firm had discovered that, like the rest of the assets, it was worthless. In the accountant's view the financial director of the company had been either irresponsible or criminal, and the auditors, a City firm headed by his old friend Ashley Brighton, had been hoodwinked. He called his office to tell his senior partner about the offer. As there was still some contention as to who had ultimate ownership, Eastcote was called into the offices of the liquidator for a meeting. His reaction, when he was told of Schellenberg's offer, was hostile and suspicious.

'That's a fraction of what I paid,' he objected.

'Yes, but you lent money to purchase a different beach,' said the liquidator.

'Who are these people anyway?'

The accountant, who was also present, told him, 'Nature conservancy in Liechtenstein.'

'It's a swindle,' Eastcote screeched, 'a tax dodge. Somebody is trying to buy my property on the cheap.'

'Mr Eastcote,' said the liquidator coldly, 'I must remind you that this land belongs to the Receiver and that you have gone on record frequently as saying that it is totally useless and has no value whatsoever. For something which you say is worthless, this is a very good offer.'

Eastcote squirmed in agitation. 'No one offers ten thousand pounds so that a bunch of fucking flamingoes can live to be four hundred,' he said.

The liquidator was becoming angry. 'We have been offered a considerable sum of money for a piece of land which for weeks you have been saying is worthless. In my opinion, it is the only offer we are ever likely to have. I fail to see how this can in any way be some form of tax evasion.'

'Anyway,' interrupted the accountant, 'flamingoes don't live in the Caribbean.'

Eastcote stared at him incredulously.

'I would suggest,' the liquidator continued, 'that it is in your own interests to agree to this sale. I think you have enough problems. You have nothing to gain by being unnecessarily obstructive.'

Eastcote got the message. Both the liquidator and the accountant were well-connected, they knew personally the men in the Bank of England and the others who were pursuing him for money. It would go easier with him if he was co-operative. Reluctantly he agreed to the sale and within a week the deeds had been drawn up and Schellenberg had flown to London with a banker's draft drawn on the Swiss bank for ten thousand pounds.

A few days before the end of January the land was, for the second time, in the ownership of the partners.

Schellenberg was staying at Brown's Hotel in Dover Street, where Woodberry had arranged to meet him after he had finished at the Receiver's office. The two men took afternoon tea in the hotel's warm, opulent lounge as the dark of a cold afternoon fell on the busy, brightly lit streets outside. Schellenberg showed his client the documents of sale and the deeds to the land. The glass-framed title deed which Eastcote had bitterly seen disappear from his office wall was wrapped in brown corrugated paper. The lawyer unwrapped it. Woodberry had not seen it before and in the dull glow of the hotel's lights the yellowing parchment with its copperplate script and great red seal seemed to remain wrapped in the mystery of its past. Woodberry studied it closely then passed it back to Schellenberg who carefully repackaged it. 'What do you wish us to do with the property now, Mr Boniface?' he asked.

'These documents should be held in the bank's vaults for now,' Woodberry replied. 'We expect that you will be contacted by an American corporation within the next couple of weeks who will want to purchase the property. We will expect you and Herr Dr Stekenmuller to negotiate its sale. You should open the negotiating at forty million dollars.'

Schellenberg, who was sipping his lapsang souchong, coughed in surprise and a few drops of the tea dribbled down his chin. He stared at Woodberry in silence as he dabbed at them with his handkerchief.

'That's just the opening price, you understand,' continued Woodberry. 'I think we could perhaps get more.'

The little lawyer regained his composure. He took off his rimless spectacles and polished them slowly with his handkerchief. 'Can I ask why the Americans wish to pay such a price, Mr Boniface?'

'Oil,' said Woodberry standing up and making ready to leave. 'The place is swimming in it.'

They walked together to the reception area where Schellenberg arranged to have the legal documents deposited overnight in the hotel's safe. Afterwards, they shook hands. 'Goodbye, Mr Boniface,' said Schellenberg. 'I shall be in touch with you as soon as the Americans have contacted me.'

'It shouldn't be long,' said Woodberry, buttoning up his Crombie. 'You know the Americans, once they decide they want something, they act very quickly.' He laughed. 'So enthusiastic,' he said as he stepped through the swing doors.

In fact as Woodberry was striding along the crowded pavements of Mayfair, Patrick Brandon, vice president of Miranda Oil, was boarding the morning flight out of Pinta Leone with a very definite lack of enthusiasm. He was not looking forward to his return to Houston and to telling his boss that the land he had gone to buy had already been sold.

'What!' shouted Fitzpatrick. 'Jesus Christ.' Big Phil's booming voice filled the great office and his hardened tones beat down like rods on the brain of the white-faced vice president.

'We've wasted a month. If this guy Portalier doesn't own it, who does? And how come he said OK to the survey team going in there when he doesn't own it?' He glared at Brandon seated opposite, his eyes as hard as gun barrels.

'Portalier says he sold it some time back to a nature conservancy trust in Liechtenstein,' said Brandon. Fitzpatrick's eyes narrowed. 'He's spent the last month trying to buy it back so he could sell at a profit to us but they won't sell.'

'Shit.' Fitzpatrick lumbered to his feet. Brandon jerked nervously in his seat and rubbed his stomach, his ulcers were giving him hell. 'So who owns it now?'

Brandon passed across a sheet of paper on which was written Schellenberg's address.

'Don't mean a damn thing to me,' said Fitzpatrick peering at it. 'One thing's for sure, if this guy Portalier tried to buy back the land, that trust must know it's valuable. Jesus, it's a mess. You'd better go to Europe tomorrow and talk to this guy.'

The other man nodded dumbly, stood up and shuffled wearily towards the door.

'Oh yeah,' called Fitzpatrick. 'This guy Portalier, what's he like?'

Brandon stopped and thought for a moment. 'Greedy,' he replied. 'Do anything if the price is right.'

'Could he be useful?' Big Phil asked. 'Keeping the local politicians off our backs, that kind of stuff?'

'Sure,' came the reply. 'He'd be good at it.'

'OK,' said Fitzpatrick. 'If you get trouble in Europe, call me and I'll fly over. Whatever happens I want that oil field. The survey team's confirmed that there's a billion barrels of fine crude down there. So you'd better get it.'

Brandon nodded once more and left the office. Fitzpatrick watched him go, his mind elsewhere. Nothing in the oil industry was simple but Caribbean land owned by a Liechtenstein trust made Big Phil Fitzpatrick suspicious. He was thinking it was time to call his friend Haines Horowitz. He was also thinking that he might take a trip to Pinta Leone to look at the property for himself and meet its previous owner, John Portalier.

Fitzpatrick was a man who usually did what he set out to do, but in one respect he was not going to realise his plans; he was never going to meet John Portalier. For at that precise moment the last of the Portalier line was about to quit the land that had given him birth. For ever.

Chapter Ten

The voice on the phone was American and vaguely familiar and for a moment Portalier thought that it was Brandon, the man from Miranda who had recently flown back to the States and who had, maybe, called with some more questions. But there was a note of panic in the voice and after a few seconds he realised who was calling. It was Joe Collioure. The desperate voice confirmed its owner. 'This is Joe Collioure. You remember me.'

'Of course,' said Portalier. 'The bond salesman.'

'You're still here.'

'Still here?' Something was wrong.

'Haven't you heard?'

'Heard what?'

'Victor's dead. They got Victor.'

Portalier felt his heart surge and his pulse accelerate. 'Wait,' he commanded. He stood still, holding the phone away from his ear as he breathed deeply and fought to control his galloping heartbeat. After a few seconds his heart began to slow down. He brought the phone to his ear.

The voice was babbling. 'Hello. What's happening? What's wrong? Hello.'

'It's all right. I'm here,' said Portalier calmly.

'What happened?'

'Nothing. Now, tell me again. About Victor. What happened?' Portalier's voice was slow and deliberate.

'He's dead. They're all dead.'

'How?'

'Look, I don't want to talk on the phone. Can we meet somewhere?'

'Meet?' enquired Portalier. 'Why, where are you?'

'At the airport, I just flew in.'

'Come here. My apartment.'

'No.' The answer was instant. 'They may be watching.'

Portalier's heart gave another surge. 'Who?'

'How the hell do I know,' Collioure squeaked. 'For Christ's sake, let's meet.'

Portalier thought for a moment and then suggested a bar in the main street of Nuvo Grado. 'Take a cab,' he commanded. 'The driver will know the place. I'll see you there in half an hour.' He put the phone down and noticed his hand was shaking.

Portalier's apartment was in a leafy suburb of the city no more than a mile from the main thoroughfare and the bar where he had arranged to meet Joe Collioure. He decided to walk to the meeting. He emerged cautiously from the apartment and started walking slowly towards the city centre. The feeling that there were perhaps unknown and malevolent eyes watching made his flesh crawl. He had not felt so exposed and vulnerable since his days in Mexico, running guns and drugs for the Mafia. But he had also remembered the lessons; suddenly he turned on his heel and walked rapidly in the direction from which he had just come. There was nobody following him, there were no unknown cars cruising slowly behind him, no sauntering strangers on the other side of the street. When he had covered about a hundred yards, he turned again towards the city. He was convinced that no one was watching him and he was sure he was not followed as he sauntered into the centre of the city.

He had chosen a pavement café on the main avenue in Nuvo Grado. It was a busy place, thronged with locals and off-duty British soldiers, most of whom sat at the tables set out across the pavement. Collioure had not yet arrived when he got there. He chose a table inside the café and at the back. It was dark and cool, impossible to see from the sunny pavement outside.

A cab pulled up outside the café and the bond salesman emerged. He paid the driver quickly and scurried furtively across the pavement into the café. For a few seconds he stood blinking like a rabbit, his eyes unused to the gloom. Portalier stood up and rapped the table with his knuckles; attracted by the noise, Collioure shuffled towards him, peering intently, and it was only when he was a few feet away from Portalier that he recognised him. Portalier noticed that he wasn't wearing his gold-rimmed spectacles and that his appearance was quite altered from that of the urbane salesman whom he had last encountered. Collioure was wearing a bright casual shirt and blue slacks, his hair was tousled, combed somehow differently, and his thin pencil moustache had disappeared. It came as something of a shock to Portalier to realise that the man had evidently tried to alter his appearance.

'Christ, I need a drink,' he said.

Portalier motioned him to sit down and beckoned to one of the white-aproned waiters. The man's teeth flashed as he smiled and the bright sunlight from the street shone on his polished ebony skin. Portalier ordered coffee and two large cognacs. 'I must say,' he said trying to keep the tone of his voice conversational, 'you look a little different from when we last met.'

'Good,' said Collioure. 'That's the idea.' He peered around the café. 'Is this safe?' he asked. His face had a hunted look and his body was hunched like a cowering animal.

'Perfectly,' said Portalier.

'What about you? Were you followed?'

'No, I'm certain that I wasn't.' Collioure stared hard at him. 'I'd know if I were being watched. There's nothing unusual going on. It's all quite normal.'

Collioure nodded. 'You guys haven't heard then?'

'Heard what?'

'I figured maybe they might miss this place,' said Collioure, almost to himself. 'Not too many people knew about it. Whoever got Victor didn't know, that's for sure, though I guess it won't take them long to find out. We don't have long to do it.'

'Before we do anything,' said Portalier, 'tell me what happened.' The coffee and cognacs arrived. Collioure drank his cognac down in one gulp and Portalier nodded to the waiter to bring more.

'Who'd have figured it?' Collioure said. 'They totalled Victor and the whole family. All the lawyers, their families; they got the lot. Everyone.'

Portalier felt his heart leap again. 'Everyone?'

'Anyone even remotely connected with Victor.'

'How?'

'Birthday party. It was Victor's seventieth.'

Portalier nodded. He'd been sent an invitation but had turned it down, though not without trepidation; he had no wish to offend Victor, so had pleaded illness. He had thought it more important to see the man from Miranda.

'Everybody was there,' said Collioure. 'The whole of the penthouse floor was full of family. The lawyers were there and their families. All Victor's personal assistants, the lieutenants, the captains of the regimes, the place was full of people. It must have been a great party.'

'So what happened?'

Collioure shrugged. 'Whole bunch of guys moved into the two floors beneath them. They were supposed to be attending some convention. They looked OK and anyway, all the entrances to the penthouse were guarded. They started moving in a couple of days before the party, just moved in with their luggage, a whole bunch of cases, made a lot of noise, like any convention crowd. No one noticed that they had a lot of luggage. Anyway, the police figured that those suitcases were full of plastic explosive and that stuff that burns. What is it?'

'Napalm,' said Portalier.

'Right. They figure that the floor beneath the penthouse was packed with the stuff. Thousands of pounds of it. And right in the middle of the party, BANG. The top four floors of the hotel just disappered. Bits of Victor and the rest must have been raining all over Miami Beach. There's not enough left to identify anybody. These guys knew what they were doing because that napalm made a giant fireball. What didn't get blown away got burned. There's nothing left. Nothing.' He stopped, staring at the wall.

Portalier watched him and said, 'Whoever did it had a knowledge of English history.'

'What?' said Collioure scarcely listening.

'Guy Fawkes.'

Collioure screwed up his face. He didn't understand and Portalier was in no mood to enlighten him.

'But how could Victor allow anybody to get so close?'

Collioure shook his head. 'Who in hell would figure somebody would do that? A whole floor full of explosive? Whoever did it was crazy. A whole bunch of legitimate hotel guests got killed. They got close to Victor because there's been peace for so long. There hasn't been any trouble for years. Victor got careless.'

'Who did it?'

'Christ knows. None of the other families. Some of the fathers of the other families were there.'

'Who then?' Portalier was insistent.

'I don't know,' said Collioure. 'But whoever they were they knew what they were doing. The funny thing is, while Victor and the others were being blown up and fried at the same time, somebody walked into the lawyers' offices in town, quietly bumped off a couple of clerks who were there and then stole the filing cabinets with all the papers in. Every piece of paper was cleaned out of there, including the safe. They moved in with a great truck. Somebody else went to the lawyers' homes and ransacked them for papers.'

'The tax authorities?' said Portalier clutching at straws.

'No,' said Collioure, 'the Feds wouldn't do that. They couldn't. They'd need search warrants. Anyway, they don't go bumping off anybody who gets in their way.'

'I don't understand it.'

'Me neither.' Collioure fidgeted with his cognac glass. 'Why steal papers from a bunch of guys who have just been wasted? It doesn't make sense.'

The two men sat quietly in the dark cool corner of the café for a few moments, contemplating the mystery of it all.

'How was it that you weren't there?' askcd Portalier.

'I would have been but my sister in Hoboken got sick. I had to fly up to see her. I called Victor about it. He was,' Collioure paused, and there was almost a sob in his voice when he continued, 'he was real good about it. Sympathetic.'

'Lucky for you your sister was ill.'

Collioure looked up and stared at Portalier.

'Maybe,' he said, 'maybe not. But whoever did it might find out that they didn't get me. Those families who had godfathers blown away will want to know how come bits of me weren't falling on fifty states at once, like everyone else.' He shrugged. 'My sister got better. I figure I could be in a lot of trouble. Maybe you could be too.'

'The thought had occurred to me,' replied Portalier.

'I figure I ought to disappear permanently,' Collioure continued. 'But I need money. I can't sell any stock certificates because that might warn somebody, somewhere that I'm alive. But you've got a bank here,' he said, staring directly at Portalier, 'full of cash. Victor's cash. Only where he is, he don't need it.'

'You mean empty the safe?'

'What have you got to lose?'

'Victor's got three heavies guarding that money round the clock,' Portalier replied earnestly, 'all armed. I'm president of the bank but that doesn't give me the right to just walk in and grab the money. I have to return accounts to

Victor every month and they have to be absolutely accurate.'

'Where are you going to send them this time? That money belongs to whoever grabs it. I guess none of those goons know what has happened to Victor yet.'

Portalier shook his head. 'No. They report to me. But it won't be long before one of them reads a paper or hears about it.'

'So we've got a couple of days at most. How much is in there?'

Portalier thought for a moment. 'A shipment came in by sea a week ago, so there's probably over a million.'

'Half a million each,' said Collioure.

'What about the guards?'

Collioure shook his head. 'If they know about this, they'll end up killing us and each other. Guys like that are greedy. They're dumb. We've got to get them out of the way.'

Portalier stared at him. 'I'm a bit too old for violence, old boy,' he said slowly, 'firearms, that kind of thing.'

Collioure nodded. 'Me too. I've never handled a gun in my life. I'm a con man not a hit man. Where do they live?'

'In an apartment above the bank.'

'So they all eat together?'

'Yes, I think so.'

'Could we bribe someone to put something in their food? You know, knockout drops in the pizza, something like that. Bingo. Put them out for, say, twenty-four hours. That's all we need.'

Portalier's face brightened. 'Yes,' he said. 'We could do that. I supply all their women. They work for me. That could easily be done.'

'OK,' said Collioure, 'but don't kill them, just put them down long enough for us to get the morning flight and get well away. When they wake up they'll find there's no money, no Portalier, no Victor,' he shook his head, 'no future. Just a bunch of dumb guineas. Long on muscle, short on brains. No problem.'

'When?'

'Tonight,' said Collioure. 'We don't have long. Let's get the hell out of here. Can you do it tonight?'

Portalier thought for a few seconds. 'Yes,' he said.

'Good. I figure once we've done it and gotten the hell out, if I were you, I wouldn't come back – ever.'

Portalier took Collioure back to his apartment. He left him there and drove to the airport to pick up a suitcase which his visitor had deposited in the left luggage. There was no one watching and he was convinced that so far nobody had come to the island to trace either Collioure or himself. On the drive back from the airport, he thought of the man's words. There was no coming back. He would be leaving for ever. He had a rented apartment with a few sticks of worthless furniture, a 1955 Buick, and a local bank account which contained six hundred pounds. It was not much of a legacy for the last of the Portaliers to leave to Pinta Leone. His family had lived on the island for more than four hundred years, his forefathers had been powerful men, made rich on the slavery of others, yet the least valuable of all their possessions had made him as rich as any of them.

Portalier drove into Nuvo Grado, emptied his local bank account and then drove to the apartment of one of the girls who cooked and serviced the bank guards with her body. He explained what he wanted her to do and gave her three hundred pounds with a promise of more when she had done the job. It was a lot of money and she was glad to do it. Portalier was a big and important man on the island and she hated the men whom she was paid to satisfy. None of them had ever shown her gentleness or kindness; they took her body in any way they pleased and at any time. She told Portalier of a concoction made from the bark of a local tree which would drug the men for more than a day. Portalier was pleased and told her that he would leave his car for her at the airport with its papers and another three hundred pounds inside. She could keep the car but he advised her to go into the hills once the job had been done and stay out of Nuvo Grado until the men had left the island. She listened to his instructions closely. She was happy. She asked Portalier if he would care to enjoy her for the rest of the afternoon, but he shook his head and smiled politely. He had much to do and he could feel his heart pounding. He doubted if it could take the strain of frenzied sex.

The girl arrived that evening at the apartment with a basket of meat and vegetables. She would, she said, make stew. The men were coarse and playful; they whispered obscenities in her ear and slapped her buttocks and thighs hard and savagely. Two were in the apartment; the third was downstairs sitting in the office which was called the First National Bank of Pinta Leone, watching over the safe. One of the men dragged the girl into a bedroom where he threw her down and shoved himself viciously inside her. He finished in seconds with a grunt. He dragged her up and pushed her back into the kitchen. It was hard for her to keep the look of disgust and revulsion off her face, but she would have her revenge. She had not told Portalier, but the tincture she would insert in the stew would not only make the men unconscious but would also attack their nervous systems. They would not die, but for the rest of their lives they would be gnarled and crippled, little more than vegetables. She looked at them, big and heavy, sprawling about the room, drinking and laughing. She smiled as she prepared the dish of living death.

By nine o'clock they had eaten and within an hour they were unconscious. Portalier and Collioure arrived a little after ten. Portalier looked at the men; their faces were a muddy yellow.

'You are sure they will not die?' he said to her anxiously.

'I promise,' she said with a strange smile on her face. 'They will not die.'

He nodded and gave her his spare set of car keys. 'The car will be at the airport tomorrow morning,' he said. 'Do not forget what I have told you.'

She nodded and left. Portalier intended that his last act on the island should have some honour. He meant to keep faith with the girl and pay her what he had promised.

He took the safe keys and went down with Collioure to the darkened room which contained the safe. He knew the combination and opened it quickly. On the shelves were bundles of used dollars. It took them almost an hour to count and divide the money. Collioure was able to fit his share into his suitcase but Portalier had not thought to bring a case to carry his. At the bottom of the massive safe was a large locked holdall. He prised it open. In it were a number of files, full of papers. Portalier put the money on top of the papers, it filled the holdall completely. They relocked the safe and left the bank, locking the street door behind them. They spent the rest of a nervous night in Portalier's apartment.

The following morning they flew to Panama. As the plane banked over the island, Portalier could see, far to the north, the beach where the shimmering ocean met the grey line of the mountains. He felt no remorse about leaving his homeland for the last time; what mainly preoccupied his thoughts was how he was going to get half a million dollars through Customs and into his bank in Zurich where it would join the millions already there.

He and Collioure parted at Panama airport. They shook hands without ceremony and Portalier watched him disappear rapidly into the crowd. He booked a flight to Zurich via Mexico City and Washington; as he was in transit at both airports his luggage was not inspected, and at Zurich airport Swiss Customs waved him through without a second glance.

The clerk at the bank didn't blink an eye when Portalier opened the holdall and showed him the half million dollars nestling inside. The money was taken out, counted and credited to Portalier's account and the bag with its papers placed in a deposit box. Portalier had an idea that they might be important but he had no time to study them. He was anxious to leave Zurich and to lose any possible pursuers. Throughout his journey to Europe, he had been worried that the bank guards, once conscious, might have tried to contact the organisation in Miami and may have alerted whoever had destroyed Victor. His vital need was to keep moving. He stayed that night in a small hotel near the station and the next day took the train to Strasbourg and then on to Amsterdam. He stayed at L'Europe but made no attempt to disguise his presence. And the next day he did not try to hide his purchase of an air ticket to Sydney. After he had bought his ticket he hopped a tram and rode down to the docks. It was bitterly cold; he was glad he had thought to bring warm clothes from Pinta Leone. It took him a couple of hours to find what he was looking for, a ship's master who, for sufficient cash, was willing to take him to England with no questions asked. They sailed that night and although his cabin was uncomfortable, Portalier was content in the certainty that if anyone had followed his trail, they would spend weeks at the other end of the earth searching for him. That would allow sufficient time for the money from the sale of Miranda to come through and for him to decide where he wished to spend his rich and opulent exile.

Big Phil Fitzpatrick flew into Zurich in the middle of a raging blizzard. He had come in response to a message from Brandon, who after his meeting with Schellenberg in Liechtenstein had returned to Zurich and telexed his boss to tell him that the land on Pinta Leone could be purchased for fifty million dollars. The moment he read the stark message, Fitzpatrick made arrangements to fly to Switzerland. He arrived in a towering rage. His plane had been laid over for six hours in Paris until the runway at Zurich airport had been cleared of snow. He vented his wrath on Brandon in the back of a cab taking them to the city.

'Fifty million, for Christ's sake,' he growled. 'These guys have got to be nuts.'

Brandon shrugged. 'This lawyer is cute. He's got a pretty impressive set-up.'

'So who's at the back of him?' snapped Fitzpatrick. 'Who's he fronting for?'

Brandon shook his head. 'He won't say, and it's no use trying to find out. We either deal with him or we don't deal at all. It's as simple as that.'

Fitzpatrick glowered at the swirling snow in the headlights of the cab. 'Why do they want so much?'

'They know there's a lot of oil down there and they know it's fine crude. I guess they figure that's what it's worth. Schellenberg said if we didn't want to pay the price, he knew somebody who did.'

'To hell with that,' raged Fitzpatrick. 'That field is going to belong to Miranda, but I'm damned if I'll pay fifty million for it.'

Nor did he. The following day he and Brandon hired a car and drove from Zurich to Vaduz. He was in no mood to be impressed by the scene of the snow-covered little capital with its castle jutting out of the rocks high above the square. He was, however, impressed by Schellenberg's organisation and by the tough German who politely but efficiently searched him before he was shown into Schellenberg's office.

'Jesus Christ,' he muttered to Brandon. 'What is this place, Fort Knox?' Fitzpatrick had always rated himself a hard bargainer, but after two hours with the little lawyer he had to concede to himself grudgingly that the little runt was a better negotiator even than he. He had been able to reduce the asking price by only five million.

They returned to Zurich from where Fitzpatrick telexed Miranda's lawyers who quickly set about completing the deal. Forty-five million dollars was transferred from a Miranda account in a bank in Basle to the trust's bank in Zurich. The deeds of sale and the other rights to title were drawn up by Schellenberg and sent by special courier to Miranda in Houston where they arrived five days after Fitzpatrick's return. One of his lawyers brought in the framed title deed to show Fitzpatrick, who was sufficiently impressed to have it hung on his office wall. It had been an expensive purchase. More expensive than Fitzpatrick had expected, but it was worth it. It would be easy enough to justify to Miranda's stockholders once work began on it; ultimately the field would be worth more than ten times what he had paid. He had, as always, got what he wanted and was aware that he had also done Uncle Sam, in the shape of Haines Horowitz, a favour. He intended to make sure that Haines knew the full story of how he had purchased the field, and how much his loyalty to Uncle Sam had cost in dollars.

Schellenberg wrote to the accommodation address in Paddington. Woodberry picked up the letter a couple of days later. He telephoned Addingham in his chambers. Addingham was quietly delighted. 'Forty-five million. I think our lawyer friend has excelled himself. You say the money is through already?'

'Yes,' said Woodberry.

'I suggest we make an *ex gratia* payment to Schellenberg of a million dollars. Then half a million to Stekenmuller, who should divide the rest equally and deposit it in our accounts. Tell Schellenberg to disband the trust. We no longer need it. Perhaps you might see if the others agree.'

Woodberry phoned the other partners who unanimously concurred with Addingham's suggestions; he saw no point in contacting Portalier whom he presumed to be in Pinta Leone, so on the instruction of his five partners, he sent letters to Schellenberg and Stekenmuller giving precise and final instructions. A week later, when Woodberry phoned the accommodation address, as he had done often over the past few months, he was told there was a package waiting. He caught the London train the following day. Inside the package was a letter confirming his instructions had been carried out: the trust had been disbanded and its executors had taken their share of the spoils. Also enclosed in the package were six envelopes, each addressed to an archbishop. Woodberry opened the one addressed to Mr Boniface. The short statement inside declared that one-seventh of forty-three and a half million dollars had been deposited in his account which, as of that date, stood at a total of £4,645,168. Each of the other envelopes, he knew, would contain the same information. He gave the seedy little man who owned the accommodation address fifty pounds in used notes and told him that he would no longer be needing his services.

He left the premises and walked round the corner into Craven Place and then realised that there was no envelope for Portalier. He hailed a cab which took him to his club in Piccadilly. From there he telephoned Stekenmuller in Zurich. Yes, that was quite correct, Stekenmuller told him. Mr Cranmer had called personally at the bank and had made a further deposit in dollars. He told the bank that he wished the account to be denominated in dollars. He had changed his account number and the name under which it would be operated, and had requested that his statements and all correspondence be retained by the bank until he contacted them. Therefore the payment to Mr Cranmer of almost six and a half million dollars had been credited to his changed account. Stekenmuller hoped that was in order.

'Absolutely,' said Woodberry, puzzled and faintly embarrassed that he had had to ask.

Woodberry spent the rest of the day delivering the sealed envelopes to the partners. Frimley-Kimpton when he read the contents suggested another lunch to celebrate, but none of the others seemed interested. The partnership had disintegrated. They had received the final pay-off and although they were now enormously rich, they were professional men and busy. They had no time for further frolics in celebration of their wealth; their attitude to the accumulation of riches was the same as their attitude to everything else in their lives. They were neither surprised nor overly elated that they were now multi-millionaires; they had expected to be rich, and they believed they deserved it. The celebration lunch they had enjoyed at Woodberry's club had been sufficient; another one would have been overdoing things.

Addingham was the last one to be visited by Woodberry, who delivered the envelope to his chambers in the Inner Temple. The Queen's Counsel read its contents, then put it in an inside pocket. The two men chatted for a few minutes, but Woodberry could see that, like the others, Addingham was no longer concerned about the partnership. As he made to leave he told Addingham what he had heard about Portalier. The barrister registered a mild flicker of interest.

'Made another deposit? Maybe he's transferring money from accounts in America.'

'Strange he was in Zurich, yet didn't contact any of us,' observed Woodberry.

Addingham gave a short laugh and turned his attention to the papers on his desk. 'Everything John Portalier does is strange,' he said as Woodberry opened the door to leave. 'He's probably gone to ground for a while. He'll surface again, sooner or later.'

'I'm sure you're right,' said Woodberry and closed the door behind him.

Addingham was only half right, though he wasn't to know it for sure, not for more than twenty years.

Lauren sensed his growing intensity. There was a vein at his temple, inches from her face, which had been gently fluttering; suddenly it began to pulse rapidly. Inside her, she felt his penis grow bigger and harder and she could feel the ridges round its tip as it expanded. Then she felt the throb deep within his organ as he began to come. She shifted her position slightly on the bed; he was big and heavy and was bearing down hard upon her. She gripped him tightly and closed her eyes.

Lauren loathed the feeling of a man coming inside her when he wasn't wearing something; it made her feel vulnerable. Usually she insisted that her clients used a condom, but the man on top of her had paid her well for the privilege of not wearing a rubber. She gritted her teeth as she thought of the unsheathed penis deep inside her. God knows, she thought, what diseases he may have or what malevolent microbes floated within the hot liquid pumping into her vagina.

She moved her hands down to his buttocks and pressed them firmly. 'Come, lover,' she whispered hoarsely close to his ear. 'God, that's good. Do it, do it. Oh, fuck me. Please fuck me, harder.' Her voice was filled with fabricated passion. His loins banged repeatedly into hers, forcing her to spread her legs even further apart. Their bellies slapped together rapidly and she felt another surge of warm fluid squirt into her. The man heaved up and stared down at her. His dark eyes were bulging, the pupils surrounded by a fine tracery of bloodshot veins, and his rich brown skin was gleaming in a sheen of perspiration. He let out a long, low groan of passion as the great gush of semen poured from him, which he followed with a series of wild animal grunts. He hung for a few seconds, suspended in his ecstasy, until his eyes rolled up into his head and he dropped heavily back onto her breasts.

Lauren moved her hands up his body and peered over his right shoulder to look at her wristwatch. She had plenty of time, she could afford a few more minutes yet of bearing his weight. He had paid her handsomely and if she was good to him he might want her again. She stroked his back, moving her hands slowly over his shoulder blades, down his spine to his buttocks which her fingers sought to ease aside in order gently to caress his anus.

'Jesus Christ,' she whispered, 'that was great. God, you're good. You're so big. I've never had it like that before. Christ, what a lover. I love it.' She waited for the usual response when he would raise himself up, beam at her and say 'Really?' and she would lie with great sincerity. Instead the man lay still, panting hoarsely.

Suddenly he jerked violently, ramming himself deeper into her body. She let out a yelp of pained surprise as the heavy body crushed her into the mattress. The man gave another great heave and cried out. He began to convulse, seemingly eager to push himself further into her. His back arched like a cat's as he buried his face into the base of her neck, from where he let out a series of hot panting cries. To Lauren it seemed that he was reaching a second and even better orgasm. She did what she always did when a man was coming; she hung on tightly and whispered sweet obscenities in his ear.

'Move lover, give me more. My pussy wants more.' Her clinging arms were white against the dark skin of his shoulders. 'Jesus, what a cock. Oh God, it's big. Give it to me, lover.' His body was trembling, his skin felt cold and clammy as Lauren hung on. He seemed to want to pull away from her, pushing up with what feeble strength was left in his arms, but she clung on like a limpet speared by his penis, her arms and legs wrapped round his shaking body like lily-white tentacles. He gave a final gasp and a tremendous spasm passed through him. She couldn't tell if he had come again, her vagina was a soggy mess of semen, numbed from the pummelling the man had given her.

With an effort he pushed up from her sweaty breasts and she saw his face. It had turned to the colour of ashes, his mouth was surrounded by bubbling froth and his eyes were bulging almost out of their sockets. She watched transfixed, pinioned by the weight of his body as his mouth opened and closed slowly like a fish's. She caught the smell of his breath and turned her face in disgust for it smelled like rotten eggs. Slowly, his great leonine head sank onto his chest and from deep within his throat she heard a long, dry rattle. His body appeared to crumple above her; his shoulders sagged and his glistening belly rolled slackly over hers. Almost casually, he collapsed upon her, his great dark head banging down into the pillow beside her face, the eyes wide and staring. It was then she knew that he was dead.

For a few seconds she clung on to the corpse, burying her face into its shoulder, filling her open mouth with its flesh in order to choke back the screams and the rising terror. She wanted desperately to vomit but instead the mental discipline necessary to a professional prostitute prevailed and she hung on, forcing her mind to control her feelings. Gradually the terror subsided. She began to take in the full measure of her situation. The big man who only minutes before had been coming in ecstasy, was now no more than two hundred and forty pounds of flabby dead meat. She remembered the fables; perhaps he had grown big and rigid and perhaps she was now permanently skewered by his lifeless cock. She whimpered at the thought of being locked into a corpse and struggled frantically to extricate herself from the dead weight above her. She pushed against his loins and his penis plopped out. The once proud and beautiful organ was now no more than a lifeless, fat worm. She rolled free, swinging herself off the bed to stand staring at the man lying face down on top of the sheets. He looked like a man in a deep sleep. As she watched, the body twitched as the nerves relaxed. The sudden tremor startled Lauren; she backed away and slumped heavily into an armchair on the other side of the room. She needed to think and to decide how best to deal with the situation. She looked around.

It was a large and well-appointed suite in a fashionable hotel in Bayswater. The man had contacted her through her agency who, for their usual fee, had given her his number.

She'd called him and he had told her what he wanted and how much he would pay and she had agreed to come to his room. He had told her his name was John. She'd been surprised to find that he was black; not that she cared, it was the colour of his money that interested Lauren. But his voice on the phone had been cultured and very English; the few West Indians who could afford Lauren had made their money out of crime and were of a different class. This one was, or at least had been, a gentleman. She looked again at the body. She needed a cigarette and stood up to get one from the bedside table. The movement disturbed the pond of fluid inside her vagina and she felt a sudden hot gush of semen. The sensation of the warm sticky fluid seeping down the inside of her thighs reminded Lauren of the detailed considerations which attended her profession. The man on the bed might be dead, but the stuff inside her was probably very much alive. She had no wish to bear any posthumous bastards nor to undergo the risk and expense of an abortion. She crossed the room and took out of her small overnight bag a rubber douche, which she carried into the bathroom. Like the rest of the suite, the bathroom was large. Staring at the big bath, she decided to have a long, hot soak. She turned on the taps.

Lauren was a child of her age. It was a cynical time and Lauren was a beautiful and cynical young woman. The man in the other room was dead. She had quickly adjusted to the fact. He wouldn't be bothering her and she knew he had hung a 'Do Not Disturb' sign on the door soon after she had arrived. She needed to think and she preferred to do that undisturbed and in comfort. She douched herself and then sank into the bath. As she lay in the hot water, Lauren began to see a way out of her predicament. Nobody had noticed her walk through the lobby of the busy hotel. She didn't look like a prostitute, she was much too young and pretty. Nobody knew she was there, nobody except her agency, and they weren't likely to tell anyone, for that would have meant exposing the service they provided for rich visitors to

London. The agency was quite safe, which meant that she could walk out of the hotel with nobody ever knowing that she had been there. As that was the situation, she decided she wasn't going to walk out empty-handed.

She finished her bath, dried and wrapped a towel round herself. She walked back into the bedroom and stared for a moment at the body on the bed. She found his wallet in an inside pocket of a suit hanging in the wardrobe. It contained two hundred pounds in notes and some credit cards. The name on them was John Portalier. She dropped it into her overnight case and contemplated the suits hanging in the wardrobe. They were expensive, like the shoes placed neatly beneath them. She knew where she could get a good price, with no questions asked, for clothes like that. It was then that she decided to take everything. It was a simple answer, it would make the police concentrate on establishing the identity of the man rather than the girl he had been with.

It took her twenty minutes to pack everything the man owned into his two matching suitcases. She took his gold watch and cigarette case off the bedside table and put them into her handbag. She tried to take the signet ring off his little finger but it wouldn't move, it seemed almost to be part of the man. Finally, she gave up the struggle. The ring was probably valuable but she was feeling queasy about touching the body. She dressed herself and took one last long look around the hotel suite for anything belonging to the man. There was nothing. She carefully packed her own belongings and manhandled the luggage out of the room. She made sure to close the door firmly behind her before staggering along the corridor to the lift.

Lauren was warmly dressed against the winter cold. The collar of her knee-length fur coat was pulled up round her face and her matching fur hat was pulled well down. The porter who carried her luggage across the lobby and into a taxi could barely see her face and assumed she was a

departing guest. She tipped him ten shillings, which was
enough to make him grateful but not enough to make him
remember her. The taxi took her to Paddington station
where Lauren deposited the cases in the left luggage office.
She intended to pick them up in a week or so, once she was
sure nobody connected her with the death of the now anonymous man in the hotel. She took the Underground back to
her flat.

It was thirty-six hours before a maid discovered the body,
by which time the contents of Portalier's bowels had seeped
out of his lifeless form and the room was filled with a
putrid stink. The hotel manager was anxious to hush the
matter up, his major problem being to calm an hysterical
housemaid. He called the police and a doctor who under-
took a preliminary examination of the body. The doctor
told the police it looked like a heart attack. The police
were surprised to find nothing in the room, not even a suit
of clothes, and checked the name under which the man had
registered. It was John Porter, but the address he had given
in Finchley didn't exist. They waited for the coroner's
report which, when it arrived, stated that the man had
died of a massive coronary shortly after ejaculation. The
report occasioned some mild humour among the detectives
handling the case; the man had evidently died on the job,
which they all agreed was decidedly the best way to cash
in one's chips. The girl he was with, if it had been a girl,
had panicked and decided to rob him. It wasn't a serious
case. There had been no foul play. The unknown man had
died of natural causes. All the detectives had to clear up was
a minor case of petty crime. They shrugged; they weren't
about to bust a gut searching for some cheap tart who had
robbed a West Indian of ten quid and a couple of suits. The
case was never officially closed, but no one bothered much
about it.

Portalier's body lay in the West London morgue for a few
weeks and then, as there were no claimants, it was finally

buried. The last of the Portaliers went to earth in an unmarked corner of Kensal Green cemetery.

The case of George Rupert Stansgate came to trial in April at Birmingham Crown Court. Stansgate's lawyers had advised him to plead guilty as the evidence against him seemed conclusive, but Stansgate refused to listen. He had a naive belief in justice and a foolhardy notion that the judge and jury would see through the mass of damning evidence against him to the purity of his innocence. He was mistaken. By the time the prosecution had finished, all anyone could see was the extent of the mud sticking to his assassinated character. Chief among those who destroyed Stansgate's credibility was Nigel Eastcote, who spoke with all the squeaky rancour of a man who truly believed that he had been wronged. He told the court how he'd come to learn of the land deal and how Richard Thornbury had insisted that Stansgate accompany him to Pinta Leone.

'It's obvious,' he said bitterly, 'that Richard Thornbury was in on the plot.' The defence objected and the judge told Eastcote that no plot had been proven and that Thornbury was not in court to defend himself. He instructed the members of the jury to disregard Eastcote's remarks which, of course, they did not. Eastcote recounted how Stansgate had introduced him to Gonzales and Portalier and how he had taken the lead in explaining the accounts of the Caicos and Caribbean Company and the Bank of Nuvo Grado. Gonzales and Portalier, he said, had remained in the background. Stansgate had taken him to a beach on the northwest coast of the island and had told him that it was the beach Thornbury Engineering intended to develop with his financial backing. Stansgate had proved the beach's location with a compass. Eastcote had since learned that it was easy enough to rig a compass with a small magnet set within it. The defence lawyer tried to cast doubts on Eastcote's evidence by referring to his attempts to avoid exchange controls and the problems he was having in paying back the huge sums he owed the Bank of England and his creditors. The judge would have none of it. Eastcote, he said, was not on trial.

The circumstantial evidence against Stansgate was overwhelming. He admitted that he had ringed the beach on the north-west of the island on the map and had also marked on it routes to the north-west. 'Therefore,' the prosecution alleged, 'he must have known of the existence of the north-east beach.' Stansgate's denials seemed hesitant and evasive. He couldn't explain the surveyor's report, evidently typed outside his office, nor the flight to Switzerland booked in his name, nor the deposit of five thousand pounds made into the Zurich bank on the same day. Nor could he explain the regular deposits from Switzerland into an account in his name in Piccadilly. He didn't, he insisted, have an account at that bank.

The little printer from Wealdstone couldn't swear that the man who had ordered the printing of half a dozen expensive brochures was Stansgate. To the printer, all toffs looked alike, but he did remember that the man was tall and bulky and that he called himself Stanstead or something like that.

Stansgate's story sounded weak and unconvincing. It was the truth but it didn't sound like the truth. His claim that Gonzales and Portalier had taken him to the beach on the north-west and told him that it was for sale was denied by their written statements which were read out to the court. His claim that he hadn't checked the location because he had believed that both men were gentlemen who could be trusted sounded pathetic to the twelve ordinary men and women on the jury. His denial that he knew about the bank accounts was completely unbelievable. Nobody, thought the jury, could have that much cash in a bank account and not know about it.

As far as they were concerned, he was as guilty as hell.

Edward Addingham's cynical view of juries was right; none of them had understood the first thing about the land deal or Thornbury's bankruptcy or the intricacies of conspiracy to defraud. All they could see was an overweight, pompous, public-school accountant who had tried to cheat the system. They listened intently as the prosecution barrister tore Stansgate and his story to pieces. They watched impassively as Stansgate, isolated and alone in the elevated witness box, surrounded by a sea of accusation, began to cry. They retired for less than twenty minutes before they returned a unanimous verdict of guilty.

Stansgate, said the judge, had been found guilty of conspiracy to defraud and of avoiding exchange controls. His actions had caused the bankruptcy of a well-known company and his criminal activities had resulted in a property speculator losing eighteen million pounds. The judge made no comment as to where the money might have gone; like everyone else, he wasn't interested. Stansgate, he continued, had come from a privileged background, educated to possess superior intelligence and moral fibre and trained to set an example. He was a professional accountant who had betrayed his trust and it was for that reason that he was sentencing the prisoner to five years in custody.

It was a savage sentence and Stansgate took it hard. His great bulk seemed to crumple and his florid jowls quivered as he tried to fight back more tears. He stood staring at the judge, his watery eyes bright and unfocused. He was like a rabbit caught in the headlights of a speeding car, mesmerised, uncomprehending.

The clerk of the court declared the case over and the court ushers gently led the prisoner down to the cells to await transfer to the smells and terror of Winsom Green Prison.

The case was given a couple of paragraphs on the inside pages of the following day's press. Only Woodberry read about it; the others were too busy to notice.

Chapter Eleven

The years came and went. During the sixties, as the Vietnam war was fought and lost, the world discovered that if God was on the side of the big battalions, then Mammon was on the side of big business. Corporations were merging and remerging, taking over and being taken over; nationally and internationally the gospel was economy of scale, the bigger the better. International business empires were welded together overnight and in all the frenetic activity, the people whose productivity genuinely increased were the bankers, the lawyers and the accountants.

All the partners prospered as they took on the business of corporate marriage-broking and the birth of the new multi-nationals; each of them used their wealth to enhance their careers and realise their ambitions.

Edward Addingham became a judge, a role for which he was well suited and in which he performed with distinction, so much so that in the mid-seventies he was elevated to the peerage, becoming, as Lord Addingham of Upham, one of the ten Law Lords. Part of his rise was due to his money; he could afford to entertain the right people, and his life style, though unobtrusive, was expensive. Another reason for his success was his marriage, for he had taken, albeit posthumously, John Portalier's advice, and found himself the right woman. His wife was a tall willowy lady of anaemic appearance and refined demeanour. She was unattractive and, having reached the age of thirty-six unmarried, had thought that she would remain a spinster. She accepted

Addingham's offer of marriage with alacrity. Neither of them was in love, nor were they sexually allured by each other. They attempted intercourse only once; two lanky and unattractive bodies awkwardly and briefly coupling. It was not a success. Addingham had difficulty achieving penetration and when at last he did, it seemed like poking a hollow of dead leaves with a dry withered twig. Neither of them reached orgasm, and they never again contemplated sex with each other. It was a successful marriage. Addingham's wife was the daughter of a well-established county family. She understood instinctively her role in the promotion of her husband's career and she fulfilled it perfectly. Addingham bought a large country house in Upham where he had had his weekend cottage. It was there that he and his wife entertained. The combination of Addingham's undoubted brilliance, his money and Lady Addingham's social abilities paid off. Ten years after becoming a Law Lord he was appointed Lord Chief Justice, the most eminent and powerful judge in the country.

Oliver Blackmore too had his sights aligned on high office. In the mid-sixties he resigned his senior partnership with Warminger, Poister and Blackmore and read for the Bar. He had little intention of practising as a barrister, but he knew that the high legal appointments in government traditionally went to barristers rather than solicitors. He passed his Bar exams with ease. In the ensuing years he held a number of ministerial positions and was an exceptionally effective politician both in government and in opposition. He was finally appointed Attorney General, the highest law officer in the land, and was knighted in the following year.

Henry Dundonald's career was also a spectacular success. His adroit handling of the Thornbury affair had been noted. He was made chairman of Smithson-Perez in the late sixties and was knighted in the following year's birthday honours. His reputation grew. He was a banker's banker, respected by the presidents of powerful banks in Europe,

America and the Middle East. He was personally involved in the politically sensitive negotiations surrounding rescheduling of developing countries' sovereign debts, and was thought to have been instrumental in avoiding a major international banking crisis. Like Addingham and Blackmore, his brilliance was accompanied by an elegant and expensive life style. With such a reputation it was only natural that when the opportunity arose, Sir Henry Dundonald was made Governor of the Bank of England.

Ashley Brighton's career was less public than those of some of his former partners but nevertheless his achievements were, within the context of English professional life, significant. He became the president of his accountancy institute and was instrumental in introducing a number of major improvements in the profession, particularly concerning the detection of fraud. He was for a year, in the seventies, Lord Mayor of London, and as such was appointed a Knight of the Realm. In the late seventies he retired as senior partner of his firm, Glynnis & James, which by then was one of the foremost international accountancy practices. He was still comparatively young, only sixty-five, but his health had not been good and he wished to devote more time to writing books on accountancy.

Jeffrey Frimley-Kimpton remained a member of his club, the House of Commons, throughout the sixties. By the end of the decade, however, his reputation as a member who sat on the fence on every issue had become generally known. Even his most loyal constituency workers could see he was no more than lobby fodder, toeing the party line on every issue; in politics only for what he could get out of it. He sensed the rising discontent in his constituency and decided it was time to get out before he was pushed. He resigned his seat shortly before a general election, when his constituency party was about to pass a vote of no confidence.

During the business boom of the sixties, his public relations company prospered greatly and in that time Frimley-Kimpton discovered a new and lucrative line of work. He became a television personality. He developed the ability to ask what appeared on the surface to be tough and incisive questions but which were in fact easily handled by politicians. As the seventies unfolded he became one of the best known and most respected political commentators in the media. His knowledge of the actual politics was strictly limited; what he knew was supplied by a team of researchers from his programme staff, all of whom were female graduates and most of whom he took to bed. But knowledge of the scandals and personalities in the political arena ensured that politicians who would not normally allow themselves to be questioned appeared willingly on his programme. He became famous and very powerful and his only regret was that no matter how hard he tried and how much of his personal fortune he spent on the right people and charities, he was never given a knighthood.

Simon Woodberry went back to his life in the country. He used much of his fortune to purchase more land around his estate and to renovate his lovely manor house in the Cotswolds. His life style remained as rustic and unobtrusive as it had always been; he occupied himself with hunting and the care of his estates though he did invest in some commercial enterprises in the Midlands. He even continued his modest work as a solicitor.

Herr Dr Stekenmuller died of a heart attack in 1972. He was on holiday in Venice and dropped dead one hot afternoon as he wandered across the baking expanse of St Mark's Square. The bank which had been his life mourned him for a week, appointed a new president, and quietly got on with making money.

The lawyer, Schellenberg, continued to grow rich. By the time he was forty he was a multimillionaire. After 1973 much of his work was for rich Arabs who wished to divert some of the massive profits OPEC was making out of the rise in oil prices into their own trust funds. Schellenberg was, as always, pleased to accommodate their greed.

Max Gonzales, too, continued to find profitable employment, at least for a while. In the early sixties numerous loans were made by international lending agencies to Latin American countries for major social and industrial projects. Gonzales found methods whereby large sums of money could be creamed off the top of the loans and poured into the pockets of government officials. A fair amount of the money intended to provide a better life for the peasants also found its way into Max's pocket. In 1967 he got careless and was almost caught syphoning funds out of a World Bank loan to Mexico. With the help of some American officials, he decided to retire. He sold up his large house in Panama and moved to California.

With his customary energy Big Phil Fitzpatrick ploughed ahead with the development of the oilfield on Pinta Leone. Within eighteen months rigs were in position dotted throughout the whole area, both in the swamps and in the shallows out to sea. Shanty towns grew up at the bottom of the mountains as the rigs were assembled and the fine crude was drawn out of the earth. The island's economy began to prosper as Miranda 811 came on stream. Her Majesty's Government in the shape of the Department of Trade was aggrieved that an American company had acquired the land and with it the oil. Two years later it was the turn of the Foreign Office to feel peeved when the island underwent an efficient and almost bloodless revolution. All connections with Britain were finally severed, what few troops remained on the island were recalled and Pinta Leone for the first time in its history declared its complete independence. For a while both Russia and China courted the island's new leaders but, surprisingly, within a few months the revolutionary government accepted aid from America and guaranteed in return to protect American investments on the island. It had been a well-organised coup, orchestrated by Haines Horowitz. There was nothing attractive about the island's new government. They were greedy, corrupt and stupid. A year after they appointed a Minister of Posts and Telecommunications, he was executed for incompetence when it was discovered he could neither read nor write. The only thing that recommended the island's new leadership to the men working out of Langley was the fact that they were prepared to watch over Uncle Sam's back door.

The coup on Pinta Leone revived the interest of the British press in the island. Some of the papers discovered that the large oilfield in the north-east was the same piece of land that had bankrupted Thornbury Engineering four years before. None of them, however, made any connection, they merely pointed out the irony of the situation and then lost interest.

Nigel Eastcote saw a connection, or thought he did. Again he tried to revive official interest in the affair, claiming loudly, as he had done before, that in the debacle of the fall of Thornbury Engineering and the demise of his own company he had been defrauded of eighteen million pounds. No one was interested. Eastcote's property company had finally been forced into receivership by the Bank of England and his major creditors. He was lucky to escape criminal charges. He later tried some minor property speculation in the north of England but without success. Eastcote had become a commercial pariah. Other property speculators avoided him like the plague; his failure had revealed just how vulnerable was their business and none of the lending institutions would touch him, even with someone else's barge pole. When it finally got through to him that no one cared about his predicament, he left the country and went to Torremolinos where he set up a small business developing holiday apartments. In 1973 his car, with his mangled body still in it, was found at the bottom of a cliff in the Sierra Nevada mountains on the road between Malaga and Granada. It was never really known whether it was an accident or whether his mind had finally cracked and he had driven the car over the edge deliberately.

As agreed between the Bank of England and the Treasury, the financial institutions which had loaned Eastcote the eighteen million were bailed out by the Bank. None of them incurred a loss.

Big Phil Fitzpatrick collapsed at his desk in 1968. He died four days later. He had not groomed a crown prince to take over his kingdom and the internecine war which broke out between groups of stockholders over his succession was bitter and protracted. It weakened Miranda and made it a vulnerable takeover target for one of the US oil majors. In 1970, Miranda was merged with one of America's largest oil companies and the Miranda 811 field on Pinta Leone was taken over by new and bigger masters.

Camilla Billingham married well and her wedding was written up in Jennifer's Diary.

During the sixties, Haines Horowitz worked on the south-east Asia desk in the Agency. The debacle of Watergate improved his career and he moved up the ladder at a steady pace.

It was never discovered who had blown Victor Maggiore and his people to bits. After they had recovered from the shock of his assassination, the godfathers amicably agreed to share out his empire, and Maggiore's vast business of drugs and prostitution was peacefully appropriated. After a few years, speculation about the bombing died.

Joe Collioure finally settled in Buenos Aires and became a rich and well-respected member of its Italian community. He died in his bed more than twenty years after arriving in the city. No one from the old days in Miami ever found him because no one from Miami ever looked.

George Stansgate was released from open prison in the autumn of 1967 having been given remission for good behaviour. He was thinner, three years without alcohol had taken pounds off him, but he had lost much of his hair. His pompous manner had gone, he walked with a stoop and he had an air of servility. His wife had divorced him as soon as he had gone to prison and by then she had remarried and was living outside Birmingham. Stansgate travelled north to Birmingham in the hope of seeing what once had been his family. Two weeks later he was dead.

In the same year, in a small house in Harrow, not far from where Stansgate had once lived, another death occurred. Evelyn Lesley Pilgrim, after a long and painful illness, finally passed away. The chief mourner among the handful of people who attended the funeral service at the crematorium was her son, her only surviving relative.

Book II

Chapter One

Jeremy Paul Pilgrim was twenty. He was slightly less than average height, of medium build, with blue eyes and mouse-brown hair. His appearance, like his background, was unremarkable.

His parents had married during the war. His father went to sea as a naval officer and in 1944, in an engagement in the Mediterranean, he was badly wounded; his left leg was blown off and back at the hospital in Gibraltar the surgeons were forced to amputate his injured right arm. He died two years after his son was born, hopping his way to God wondering whether the preservation of England and her Empire had been worth the price he had paid. Pilgrim's mother worked long hours in a shop six days a week. She was too proud to seek assistance from the state, she wanted to remain middle class and independent. She never remarried; instead she turned to religion.

As a child Jerry Pilgrim was taken to innumerable places of worship as his mother sought to find the answer to why things were as they were. He was a lonely boy, spending much of his time reading in public libraries or fidgeting in churches next to his enraptured mother. He heard a lot of sermons.

Pilgrim left his local grammar school at seventeen and took a job on a local paper. It was one of the more fortunate events in his life for he turned out to be a good reporter; he was well-read from his hours alone with books, he was curious about people and their lives, and he possessed the slightly dishonest ability to make people reveal more about themselves than they intended. When Pilgrim was nineteen, his mother contracted leukaemia and died painfully within fifteen months.

After he had disposed of his mother's effects, Pilgrim moved to another paper. By the time he was twenty-three he was a senior reporter. His character was eminently suitable to the practice of journalism; he was devious, cynical and basically dishonest. His desire to know the truth was only so he might embellish it and turn it into a good story. He was highly thought of.

He married Patricia when he was twenty-five; she was a teacher from Bradford. He was quite fond of her and anyway he had made her pregnant so it seemed like a good idea at the time. Within six months he was back to sleeping with other women.

He liked his children even when they were babies. He had a capacity for gentleness and a compassion which manifested itself not only in a fondness for children but also, surprisingly, in an ability to relate easily to women. Unusually for a man, he liked women. Over the years he had a number of deeply intimate love affairs.

Three years after his marriage and just after the birth of his second child, a daughter, he went to work on a provincial daily in the West Midlands. The paper was independent, owned by local businessmen, and judged to be one of the best newspapers in the country. Though not in the same league as Addingham, Dundonald and the others, his career, like theirs, was developing well.

A few months after joining the West Midlands paper his editor called him into his office. 'Derek Hopkins is our biggest individual shareholder,' he said, 'and an influential proprietor. His daughter wants to be a journalist. I want you to train her.'

Pilgrim was not enthusiastic. 'Christ, Bob,' he said, 'I haven't time for some boss's spoiled brat trailing after me.'

Susan was introduced to him the following day. Pilgrim was right, she was a spoiled child. But she was also lovely. She had long, red-russet hair which framed an oval face of perfect proportions. She had dark brown eyes and long eyelashes, good breasts, high and firm, a narrow waist and well-shaped legs tapering from her small rounded bottom. She had been educated at a private school in Ashford and then finished at an academy in Switzerland. She was elegant and cultured; she spoke both Spanish and French fluently. She was rich. She was the boss's only child and although he was only her stepfather, he loved her deeply and spoiled her atrociously. He had given her an expensive sports car for her birthday. She had everything, and Pilgrim didn't like her. But he soon discovered that although she was spoiled, she was also intelligent and quick to learn. She had a talent for the job, she was strong and capable and she was brave. Quietly he began to respect her; if she had it all, maybe it was because she deserved it.

Susan, for her part, soon came to understand Jerry. He was weak and greedy, always searching for ways to pad his expenses and to dodge uninteresting assignments. But he was a good reporter, he got people to tell him things they wouldn't have told anyone else and he researched everything he was told. He never believed anything until he'd checked. She was surprised at how many times they were told lies which she would have believed. She liked his mild, almost benevolent cynicism.

'Everybody lies,' he told her. 'It's natural, especially lying to newspapers. If it's plausible or logical or makes sense, it's probably a lie. The truth is awkward and it rarely sounds like the truth. Newspapers don't want the truth, they wouldn't know what to do with it. They want the facts. That's quite a different matter. The facts and a good story. I spent my childhood listening to lots of different versions of the truth. They all claimed to be the only truth. Basically, the truth is what you want to believe.'

Slowly they came together and began to indulge in that most dangerous and intimate of all human activities; they began to talk, deeply, personally, about themselves. And then they became lovers. They met every day and made love as often as they could. Sometimes they had nowhere to go and would resort in their frustration to making love in the back of the car somewhere in the country. They borrowed friends' houses or flats; a number of times Susan took Jerry to her parents' great house in Warwickshire when they were away.

They began to think of living together. There would be problems but, they agreed as they lay together in some strange bed, they could all be reconciled. Their love would overcome everything. Those of their friends who knew would help and the rest of the world when it came to know would understand. Susan's parents would be a problem and of course there was Patricia. Susan was frightened of telling her parents. They had expectations of a successful marriage for her, but she would brave anything just to be with Pilgrim and he felt the same, or at least he said he did. He knew he didn't love Patricia and he thought he loved Susan. He was definitely going to leave Patricia but, he said, he would have to choose 'the right moment'. He didn't want to hurt the children. Susan said she understood, though really she didn't. Nor did Jerry. He'd never been involved in anything so desperate. He had never thought that he might be tempted to leave his children.

Of course the rest of the world, or almost the rest of the world, already knew. The editorial hall of a busy newspaper is about the last place on earth in which anything can be kept secret. Everybody on the paper had known about Jerry and Susan almost immediately but it took six months for the news finally to reach the ears of her parents.

Her stepfather confronted her. Was it true? She admitted it. Her mother was shocked. There was an ugly scene: Susan protesting her love, her parents alternately shouting and pleading.

Finally she rushed to her room in tears. Her stepfather

came to her. He knew how to manipulate her. He understood, he said. If she really loved this man then he would accept it but he wanted her to go on holiday with her mother for a few weeks just to give herself time to think. At first she said no, but she loved him, he had always been good to her and so finally she agreed.

She saw Jerry and told him what had happened. He was shocked. He felt under pressure, he wanted her, but he wanted her in his own time, when he was ready. Events seemed to be overtaking him. Secretly he was glad she was going away, it would give him time to think.

Susan was away five weeks and in that time Jerry had his own problems. Patricia received an anonymous letter which described the affair in detail. She was hysterical and Jerry, scared and angry, denied everything. He told her that he had been fond of Susan, had liked her a lot, but he hadn't slept with her. The letter was a poisonous lie. In the end she accepted what he said, though whether she really believed him he couldn't tell. But at least it stopped her crying, threatening to take the children away. Afterwards, he regretted his betrayal and was ashamed.

Susan got back from northern Spain and called him at work. While she had been away, her parents had made arrangements for her to go to America to stay with distant relations. She was angry, she wasn't going, she said. Now was the time for both of them to break away and start their lives. They arranged to meet at a friend's flat. The moment Jerry walked in, Susan knew that it wasn't going to happen. Somehow, somewhere, she knew Jerry had denied her. For the first time in their relationship they had an available bed which they didn't use. He did want her, he said, but he couldn't just walk out. By the time she got back from America things would have worked out, he would have arranged a smooth and painless separation. She saw through it; he wanted her, but he also wanted his easy and comfortable life. He didn't love Patricia but he was frightened of what she might do or what she might say to the children. He was weak, he wanted it all. He wanted Susan and his children.

She screamed, she ranted, she raved. She wept like an inconsolable child, which was what she was, and all the while Jerry shuffled from foot to foot trying weakly to placate her. Finally, she stormed out and drove home at breakneck speed hoping she would crash. She locked herself in her room, drew the curtains, sat on the floor and wept for hours, imprisoned in the half-mad world of the rejected lover.

She flew to America three days later in the company of her mother. Throughout the journey she spoke hardly a word, surrounded by a wall of pain. She spent her time staring at infinity through the cabin window, fervently wishing that the plane would fall out of the sky and end her misery.

At first Jerry didn't notice what was happening, but finally in a week when his most notable job had been to interview a man who claimed to have a cure for the hiccups, he realised that he was no longer being given any of the good assignments. In a stormy meeting with his editor, Pilgrim's suspicions were confirmed; he was being eased out. 'Old man Hopkins wants you off the paper,' he was told.

Pilgrim was shocked. 'Why?'

His editor sighed wearily. 'Because, Jerry, you stuck your dirty little working-class willie into the public school pussy of our most powerful proprietor's only daughter. That's why. Oedipus, you've heard of him?'

'Stepdaughter,' Pilgrim corrected him.

'Same difference,' responded his editor. 'One day she's going to be very rich. If you had stuck with her, Jerry, you might have owned all this. Instead you decided to play it safe, stay as you are, mediocre.'

'I never ever thought about her money.' Pilgrim was offended.

'Well, maybe you should have done. Maybe you should try thinking with your brains sometimes, instead of your cock. Anyway, you're finished here, I'm afraid. It's one thing to screw the boss's daughter, it's another thing to screw up her life. They say she's had a nervous breakdown in New York. Hopkins will never forgive you.'

He left the paper a month later. He had decided to quit journalism and take his editor's advice and think about money. Up until then money had not been a prime mover in his life, but as he'd opted for the mediocre he resolved to be rich while he was being ordinary. He telephoned Nick Byers. 'Nick,' he asked, 'that offer of yours, does it still stand?'

Nicholas Byers had worked with Pilgrim during his early days in newspapers. They had come to know each other quite well before Byers had moved to another paper. Within a few months he had moved again and within a year had moved once more. Byers stayed in a job only as long as it took for his reputation to catch up with him. At about the time that Pilgrim had moved to the West Midlands, Byers had decided that he would become a public relations man. Byers was as shallow and mindless as tinsel and in a short time achieved some success in the world of PR. However, he discovered that in order to survive he needed someone who had a talent for writing and who had good contacts within the media. He had called Pilgrim a number of times over the past year, each time offering him a larger salary and a bigger shareholding as an inducement to join his new company.

Pilgrim moved to London and the name of the consultancy was changed to Byers-Pilgrim. He took a flat in Chelsea and commuted back to Patricia and the children every weekend. During the week he took a great many women to bed. Always they were young and fresh, girls just out of good schools, who worked for advertising agencies and publishers, all fresh as flowers with skin as soft as butter. They were noisy and articulate, exciting and meaningless. It was the good life, he earned a lot of money, made a lot of friends and travelled considerably.

After about a year he moved Patricia and his children south and buried them in the Hertfordshire countryside. He purchased a big house and a large white Mercedes, bought his daughter a pony which she didn't want and spent a small fortune having the kitchen modernised. His wife's cooking didn't get any better.

He kept his flat in Chelsea and continued to fornicate mindlessly. Although he was a lesser luminary than Addingham and the others, his star, like theirs, was in the ascendant. As Byers-Pilgrim prospered, his life style became richer and sleeker. For seven years it was a very good living until one bright sunny morning in early September it all came to a shuddering stop.

He had arrived at their new offices in Jermyn Street at about ten and was going through his mail when Byers walked in and closed the door behind him.

'Morning,' he said abruptly. 'Look, I'm afraid we're in a spot of bother. It looks like Bigland Motors are going to sue us.'

Bigland Motors was a well-known firm of truck and lorry manufacturers and was one of their largest clients.

Pilgrim was shocked. 'What the hell for?'

Byers took a deep breath before explaining how he had induced Bigland Motors and four other major clients to put money up front for various PR campaigns, none of which had been organised. In all, they had more than a quarter of a million pounds of clients' money unaccounted for. Pilgrim guessed that Byers had spent some of the money expanding the company into Europe. They had opened an office in Amsterdam but it had proved to be an expensive mistake. Just how expensive Pilgrim was now learning.

He was angry. 'Hell, Nick, you were supposed to take care of the business end of things.'

Byers' response was bleak. 'You're a director of the company too. You're just as responsible legally as I am, Jerry.

It's no use getting angry, we've got to hang together on this.'

The following day they sought legal advice. After reviewing the papers the solicitor was faintly contemptuous. 'The company looks successful,' he said, 'but there's nothing to it, no substance. You've been living off the cash. The business is probably insolvent. What's more, you could face criminal charges for fraudulent conversion. There is a faint possibility you could go to prison.'

Pilgrim felt his skin go cold.

'You see,' said the solicitor noting his reaction, 'these companies feel they've been deliberately misled, tricked into giving you money for nothing.'

Afterwards the partners had a bitter row. Pilgrim was frightened.

'It's all your fault,' he accused. 'You got us into this mess. You get us out of it.'

Byers stared angrily at him, turned on his heel and walked away. It was the last time Jerry ever saw him.

When after three days he hadn't come to the office, Pilgrim phoned his ex-wife to find out where he was. She had no idea. He went to Byers' flat only to learn that he'd given it up the month before. It took him ten days to find out that Byers had flown to South Africa with his girlfriend. Byers, it seemed, had decided that he was not, after all, going to hang together with Pilgrim but was rather more inclined to let Pilgrim get hung all by himself.

Within a few days word had got around that the company was in trouble and everybody to whom it owed money was angrily demanding payment. It was, for Pilgrim, the worst time in his life.

He attended a meeting of his creditors. They were icily polite. What did Pilgrim, as a director of the company, intend to do in order to pay them what was owed? they asked. There wasn't vey much he could do, he told them; he was sorry but the money had disappeared and the company had no assets. There was silence. The meeting broke up in an orderly fashion; there were no hard words and no recriminations. The following week Byers-Pilgrim received a series of writs and a visit from the police. The creditors had decided to apply for a winding up order and Bigland Motors with some of the others had made allegations of fraud.

Pilgrim called his staff together and told them what had happened. Many of them were women with whom he had been to bed. The next day four very large men appeared at the offices and took all the leased furniture away. After they had gone, Pilgrim wandered from one empty office to another. The phones sat silently on the floor, their cords snaking across the beige carpet, and a few abandoned posters remained stuck to the walls. He stared at a carpeted spot upon which he and a secretary had taken each other one evening in a fit of lust; he had been so frenzied in his passion that the carpet burn on his knees had taken a week to heal. He stayed there for hours remembering the good times.

He was invited to Scotland Yard to answer some questions. He went, quaking with fear, accompanied by his solicitor. He remained there all day answering their polite but searching enquiries.

The company was put into liquidation. Pilgrim spent long hours at the liquidator's offices going slowly and methodically through its affairs with the accountants.

'I see, Mr Pilgrim,' said the liquidator, 'that the company pays the rent of a flat in Chelsea. I'm afraid it can no longer continue to do so.'

Pilgrim nodded. The flat would be no great loss. He had been so numbed by what had happened that it seemed his sexual feelings had been eradicated.

'Also, Mr Pilgrim,' continued the liquidator, 'as your car is leased by the company I shall need the keys. Tomorrow.'

Pilgrim agreed to bring the car in the next day.

The following morning he drove down the gravel drive of

his house and along the Hertfordshire lanes on his way to London. A few miles from the house he parked the car on a quiet and grassy common and for the first time since Byers had told him of their predicament, he wept. He wished then that he had never given up Susan, that he'd never left newspapers, that he'd never met Nick Byers. His mind ranged over all his missed opportunities, over all his mean and petty acts. He was weak and he shed the tears the weak shed when good things go bad, when their paper planes will not fly. The car would be the first of many things he would lose; the prospect of poverty and humiliation was staring dolefully at him from beyond the steamed-up windows of the Mercedes. There was no way that he could see of avoiding his fate. Except one. He could kill himself. Suicide, he reasoned with his disturbed mind, was the answer. It avoided guilt, carried no fear and in fact seemed a wonderfully benign solution, for it provided escape to a place where none of his accusers could follow. It would be his penance, paid to all those whom he had betrayed. His discovery that death could solve all his problems brought a grim satisfaction.

That evening, when he got home, Patricia told him that there had been a man at the house, asking for him. The man returned at nine o'clock and slapped a writ into Pilgrim's hand. His five biggest creditors had decided to sue him, personally. He stood in the large hallway of his house, shaking as he read the long legal document. Patricia wanted to know what was wrong, what it was all about. Until that moment, he had told her nothing of the events of the past five weeks; as always he had kept her in ignorance of his life in London. He explained why he no longer had the Mercedes and went on to tell her the full extent of their troubles. She began to cry. It was all his own fault, she accused. He had always wanted too much, never been content. He was angry and frightened; everything he'd done, he shouted, he'd done for her and the kids. It was all for himself, she wailed, he was selfish. He didn't love her. She knew he didn't. He'd been to bed with other women. Yes he had, he said spitefully, with intelligent women, who were young and interesting.

They tramped from room to room hurling sharp and bitter words, ripping away at the layers of protection each had laid down to cover the emptiness of their life together. Their throats ached from the bitterness of their tears and the intensity of their lowered tones, for in all the fighting they had never raised their voices. Neither of them wished to wake their children and have them witness the demolition of a marriage and the destruction of all they thought secure, nor to have them observe the banal and pathetic spectacle of their parents skinning each other alive.

In the end they were both just too tired to go on. Patricia stumbled to bed and Jerry slept in the spare room. There was no thought, the following morning, of patching things up. There was nothing left to patch. Patricia packed a couple of suitcases, while Jerry watched silently from the kitchen. She bundled the children into the car and before driving north to Bradford told him that she wanted her share of the house and everything else.

It took six months to sell the house. He managed to get himself a job writing copy for a small sales promotion company. It wasn't much of a job and it wasn't much of a company; its one saving grace was that it knew nothing about Pilgrim or his circumstances. The salary barely covered his legal costs. The mortgage on the house got into arrears and twice the electricity was almost cut off.

He spent that autumn and winter in a trance. In London, to save money, he walked everywhere, watching the cabs in which he had once ridden glide past. As he plodded the streets he could feel the weight of guilt and fear press down on his shoulders; there was constant pain in the small of his back, even his calf muscles ached.

He was petrified. The police had interviewed him twice

more, asking him the same questions as at first. He thought about his suicide. The ideal way would be a hosepipe attached to the exhaust of a car: it would be painless enough to settle down with a bottle of whisky and let the poisonous fumes do their work. He knew a place where they sold rubber hose; the problem was that although he could afford the hosepipe, he couldn't afford the car, nor scarcely the bottle of whisky.

But it was thoughts of his children which most preoccupied Pilgrim. Most of his guilt was centred round them for he had, through his greed, condemned them to poverty. The realisation that he had betrayed them dragged him down. And yet it was the thought of his children which prevented him from actually attempting his ultimate exit. He knew that to kill himself would, for them, solve nothing. While he was alive there was always a chance something might happen.

Early in the New Year he was invited once more to Scotland Yard. They asked him more questions about the company and then asked him to surrender his passport. Just a precaution, they said, but Pilgrim was convinced he was about to be arrested. The costs of his solicitor and numerous conferences with counsel in chambers were forcing him into further debt.

Winter began to turn to spring. His fear and the imminence of prosecution had sharpened his perception. As he walked the streets he noticed the faces of the strangers who passed him, the men whom he had once despised. Ordinary men, who did not take risks, who did not strive to be rich, who lived in suburban houses, drove ordinary cars and lived ordinary lives. The men who had unexciting jobs and unexciting wives, who had security and a place of comfort to which they could go home. Now he envied the uneventfulness of their lives, the very thing he had once looked down upon. He would gladly have traded the knocking fear inside him for a job as a van driver.

The house was sold at the beginning of March. After paying off the mortgage he had twelve thousand pounds. He put the furniture in store for Patricia and sent her a cheque for ten thousand. It eased his conscience a little, for he reasoned that when he was finally cornered, his accusers would strip everything from him. It was better for Patricia and the children to have the money.

He took a dingy bedsit in Gospel Oak. The next week he was fired from his job. His solicitor wrote to say his case was set down at the Royal Courts at the end of the month.

It was the blackest time. Pilgrim bought a long length of hosepipe and a bottle of whisky. He had decided to hire a car, it wouldn't matter that his cheque was no good, they couldn't do anything about it where he was going. As living was such pain, dying, he thought, should be a pleasure.

The morning of the day he decided to terminate his life was bright and sunny. Pilgrim washed and shaved and made coffee, his mind fuzzy at the prospect of eternal dark. He left his room and found a large white envelope addressed to him in the communal hallway. It was his passport and a letter from his solicitor. The police, it said, had no further interest in him. They were satisfied that he wasn't involved with Byers and that he had not been party to the fraud. He took the letter upstairs to his room and sat on his bed, reading it again and again. It was the first piece of good news in more than six months. He noticed, when he looked up, that the sun was dappling the brick wall outside his window. Whatever happened, he realised, it was worth staying alive. The following day he went to see his solicitor at his offices in St John Street to discuss his case.

Two weeks later, just after nine thirty, he arrived at the Royal Courts of Justice in Holborn. It was a bright sunny day, the Thursday before the Easter bank holiday, and everywhere there was an atmosphere of happy expectation. Pilgrim found his solicitor and barrister standing in the long corridor which ran outside the courtroom. Some distance beyond them was a flock of dark-suited men, his creditors and their legal representatives.

'We've got a chance of a settlement,' his solicitor, David Yeadon, said as soon as he joined them.

'The opposition are pretty peeved to learn of your financial status, Mr Pilgrim,' his barrister told him. His name was Andrew Caiesdykes.

'I'm not all that happy with it myself,' replied Pilgrim. For some reason he felt a sense of euphoria. Caiesdykes smiled quietly.

'They are threatening to force you into bankruptcy. I've told them that to do so would achieve nothing. If they agree to settle, they could at least get something. The question is, what could you afford?'

Pilgrim put his hand in his pocket and pulled out a few coins. 'About forty-five pence,' he said.

'Christ,' Yeadon exclaimed in a deep voice, 'be sensible, Jerry.'

'I am being sensible,' he replied. 'I've enough to pay both of you up to today and that's it. Tell them to go ahead. Bankruptcy isn't the end of the world.'

'Mr Pilgrim,' said Caiesdykes dryly, 'bankruptcy is a serious affair. It will affect the rest of your life. It is not a circumstance into which anyone with sense should seek to fling themselves. I strongly advise you to reach a settlement.'

'But I haven't any money,' said Pilgrim.

'There are people who will lend you money in these circumstances. They are not reputable people, their rates of interest are extortionate and you must insure your life in their favour, but nevertheless, it is preferable to being bankrupt.'

Pilgrim stared at the great double doors of the courtroom standing tightly shut. Caiesdykes followed his gaze. 'I didn't take up the law,' he said, 'to stay outside courtrooms and effect settlements in draughty passages. But in this case, Mr Pilgrim, I strongly recommend that we don't go into court.'

'All right,' said Pilgrim finally. 'Whatever you say.'

It took the barrister two hours to negotiate the settlement. He and the opposing barrister flapped back and forth along the corridor in their black gowns, meeting and muttering halfway between the two groups. Finally they agreed a sum of sixty thousand pounds.

'It's the best we can do, but they insist they get their costs as well,' he announced finally.

'Christ,' muttered Pilgrim. 'How much will they be?'

'About ten thousand pounds, I would guess.'

'You fellows don't come cheap,' said Pilgrim bitterly.

'Their QC is very expensive,' his solicitor told him.

Pilgrim glanced at the opposition barrister, a short, dark-haired man. 'So they want seventy thousand pounds.'

'Yes, I'm afraid so,' replied Caiesdykes.

Pilgrim stared at the men standing in a huddle along the corridor. 'All right,' he said finally, 'I agree.'

The barrister made to walk away.

'Perhaps,' continued Pilgrim, 'you would ask their barrister if he would mind coming over here and giving me a kiss.'

Caiesdykes stopped dead and both he and Yeadon stared in amazement at him.

'Why not?' said Pilgrim grinning broadly. 'I like to be kissed while I'm being screwed.'

With some difficulty Pilgrim was able to raise the seventy thousand pounds from a back-street moneylender who charged crippling interest. For the next two years he did no more than survive just above the poverty line. His whole existence was centred round keeping up with the massive repayments he was forced to make on his debt. He sent what money he could to Patricia who had found a job teaching in Bradford. Since their separation he had seen his children only once.

He took a succession of jobs. Occasionally he got free-lance work from some of the European scandal magazines. It was pretty sordid reporting but it paid well and he was glad of it. Sometimes he was able to get a few freelance copy-writing assignments but his main livelihood was selling insurance. He wasn't very good at it, he couldn't summon up the necessary fervour to be really successful, but he did well enough to survive. He lived in a series of dingy bedsitters and had affairs with a succession of equally dingy women. It seemed almost as if the women were rented with the apart-ments. Emotionally, he lived in a state of suspended anima-tion; a state out of which he was jolted one Saturday afternoon in the Fulham Palace Road.

He'd recently moved into a bedsit near the Charing Cross Hospital. He was sitting in a pub. Earlier, at lunch time, it had been crowded but by half past two there were only a few people left; Fulham were playing at home and most of the crowd had gone to see the match. Someone had left a news-paper behind and Pilgrim, seated on a red moquette bench, was quietly reading. Gradually he became aware that some-one had sat down further along the bench. He looked up.

It was Susan. He could not have been more surprised if it had been his mother, risen from the dead. His mouth dropped open and he stared at her dumbstruck. She was seated demurely, as always, her back straight, her feet together, her hands lightly clasped, resting in her lap.

'Jesus Christ,' was all he could manage to croak.

'Hello, Jerry,' she said simply. He continued to stare at her. She was wearing a white polo neck jumper and a light tan skirt. Her russet hair fell in waves about her face and reached down to her shoulders. She looked stunning. What few pairs of eyes were left in the saloon bar were riveted on her.

'You seem surprised,' she said. Her face held a look of casual concern. It was as if she was addressing a child.

'I am.'

'Let me buy you a drink.'

He recovered his composure a little. 'No, no, let me buy you one.' The words stumbled out.

'Why?' she said. 'I offered first.' She bought him a large Scotch. From what he could see as he watched her standing at the bar, her body was as firm and beautiful as when he had known her. He noticed that she bought herself a tonic water. She walked towards him carrying the drinks and for a moment he half expected her to throw the Scotch into his face but she placed his glass carefully in front of him and seated herself as pertly as before. 'Cheers,' she said.

He noticed that she wore a wedding ring. He raised the glass in salute. 'I never thought to see you again,' he said.

'Evidently,' she replied. 'You look as if you've seen a ghost. Drink up, it'll help you get over the shock.'

'What does your husband do?' he asked.

She smiled briefly. 'Not a lot. He's in the City. He's an underwriter at Lloyd's and he's on the board of a few companies.'

He nodded. 'You've done well. I'm glad. You look fantastic.'

She stared at him. 'You're thinner,' she observed, 'and your face is very drawn. At least,' she said cheerily, 'you've kept most of your hair.'

She wasn't as he had remembered her. Certainly she was as beautiful, probably more so, but she was also more mature, more relaxed and self-possessed. He felt uncomfortable as she surveyed him with a steady gaze. 'Do you have any children?' he asked finally.

'I have a little boy,' she replied. 'Anyway, how are you?'

'Like I look. A mess.'

She shrugged. 'I'm sorry.'

He looked directly into her lovely brown eyes and knew that she meant it. The bitterness inside him evaporated. His voice was quiet. 'I had it coming,' he said. He shrugged as she continued to stare at him and there was another long silence. 'Look,' he said finally, 'I'm sorry about what happened. I suppose you must have thought I was just leading you on. I wasn't. I've been wanting to apologise to you for years. I didn't mean you any harm.'

'You didn't do me any bloody good,' she replied evenly.

'I heard,' he said.

'Anyway,' her voice brightened, 'that was a long time ago. Tell me what happened to you.'

Briefly he told her, from the time he'd come to London. He recounted the story of his rise and fall factually and without bitterness. 'So here I am,' he said.

'So I see. Well, I am afraid I must go.' She rose. Pilgrim hurriedly stood up, downed the last of his whisky and followed her outside. She hailed a passing cab which was going south towards the river. They crossed the road to where it had parked at the kerb. He opened the door for her. 'Will I see you again?' he asked.

She turned and stared at him. 'That's up to you.'

'How do I know where to find you?' he said as she climbed in.

'I found you,' she said and shut the door, motioning to the driver. The cab moved off.

For the rest of that afternoon Pilgrim was in a daze and by the following day he had begun to believe that the whole incident had been a dream. There seemed to be no logical reason why Susan should seek him out. The bond that had once been between them had long gone. She was rich, attractive and in charge of her life. He was none of those things. But he was curious, her parting words seemed to be a challenge. He decided to track her down.

It took him a week to find out that her married name was Bronwyn-Taylor and that she lived at the fashionable end of Elizabeth Street, near the corner with Eaton Square. He called her and she agreed to go for a lunchtime drink. They went to a small pub in Westminster on the corner of Medway Street, behind the towers of the Department of the Environment. They were there until the place closed, during which time, Susan told Pilgrim her story.

'It took me a long time to get over you,' she said. It made him sound as if he was pneumonia. She'd taken a series of jobs and various lovers until after a couple of years she had a serious love affair. 'He was Jewish,' she said. 'A rich oversexed New Yorker. It was good while it lasted. He liked women, he was interested in them. He reminded me a lot of you.'

They had lived together for two years, but in the end it hadn't worked out and it was she who had left him. 'In some ways,' she said, 'because he reminded me so much of you, I began to think that perhaps our parting had been a good thing. Maybe you and I wouldn't have worked out.'

Pilgrim smiled wanly and stared at the wall behind her, wondering at the perversity of a life in which, for the past years, he had been regretting their separation while she had been thankful for it.

After that she moved to California where she had an affair with another woman. 'I was sick of men,' she said. 'Sick of macho males who thought all I wanted was a few inches of prick and plenty of pump action. Guys who allotted me three minutes to reach an orgasm and if I couldn't make it, gave up and looked after themselves. So I thought I might get what I wanted with another woman.'

'What was that?' he asked.

She thought about it. 'Tenderness,' she replied. 'I hadn't had much of that. Except maybe from you and the guy in New York. But it hadn't worked out with either of you and in the end it didn't work out with her either.'

By then she had been in America for five years and for some time her parents had been urging her to come home. She found on her return that her parents were even more anxious to see her married well. So she became a member of the county set, a hunt ball groupie who throughout the following year went to countless dinner parties where she was introduced to all the right men. She met David, her husband, at a ball in Shropshire. His family owned vast acres of land on the Welsh border; the Bronwyn-Taylors could trace their pedigree back to Henry VII. He was exactly the kind of man her parents wanted her to marry and as he evidently agreed with them, she said yes.

'Did you love him?' asked Pilgrim.

'No, not really,' she said. 'I needed a rest. I hadn't made it in America and as soon as I come back to England my mother started parading me in front of eligible men like a prize heifer. I was tired. David offered peace and security. He is very rich, you know.' A year after they married she had given birth to her son.

'Why did you search me out?' he asked suddenly.

She thought for a while. 'I wanted to find out what had happened to you. To see whether you had changed.' Pilgrim was silent for a few moments, he had the impression that Susan's life was so full of peace and security that she was bored.

'You know,' he said, 'a few years ago I used to wish that we could meet, so you could see how well I'd done, the house, the car, all that.'

'I'm glad we didn't,' she said. 'I wouldn't have liked you rich.'

'You're rich.'

'I was brought up to it.'

'How did you know where to find me?' he asked.

'It wasn't easy but I remembered some of the things you'd taught me.' She laughed.

They met almost every day and gradually began to recapture something of what they'd had: she was wiser about the world and he was wiser about himself; much of what had attracted them to each other was still there.

A month after their first meeting in Fulham, they went to bed. Susan planned it all. She booked a room in a small hotel in Ebury Street, just round the corner from her house, for a weekend when David had to go to Wales. She told him that she would come to his room on Saturday at midday, stay until late in the evening when she would walk back to her home, and spend the night with her son. She would reappear on the Sunday morning and spend all day with him.

Lying with her face framed by the mass of russet hair spread loosely on the pillow, Pilgrim wondered at her beauty. Her face had hardly changed, and her body, although she had borne a child, was almost exactly as he remembered it. Her breasts were still high and firm but full, like her belly, more womanly than before. She was different in bed. As she held him, he could tell that she had become technically expert in the art of making a man happy. A lot of men had taught her what to do with their bodies.

They made love, grappling to pull each other tightly together. She was the most beautiful and giving woman he had been to bed with in years and a large amount of gratitude was mixed with his passion.

After a few minutes Susan jerked rapidly for a few seconds. 'Oh God,' she whimpered in his ear, 'I'm coming.' Afterwards Pilgrim lay quietly for a few minutes and then rolled out of her. He was still hard. 'What's wrong?' she asked.

'You faked it,' he said.

She stared at him. 'I thought men weren't supposed to know when women do that.'

He leaned up on one elbow and looked at her. 'That's only when they don't care.'

'Coming isn't something I do much of these days, not unless I do it myself,' she said.

He nodded. In learning the mechanics of giving, she had somehow lost the gift of receiving. For all her openness with her body, her mind was closed; her flesh was wanton but her spirit was frigid. He tried later to coax an orgasm out of her but after more than an hour he gave up. They were both trying too hard. 'I'm sorry,' he said. She shrugged perfunctorily. He saw that there were tears in her eyes. They lay close and held each other tight until she had to go. She returned on the Sunday morning and they repeated the performance. Again, she was unable to climax. Pilgrim felt slightly guilty. Susan was paying for the room but it was he who was getting the pleasure. He said as much.

She drew her hand down his rib cage in affection. 'I enjoy it, Jerry,' she said. 'It's lovely. Like the old days. It's just that I've had too many men give up when I was about to come. Men abandon me when I need them most.'

After that weekend they went to bed as often as they could. Always it was in his bedsit, which Susan managed to brighten up with some curtains and a couple of pictures. Even so, it was still dingy. Pilgrim was self-conscious about it, but she was more practical. 'It's a bed,' she said, 'and it's ours.' What he disliked most about the place was her absence, for without Susan it was barren and lonely. It seemed to come to life only when she was there.

She was there one afternoon, lying in the bed while Pilgrim gently licked her. He was tired and was almost falling asleep, when suddenly she started to writhe. 'I'm coming,' she gasped.

It had happened quite by chance, the feeling had boiled up within her in seconds. It was a minor climax but a major event. Afterwards they talked about it excitedly. From there on it began to happen more frequently until she had become accustomed to reaching orgasm again. It wasn't something that happened every time they made love, but the fact that it happened at all made them both immensely happy.

About a month after they had become lovers, as they were lying in the narrow bed in his room, Susan asked, 'What do you intend doing with your life, Jerry?'

Pilgrim was leaning back on the pillow, his hands behind his head, staring at the ceiling contemplating the same question. 'I've no idea,' he said. 'There's not much I can do. I just have to hope something will turn up. You turned up.' He smiled at her.

'You ought to get out of this.' She nodded at the room. 'Out of London.'

'I wish I could,' he said, 'but I owe nearly seventy thousand pounds. It's a dead weight. I can't move, it grinds me down.'

'You could rebuild your life and pay it off.' She sat up in the bed and turned to him. 'Some friends of mine have a cottage in a village in Northamptonshire. He's a vet and he's taken a job in New Zealand for three years. They want to lend the place to someone who'll look after it.'

'How do I earn a living?'

'I know hundreds of people in business all over the Midlands and the south. You're a good writer, Jerry. I could get you work copywriting for advertising, PR, that kind of stuff. We could start a business.'

Pilgrim stiffened. 'I don't want to go into business, not again.'

'Christ, Jerry,' she laughed. 'I wouldn't let you run it. I wouldn't let you near it. I'll form the business and you can work for it. I'll find you the contacts, you do the work.'

A couple of weeks later she took him to see the cottage. He liked it. If she could find the work, he said, he would love to move. Within two weeks, Susan had found nine writing assignments. He came to the conclusion that if he'd gone into partnership with Susan rather than Nick Byers, he really could have been rich.

One morning in early June he packed his clothes into an old suitcase and his books into a few cardboard boxes. He piled them into the boot of Susan's Jaguar and moved them to his new life in Northamptonshire. As the car purred north along the A1, Pilgrim realised that it was almost exactly ten years since he had moved to London. It had been ten years of triumph and tragedy, a life of shallow success and total failure, a life that he was now shrugging off as easily as a snake sheds its skin.

Susan bought an inexpensive word processor and kept him supplied with a constant stream of work. He earned more than he had been earning in London and he wasn't paying rent, all of which meant that though he was still poor, he was somehow less enslaved by his poverty. The cottage was small and warm. He went for long walks in the countryside and slowly began to regain his health. He stopped smoking, at least he stopped buying cigarettes, though he occasionally bummed a cigarette off Susan. He joined a local yoga class and the regular practice of yoga helped to calm him. Susan came to see him often, making a detour on her frequent visits from London to her parents in Warwickshire. The business prospered in a modest sort of way and with Susan's help, Pilgrim bought an old second-hand car. He began to relax and settle in to his new life. The villagers were friendly and he found a local pub.

In London he had been faithful to Susan, but once he had established himself in his new home, he began cautiously to appraise the local females. He decided to seduce Trixie Hayhoe who worked at the local stables and was a regular at his pub. It was easy to persuade her into bed. She provided a counterpoint to Susan, the bit of fun when she wasn't around. It wasn't that he wasn't grateful to Susan, he was. He'd been lucky, Susan had pulled him out of his meaningless existence and given him a new start. He was still poor, still saddled with a debt that would last for the rest of his life, still the father of children he couldn't properly support. But his life was more comfortable and, for the first time in years, fun. He had his work, he had Susan and, on the side, Trixie. And he truly appreciated it all.

Unlike the men in the Archbishop's Enterprise whose careers had become blueprints for success, Pilgrim had in the past few years been steadily climbing down the ladder of success. It had changed him, changed him a lot, but it hadn't changed him completely. When he could, he still liked to have his cake and eat it too.

Chapter Two

The village of Gretton lies hunched upon a south-western flank of the hills overlooking the broad, shallow valley of the River Welland, along which once had sailed the dragon-prowed ships of the Norsemen, quietly slipping through the mists of the great forest of Rockingham, on their way to Market Harborough. Fourteen centuries ago, men in the village of Corby had worked the iron extracted from the local stone; the stone with which King William had built the great castle at Rockingham, yellow and orange marlstone and sheep-grey Cotswold stone, which characterised the local towns of Stamford, Uppingham and Oakham.

From the squared kitchen windows of the mellow stone cottage, Pilgrim could see across the Welland almost to the roofs and chimneys of the country town of Uppingham, five miles distant on the opposite slope of the valley. It was a cool day in September. The light was good and Pilgrim stared out of the window for a long time. He was supposed to be writing sales copy for a company in Peterborough, his deadline was close and he had hardly begun to work. He found it difficult to concentrate; it was a boring assignment and the prospect of Susan's arrival excited him.

Thoughts of Susan reminded him of the crumpled state of the bedroom. He got up from the stripped pine table at which he had been working and walked from the kitchen along the short, stone-floored passage to the cottage's only bedroom. The wooden shutters were still closed, what little light filtered through their slats revealed crumpled bed sheets and the duvet on the floor. He opened the shutters and the window, pulled the sheet off the bed and shook it vigorously. After he had put it back he examined it minutely for pubic hair.

The night before he had taken Trixie to bed. Trixie was nineteen. She had the young, solid flesh of the robust outdoor girl; her skin was tanned and she had a mop of dark curly hair and throughout their frequent bouts of bumping and grinding, squeaking and coming, she managed to shed over the sheets a fair amount of coarse, black pubic hair. Susan's pubic hair on the other hand was fine and fair and as soft as silk. Pilgrim was anxious that she did not discover that he was regularly taking an energetic and talkative teenager whooping into bed.

He finished his housework in the bedroom and retraced his steps along the passage. He checked the lounge and then the bathroom before returning to the kitchen to make coffee. He sat at the table with a coffee mug and stared at the work before him. He couldn't be bothered, not with Susan's arrival imminent. Suddenly he heard the sound of tyres on gravel and the deep, affluent purring of £35,000 worth of motor car. He stood up and from the kitchen window saw Susan manoeuvre the Jaguar XJS HE perilously close to the low, stone garden wall. He watched as she got out of the car and walked round the side of the cottage. She was carrying a burgundy briefcase. A few seconds later he heard the clatter of her heels on the stone flagging of the passage. Suddenly she was there, framed in the doorway of the kitchen. 'Hello,' he said.

'Hi,' she replied. She was, as always, expensively and simply dressed, in a navy blue pleated skirt and a cream silk blouse.

'You look great,' he said. 'Coffee?' He moved towards the gas cooker.

'No thank you.'

He put the kettle back on the cooker and looked at

her across the room. She hadn't moved. 'How was the journey?'

'All right.'

'How have things been?' He hadn't seen her for more than a week.

'Okay,' she replied nonchalantly.

He nodded. There was an awkward pause. Still Susan had not moved from her position in the doorway and Pilgrim was faintly puzzled. 'Good,' he said at last.

'Look,' said Susan suddenly, 'are we going to stand around here all day or are we going to fuck?'

The previous night with Trixie had taken the edge off his sexual appetite. He wanted Susan more than he wanted sex, he was in the mood to give pleasure rather than get it for himself. He took a long time over her. She was anxious to have him inside her but he resisted her blandishments, the gentle fluttering hands tenderly yet urgently grabbing for his penis. He caressed her everywhere with his fingertips and with his tongue, everywhere but the one place where she most wanted to be touched. She moaned at the gentleness of his caresses and the exquisite sensation that his denial brought to her vagina. He played with her until, moaning softly, she gently touched his face. 'Come inside me,' she said, 'inside.'

She opened her arms like a supplicant and he grinned as he crawled up her body. Her gentle trembling hands guided him inside her. They moved together calmly at first and then as their senses drowned in their desire they clashed more urgently, jabbing and stabbing their loins at each other, their hands clutching at sweat-soaked flesh. Pilgrim felt the orgasm rise inside and slowed the insane pace of his hammering pelvis; Susan moaned in disappointment, sorry to lose the feeling that their desperate urgency gave within her. She was lying flat on the bed, her head thrown back, her face fixed in a rictus of sexual pleasure. Her eyes were half rolled up in her head, and her lips pulled back in a snarl of passion. Pilgrim's rising orgasm was not diminished as he stared into her face of animal sensuality. He stopped for a few seconds and Susan slightly shifted her position so that she might extract every tremor of pleasure from the rigid, succulent muscle that throbbed inside her. Slowly Pilgrim started again and it was then that Susan came.

She came on a rising sigh and at its peak her orgasm teetered for what seemed an eternity; she was held in the balance, ecstatic, until finally her orgasm swooped down on a falling moan. At that moment, as if in sympathy, Pilgrim came too. He shouted her name and then held her tightly to him as the feeling rattled him as a dog might shake a rabbit.

It was the closest they had come to mutual orgasm. Afterwards they wrapped themselves round each other and drifted off into sleep. They slept for almost an hour and when they awoke were greedy for more. The second time was more playful; it was too soon for Susan to come again, but to his surprise Jerry climaxed quite quickly. Recalling his time with Trixie the night before, he realised he'd reached four orgasms in less than twelve hours. As he lay by Susan's side, gently caressing her coccyx, he felt pleased with himself. She leaned up. 'That's lovely,' she purred, 'but I'm dying to go to the loo and I'd love a cup of coffee.'

Slowly he got off the bed. The day had brightened and sunlight was filtering through the slats of the half-closed shutters. It had become warmer. Both of them were damp with perspiration. He put a towel round his middle and went into the kitchen to make coffee. As he was waiting for the kettle to boil he heard Susan padding along the stone floor to the bathroom. He came back to the bedroom with two large mugs on a tray. Susan was sitting up in bed with the pillow propped up behind her. Her briefcase was lying on the duvet beside her. He handed her a mug and climbed in beside her.

'More work?' he enquired looking at the briefcase as she sipped her coffee.

She placed her mug on the floor beside her. 'Did I ever tell you about my Uncle Simon?'

'No, I don't think so,' replied Pilgrim, lolling back against the pillows.

'Well, he wasn't really my uncle, just a very close friend of the family. He was my stepfather's solicitor and business adviser. They were very close. He had a lovely old manor house and an estate of thousands of acres in Gloucestershire. He was really quite rich.'

Pilgrim smiled to himself. All of Susan's friends were 'really quite rich'. He was convinced that the only person she knew who was worth less than a million was himself.

'He died a few weeks ago,' she said

'I'm sorry.' Pilgrim offered the traditional response.

'I used to like him though I hadn't seen much of him lately. There was a time, when I was young, when I stayed at his house a lot and played with his children. They were like cousins. One of the places we used to play was in a big hayloft in the barn attached to the house. Ian, Uncle Simon's son, fancied me and he would take me up there and try to touch me up. I was only about twelve.' She smiled at the recollection. 'I don't know if you know,' she continued, reaching for her mug of coffee, 'but they used to build houses and barns from old ships' timbers. Uncle Simon said that his house was built from the timbers of a Spanish galleon from the Armada which had been wrecked off the Dorset coast. Some of the timbers were hollow inside from dry rot and Ian and I used to leave each other love letters inside the beams.

'Anyway, a couple of weeks ago my Auntie Felicity, Uncle Simon's widow, asked me over to the house. During the afternoon she had to go off somewhere so I decided to wander around for a couple of hours. I thought I'd visit the barn and see if there were any of our old love letters still in the timbers. I felt all around the places in the hayloft where I used to leave them but there was nothing. I had about given up when I thought I might try the furthest corner. It was dark and I had to bend almost double and reach up. I thought, This is silly, then I felt something, only when I tried to pull it out I found that it was quite heavy. After a struggle I discovered that it was a bundle of papers, rolled up. Whoever had put them there evidently wished them to be hidden.'

By now Pilgim had become interested in her story. He waited impatiently as she took a sip of coffee. 'Well?' he said. 'What happened?'

She put her mug down, opened her briefcase and pulled out a wad of paper. 'This is what I found.' She handed it to Pilgrim.

He examined the wrapping. 'Greaseproof paper,' he said. 'I haven't seen that since I was a kid. Well, whatever they are, they aren't very old.'

'Over twenty years.'

He looked at her. 'Have you read them all?'

She nodded.

'So, what are they about?'

She shook her head slowly. 'You read them.' There was something in her voice, a kind of excited intensity. He undid the string that held the bundle together. Inside the protective covering of greaseproof paper were a dozen or more sheets of fine spidery handwriting, a number of papers with figures listed in columns, some miscellaneous receipts and a writing pad which was filled with bold handwriting. It appeared to be some kind of diary or narrative.

It took him forty minutes to read everything. Susan sat quietly watching him. On a few occasions Pilgrim stopped reading and turned to stare at her but they didn't converse until he had finished and had put the last of the papers down on the duvet. She was watching him closely.

'Well,' he said, 'now we know how come your Uncle

Simon was so rich. He was a gangster. He made almost five million pounds out of nothing, and that's the least of it.'

They were silent for a while, Pilgrim staring at the papers spread before him on the duvet, Susan leaning her naked breast against his arm as she looked over his shoulder. 'You realise who these people are?'

'Well, I know Frimley-Kimpton,' Pilgrim replied. 'From what I've seen of him on the box I could believe this of him.'

Susan pointed an elegantly manicured fingernail at the spidery writing. 'That was written by Addingham. He thought it up,' she said, 'only he now happens to be Lord Addingham, Lord Chief Justice.'

'Christ.'

'Sir Henry Dundonald is Governor of the Bank of England. Actually, I've met him.'

'Yes, you would have,' said Pilgrim mildly. 'Blackmore, isn't he the Attorney General?'

'Yes.'

'I know the name Brighton,' he continued, 'but I can't place it.'

'I checked,' said Susan. 'He was Lord Mayor of London a few years ago. He started one of the biggest accountancy practices in the country. Why on earth do you think Uncle Simon wrote it all down?'

Pilgrim carefully leafed through Woodberry's narrative. 'I'm not sure,' he said slowly, 'but I have the impression that he got scared after the lunch they had at his club to celebrate the success of the scheme. When he guessed Richard Thornbury had been murdered he must have realised that he was an accessory. He may have been frightened that something was going to happen to him. He knew that Addingham didn't like him. I think he wrote it as a precaution. You notice he started it in December 1963.'

'But he had nothing to be frightened of,' Susan observed.

'Of course not, and within a few weeks he'd doubled his

money. I expect the fact that Thornbury had been murdered came as a shock at first, but you can see from what he wrote that he soon got used to the idea.'

'So then why did he go on writing it down, why did he want to keep all these records, receipts, accounts, and things?'

'That's easy,' Pilgrim responded. 'He's a lawyer.'

'What do you mean?'

Pilgrim contemplated the papers spread before him on the bed. 'These men,' he said, 'are some of the most powerful in the country. They are also a bunch of evil bastards. But more important than that, they're bureaucrats, lawyers and accountants and bankers, and they're brainwashed into keeping records. They can't help it. They're trained to detail everything they do, everything they spend, everything they say. They can't break the habit. The Nazis kept immaculate records of all the people they stuffed into the ovens. Look at Watergate. Nixon and all his people. They were mostly lawyers and look at their records. They kept tapes. Bureaucrats have a compulsion to keep records, it's in their blood and they don't lose it just because they become crooks, which,' he continued after a pause, 'is great for us because this, my darling, is a fantastic story. This is going to be our Watergate.' He was gleeful. 'This will be the newspaper story of the decade.'

'You think you could get it printed?' she asked quietly.

'Not in Britain, not straightaway,' he told her, 'but I could syndicate it to the French, Italian and German scandal magazines. When the British press picks it up they'll have to come to me. I could get a job out of this and make a lot of money.' His delight at Susan's discovery and what it would mean to his prospects was like a child's, he was almost bouncing on the bed. Susan did not appear to share his excitement.

'How much money could you make?' she asked.

He thought for a moment. 'Maybe ten thousand,' he

said. He glanced at her and noticed her lack of enthusiasm 'Of course,' he added hastily, 'we'd divide it.'

She continued to look thoughtful. 'Ten thousand pounds?'

'Maybe,' he replied.

She nodded slightly and was silent for a few seconds before she announced, 'Jerry, I'm hungry.'

'So am I, famished. There are some eggs in the fridge and some sausages.' He turned to the papers on the bed while she stared at him.

'Well?'

He looked up and smiled at her. 'Well what?'

'You don't expect me to cook, do you?' she said. There was anger in her voice. 'God, I hate cooking, especially cooking for a man. It's so,' she paused, searching for the word, 'demeaning. Christ, I'd rather go down on a man than cook for him.'

The grin on Pilgrim's face broadened. He pushed the papers out of the way and threw back the covers. 'Okay,' he said. 'Forget cooking.'

She looked disdainfully at his loins. 'I'm not in the mood for little fat worms,' she said. 'If I get my mouth anywhere near that thing, I'll chew it off.' She bent suddenly and snapped her teeth dangerously close to his testicles. He leapt out of bed.

He cooked a large plate of scrambled eggs. It was one of the few dishes that he could do well. He opened a bottle of white wine. They ate in the kitchen. He had put on a shirt and a pair of jeans, and she wore a white towelling dressing gown that she had bought him as a present. She watched as he ate. 'Do you really think you can get a job out of the story?'

'Why not? It's the best story for years.'

She looked at him and shook her head pityingly. 'You're out of your mind, Jerry,' she said. 'You might make a few thousand from the Continent but you won't get a job on

Fleet Street. They'll take all that stuff,' she jerked her head towards the bedroom where they'd left the papers, 'and run the story themselves. What's more, you'll be a marked man. If you think you've been in trouble before, it'll be nothing to the trouble you'll have over this. No one's going to thank you for this story. The establishment will get you somehow. I'm part of that scene, Jerry, I know how it works. It's a club. They'll all close ranks. If you topple some of their people, they'll find a way to bury you.'

Pilgrim was annoyed. 'All these top people, these eminent and powerful men, are nothing but gangsters. The public should know about them and if I can make some money telling the public, well, fine.'

'The public won't care,' she said. 'The fact that these men are thieves and murderers wouldn't come as any great surprise. The public believes all politicians are bent anyway. It would be a juicy story for a few weeks and then it would be forgotten. OK, so you would ruin a few careers. They'd all be forced to resign and there would be an outcry about how they ever got to the top. By then they'd have disappeared to some sunny island to live off their fortunes, and write their memoirs. In five years' time, they'd be back appearing on TV chat shows.'

Pilgrim frowned in disagreement.

'In the meantime,' she continued, 'someone would have decided that you did defraud those people at Byers-Pilgrim and you would be prosecuted. They'd dig everything up. They'd destroy you.'

'Addingham and his cronies wouldn't get off that lightly. This is a serious affair, Susan. Men died.' He jabbed a finger at her. 'The British public doesn't like its soldiers being chopped to bits, especially when the people who deliberately set them up are a bunch of bent politicians who did it for their own private ends.'

Susan laughed. 'Who the hell do you think sends the boys to Belfast, and for what reason? The British public has got

used to soldiers dying. They're not going to be that bothered about a bunch of squaddies who've been dead for
more than twenty years. That's if you could prove any
connection.'

He looked at her in disbelief. 'You don't mean to say that
you want to protect these people? I know you're part of the
bloody club, but even you can't like what they did. They
ought to be exposed, Susan. Christ, you must see that.'

'Why must I? Just because you entertain some naive
notion of routing out corruption in high places doesn't
mean that I have to agree.' Her voice was raised in irritation. 'Fearless reporters searching out the truth are out of
fashion. You see yourself as some kind of fucking white
knight in shining armour, don't you, all pure and noble.
Well, you're not, so forget it. Anyway,' she said more
calmly, 'the dragons are all dead, Jerry.'

There was a long and strained moment as they faced each
other across the table. Pilgrim had been shocked by her
outburst. 'But it's such a great story,' he said pleadingly.

'I know, but I won't agree to let you use it.'

'What do you mean?'

'Those are my papers. I found them. I've let you read
them but I won't let you use them. If you used them for a
story, a lot of people would want to know where you got
them. They might establish a connection between us. I love
you, Jerry, in a funny kind of way,' she said it softly,
'though God knows why, you're such a dumb bastard
sometimes, but I'm not going to have you screwing up my
life again.'

He could see that she meant it. 'So that's it,' he said with
defeat in his voice. 'We know what they did but we're going
to let them get away with it.'

'No, I didn't say that. There is another way. We could
make them pay for what they've done.'

'How?'

'Just that, make them pay.'

Pilgrim was too preoccupied to understand. 'Don't be bloody silly, Susan,' he said bitterly. 'Those people won't part with money. They're the professional classes, they don't pay for anything unless they have to. You don't seriously expect them to say they're sorry and give it all back, do you?'

'Addingham would pay you,' she insisted quietly.

'Me? Why should he pay me? Addingham is a lawyer, which means he's about as altruistic as a maggot. He wouldn't give a bloke like me the time of day, not even if he had Big Ben in his pocket.'

'He'd pay you to keep it quiet, Jerry.'

His head jerked back as he realised what she was saying. 'But that's blackmail,' he said weakly. 'Pay up or I'll publish.'

She nodded.

'I'd never get away with it.'

'Why not? They'd expect you to do it. They'd never understand your selling it to a newspaper. They'd expect you to sell it back to them. They're lawyers, they're always doing deals like that.'

Pilgrim felt a frisson of fear scamper down his backbone. He'd not experienced that feeling since the early days of the collapse of his company. 'Christ, Susan,' he said. 'I only just managed to escape one lot of trouble and I'm going to be paying for it for ever. Now you want me to get into something really serious. Blackmail is a crime.'

'It's the best chance you're ever going to get,' she said. 'You could clean the slate and start again. Pay off all your debts, settle Patricia and the kids.'

'It won't work, Susan. They're not going to let me walk in there and say "Hi, I'm Jerry Pilgrim. I'd like some money to keep quiet, please." How much money do you think I'd get out of that?'

'Six hundred thousand pounds.' Her answer came swiftly.

Pilgrim's forkful of scrambled egg stopped halfway to his open mouth. 'How much?'

'One hundred thousand pounds from each of them.'

'They'd never stand for that.'

'I would,' she said, 'if I was rich and had their kind of life. It would be a cheap price to pay to keep it all. It's only about two and a half per cent of what they made. That's not a lot.'

Pilgrim sighed. When Susan was in her business mood she was like all the others; she saw everything in terms of percentages.

'And you wouldn't be Jerry Pilgrim,' she said. 'You'd call yourself Richard Thornbury.'

He watched her as she placed her knife and fork neatly together on the plate. She looked at him and smiled sweetly. 'That would make them listen.'

Pilgrim eyed her suspiciously. 'You've been thinking about this,' he said accusingly.

'Darling, of course I have,' she replied brightly. 'About ten minutes after reading those papers I began to see the possibilities. We could make a lot of money quite easily. Money for nothing, Jerry.' She raised her glass and finished the last of her wine.

'You can't blackmail those kind of people.'

'You can blackmail anybody who's got money and something to hide. These people have got a lot of both.'

He sat quietly for a few seconds, searching for objections to her crazy idea. Finally he said, 'What you've forgotten is that these are powerful people. They're surrounded by security men. I'd never get near them.'

'Some of them are protected in public certainly, but a security man isn't employed to stop old friends coming to visit. You're an old friend, from twenty years back.'

'I am?'

'The last thing that Addingham and the others will want,' continued Susan, 'is some Special Branch detective sitting in on a conversation with a man they thought they'd murdered.'

'You've got it all worked out, haven't you?' His voice was resentful.

'Yes, I have, and I've written it down. Come and see.' She rose from the table and padded out of the kitchen. Pilgrim followed her into the bedroom. They sat on the edge of the bed and Susan took out of her briefcase a small notebook. It was mid-afternoon and the warm sunny light was already beginning to fade. Pilgrim pushed the shutters open to read Susan's notes.

'It looks good on paper,' he said when he'd finished.

'I took a leaf out of Addingham's book,' she explained. 'He wrote down his plan and then he wrote down everything he thought might go wrong. You've got to admit it worked.'

'They had to murder a few people in the process,' said Pilgrim coldly. 'You forget these men are killers, yet you want me to go trotting along to demand money from them. What's to stop them having me bumped off? They've done it before.'

'The fact that someone else holds the originals of these documents.' Her voice was definite. 'If anything happened to you they would be sent to all the newspapers. Once they know that, they wouldn't take the risk. You're not asking a lot from them, Jerry. Much safer to pay you off.'

'Yes, but if you're wrong I might end up dead.'

'I'm not wrong,' she said simply.

Pilgrim turned and looked at the papers spread upon the crumpled bed. 'I don't like it,' he said.

'It'll be all right.' Gently she placed her hand between his legs. She felt him move beneath her fingers. 'I enjoyed the lunch, darling,' she said, 'but I'd like some pudding.' She grinned.

He chuckled. 'What did you have in mind?'

'Well, I wonder what has happened to that little fat

worm.' Her fingers caressed him. 'Do you think it may have grown?'

She stood up and took off the dressing gown as he wriggled out of his jeans and shirt. He lay upon the bed as Susan turned her body opposite to his, her head between his legs. She swung one of her slim thighs over his head and gently lowered the soft, damp mat of her vagina upon his face.

He didn't see her again for a week. She took the papers with her and left him nothing but the outline to think over. He had to admit that she made it look easy. In a few days he could make six hundred thousand pounds.

Then she telephoned early one morning 'I'll be up in a couple of hours,' she said. 'I've got everything ready.' She hung up before he could reply. It was a wet, blustery day, and the wind was shrieking up off the Welland like a hooligan. Susan burst into the cottage kitchen at eleven o'clock, violently shaking the rain off her russet hair. She kissed him lightly on the mouth.

'How about coffee?' She was affectionate but businesslike and it was evident that sex was a long way from her thoughts. He brought over two mugs of coffee and sat next to her at the table.

'Bad news,' she told him. 'I can't locate Portalier. You've no idea how hard it is to trace somebody after more than twenty years. Apparently he left Pinta Leone quite suddenly and has never been back. God knows where he is now. I'm afraid we'll have to settle for half a million.' She was blatantly confident that he would participate.

'I've researched the others,' she continued. She picked a paper out of the small pile she had placed upon the table. 'Sir Ashley Brighton lives quietly in Hampstead with his wife. His health hasn't been good. He'll be easy to get to. Here's the address and telephone number.' She took another paper from the table. 'Frimley-Kimpton has a house in Chelsea, but he entertains there a lot, mostly women. I don't think you can go there and you can't see him at his offices at the television company.' She paused. 'I found out he has a house near Camberley and he usually spends Fridays and the weekend there. That's the place to get him. Here's the address and phone number. Now, Sir Henry Dundonald. The Governor of the Bank of England has an official residence at New Change near the Bank but he's protected. He's not considered a prime security target so he only has one detective guarding him, but I don't think you could get to him very easily in London. He has a big house and an estate in Hertfordshire. He's there quite a lot, weekends mostly.' She put another paper in front of him.

'You've done well,' he said.

She turned and grinned at him. 'I've enjoyed it. It's a bit like the old days. Oliver Blackmore,' she continued. 'He gets a lot of protection. He has two, perhaps three, Special Branch men around him, all armed. He lives in Lord North Street, near the Houses of Parliament. That's the best place to get to see him. The security men sit in a car outside the house. They'll see you, of course, but if you've been invited there officially they won't take a lot of notice.'

'He'll probably tell them to bump me off,' said Pilgrim dolefully.

'Not likely, darling. Blackmore seems to be the coolest of the lot. He'll tell them you're a long lost friend. Whatever happens, he'll want to see you alone, he'll want to hear what you've got to say. Finally, Lord Addingham. Although he's a judge he still has his chambers and they are the best place to see him. He has a flat in Knightsbridge but a security man actually stays in the flat when he's there. He has a house in Upham, that's miles out of London. I have the telephone number. You should have no problem if you see him in his chambers. That's it,' she said. 'You should start with Addingham or Blackmore. Once those two understand what you're after, they'll persuade the others to co-operate.'

Pilgrim was impressed. 'How did you get all this stuff so quickly?'

'With great difficulty,' she replied. 'You always said I was a good researcher. I must admit that David and some of his friends were invaluable, though of course they didn't realise it. You won't find any of those numbers in a directory,' she added. She stood up and leaned across the table to gather together the papers. 'It's funny, isn't it,' she said, 'how they've all done so well. Even with the money, you wouldn't have expected them all to be famous. Uncle Simon was the only one who wasn't well-known.'

'What do I say when I go to see them?' asked Pilgrim.

Susan reached across to her briefcase and extracted five sets of papers 'Here are photocopies of all the documents I showed you. You just walk in, drop these in their laps, tell them you know the whole story and that you want a hundred thousand pounds.'

'Just like that.'

'Of course. You're not there to ask after their health,' she said brightly. 'They'll understand perfectly. But there's something else you must tell them.' Her tone became more serious. 'You must tell them that the originals are with a friend. If anything should happen to you, they'll be sent to the papers.'

'Great,' he said. 'And if they don't believe me I'll end up like the real Richard Thornbury.'

'Don't be so nervous, darling,' she said. 'They'll believe you, they're not stupid. They may call you a few names but they'll cough up. You'll need this.' She reached across to the case and took out a slip of paper upon which was written the name and address of a bank in Geneva and a number. 'They are to pay the money into that account,' she said.

'How did you fix this?'

'I flew over a couple of days ago. It's a joint account in the name of Mr and Mrs Thornbury and it will need both our signatures to withdraw money.' She looked directly at him and smiled.

'Nice to know you trust me.'

'I love you, darling,' she said continuing to smile, 'but I'd never trust you.'

He frowned. He was slightly hurt by her words.

She leaned over and put both her arms round his neck. 'Cheer up,' she said. 'What do you think of the plan?'

He shrugged slightly. 'It's great on paper but will it work? If it goes wrong, it's my neck.'

She stared intently at him. 'Then,' she said, 'let's go to bed.'

It was frenzied, as if they were both trying to forget the commitment they had to make. Afterwards she took a cigarette from her handbag. She sat up in the bed, nervously flicking the ash into an ashtray. Her voice when she spoke was quiet and serious. 'It's make or break time, Jerry. This is the second best chance you've ever had. You threw the first one away; you're lucky to get another. There won't be any more. This plan could set you up for life. You can't stay here for ever. You're forty, Jerry, you've got to do something with your life and you can do a lot more if you've got half a million pounds. I'm not going to hang around for ever, not if you choose to stay poor. It's a good plan.'

She turned to him as he lay on his back with his hands behind his head. There was a long silence. He leaned forward, plucked the cigarette from her fingers and took a long drag. He returned it to her and lay back against the pillows to stare at her. Her skin was still slightly tanned from her summer holiday; his eyes followed the curve of her back as it swept down into her waist and rolled over her hips. Her right arm moved forward as she put the cigarette to her lips, revealing the sweeping curve under her breasts. She was beautiful.

'You know me,' he said. 'I never could say no and I could never turn down the chance of easy money. It's just that the thought of trying to extract money from these people scares me shitless. But you're probably right, they'll pay up. Anyway, I'll do it, Susan, I don't want to lose you.' He smiled at her and the tension broke.

She laughed and hugged him. 'It will be all over in two weeks at the most,' she declared. 'I'll tell you what, we'll go away for a few days, maybe a week, abroad. To celebrate.' Her delight was obvious.

They agreed that he would go to London the following week and stay there until he had made contact with all the conspirators. Before she left, Susan gave him an envelope. Inside was five hundred pounds in ten-pound notes.

'You'll need that,' she said. 'Pay everything in cash; make all your calls from pay phones; stay at cheap hotels and remember, you're Richard Thornbury. Keep in touch, darling,' she said as she got into the car. 'Good luck.'

The Jaguar roared away down the hill towards Rockingham and the Al to London.

Pilgrim spent his last few days completing the writing assignments Susan had left him. He felt jittery and spent his nights dissipating his nervous energy inside the young and solid body of Trixie Hayhoe.

Chapter Three

He drove to London on the following Sunday. The day was sunny and fresh and everywhere along the route the trees were turning to gold and yellow. He had doubts about the ability of his Morris 1100 to make the journey but as it turned out, it purred sweetly all the way down the Al. The car had no radio so Pilgrim kept an ancient cassette recorder on the passenger seat on which he played his favourite tapes.

He had deposited his passport inside the car's glove compartment in anticipation of the holiday with Susan which was to be his reward. He had also thought it prudent to take it with him in case things went wrong; there was always the possibility that he would have to get out of the country quickly.

He checked into a small and anonymous hotel near King's Cross station. Like the others in the square it boasted a large garish sign but inside it was cramped and seedy. He was shown to a small room on the third floor, filled with solid pieces of heavy, dark furniture, all of which had been made to suit a room of far more generous dimensions. The double bed looked tacky and well-used. He unpacked his few things, went out and bought himself a double whisky in a nearby pub. He could have drunk more but decided that one was enough. The sun was bright, he could sense a touch of chill in the air and he felt like walking. He was wearing a grey tweed jacket, navy slacks and a navy woollen polo neck. He sauntered southwards, through Russell Square past the British Museum and into Covent Garden. It was an eerie sensation, wandering through the streets in which the last time he had walked he had seriously contemplated killing himself. He could recall his feelings distinctly and in some ways he didn't feel so very different. He felt as if he had moved away, but not as if he had moved on. Here he was, back in London, still hustling to make a living, still outside the mainstream, still different from the ordinary people who worked in normal jobs, who went home to normal families, who spent Sunday afternoons digging the garden.

It was almost time for the pubs to close. He had another small whisky and then decided to make his first call. He chose the call box carefully; it was in a quiet side street where there was little traffic noise to distract him. He took out his notebook and dialled a number in Upham. He breathed deeply as he waited for the phone at the other end to be lifted.

'Hello.' It was a young man's voice.

'May I speak to Edward Addingham.' Pilgrim adopted his most superior tone. There was a pause on the other end.

'Do you mean Lord Addingham?' the voice enquired.

'Yes,' said Pilgrim.

'Are you sure you have the right number?'

'Of course I have,' said Pilgrim as if talking to a small child.

'Who is this?' asked the voice.

'I'm an old friend of Edward's.' Pilgrim was warming to his task. Partly it was the effects of the whisky and the walk in the brisk air and partly it was the recollection of all the dishonest tricks he'd once used as a journalist.

'May I have your name?'

'Tell him it's Richard Thornbury,' said Pilgrim. 'He'll remember me. He and some friends used to call me Becket, and I recall we used to call him,' Pilgrim glanced at the notebook in front of him, 'Bouchier.'

'Bouchier,' repeated the voice deliberately.

'Yes,' confirmed Pilgrim. 'Tell him, he'll remember.'

'I'm afraid Lord Addingham isn't in the house at the moment,' said the voice. 'Perhaps he could call you.'

'Not possible, I'm afraid,' said Pilgrim. 'I'll call again. What would be the best time?'

'I really can't say.' The voice was defensive.

'I expect he'll be there about six, won't he? Tell him Richard Thornbury will call then.' Pilgrim put the phone down. He remained in the telephone kiosk for a couple minutes. He noticed that his hands were shaking but he was pleased with himself.

He had three hours to kill. He wandered into Trafalgar Square and watched the crowds for a while before going into the National Gallery. By the time he came out it was dark and after a snack in a café, he wandered past his old offices in Jermyn Street before he found another telephone kiosk. He called the number again; it was the same voice.

'This is Richard Thornbury.'

'Ah yes,' came the reply promptly. 'Please wait.'

'This is Lord Addingham.' The voice was older, more measured, more imperious. 'Who is this?'

'Richard Thornbury.'

There was a short pause. 'I see.' There was another pause. 'How is your mother?'

Pilgrim was heartily glad Susan had done her research thoroughly. 'My mother died four years ago,' said Pilgrim. 'I'm surprised you didn't know that.'

'I did,' said Addingham. 'I merely wished to see if you knew it.'

'I think we ought to meet,' said Pilgrim.

'Why?' Addingham replied. 'I see no reason why we should.'

'We can talk of old times,' said Pilgrim. 'Anyway, I've got some papers of yours.'

Pilgrim could hear a strange smacking noise as if Addingham was eating. 'What papers?'

'Some notes that you wrote about that island, what's it called?' Pilgrim was enjoying himself. 'Pinta Leone.'

'I see.' The voice held just a slight note of strain. 'Where and when do you suggest we meet?'

'At your chambers?' said Pilgrim. 'Tomorrow afternoon.'

'I have a flat in London,' said Addingham. 'That would be more convenient.'

'You also have a security man staying there,' said Pilgrim. 'I don't mind if he listens but you might.'

'Very well,' said the voice icily. 'As you seem so remarkably well informed, I presume you know where my chambers are. I shall meet you there at five thirty tomorrow afternoon.'

The line went dead. Pilgrim stepped out into the chilly night. He was elated. It had gone better than he could have wished, though the thought of actually meeting Addingham face to face filled him with trepidation. He walked a few yards, before suddenly deciding to cash in on his good luck. He would phone the others who lived in London. It wasn't in Susan's plan and he knew he was rushing things but with some luck he thought he could be finished and out of London by Tuesday night. He retraced his steps to the call box and phoned Oliver Blackmore's number. There was no reply. He tried it again but still no answer.

He decided to phone Ashley Brighton. A woman answered, it was Lady Brighton. He told her his name.

'How curious,' she said. 'My husband and I knew a young man by that name many years ago.' Pilgrim froze, he had forgotten Woodberry's notes. Brighton had known the Thornbury family. It was obvious that his wife would also have known them. Only Susan had missed it.

'What can I do for you?' she continued.

He had no idea what to say. Everything was a mistake, he wanted to put the phone down, rush away, leave London. Finally, he blurted out, 'I'm a reporter. I was hoping to interview your husband.'

'Another one,' said Lady Brighton. 'Goodness, he is popular. Well, when would you like to see him, Mr Thornbury?'

'As soon as possible.'

'Please wait while I get his diary.'

He was shaking and something inside was clawing to get out of his stomach. All thought of talking to Brighton had gone out of his mind. He was scared that she'd gone to get him on the phone. He hung on with baited breath. She came back on the line. 'You can see him Tuesday morning. Would that be suitable?'

He told her it would.

'Ten thirty then. Do you know where we live?'

He said he did, thanked her and hung up. He felt sick. His legs could barely carry him round the corner into the nearest pub. After a couple of stiff whiskies he felt better. He concluded that no real harm had been done. In fact, it had been better that he had not spoken to Brighton, his story that he was a reporter was a good one.

He left the pub and hailed a taxi, which whisked him through the dark, past the Houses of Parliament, and dropped him at the corner of Horseferry Road. He walked through Smith Square and along the sedate and dimly lit Lord North Street. There were a few pedestrians in the street, making their way towards the brightly lit church in the square. Slowly, he sauntered past Blackmore's house. It was in darkness. A few yards beyond the house he passed a car parked at the kerb. The two men inside kept their eyes fixed on him as he strolled by. It seemed that Blackmore and his family were away for the weekend, but even in their absence security maintained its constant vigil. He treated himself to the luxury of another cab. He had meant to return to his hotel but as they drove past the Haymarket, he noticed the crowds making their way towards the cinemas and he decided that he would join them. He stopped the cab and walked into Leicester Square.

He slept badly. The room was damp, and the bed was cold. The hotel was full of odd noises and creaks and the bright orange glow of the sodium lamp in the square beamed through the thin curtains of the bedroom. He got up feeling tired and faintly depressed. Along the darkened corridor from his room the bathroom was grubby and uninviting; a large black spider was crawling around in the stained bathtub. Pilgrim decided that he was likely to stay cleaner and healthier if he didn't have a bath. He shaved as best he could in the lukewarm water which dribbled into the grimy sink in his room, dressed and went down. He rarely ate breakfast and that morning was no exception; he decided to allow his bacon and eggs to continue swimming in the grease on his plate. He took a sip of his coffee, which was the colour and temperature of the water in which he'd shaved, and went out.

The fine spell of weather continued. The morning was sharp and bright, filled with colour and thousands of Monday morning commuters pouring out of the mainline stations; St Pancras with its great orange and cream façade and its high turrets reared up over the houses at the far side of the square like a Renaissance palace. He bought coffee and rolls in the station buffet and idly watched the commuters scurrying past. He felt better, the food and the brisk air had revived him, and that morning he was glad that he was not one of the normal people, one of the herd jammed into Tube trains rushing to get to the office on time. It was after ten when he left the buffet. He wandered south into Bloomsbury and chose a quiet call box near the British Museum to call Blackmore.

'Hello.' It was a young woman's voice.

'This is Richard Thornbury,' he said, 'I'm an old friend of Oliver Blackmore's. Is he there?'

'Do you mean Sir Oliver Blackmore?'

'Yes.'

'Are you sure you have the right number?' Evidently this was the standard response to unknown callers.

'Yes, I have the right number.'

'Please hang on,' she said.

'This is Blackmore.' The voice at the other end sounded deep and heavy, like a great slab of granite. Pilgrim's heart began to sink. 'I was expecting you to call,' the ominous voice continued.

'Then you know why I am calling.'

'Not exactly,' said Blackmore. 'You claim to be Richard Thornbury and you claim to know something of my affairs more than twenty years ago.'

'I know enough,' said Pilgrim. 'I know that Edward Addingham and I used to call you Lanfranc and that we all had a pretty good deal going on Pinta Leone.'

'Yes, but can you substantiate any of that?'

'I've got enough,' said Pilgrim, hackles rising, 'to make every newspaper in the world grab at it.' There was silence. 'I think we ought to talk.'

There was a contemptuous snort at the other end of the phone. 'Very well,' Blackmore said sharply. 'I'm due at the House at twelve. Be here by eleven thirty.'

Pilgrim was surprised. 'What, this morning?'

'Of course.'

'How do you expect me to get past your tame guards?' asked Pilgrim, trying vaguely to recover his composure. He was conscious that the clipped and superior accent he had adopted had slipped a little in his surprise.

'You'll be expected.' The phone went dead.

It was another surprising turn of events. Pilgrim had not anticipated seeing any of them so quickly. He felt grubby, he needed to change his clothes; a polo neck jumper and spórts jacket were not, he felt, appropriate attire for black-mailing the Attorney General. He retraced his steps to the hotel. It seemed that after all he would have to use the grimy bath. He stripped off in his room and padded down the corridor carrying his toilet bag, a towel wrapped round his middle. The water was cold but he gritted his teeth and bathed and washed his hair as quickly as he could. He took ages to dry himself, the small towel was as thin as tissue paper. He returned to his room and put on a blue shirt and a navy blue suit, the only one he had. When he had finished dressing and had polished his shoes on the candlewick bed-spread he appraised himself in the wardrobe mirror. He looked good enough and, more important, he look anony-mous. There was nothing to distinguish him from any of the other thousands of men abroad in the streets of London. Carefully he checked his wallet, bulging with the money Susan had given him, and then went through his pockets in accordance with Susan's instructions. He had money, a pencil and some paper. And that was all. He had nothing in the wallet or on his person which could identify him as either Pilgrim or Thornbury. He left the hotel and crossed the road to St Pancras station. The previous day he had deposited a locked briefcase in the left luggage depart-ment. He retrieved the case, and in a quiet, unobserved corner of the station rotated the combination locks and extracted three separate envelopes, each containing one set of the Woodberry papers and details of the Swiss bank account. He relocked the case and, again in accordance with Susan's instructions, walked the few yards to King's Cross station where he redeposited the case in the left luggage department. He slipped the claim form into the back of his wallet.

He took a cab from the station, which dropped him at the corner of Marsham Street. He walked along Great Peter Street and turned into Lord North Street. The car was parked in the same place as the previous evening although this time he was approaching it from behind. As he walked past he was acutely conscious of two pairs of eyes boring into the back of his head. He stopped at Blackmore's front door and rang the bell. He was shaking with nerves yet he knew that it was important not to appear frightened or suspicious. He did not look in the direction of the men in the car, nor did he deliberately turn his face away: they were able to see him in profile, but no more.

The door was opened by a tall good-looking young woman with red hair who was wearing a Christian Dior suit. Pilgrim noticed the Gucci belt and gold necklace. 'Yes,' she said, staring down at him.

Pilgrim swallowed. 'I'm Richard Thornbury.'

'Yes.' For one awful moment Pilgrim thought she was going to ask what he wanted. She looked at him coldly and then commanded, 'Come in.'

He entered a small lobby, the inside door of which led into a large square room. Halfway along its left wall was a stairwell leading down into what Pilgrim guessed were the kitchens; next to it a staircase led to the floor above. Its solid wooden banister was the same deep hue as the panelling throughout the house. To the right of the staircase, at the far end of the room, were two large double doors. They were closed. On a chintzy couch to Pilgrim's right sat a heavy, dark-haired man who stood up as he entered. The man said nothing but considered a typed sheet of paper attached to a clipboard.

'This is Mr Thornbury,' said the young woman. 'He's expected. He's an old friend.'

The man stared hard at Pilgrim. Although he was built like a bull, his eyes were small and piercing. The double doors at the far end were thrown open and another large man strode into the room. Pilgrim recognised him immediately. It was Blackmore. 'Jane,' he commanded, 'I want . . .' He stopped as he noticed Pilgrim. There was an awkward pause as the young woman turned to Blackmore, a puzzled expression on her face.

'This is Mr Thornbury,' she said.

Blackmore was superb; although he had never seen Pilgrim before in his life, his reaction was instantaneous. 'Richard,' he said, 'of course, I didn't recognise you. It's been so long. Do come in.'

The security man ponderously lowered himself onto the settee as Pilgrim walked across the room into Blackmore's study. Blackmore allowed him to go first and as he passed, Pilgrim was conscious of the man's size; Blackmore towered over him ominously. He followed Pilgrim into the small book-lined study and closed the doors. In the middle of the room was a large old-fashioned desk. Outside, beyond the leaded windows, was a small paved garden, surrounded by high whitewashed walls festooned with plants. Blackmore seated himself in a well-used wing chair behind the desk. Pilgrim sat opposite.

'You won't mind if I don't offer you a drink.'

Pilgrim shook his head, deciding for the moment to say nothing.

'My time is limited,' Blackmore continued brusquely. 'If you've got something to say, you'd better get on and say it.'

Pilgrim glanced at the double doors on his right. Blackmore followed his gaze. 'They are South African sapele,' he said, 'very solid and absolutely sound proof. I don't suppose you intend to shout anyway.'

Pilgrim made an effort to control his racing heart. He was conscious that his hands were shaking as he held the envelope containing the photocopied papers. 'I don't need to say a lot. These say it all.' He dropped the papers onto the desk. For a few seconds Blackmore continued to stare at him and then his pale blue eyes dropped to the envelope. He picked it up, ripped it open, unfolded the papers and scanned them.

'How do I know these are genuine?' he asked.

'You know they are,' said Pilgrim. 'Addingham's plans, the expenses, the bills, you've seen them all before. The only thing you haven't seen is Woodberry's little account of your misdeeds and that's authentic enough. Lots of detail. Right down to how much it cost to murder Richard Thornbury.'

'You could never prove that,' said Blackmore. There was a defensive edge to his voice.

'Maybe I could, maybe I couldn't, but Woodberry believed it and he was one of your lot. There's enough circumstantial evidence to link you with Thornbury's disappearance as well as the killing of those soldiers on Pinta Leone.'

'I,' announced Blackmore, 'am the Attorney General. I don't need someone like you to tell me about circumstantial evidence.'

'And I'm a reporter,' responded Pilgrim, 'and I don't need someone like you trying to tell me these papers are forgeries. They're genuine. Anyway, if this story got out people would believe it because they want to believe it. You've got enemies, they'd love to get their hands on all this, and the public always enjoys seeing some high and mighty politician fall on his face.'

'I see.' Blackmore's eyes were filled with hate. 'So you think you could make this public. The newspapers would never publish it.'

'We're not that stupid,' said Pilgrim. 'Firstly we'd send copies to the European magazines. Once they published, the British press wouldn't be able to ignore it.'

Blackmore's face changed. He was frowning. 'We?' he enquired. 'Who are we?'

'I have a partner,' said Pilgrim, 'who holds the originals. If anything should happen to me, if I should have an accident,' he emphasised, 'she would send copies straight to all the newspapers.'

'They would want to see the originals,' Blackmore observed.

Pilgrim smiled slightly. Although his heart continued to pound he was beginning to feel more at ease. 'That's no problem.'

There was silence as the two men stared at each other across the desk.

'Is that what you intend to do?' asked Blackmore finally.

'Perhaps,' said Pilgrim.

There was another pause. 'What do you really want?'

'Money.'

Blackmore stared hard at him and then leaned back in his seat with some sense of relief. 'Well, I can handle that,' he said, 'that's straightforward enough. How much?'

'Two hundred thousand pounds.'

That was the sum which on his journey south Pilgrim had decided to demand. As Susan's plan was so good he had made up his mind to cash in on it for himself: he was sure that if the partners could afford to pay one hundred thousand pounds then they could afford to double it. It had occurred to Pilgrim that although having a joint account with Susan in the sum of half a million pounds was an excellent idea, having another account with the same sum in his own name, and unknown to Susan, was an even better one.

Blackmore looked surprised and Pilgrim smiled. 'I know it isn't very much,' he said, 'but that is the sum that I intend to obtain from everyone. There were seven of you. Woodberry is dead and I can't find Portalier anywhere. So that leaves just the five of you. Which means I make a million. A million should keep me comfortably for the rest of my life.'

'Are you trying to tell me this is a once only visit?' Blackmore was sceptical. 'What is to stop you coming back for more? Putting the black on all of us, year after year?'

'Nothing, I suppose,' Pilgrim replied. 'But once I've got the money then I'm implicated along with you. A million pounds should last me.'

'I should bloody well hope it would.' Blackmore's tone was bitter. 'It's a lot of money.'

Pilgrim recalled Susan's words. 'It's less than two per cent of what you made and that's not counting inflation. It's probably about one per cent now.'

This was language Blackmore understood. He nodded. 'So if I pay you'll keep out of the way?' he said. 'No more calls, next week, next month or next year?'

'You haven't heard from Richard Thornbury in twenty years,' Pilgrim observed. 'There's no reason why you should ever hear from him again.'

Blackmore conceded the game. 'Very well,' he said 'What do you want? A sack stuffed with money, I suppose.'

'No.' Pilgrim indicated the slip of paper containing details of the Swiss account lying on the desk. 'I want a hundred thousand pounds passed into that account in Geneva. You can switch it from one of your own accounts over there. Also, I want a banker's draft in the sum of one hundred thousand pounds made out to Richard Thornbury. I shall collect that here.'

Blackmore looked puzzled. 'I don't understand. Why do you want it in two lots?'

'That's my business,' said Pilgrim. 'That's the way I want it done.'

'And what exactly do I get for my money?'

'You get to keep those.' Pilgrim nodded at the papers.

'I intend to do that anyway. What else do I get?'

'You get silence. You get me living far away somewhere in the sun, killing myself laughing every time I read some pompous statement of yours in a paper.'

Blackmore reddened with anger and Pilgrim felt a slight lurch of fear in his belly. He realised that it was foolish to antagonise the big lawyer. 'You and your partner,' said Blackmore contemptuously, 'living off the fat of the land until the money runs out and you come slithering back for more.'

'No, just me,' Pilgrim said plainly. 'I won't be living the

high life. I drink a bit but I don't gamble. It'll be a simple
life with no money worries. I don't think you'll see me
again.'

'I have to be assured of that,' said Blackmore.

'You come up with the money and you can be pretty
sure.'

Blackmore stood up and put the papers into the envelope. He put the note of the bank details into his pocket.
'When do you want your banker's draft?'

'As soon as possible.'

Blackmore thought for a moment. 'Be here Wednesday
afternoon, at one o'clock.' He pulled open the double
doors of the study and immediately his voice changed.
'Goodbye, Richard,' he said heartily. 'It was good to see
you again after so long. See you Wednesday at about one.'

The heavy security man lumbered to his feet as Jane, the
secretary, trotted down the stairs. The man opened the
front door for Pilgrim and the secretary gave him a frosty
smile as he left. He was out. He walked unsteadily away
from the door and the parked car. Once out of sight in
Smith Square he stopped. His legs were trembling and he
could hardly walk. He breathed deeply to calm his racing
heart. It had gone well, better than he could have hoped. He
thought he had handled it superbly; Susan would have been
impressed.

After he had regained his composure, he crossed the
square into Horseferry Road and, turning away from the
river, walked past the Magistrates Courts to Victoria Street.
He badly needed a drink. He wandered into the ornate
Edwardian bar of the Prince Albert, where he spent the next
hour calming his nerves on large whiskies. Afterwards, he
ate lunch in the salad bar of the Army and Navy Stores. He
had the afternoon to kill. He sauntered along Victoria
Street looking at the shops and then cut through Buckingham Gate. He marvelled that even at that time of year
there were still tourists clinging to the railings outside the

Palace. He wandered across Green Park and turned right at the Ritz to walk along Piccadilly to the Circus. He walked northward along Regent Street, idly window shopping. By the time he reached Oxford Circus he was weary and he caught a bus back to Bloomsbury where he whiled away the remainder of the afternoon in the British Museum before making his way to the Inner Temple and Addingham's chambers.

He was surprised to find them quite busy. He cautiously mounted the wooden stairs to the first-floor landing, opened the solid wooden door to find a long book-lined corridor crowded with solicitors and their clients. Leading off both sides of the corridor were a number of doors to offices in which litigants consulted with counsel. The surroundings did not evoke happy memories; they reminded Pilgrim of the time when he had been embroiled in litigation. At the far end of the corridor was an open office in which sat the clerks. Pilgrim tentatively sidled past the huddled groups to the office.

'Yes, sir,' said a clerk.

'My name is Thornbury,' said Pilgrim. 'I am here to see Lord Addingham. I'm an old friend.'

The clerk gave Pilgrim a curious look. 'You'll know where to go then,' he said.

'Isn't he here?'

'Here? The Lord Chief Justice has his own establishment,' said the clerk, incredulity in his voice. 'These were his chambers when he was practising at the Bar. Percy,' he called across to one of the other clerks. 'Accompany this gentleman to His Lordship's chambers. He's expected.'

Pilgrim followed the aged clerk as he led him down and out into the falling light of the October afternoon. They walked a few hundred yards until they came to another, discreetly placed entrance. They climbed more stairs, at the top of which was another heavy door. The clerk knocked loudly and the door was opened by a large man who could have been the brother of the man guarding Blackmore.

'Richard Thornbury to see His Lordship,' said Percy. The security man consulted a notepad. 'All right,' he said, 'sit there.' He motioned Pilgrim into a chair. The room was traditionally furnished with leather-upholstered chairs and heavy wooden desks. Hanging on a wooden clothes stand in the corner was a scarlet robe. A couple of clerks were busily sorting papers at a desk in the far corners. After a few minutes one of them spoke to Pilgrim. 'Please follow me,' he said.

They walked down a short corridor to a door on which the clerk knocked before entering. Addingham was standing behind a desk in the centre of the room. The Lord Chief Justice was as tall as his partner in crime, the Attorney General, but whereas Blackmore was heavy and powerful, Addingham was thin. He was almost completely bald and his scalp was dotted with large brown freckles. The beak of his nose hung above a thin-lipped mouth curved like a scimitar, while his scrawny neck dropped in folds over his collar. The eyes that stared at Pilgrim were bright with contempt. 'You're not Richard Thornbury.'

Pilgrim had expected such a greeting. 'None of us look what we are,' he said pointedly.

Addingham's response was immediate. 'I disagree. You look exactly the type of guttersnipe who'd stoop to blackmail.'

Pilgrim was shocked by the remark. He felt his face redden and watched Addingham's thin mouth smirk. Already the Lord Chief Justice had gained the initiative.

'And you look exactly the type of hypocrite who'll pay it,' he responded, 'so the world won't know what a crook you really are.'

It was Addingham's turn to be surprised. 'I sincerely hope that someone, someday soon, will cause you grievous harm.' He said it with feeling.

'I wouldn't wish for that if I were you. If anything happens to me, then these,' Pilgrim dropped the envelope onto the desk, 'will be sent to every major newspaper in Europe. There are enough nails in there to crucify you ten times over.'

Addingham sat at the desk and picked up the envelope. As there was no chair on his side of the desk, Pilgrim remained standing. He watched as Addingham examined Woodberry's narrative; as he did so he began to smack his lips together. It was a predatory sound and it made Pilgrim uncomfortable. Finally, Addingham dropped the papers onto his desk. 'That bloody farmer.' His voice was like broken glass. 'I never wanted him in the first place. He was supposed to destroy all this, instead he writes a history. God rot his soul.' He looked up at Pilgrim. 'I take it you came by these after Woodberry died? What connection did you have with him?'

'None,' replied Pilgrim. 'He was a thief and an accomplice to murder. I'm neither.'

It was Addingham's turn to redden slightly. His lips smacked together noisily. 'You're a blackmailer, though. How did you come by these papers?'

Pilgrim ignored the question. 'You accept they're genuine then? Your good friend, Sir Oliver Blackmore, tried to suggest they were forgeries.'

'I understand you want two hundred thousand pounds for them.'

'I want a hundred thousand pounds transferred to that bank,' Pilgrim nodded to the account number, 'and a hundred thousand pounds in a banker's draft made out to Richard Thornbury.'

'And for that,' said Addingham, 'I understand we buy your silence. Permanently.'

Pilgrim nodded.

Addingham looked at the bank account details. 'It appears that these days anyone can have a Swiss bank account.'

'If they have enough money.'

'It's hardly your money,' said Addingham.

'Nor yours. You stole it, remember?'

The two red spots high on Addingham's cheekbones grew larger. 'It was an acceptable business transaction,' he said.

'Just illegal.'

'It was perfectly legal with the Americans.'

'Except by that time you had murdered Richard Thornbury, arranged the butchery of a bunch of soldiers, contravened exchange control regulations and defrauded both Thornbury Engineering and Nigel Eastcote. And I bet you didn't declare any of it for income tax.'

'Eastcote was a greedy fool,' Addingham observed coldly. 'Like all fools he was easily parted from his money. It wasn't even his money in the first place.'

Pilgrim smiled as he stared down at the bald, brown-speckled head. He couldn't resist the temptation to sneer at the judge. 'Well, now it's your turn to be parted from money which isn't yours.' He chuckled for a moment and then stopped abruptly. Addingham's thin frame was shaking with rage, his lips slapping together furiously. Specks of foam appeared at the edges of his mouth. 'How dare you,' he whispered. 'How dare you. I am the highest legal officer in the land. How dare you speak to me like that.'

Pilgrim's heart began to race. Although Addingham did not have the bulk or the physical presence of Blackmore, Pilgrim could feel the man's power to do him harm. He gulped slightly but said nothing.

'How dare you believe that you can blackmail me,' the voice grated in loathing. 'I have the power to send you to prison for the rest of your life.'

Although he was standing, Pilgrim felt overawed by the elderly man sitting at the desk. 'You won't do that,' he croaked. His throat had dried up. 'If you were going to do that you would have called the police. No, your friend Blackmore has told you that it's best to pay me off. What the hell, two hundred thousand is nothing to you. It's a one-off payment. Pay me and I'm gone.' Despite himself, Pilgrim could hear the whine creeping into his voice. He watched Addingham make an effort to control himself. For almost half a minute the judge sat silently glaring up at him. When finally he spoke his voice was, once again, composed.

'A one-off payment, you say. And if I pay you, when do you want your dirty money?'

'Forty-eight hours. I want the money in the bank and a banker's draft ready for me to collect by Wednesday.'

There was another long pause.

'Very well. I shall pay you, but only once. There will be no further payment. Come to these offices at eight o'clock Wednesday evening. The banker's draft will be ready.' He paused and looked at Pilgrim with a puzzled expression. 'How are you going to explain your ill-gotten wealth to your friends and relatives or do you intend just to walk out on everyone?'

'There's no one to walk out on. I won't have anyone asking me awkward questions, if that's what you mean. I'm just going to disappear quietly with my million and live a nice simple life.'

Addingham stood up. He pressed a bell push set into the wall. 'So long as you live the rest of your despicable life well away from me,' he said, sneering down at Pilgrim. 'After Wednesday I never wish to see you again.'

'Don't worry,' said Pilgrim with some relief, 'you won't.'

There was a tap at the door and one of the clerks entered. 'See Mr Thornbury out,' Addingham commanded.

The clerk escorted Pilgrim past the security guard and down the wooden staircase. Outside it was dark, the cold grey mist rising from the river was lazily curling itself about the deserted courtyards. Pilgrim pulled his jacket closer to his body and wished that he owned an overcoat. He made for Fleet Street and the warmth of a taxi. He felt shaky, not only from the cold but from his confrontation with Addingham. It had been a frightening ordeal with the Lord Chief Justice. Pilgrim felt as if he had been trapped in the same room as a cobra.

Yet he had come through and the mere fact of his survival sustained him. He had seen the two chief figures in the conspiracy and had persuaded them that his was a serious threat which could only be averted upon payment of a lot of money. He was sure that they would pay him. Yet what he had forgotten as he stood trembling at the kerbside searching for the orange light of an empty cab, was that a cautious man, when answering lawyers' questions, says as little as possible.

Chapter Four

That night he slept soundly; after a good meal he had returned to his hotel with a bottle of whisky, which ensured him eight hours' solid sleep.

Tuesday dawned bright, though more chilly than the previous two days. It occurred to Pilgrim as he drank his coffee in the St Pancras buffet that since he had come to London, even the weather had been on his side. He telephoned Susan from the buffet; it was impossible for her to talk so he told her rapidly that he'd seen Addingham and Blackmore and rang off. The third envelope containing the documents was in his inside pocket and by ten fifteen he was driving his car out of the car park behind the station. He headed north, through Camden, up Haverstock Hill, past Hampstead Pond and Jack Straw's Castle into Spaniards Road.

Brighton had a house in the Bishop's Avenue backing onto Highgate golf course. Like the rest of the properties in the avenue, it was large and opulent. Pilgrim decided to park his decrepit car a few hundred yards away from the house. He was faintly puzzled to see, as he walked up the broad drive, that all the curtains were closed. He rang the bell. He felt slightly nervous, though he was much less scared than he had been the previous day. He waited impatiently in the chilly sunshine for someone to come and was about to press the bell for the second time when one of the double wooden doors was opened by a middle-aged woman. She was wearing a dark dress and her fair hair was tied back in a bun. The most noticeable aspect of her appearance was her face, which was drawn and blotched. It was obvious that she had been crying.

'Good morning,' Pilgrim announced. 'My name is Richard Thornbury. I've come to interview Sir Ashley.'

The woman's lifeless eyes stared at him. Her mouth opened and closed a few times before she managed to speak. 'I'm sorry.' Her voice was low and hoarse. 'My father died yesterday.'

Pilgrim blinked. He heard the stark words but they meant nothing to him. It was as if the woman had told him that Brighton had gone off to play golf. 'But I had a meeting with him. This morning, at eleven.'

He and the woman stared at each other across the threshold in mutual incomprehension. When at last she spoke her voice was glazed like her eyes. 'Yes. I'm sorry. He's dead.'

The message finally sunk into Pilgrim's surprised mind. 'I'm sorry,' he said. 'Please accept my . . .' he searched for the word.

'Yes. Yes,' said the woman curtly. It was clear she was emerging from her trance and was impatient to get back to her sombre duties in the house.

Pilgrim persisted. He could not come to terms with the fact that two hundred thousand pounds had just passed away from him. 'He seemed fine when I telephoned him on Sunday. What happened?'

'My mother returned to the house yesterday evening,' said the woman, 'and found my father dead. He'd had a heart attack. Now if you will excuse me.'

The big wooden door swung smoothly and purposely shut. Pilgrim walked slowly down the drive and along the avenue to his car. He felt cheated, as if Brighton had died owing him a debt. He got into the car. He drove slowly through Highgate village and turned towards Hampstead. He had agreed to telephone Susan that morning to give her a progress report. He parked the car outside a coffee shop in Hampstead and telephoned from a nearby call box. Susan's daily cleaner answered the phone.

'Can I speak to Mrs Bronwyn-Taylor?'

Susan came on the line. 'Hello, Jerry.' Her voice was bright. 'How's it going?'

'Brighton's dead,' he blurted out.

'Dead? What do you mean dead?'

'I mean dead. Pushing up daisies dead. Rigor mortis dead. That kind of dead.'

'All right. All right,' said Susan. 'What happened?'

'Heart attack. Yesterday, for Christ's sake. He could have waited another couple of days, couldn't he?'

'Look,' said Susan in an effort to calm him. 'You'd better come round. I'll meet you in the wine bar.'

It was early and the bar in Ebury Street was almost deserted. They sat at a round wooden table in a far corner. Pilgrim told her briefly what had happened since his arrival in the city on Sunday.

'So everything has gone well,' said Susan. 'Better even than we'd hoped.'

'Except Brighton is dead,' said Pilgrim mournfully. 'He shuffled off owing me –' He stopped. He'd been on the verge of revealing the true amount he had intended raising from the dead accountant. 'Owing me one hundred thousand pounds,' he finished.

Susan shrugged. 'It can't be helped. You'll have to settle for four hundred thousand instead.'

'It would be all right if we could find this fellow Portalier,' said Pilgrim morosely.

'I've been trying,' said Susan. 'He's not to be found. He could be anywhere. Forget it, Jerry. Four hundred thousand is still a lot of cash. So today is the big day,' she said, changing the subject.

'What do you mean?'

'Addingham and Blackmore will be transferring the money to Switzerland. I'll phone the bank tomorrow morning and check that the money has gone in. What are you going to do?'

'Not very much,' he lied. 'I could try to see Dundonald and Frimley-Kimpton.'

Susan shook her head. 'No, that's not the plan. You can only get to them at the weekends. You couldn't get through all the people that surround them in their offices.'

'They might be dead by the weekend.'

'Stick to the plan, Jerry. Why don't you go back to Gretton? You've got plenty to do there.'

'Christ, what a slave driver you are,' Pilgrim responded. 'I'll go back tomorrow.'

'I'll call you on Thursday about lunch time,' said Susan. 'I've got people coming this afternoon. They'll be staying until tomorrow.' She kissed him lightly and left him to while away the afternoon and evening at the cinema.

The hours on Wednesday morning before he was due to see Blackmore he spent wandering around the men's shops in Jermyn Street. He had decided not to check out of his hotel yet; he intended to treat himself to one more night in London on Susan's money and to drive north the following morning, with two hundred thousand pounds in his pocket.

The weather remained bright, and just after twelve Pilgrim retraced his steps across the parks and through Queen Anne's Gate towards Lord North Street. As he walked, he again felt the nervous excitement bubbling inside him. When he was close to the house he screwed up his courage to undergo the scrutiny of the men guarding Blackmore. It was therefore a surprise when, on rounding the corner of Lord North Street, he discovered that they weren't there. He walked slowly, noting that what few cars were parked along the street were all empty. Immediately outside Blackmore's front door was a dark blue Rolls-Royce. It was being slowly and absentmindedly polished by a uniformed chauffeur. Pilgrim nodded to him as he rang the doorbell of Blackmore's house; the door was opened by the tall red-headed secretary.

'Morning,' said Pilgrim breezily. 'Richard Thornbury. I have an appointment to see Sir Oliver at one o'clock.'

The girl stared at him blankly.

'Perhaps you don't remember me,' Pilgrim continued. 'I came here a couple of days ago.'

'Yes,' the girl replied. 'I remember you. I am afraid you can't see him.'

Pilgrim was slightly affronted. 'But I have an appointment. He wanted to see me.' As he said the words, Pilgrim had a sudden impression of *déjà vu*. He had said almost the same thing on Brighton's doorstep the previous morning.

'I'm afraid you can't see him,' the girl said again. Pilgrim noticed that her face showed signs of strain. 'Sir Oliver has had an accident.'

Something cold crawled up Pilgrim's spine. 'What kind of accident?' He was almost afraid to ask.

The girl looked at him, scarcely hearing the question. 'You were a friend of his, weren't you?'

Pilgrim nodded dumbly. The girl had used the past tense. 'I was a close friend some years ago,' he mumbled. 'What's happened to him?'

'We've been told not to say anything,' she said and hesitated. 'But the fact is,' she continued hurriedly, 'Sir Oliver is dead.'

'Dead!' It was the second time in two days that the word had dropped onto Pilgrim like a mortuary slab. 'How?'

The girl looked puzzled. 'We really don't know. He had an accident yesterday afternoon and that's all I know. Actually, I've been told not to tell anyone so please keep it to yourself. On no account must the press know.'

'But how did it happen?' Pilgrim persisted.

'I am sorry. I just don't know. No one knows.' She closed the door.

Pilgrim turned away and just ten feet across the narrow pavement the chauffeur, still mournfully polishing the car, gave Pilgrim a look of puzzled sympathy. Pilgrim walked slowly away from the house.

He wandered into Smith Square. The white Portland stone architraves of St John's shone dully in the weak rays of the autumn sun. From inside the ugly Queen Anne edifice came the music of a morning concert. He walked across the square, crossed the Embarkment, busy with the lunchtime traffic, and wandered into Westminster Tower Gardens. The chilly sunshine had brought some office workers out into the gardens; a few joggers were loping across the lawns and a number of people were wandering idly between the freshly dug flower beds. There was even, Pilgrim noticed, a pair of brave and desperate lovers lying huddled together on a raincoat spread on the damp grass. He crossed the gardens to stand leaning against the solid stone parapet above the bank of the Thames. He watched the grey waters as they flowed gently downstream, past the Palace of Westminster to the bend in the river at Waterloo. Across the river, the tower of St Thomas's Hospital glinted in the sun. He remained there for more than twenty minutes trying to make sense of what had happened in the past two days.

Something was wrong. It was an unbelievable coincidence that two men who had been partners in a crime more than twenty years old should die within hours of each other. Ashley Brighton may have died naturally, but the reason for Blackmore's sudden fatality was a mystery. It wasn't easy to accept that Blackmore was dead. He had overawed Pilgrim; his vigour, his bulk, the power in his voice and body had made him seem indestructible, like a fortress. Yet now he was laid waste. How?

The prickling sensation that Pilgrim felt at the back of his neck had nothing to do with the cold air rising from the river. He thought about the fortune that he had lost, the money he had expected to extract from the two dead men. Yesterday, he had been resentful about Brighton's sudden departure; today, although his losses were doubled, the money for the moment concerned him less. He wanted to find out what was going on.

He realised he was cold. He turned from the river and retraced his steps back into St John's Square. Close to one of its corners was a pub, the Marquis of Granby, and Pilgrim decided that he needed a drink. The place was crowded. He squeezed his way to the bar and ordered a large whisky and a heaped plate of shepherd's pie. By the time he had finished, most of the crowd had gone and the pub was quieter. He went to the bar to order another drink and noticed, seated in a gloomy corner, the chauffeur who had been polishing the Rolls. He wandered across. 'What are you having?'

The man looked up from his newspaper. He had a thin, sharp face, like a rat's. His shifty eyes noticed the tumbler in Pilgrim's hand. 'I'll have a whisky,' he said. He had a Scots accent. Pilgrim nodded and turned to the bar as the man added, 'A large one.'

Pilgrim placed the whisky on the small round table next to the chauffeur's empty half-pint glass and sat down. 'So,' he enquired conversationally, 'what's going to happen to you?'

The man took a hefty gulp of whisky. 'What do you mean?'

'Now your boss is dead. You work for Sir Oliver Blackmore, don't you?'

'Did,' said the man morosely.

'So, where does that leave you?'

The man shrugged. 'What are you, the papers? I'm not supposed to talk to the press.'

'No, I'm not the press,' said Pilgrim. 'I'm an old friend. I knew him before he was Sir Oliver.'

The man continued to eye Pilgrim suspiciously.

'I had some business dealings with him and a few other people. My name is Richard Thornbury.'

The man nodded slightly.

'Another one?' asked Pilgrim indicating the empty glass.

'Aye, the same.'

He bought the chauffeur another double and added a liberal helping of water to his own small measure.

'So, what was he like?' Pilgrim asked when he sat down again.

The man flung the contents of his glass down his throat. 'He was a bastard. He may have been a friend of yours, but he was no friend of mine. He treated me like dirt, I was just the part of the car that made it go. He treated all the others the same.'

'The others?'

'Aye, he only used the Roller for private business, he had a government car for official trips and he had government drivers. He treated us all like dirt. All security-trained, they were, how to escape a terrorist attack and all that.' The man laughed. 'If terrorists had attacked him when I was driving, I'd have buggered off and left them to it.'

'Do you think that's what happened?' Pilgrim asked. 'He's been kidnapped or something?'

'No.' The man shook his head. 'It was me who was driving him yesterday afternoon. Off on one of his little jaunts, he was.'

There was something in the way the man said the last few words that caught Pilgrim's ear. The chauffeur raised his empty glass to his lips.

'Let me get you another,' said Pilgrim hurriedly. When he returned, the chauffeur's spite had settled on a different target.

'He was bad enough,' he whined, 'but her, her ladyship, she's a real cow. Treats me like shit she does. Has me trotting after her in Harrods like a dog, carrying all her fucking parcels.'

Pilgrim listened quietly, waiting for the chance to get back to his questions. The whisky was taking effect, fuelling the man's resentment, and Pilgrim's opportunity came when the chauffeur took another gulp from his glass. 'So Oliver was still going on little jaunts?' he asked nonchalantly. 'He used to do that quite a lot when I knew him.'

'Aye,' said the Scotsman. 'It was a regular thing. The Right Honourable Member was a kinky bastard. I bet his voters didn't know.'

'Really?' Pilgrim tried to keep the keen interest out of his voice. 'I didn't know that. He didn't seem kinky to me.'

'They never do,' said the man, 'not people like him who look so respectable. But he wasn't, not by a long chalk. I know.' He tapped his temple with his forefinger. 'When you've got money, you can have whatever you want, as often as you want it. The bastard used to have a regular session every Tuesday afternoon except for yesterday.'

'That would be the woman in Shepherd's Market,' said Pilgrim, guessing in order that he might learn the truth.

'No, no, she wasn't in Shepherd's Market. She lived in Davies Street, fabulous place, near Claridges.'

'You've seen it?'

'Aye, I have.' The chauffeur emptied his glass. Pilgrim crossed to the bar as quickly and bought two large whiskies. It was almost closing time.

'So,' said Pilgrim sitting down. 'What was Oliver's little lady like?'

'His whore, you mean? Christ, he must have paid her a fortune. Her place was stinking with money. They all live in the lap of fucking luxury those people, and the hell with the rest of us.'

'So when did you see the inside of her place?'

The man was diverted from his self-pity. 'A couple of years ago. I had a phone call in the car. Blackmore was wanted urgently, at the House. I was parked in Berkeley Square waiting for him.'

'So how did you know where to go?'

'He always told me where he was,' said the man, 'he had to, just in case he was ever needed in an emergency. But he told me to keep my mouth shut too. Anyway, this was an emergency. I went up to the apartment, it was on the fourth floor, and rung one of those things where you have to announce yourself. After a while some woman's voice came on and asked who I was and I said Blackmore was wanted urgently. After a few minutes the door opened, just slightly, and there was this bird with fabulous tits, like a nurse only with a short skirt and black stockings. You know what I mean.'

The woman had obviously made a deep impression on the chauffeur. 'Christ, she was a looker,' he continued. 'I damn near came in my pants looking at her. I told her that Blackmore was wanted. She just stared at me without saying a word. Her face was covered in sweat and I could hear this noise in the background.' He stopped.

'Well?' said Pilgrim.

'It was him, Blackmore, kind of panting and crying at the same time. I think she had been whipping him.'

'Charming,' said Pilgrim.

'Like I say, he was kinky. He used to come out of that place looking like he'd been on a ten-mile run. Christ, I bet that whore sucked him dry.' His voice was hoarse.

'But you said that yesterday he didn't go for his weekly thrashing,' said Pilgrim. 'So where did he go?'

There was by now just one Scotch left on the table. The chauffeur's bleary eyes turned to Pilgrim. 'You sure you're not the press?' His pinched face was tinged with suspicion.

Pilgrim grinned broadly. 'No. I'm not the press,' he said. 'If I were, I would be writing all this down, wouldn't I? I'm just interested. After all, you've got to admit it's strange. Every Tuesday Oliver goes to get beaten black and blue. Yesterday, he decides to give it a miss. Now why should he do that?'

'God knows,' said the chauffeur. 'But he was up to something. That's for sure. I dropped him off at Swiss Cottage Tube station. I've never dropped him at a Tube station before. I asked how I was supposed to get in touch if there was an emergency and he said he'd phone me later. He told me to cruise round Regents Park until I heard from him.'

Pilgrim look at him enquiringly and the man stared back. 'I never heard.'

'And the next thing you know, he's dead.'

'That's right,' said the man. 'Nobody tells me how or why. Just that he's dead and don't talk to the press. Are you sure you're not the press?' he asked again, glaring at Pilgrim.

'No, no,' said Pilgrim dismissively. 'Swiss Cottage Tube. It doesn't sound like Sir Oliver Blackmore, does it? Yet it's anonymous.' He was thinking aloud. 'It's not likely anyone would recognise him and he could go anywhere from there.' Pilgrim felt worried. Perhaps Blackmore's disappearance was connected to his visit and his attempts at extortion. 'Are you sure he's dead?'

The chauffeur shrugged. 'I haven't seen the body but there are plenty of long faces and people whispering in corners. Something's up.'

The whisky was finished. Time had been called and the glasses were being cleared rapidly. Pilgrim had one last fact to learn. 'Listen,' he said, 'this lady of Oliver's in Davies Street, what's the address?'

The chauffeur looked at him shiftily. 'Why? What do you want to know for?'

Pilgrim smiled. 'Maybe I'd like to sample some of what she's got.'

The chauffeur snorted. 'She's more than you could bloody afford.'

'Don't be so sure,' said Pilgrim. He pulled the wallet stuffed with Susan's money from his pocket. The chauffeur'e eyes bulged. Pilgrim pulled out a ten-pound note. 'If I want it, I can afford it,' he said. He laid the note on the table with his hand half covering it. The man looked at it greedily.

'If you can afford a tart like her,' he said viciously 'you can afford to pay more than that.'

Pilgrim shook his head slowly. 'That's a good price.'

'What's to stop me taking that money and giving you the wrong address?'

'What's to stop me telling Joanna Blackmore everything you've told me about her,' replied Pilgrim with a wry smile. The man's face changed. 'I'm an old friend of the family, don't forget. If I found myself knocking on the wrong door, you would find yourself unemployed.'

'Shit,' said the chauffeur viciously. 'You're all the same, you bastards. You think money'll buy anything.'

'It does. Do you want this money or not?'

'She calls herself Beverley, some double-barrelled name.' He repeated the address and Pilgrim wrote it down.

'Describe the place to me,' said Pilgrim, keeping his hand on the money.

The man told him in which building in the street the flat was situated and on what floor. He described what he had seen of the interior, which sounded authentic. Pilgrim took his hand off the note and it disappeared in a flash into the man's pocket. They were the last people in the pub. A man behind the bar was glaring at them.

'You'd better drink up,' said Pilgrim. 'I think they want us to leave.' The chauffeur drained the last few drops of whisky and stood up unsteadily. 'It's been nice talking you,' said Pilgrim, moving away.

'Aye,' said the chauffeur tipping unsteadily forward against the table. 'I hope you get what you want from that whore.'

'So do I.'

The man staggered again as he walked towards the door.

'If I were you,' said Pilgrim sweetly, 'I wouldn't try driving the Rolls this afternoon.'

'Ooh that's no problem,' said the man as he crashed into the wall.

Pilgrim hailed a cab on the corner of Horseferry Road and told the driver to drop him in Berkeley Square. It felt like the old days; he was in hot pursuit of a story, on the inside track, knowing facts which no one else knew, facts which his particular brand of shallow charm had easily extracted from a resentful drunk.

The hall of the building in Davies Street was quietly luxurious with deep-pile carpets and elegant vases. Pilgrim had visited similar places before and he knew that, apart from their living accommodation, they were frequently used as office suites by large American law practices, international oil brokers and prestigious management consultants. They were the last word in chic. Any woman who practised as a professional harlot from such premises, thought Pilgrim, had to be at the very top of her profession.

A uniformed attendant accompanied him in the small mirror-lined lift to the fourth floor. Pilgrim waited for him to descend before he made a move. Down the stairwell he heard the lift arrive at the ground floor. He padded across the thick carpet to the door of a flat. The name above the bell was Beverley Brandon-Burke. He pressed the buzzer. A metallic voice came through the loudspeaker. 'Yes, who is it?'

'My name is Richard Thornbury,' said Pilgrim. There was a pause.

'Do you have an appointment?'

'No,' said Pilgrim flatly. 'I've come about Oliver Blackmore.'

There was an even longer pause. 'I have spoken to somebody about Sir Oliver already.'

'I know,' said Pilgrim, keeping the surprise out of his voice. 'I have a few questions.'

There was a sigh of exasperation and the buzzer was silent. Pilgrim stood facing the middle of the door so he could easily be seen through the spy hole. After a few seconds the polished wooden door swung noiselessly open. Standing in the hallway was a tall, blonde and exceptionally beautiful woman in her late twenties. She was wearing a pair of very tight trousers made of soft leather and a white open-necked blouse. Her hair was pulled back tightly from her face and tied in a bun at the back of her head. The severity of the hairstyle only served to heighten her arrogant beauty. 'Well?' she asked.

'Can I come inside?' said Pilgrim. 'I don't want to talk about Sir Oliver out here.' His voice was deliberately loud. The woman grimaced but stepped to one side and motioned him in. She closed the door and led the way into a large sitting room. She turned to him, her back to the windows.

'What time was Sir Oliver due to see you yesterday?' asked Pilgrim.

'Two o'clock,' she replied.

'Why didn't he keep his appointment?'

'I don't know,' she said impatiently. 'He phoned and said he wasn't coming.'

'Had he ever cancelled an appointment before?'

'No.' She was staring at him, a frown of doubt on her face. The look made Pilgrim feel uncomfortable, as if his flies were open. 'Who did you say you were?' she asked.

'Same mob as before,' Pilgrim replied nonchalantly. 'My guv'nor wants me to check your story.'

'You're not security,' she stated, 'you're not the type. For one thing, you're not big enough. Let me see your warrant card.'

'No. I'm not security,' Pilgrim replied. 'Actually I'm doing a story on Sir Oliver for a couple of . . .'

'Oh my God, the press. I'm not talking to you. The security men were insistent that I shouldn't talk to the press. Anyway, they said the press didn't know about him being dead. You'll have to leave.' She brushed past him, making for the living room door. She looked over her shoulder. 'Come on,' she ordered, 'get out.'

Pilgrim remained where he was. He had caught sight of some magazines on a coffee table and even from where he was standing he could see what they were. He moved towards them. Beverley Brandon-Burke flounced back into the room. She stopped when she saw that Pilgrim was flicking through a journal which depicted, in graphic detail, scenes of sexual bondage. 'Look,' she said, her voice rising, 'put that down and get out. If you don't go, I'll call the police. Now. Out.' Something in her voice made Pilgrim look up. The elegantly modified tones were less perfectly pitched; the elongated vowels were flattened just slightly in a way which he instantly recognised.

'OK,' he said, casually dropping the magazine onto the table. 'We'll run the story and say that Miss Beverley Brandon-Burke who keeps dirty books in her flat and who used to regularly entertain Sir Oliver Blackmore refused to comment.'

'You can't do that. Jesus Christ, you wouldn't.'

'We can and I expect we will,' said Pilgrim. 'By the way, where are you from?'

'If you print my name in the papers, I'll be finished,' she said. She moved towards him in the manner of a supplicant. 'For Christ's sake, I had nothing to do with him dying. Why do you want to involve me?' With every sentence the accent was moving further away from the received Roedean she had affected when he first walked in.

'Newcastle?' said Pilgrim. 'Somewhere up there, in the north-east.'

She had come close to him, staring intently into his face, her eyes pleading. 'Sunderland,' she said flatly.

'Brandon-Burke? That's not your real name, not from Sunderland?'

'It's Hardcastle,' she replied. 'Ann Hardcastle. Now you know. I'm just a working girl from way out in the sticks. Trying to make a living.'

'It's a pretty good living,' observed Pilgrim looking at the expensive furnishings in the room.

'It's fucking hard work,' she replied. 'And it isn't going

to last for ever. I've got a few more years. After that I'll start losing business. They'll want someone younger. I've got to make the money now and if you put my name in the papers that will be it. Finished. A lot of the people who come here are well known. If there's any publicity they'll just disappear.' The look of pleading stayed in her deep blue eyes.

Pilgrim nodded. Now that he knew something of the real person behind the polished façade he quite liked her. 'Look,' he said, 'all I really want to know about is Blackmore. There's no need to bring you into it if you can tell me about him.'

Beverley breathed a deep sigh of relief. She moved to a small table and picked up a silver cigarette box which she opened and proffered to Pilgrim. He was tempted but shook his head. 'Blackmore, what was he like?' he asked as she lit a cigarette.

She inhaled and then blew a long stream of smoke towards the ceiling. 'A bastard,' she replied. 'An absolute bastard. Some of them who come here are just lonely or need a bit of affection. Not him. He was completely cold. Not an ounce of feeling in him.'

'He liked to be whipped, didn't he?'

She looked at him in surprise. 'How do you know that?'

Pilgrim smiled enigmatically but said nothing.

'He liked pain,' she continued, 'giving it and getting it. Ropes, rubber, torture, all of that stuff. He was an animal.'

'And you gave him what he wanted? You did what he asked?'

'Of course,' she replied. 'He was a big payer. He got all he wanted and more. He loved it. Sometimes he could barely walk when he left here.'

'If he loved it so much why did he cancel yesterday?' asked Pilgrim.

'God knows,' she answered. 'He was as regular as clockwork. Every Tuesday afternoon. It must have been important, whatever it was.'

'Didn't he say when he telephoned?'

'No. He called about midday and said he wasn't coming this week. He'd never done that before, he was always so well-organised.'

'What else did he say?'

'I can't remember. Not very much, I don't think.' She paused. 'Maybe he'd found someone else to give him what he wanted.' She laughed; a quicksilver sound.

'So what about the people who came to see you this morning. Who were they?'

'Security. That's all they said. One of them flashed a card under my nose but I didn't get a chance to read it.'

'But what do you mean, security? Were they Special Branch or what?'

'God knows.' She shrugged. 'They weren't ordinary policemen, that's for sure.'

'How do you know?'

'Girls in my line of work get the business from policemen. They look at you with a kind of lecherous sneer; they feel superior but they fancy a free screw. These blokes weren't like that. Christ, they were hard, they looked at me like I was a corpse.'

A thought suddenly occurred to Pilgrim. 'How did they know about you and Blackmore?'

'I don't know,' she replied. 'How did you know? And they knew what he was into as well, the whips and everything. Like you. I don't understand it. Suddenly, everyone knows my business.'

Pilgrim could see she was getting agitated. 'Did they say how he died?'

'I can't remember. I was too scared. I think one of them said he'd had an accident but I'm not sure.'

'An accident,' Pilgrim repeated. 'Did they say whether they had actually seen him. Dead, I mean. His body?'

'No.' Beverley looked puzzled. 'Why, don't you think he's dead?'

Pilgrim shrugged. 'I don't know. I suppose he is. It's just

unusual, the way it's being handled. Why do they want to keep it from the press? If he'd fallen under a bus or something they wouldn't bother to hide it. Why all the secrecy?'

'They said the press wouldn't know about it, not for a couple of days, not until they had finished their investigations. Anyway,' her voice became tinged with sarcasm, 'they said the press wouldn't find out about me.'

'They probably won't,' said Pilgrim.

'You did. You seem to know a hell of a lot about Blackmore and me.'

'I'm different,' he replied. 'Can you remember anything else they said?'

She shook her head. 'No, I don't think so.'

Pilgrim felt frustrated. It seemed he had wasted his time. Ann Hardcastle, the girl from Sunderland, who had made good by being bad had been unable to tell him anything, except to confirm that Blackmore was probably dead. 'Look,' he said, 'if you do remember anything, anything at all, I want you to telephone me.' He took out a pencil and a piece of paper and told her where he was staying in London as he wrote down his assumed name, and the name and number of his hotel.

Beverley looked at it dubiously. 'I don't know,' she said. 'I'm not supposed to be talking to you. And I told you, I don't want my name in the papers.'

'It's all right,' Pilgrim placated her. 'No one knows you've talked to me. You won't get your name in the papers. I promise.' He smiled at her and moved to where a telephone sat on a small table. He wrote down her number.

'Hey,' she said sharply. 'What do you think you're doing?'

'Taking your number. If I'm not there when you call, leave a message and I'll call you back.'

'I don't want you wandering around with my unlisted number.' Her voice had slipped back into its polished accents. 'It's private. Only my special friends know it.'

'Don't worry.' Pilgrim's tone was calm. 'I'm not going to advertise it. Anyway, I'd like to stay in touch with you.'

She looked at him suspiciously. 'Why?'

'Because,' replied Pilgrim, walking slowly towards the door, 'when you decide to get out of this business, I could help you make a lot of money selling your story to a couple of magazines I know on the Continent. I've got some very good contacts.'

The beautiful face looked at him shrewdly. 'Oh, yes? How much money?'

'Depends on how many well-known clients you've had and what they liked to do. But with me writing it you could make fifty thousand pounds.'

She looked interested. 'Really?' She opened the apartment door.

'Sure,' he replied. 'Anyway, if you remember anything else about Blackmore, call me.'

'Don't hold your breath waiting,' she replied. 'I'm going on holiday to the Seychelles. For a month. My friend and I are leaving the day after tomorrow.'

'Nice,' responded Pilgrim with a grin. 'Who's the friend? Anyone I know?'

'I doubt it,' she replied haughtily. 'He's a Syrian gynaecologist. Makes lots of money giving rich ladies abortions.'

She closed the door leaving Pilgrim to stare blankly at its richly glossed varnish. 'That's like taking your own mechanic on a motoring holiday,' he said peevishly to his reflection in the lift mirror.

Outside, the sky had become grey and overcast and a fine drizzle was falling. The weather fitted his mood. He was dejected. He had come to London in bright sunshine in a mood of excited anticipation, certain he would make a fortune. He had been there more than three days and he hadn't made a penny, while two-fifths of his prospective fortune had disappeared for ever. His only immediate hope was the

369

meeting he had arranged with Addingham for that evening. And the prospect of another confrontation with the Lord Chief Justice depressed him even further.

The man in the brick-lined cellar in the anonymous building near Vauxhall station took off his earphones and picked up the phone next to the tape recorder. A hard, flat voice answered. 'Yes?'

'That target you've been trying to track,' said the man in the cellar, 'the one who's been visiting some of your special people.'

'Yes?'

'He's just left a trail. He called on the woman at her flat and left a phone number.'

'Did you get everything on tape?' asked the voice.

'Yes.'

'Right, we'll get on to it.' The phone went dead.

Chapter Five

Pilgrim arrived at the Inner Temple a few minutes before eight o'clock. He was wearing an old anorak which he had zipped up tight against the chill of the night. Despite a few whiskies and a large plate of Madras curry, his mood of depression remained; it enveloped him like the fine drizzle which had continued to fall throughout the miserable afternoon. He was anticipating some difficulty in dominating the interview with Addingham. He didn't feel in control; he knew he didn't look in control, he was damp and bedraggled.

The euphoria with which he had come to London had evaporated. As with everything in his life, he had expected it to be easy; to extort one million pounds and disappear, grab the money and run. Predictably, it was proving more difficult, and as always when things began to go wrong, all Pilgrim now wanted to do was run. Only the thought of the money kept him walking towards Addingham's chambers. All he wanted was just one successful coup, for just one of the conspirators to come across with the money. He no longer had thoughts of sweeping the board and taking it all. He would settle happily for a hundred thousand as long as he could get it quickly and get out.

He rounded the corner of the Inn and walked to the entrance of Addingham's chambers. The heavy door which led directly from the pavement up the stairs to Addingham's rooms was closed. He pushed it. It was locked. He tried again but it was unyielding. He looked around for a bell but saw none. He rapped loudly on the door. He waited for a while but could hear no movement. His heart sank even further. He stepped back to see if there was any sign of life behind the dark, leaded panes of the first-floor windows. Nothing. Then, as he stood perfectly still in the dark and silent drizzle, his hands deep in his pockets, staring at the blank unyielding door, he became aware of the presence of someone close by. He turned. Standing just a few feet away was a tall, powerfully built man, wearing a dark overcoat. Next to him was a shorter though equally bulky man who, like Pilgrim, was dressed in an anorak. Pilgrim's heart gave a surge of fear. Whoever they were, they meant him no good.

'Are you Richard Thornbury?' asked the big man.

Pilgrim didn't answer. In the dim street light of the Inner Temple he was trying to make out their faces, trying to see somehow if they had the look of policemen, though something in his frightened mind told him they were not. The shorter of the two men moved towards him menacingly. 'Well,' he asked, 'are you Thornbury?'

'We've got a message for you,' said his partner.

'What is it?' asked Pilgrim, backing away slightly.

'You're Thornbury, yes?' asked the man closest to him.

Pilgrim nodded faintly. 'Yes,' he said hesitantly, 'but who are you?' He saw the man shoot his partner a swift glance. 'What's the message?'

The shorter man stepped another pace closer and in the half-light Pilgrim saw him smile, though perhaps it was a snarl. He never knew. At that instant something exploded against his stomach. The force crashed him back, arms flailing, against the heavy door. With the piece of his mind that still worked, he realised the man had hit him. The blow had landed on his solar plexus. It had driven all the wind out of his body. He tried to cry, to shout, to plead with the man to stop but all he could manage was a rasping croak. He saw the blur of the man's fist come whirring out of the darkness towards his face. The blow caught him high on the left side of his head. He began to slide down the door and would have collapsed in a heap had not the big man grabbed him and jerked him violently to his feet. He couldn't breathe, he couldn't think, he couldn't see; all he could feel was the pain in his head and body and the agony of fighting for his breath. Rough hands grabbed his arms, lifted him almost off his feet and propelled him forward. He would not have been able to resist them even at his best; as it was, they took him as easily as children would carry a broken doll.

Their car was parked on the Embankment. They bundled him into the back seat and the big man shoved himself in beside him. They drove off heading east.

Pilgrim was terrified. He ached everywhere, the pain in his stomach had spread to every muscle and joint in his body, and his head throbbed like a piston. He sat huddled with his knees close together, scared lest at any moment he should fill his trousers. The big man grabbed his arm and viciously twisted it. Pilgrim yelped with pain.

'Right, you little bastard. You got some papers that belong to someone else. We want them.'

'I haven't got any papers,' Pilgrim gasped. The man's grip was forcing him forward, face down to the floor.

'Don't give us that,' said the man in the front.

'We want them tonight,' said the man next to him, twisting his arm harder. 'Not copies, the real thing. And we want to know who you're working with.'

'I haven't got any papers.' Pilgrim's eyes filled with tears from the pain. Suddenly he realised that nestling in an inside pocket of his jacket was the envelope containing the papers that he had meant to leave with Ashley Brighton.

'Don't worry, you're going to tell us,' said the man. 'We're going to take you somewhere nice and quiet and then my friend here is going to start cutting little bits off you until you tell us.' The man driving the car let out a low, evil chuckle.

'We want those papers and we want your friend.' The big man twisted Pilgrim's arm again.

Pilgrim could hear himself sobbing with the agony.

'Leave it out,' the driver ordered sharply. 'Someone will see.' The man let go of Pilgrim's arm and yanked him back to an upright position in his seat. They were waiting at a set of traffic lights somewhere in the City: drawn up on their offside was a dark Ford. There were three men in it; the two in front seemed to be in conversation but the man in the back was looking vaguely in their direction. Pilgrim could barely focus through the tears in his eyes and the pounding in his head but for a moment he thought about crying for help. He heard a metallic click next to him and felt something sharp press into his back.

'Don't even think about it,' his captor growled. 'Just one squeak out of you and I'll slice your kidneys in half.' The car moved off from the lights.

'Leave him alone till we get there,' said the driver. 'We don't want attention.'

The rest of the journey was made in silence. The man let go of Pilgrim's arm and left him alone with his pain and terror. He imagined the knife cutting into his flesh, sawing off each of his fingers, one by one, then his toes or ears or, most shocking of all, his penis. He knew that as soon as they laid hands on him he would tell them everything; he would beg them to believe him about Susan, about the papers, everything.

They drove out of the City, the Tower and Tower Bridge on their right. They stayed north of the river and drove into Wapping, along dark, deserted streets. There were only a few cars about and no pedestrians. Finally, they turned down a street with wasteland on either side and at its end derelict warehouses.

'This is it,' said the man next to Pilgrim. The car slowed to a halt in the deep shadow of the warehouses. Pilgrim lost his battle to control the fear in his body. Somehow he managed to keep his sphincter muscles shut but the quaking terror in his stomach could not be denied. His stomach erupted and with projectile force Pilgrim vomited its contents all over the man seated next to him.

'Jesus Christ!' The man jerked away from Pilgrim as the gooey mess slid down the front of his overcoat and oozed into his lap and down his trouser legs. 'You dirty bastard,' he snarled, torn between smashing Pilgrim's face to pulp and his revulsion at the warm sick seeping through his clothes. The car was filled with the smell of vomit. 'I'm going to kill that bastard.' He opened the car door violently and edged his way out. He stood next to the car, his face screwed in revulsion and his legs bowed, watching the contents of Pilgrim's stomach dribble slowly down to his shoes.

The man in the driving seat jumped out of the car, opened the rear door and grasped the white and shaking Pilgrim by the front of his anorak. He pulled him from the car and threw his limp body almost a dozen feet. Pilgrim crashed against a chain-link fence like a ball against a net and slumped at its base, staring dazedly at the men who were about to destroy him. He knew he was finished, and somehow he didn't care. His stomach was empty and his head was light; nothing mattered any more.

It was then, when Pilgrim had given up hope, that with a screeching of tyres a car rounded the corner of the street and roared towards them, headlights glaring. It slammed to a halt in a spray of dirt and water, just inches from Pilgrim's two assailants who were as shocked as he at its dramatic appearance. They stood in a frozen tableau as three men leapt from the car. Pilgrim watched stupidly as two of them ran towards the man who had thrown him from the car while the third closed with the big man. The driver lashed out with his foot at the first of his attackers who staggered away, clutching his genitals. The second man was immediately upon him and the two fell to the ground, kicking and punching. On the far side of the car, the big man's attacker had recoiled in horror when his hands had slipped on the loathsome mess covering the thug's coat. The two were now punching each other with intense ferocity.

Pilgrim's painful brain tried to make sense of the violent scene. He had no idea who the newcomers were; it was evident that they were his enemies' enemies, but did that mean they were his friends? It was too difficult to work out. All he knew was that he had to get away. He tried to stand but fell over to his side. He felt the fence give. In the lights of the newly arrived car he saw that the bottom of the fence was loose and that something, children or animals, had burrowed beneath it, making a gap large enough for a man to get through. He half scrambled, half crawled beneath the fence onto the wasteland beyond. He stood up and groaned; his body was a mass of aches. He turned to look at the five men, still punching and kicking each other, beside the cars. The man who had been kicked in the genitals had rejoined the fray and in the lights Pilgrim recognised him. He was the man who, only minutes previously, had stared vacantly at him from the rear seat of the dark Ford. Bent almost double, Pilgrim stumbled through the dark waste ground.

It seemed as if he was in the gloomy wilderness for hours. Countless times he fell, tripping over paint tins and rusty junk into puddles and mud. Yet after a while he began to think more clearly and to regain a sense of direction. He calculated that beyond the dark mass of abandoned warehouses to his left was the river and that if he kept the river to his left, he would be travelling west, back towards the City and the safety of bright lights. Far away to his right was a line of amber street lights strung out like beads. He made towards them, staggering diagonally across the wasteland. At last he reached the brightly lit road. There was a fence between it and himself but it had been sufficiently well vandalised to allow him to get through without much difficulty.

He had no real notion of where he was. It could be Wapping, he thought, or perhaps Chadwell, even as far east as Millwall and the Isle of Dogs. All he knew was that he was standing by a fence in the middle of a long, straight stretch of road with just a few cars passing. He turned towards the west and the City. He was desperate to get out of sight, to get off the road. As the only pedestrian around, he felt painfully conspicuous. He unzipped his anorak and felt inside his jacket pocket. He still had his wallet. He stayed in the shadows, trembling at the approach of every car, ready at an instant to stumble back over the fence and into the blackness of the waste ground should one screech to a stop. He walked for what seemed an eternity; a few occupied cabs passed him and then, at last, salvation in the shape of the orange light of a vacant cab hurtled into sight.

The driver gave Pilgrim a strange look as he gave his destination but it was only when he climbed into the back of the taxi that he understood why. His anorak was soaked through and torn in a dozen places. So were his trousers; there was a large hole in the knee of one of the legs, the cloth flapping against his scratched knee. His face and hands were covered in dirt.

He sat huddled in the corner of the cab, peering furtively at any cars that overtook them. Within a few minutes the cab was driving past Catherine's Dock and the Tower of London. Pilgrim looked at his watch and was shocked to see that it was barely nine o'clock. It seemed a lifetime since he had passed those same lights going the other way, yet it was less than sixty minutes. Suddenly, he began to shake uncontrollably. The thought of what had happened to him in those sixty minutes and, far worse, the insidious imaginings of what might have happened to him, finally came home. He buried his chin in the collar of his anorak to muffle his sobs as the tears flowed down his dirty face. He tried to pull himself together as the taxi arrived outside his hotel but his hand was shaking like a leaf in a storm when he handed the cabbie a fiver. Teeth chattering, he muttered to him to keep it; there was no way he would have been able to keep hold of his change.

He retrieved his room key from the sour and anorectic

woman who worked behind the tiny reception desk in the hotel's narrow hallway and stumbled to his room where he fell on his bed, quivering. After a while he remembered the bottle of whisky he had bought the previous night. He got up and retrieved it from a drawer. He thought he might vomit again as the fiery liquid swirled around his stomach, but as he sat on the edge of the bed, slowly the shakes began to subside. Finally, and with still trembling fingers, he undressed. He did the best he could to dry himself down with the limp hotel towel before crawling under the bedcovers with the whisky bottle and the glass.

He soon dispensed with the glass, it was easier to drink straight from the bottle. The alcohol anaesthetised him, deadening the aches in his body and head, and calming the turmoil in the pit of his stomach. He began to feel drowsy. He laid his head on the pillow and gradually fell into a deep sleep.

He awoke with a start and for a few seconds lay blinking at the patchy ceiling, trying to remember where he was. Suddenly, his memories of the night before flooded in and he closed his eyes with a groan. His head throbbed and he felt exhausted; his sleep had been filled with nameless fears and nightmares. The capless bottle of whisky by the side of his bed was almost empty.

Gingerly, he eased himself out of the bed. There was a dull ache in his stomach where the man had hit him but it was the pain in his head which hurt most. His left eye was half closed, the flesh around it felt swollen and tender. Looking in the mirror he saw it was purple and black. He sat on the edge of his bed, waiting for the pain in his temple to ease, but the room was cold and he was naked, and he was soon forced to move about and get himself ready. His face was streaked with mud and tears, his hands were filthy and he noticed that his right knee was gashed and covered in congealed blood. He slouched down the corridor to the depressing bathroom where he bathed and washed his hair.

The water, if anything, was colder than it had been previously, but it served to revive him. He felt better when he was clean and even the pain in his head subsided. He shaved and examined his clothes. The trousers of his suit and his anorak were beyond repair. He put on his slacks, polo neck jumper and grey tweed jacket. He still had a great deal of Susan's money. He decided to use some of it to replace his ruined clothing. It was all her fault anyway. None of it, he reasoned, would have happened if he hadn't listened to her.

He emerged from the front door of the hotel. The morning was grey and overcast but the drizzle of the day before had stopped. He felt cold and he walked as briskly as he could out of the square towards Gray's Inn Road.

The two men in the nondescript van parked a few doors down from the hotel watched him. The driver started the engine and slowly the van moved out from the line of parked vehicles to cruise gently well back in the wake of the hurrying Pilgrim.

He reached Gray's Inn Road and saw a bus stop. Travelling northward was a bus with its indicator board showing Oxford Circus. Pilgrim climbed aboard. The bus was crowded and he stood with the other passengers on the lower deck. The van eased into the queue of traffic three or four vehicles behind the bus. The bus remained in the nearside bus lane, ready to turn left out of Gray's Inn Road into Euston Road. Suddenly there was a gap in the queue of traffic ahead and the bus accelerated. The space it left behind was immediately filled by taxis filtering from the right out of Swinton Street and the men in the van found themselves positioned almost a dozen vehicles behind their quarry. 'For God's sake,' said the van's passenger, 'don't lose him.'

The bus conductor, a young cheerful West Indian, came rattling down the stairs.

'Oxford Circus,' said Pilgrim.

'We're not going to Oxford Circus.'

'You've got it on the board.'

'That's where we've been, man.' said the conductor, his face breaking into a grin. 'It ain't where we're going.'

Pilgrim pulled a face and the man's smile broadened.

'Jump off here, man,' he said. 'I won't charge you for riding one stop.'

As Pilgrim squeezed past him in the narrow gangway, the conductor nodded at Pilgrim's black eye. 'What happened to you? Did her old man come home and catch you plonking your joy stick in her honeypot?' He laughed, showing a row of white even teeth.

Despite himself and his mood, Pilgrim laughed as well. There was something about the conductor, his vitality, his love of life, that wasn't to be denied and the smile remained on Pilgrim's face as he leapt off the bus which was slowing for the next stop. He mingled with the throng of pedestrians who were waiting on the pavement to cross the busy road. The two men in the dark van speeding past in the flow of traffic did not notice him. In the few seconds that it had taken him to jump off the bus, he had been out of their sight, round the corner in Euston Road, while they fumed in the line of traffic, still waiting at its junction with Gray's Inn Road.

The van caught up with the bus at the next stop. Its passenger leapt out, boarded the bus and quickly scoured both decks. He reappeared on the platform and his colleague, driving closely behind the bus, could see from the look of consternation on his face that they had lost their quarry. By that time, Pilgrim was on the Tube, halfway to Oxford Circus.

He was slightly cheered by his new anorak and was more heartened after he'd eaten a couple of Danish pastries in the coffee shop of the store where he had purchased it. He had noticed the few early shoppers in the store looking quizzically at his black eye and he realised, as he lingered over his second cup of coffee, that he would have to find a believable explanation to give Susan. He didn't think that he could tell her the truth; his horrifying experience would sound too far-fetched. He had also begun to admit that what had befallen him the night before had been largely the result of his own greed. If he had followed Susan's plan he would not have had to return to Addingham's chambers. He had set himself up, easily allowed himself to be ambushed. Addingham must have guessed that he would talk. But how could Addingham know men like that? And what would they have done to him, once he had told them about Susan and the whereabouts of the original papers? The thought of the two men and what they had threatened brought on another attack of the shakes and his coffee cup rattled as he put it in the saucer. Pilgrim forced himself to breathe deeply and after a couple of minutes brought his nerves back under control. Whatever else he told Susan, he meant to tell her that he was finished with her crazy idea.

He got up and left his table, moving cautiously among the shoppers. He had the feeling that at any moment the two large men would emerge out of nowhere and carry him off. Although Oxford Street was crowded he felt vulnerable; he tried to control his fear. He returned to the Tube station and took a train to Victoria where he telephoned Susan.

She sounded surprised when he told her he was round the corner from Elizabeth Street. 'The house is empty until five. You'd better come round now,' she instructed him.

He said he would be there in five minutes. He walked the length of Elizabeth Street, slowly passing the fashionable restaurants and chic boutiques, composing the story he would tell her.

She opened the door immediately he'd rung the bell. 'God,' she exclaimed. 'What happened to you?'

He stepped inside the hallway and she closed the door behind him.

'I got mugged,' he said.

'Didn't you go back to Gretton on Tuesday?'

He shook his head.

'Oh, for God's sake, Jerry.' She sounded annoyed. 'You're supposed to stick to the plan.' She looked hard at the purple bruise round his eye and then kissed him. He followed her down the hallway to the large, high-ceilinged sitting room at the rear of the house. 'Drink?' she enquired.

He nodded and she poured him a glass of white wine. He sat down on a sofa and she sat close to him, her hands in her lap, her back straight, her face full of enquiry. 'What happened?'

'I telephoned the bank yesterday morning,' Pilgrim lied, 'to see if any money had been transferred. It hadn't.'

'I know. I called this morning. They haven't received anything.'

'I don't think they're ever going to,' said Pilgrim morosely.

'Why not? What's gone wrong?'

'When I found out there was no money in the bank I called Blackmore's house. They said he was dead.'

'What?'

'He's dead,' he repeated.

'You weren't supposed to call him after you'd seen him. That's not in the plan.'

'He's not supposed to be dead,' Pilgrim retorted. 'That's not in the plan either.'

'But there is nothing in the papers about his death,' said Susan.

'I know. They said it was a security matter. They weren't telling the press. So then I phoned Addingham to find out why he hadn't transferred the money. He said everything had changed. Blackmore was dead and Brighton was dead. He asked me to go round yesterday evening.'

'You didn't go?' asked Susan incredulously.

Pilgrim shrugged. 'Yes, I did, and I got mugged outside his chambers.'

'What?' Susan's voice was even more incredulous. 'Nobody gets mugged in the Inner Temple.'

'Well, I did,' said Pilgrim.

'Do you think Addingham is responsible?'

'I don't know. It's a bit hard to believe that the Lord Chief Justice hires hit men.'

'Don't be naive,' said Susan. 'Anyone with money can hire people like that. There are men who will arrange everything and protect the identity of the hirer.'

'You seem to know a lot about it,' Pilgrim observed.

'I've heard David and his friends talk about it. It usually happens when someone finds his wife is playing around. The boyfriend finds himself with a couple of broken legs.'

Pilgrim tried to look shocked. 'You don't think it's your husband?'

'David? No. If he knew about you he would have beaten hell out of me before he got round to you.' She shook her head. 'No, David doesn't know about us.' She stood up abruptly and took a cigarette from a packet which was lying on top of a polished walnut writing bureau. She lit it. 'I think it was Addingham,' she said walking to the window which overlooked the small garden.

'Maybe.'

'Well, did they say anything?' Her voice had an edge.

'No.'

'It doesn't make sense.' She was speaking almost to herself. 'Why should he take the risk of beating you up. All you want is a hundred thousand pounds. Easier to pay you off. Why risk it?'

'He wasn't very pleased to see me.'

'That doesn't mean that he wasn't going to pay up.'

'It's a lot of money.'

'It's not a lot of money to him. Unless . . .' she paused and stared at Pilgrim, 'you were asking for more.'

Pilgrim tried his best to look hurt and innocent but it was difficult with his bruised eye.

Susan continued to stare at him. 'I must say,' she said, 'you got off very lightly.'

'What do you mean?'

'If those men were professionals, you would have woken

383

up in hospital in a plaster cast with your jaw wired up. All you've got is a black eye.'

'I've got a lot more than that,' he said plaintively. 'I'm bruised all over.'

'You can still walk.'

'I fought them off.'

She laughed shortly. 'Don't give me that. You don't fight off men like that. You may be a good lover, Jerry, but you're not a fighter; you couldn't punch your way out of a paper bag.'

He felt the resentment rise within him. 'Well, this time I did,' he said sharply.

'How much money have you got left?' she said, changing the subject abruptly.

'About three hundred and fifty. I had to buy another anorak, the other one got ripped to shreds.'

'Strikes me that they did more damage to your anorak than they did to you,' said Susan. 'And they didn't rob you. Some muggers.' She turned her back on him to stare out of the window.

'Look, Susan,' he said addressing her back. 'Let's face it, it's all gone wrong. It was a good idea but I never thought it would work anyway. Brighton's dead, Blackmore's dead and none of the others are going to pay me a penny. Let's just forget it.'

Susan continued to stare out of the window for a few moments and then rounded on him sharply. He was shocked to see that her face was fixed in fury. 'I don't believe a word of it.' Her voice was strained. 'It's a pack of lies.'

'What do you mean?' Pilgrim said defensively.

'Christ, Jerry, you're such a liar. I could never trust you. Ever. What really happened?'

'I've told you.'

'Oh God. You must think I just got off the banana boat. You've messed it up,' she stated flatly. 'I know you. You didn't stick to the plan. You got greedy. You tried to do a deal for yourself and now you've screwed everything up.'

'That's not true.' He was beginning to get scared. 'I tried to stick to the plan. It's not my fault it's gone wrong.'

'Shit,' she said vehemently. 'There's nothing in the papers about Blackmore's death. If they were keeping it quiet, why should they tell you, a stranger, over the phone.'

Pilgrim was thrown. He hadn't thought of that. 'Well,' he stumbled, 'it's because I'd called on him on Monday. I'm an old friend, Richard Thornbury, remember?'

She sneered. 'You are nothing but a lying shit. And a coward. You can't go through with it. You're too scared.'

'Susan, I know you're upset. It was a good plan and I tried to make it work. Really I did.'

'You didn't try at all. You could have made a lot of money. All you had to do was stick to the plan. Just do what you were told, for once in your life. You could have been straight for life. But no, you had to do it your way. You got greedy. And now you're scared. I know you.'

Pilgrim stood up and moved towards her. 'Come on, Susan.'

'Don't come near me,' she said. 'Don't touch me.' The anger was flaming in her face. 'I set you up in the cottage. I got you work. And I gave you the chance to make some real money. It's always been me who did things for you. What have you ever done for anybody? Except cheat on them. Well, that's it, Jerry. I've had enough, enough of you and your lies. You're on your own now. You can manage without me.'

Pilgrim felt himself go cold. 'Jesus Christ, Susan, it's not my fault it's gone wrong. I've told you the truth. God, I couldn't manage without you, it would mean going right back to where I was. I need you, Susan.'

'Well, I don't need you,' she said. 'You'd better go. Go on, take your new anorak and go.' She walked towards the living room door with Pilgrim stumbling after her.

'For God's sake listen. I've worked bloody hard on this. It was me who had to do everything, not you. It's not my fault that nothing's happened. I've been five days in this shitty city and I haven't made a penny. All I've got to show for it is this.' He pointed to his swollen eye. 'And it bloody hurts.'

'Serves you right,' she said coldly. She pulled his anorak off the stand in the hall and thrust it at him. 'You can keep the rest of the money I gave you. That's the last you're going to get out of me. Ever. Now, just go.'

Pilgrim found himself on the doorstep with the black gloss-painted door shut fast behind him.

He did what he always did when he'd been caught out in a lie. He went looking for a drink. Numbly he wandered the streets of Belgravia until he found a pub which he recognised. It had been a favourite watering hole in the days of his long gone affluence. It was a place in which he had frequently picked up women. The people drinking in the crowded bar were the same type that had frequented the place in his day; young, well-heeled piss artists, noisy and spiteful.

He sat morosely in a corner of the bar, nursing a large whisky, watching the crowd. Once he'd been like them; now he was neither young nor affluent, and he wasn't even a good piss artist. Susan had seen right through his pathetic lies. She hadn't believed anything he had told her, even the parts which were true. Pilgrim hovered between resentment at Susan's lack of sympathy for his battering, and cold fear at the prospect of losing the cottage in Gretton and the work she supplied. The pain in his head grew steadily worse. Once more he had betrayed Susan, only now she meant to abandon him, to throw him to the dogs. He knew her well enough to know that she meant it. He got up from his seat and called her from a pay phone in the bar. He put one hand over his ear to blot out the careless noise of the other drinkers as he heard her sullen voice answer.

'It's me.' That was as far as he got.

'Fuck off.' She said it dully and without emotion and the phone went dead.

There was no point hanging around the bar. The place depressed him. He walked out into the grey, drab afternoon and caught a cab back to his hotel.

The men in the van parked innocently in the square were relieved to see his return. Once they knew that they had lost Pilgrim, they had returned to his hotel. Quite easily and without the knowledge of the management, they located and broke into his bedroom. They searched it thoroughly but found nothing which could identify their quarry, only a wet and torn anorak, a suit with trousers in shreds, a couple of shirts, a tie and some shaving gear. There was nothing to tell them about the man they were shadowing. They had checked that the address Richard Thornbury had written in the hotel register was false. So they had sat tight and waited. The hotel was their only lead to the man. And their patience had been rewarded.

They watched with hard eyes as he disappeared through the front door of the hotel. Within minutes he re-emerged carrying his suitcase; it was obvious he'd checked out. They followed him at a safe distance as he walked across Euston Road towards King's Cross. They trailed him to a car park behind the station and watched him drive out in a G registered Morris 1100. That was their first tangible clue to his true identity; the passenger in the van noted the car's registration number. The 1100 turned north and the men in the van settled back. This time they would not lose their quarry.

Pilgrim headed north along Camden High Street. As he drove he remembered the case waiting in the left luggage department at King's Cross. He shrugged, he didn't care if someone, someday, found the papers. It was nothing to do with him any more. As he breasted the small rise at Camden Lock he saw above the dark buildings an expanse of grey sky which seemed to be the colour and texture of a paving slab;

it seemed to Pilgrim that he was driving straight at it, aiming the car and his life straight into a block of concrete.

He stopped halfway up Tavistock Hill and bought another bottle of whisky from an off-licence. There had been an accident on the North Circular Road and the traffic was a mess. He was caught for almost an hour in the jam. When at last he started moving again, he realised he was in the wrong lane and instead of heading north on the A1 found himself on the motorway. He shrugged. It didn't matter. It didn't make any difference. Every turning he had ever taken in his life had been the wrong one. It was a small matter that he was on the wrong road; indeed it seemed a miracle that he was even going in the right direction. The motorway lights stretched for miles into the distance. They looked like a giant zip, pulling the black night tight over the dark earth. He took the ring road round Northampton and arrived at the cottage just after eight o'clock.

The house was cold. The stone-flagged hall was littered with letters, most of which were final demands for the payment of bills. Pilgrim leafed through the envelopes before throwing them all onto the kitchen table. He decided to lay a fire in the empty stone fireplace of the little sitting room. He found some sticks and logs in the yard but was short of paper to start it. Finally he used the bills he had thrown onto the table. It didn't matter if they weren't paid, he reasoned; Susan would be kicking him out soon enough anyway. He went in search of some food. There was a chunk of Edam cheese and a yoghurt in the fridge. He ate them both and made himself a black coffee before settling down with his bottle of whisky in front of the small fire and the TV set. He was glad to be back; he felt secure and safe in his comfortable armchair in the familiar sitting room, miles away from London. The whisky, the warm fire and the flickering images on the screen anaesthetised him and for the moment erased his fears about the future. He went to bed after midnight and did not awake until mid-morning.

He crawled out of bed reluctantly but after he had shaved and bathed he felt better. He spent a solid four hours completing his copy-writing assignments and arranging his work for the next couple of weeks. As he worked, part of his mind wrestled with his problems. He was sure Susan meant it when she said she was finished with him. The prospect of having to leave the cottage which he had come to regard almost as his own made him miserable. He had to think of some way of ingratiating himself with Susan. His only option seemed to be to go on with her plan and be successful. The thought of going back south to renew his attempts at extortion and the memory of his narrow escape from mutilation made the hairs on the nape of his neck stand on end. But he had to do it; he had to persuade either Sir Henry Dundonald or Jeffrey Frimley-Kimpton, or better still both of them, to part with one hundred thousand pounds. He had to convince them that he was serious. If he could do that he might, he thought, even be able to go back to Addingham; either way, some money in the Swiss account would bring Susan round. His concentration on his work allowed his subconscious to wrestle with the problems; by the middle of the afternoon he had come up with a plan. He waited until about four o'clock and then dialled the number of Frimley-Kimpton's house in Surrey. A woman answered the phone.

'Can I speak to Jeffrey?' he asked heartily.

'I'm sorry,' said the woman, 'he's away this weekend.'

Pilgrim's heart sank. 'When do you expect him back?'

'He'll be back in London on Tuesday.'

Pilgrim remembered that Frimley-Kimpton spent only his weekends in Surrey. 'When do you expect him back at the house?'

'He'll be back here a week today, Friday.'

'I'd like to come along and see him for a few minutes,' said Pilgrim.

There was a pause at the other end of the line. 'He's got quite a busy day,' she said. 'What's it in connection with?'

'I'm an old friend. My name is Richard Thornbury. I'm sure he will want to see me.'

There was another pause. 'I've got his diary here. He could see you about noon for a few minutes, if that's all right?'

Pilgrim told her that it was and added that he would phone to confirm on the Friday morning. He put the phone down. He felt cheated but there was nothing he could do. He didn't want to see Frimley-Kimpton in London. This time he would stick as closely as he could to Susan's original plan.

He dialled Dundonald's number in Hertfordshire. An older woman answered. He asked for Henry.

'Can I ask who is calling?'

'Please tell him it's Richard Thornbury.'

He waited for about half a minute until he heard a sharp and precise voice at the other end. 'This is Sir Henry Dundonald. What do you want?'

'I think you know what I want,' said Pilgrim evenly.

'I understand you claim to have some papers which you say implicate me in some business transaction.'

'That's right and I've still got them.' Pilgrim glanced across to where his jacket was hanging on a chair. He could see the envelope meant for Ashley Brighton sticking out of an inside pocket. 'You can tell your friend Addingham that the two thugs he hired to take them off me failed.'

'I don't know what you mean,' said the voice.

Pilgrim snorted. 'I bet you don't. Addingham hired a couple of heavies who were told to chop bits off me until I told them where the originals of those papers were. Only I've got friends too, so it was his blokes who got beaten while I still have the evidence which could put you in prison.'

There was silence at the other end of the phone before the sharp voice enquired earnestly and with some strain, 'What's happened to Blackmore?'

Pilgrim had no idea but he wasn't about to tell Sir Henry that. 'Why, what's it to you?' he asked.

'For God's sake, he's disappeared and his family isn't talking to anyone. Are you responsible for this? What have you done to him?'

Pilgrim thought quickly. 'That's my business.' he said. 'Don't worry about Blackmore. He's being taken care of.'

'Listen,' said Dundonald quickly, 'we're all business-men. We'll listen to a reasonable proposition. There's no need to abduct people.'

'Tell that to your friend Addingham. His friends tried to abduct me, they were going to cut me to ribbons.'

'I don't know anything about that,' said Dundonald. 'Look, I am quite prepared to pay a reasonable price for those papers. I believe you are asking two hundred thousand pounds.'

Pilgrim raised his eyebrows. Maybe he could recoup more money than he thought. 'Yes,' he said quickly.

'Very well,' said Dundonald. 'I shall need to see the papers first.'

Pilgrim recoiled. 'You're joking. I'm not coming to see you. I went to see Addingham and got beaten for it.'

'If those papers implicate me as is suggested, then I insist on seeing them,' said Dundonald imperiously. 'You can take my word that there will be no double dealing. I shall ensure that I am completely alone when you come.'

Pilgrim thought about it for a few seconds. He knew he had no real option; if he wanted to get Susan back he had to take the risk.

'All right,' he said. 'But remember that I've got friends too. You can check with Addingham. His heavies got sorted out.'

'There'll be no violence,' Dundonald said. 'There'll be nobody here. However, I insist that you tell me where Oliver Blackmore is when you come.'

Pilgrim could see that the fate of Blackmore worried

Dundonald and that he could use it to safeguard himself. 'When I've got the money,' he said, 'I'll tell you where Blackmore is but if you've got any ideas about double-crossing me, then you'll never know. And what's more, I'll send these papers directly to some friends of mine in the press.'

'Very well,' said Dundonald.

Pilgrim felt more confident. 'I want a banker's draft made out to Richard Thornbury to the value of one hundred thousand pounds. The other one hundred thousand pounds will be transferred to an account in Switzerland. I shall give you the details when I see you. You must have the banker's draft ready then.'

'Very well,' Dundonald said again. 'I will have a banker's draft ready on Monday morning by . . .' he paused, 'by eleven o'clock.'

'All right,' said Pilgrim. 'But remember I'll have friends watching just in case there are any tricks. Eleven o'clock on Monday.'

He put the phone down. He wondered if he was doing the right thing in meeting Dundonald but Susan had said that none of them would pay out until they saw the papers. He had no option. The prospect depressed him but his hope that this time he might be successful encouraged him. It might turn out to be a better weekend than he had expected. He thought of something that might help him pass the time over the next couple of days. He dialled the number of the local stables. A woman with a voice like sheet metal answered.

'Hello,' said Pilgrim, 'can I speak to Trixie?'

'No,' came the flat, metallic voice. 'Trixie's gone with Danny and Bobby and Kim and Patsy and Sammy to Stamford. They won't be back for hours.' The phone went dead. Some of the names the woman had reeled off were people and some were horses, but except for Trixie, he didn't know which was which. He shrugged. He'd call Trixie later. He cleared up after his day's work, then set about cleaning and tidying the cottage. When he'd finished, he decided to buy groceries; he still had Susan's money and he figured that it was wise to stock up on food while he had the opportunity.

Dusk was falling as he slammed the low wooden door of the cottage behind him. The dull orange glow of the setting sun was smeared over the low hills on the far side of the valley. Pilgrim walked down the lane in the failing light, passing within a few feet of a van parked on the corner. He turned and continued walking for a couple of hundred yards until he reached a small grocery.

The men cramped in the rear of the van watched him disappear inside the shop. They had been on watch for more than twenty-four hours, taking it in turns to sleep on the mattress in the back of the van. They had learned how difficult it was to maintain surveillance in a small village; almost all the people who had walked past the vehicle had glanced at it curiously. It was tedious to be an object of interest to the natives; in a big city, no one would have taken any notice. One elderly busybody had circled the van with suspicion, peering through the windows to see if she could learn to whom the unknown vehicle belonged. Although she could see nothing, the men in the darkened rear could see her easily for the van had been specially modified for surveillance work. The men cursed the nosy old woman under their breath as they watched her face contort itself against the glass of the van.

'Christ, the old cow's taking our number,' whispered one. 'I hope she doesn't call the police. That's all we need.'

They were due to receive extra help that evening; one of them had made a phone call soon after reaching Gretton and had been told that more men would be despatched to help keep watch on Pilgrim.

They saw him emerge from the store carrying two large plastic bags filled with groceries. He struggled back to the cottage and disappeared inside. Almost immediately the lights came on and the curtains were drawn. Just over an hour later he re-emerged. By that time two other men had joined those watching; all four were crowded in the back of the van. One of them got out and followed Pilgrim at a discreet distance as he walked through the village to a pub on its outskirts. The man followed him inside and stood waiting to be served at a corner of the bar. Some of the more elderly patrons eyed him speculatively but Pilgrim, who had taken off his jacket and was seated by a roaring fire at the far end of the room joking with two men, gave him only a cursory glance. The man finished his drink quickly and returned to his companions. 'It's his local,' he told them. 'It looks like he's settled there for the night.' The others cautiously emerged from the van and while one of them kept watch for Pilgrim's return, the other three stole up the darkened lane to the cottage. The lock on the door presented no problem; within seconds it had been picked and they were inside.

They were there for almost two hours and they searched the cottage thoroughly. They photographed Pilgrim's work and his personal papers which they found in the bottom of the wardrobe. In every room they planted small but highly sensitive listening devices and inside the phone they put a tiny electronic bug which would allow them to monitor all Pilgrim's calls. They looked behind the furniture, beneath the sinks; they probed every nook and crevice. They checked his mail, carefully opening and photographing all the correspondence. They finished at last and departed, leaving the cottage just as they had found it.

Two men stayed to keep vigil throughout the night in the back of the van; the other two drove the five miles across the valley to Uppingham, where they took two rooms in a small hotel. Even if the five miles between Gretton and Uppingham had consisted entirely of brick wall, the electronic equipment they had planted in Pilgrim's cottage and the receiving equipment they set up in one of the hotel bedrooms would have allowed them to hear everything that was going on. As it was, with an almost uninterrupted line of sight across the darkened valley, the men would be able to register every breath Pilgrim took.

Pilgrim returned to the cottage after midnight. He'd spent a convivial evening drinking after hours with the pub's landlord and a few friends. He'd called Trixie from the pub; she'd told him that she had to go to her parents' house in Tixover, a village further down the valley, but that she would come to the cottage at about midday on Saturday.

He slept late; it was almost eleven o'clock on the Saturday morning before the men in Uppingham heard him moving about in the cottage. Just after twelve, they were surprised to hear a female voice. One of them called his companions in the van on a shortwave radio.

'Who's the woman?'

'What woman?' said his surprised colleague. The men in the van had no listening equipment; their job was merely to watch.

'There's a woman in there, for Christ's sake,' said the man in the hotel.

'Well, she didn't come in the front door.'

The men in the hotel glanced at each other. 'Who the hell is she?' asked one.

'I don't know,' the other said. 'Keep listening.'

For more than thirty hours they listened and in that time found out that Trixie Hayhoe had three interests in life, sex, food and horses. Within minutes of Trixie's arrival the man with the headphones was bombarded by the sound of vigorous and noisy copulation.

'Jesus Christ,' he said, turning down the volume on the tape recorder. 'They're going at it like grasshoppers in a matchbox.'

'Ah, oh, oh, Jerry.'

'Christ, no wonder he lives in the middle of the country. Civilised neighbours wouldn't stand for all that roaring and screaming. It's like living next to a zoo.' He threw his earphones down on the table in disgust. 'I hope this isn't going to go on all fucking day,' he complained.

'Just keep listening,' his partner ordered.

The man put the headphones back on reluctantly and screwed· up his face as the sensitive electronic bug hidden beneath the chest of drawers picked up the frenzied sounds of sex. Afterwards there was a blessed silence before the girl said, 'Jerry, I'm hungry.'

'So am I,' Pilgrim replied. 'What about some fish and chips?'

'Super,' said the girl with enthusiasm.

'Well off you go then,' said Pilgrim, 'get two portions.'

'Why me?' Trixie was petulant. 'If I go, that old busy-body across the road will see me. She knows my mother. She'll tell her I've been here.'

'Go the way you came, across the smallholding and along the footpath.'

The man heard the rustling of the clothes as they dressed.

'Have you got any money?' asked Pilgrim.

'Yes.'

'Then get a few cans of lager as well.'

The man in the hotel contacted his colleagues in the van. 'The girl's leaving the cottage by the back door. See if you can get a look at her.' One of the watchers left the van and hurried along the main street of the village. Halfway down, a footpath ran between two of the stone cottages. Marching down it in a pair of mud-spattered riding boots was a girl in her late teens. She had shoulder-length black hair and was well built with heavy breasts and broad hips, across which was straining a pair of riding breeches. The watching man had no idea what had gone on between the girl and Pilgrim but he noticed as she passed that she wore upon her face the look of a woman well-satisfied. She climbed into the battered Mini parked at the end of the footpath and drove off. The man made a note of the number and strolled slowly back to the van.

The four men took it in turns, either in the van or the hotel room, to monitor events inside the cottage. They heard Pilgrim and the girl eat their fish and chips and afterwards listened to the shrieks and clattering as he made love to her on the kitchen table.

Later that afternoon they heard them go to bed, first to copulate and then to sleep. In the evening the men watching from the van saw them leave the cottage and make their way to the local pub where they stayed until well after midnight. They returned to the cottage and fell into bed where the girl induced a wearily complaining Pilgrim to perform yet again. The listeners heard no more except for the long sonorous snores of the girl until late on the Sunday morning when they overheard the noises of a leisurely awakening; the pad of feet upon stone, the tinkling of urine on water, the flushing of a lavatory cistern. And it wasn't long before they heard the girl enthusiastically urging Pilgrim to 'do it again' and soon the now familiar rhythmic squeaking of the bed and the raucous moans of orgasm began again.

Later, they heard Pilgrim tell the girl that he wanted the Sunday papers. The men in Uppingham radioed their colleagues in the van to watch out for him. A few minutes later, he plodded past, his eyes blinking in the bright grey daylight. They chuckled when they saw his face, haggard and drawn from his sexual excesses. 'He won't last another night,' laughed one of the men. 'He'll be dead before morning. Look at him, he can hardly walk.' They observed his slow return, carrying the papers and a couple of bottles of milk. No sooner had he disappeared back inside the cottage than the listening men heard the girl enticing him back to bed. Pilgrim told her angrily that he was hungry and that he wanted breakfast. They listened as he fried bacon and eggs and the girl chattered incessantly about horses and her friends' horses.

'Christ,' said one of the men in the hotel room. 'This woman is only interested in what she can get between her legs.'

There was one small incident that made the men listening

prick up their ears. Pilgrim and the girl were eating breakfast, she was continuing her incessant chatter while he, obviously preoccupied with reading the papers, was silent. Suddenly they heard him exclaim.

'Bloody hell.'

'What is it, Jerry?'

'Oh nothing.'

'What?'

'It's nothing. I've just read about somebody's death.'

'Oh.'

The man in the hotel radioed his colleague. 'What papers did he buy?'

'*The Sunday Times* and *Observer*, I think,' came the reply.

'He's read something in one of them. About someone being dead. Get them and find out what it was.'

As the man in the van went to buy newspapers, the two in the hotel turned their attention to events in the cottage. They were in time to hear Trixie ask, 'Jerry, after breakfast, can we do it in the living room, you know, like we did it before?'

Pilgrim didn't answer.

Later that afternoon they did as she had asked and the men heard them indulging their favourite pastime on what was evidently an extremely well-built armchair. They slept for a while and coupled once more, just before the girl left. The men heard her take her leave and the cottage at last went quiet, except for a long, drawn-out sigh of relief from Pilgrim.

Chapter Six

He left the cottage early the next morning. He had gone to bed soon after Trixie had left, and had slept long and soundly. Even so, he felt bleary and exhausted as he climbed into his car. Trixie had served her purpose, the weekend had passed quickly and the time that he had spent pumping her robust flesh had taken his mind off his problems. He had scarcely given a thought to his imminent meeting with Sir Henry Dundonald. But Trixie had taken her toll. Her voracious sexual appetitie had left him as limp as a dead fish. He felt dry and hollow, his eyes were out on stalks, his loins were bruised and tender and his back hurt like hell. He felt like death. He slumped into the driving seat and after a few false starts managed to get the engine to gurgle into life.

He took the road to Oundle and thence onto the A1 where he stopped at a roadside diner. The hot food and coffee revived him and he felt much better when he set off again, heading south. He turned off the A1 at Hatfield and drove through St Albans and then to Harpenden. He was in familiar territory, the big house in which he and Patricia had lived only a few years before was less than ten miles away. He knew Harpenden, it was one of those small, rich and privileged towns which encircle London like pearls around a throat. He drove past the great expanse of green common on the town's outskirts and onto the High Street which seemed entirely made up of half-timbered pubs, banks and building societies. He stopped the car and asked a middle-aged woman who was getting out of a Volvo estate for directions. She gave both Pilgrim and his decrepit car a disdainful look and informed him that where he wanted to go was somewhere in the direction of a village called Wheathampstead. Pilgrim saw a signpost and headed for the village, where he stopped at a shop and asked for directions again. The man told Pilgrim that the house was set in its own grounds and was difficult to find. He kindly drew a small map which outlined the network of narrow roads crisscrossing the countryside beyond the village. Pilgrim set off, the map resting on the passenger seat.

He drove for about three miles through the narrow lanes. Sometimes they were bordered by high hawthorn hedges but more often by the gently undulating fields, newly ploughed and speckled with pudding stones. Along one lane was a long line of copper beeches with leaves of burnt yellow and gold, fiery in the watery sun of late autumn. He came to a T junction and knew from the map that he was less than half a mile from his destination. He turned right and had driven no more than a couple of hundred yards when an ancient grey Peugeot 304 hurtled into sight. He pulled his car as close as he could into the nearside hedge. The Peugeot rocketed down the narrow lane and ploughed past his car with only inches to spare before careering out of sight round a bend. Pilgrim cursed the driver.

He drove slowly along the lane until he came to the gates leading to Dundonald's house. He turned into the drive and followed it in a gentle curve for about a hundred yards until he came in sight of a large, late-Victorian house, built of red Hertfordshire brick. Pilgrim parked close to an ornamental flowerbed and walked to the front door, his feet scrunching upon the gravel. The place, as Dundonald had promised, seemed deserted. He pressed the doorbell and waited. There was no sound from within. He pressed the bell again but still there was no response. Fixed to the front door was an ornamental lion's head made of brass with a circular knocker hanging from its jaws. Pilgrim grasped the knocker and rapped on the door sharply. The sound echoed through the house as the front door swung slowly open. He remained standing on the door-step in surprise, wondering what he should do. He hadn't expected Dundonald to leave the front door open for him and his suspicions were aroused. Perhaps, he thought, it was another trap. There was no sign of life in the large square hall beyond the open door.

'Hello,' he called. 'Is anyone there?' There was no answer.

He pushed the front door open wide and stepped into the hallway. At any moment he expected two large men to leap out at him. Slowly and very cautiously, he moved along the hall. On his right was a wide staircase. He stood at the bottom of the stairs and looked up.

'Hello,' he called. There was no sound or movement from the upper floors. He had an uncanny sensation that he was being watched. He edged his way further into the house. To his left was a door, slightly ajar. He pushed it open. Inside was a long dining room, empty. He opened a door at the far end of the hall. The room was a large and well-appointed kitchen, sufficiently cluttered to tell Pilgrim someone had used it that morning. To the right of the hall was another door. It was open. Pilgrim eased himself into the room step by step. It was a sitting room, at least forty feet long and almost as wide, scattered with armchairs and sofas. At the far end was a great Yorkshire stone fireplace; along the left side was a series of French windows which overlooked the ornamental gardens. The walls were decorated with a pretty wallpaper of little green flowers on a white background. In among the green flowers were dots of vivid red. There was something about the red dots on the wallpaper that caught Pilgrim's eye; somehow they didn't fit in. They were badly done. Some of them were smeared and even as he watched one big red blob slid down the wallpaper, smearing a pink trail over the little green flowers. Despite his feeling that he was being watched, and his anxiety at being alone in a strange house, he felt a strange sense of curiosity about the red spattering on the walls. He moved further into the room to take a closer look and his foot kicked something hard on the floor. Lying in the deep pile of the carpet was a shotgun. Pilgrim recoiled with a grunt. He was already as nervous as a colt and seeing the gun's twin barrels gleaming dully in the morning light did nothing to calm his fears. He was about to turn away when he noticed something puzzlingly familiar about the weapon. He knelt closer to examine it; like the wallpaper it was speckled with tiny blobs of red. He tentatively ran a finger along one of the smooth black barrels and looked closely at the red smear which appeared on his skin. It was blood. It took him a few moments to grasp the implications; he had walked into a house which had a gun on the floor and blood on its walls. While he was kneeling close to the gun, his eyes widening in fright, he became aware of something intruding slightly into his vision from the left. He turned his head. It was a man's leg. Pilgrim let out a small cry and leapt up and sideways. When he had first entered the room, he'd not seen that the high-backed chair with its back to the door was occupied.

'Hello,' said Pilgrim nervously. 'Hello.' From where he was standing, slightly behind and to the right of the chair, he could see a pair of legs dressed in brown tweed trousers and stout brogues. The legs were stuck out from the chair at an angle which suggested that their owner was asleep.

'Hello.' Pilgrim raised his voice. The legs did not move. Pilgrim's hands were clammy. He moved from one foot to the other, unsure whether to run from the room or approach the recumbent figure. Finally, he screwed up his courage and edged round to the front of the chair to face the man. The sight which confronted him would remain with him for the rest of his life. The long body of a man was slumped in the armchair. The upper part of the body was clothed in a brown tweed jacket and a check shirt. Round his neck was a knitted tie. Above the neck there was nothing. Nothing except a red, pulpy stump of blood and brains and slithers of flapping skin. The pretty white and green wallpaper behind the wing-backed chair was plastered with blood and brains.

Pilgrim did nothing. He neither cried out nor moved. He froze in abject terror. It was his first sight of violent death. He stared at the bloody mass and watched, riveted by revulsion, as blood and mucus slipped slowly down the front of the check shirt. Someone, perhaps the man himself, had stuck the shotgun beneath his chin and let off both barrels. Most of what had been the man's scalp was stuck firmly to the blood-spattered ceiling of the living room. Pilgrim backed away from the sight in a daze. He got as far as the doorway before the terror caught him. For the second time in less than a week he felt his stomach heaving and just reached the kitchen sink before his breakfast made it to the open air. He hung on to the stainless steel bowl and vomited. Each time he paused he thought of the faceless, shattered head in the room next door and immediately heaved some more. At last he stopped. His stomach was empty and his legs were trembling. With a shaking hand he turned on the tap and, cupping both hands, gulped down the cold water. The effects of the water sliding into his stomach and splashing his face revived him. Gradually his trembling lessened and he felt his muscles start to function once more. He shook his face free of water, dabbed a towel on it and stumbled out of the kitchen to the front door.

Still there was nobody about. He tottered across the gravel drive, scrambled into his car and after three terrifying attempts managed to start it. He drove off, roaring round the gravel drive which circled the ornate gardens, accelerating as hard as he could away from the ghastly sight in the sitting room. He barely stopped at the end of the driveway before swinging the car viciously into the narrow country lane and accelerating away hard. In his panic he didn't notice the transit van parked in the lay-by close to the gates of the drive. Pilgrim drove like a man demented, desperate to put as many miles as he could between himself and the faceless corpse. He came to a major road and, turning into it, soon found himself driving back through the village of Wheathampstead from where he followed the signs to the A1. He drove the rattling 1100 as fast as he could, which was no more than sixty. Despite the increasing distance between himself and the house, his mind was continually drawn back to the violent bloody sight that he had encountered in that quiet comfortable room. He took a series of deep breaths in order to calm his nerves.

He came off the A1 at the Leicester turn and drove west along the A47. Turning south off the main road he breasted the hill overlooking Haringworth and was comforted to see the great railway viaduct traversing the valley below. He drove down the hill and through the Gothic arch formed by the massive columns of the viaduct more than forty feet apart. The brittle light of early afternoon filled the arch like a window in a cathedral.

He arrived at the cottage. He wanted urgently to talk to Susan. He picked up the phone; he heard a crackle and a buzz on the line and then nothing. He jigged the receiver a few times but there was no response. Then he remembered, one of the final demands he had used to start the fire when he had returned from London was for the telephone. Sometime over the weekend they had cut off his phone. Cursing bitterly he slammed the handset back onto its cradle and drove the few hundred yards to the Dutch Mill. It was a few minutes before closing time, the regulars had left and the bar was empty and quiet. One of the tables close to a window of leaded panes was crowded with empty bottles. Dark brown and black, they stood like chess pieces on the small square table. Malcolm, the landlord, was polishing glasses behind the bar.

'Afternoon, Jerry,' his voice was friendly. 'Didn't expect to see you in today. The usual?'

'Make it a bloody big one.'

Malcolm leaned across the bar and peered at him. 'You look like you've seen a ghost. What's wrong?'

Pilgrim shook his head. 'Nothing,' he said quickly. 'I nearly had an accident in the car, that's all.'

Malcolm grunted and moved away to pour his drink.

'Look, Malcolm, can I use your phone? Mine's on the blink and I've got to talk to someone urgently.'

'Sure.' Malcolm handed him his drink.

Pilgrim walked round the bar and squeezed himself into the little cubby hole which housed the telephone perched on a pile of torn directories. The walls were yellow with age and cigarette smoke, and covered in telephone numbers. He dialled Susan's number and took a long gulp of whisky as he waited. He hoped that she was in and would answer the phone herself.

'Hello.' It was Susan.

'Don't hang up. It's me.' Though he didn't know it, there was a note of genuine and desperate need in his voice.

'What do you want?' Susan's voice was unemotional.

'I went to see Henry Dundonald this morning.' Pilgrim spoke quietly. 'Strictly according to the plan, your plan. Only when I got there someone had blown his head off.'

He heard Susan let out a slight gasp and then there was silence.

'Susan. Susan, are you still there?'

'Come on, Jerry,' she said.

'I'm not kidding. It's absolutely true. Somebody had blown his brains all over the walls.'

'Are you serious?'

'I've never been more serious in my life. Christ, it was awful, there was nothing left of his head or his face.'

'How do you know it was Dundonald?' she asked. 'If he had no face?'

The vision of the bloody mess that he had seen rose before him, crowding him in the cramped space. He took another gulp of whisky. 'I don't know,' he replied. 'I just do. He was tall and thin and wearing an expensive tweed suit. I know it was him.'

'Why did you go there anyway?' she enquired.

'I wanted to carry on with the plan.'

'It wasn't in the plan to go on Monday morning. Anyway, there isn't a plan,' she said forcefully, 'not any more. You ruined it. I suppose you were just trying to make some money for yourself.'

'No I wasn't. I was trying to save something out of the original idea and make some money for both of us.'

'You aren't lying about all this, are you, Jerry?'

'Jesus Christ,' he reacted. 'Nobody would tell lies about what I've just seen. I am telling you he's dead. He was shot. Or he shot himself.' There was another pause. 'Did you see that story in the paper about Blackmore?'

'Yes,' she said. She sounded puzzled. 'It said he died on Friday; an accident at home.'

'I know.'

'But you said he was dead on Wednesday.'

'That's when I was told he was dead. I think he died on Tuesday. And I'm pretty sure he didn't die at home either.'

'How do you know all this?'

'I made some enquiries. I was telling you the truth when I came to see you, Susan.' He was emphatic.

'I don't know,' said Susan doubtfully.

'I told you on Thursday, for Christ's sake. That's at least twenty-four hours before he was supposed to have died. It's a cover-up, Susan.' His voice had grown more confident, she hadn't hung up and the whisky was beginning to work. 'I think we've stumbled into something that we shouldn't have. At least three of the people involved in this conspiracy are now, all of a sudden, dead.' As he spoke a vague thought rose like a mist at the back of his mind. His brain couldn't grasp it. He was unable to focus on it before it disappeared. His attention jerked back to the conversation. 'We've got to meet and talk. I think we're into something dangerous.'

There was another pause before she agreed. 'Yes, all right. I have to go to Daddy's tomorrow. We can meet somewhere on the way.'

'What's wrong with coming to the cottage?'

'I am not coming to Gretton, Jerry.' Susan's voice was stern. 'Not until you've explained to me what actually happened in London.'

'All right. All right. It doesn't matter where we meet. So long as we talk.'

'Meet me at the pub in Naseby, two o'clock.'

Pilgrim told her he would be there.

'I'll see you tomorrow.' Her voice was softer.

'OK,' he said warmly. It was then, just as he was about to put the phone down, that the vague thought which had eluded him earlier rose in his brain like a ghoul from the grave. He jerked the phone back to his ear. 'Susan,' he shouted urgently. 'Susan.'

'Yes, what is it?' She had been on the point of putting down the phone.

'Your uncle, Woodberry.'

'Uncle Simon.'

'That's right. How did he die?'

'He had an accident.'

'What kind of accident?' Pilgrim felt a familiar tingle running up his backbone. 'What happened?'

'No one knows for sure. It was some kind of hunting accident. They found him. Dead. He'd been shot. You don't think . . .' Her voice trailed off.

'How was he shot, who shot him?'

'They don't know.' Susan's voice was weaker. 'They found him with a bullet in his head. High velocity. The kind they would use to kill a stag. Everybody said it was a tragic accident. Some other hunter must have been out on the moor. He could have been more than a mile away. He could have shot at something and missed and never known that he had hit Uncle Simon.'

'Did they find out who it was?'

'No,' she said slowly. 'They never did.'

'Why didn't you tell me this before?'

Her voice sounded frightened. 'Everybody thought it was an accident.'

'Everybody thinks Blackmore died on Friday,' said Pilgrim bleakly. 'That makes four.'

'What?'

'Four of them dead. And at least two of them were shot. We'll talk tomorrow.'

'Yes,' she said.

'Susan.'

'Yes?'

'Just,' he paused, 'be careful.' The phone went down.

He finished his whisky and had another with Malcolm but he was in no mood for leaning on the bar and swapping jokes. He left and drove back to the cottage. A few minutes later, a dark blue Ford purred slowly through the village and parked at the corner of the lane close to the spot where, for the past three nights, a Ford transit van had been parked.

Pilgrim arrived at the pub in Naseby a little before two o'clock. He had spent the previous evening thinking hard about the events of the past week, trying to make some sense of them. He'd been unsuccessful. The Tuesday morning had turned out dry and sunny and he'd made good time driving westward across the Leicestershire hills. He parked the car, got himself a drink and settled in a corner of the large, square lounge. He opened the newspapers that he'd bought on his way. All three, the *Telegraph*, the *Guardian* and the *Mail*, prominently featured the tragic death of the

Governor of the Bank of England. All the stories said that the death was being investigated but that it appeared that the Governor had committed suicide. He had, said the *Telegraph*, been under considerable pressure of work.

Pilgrim looked up to see Susan glide through the double swing doors at the far end of the lounge. He waved a paper to attract her attention. Two large men, seated at a table a few yards away, were attracted by his signalling. They gave Susan a long appraising look. Pilgrim smiled to himself; it often happened that men gazed longingly at her and in wonder at him, trying to work out what such a good-looking, classy woman could see in such an ordinary, nondescript man. Susan was, as always, looking beautiful. She was wearing a pair of soft wine-coloured leather boots, a dark blue flared knee-length skirt and a white blouse underneath a sheepskin coat. Pilgrim noticed as she approached him that her face was lined with concern. She looked at him coolly for a moment and then kissed him affectionately, on the cheek. 'What are you having?' he asked.

'Vodka and tonic. Have you seen the papers?'

He nodded and walked to the bar. By the time he'd returned she'd read the articles. 'It's the same story in *The Times*,' she told him. 'What do you think, Jerry?'

'Christ, I don't know. Maybe he did it himself, though there must be an easier way. I've never seen anything like it.' He shuddered.

Susan was sympathetic, she leaned across the table and held his hand. Pilgrim noticed the two men watching him. 'Poor darling, it must have been ghastly for you.' Her big brown eyes were filled with concern. Then her expression changed abruptly. She let go of his hand. 'Now,' she said sternly. 'I want to hear the truth about what happened last week in London. I don't want to hear any more stories about you being mugged.'

Pilgrim pulled a face. Although the bruising round his eye had gone down, the flesh was still tender. 'It's not a story. I got beaten up. I think the blokes who did it meant to kill me.'

Susan stared at him, her face a mixture of disbelief and fright.

'I mean it,' he said earnestly. 'Look, I stuck to the plan pretty well. I did embellish it a bit, but that's all.'

'I thought so,' she said. 'Come on, tell me.'

He told her everything that had happened from the Sunday when he had first arrived in London. She listened quietly, her hands in her lap, her face expressionless. When he told her of his attempts to extort more money by doubling the price of his silence, she shook her head slowly, like an indulgent mother with a wayward child, though when he told her of his visit to Ann Hardcastle, her gaze changed to one of deep suspicion. When finally he recounted the tale of his kidnap and subsequent rescue by the three unknown men, her lovely face took on a puzzled look. He could see that she believed him. 'And that's it,' he finished. 'I saw you on Thursday and then came back to Gretton. I had a quiet weekend just thinking about things and I decided I would try it your way. So I arranged to see Dundonald.'

'You should have told me.'

'You weren't talking to me, remember.'

'You should have done it my way from the beginning,' she said reproachfully.

'Maybe. I might not have been beaten up if I had. But whatever, I think they would all have been dead just the same. I think that by getting into this, we've triggered something off.'

'What do you mean?'

'I don't know, but the odds against Brighton, Blackmore and Dundonald dying within a few days of each other must be hundreds to one.'

'Do you think someone is doing it, killing them, I mean?'

He shrugged. 'The papers don't think so. Nor do the police.'

'Do you want to tell the police?'

'What could we tell them? The only crime we know about

is our own. Blackmail is serious business. You'd be dragged into it, Susan. You've got too much to lose.'

'So, what do you think we should do?'

'Forget it. Get out while we're still in one piece. There's only Frimley-Kimpton and Addingham left, and I'm sure it was Addingham who put those heavies onto me. Let's leave it. It was a great idea, but it's turning out to be dangerous. Those two blokes meant to kill me.'

They were silent for a while.

'What about the other three?' she asked. 'Who were they?'

'I don't know. I'd never seen them before.'

'Maybe they were after you too.'

'Why should they be after me?'

'Perhaps they followed you from your hotel.'

'They couldn't have done. Nobody knew I was staying there. They would have . . .' His voice trailed off.

'What is it?'

'I told that woman.' His voice was aghast. 'Beverley Brandon-Burke. I told her where I was staying.'

'Why?' Susan asked suspiciously.

'In case she remembered anything else about Blackmore.'

'Maybe those three men were friends of hers. Maybe they were after you so they could shut you up.'

'Oh Christ,' said Pilgrim. 'Don't say that.' He wanted to crawl into a corner and hide. It seemed that the whole world was seeking to do him injury.

'Are you sure they didn't follow you, after you were attacked?' Susan asked earnestly.

'No,' said Pilgrim. 'I was really twitchy on the day I came to see you. I'm sure nobody was following me. I checked. And I'd have known if I was followed back to Gretton.'

One of the large men who had given Susan such an appraising look brushed against their table on his way to the lavatory. The barmaids were calling time.

'Another?' asked Pilgrim.

Susan shook her head. 'I'm hungry, let's find somewhere to eat.'

Pilgrim looked at his watch. 'We'll be lucky. It's two thirty.'

'A roadside diner, somewhere like that will do,' said Susan.

They stood up and walked towards the lounge bar doors. The big man emerged from the toilet behind them and stood by their table watching them go. They passed his friend who was talking on a payphone near the entrance to the bar. The car park was almost empty. 'Where's the car?' Pilgrim enquired.

Susan was sheepish. 'I had a slight accident.'

'Not another one?' Pilgrim laughed. 'You have a bump once a month.'

'Well, it wasn't my fault,' she said crossly. 'This idiot of a man stopped dead in the middle of Sloane Square. I couldn't avoid him.'

Pilgrim continued to smile.

'I don't think it's funny, Jerry. David was very angry and when I told Daddy he was most unsympathetic. In fact, he was quite cross.'

'I am not surprised. He must spend thousands on repair bills.'

'It's not my fault, there are so many stupid drivers. Anyway, Daddy wouldn't lend me another car. He refused point blank. The only thing he said he'd let me drive was that.' She pointed to a battered Volkswagen van, on the side of which was written 'S. NEWTON – FLOWERS AND PLANTS'. Pilgrim laughed loudly.

'What a come-down.'

'I think it's quite beastly of Daddy to expect me to drive that.'

'Where did he get it?' asked Pilgrim.

'He owns the company. You try driving it.'

'God, no wonder he can afford to keep you in repair

bills,' said Pilgrim, climbing into the front seat of the van. 'He owns half the country.' He adjusted his seating position as Susan got in beside him. It was a strange feeling to be so high and so far forward in a vehicle; the absence of a bonnet made him feel exposed, all that stood between him and everything else on the road was the flat front of the vehicle and the spare wheel fixed to it. He adjusted his interior mirror, only to find there were no windows in the rear doors. 'How are you expected to reverse this thing if you can't see what's behind you?'

'No idea.' said Susan. 'I hope I never have to find out.'

Pilgrim peered into the wing mirrors and cautiously edged the vehicle backwards. He was too preoccupied to notice that the two men in the pub had followed them out into the car park and were watching his cautious reversing with great interest. One of the men had written down the number of the van on a piece of paper. As Pilgrim drove slowly out of the car park, a big dark blue Ford which had been half hidden in a far corner cruised smoothly forward. It stopped long enough for the two men to clamber in before moving off again in the same direction as the van.

'What did he say?' asked the driver of the car.

'We've got to pick them up,' said the man who had made the telephone call.

The other man nodded. 'As soon as we find a quiet place, we'll take them.'

Susan and Pilgrim drove westwards for a few miles expecting at any moment to come across a roadside diner. They were disappointed and Pilgrim was becoming increasingly uncomfortable driving the unfamiliar van. He became irritable. 'This is hopeless,' he said. 'If we ever find anywhere to eat, I'll still have to drive this thing all the way back to get my car.'

Susan nodded. She felt nervous with Pilgrim driving the van. 'Let's go back. I can get something to eat when I get to

413

Warwickshire. Turn off on one of these side roads. You can turn round and drive back.'

Pilgrim glanced anxiously into his wing mirror. It was a large, oblong piece of glass which magnified the size and closeness of the vehicles behind. It made him nervous, for it made the car behind, which was at least a hundred feet away, seem to be almost on his tail. The car behind him was a dark blue Ford. He stared intently at its reflection in the mirror with only half an eye on the road ahead. Susan's question about being followed came back to him. He peered closer at the wing mirror. The man in the passenger seat looked like one of the men he had seen in the pub just a few minutes before. There was also something familiar about the driver.

'Careful,' Susan cried. 'You'll have us in the ditch.'

Pilgrim's attention jerked back to the road ahead. His heart gave a lurch and at the same time his brain locked onto where he'd seen the driver of the car. The last time he'd seen the face he'd been escaping into the blackness of the Wapping wasteland. The driver was the one who had been kicked in the groin.

'Oh dear God.'

'What's wrong?'

'I think we're being followed. The driver of that car behind. He's one of those three blokes. The ones who attacked the men who beat me up.'

'Are you sure?' asked Susan staring at the car through the nearside wing mirror.

Pilgrim slowed the van and the Ford closed up. 'Absolutely,' he confirmed. 'The fellow next to him looks like a man who was in the pub.'

'Maybe it isn't the same man. Maybe he just looks like him,' said Susan hopefully.

'I don't think so. That's the guy I saw. I'm sure of it.'

'Maybe it's just coincidence. Maybe they're not following us.'

'Why else would he stay back there?' Pilgrim snapped at her. 'He could go faster than us driving backwards.' Pilgrim was doing no more than forty-five, the traffic was light; the Ford could have overtaken easily.

'What do they want?'

'How the hell do I know?'

'This is all your fault, Jerry,' she cried angrily. 'You had to give that bloody tart your address. Christ, I don't want these people following me back to Mummy and Daddy's.'

'It's not you they're following. It's me.'

'You don't know that. Maybe it's me they want.'

'Why do you always have to be the centre of attraction?' Pilgrim said irritably. 'You always want all the attention. It's me they're following. Why the hell should they want to follow you?' He paused for breath. 'If only we had the Jag. We might have lost them.'

'Turn off the road, Jerry,' Susan commanded. 'They may not be following us. We could have got it all wrong. Look.' They were rapidly approaching an intersection on their left. 'Turn here.'

Pilgrim immediately swung the van to the left, scarcely braking. They were fortunate that there was nothing coming the other way, for they found themselves in a narrow country lane hardly wider than the van. It was bordered on both sides by high hawthorn hedges. They both watched through their wing mirrors, hoping against hope that the big Ford would pass the end of the lane without turning. Their hearts sank as they saw it turn menacingly into the lane behind them.

'I think they've spotted us,' said the man in the front passenger seat.

'I can't take them here,' said the driver. 'There's no room to pass.'

'We can't hang about in the middle of nowhere all day,' said the man at the back. 'We need to take them quickly. Push them into the hedge.'

'What?'

'It's lonely enough here. Make them stop anyway you can. Then we can take them.'

The driver accelerated. The car leapt forward and crashed into the rear of the Volkswagen. Susan screamed. The van shot forward and skidded towards the hedge. From the rear came a loud sound of crashing and smashing plant pots. Pilgrim fought to keep control of the wheel.

'Jesus, they're trying to put us off the road,' he shouted.

'Oh my God,' Susan sobbed. To brace herself against the Ford's next assault, she put both her feet up on the dashboard. Her dark blue skirt fell away from the tops of her boots and folded itself round her hips, exposing her slim thighs in their light brown tights. The Ford hit them again. The van rocketed forward with another great crashing of plant pots from the interior. Pilgrim struggled to control it but it skidded into the hedge on his left, branches scraping and gouging the paintwork mercilessly along its side. Somehow Pilgrim straightened up the vehicle. Susan screamed again. She could see the Ford coming at them fast. Pilgrim was also watching in his wing mirror. The van's acceleration was not sufficient to allow it to shoot forward at the right moment and lessen the impact. The car hit them squarely, punching the van violently forward. Pilgrim braked hard and then crashed his foot onto the accelerator to lessen the impact of the next shove.

'They're trying to kill us,' Susan screamed. 'They're trying to murder us.'

'They want us to get off the road,' said Pilgrim.

The Ford hit them again, but this time Pilgrim was more prepared and he was able to steer a straighter course. He had no idea how he could get them out of the situation. Sooner or later the other car would force them off the road. His arms and wrists ached from fighting to control the steering wheel, which was wet with the sweat from his palms.

He glanced across at Susan. He could scarcely believe

what he saw. Both of Susan's slim thighs were fluttering like the wings of a butterfly and while her left hand was pressed against the roof of the van to steady herself, her right hand was shoved deep inside her tights, scrabbling at her vagina. Her eyes were wide open and fixed straight ahead, though whether in terror or passion he couldn't tell.

'Jesus Christ, Susan.' He was riveted by the sight of her desperate masturbation and was gaping at her when the Ford hit them again. He lost control; the slippery steering wheel bounced out of his hands and the van plunged towards the right-hand hedge. They hit it at a shallow angle and raked along it for a few hundred feet. Pilgrim managed to grab the wheel and hang on. Somehow, after what seemed an age of crashing and tearing, he pulled the vehicle away from the hedge and branches, back into the centre of the narrow lane. The car had fallen some distance behind. The driver had slowed, evidently believing that the last assault had finally pushed them off the road. Pilgrim accelerated to put more distance between him and the men in the car. He looked at Susan. She had sunk deeper into the passenger seat, her feet pressed hard against the dashboard. Her thighs continued to quiver, only now both her hands were fluttering deep within her tights. She was staring straight ahead. Suddenly, she cried out. 'Oh my God, look.'

They were at the top of a steep hill, the road wound down between hedges into a valley and then ascended the hill on the other side. At the top of the opposite hill, just beginning its descent, was a large heavily loaded truck. They watched desperately as it began to hurtle down the opposite slope towards them. The Ford crashed into the van again and shot them forward. Pilgrim rammed the accelerator down and they were off, roaring down the hill. He glanced at the speedometer; they were touching seventy. The broken pots in the back banged noisily against the van's metal walls. On the opposite slope he could see, between gaps in the hedges, the lorry thundering towards them. Susan began to wail, a long, continuous squeal.

The downward bend of the steep lane was straightening out. He could see the bottom of the valley where the lane curved gently before beginning the ascent of the hill opposite. He could see the truck pursuing its downward course like a bat out of hell. He pressed the horn in a vain attempt to attract attention, but he knew it was useless, he could scarcely hear the horn himself above the racket of the engine. The Ford hit them again and they shot forward, though Pilgrim managed to keep the van straight. The hedges on either side of the lane were lower and he could see that they were within a few hundred yards of the speeding truck. Susan's squealing grew louder and more shrill.

As they sped downwards, Pilgrim saw that the surface of the road at the bottom of the hill was discoloured, the bend was covered in a layer of greasy mud. There were tracks in the mud leading to a wooden gate set back in the left-hand hedge, just on the bend of the curve. Instantly Pilgrim saw that the gate was their only possible line of escape. If he could reach it in time and smash the speeding van through it, they might, just might, escape being crushed as flat as a fly on a wall. He pressed as hard as he could on the accelerator. Susan's scream rose to a crescendo and despite his fearful need to concentrate he shot her a quick glance. She was at the point of climax, her thighs and arms as rigid as the unyielding rod of muscle straining to break free between his legs. Her face, too, was fixed rigid in a mask of fear and frenzy. He glanced in the wing mirror. The car was some distance back, gathering speed to hit them again. In front he could see the face of the lorry driver, showing fear and surprise; he had only just seen the Volkswagen.

Pilgrim aimed for the wooden gate and prayed. He felt the van's wheels slither on the mud and through a supreme effort of will he kept his right foot off the brake and hard on the accelerator. The truck was less than thirty yards away, the driver trying to check its insane impetus as it too slid into the mud. Pilgrim kept his foot down. He didn't know which he was going to hit first, the truck or the gate. He closed his eyes. His head was filled with the screaming of the engine, the crashing in the back of the van and Susan's never-ending shriek.

They made it to the gate with no more than a dozen feet to spare between them and the truck. There was a thunderous crash and they felt a brain-quivering jolt as the spare wheel at the front of the Volkswagen took the full impact of the rotten wood of the gate. Pilgrim opened his eyes to see shattered chunks of wood flying everywhere, crashing on the roof of the van and against the sides. The Volkswagen skidded sideways and then bounced violently up and down as it tore along the grassy ridges of the field. Luckily it stayed upright and within a few seconds it began to slow down. Pilgrim pressed the brake pedal gently and brought the vehicle to a halt. Immediately the engine cut out.

For the first time in what seemed a lifetime, he was not being banged about inside the van. Susan was at last silent. He leaned back in his seat and let his hands drop from the steering wheel. They were shaking violently and his sweaty palms were burning from the grip of the wheel. He closed his eyes, his ears ringing from the screaming of the engine. He looked across at Susan. She was huddled in the corner, great silent tears rolling down her cheeks, and she was shivering. Pilgrim leaned across and held her awkwardly. 'It's all right,' he said gently. 'We're all right.'

She nodded but said nothing. After a while he let her go. He looked in the wing mirror expecting to see the occupants of the mysterious car converging on the van, but there was no one. He could see in its reflection the wreckage of the gate lying at a drunken angle, but beyond that nothing. He watched and waited patiently for the men in the car to come for them, too shaken to resist. He was prepared to accept whatever their fate would be. But no one came and they just sat, Pilgrim staring dazedly into the wing mirror of the van.

At last he came out of his stupor. He turned the ignition key. The engine did not start. It took half a dozen attempts before it finally clattered into noisy, overstrained life. Cautiously, he put it into gear and turning it in a wide sweeping circle, they bounced slowly towards the wreckage of the gate. He stopped at the entrance of the field and got out, his shoes squelching in the mud. Slowly, he walked out into the narrow lane, then stopped as he saw the reason why the men had not come for them. Nothing and nobody was ever going to come out of what was left of the dark blue Ford. It had smashed head-on into the front of the truck. Its speed had taken it into and underneath the front of the truck; its engine had been shoved back into the passenger compartment and the roof at the front was crushed flat. It looked to Pilgrim, staring shakily at the awful wreck, as if the Ford was some metal bug which had been half swallowed by the monster lorry. The sight curled his testicles, they grew hard and small like walnuts. The combined speed of the impact must have been over one hundred and twenty miles per hour. The cab of the truck was empty and its windscreen had evaporated. Both the sun visors were pulled down. Pilgrim spied the crumpled body of the driver in the road, yards beyond the rear of the Ford. He walked unsteadily towards the body. It was lying very still. The head was turned at a strange angle and with a shock Pilgrim realised that the man's neck was broken. He heard a noise behind him and turned. It was Susan. She was staring numbly at the mass of twisted metal.

'Christ,' she said and started to move towards the wreck.

'Don't go near it, Susan,' Pilgrim cried out. There were wisps of smoke coming from the inside of the car. 'I think they're all dead.'

She looked at him blankly. 'Good,' she said quietly. 'I'm glad.' She turned back towards the van.

Pilgrim made to follow her but stopped to stare again at

the wreck. Then he turned and contemplated the hill down which just minutes before he and Susan had raced so terrifyingly. The sun, lying low on its brow, blinded him, as it must have blinded the truck driver. With his sun visors down, he would not have seen any vehicle high on the opposite slope until it had reached level ground. Pilgrim felt himself go cold as he realised just how close he and Susan had come to joining the men in the car.

Despite the smoke which was rising more thickly now from the wreck, he moved closer to what was left of the car, yanked open a rear door, and peered inside. There was little to be seen of the driver, parts of the hot, smoking engine had been shoved into his stomach and the roof had smashed down on his head. The front passenger had been thrown far back into the car; the top half of the body was lying at a drunken angle. Sharp metal had sliced through the dashboard, ripped away the man's testicles and partially amputated both his legs below the hip. In the time it had taken Pilgrim, sitting in the van, to regain his composure, the man had bled to death from a severed aortic artery. His blood was seeping over the door sills and onto the road. The man in the back seat was propped up in a corner of the car; his neck, too, had been broken. The interior of the car was a shambles. Yet the sight of the mangled bodies left Pilgrim unmoved. He was fast becoming used to scenes of violent and bloody death. He was about to turn away when an object, sticking out from underneath the jacket of the dead man on the rear seat, caught his eye. Cautiously, he reached into the car and tugged at it. It was a gun. Pilgrim examined it for a few seconds and then looked at the face of the dead man. He felt inside the dead man's jacket. He found what he was looking for – a wallet. He put it in his anorak pocket. He hurried round to the other side of the wreck and pulled at the door. It fell open. Wrinkling his nose at the scene inside, Pilgrim reached across and felt inside the jacket of the corpse with half-severed legs. It too had a gun nestling in a holster, just below the armpit; Pilgrim pulled it out and pocketed it before relieving the dead man of his wallet. He leaned forward to the front seat and felt around in the narrow space under the caved-in roof. His hand groped at the smashed torso of the driver until he detected the bulky lump of his holstered gun. He pulled it free. His hand was red and sticky from the blood. He wiped it as best as he could on the upholstery of the rear seat. He decided not to search for the man's wallet and backed out of the smashed and jumbled mess. He moved away from the car and slipped slightly on the wet surface. The blood seeping out of the wreck had made the layer of greasy mud even more slippery; some of the blood had dripped onto his shoes.

The interior of the car was filling up with smoke. He hurried back to Susan who was standing forlornly by the side of the Volkswagen. Her face was streaked with tears and she was shaking.

'Come on, Susan,' he said gently. 'Let's get out of here.'

He helped her into the passenger seat and then squelched through the mud to the back of the van to survey the damage. The rear bumper and the lights had been smashed completely. The doors had caved in at the bottom and had come adrift from the hinges at the top. Both sides of the van were pitted and scarred from scraping against the hedges and the spare wheel at the front had disappeared. The bodywork at the front was dented and chipped by pieces of flying wood.

Pilgrim climbed into the driver's seat and drove slowly out of the field. He edged the vehicle past the prone body of the truck driver and drove cautiously back the way they had come.

Compared to their nightmare descent, their return journey back up the hill was sedate but as they reached the top they heard a dull boom from the valley below. Pilgrim stopped the van and got out. The wrecked Ford had exploded into flames, a pall of black smoke was rising into the misty afternoon sky. Pilgrim quickly returned to the van and drove as fast as his nerve would allow back to the main road. Throughout the entire time they had been in the country lane, they had encountered no other vehicles.

Susan sat quietly, saying nothing though smoking constantly. They drove into a village and Pilgrim stopped outside a small supermarket. He left the van and disappeared inside. He returned a few seconds later carrying a bottle of whisky. They drove off. After a few minutes he spotted a secluded lay-by into which he drove the van.

He handed Susan the bottle. 'Drink,' he said. She put the bottle to her lips and tipped back her head, taking a long pull at the amber liquid. Pilgrim did likewise and then passed the bottle back to her. She took another gulp and then fished two cigarettes from her bag. She lit them both and handed one to Pilgrim who took it without a word.

'What do we do now?' she asked.

Pilgrim felt surprisingly calm. His stomach was protesting noisily at the whisky but he'd stopped shaking and his brain was clear. 'You've got to get home before it's dark,' he said. 'The rear lights are smashed. You don't want to be stopped by the police. They might think this heap of junk had something to do with the smash.'

'It almost did,' said Susan quietly. She turned to face him. 'You were marvellous. God knows how you got us out of it.'

'Luck, I suppose. It wasn't easy. Especially with you wailing like a fucking banshee all the way down the hill.'

'My God, Jerry.' Her voice grew intense. 'I was convinced we were going to die. I just kept coming, time after time, all the way down that hill. I couldn't stop it.'

'That's a great help in a crisis,' he observed dryly. He felt the tube of muscle between his legs grow long and solid again. 'I could hardly take my eyes off you. God, you were sexy.'

423

'I still am.' She was staring straight at him. They stretched across the engine compartment and kissed fiercely. Susan took his hand and pulled it under her skirt. Her tights had been ripped by her frantic hands; his fingertips found the hot, soaking lips of her vagina. The van was filled with the smell of her.

'Where?' he said urgently.

'Anywhere.' Her eyes were glazed.

The hardboard partition behind them was cracked and bent. He pushed it violently and it fell back into the rear of the van. The interior was littered with bulbs and soil and bits of broken terracotta pots. Pilgrim shrugged off his anorak. They scrambled, panting, into the back of the van. In one corner was a jumbled pile of sacks. Bending almost double they kicked a space free of dirt and broken pottery and pulled the sacks into the centre of the floor. Susan fell back on them and hitched her skirt up round her thighs. Pilgrim pulled at her tights. 'Off,' he grunted. 'Get them off.'

'No,' she moaned. 'No time, go through.' She pulled desperately at the seam of her ripped tights as Pilgrim helped her. They yanked at the nylon until they'd pulled a large gaping hole in her crotch. They ripped away the soggy white cotton of her panties beneath.

'Come on,' she shouted desperately. 'Come on. Jesus, do it.'

He unzipped his flies and she pulled at him painfully. He got his trousers halfway down. She lay back, her legs bent up in the air, and he shoved the rigid stick of muscle into her, desperately, blindly, cruelly. He felt the soft leather of her boots wrap tightly round his hips. 'Do it,' she commanded. 'Fuck me. Fuck me.' Her voice was rasping. She continued in a low monotone, an incantation of obscenities. Pilgrim thrust as hard as he could into her. There was no feeling in him for her. There was no feeling in him for himself, only a desperate urge to push and shove, push and shove, push and shove, until the world exploded. He felt himself coming, like a long low howl of wind, growing in strength and intensity with every second, roaring in behind him until he became a whirling tornado of energy and passion and lust which exploded from his penis in a great hot geyser of semen. As he came, so too did Susan. She screamed obscenities and blasphemies as she gyrated her hips like a whirling dervish, pumping and sucking the juice out of him. The leather of her boots, rubbing like pistons along his hips, was scoring and burning his flesh. They writhed and jerked together until the awful passion ebbed, and then held each other tightly. They were like fearful, quaking children, locked together for comfort, quelling the spectre of an evil dream. They had mounted and ridden the beast with two backs, whipping, thundering, roaring, until their fear, mixed with their passion, had exploded into infinity.

They lay in the back of the van for some minutes, quietly holding on to each other. Finally, Pilgrim withdrew his now diminished penis. Susan looked a dishevelled wreck, her hair was tousled and her face streaked with tears, her clothes crumpled and smudged with soil. Pilgrim got to his knees and helped her brush her skirt. She sat up and clung to him tightly. 'That was the best orgasm of my life,' she said softly.

They scrambled back into the front of the van. Pilgrim leaned over to pick up his anorak. Its weight surprised him and he remembered the guns. He took one out of the pocket. 'They were carrying these.'

Susan's eyes opened wide in surprise. She reached across to take it from him.

'Careful,' he said.

'It's all right,' she assured him as she lifted the gun from his hand. 'The safety catch is on.'

Deftly she extracted a full magazine from the butt of the gun before sliding the jacket of the barrel backwards and

425

ejecting a small gleaming bullet onto the floor of the van. 'This is a nine millimetre automatic,' she said. 'You don't carry one of these unless you mean business.'

Pilgrim was surprised. 'How the hell do you know about guns?'

'One of the men I lived with in America taught me a lot about them.'

'All those guys following us had one,' he said. He dug into the pockets of the anorak and pulled out the other two automatics. Susan examined them.

'They have consecutive serial numbers. Look.' She showed him the numbers stamped on the undersides of each weapon. 'I don't understand it. Why were they after us? Who are they?'

Pilgrim took the two wallets from his pocket. 'I took these off their bodies.'

They each examined a wallet. Both of them contained over a hundred pounds. Susan took the money in the wallet she was examining and gave it to Pilgrim. 'Here. You had better have this.'

There was little else in the wallets. One of the man was called Eric O'Kelly, the other one Bob Mair. Eric had been married; there were a few letters, photographs and credit cards, and not much else. Except that they both had business cards which showed that they were representatives of an export trading company called Foster Rowles. The company had offices in South London. 'Where's SW8?' asked Susan.

'I think it's Lambeth or somewhere round there,' replied Pilgrim.

'Foster Rowles, I've never heard of them.' She dropped the wallet onto her lap. 'It's all beyond me,' she said wearily.

'You look tired,' said Pilgrim. The lines which he had seen on her face in the pub were now more deeply etched. 'Come on, we'd better get going.'

They put everything back into the wallets and Susan returned the gun and wallet she was holding to Pilgrim, who pocketed them along with the snub-nosed bullet which had dropped to the floor. They each took a gulp from the whisky bottle and lit a cigarette before they set off.

The van had developed a concerto of alarming rattles and the engine sounded strained. Pilgrim kept to a steady thirty and hoped that it wouldn't blow up. 'How are you going to explain this wreck when you get home?' he asked.

Susan was slumped in the corner of the cab, her head back, her eyes closed. She opened them slowly.

'I don't know.' Her voice was lifeless. 'I'll tell my parents I was forced off the road by some maniac.'

'Do you think they'll believe it?'

'It doesn't matter,' she sighed. 'It was an old van anyway. They won't be bothered much.'

'They'll be bothered about you,' said Pilgrim. 'You look a wreck.'

'Thanks.'

'You'll have to clean up a bit,' he continued. 'You look like you've been pulled through a hedge backwards.'

They both laughed, on the edge of hysteria.

'Thanks for getting us out of it, Jerry,' Susan said finally. Her voice was low and warm. 'I don't know how you did it. You were great.'

'Maybe if I'd stuck to the plan I wouldn't have got us into this mess in the first place.'

They drove in silence. The road took them over the motorway; from both directions continuous ribbons of steel converged and thundered beneath the bridge. They drove south-west.

Suddenly Pilgrim asked, 'Do you have a safety deposit box?'

Susan was startled. 'No.'

'Could you get one? I mean without David or anyone else knowing?'

'Of course.'

'Then get one. I want you to write down everything that has happened to us since we got into all this, including everything I told you happened in London. Then I want you to put what you've written into a box along with the original papers you found at your uncle's as well as a wallet and one of the guns. Do it soon while you can still remember it.'

Susan's face was puzzled.

'Put it all in the deposit box and then either give the key to someone you trust absolutely, or better still, to a solicitor with instructions to open it if anything should happen.'

'What do you mean, if anything should happen?'

'To you. If you disappear or something like that.' He looked across the cab at her and their eyes met. 'It's an insurance policy. Just in case.'

'In case of what?'

'I don't know, but you must do it, Susan, and quickly. Get everything incriminating out of your house.'

'All right' she said. 'I'll do it as soon as I get back to London.'

'When will that be?'

'In a couple of days.'

They were silent for a few more miles. 'What are you going to do about your car?' asked Susan. 'How are you going to get back?'

'I'll drop you and take a train to Market Harborough.'

'Supposing someone is watching your car?'

'It's a risk I'll have to take. I need the car.'

He drove into the car park of Warwick railway station. It was nearly five o'clock. 'You should just make it before it gets really dark,' he said. 'Here take these.' He peered around to make sure no one was watching, then took a wallet and two of the automatics out of his pocket. 'Get rid of one of them, put the other in the safety deposit,' he instructed. He passed them quickly to Susan who jammed them into a pocket of her sheepskin coat. She nodded. He leaned across and kissed her tenderly on the lips. 'Whatever you do,' he said as he made ready to get out, 'don't call me. Don't come near the cottage.'

'How will I see you?'

'I'll contact you.' He opened the van door and then pulled it shut. 'One more thing.' He took the remaining automatic from his pocket. 'Do you know how to take one of these things apart?'

Susan looked surprised. 'Why?'

'Do you know?' he insisted.

'Yes, I think so.'

In the car park of Warwick railway station, Susan showed Pilgrim how a nine millimetre automatic could be broken down into small parts. He insisted that she showed him twice. 'OK,' he said finally. 'I think I've got it.'

'Why do you want to know?'

'I'll tell you in a few days.' He kissed her again, lightly. 'Take it easy going home. I hope your parents aren't too angry.' He leaned across the cab and retrieved the bottle of whisky. 'Do you want this?'

She shook her head. He put it into the pocket of his anorak as Susan climbed out of the cab and walked round the front of the van. He got out.

'You're a mess too, Jerry,' she said. 'You look like a tramp, especially with that bottle sticking out of your pocket.'

He smiled. 'Never mind. I'm alive.'

Chapter Seven

Pilgrim knew that he looked dishevelled but he was two hundred pounds better off than he had been a few hours before and he had very definite plans about what he was going to do for the next few days. He found a chemist and purchased some shaving gear and a toothbrush. He looked for an overnight case but the shops were expensive so he made do with a carrier bag into which he put the toilet articles and the bottle of whisky. The journey to Market Harborough was long and tedious. He caught a succession of slow trains; first to Coventry and then Birmingham, from where he rattled slowly across country to Leicester. There he changed finally to a train for Market Harborough. It was after nine when he arrived. It cost him nine pounds and a lot of persuasion to get the taxi driver to drive him the seven miles to his car.

It was dark and the car park was crowded. He couldn't tell if there was a silent watcher hidden in one of the darkened cars. He drove out of the car park and stopped a couple of hundred yards along the road. No one followed him out. He started off again. The road was quiet; what few vehicles were going in his direction swept past his slowly moving car. The further he drove, the more he became convinced that he wasn't being followed. He reached the motorway and turned south towards London. He stayed mainly on the inside lane, keeping a sharp lookout for any set of headlights which stayed for too long behind him, but in the constantly shifting pattern of lights in his mirror, it wasn't easy to check on any one vehicle, though he remained fairly sure that no one was on his tail.

It took over an hour to get to London. He stopped at a call box in Finchley and phoned to book a room.

By the time he had parked his car outside the hotel in Ebury Street it was long past eleven. He liked the hotel. It was small and anonymous and held memories of Susan. The woman at the reception desk looked at him curiously. He was dirty and unkempt and his only luggage was a carrier bag. However, he paid for two nights in cash and gave her a lovely smile so she seemed happy enough. He asked for a plate of sandwiches and a pot of coffee to be brought to his room. He had a bath and cleaned up as best he could and then he lay on the big double bed in the warm room with a glass in his hand and his whisky bottle by his side, thinking about his plans for the next forty-eight hours; about how he could make the most of the money he had left, about the terror of the day, and about the threatening and dangerous mystery into which he and Susan had trespassed.

The effort of trying to piece together the bits of the jigsaw was too much. He grew tired and crawled beneath the sheets. During the past twelve hours he'd been constantly on the move. His body ached. He'd been through yet another terrifying experience, the third in less than a week and he was beginning to learn that the dregs of terror made him weary to his bones.

By nine o'clock the following morning he was walking to Victoria, having slept deeply. He'd been awake for over two hours and had been busy. He'd started to write an account of everything that had happened to him since Susan had first shown him the papers. Just after eight thirty, he asked the hotel switchboard to get him a number in Amsterdam; he was on the line for no more than three minutes but it was sufficient time for him to make the necessary arrangements.

432

He left the hotel and retrieved his passport from the glove compartment of his car.

He bought a cheap overnight case from a shop near the station. From there he walked down Victoria Street to the Army and Navy Stores. He needed some new clothes; the ones he was wearing were desperately in need of cleaning and, more importantly, he wanted something to put in the overnight bag. He bought a plain navy blue suit, two shirts and a tie. They were expensive. He winced when he handed over the money but his plans required him to look reasonably well-dressed. He kept his new clothes on beneath his anorak and went in search of a dry cleaners who would promise to have his tweed jacket, slacks and polo neck jumper cleaned and ready by the evening. Afterwards, he wandered around until he found a travel agent, where he negotiated the cheapest flight possible to Amsterdam for the following day. He was satisfied. It had been a successful though expensive hour's work.

He returned to his hotel and deposited his new travel case in his room. While he was there, he checked in the telephone directory to see if Foster Rowles was listed. It wasn't. He borrowed a street map of London from reception. The address on the card from the wallet was in a short street just behind Vauxhall station. Conscious of his dwindling cash, he decided to walk; it took him less than half an hour.

The street was narrow and derelict; some of the properties in it were late-Victorian houses which had been converted to shops and were now empty and boarded up. The rest of the street was made up of abandoned warehouses. Slowly he strolled along the pavement, feeling the now familiar prickling running up his spine. The street was deserted. Halfway down its short length was a large warehouse in no better repair than the surrounding properties. Next to its narrow entrance door was a weatherbeaten sign: 'Foster Rowles Trading Co.' Pilgrim casually sauntered past and crossed the road. He turned to look at the windows on

the warehouse's upper floors. They hadn't been cleaned in
years, and there appeared to be no sign of life behind them.
Whatever Foster Rowles was, it wasn't a booming business.
He continued slowly to the end of the street. He felt a
strange and uncanny sensation carrying in his anorak
pocket a gun and wallet belonging to a man who must have
once known this street and who was now no more. At its far
end, the street formed a junction with Kennington Lane
and some other roads. At the junction was a group of
brightly coloured yellow lorries; cable layers were digging
the road. The racket from the road drills was horrendous.
On the corner was a small tobacconist next to a Greek
restaurant. The persuasive smell of the spicy food made
Pilgrim feel hungry. He wandered into the tobacconist and
took his time choosing a bar of chocolate. Afterwards, he
stood at the corner, eating his chocolate and watching the
workmen, for as long as he could tolerate the noise. Then,
having killed enough time, he wandered slowly back along
the street on its opposite side. The premises of Foster
Rowles remained deserted. He was tempted to stay around
for a while and watch the front door but was frightened that
someone behind the dirt-encrusted windows was watching.
He walked back to the arches beneath Vauxhall station and
found a telephone kiosk. He called directory enquiries who
told him they had no record of any company of that name
having a telephone number. He took the wallet from his
pocket and dialled the number on the card.

A man's voice answered. 'Foster Rowles.'

'Is that Fred?' asked Pilgrim, adopting a broad Cockney
accent.

There was silence from the other end.

'Is that Fred?'

'No,' said the voice.

'Well, who is it then?' There was another silence and then
the line went dead.

Pilgrim scurried away from the phone box. There had

been something ominous about the long silence at the other end of the phone. He wanted to get away. The area had become alien, it seemed like enemy territory. He leapt aboard a passing bus heading towards the bridge.

Back in Victoria, Pilgrim bought some black tape and a large brown envelope and went looking for his next purchase. It took him some time. He scoured the ironmongers and do-it-yourself shops until he found what he wanted; a tool box filled with spanners and socket wrenches, which would fit into his suitcase. Back in his hotel room he used a screwdriver to disassemble the gun and then positioned its various parts in empty receptacles in the box. The barrel and the stock looked in place; although they were of a different colour metal, they could at a swift glance be taken for tools. The trigger mechanism was too obvious. He masked it with black tape and did the same to the ammunition clip. The gun's handle, by itself, looked innocuous.

He surveyed the tool box. It wouldn't have fooled an experienced Customs official, but Pilgrim fervently hoped that it wouldn't have to. If the case had to pass through an x-ray machine somewhere on its journey, he was fairly sure that the separate parts of the gun would look like tools in a tool kit. He sat down at the small desk in the bedroom and finished writing his account of the last few days.

Just after five, he walked to the dry cleaners in Victoria Street and collected his clothes. On his way back he drove his car out of the car park in which he had put it that morning and parked it outside the hotel, ready for an early start.

By seven o'clock the following morning he was heading west along the M4. He had packed his suitcase carefully, laying his spare clothes over the tool box and then putting on top of them the envelope filled with the papers. He had inspected himself in the mirror just before leaving and had decided that he looked presentable enough in his new suit and shirt. He appeared at least as well-dressed as the dark-suited businessmen who crowded around the check-in desks at Terminal One.

He checked his baggage in at the desk. 'Do you only have one piece, Mr Pilgrim?' the girl asked.

'No,' he smiled at her broadly. 'I have some hand luggage too, my wife is looking after it.' He waved vaguely in the direction behind him. The girl nodded and ticketed his case through. He bought copies of *The Times* and the *Economist* in the hope they would make him appear more respectable and read them on the uneventful flight to Amsterdam. It was as he was being carried effortlessly along the mechanised walkways of the long corridors of Schipol that he began to panic. He was smuggling a lethal weapon into a foreign country. If he was stopped at Customs and searched, it would be discovered. He began to feel sick as he thought how crude had been his attempt to disguise the weapon.

He and his fellow passengers were quickly shunted through passport control and emerged into the baggage reclaim area. Most of them, carrying only hand baggage, bustled straight through Customs and only a few were left, like Pilgrim, in the empty arrivals hall, staring at the immobile baggage carousels. The palms of Pilgrim's hands grew sweaty as the weaknesses in his plan loomed large. He would have to walk through Customs with a small bag which he could easily have taken with him on board the aircraft. Any quick-witted Customs official would wonder why he had not taken it with him through the security checks. With a clank which startled him, the carousels began to move and upon its signal board was flashed the number of his flight. As he stood with the small knot of passengers waiting for their baggage, Pilgrim felt that all eyes were on him. He was marooned in no-man's land; he couldn't go back and if he went on through Customs he was sure he would be stopped.

An Air France flight number was flashed up on the signal

board. Suddenly, the arrivals hall was invaded by a large and voluble crowd of Frenchmen, just off the flight from Paris. Many of them were, like Pilgrim, dressed in suits and carrying small cases; almost all of them were hurrying towards the green Customs channel. It was his chance. Pilgrim grabbed his case and joined the hurrying throng.

'Pardon, monsieur,' he said to one of them. The man, who was clearly in a hurry, continued walking towards Customs as he inclined his head towards Pilgrim who asked him, in his execrable French, if there was a bus to the city. It was evident that the Frenchman had not understood. A concerned look came over his face as he replied in rapid French. As they hurried with the other passengers through the Customs hall, Pilgrim glanced quickly at the Dutch Customs officials who were idly surveying the group. Pilgrim and the Frenchman had just a few yards further to go before they were through. Pilgrim grinned broadly as the Frenchman continued to talk rapidly at him. His smile perplexed the man, who frowned in bewilderment. They walked the last few steps out of the Customs hall.

'Merci, monsieur,' Pilgrim said to the man and hurried away, towards the blue KLM bus which would take him to the city. The Frenchman raised his eyebrows and shrugged his shoulders as he watched the mad Englishman go. He was convinced that the man had told him that his daughter had been run over by a bus that morning, yet when he had offered his condolences the man had grinned.

The bus took Pilgrim into the centre of Amsterdam. He changed a few pounds into guilders at a bank before walking to an address in the Kaiserstrat where he spent all morning in the company of his old acquaintance the Dutch lawyer Sjef de Bok. Jerry had first got to know Sjef when Byers-Pilgrim was attempting its abortive expansion into Europe, and had appointed De Bok the company's European lawyer. Recently divorced, he had been pleased to spend his evenings touring the bars and fleshpots with

Jerry, on Pilgrim's numerous visits to the city. They had become friends and although Pilgrim had seen little of him since the demise of Byers-Pilgrim, he had maintained contact. De Bok had been surprised to hear from him, but intrigued by the cryptic phone call.

The two men sat at a table drinking dark coffee and mineral water close to the first-floor windows of Sjef's offices overlooking the placid canal. Pilgrim took more than two hours to tell Sjef his story. After he had finished he handed the Dutch lawyer the sealed envelope which contained his account of everything that had happened, with copies of all Woodberry's papers and the wallet which he had taken from the dead man. Then to Sjef's surprise he opened the case, took out the tool box and reassembled the automatic. He passed the unloaded gun and its ammunition clip to the startled lawyer who put them, along with the bulky envelope, into his safe. Later the two men left the offices, emerging into the late October sunshine. They took Sjef's car and drove across the city to a restaurant close to the Van Gogh Museum where Sjef treated his visitor to lunch. They didn't leave until the middle of the afternoon when they drove back into the centre of the city. Sjef dropped Pilgrim at the KLM bus terminal and they shook hands. Pilgrim confirmed the arrangements he had made with the lawyer and promised that a retainer would be sent from England within the next few days. De Bok drove away and Pilgrim caught the bus to Schipol.

The following morning he made two phone calls. The first was to Susan. 'Can you talk?' he asked when she picked up the phone.

Her voice was startled. 'Not really. Where are you?'

'I'm round the corner,' he replied. 'At the hotel in Ebury Street.'

'What are you doing there?'

'It's somewhere to stay. It's safe and it's close to you. Can I see you?'

'No.'

'Only for a minute,' he pleaded.

She was quiet for a moment. 'Jerry, I can't. My parents are here. They've made a fuss about the van and what happened to me. Daddy wanted to get the police over to see me. I don't think he believes my story entirely, he keeps giving me funny looks. And when David came up in the Rolls to get me on Wednesday he didn't seem at all concerned about me, he just looked at the van and said it was a typical example of my driving.'

'Did you do what I said?' asked Pilgrim. 'About the deposit box?'

'Yes. Everything's in a safe deposit box in a bank.'

'What about the key?'

'I've posted it to my old English mistress. She's retired now and lives in Weybourne in Norfolk. I've written her a note saying I'll go up and see her soon and explain. She probably thinks I'm having an affair.'

'Good,' said Pilgrim. 'When can I see you?'

'I don't know. Look, I have to go now. Call me,' she pondered, 'Sunday morning. I should be able to slip out for a few minutes then. I must go.'

Her phone went down. Pilgrim stared at the handset for a few seconds then took a deep breath and cleared the line. He dialled a number in Surrey. A woman answered.

'This is Richard Thornbury,' said Pilgrim in his public school voice. 'I am phoning to confirm my appointment with Jeffrey Frimley-Kimpton. Has he returned safely from his trip abroad?'

'Yes, of course,' said the voice, clipped and precise. 'You're in the diary to see him at midday. He has said specifically that he wishes to see you alone. I would be grateful if you could be on time, he has a very busy morning.'

'Certainly,' said Pilgrim. 'Goodbye.'

He remained standing by the phone, staring at the

wallpaper. A few minutes later he checked out of the hotel, retrieved his car from the car park and headed through Belgravia and onto the Brompton Road. Instead of turning south for the M30 at the Hogarth roundabout, he continued driving towards the M4, taking the same route that he had taken the previous day. He drove past the airport which was busy with the mid-morning rush of transcontinental flights. He watched as every few seconds another plane climbed majestically into the sky, heading nose up in the same westerly direction as he was driving.

He turned south off the M4 at Windsor and drove leisurely through the Great Park to Ascot, from where he took the road to Bagshot, driving between the thick woods of conifers which bordered both sides of the road. He continued through Bagshot and on to the windswept heath. He knew he was close; Frimley-Kimpton lived somewhere off Chobham Ridges. He found a road signposted Camberley and soon came across the Chobham Ridges road. Minutes later he'd found Frimley-Kimpton's country retreat, a large Edwardian house set well back off the road and surrounded by conifers and rhododendron bushes.

He decided not to risk taking his car into the grounds; he found a parking spot about a quarter of a mile away from the entrance and walked back towards the house. He left his anorak in the car. He was wearing a blue shirt and a navy knitted tie, dark slacks and his tweed jacket, in the pocket of which nestled the envelope of papers he had originally intended giving to Ashley Brighton, eleven days previously. He reached the gates of the house and stopped to survey the grounds. Trees and clumps of bushes were interspersed between well-kept lawns. There was plenty of cover for anyone who meant him harm. He wrinkled his nose, trying like a dog to sniff the air for danger. It all looked innocent enough, the bushes moved gently in the slight breeze and the bright sun dappled the lawns. Pilgrim slowly walked down the drive and rang the front doorbell as icy fingers played with the hairs at the back of his neck. A middle-aged woman wearing a fawn twin-set opened the door.

'Richard Thornbury,' he announced. 'I'm here to see Jeffrey.'

'Ah yes,' said the woman. 'I spoke to you on the phone.' She surveyed him with a kind of arrogant curiosity. He was clearly not what she had expected. 'Come in.'

She led him down a wide hallway to a large room at the rear of the house which was Frimley-Kimpton's study. Its walls were lined with books and a large antique table in the centre was cluttered with papers and two telephones. The room was filled with sunlight yet cold; the French windows were standing wide open. The woman momentarily raised her eyebrows in surprise, before her face took on a look of resignation. 'I think my husband may have taken his earlier visitor out into the garden,' she said.

She left Pilgrim standing in the middle of the room. He glanced cautiously at the papers on the desk but found nothing of interest. He examined the books on the shelves. After about five minutes Frimley-Kimpton's wife returned. 'He hasn't come back then?'

Pilgrim shook his head.

'Very well. Then I suggest you go and find him in the garden.'

Pilgrim felt uneasy at the suggestion. The discomfort showed on his face.

'He won't mind. After all, you are an old friend,' she said. 'And he did say that he was anxious to see you. He's five minutes late already and he's got a very busy schedule. I think you ought to go and find him.'

They stepped out onto the patio together. 'There's a gate in the garden wall about a hundred yards down on the right,' she announced. 'It leads out onto the lane. My husband may be showing his visitor out through there. Beyond the rhododendrons.' She pointed to a massed bank of bushes into which the flagstoned garden path disappeared. She turned and retreated into the house.

Pilgrim descended the few steps of the patio and followed the path. The garden was enormous. Thirty yards or so to his right was the high wall which he guessed bordered the lane. It was covered with the flaming red leaves of Virginia creeper. Through the first bank of bushes, he came to an open space of well-manicured lawns planted with willow trees. The path led between more bushes, high and dark; they shut out the sun, making that part of the garden seem like a cold sombre valley. Further on, in a grassy area surrounded by the dark whispering leaves of the massed bushes, he came across a small, wooden gardening shed. The door was open, swinging backwards and forwards in the slight breeze. Pilgrim wondered whether Frimley-Kimpton was inside.

He moved close to the door and cleared his throat. There was no sound from within. Carefully he stepped over the threshold into the gloom. The dark interior smelled of earth and decaying vegetation. He took another step and stumbled over something on the floor. His heart leapt but it was merely a rake left lying on the wooden boards. Pilgrim noticed, before he turned to leave, that various gardening tools had been scattered about the floor. Whoever did the gardening, he thought, clearly kept the grounds in much neater order than they kept the gardening shed.

He re-emerged into the light and continued along the path. His anxiety was beginning to grow, the familiar cold fingers playing the scales along his backbone. He wished he could find Frimley-Kimpton and get on with what he had come to do. He began to feel as though he'd been wandering in the garden for ages.

A few yards further on, the path divided; to the right it wound its way towards the wall bordering the lane; to the left it disappeared behind another thick clump of bushes. He stopped, undecided which way to go. Then slowly, but with an absolute certainty, there came over him the sensation that someone was silently watching him. His scalp tightened and the skin on the back of his neck started to crawl. He turned suddenly, but there was no one, merely the menacing garden, filled with chilly sunlight. He took a deep breath and shook his head, vigorously trying to dispel his unease. He started along the right-hand path but had scarcely moved more than a dozen feet when he heard from his left a scuffling in the undergrowth. He stopped and stared but could see nothing. Then, as he was looking for he knew not what, he heard a ghastly noise. It was a dry croaking gargle, the sound of a parched, arid wind escaping an empty hollow tube. It didn't sound as if it could have been made by anything human or animal. It had come from the clump of bushes in which he'd heard the scuffling. Pilgrim moved across the grass. He edged his way round a clump of rhododendrons. There was nothing. The small area of grass between the encircling bushes was empty.

He stopped and tried to get a grip on his quivering nerves. It was, he told himself, a sunny day in a suburban garden. He was searching for the ageing owner of that garden, who had come out into the sunshine. He had no reason to feel uneasy. It was daylight in Surrey, not darkness in the Inner Temple. He took a deep breath then strode purposefully across the lawn and between the two high dark bushes.

Just beyond the bushes, beneath the leaves of a variegated laurel, was the portly figure of a man lying face up to the sky. A gardening fork was embedded all the way up to its hilt in his soft and ample belly, and he was dead, stuck like a pig. The man was Jeffrey Frimley-Kimpton. His open-necked blue shirt had about half a dozen holes in it, from which oozed dark blood. The fork's long, wooden handle swayed slightly as the nerves within the punctured gut twitched and jumped.

Pilgrim shivered in the chilly air. Yet he was barely shocked; the blood and violence of the past few days had begun to desensitise him. He noticed the thick trickle of blood escaping from the body's slack mouth, the sightless eyes gazing at the sky; the scuffed soil where Frimley-Kimpton had kicked his last pathetic steps as his life ebbed away; the white flabby hands, tightly clutching the soil in an effort to hang on to the world. Pilgrim viewed it all with dispassion, almost with relief. It was all over. Yet again, someone else had got there first. He had arrived only in time to hear the rattle of death escape the black, bloody rictus of the late Jeffrey Frimley-Kimpton. Pilgrim's last chance, his final prospect, was lying like a tossed heap of horse manure, skewered by a garden fork, abandoned to rot in a corner of a Surrey garden.

He pulled himself out of his trance; he had to get away, make for the gate that was somewhere in the wall bordering the lane, and get back to the car as quickly as possible.

He turned and found himself staring down the barrel of a gun, the end of which was being held as steady as a concrete block three inches from a spot between his eyes. He jerked his head back, blinking rapidly, and the gun's barrel smoothly moved closer to his forehead. He squeaked, a high-pitched sound of emasculated terror. He waited for the sudden, dreadful pain and the explosion of bright lights which would mean the end of his world. Nothing happened. He felt as if his face was being shoved into the back of his head. His eyes were crossed, focusing on the barrel of the evil-looking weapon and the hand that held it. Long, strong, tanned fingers ending in well-kept, clear-polished nails. A woman's hand. A hand he knew well. Susan's hand. The barrel of the gun moved back slightly from his forehead and Susan's face came into focus. 'What the hell are you doing here?'

He was speechless. His brain had lost the power to form words. He stared at her aghast, the barrel of a familiar nine millimetre automatic inches from his eyes. He noticed, almost incidentally, that she was looking as beautiful as always. The sun was glinting on her slightly tousled hair and she was wearing a cream sweater and a pale blue floral skirt.

It was then that he knew that she was the one who had just ruptured Jeffrey Frimley-Kimpton's vital organs with three long tongs of stainless steel; that she had blown the Governor of the Bank of England's brains all over his Laura Ashley wallpaper, and that now she was about to repeat the performances, by blowing Pilgrim's brains all over the Surrey/Hampshire border. For speckling her skirt and stockings and her pretty cream shoes were drops of blood.

'Why?' he croaked at last.

She remained holding the gun rigidly close to his forehead. Beyond it her deep brown eyes were hard, shining like polished stones. Her face was grim. She was about to speak when from the direction of the house came the sound of a telephone ringing. They both listened intently. The ringing stopped and a few seconds later they heard Frimley-Kimpton's wife calling her husband's name. Susan's eyes widened momentarily in fear, then she let the hand holding the gun fall to her side and with the other grabbed Pilgrim by his lapel.

'Come on,' she ordered, pulling him towards the path which led to the garden wall. Pilgrim shot one last glance at the rounded heap of Frimley-Kimpton's spiked carcass before stumbling between the rhododendrons to a wooden door set within the high garden wall. There was a key in the lock.

'Open it.'

Pilgrim obeyed. He was aware that, although Susan was no longer pointing the gun at him, she continued to carry it, tightly gripped, at her side.

They emerged into a narrow gravelled road.

'Close it.'

Pilgrim turned from shutting the door behind them to see Susan carefully depositing the gun into a bulky cream-coloured leather bag hanging from her shoulder. He noticed ominously that she kept a grip on the strap close to the bag's top.

'This way.' She jerked her head in the direction they were to take and grabbing Pilgrim's arm hurried him along the deserted lane. Their feet scrunched noisily on the loose stones. After about two hundred yards they turned off the lane into a small road in which, parked beneath some trees, was an old, grey Peugeot 304. Susan motioned him to the driver's seat. 'You drive,' she said.

'Where to?'

'Just drive. I'll tell you where,' she snapped. Her voice was filled with anxious authority. Pilgrim got into the car, Susan beside him. The leather shoulder bag lay casually on her lap, her hands resting lightly on it. She directed him to turn right out of the road and then, a few hundred yards further, to turn right again. Soon he found himself driving back along the Chobham Ridges, from where she directed him onto the motorway going north. They were heading for London.

Chapter Eight

He drove badly. The car was strange, its acceleration was sluggish and the brakes soft and spongy. He couldn't adjust his driving position and the rear-view mirror was awkwardly placed; not that it mattered a lot, Susan's attention was almost wholly taken up with checking behind to see what vehicles were following them. She'd ordered him to keep below forty which meant that everything else on the motorway roared past them. Susan watched them all with suspicion.

Pilgrim tried to talk. 'It was you, wasn't it? I mean all the others.'

'Not now, Jerry,' she rapped. Her sweeping gaze paused momentarily, focusing on him before moving on to track the overtaking vehicles. He was quiet for a couple of minutes.

'But why?' he exclaimed suddenly. 'Why? I don't understand it.'

'Jesus Christ, not now. Not now,' she shrieked at him. She raised her clenched fists to her ears, her eyes screwed tight to shut him out. He was so shocked at her outburst he turned the steering wheel, as if to escape from her, pulling the car out into the fast lane and into the path of an oncoming refrigerated lorry. With horror, Pilgrim saw the dark bulk of the lorry bearing down upon them, its headlights flashing. He pushed down upon the accelerator but there was no response as the lorry, its wheels locked and tyres smoking, began to slide to the right. Pilgrim pulled the

Peugeot back into the slow lane and watched, with Susan, the cars behind weave and swerve in their efforts to evade the skidding lorry. Miraculously all the vehicles managed to avoid each other and somehow steer themselves back into an orderly formation. Some of the cars' drivers gestured angrily at him as they overtook, the refrigerated lorry thundered past, its horn blowing and lights still flashing.

They sped off the end of the motorway at Sunbury and drove up the Chertsey road, past the rugby ground and through East Sheen. Susan continued to scrutinise the following traffic as they crossed the river at Putney Bridge and drove onto the Fulham Road. They turned left just after the football ground, into Ifield Road. A few yards along it, Susan instructed him to stop. He parked on the right-hand side of the road and they got out. Susan took the keys from him, locked the car and then stood scrutinising the traffic in the street and carefully checking the parked cars and the windows of the houses all around them. Finally she turned to Pilgrim. 'It looks all right.' She gave him a tight, tired smile. 'Come on.'

She led him to a house in the middle of a long terrace, close to where they had parked. In its porchway were two doors, one for the flat above and one, which Susan unlocked, for the flat downstairs.

Inside was a short, narrow hallway painted a dirty shade of white. The first room off to the right was a cramped sitting room, furnished with a worn carpet and an old and bulky three-piece suite. The next room, also on the right, was a small bedroom entirely taken up by a double bed and a large old-fashioned wardrobe. The room was dark and lifeless. At the end of the narrow hallway was a small kitchen; beyond that, Pilgrim could see a tiny bathroom. He followed Susan down the passage to the kitchen. Standing on a cheap kitchen dresser was a bottle of brandy. She took a couple of glasses from the dresser and poured an enormous measure into each of them. Her hand was shaking and the bottle rattled against the rim of the glass. She raised her glass briefly in salute and downed half its contents in one long gulp. Pilgrim did the same. Susan coughed a couple of times as the brandy flowed down her throat, then leaned wearily against the dresser and contemplated her glass.

'Where are we?'

'Fulham.'

'I know we're in Fulham, for God's sake.' Pilgrim's anger was coming to the surface. 'But why? Whose place is this? What are we doing here?'

Susan sighed and looked up at him. 'Let's go and sit down,' she said. She picked up the brandy and, with Pilgrim following, walked along the passage to the sitting room. She placed the bottle on a scratched coffee table set in the middle of the floor before closing the faded yellow cotton curtains. They allowed enough daylight into the room to fill it with a sombre twilight, the kind of light Pilgrim guessed they had in a morgue. She flopped onto a worn green moquette settee and Pilgrim seated himself opposite in an armchair. He noticed that she kept her shoulder bag close to her side.

'This is my place,' she told him. 'I rent it.'

'Why?'

'Privacy. Somewhere to come when I want to be alone.' She guessed his thoughts. 'No, Jerry, I don't bring lovers here. You're the only other person who knows about the place.' She reached across and helped herself to more brandy. Her hand was steadier. She lit a cigarette and passed the pack and her lighter to Pilgrim. They were silent for a few moments.

'I'm sorry I screamed at you in the car,' she said finally. 'I was very overwrought.'

'It's not surprising. Not after . . .' Pilgrim paused as he recalled the sight of Frimley-Kimpton's body. 'I can't believe it, I can't believe you killed him, Susan. Murdered him.'

'He was a murderer,' she replied evenly. 'What about those soldiers on Pinta Leone, what about Richard Thornbury. What about . . .' she paused. 'He had it coming. He killed people, just to get rich.'

'But like that, why do it like that?'

'The lecherous bastard was showing me round the garden and I thought the gun would be too noisy. He got me to go into the garden shed with him. He was trying to have a grope. We were stumbling around among all the tools when it suddenly occurred to me that I could use one of them to hit him on the head. I grabbed something. It was only after I'd rushed outside I realised it was the gardening fork. Frimley-Kimpton came out after me, like an old tomcat on heat. You should have seen his face when I pulled the gun on him. I made him walk behind the bushes and then I hit him on the head with the handle.'

'And then you shoved that fork into him. Just like that.'

'He was lying on the grass moaning, looking up at me in total surprise. And I thought, You fat lecherous murdering swine. So, I stuck him.'

He stared at her in horror. 'You're crazy.'

'No, I'm not,' Susan's voice was calm. 'Not at all. You'd have done the same. It was easy. I got one of the prongs jammed in his ribs the first time and it was hard to pull it out but after that it was like sticking a fork into blancmange.'

Pilgrim felt sick. 'How did you get to see him?' he asked weakly.

'I'd called him on the phone a few days ago and said I wanted to interview him. I've still got a press card, after all these years. Anyway, what were you doing there?'

Pilgrim's voice remained weak. 'I went to show him the papers.' He tapped his inside jacket pocket. 'I wanted to make him pay up. That was our original idea, you remember, the plan.'

'We dropped that plan last week. God, Jerry. You're so inconsistent. First you don't stick to the plan, then when we abandon it, you go back to it. You've no idea what a shock I got when I saw your car on the way to Dundonald's place.'

'So it was you!' he said incredulously.

They were silent for a moment until her words got through.

'*You* got a shock,' he exclaimed suddenly. 'What the fuck do you think I got? I was throwing my guts up all over his designer kitchen. And to think you did that.'

Susan stared intently at him as he reached across to the coffee table and helped himself to another brandy.

'The papers say he did it himself,' she stated.

'I don't know how anybody can believe that, especially the police. How did you do it?'

She shrugged. 'Another interview. I knew he'd be alone. He talked about shooting, so I asked him to show me his guns. He showed me how to load a shotgun.'

'And then you blew his head off.'

'He was another of them. He deserved it. It took a long time but he had it coming. I didn't think there would be such a mess. Blood everywhere.'

Pilgrim grimaced as he recalled the horror.

'That reminds me,' Susan said. 'Come on.' She stood up, picked up her shoulder bag and with Pilgrim behind her marched into the small sombre bedroom next door. She motioned Pilgrim to sit on the creaky double bed as she began to take off her clothes. She examined her skirt and stockings carefully for blood. From the big old-fashioned wardrobe she pulled out a black plastic bag already half-filled with clothes. 'Pity about these,' she said, examining her shoes before throwing them, along with her skirt and stockings, into the bag.

'Did you come here after you shot Dundonald?'

'As a matter of fact, I've come back here after all of them.' She was pulling on a new pair of tights. 'But I had to hurry after Dundonald. I knew you'd call. I only just made it back to Elizabeth Street in time.'

'All of them?' He looked at her with renewed horror. 'For God's sake, don't tell me you killed Blackmore too?' She ignored his question. She was wriggling into a skirt of Black Watch tartan. 'Jesus Christ, Susan!' He leapt up from the bed and rushed out into the hall. He had moved no more than a few paces when he heard her voice.

'Where do you think you're going, Jerry?'

He turned. She had followed him out into the hallway. In her left hand she held her shoulder bag; her right hand was stuffed deep inside it, holding something. He knew what it was. He stared at her face for a moment, then at her hands.

'To get a bloody drink,' he said and turned into the living room.

She followed him in a few moments later. He was in the same seat as before, nursing a large brandy and smoking one of her cigarettes. 'You'd shoot me too, wouldn't you?'

'If you made me.'

'What does that mean?'

'If you tried to do something silly, like go to the police or leave here or something like that.'

'I see,' said Pilgrim. 'So I'm a prisoner. What happens to me when you leave? Aren't your parents at your place? They'll be expecting you back soon.'

Susan shrugged. 'I told you that so I wouldn't have to see you today. My parents are actually at home in Warwickshire and Nanny has taken my son to stay there for a few days. David is away, on a business trip. We'll stay here tonight.'

Pilgrim looked around the room. 'Terrific,' he said. 'So you'll keep watch over me. Like a warden.'

'Jerry, it isn't like that. I don't want you doing anything stupid, that's all. Like panicking.'

'Panic, why should I panic? I'm only running around with a woman who's wiped out half the top men in the country.' They were silent for a while. 'Did you kill Blackmore?'

She nodded.

'Dear God,' he said softly. He stared at her. 'What happened?'

'I got David to take me to some parties where I expected him to be. He picked me up, he likes redheads. I saw him for drinks a couple of times, then we agreed to take a room somewhere.'

'You slept with him?' Pilgrim was incredulous.

She nodded. 'I booked a hotel room in Hampstead and he came to me. He told me that he had a regular meeting every Tuesday afternoon.' She paused. 'I didn't know it was with that woman, the one you saw. Anyway, he had no security men with him, they didn't expect him to break his routine. No one recognised him and no one was interested in me.'

'So you went to bed.'

'He was just like all the others, he looked after himself. He didn't care about how I felt. I don't actually think he liked me that much, not in bed anyway. He was into some bizarre rituals.'

'I heard,' Pilgrim mumbled. He felt strange. Something inside him had started shaking. Blackmore had seemed indestructible.

'I hadn't gone there with the intention of killing him,' she continued. 'I don't know what I intended. I wanted to find out what he was like, I suppose. Maybe tell him I knew about what he'd done. You'd called me, if you remember, and told me you'd seen him, so I presumed he'd already transferred the money. I didn't know you'd changed the plan.' She glowered at him.

'Go on.'

'Afterwards he wanted a bath. And then I saw my chance. I had my travelling hairdryer with me, it has a long lead. I plugged it in and walked into the bathroom. I was going to tell him why, but I couldn't be bothered. I just dropped it into the water.'

'Poor bastard,' said Pilgrim grimly. 'Still, at least in the end you gave him a buzz.'

'I don't think that's very funny.'

'I don't suppose he did.'

She frowned at him.

'How in hell did you get away with it?'

She shrugged. 'Emptied the bath, wiped my fingerprints off everything. I'd given the hotel a false name and address and I left without paying. The place was in chaos anyway, most of the power was out.'

Pilgrim let out a hollow laugh. 'I bet when you asked him if he wanted a bang he didn't expect you to use half the fucking national grid.'

She ignored the remark and remained silent, stone-walling him with her unflinching gaze.

'Jesus Christ.' He put his head into his hands. The brandy was churning his emotions. Despite himself he admired her, slim, beautiful, elegant, yet as tough as tensioned steel. She had coolly and violently done to death some of the country's great men. She had also been to bed with one of them. He didn't know if he hated her or loved her. He knew he feared her. He looked up. 'That day I came to see you, after I'd been beaten up. What a bloody act! Giving me hell because I'd changed the plan. What about you? All I wanted was a bit of extra cash, at least I meant to leave them breathing.'

'If you hadn't changed the plan, I might not have gone to see Dundonald and Frimley-Kimpton and they might still be alive.' She reached for the brandy bottle and poured the last drops into her glass.

'What are you telling me? That it's my fault? To hell with that. It's nothing to do with me, Susan. I'm not involved.'

She stood up, walked across the room and pressed the light switch. The room was drenched in a harsh unyielding light. It hurt Pilgrim's eyes. 'As a matter of fact,' she told him in a quiet, deliberate voice, 'it is your fault. All your fault. And make no mistake, Jerry, you're in it, all the way, with me.'

'How do you make that out?'

She sighed and leaned against the wall, close to the door. 'Your car,' she said simply.

'What do you mean?'

'Your car is parked near Frimley-Kimpton's place. Sooner or later someone is going to think it suspicious. And if the police examine it, are they going to find Woodberry's papers? Did you leave any in the car?'

He leaned back in his chair and closed his eyes. 'Oh God,' he moaned. 'I don't know. I can't remember.' He was silent for a few moments. 'I don't think so.'

'Well, even if you haven't, you'll have to explain why your car is there. And there's something else.'

'What?'

'Every one of those men who died was visited by someone called Richard Thornbury. That name will be in all their appointment diaries.'

'So what? He doesn't exist. He's nothing to do with me.'

'Lord Addingham can say otherwise. He's seen you. He can identify you as Richard Thornbury. He's the only one left who can.'

Pilgrim jumped up from his seat. 'For Christ's sake,' he shouted. 'You've dropped me right in it. I could be the number one suspect for a whole bunch of killings done by you.' He pointed an accusing finger at her.

Susan moved across the room closer to the settee and to her shoulder bag lying carelessly on it. 'Look, Jerry,' she said. 'It's no use shouting at me. We're both involved in this. We've got to stick together.'

'The last person who said that to me didn't stick too long. He pissed off to South Africa and left me to get stuck with all the shit.'

She tried to mollify him. 'Let's go out for a drink and something to eat. The brandy is finished and there's no food in the flat. We need to get something for tomorrow's breakfast anyway.' She picked up her bag and moved towards the door.

'But why did you do it? I mean, why murder them?' Pilgrim was insistent. 'We had a perfectly good plan to take half a million off them. Why kill them?'

'If you had stuck to the plan,' said Susan walking out into the hallway, 'we could have accomplished both.'

'But why should we want to? Why kill them?'

She turned to him. 'Because they deserved it,' she said emphatically. 'They were murderers.'

'I know they were,' Pilgrim replied, 'but you yourself said that nobody now would care about a bunch of dead soldiers on Pinta Leone or about Richard Thornbury.'

'I care.' Susan said. 'I care about them and I care about my father.'

'Your father? What the hell has he got to do with it?' Pilgrim was nonplussed.

'They murdered him,' she said simply.

'What?'

'They murdered my father.' Susan turned to open the front door.

'I don't understand.'

She looked at him over her shoulder as she opened the door. 'My father was George Stansgate.'

They walked in silence, turning left into the Fulham Road and heading east towards Chelsea. They found a pub after a few hundred yards; it was early, just after six, and the pub was quiet. Pilgrim bought them both a glass of red wine and they settled in a corner. He looked at her expectantly, waiting for an explanation.

'Now you understand,' she said simply.

'No, I don't, not at all. Does that mean you've known about the Archbishop's Enterprise all along?'

'No.'

'You said they murdered your father. Woodberry doesn't say anything about that. He just says that Stansgate, I mean your father, went to prison.'

'He wouldn't. My father was killed after Uncle Simon had finished writing his account. But they murdered him all the same.'

'How can you be so sure?'

'My father got out of prison in 1967. He contacted my mother and begged her to let him see me.'

'Wait a minute,' Pilgrim interrupted her. 'Didn't Woodberry write that you had a brother?'

'He died a few months after my father went inside. Meningitis. My mother always blamed my father for his death. That's one of the reasons why she refused to see him.'

'But you wanted to see him,' Pilgrim prompted her.

'Not especially,' she replied. 'I was eleven. I'd forgotten nearly everything about him. My mother had been married to Daddy, I mean my stepfather, for a couple of years by then. We were all ever so happy, it was much better with my stepfather. The irony of it is that it was Uncle Simon who introduced Daddy to my mother. He and my stepfather had always been close business associates.'

'Yet in the end your mother let him see you.'

'Twice,' she replied. 'The second time he took me for a walk and talked to me about what had happened to him. The following week he was knocked down and killed by a hit and run driver.'

'That doesn't mean that he was murdered. It could have been an accident.'

'The car had to mount the pavement to hit my father and the driver didn't stop. The police never found out who did it, they always reckoned it was a drunk. I'm pretty sure that it was my beloved Uncle Simon driving that car. Or Ashley Brighton.'

'Why? Why should they kill him three years afterwards.'

'Because one of the last things my father said to me was

457

that he was going to talk to both of them about certain conclusions he had come to in prison.'

Pilgrim looked puzzled.

'My father was a weak man. And greedy. But he wasn't a criminal. Being sent to prison was a terrible thing to happen to him. It was very hard for him. After a while he began to think about everything that had happened and he began to realise that he had been made a scapegoat.'

'How?'

'To begin with, the only people that he knew for sure were involved in the plot were Max Gonzales in Panama and John Portalier in Pinta Leone. He also suspected Richard Thornbury, only by then he'd disappeared. But he had plenty of time to think in his prison cell and after a while he began to remember things, little things but significant. He told me that on the day he had been offered the job at Thornbury's, he had phoned to thank Uncle Simon for giving him the introduction. Only he wasn't there. Felicity told my father that he'd gone to Panama on business. He didn't think anything of it at the time but in prison he began to suspect. After that he thought about Ashley Brighton. Somebody must have planted all that false but incriminating evidence in his desk. My father remembered that Brighton had been around for a bit in the days after Thornbury Engineering went bankrupt. It all began to make sense. Woodberry had introduced him to a good job, which Brighton had offered to him all too easily. Then Thornbury had sent him out to Pinta Leone almost immediately. Everything had been done in a hurry; all that expense-account living went to his head.'

'Poor bugger,' said Pilgrim with feeling. He remembered how invincible he had felt when times had been good and expenses unlimited.

Susan nodded. 'They used him.' She sighed. 'But I was eleven. I didn't understand what he was talking about. After all, he was practically a stranger. I was happy with my stepfather and I liked my Uncle Simon, I didn't take much notice. When I got home I told my mother that he was boring and that I didn't want to see him again. Well, I didn't. Uncle Simon saw to that.'

They were quiet for a few moments. 'I'll get us another drink,' Pilgrim said softly. The pub was becoming crowded but he was quickly back with two more glasses of wine. 'Despite what you've told me,' he said, 'I can't believe they'd take the risk of murdering him. He was right but he couldn't prove any of it. He couldn't hurt them.'

'He'd guessed enough to get himself killed,' Susan said flatly.

'What made you get involved, after all this time?'

'Going to America,' she told him. 'Breakdowns do funny things to you.' Pilgrim felt himself flush as he recalled the cause of her disorder. 'For the first time in my life I began to think about my father and what he had told me the last time I saw him. After a couple of years I decided to trace Gonzales and find out whether what my father had said was really true. I suppose it was a kind of whim, trying to make up for not being nicer to him when I was a child. I went to Panama but it was very difficult. Gonzales had left years before, and it took me ages to find someone who knew where he'd gone. After weeks of searching I traced him to Santa Cruz just south of San Francisco. You'd have been proud of me, Jerry, it took every trick you ever taught me to find him.'

He smiled briefly at the compliment.

'He was living in a condominium, close to the ocean. I called him and told him who I was. He was very concerned to know how I'd tracked him down and he asked me over to his place to talk. He was alone. The funny thing was, he was quite open about what he'd done. He must have known that my father had gone to prison, yet all he could talk about was what a clever idea it was. He told me that the man who had flown out there and briefed him about the plan had been Simon Woodberry. He'd called himself Boniface, but Gonzales had bribed a receptionist at Uncle Simon's hotel to tell him his real name. So my father had been right, Uncle Simon had set him up. Gonzales was completely frank about it. It didn't bother him at all. When I asked why not, he laughed and said that he'd been involved in a big fraud on the World Bank in the sixties. Some Americans had got him out of it, promised him immunity and moved him to California. He obviously thought that he'd got away with everything.' There was a hard edge to her voice.

'What do you mean?' he asked suspiciously.

'You're right about lawyers, Jerry,' she told him, 'they do write everything down. That's what made me look for Uncle Simon's papers later on. Gonzales said he'd kept all his papers; he went rummaging about for them in a bureau. In one of the drawers was a gun. When he went searching for the papers somewhere else I took it out.'

Pilgrim caught his breath. 'You don't mean . . .'

She nodded. 'I really, honestly only meant to scare him. I told him my father had been murdered by Simon Woodberry but he wouldn't believe it. He said Uncle Simon wasn't the type and anyway it was all a long time ago. He was such a cocky self-satisfied little man. Just because some American official had done a deal with him he thought he was safe. He laughed and told me the gun wasn't loaded. So I pulled the trigger just to see if he was right. He was wrong. It wasn't a very loud bang. Gonzales looked at me with a ludicrous expression of surprise, then he sat down on the sofa. And that was it. He rolled over quite slowly and slipped to the floor. He was dead. I was so scared, I picked up his papers and got away as fast as I could. I threw the gun into the Pacific and flew back East. Every day I expected to be arrested for murder but nothing happened.' She paused. 'It took me a little while to get over it but it's amazing how easy it is to kill someone, and after a while you get used to it. I can't say that I felt any satisfaction that I'd killed him, I didn't feel anything really. At least not then. What pleased me most was that I'd been able to track him down. So about a year afterwards I decided to find Portalier.'

'You said he couldn't be traced.' Pilgrim recalled their conversation in the cottage.

'That's right, I failed,' she admitted. 'I went to Pinta Leone. What a dump. Nobody had seen Portalier in more than twenty years. Finally I located a woman who said she'd done him a favour. She'd got some men out of his way so he could leave the island with money from a bank. He told her that he was going to Switzerland. Pinta Leone was a dead end. Gonzales had told me that Portalier had used the name Thomas Cranmer so, after I came back to England a couple of years later, I was able to trace him to Zurich. After that, nothing. I'm sure he came to London but,' she shrugged, 'twenty years is a long time.'

The pub had become noisy and crowded and their glasses were empty. 'Let's get something to eat,' Susan suggested. Pilgrim didn't feel hungry but he was glad to get outside, into the cool night air. The Fulham Road was busy, but they found a small Indian restaurant which at that time of the evening was almost empty.

Susan took her time in ordering, choosing her food with relish. Pilgrim said, dully, that he would have the same as her. She ordered a bottle of red wine.

'So you knew about everything years ago,' he said as she poured the wine.

'No, not really. I only knew part of it. Uncle Simon, on the other hand, knew everything, so when I came back to England I made a point of getting close to him. I visited the big house often. I even tried to get him to talk about my father, my real father, but he always avoided the subject. After a while I was too busy getting married, setting up the home and having my baby.'

'I see, you couldn't fit it all in. It's only now you've been able to get round to killing everyone.' Some of Pilgrim's fear and resentment at being framed was surfacing again.

'For God's sake, don't keep talking about killing,' she replied crossly. 'I didn't even know who any of the others were until a few months ago.'

'When you found the papers?'

'No, I knew about all the others before that.'

'Before you found the papers?'

'Yes.'

'How?'

'David had been proposed for Uncle Simon's club. In fact, Uncle Simon was a seconder. David was delighted, he wouldn't stop talking about it. It made me recall something my father had told me. It hadn't seemed important at the time, so I'd forgotten it. He told me that on the day after he was arrested, when they released him from the police station, he had phoned anybody he thought could help him. He was desperate. He called Woodberry, and Felicity had told him that Uncle Simon was in London. He'd gone up to have lunch at his club. She said it was some kind of celebration. Later he called Ashley Brighton. His wife told my father practically the same story.' She shrugged. 'My father believed that they had gone to celebrate his arrest.'

Pilgrim nodded. He remembered his paranoia when he thought the police were about to charge him with fraud. It was a time when he could believe that a couple of strangers looking at him across a bar were laughing at his misfortunes. It would be easy for Stansgate, locked up for years, to convince himself that the two men had rejoiced in his troubles.

'It wasn't much to go on,' she continued. 'But I thought I'd follow it up. After all, it was a very strange day to celebrate anything.'

Pilgrim looked puzzled. 'Why?'

'It was the day after they'd shot Kennedy, 24 November 1963.'

Pilgrim nodded in understanding.

'A friend of mine,' she continued, 'runs a small magazine. I persuaded him to let me do a human interest story about the weekend of the shooting. I went to Uncle Simon's club and told them what I was doing. I asked to see their records for that weekend so I could interview some of the members. They were very reluctant at first but my friend backed me up and I told them I knew quite a lot of the members, including Uncle Simon, so they let me see their records. An old man took me down to a cellar and found a big dusty leather-bound book. There it was.' She stopped and Pilgrim waited for her to continue. 'All the names, and Woodberry had even written in the reason for the lunch as the Archbishop's Enterprise.' She shook her head in silent amazement. 'They never expected to be traced. It never occurred to them, did it? Every single one of them had signed himself in by his real name. Woodberry was there, Brighton, Portalier too, so I knew that all the others must have been part of it.'

Pilgrim shook his head slowly. Again he was forced to admire her, she'd done a very professional job in tracking down the men. 'If they'd never had that lunch,' he said, 'you'd never have known. No one would ever have known. Woodberry wouldn't have become suspicious about Thornbury's death and he'd have never written his account.'

'Perhaps not.'

'Nobody would ever have known,' insisted Pilgrim.

'Maybe,' she replied hesitantly. 'Yet, somebody had been there before me.'

Pilgrim didn't understand. 'What do you mean?'

'Someone had written all those names down before.'

'How do you know?'

'It was an old-fashioned book,' she said, 'the pages were very thick.' She rubbed her thumb and index finger together trying to give an impression of the paper. 'Cartridge paper,' she said. 'The kind of paper that is easily impressed.'

Pilgrim nodded.

'Somebody had rested a piece of paper on the page

opposite and used a ball point pen to write down all the names. I could see the impression clearly on the paper.'

'Maybe it was somebody at the club.'

'Maybe.' She sounded doubtful. 'A few days later I had a phone call from Uncle Simon. Some official at the club had mentioned to him what I'd been doing. He sounded very agitated.'

The food arrived. Pilgrim waited as patiently as he could until the waiter had gone.

'I drove over to Gloucestershire the following day. I could tell he was very disturbed. He asked a lot of questions about the story I was writing. I told him something about it but I could see that he wasn't convinced. He was still very suspicious. So I decided to tell him the truth.'

'Good God! All of it?'

'Of course not. I didn't tell him about Gonzales although I did say that I'd seen him, and I showed Uncle Simon the papers. He asked me how I'd got hold of them. I told him Gonzales kept them in a bureau and I'd taken them. He wouldn't believe me, he said no lawyer would leave papers lying around where they could be found. So it was obvious they weren't incriminating, if they had been, Gonzales would have hidden them where nobody could find them. He was very angry, he said I'd been spying on him. Imagine that, he frames my father, then murders him, and yet accuses me of spying on him. I told him as much. I hadn't realised what a talent he had for acting. He played the injured innocent to perfection when I accused him of murdering my father.'

'You can't be sure that he did,' Pilgrim interjected.

'He certainly protested his innocence long enough. Anyway, I think he did it, or if he didn't, he knew about it and that's the same thing. He acted as guilty as hell – you know, like men do when they've been caught out, all loud and angry and red in the face.'

'Well, he would be, wouldn't he? You just caught him

out in a crime he'd committed more than twenty years before. He'd probably forgotten all about it until you raised the matter. So what happened?'

'He asked me what I intended to do,' Susan replied. 'I thought I could frighten him. I said I might go to the police. He laughed. He said I didn't have anything to go on. Gonzales's papers weren't incriminating and everything else was guesswork. The fact that I was accusing Lord Edward Addingham, Sir Henry Dundonald, Sir Oliver Blackmore and the others made it even worse. They'd put me down as some paranoiac female. He was right, of course. I didn't really have any proof. He told me that he was going to Scotland for a few days' shooting and that we'd meet when he got back. I felt a bloody idiot. I'd overplayed my hand. I realised that I'd only got one course of action left open.' She paused. Pilgrim, sitting across the table, had been watching her intently. For a moment their eyes locked and then she glanced away.

'It was you who shot him,' he said quietly.

'What else could I do?' she asked. 'I'd made such a mess of it. I'd exposed myself. If Uncle Simon told any of the others, they would put pressure on him to get rid of me. Just to protect themselves. I would be the next one in my family to have a fatal accident.'

'You couldn't be sure of that.'

'Couldn't I?' she retorted. 'Who do you think those two men who kidnapped you were working for? What would they have done to you if you hadn't got away?'

Pilgrim shivered.

'What about those three in the car? Who the hell do you think sent them? No, Jerry, it was either him or me and I decided it had to be him. I worked it all out driving home. As soon as I got back I rented the flat with a cash deposit, giving a false name. Then I bought the Peugeot. A couple of days later I drove to Perthshire. It was quite different with Uncle Simon. With Gonzales I'd been close enough to see his face when I shot him, Uncle Simon was almost a mile away. With him it was,' she searched for the word, 'technical. Just one shot. Actually,' she added, 'I'm a very good shot.'

Pilgrim pulled a face. 'So how did you find the papers?'

'After the funeral I spent a lot of time with Felicity at the house, helping her sort things out.'

'Christ, you're a hard bitch,' said Pilgrim. 'First you make her a widow, then you help her get over it.'

Susan ignored the remark. 'Uncle Simon had said Gonzales wouldn't leave incriminating papers around where anybody could find them. That made me think that Uncle Simon might have kept papers, but if he did he would have put them somewhere unusual, not somewhere where anyone could find them when his estate was being wound up. Certainly they didn't come to light in any of his deposit boxes or in his safe in the house. I spent a lot of time thinking about where were they might be. Felicity was happy to let me come and go pretty much as I pleased. So I started looking. It took me some time to get round to the barn but that's where I found them. Just as I told you. Of course, I didn't expect to find such a goldmine, such an explicit account. I thought I'd find maybe a few notes.'

'So, after that, you got me to join in your crazy plan to blackmail them,' said Pilgrim.

'You were eager enough at the start, when you saw a chance of some easy money.'

'Easy money,' he repeated. 'There's been nothing easy about any of this affair and there's been no money either. Not a penny. It has to be the worst blackmail plan in the history of the world. Half a million pounds you said we'd make and we haven't made a penny. You were killing them quicker than I could get to them.'

'Maybe,' Susan agreed, 'but at least they didn't get away with it. One way or the other they've paid for what they did.'

'They've paid all right,' said Pilgrim. 'Brighton's the only poor sod who's been allowed to die in peace. Don't tell me you had something to do with that?'

She looked directly at him and shook her head. 'No, that was a surprise. I met him at Uncle Simon's funeral. I knew he wasn't very well then. I did drive up to Hampstead on the day before you phoned to say he was dead.'

'Why?'

'Just to get the lie of the land.' She continued looking intently at him.

Pilgrim let out a cynical laugh. 'He snuffed it just a bit too soon, eh? He beat you to it. Now they're all dead.'

'Not all of them,' said Susan. 'Addingham is still left.'

The waiter brought the bill, which Susan paid. They emerged into the Fulham Road. It was after nine o'clock. Susan reminded them that they needed food for the next morning so they found a late-night supermarket where they bought cereal and milk, cigarettes and another bottle of brandy. Susan bought a late edition of the *Evening Standard* at the check-out desk. They walked slowly. Occasionally Susan glanced behind to check if anyone was following but no one showed any interest in them.

They let themselves into the harsh, stark light of the flat. Susan disappeared into the kitchen for a moment then returned to the living room with a small transistor radio. 'It's almost time for the news,' she explained.

Pilgrim looked surprised.

'I want to hear what they say about Frimley-Kimpton.' She turned the volume on low and settled down to examine the contents of the newspaper. 'There's nothing about him in here,' she said after a few minutes.

'The story would have come through too late,' Pilgrim observed. 'It will be on the news,' he said ominously, nodding at the radio. The news came on a few minutes later; it was an extended summary lasting half an hour, but no mention was made of Frimley-Kimpton. Susan got up and turned it off. She looked puzzled.

'I would have thought they would have said something,' she said.

'So would I,' agreed Pilgrim. 'Either the local reporters aren't doing their job or the police are sitting on it.'

'Why should they do that?'

'Maybe they've got a lead to whoever did it,' Pilgrim said pointedly.

Susan was calm as she considered what he'd said. 'They've not got much to go on,' she replied finally. 'Everywhere I went, I wore these.' She reached for her shoulder bag and pulled from it a wig of short dark hair and sunglasses. Expertly she scooped her own hair up into a ball and pulled the wig over her head. She put the sunglasses on. Her appearance was dramatically different. 'And I talked like this,' she said in an authentic East Coast accent. She laughed at Pilgrim's surprise.

'That's great,' he said angrily. 'They may not know what you look like but they've got a bloody good description of me.'

Susan pulled off the wig and the sunglasses and stuffed them back into her bag. She ignored his anxiety. She sat down, picked up her glass and stared at it thoughtfully. 'Jerry, doesn't it strike you as strange that the media haven't made more of a story about their deaths?'

'What do you mean?' He sat down next to her.

'Dundonald and Blackmore were important men. Blackmore was killed on Tuesday. That woman told you security was investigating his death, yet the story, which didn't come out until Sunday, is that he died of an accident at home. You said earlier that it was hard to understand how the police could believe that Dundonald's death was a suicide but that was the story they immediately put out. I wonder what they're going to say about Frimley-Kimpton when the news comes out. If the news comes out.'

'For God's sake, you've murdered all those people and now you're worried about what stories the newspapers put out. It doesn't matter what the papers say, our problem is not being caught, especially me.'

'According to the papers, nobody is looking for us.'

'You know better than to believe anything you read in the papers. The police have plenty to go on. Frimley-Kimpton's wife got a good look at me and as you so graciously pointed out, Edward Addingham, who only happens to be the Lord Chief Justice, could confirm that I'm the person calling himself Richard Thornbury.'

'Yes, that's quite right,' Susan said thoughtfully. She left the room for a few seconds and returned with a map which she opened out on the coffee table. 'Where's Upham?' she asked.

'Why?'

'Just show me,' she demanded.

Pilgrim examined the area between Winchester and Southampton. 'There.'

Susan ringed the name with a black felt-tipped pen. 'That's not far, it would take us about an hour and a half at most.'

Pilgrim stared at her.

'We'll go tomorrow morning.'

'I don't believe I'm hearing this,' Pilgrim said. 'Upham is the last place on God's earth that you and I want to go. Addingham has got security people there and if he or anyone else has made the connection between him and the deaths of the others, he'll have a brigade of guards dug in around him by now.'

Susan shook her head. 'The papers say that the others died naturally. No one has made any connection. Addingham only has one security man with him at Upham.'

'What the hell do we want to go there for anyway?'

'He owes us money. As you say, Jerry, we haven't made a penny out of this plan yet.'

'Forget it, he can keep his money. I'm prepared to stay poor so long as I stay out of prison.'

'Why do you always want to give up when things get tough?' Susan demanded angrily.

'This isn't tough. This is impossible. Addingham probably thinks I've got something to do with the death of the others. He can identify me as Richard Thornbury.'

'Exactly,' said Susan. 'He's the only one left who can. If we make him pay us,' she considered for a moment, 'maybe a quarter of a million, then we know he'll keep quiet. With that money you can disappear for a while.'

'Supposing he doesn't pay up? Supposing he double-crosses us like last time?'

'He won't double-cross us,' she replied. 'He won't be expecting two of us and he won't have time to plan anything.'

'How do we know he'll be there?' Pilgrim was desperately seeking a way out.

'He always goes to Upham at the weekend.' Susan was becoming exasperated. 'We'll drive down and take a look around. You can phone from somewhere local, remind him you're Richard Thornbury and arrange to see him immediately. Then we'll both go to see him.'

'And walk into a trap.'

'Jerry,' she said angrily, 'he still has everything to lose. Nothing's changed. He knows you have the papers.'

'He knew that last time. It didn't stop him putting those hoodlums onto me.'

'Last time, you let him set you up. This time you're much more dangerous. He'll see that, even if you can't. You got away from those men and now you're back, with me. What's more, all the others in his little scheme are dead. He may be wondering about that. The Lord Chief Justice has every reason to pay us and no reason not to.'

'Yes, but –'

'Look,' Susan interrupted, 'I'm not prepared to argue

about this any more tonight. I'm tired. I want to go to bed.'
She screwed the top on the brandy bottle, stood up deci-
sively and marched out of the room. After a few seconds,
Pilgrim followed her, turning off the light. Susan locked
and bolted the front door before disappearing into the
bathroom. Pilgrim realised that he had no shaving gear or
toothbrush. He wandered into the overcrowded bedroom.
A bedside light was set on a rickety chair. He turned it on.
Susan reappeared.

'You don't have a spare toothbrush, do you?' he asked.

'Afraid not,' she said.

When he returned from the bathroom Susan was already
in bed. He undressed and climbed in beside her. The bed
was lumpy and cold. Susan was wearing some kind of shirt;
he wished he'd done the same, the sheets felt damp and
clammy on his naked body.

He moved across the bed and put his arms round her. She
wriggled closer into him for warmth but he could sense a
tension in her body, the same tension he could feel in himself. There was no suppleness in their embrace, no sensuous
entwining of the limbs. Neither of them had thoughts of
passion. They held onto each other because it was cold and
there was no one else. The crimes which had united them as
partners had undone them as lovers. As the bed became
warmer, they slipped from each other's embrace. Despite
his tension Pilgrim felt himself become drowsy. The rise
and fall of Susan's regular breathing helped him drift off
into sleep.

He awoke with a start. He had no idea what time it was.
The room's blackness smothered him like a musty blanket.
Something had woken him, he didn't know what. He lay
staring up at the darkness as the events of the previous days
stamped across his brain, leaving in their wake two questions cowering in a corner of his consciousness like
wounded children. Had Susan set him up? Did she now
mean to kill him?

He had never really understood why she had come back for him. She was notorious in her contempt for losers and when she had found him, Pilgrim had lost everything. Why then had she bothered? He had persuaded himself that it was because they had something special between them, something close to love. But perhaps, he pondered, what she felt for him was quite the opposite, perhaps she hated him. For he had treated her like all the others, he had rejected her when she had most needed him. He had let her go to America, he had been the cause of her breakdown and thereby had prompted her search for her past. Everything that had followed was, ultimately, his fault.

Lying next to her, hearing her slow easy breathing, it was difficult for Pilgrim to believe that she might hate him. They had been so close, so intimate. She had been so good to him. Yet even her kindness could be questioned. Why had she so swiftly moved him out of London to bury him in the countryside? He knew no one there except Trixie and a few drinking companions, none of whom would miss him for long if he were suddenly to disappear. He knew nothing about the lease of the cottage except that he relied upon Susan to pay it. Just like he relied upon her for work. She brought the work, he did it, she paid him. He didn't even know if the companies for whom he wrote advertising copy knew of his existence. There was, when he reflected on it, nothing tangible that connected him to Susan, and if that was so, then it made sense for her to use him as a decoy.

For that was what he had become. Whereas she had inconspicuously visited her victims in disguise, he had gone obviously and openly, loudly announcing himself to be Richard Thornbury. It was him who had projected a high profile and it would be him who was remembered and described. It suddenly occurred to him that she could have booked the room in which she murdered Blackmore in the name of Richard Thornbury. He was certain that the Swiss bank account would not be in their joint names, only in hers. Her plan and its timing had been immaculate. A man calling himself Richard Thornbury had been to see the Attorney General, the Governor of the Bank of England, and a leading political television commentator. Within hours or minutes of each visit, the men were dead. With him as the focus of attention, no one would pay much attention to vague descriptions of a dark-haired American woman in sunglasses.

Now there was only one more visit to be made, to the Lord Chief Justice. Already Susan had suggested how Pilgrim might set himself up as her dummy. He would arrive in Upham, announcing himself as Thornbury, while she unobtrusively got close enough to Addingham to murder him. And then his days as a diversion would be over. For his usefulness could only be absolute if after everything he was unable to talk, unable to state any connection between himself, Susan and the murders.

Lying in the dark he could see with precise clarity that to get away with her plan, Susan must murder him. After Addingham, he had to be killed. Then she would have avenged herself upon the men who had betrayed her father and on the man who had first betrayed her.

Susan stirred. The movement made him jump. His nerves were taut. He knew that he was in bed with a very dangerous woman; he felt as if he were lying beside a coiled rattlesnake. Yet he couldn't bring himself to think of her as bad or evil; it was the men of the Archbishop's Enterprise who had been evil, who had assumed they had a God-given right to defraud others of money; to have young soldiers and greedy playboys murdered, to put men out of work, to send men to prison and subsequently murder them. They had been the evil ones, the lawyers, the accountants and the bankers, and she had made them pay for it. He knew, too, that she wasn't mad; she had a strong sense of vengeance and an iron will; she was determined to seek retribution, and that was it, nothing would dissuade her. She had also in the process made up her mind to eliminate him. He moved slightly towards his side of the bed. Susan lay still, the slow tempo of her breathing remained steady. Slowly he eased himself closer to the edge of the bed, and inch by inch moved his legs from under the covers. Then as delicately as possible he raised himself off the mattress and slipped out of bed. Susan didn't stir.

His clothes were hanging on a chair. He slipped on his shirt, then fumbled to pull on his trousers. He glanced at the dark form in the bed. Susan hadn't moved. He groped about on the floor for his shoes. Behind him he heard a delicate rustle and as he turned the light from the bedside lamp blinded him. He shot up straight like a spring and his shoes dropped back onto the floor with two dull thuds. Susan was leaning across the bed, looking up at him.

'Christ,' he muttered in fright.

'What the hell are you doing?' she asked. She said it in a sharp tone, not in the thick slurred voice of someone who had just woken up. He guessed that she hadn't been asleep at all.

He stared down at her. Her russet hair streamed across the shoulders of her pale blue shirt which, only half-buttoned, allowed her full, beautiful breasts to break provocatively loose. Her deep, brown eyes were concerned and enquiring, her lovely face glowed in the light of the bedside light. As she had leaned across the bed to switch on the lamp she had pulled her pillow out of place. Half hidden beneath it he could see the butt of an automatic pistol.

'I was going to the toilet,' he said lamely.

'Well, it's not outside,' she said crossly. 'This may be Fulham, but we do have inside lavatories. What do you want to get dressed for?' She eased herself back across to her own side of the bed, her hand moving closer to the gun beneath the pillow.

'I wanted to go out, get some air, have a think.' He said it as casually as he could.

'The back door is locked and I don't have a key, so stay inside and think instead,' she told him. 'Anyway, you've been thinking most of the night as it is. What a fidget you are, jerking and twitching.'

'You were awake?'

'How could I sleep with you performing St Vitus's dance next to me?'

He stared at her, not knowing what to say. His eyes moved to the gun butt beneath the pillow. 'Everywhere you go these days you keep a gun close by, I see. I'd forgotten I'd given you two of them.'

She glanced down. 'That's the one from my bag. I told you, the other one is in a safe deposit box in Pall Mall, and the key is safely in Norfolk.' She touched the gun. 'I need to keep this handy, just in case.' She looked up at him. 'Come back to bed, for God's sake. I'm getting cold.'

He gauged the distance between himself and the gun; she could get to it far quicker than he. And there was no way he would be able to get as far as the front door, never mind shooting the bolts and unlocking it, before she was in the hall with the gun in her hand.

'Look,' he blurted, 'what do you intend to do after you kill Addingham tomorrow?'

'Who says I'm going to kill him?'

'It's obvious to me.'

'Well, it isn't to me. The idea is to make him pay.'

Pilgrim considered for a moment. There would be more chance of escape in the morning. Somewhere on the way to Upham there would be a moment when her attention was distracted; that would be his opportunity to get away.

He shrugged. 'Forget it,' he said. 'I'll worry about tomorrow tomorrow. Now I need a pee.'

When he came out of the bathroom Susan was leaning against the wall of the small kitchen. Her blue shirt reached only to the top of her thighs and seeing her slim tanned legs caused him a momentary stab of lust, killed instantly when he saw the gun hanging loosely in her hand. She brushed past him in the doorway of the bathroom, muttering in an irritated voice, 'Now I need one.' She left the bathroom door open and so had an uninterrupted line of sight along the passage to the front door. There was no way Pilgrim could escape.

He suddenly realised how tired and weary he was. The bed was now inviting and warm and he crawled into it. Susan came back into the room and scrambled over him to her side of the bed. He caught a glimpse of the soft down of her vagina.

'For God's sake,' she muttered. 'Go to sleep.'

His last thoughts were what an extraordinary woman she was; she sounded much more like a wife, slightly bad-tempered at being woken in the middle of the night, than a killer. Pilgrim did as he was told. He slept.

Chapter Nine

Something was pulling his arm. He blinked. Grey light was streaming through the bedroom's dirty windows. He blinked again and focused on the figure of Susan standing by the side of the bed. 'Come on, Jerry,' she ordered. 'It's time to get moving.'

He moaned softly. He had slept so deeply he hadn't been aware of her leaving the bed. She looked as if she had been up for some time. She was wearing the same clothes as the previous day.

'I've found some coffee,' she said, 'and there's cereal. Come on, get up.' She left the room.

Pilgrim looked at his watch; it was barely seven thirty. He moaned again and heaved himself out of the bed. It was cold in the flat. He padded naked past Susan in the kitchen to the tiny bare bathroom. He looked at himself in an old, speckled mirror above the sink. He was a mess. He had a day's growth of beard, his hair was greasy and tousled and he had a nasty taste in his mouth. The water was no better than tepid so he decided against having a bath; he washed his face and body in the sink. He found toothpaste and a toothbrush which he presumed to be Susan's. He cleaned his teeth. There was no razor in the bathroom but there was a comb. He padded back to the bedroom and dressed quickly.

A bowl of cereal was on the kitchen dresser. He made himself a cup of instant coffee and ate the cereal standing up. He could hear Susan moving about in the bedroom. He finished his cereal, picked up his coffee cup and went to join her. She had twisted her hair up into a bun and was putting her black-haired wig into her shoulder bag.

'Did you say you have a copy of Woodberry's papers?' she asked.

'Yes, I've been carrying them around for days.'

'Give them to me.'

He felt inside his jacket and pulled from his pocket the envelope containing the folded wad of papers. He handed them to her without question and watched her stuff them into her bag. 'Are you about ready?' she asked.

He nodded, sipping his coffee.

'Good, then we'll go now. We'll be there early. You can drive.' Her tone was decisive. She looked at him expectantly. He took one last gulp of coffee, which burned his mouth, and put his coffee cup down on the chair beside the bed. She nodded to the door, indicating to Pilgrim that he should lead the way. He turned left out of the bedroom into the narrow, dirty-white passage of the flat.

He walked no more than three steps when, from outside the flat, came a tremendous crash. The solid wood of the front door shuddered violently. Pilgrim stopped, his eyes widening in fright. Another crashing impact against the front door ripped it off its hinges and sent it smashing inwards onto the floor of the hallway. Framed in the doorway were four men; two kneeling, two standing, each of them with their arms rigidly extended to their front. They were pointing at him. He realised with a shock that what they were pointing were guns. Immediately his instinct for self-preservation took over. He threw himself to the floor, his cheek rubbing painfully against the cheap cording of the carpet as he turned his head to look at Susan.

Her face was a confusion of shock and panic; she was tugging at something inside her shoulder bag, frantically trying to drag it free from the wig which was now half out of the bag. As he watched her, Pilgrim heard from the doorway a series of sharp cracks, like the sound of rulers smacking hard upon wooden tables. At the sound of the shots Susan staggered backwards to the wall and, as if by magic, four perfectly formed, bright red roses appeared on her white polo neck jumper; one blossomed high on her stomach, the other three along the upward sweep of her breasts. Yet even as the roses spread into a formless red stain across her jumper, she continued vainly trying to pull the gun from inside the bag. Pilgrim saw her lips curling in pain and desperation. The sound of more gunshots came from the doorway, and he watched in horror as Susan's face disappeared and her head exploded in a fountain of blood and grey brains. The dirty white paint on the walls of the passageway was instantly splattered in trickling rivulets of red as slivers of bone and brain pattered down upon the carpet around Pilgrim. He raised himself off the carpet. 'Susan!' he screamed.

The impact of the bullets had loosened the bun of her hair. Her long russet tresses streamed out from the bright crimson horror of what had been her face as her body, straight and rigid as a board, crashed to the floor.

For a moment he stared aghast at her still, lifeless body, then he flung himself back to the floor, wrapping his arms round the top of his head and pressing his face hard into the well-worn carpet, as if to seek sanctuary in its dirty, corded weave. He could feel his scalp prickling in expectation of the bullets smashing through the top of his skull. Suddenly, he felt two pairs of strong hands grasp him by his arms and jerk him to his feet. They pressed him forward so that he was bent double while a third pair of hands grabbed the bottom of his jacket and hauled it up his back and over his head. Led by the man holding the coat tails of his jacket, which had been so effectively turned into both a straightjacket and a hood, he was half carried along the hallway and out across the pavement to a car. The man leading him by his jacket climbed into the back of the car and dragged Pilgrim in behind him.

'On the floor.' Pilgrim was shoved down until his stomach was pressed hard against the car's transmission tunnel. More men piled into the rear seat, their feet roughly shoving his body out of their way. The doors slammed and they roared away.

Only one feeling seeped through the solid lump of seized-up emotion inside Pilgrim. It was the now familiar, desperate urge to vomit. The transmission tunnel was hammering mercilessly into his stomach, while less then six inches from his nose, one of his captor's shoes was thickly smeared in dog excrement. Also, from underneath the hood formed by his jacket, he could see his right hand. It was spattered with blood and small dollops of a grey sludge, like porridge; little bits of matter which had once been Susan's brains.

They drove for a few minutes, then he heard one of the men say, 'You'd better sack him.'

Hands hauled him up by his armpits and pulled him to his knees. His body was swivelled round so that his back was towards his captors. Stupidly, his gaze wandered to the car's offside window; he caught a momentary sight of the square blockhouse of Battersea power station beyond the river before the world was plunged into blackness. One of the men had thrown a black cotton bag over his head. Pilgrim panicked, he tried to pull the bag away from his face but a pair of hands pulled his arms to his sides and pushed him to the floor. He felt the terrifying sensation of suffocation. The bag, smelling of stale breath, sweat and fear, was as wholesome as a flasher's mac. The fabric clung to his nose and his mouth, choking him. He wanted to scream. Instead, he forced his mind to concentrate on his breathing; he panted in short shallow breaths, pushing the air out hard to keep the bag away from his mouth.

The journey was surprisingly short. Within a few minutes the car slowed, turned right and shuddered to a halt. The doors opened, he was dragged backwards out of the vehicle and hustled away. His regular breathing had helped ease his shock; he was sufficiently aware to realise from the sounds of their footsteps that they were walking along a passageway.

They descended two flights of wooden stairs and then marched through the echoing stone passageway of what he guessed was a large basement. He heard a door open and then from behind the black hood was yanked from his head and he was pushed roughly through the doorway. The heavy wooden door was slammed resolutely shut behind him and he heard its key turn in the lock.

He surveyed his surroundings. He was in a large, stone-floored cellar. Its whitewashed walls were about twelve feet high. Along one side was a series of skylights, high up the wall and protected by strong iron bars. A fluorescent light glowed from the ceiling. In one corner was an empty bucket. There was nothing else, no bed, no table, no chair, nothing. He upended the bucket and placed it close to the wall beneath the skylights. He was just tall enough to reach the windowsills. He cursed his lack of inches. Grasping the rough brickwork of the windows as firmly as he could, he pulled himself up. He managed to get his chin to the level of the sill and peer through the filthy windows. All he could see was a small area of stone-flagged yard. He dropped to the floor, sat on the upturned bucket and looked at his hands. They were shaking. He took a grubby handkerchief from his pocket and cleaned his right hand as best he could. Afterwards, he threw the handkerchief into a corner.

He sat forward on the bucket, his forearms on his knees, staring at the cracks in the stone flagging of the floor. He tried to make his mind encompass what had happened but it would have none of it. It was as if his brain had declared independence and had decided to ignore his circumstances. Distant sounds of traffic came to his ears, mingled with another sound, recently heard and faintly reminiscent, though of what his brain didn't know, or if it did, it wasn't telling him.

He had no idea how long he remained in this state of suspended animation. The light seeping through the skylights seemed to indicate that it was still early morning when he heard the rattle of a key in the door lock. Two men walked into the cellar. They were tall and well-built, both in their early thirties, hard men with piercing eyes iced over by suspicion. Pilgrim stood up as the leading man marched towards him.

'Bastard,' said the man. Pilgrim rocked back slightly as if he'd been hit. 'The blokes in that car were friends of mine.'

'What car?' Pilgrim asked. His recent terrifying existence had been filled by men in cars.

Then the man hit him. It was a blow like the one he had taken outside Addingham's chambers; coming from nowhere it caught him high on the stomach on the point of the solar plexus. The punch lashed him back against the white brick wall. He caught his feet on the galvanised bucket which clattered away across the floor as he began to slide down the wall. He saw as if in slow motion the man draw back his foot to kick him and then dumbly watched the man's companion hustle his attacker to one side.

'For Christ's sake,' he heard him say, 'knock it off.'

The first man looked down at Pilgrim for a few seconds before bending down and jerking his limp body to its feet. 'All right,' he ordered, 'turn out your pockets.'

They dragged him into the centre of the cellar where dazedly Pilgrim emptied his pockets. The men checked that he'd given them everything, then they took away his belt and his tie. Finally, the first man grabbed Pilgrim tightly round the throat and effortlessly lifted him until he was standing on tiptoe.

'You wait,' he hissed. 'I'm going to get you back for my mates. I'm going to kick your balls through the top of your head.' His arm shot out and with a heave he slung Pilgrim hard against the wall close to the cellar door. Pilgrim's head crashed against the brickwork and he crumpled into a heap on the floor. He was barely conscious of the men's footsteps as they walked out of the cellar and locked the door behind them. He flopped sideways along the floor. The stone flags were cool on his cheek and through a small gap beneath the wooden door, a steady stream of sweet, fresh air blew. He turned his face to it, as a thirsty man might turn his face to cold water dripping down a rock. Outside the door he could hear voices. The stone walls of the building made good acoustics. The conversation slipped beneath the door as clear and distinct as the air.

'It was a bloody stupid,' said a voice. 'You know Histon doesn't like them to be roughed up, in case we have to let them go.'

'Well, our beloved colonel can go and fuck himself,' came another voice. It belonged to the man who had hit Pilgrim. 'They were friends of mine. Somehow that bastard got them killed. I'm going to break his back.'

'Well, wait until you're given the word,' said the other voice.

Pilgrim heard the footsteps receding down the passage. He lay for over an hour with his cheek and forehead pressed against the cool stone. He felt almost comfortable. The cold refreshing draught from under the door played upon his face and seemed to ease the ache of his new bruises. It also slowly began to activate his brain. And as Pilgrim began to think, he sat up and started to cry. He grieved for Susan, strong, beautiful Susan, whom he had loved, and feared. He yearned for her. It didn't matter now that she had meant to kill him; she had been his lover and his only friend. Now she was gone, destroyed. Sitting on the floor of the cellar, he hugged his knees and cried her name aloud.

When at last the tears ceased, he leaned against the wall, vacant and exhausted. And then gradually reality, the here and now, began to move into the parts of his mind and heart which had been washed empty by his tears.

After a while he got up, wiped his face as best he could on his sleeve, and gingerly felt the bits of himself that hurt. A bruise was rising on the back of his head and his back was sore from where he had crashed against the wall. He took off his jacket, unbuttoned his shirt and examined the place on his stomach where the man had hit him. There was a red mark which hurt to his touch.

He glanced up at the skylight. As far as he could tell it was about noon. It had once been his favourite time of the week, he had always felt a sense of excitement about Saturday around midday for it seemed to be the most vital time of the whole week; the time when the weekend finally got under way, when plans would start to be fulfilled. From beyond the walls of his prison came a sense of the city's vibrant life: familiar smells of cooking reached his nostrils and in the distance he could still hear the puzzling, faintly remembered sound that had earlier bothered him.

Carefully, he folded his jacket into a square and laid it the floor. Then he seated himself on it, cross-legged in the lotus position, and taking care to keep his aching back as straight as he could, he concentrated on his breathing.

He tried as hard as he could to make his mind a blank, to allow his subconscious the chance to tell him what he wanted to know. He knew that there were things deep in his subsconscious which were trying to percolate through: familiar sounds, familiar smells, overheard conversations, things briefly seen, which if only he could grasp them would help him make sense of what was happening.

He remained in the position for about twenty minutes and then relaxed and lay back on the floor, staring at the ceiling. He could not have said that he felt good but he felt better. In the final minutes of his meditation he had begun to realise the fundamental truth of what had happened to him. He had survived. Not since his late teens had Pilgrim experienced physical violence. He had sometimes wondered how he might react if he were to be attacked or physically threatened. Now he knew. In the past two weeks he had been kidnapped, threatened with torture, punched, menaced by a loaded gun at his head, sworn at, kicked and half suffocated. He had been nearly smashed to pulp in a van, had seen what was left of a man with his head blown off, the mangled bodies of men in a car smash, and the quivering torso of a man punctured by a gardening fork. He had also watched his friend and lover blown to bits in front of his eyes. Yet somehow he had survived. He was, he discovered, better and stronger and more resilient than he had ever supposed. He had undergone a metamorphosis; the shocking experiences of his recent life had hardened something inside him. He was surprised. He would never have thought it possible. Yet something told him that he might come through.

Pilgrim stood up and breathed in deeply, and as the air was drawn down into his lungs so the images in his subconscious were drawn up, clear and palpable, into his brain. The faint smell that prevaded the cellar was Greek cooking. The sound that had nagged him, half heard in the distant rumble of traffic, was the sound of road drills. He knew exactly where he was. He should have known before. He should have known from his brief glimpse of the power station that he was being taken from Fulham to a nondescript factory near the back of Vauxhall station. Some of the jigsaw began to fall into place. He was in the basement of the warehouse premises of the Foster Rowles Trading Co. The man who had hit him had been a friend of one of the men who had died in the car. He remembered the conversation he had heard outside the cellar door: the man had mentioned a name. He struggled to bring it to mind. Histon, that was it. Colonel Histon. The military rank had to mean that Foster Rowles was a front for some kind of official organisation, some kind of government security operation.

It was obvious. Addingham or one of the others had enlisted the help of a government security organisation to track them down and murder them. What fools he and Susan had been to believe that they could go up against men like the Lord Chief Justice, the Attorney General and the others. They were bound to have links to official organisations who would protect them if they were threatened. He and Susan had never had a chance from the beginning. As soon as they had started on their plan, they had signed their own death warrants.

Yet, he thought, it didn't entirely make sense. If they had meant to kill them both, why hadn't they shot him at the same time as Susan? And if the conspirators had enlisted a government agency to protect them from blackmail, then they would have had to reveal what they had done. That would have made them vulnerable. He couldn't believe they would do that. He puzzled over it. Susan had made sense when she had said they would pay up rather than be exposed. Why jeopardise a glittering career for a mere two hundred thousand pounds? Another thing puzzled him. If his captors were working for Addingham and the others, why had the three men attacked his kidnappers? After all, they were all on the same side. Addingham wouldn't have cared who disposed of him, as long as he was rid of him permanently.

Pilgrim got up from the bucket, stuck his hands into his beltless trousers and paced the floor. He had no idea how much the men in Foster Rowles knew. If they meant to interrogate him then he had to think of a story. He wandered around the cellar. The fact that Susan had ensured that there was no obvious connection between herself and Pilgrim could now, he reasoned, be to his advantage. He could deny all knowledge of her. It was a betrayal, he admitted to himself as he paced the stone flags, but not a very big one. She was dead and he was still alive, and if he wished to stay alive and regain his freedom, and even perhaps make someone pay for what they had done to her, then he had to use any method he could. Including denying her. Susan had taken Woodberry's papers from him, he could therefore deny all knowledge of the plot, tell them that he'd never heard of the Archbishop's Enterprise or Richard Thornbury. Unless Addingham was there. Pilgrim stopped. If Addingham was at the interrogation, then Pilgrim would have to tell the truth. Susan had killed them all to avenge her father and had set him up as a decoy. He stared at the whitewashed walls. It wasn't much of a story. It didn't sound like the truth. He resumed his pacing. Whatever happened, he resolved, he wouldn't go down without a fight. He would keep the bastards guessing.

They came for him in the middle of the afternoon. He was seated on the upturned bucket, listening to the rumblings in his empty stomach when he heard the key rattling in the lock. It was the same men.

'Come on,' said the man who had hit him. 'You're wanted.'

They flanked him as they walked along the stone passageway and climbed the wooden stairs to the ground floor. The warehouse was disused and dirty. They emerged into a cavernous hall. Running along its centre and disappearing into the murky far end was a row of black iron columns. The men led him through a narrow doorway in a corner and up a flight of stairs. The first floor of the building had been converted into offices. A corridor of partitioning ran along the length of the floor, off which led a number of offices. Fluorescent lights were suspended from a false ceiling. The offices looked like rabbit hutches and the place, especially on a deserted Saturday afternoon, had the tacky atmosphere of all government departments everywhere. Pilgrim and his escort climbed up two more floors, each of which had also been converted to offices. On the fourth floor the men led him towards the back of the building.

They stopped outside a pair of heavy oak-panelled doors which Pilgrim guessed had been installed when the warehouse had originally been built. The leading man rapped sharply on the doors.

'Come,' came a sharp command from inside. The man swung open both doors to allow Pilgrim and his other keeper to enter a large, unkempt room. Opposite the doors, on the room's far side, were a series of long windows which reached almost from the floor to the high ceiling and which gave a view, through their grime and dust, over the rooftops to the river and across Nine Elms Reach to Pimlico beyond. The other walls of the room were panelled in a light wood which had become pitted and mottled with age and neglect. Pilgrim and the men walked across a vast but threadbare Persian carpet to a big oak desk, on the other side of which was seated a man.

'Sit,' the man barked.

Pilgrim was pushed down onto a chair. The room's heavy doors thudded shut behind him. He turned and came face to face with his guard, the man who had hit him; he had pulled forward a chair and was sitting immediately behind Pilgrim's right shoulder.

'Look at me,' ordered the man behind the desk. It was a voice accustomed to authority. Pilgrim turned to the man, who stared at him with baleful pale blue eyes, then bent his head to consider some papers on his desk. His hair was iron grey, brushed straight back from his forehead, his features were sharp, and he seemed, although seated, to be as tall and thin as a spear. He was wearing a tweed sports jacket, check shirt and a dark knitted tie.

He looked up and pinned Pilgrim to the chair with his eyes. He leaned forward slightly in his chair, rested his forearms on the desk amd locked his fingers loosely together.

'What were you doing in that flat with Bronwyn-Taylor?'

'Who?' The question was out before Pilgrim realised that the man meant Susan. 'I spent the night there,' he said quickly.

'You spent the night there,' the man echoed. 'Why?'

'She made me go there. She forced me at the point of a gun. She captured me.'

'Captured you,' the man echoed again. 'Where?'

'At Jeffrey Frimley-Kimpton's.'

'Why were you there?'

'I'm a reporter. I'd gone there to interview him.'

'Interview him.' There was a trace of mockery in the man's

repetitions. 'You saw what she did to Frimley-Kimpton?'

Pilgrim nodded.

'Then you were a witness. Why didn't she shoot you?'

'She was going to,' Pilgrim said earnestly. 'If your men hadn't turned up she'd have shot me within hours. Look,' he continued, 'I just got caught up in all this. I don't know what it's all about. All I want is to get out of here. You've got no right to keep me.'

The man looked back down at the papers on his desk. 'She didn't shoot you,' he said, 'because you were her partner. Isn't that right?'

'No.'

The man pressed on in a cold, measured tone. 'You used the assumed name of Richard Thornbury in order to gain an audience with Sir Henry Dundonald, Sir Oliver Blackmore, Lord Addingham, Sir Ashley Brighton and Jeffrey Frimley-Kimpton.' The man narrowed his eyes as he surveyed Pilgrim. 'You went to see those men in order to murder them.'

Pilgrim's mouth opened and closed like a goldfish's. 'No, I didn't,' he managed to say.

'I think you did,' the man said bleakly. 'How else do you account for the fact that after either your seeing them or making an appointment to see them, Blackmore, Dundonald and Frimley-Kimpton were violently killed?'

'That had nothing to do with me.' Pilgrim could feel the sweat standing out on his forehead and dampening his back.

'Really? Then where were you going? This morning, with Bronwyn-Taylor?'

'I don't know,' Pilgrim lied.

'I think you do. You were going to Upham to Lord Addingham's home. There was a map in her bag. Upham was marked. Not that you would have got anywhere near him. We've had a tight security guard round him for days.'

Pilgrim felt no consolation in knowing that he'd been right when he'd told Susan there would be increased security at Addingham's. 'That wasn't my idea,' he said. 'I didn't want to go. I told you, she was going to make me. I was a prisoner.'

'Then why did she have the gun in her bag? Especially inside the flat. If she had to force you she'd have had that gun at your back. There would have been a gun fight, she might still have been alive and my men would have been dead.'

Pilgrim ruefully reflected that almost certainly he would have died in the crossfire.

'You were going to kill Addingham, just as you killed the others.'

'I didn't kill anybody.'

'I want to know who you are working for. Who else knows,' the man paused, 'about everything.'

Pilgrim scarcely heard the question. 'I didn't murder anybody,' he repeated.

'Who are you working for?' the man insisted.

Pilgrim had no notion of what he meant. 'I'm not working for anyone. I work for myself.'

'Who are you working for?' The voice was like a chain saw.

Pilgrim racked his brains trying to make sense of the question. 'I'm doing a few things for Martin and Danks in Peterborough,' he said 'and I'm writing a brochure for a legal publisher in Uppingham.'

He saw the man nod briefly to the guard seated close behind him. He turned to see what was meant by the signal. The outside edge of his guard's hand caught him a stinging blow across the top of his ear. With a yelp, Pilgrim fell forward off his chair and only saved himself from crashing to the floor by clinging to the edge of the oak desk. The pain in his ear and down the right side of his face was intense. He pulled himself up until his chin was level with the top of the desk.

'For Christ's sake,' he shouted looking up at his interrogator, 'I've told you. I don't work for anyone. I work for me. Freelance. Jesus.' He held his ear, trying to ease the pain. 'Will you tell him to stop hitting me.'

His guard lifted him bodily and pulled him roughly back into his chair. Pilgrim slumped in the seat, holding his aching ear in his cupped hand. There was silence in the room. With remote and unfeeling eyes, the man looked at Pilgrim across the desk. 'Frankly,' he said finally, 'I'm not impressed. I've seen better displays of pained innocence put on by mass murderers.' He leaned forward on his forearms, his fingers still interlaced, and contemplated Pilgrim's figure. 'To be perfectly honest, I can't make up my mind about you, Pilgrim. I can't make up my mind whether you're a professional, a real professional, a sleeper that we've been lucky enough to flush out in this business, or whether you're just a lucky amateur. If you're a pro we can maybe work something out; if you're an amateur then you really are very dangerous. Whatever you are, I intend to find out. One way or the other. Nobody knows you are here. No one is going to miss you. Your partner is dead and there isn't anyone else, is there, Pilgrim? We know that. We know all about you. Your little girlfriend isn't going to miss you for long.'

Pilgrim stared uncomprehendingly at the sharp features opposite. 'What?'

The man raised his eyebrows in a quizzical look. 'Your little horse-riding friend, Trixie.'

'How do you know about her?'

The man smiled.

'She doesn't know anything about any of this,' Pilgrim stated assertively.

'We know,' retorted the man. 'That one doesn't know about anything, not unless she can get it between her legs. But you were clever, or lucky, it took us most of the weekend to discover she wasn't the one we were after, which allowed your friend Bronwyn-Taylor to carry on with her plans.'

'You followed me,' said Pilgrim. It wasn't a question.

'Of course. We needed to know who you were. We learned a lot.' He shuffled the papers on his desk until he found the one he wanted. 'We know what you do for a living. We know your past, your background, who your parents were, your wife and children in the north. We know about that spot of bother when you were almost prosecuted for fraud. We know how much in debt you are. Yes, we know a lot about you, Pilgrim. We even know where you keep your dirty socks.'

Pilgrim felt crushed. The man held him in the palm of his hand, he had invaded his privacy and hijacked his past. There was nothing he didn't know about him. Well, almost nothing; he didn't know about Woodberry's papers or the blackmail plan. At least, for the moment. And there was something else, too, that just maybe the man and his minions didn't know.

'There are a few things to get to the bottom of yet,' the man continued. 'Who you are working for. What your connection was with Susan Bronwyn-Taylor. And how did you get hold of these? Who else knows about them?' The man held up a sheaf of papers. Pilgrim recognised them at once, the Woodberry papers.

So, they had it all. They knew who he was and what he'd tried to do. He wondered how they knew so much. 'How did you find out about me?' he asked wearily.

The man leaned back in his seat. Pilgrim noticed that the long, bony fingers remained loosely entwined, resting on the desk. 'We got onto you the first time you telephoned Addingham. We monitored the call, and the one to Blackmore.'

Pilgrim straightened up. Whoever these men were, they had to be powerful if they could tap the telephones of the mighty. Susan hadn't reckoned on that. Nor had he.

'You were using the name Richard Thornbury. That made them anxious to see you, which made us interested. You seemed to know a lot about them. We thought you were just some nasty little blackmailer, certainly Addingham and Blackmore were worried. We planned to pick you up when you went back to see Blackmore. Only your friend killed him in that hotel in Hampstead. So we missed you, we had no one watching the house; we hadn't expected you to go back after he was dead.'

'Well, that proves it, doesn't it?' Pilgrim said eagerly. 'I wouldn't have gone back if I'd been her partner.'

The man looked at him balefully. 'You went there in the first place to set him up and then you went back to retrieve these papers. Only we found them first. But like all your kind you got careless. You went to see the woman, Brandon-Burke, just to make sure Blackmore hadn't told her anything about his assignation with Bronwyn-Taylor. I suppose that if she'd known something, either you or she would have killed her. Anyway,' he added, 'you told her at which hotel you were staying.'

'And she told you.'

'Not at all,' replied the man. 'We got it on tape. We monitored everything.'

Pilgrim looked hard at the man opposite. The light from the grimy windows seemed to halo his head. He looked like a sinister spectre from the Inquisition. 'You even bug the homes of whores?'

'That lady's particular talents are in great demand by a number of very powerful people. It's important that we know what those people do and, even more, what they say. History is full of fools who talked to whores more than they ought,'

'I bet you get a kick out of listening to the action,' Pilgrim sneered.

'Not at all. I've a transcript of the weekend you spent with your little nymphomaniac. It makes very boring reading, all that yelping and shrieking. You almost burst my men's eardrums.'

Pilgrim was shocked. He recalled the time with Trixie. They had been like innocent animals. The knowledge that they'd been overheard seemed to cheapen it, to make it dirty. 'You listened in? You had my cottage bugged?'

'Please don't insult our intelligence by saying that you didn't know,' said the man wearily. 'You were there from Friday to Monday, yet after Friday evening you didn't make one telephone call. You made all your calls from the pub where you thought you couldn't be overheard. You knew we were on to you. You were a decoy for Bronwyn-Taylor.'

Pilgrim opened his mouth to deny it, to explain that the phone had been cut off, when he paused. Slowly he exhaled and closed his mouth. The man had made a mistake, a small yet elementary error. But there was no point, he thought, in denying everything. The man was convinced that he was in league with Susan. He remembered what the man had said earlier: if Pilgrim was a professional, then maybe they could work something out. He'd been playing it all wrong, telling the truth: the truth wasn't believable, at least not to the men who worked for Foster Rowles. He'd be better going along with what they believed, better trying to get the man across the desk to reveal what he knew and, and even more importantly, what he didn't know. Pilgrim shrugged and said nothing.

'Ah,' the thin man observed. 'I'm glad you don't deny it. I was beginning to lose my patience with all these pointless denials. You knew that we were on to you the night we failed to snatch you outside Addingham's chambers.'

Pilgrim nodded. 'I knew something was going wrong,' he said with feeling.

'It was a cock-up.' The man glowered briefly at the guard sitting close behind Pilgrim. 'We expected you at the chambers but instead of waiting for you there, my men, once they knew it, waited at your hotel to grab you. They were lucky to get to the chambers in time to get you away from Blackmore's thugs.'

'Is that who they were?'

The man nodded. 'These papers had Addingham and Blackmore worried. They telephoned each other after you'd seen them. Between them they put together a picture. From

494

what you'd said, they guessed that your partner was a woman and that you were double-crossing her by asking for half the money in Switzerland and half the money in England. They calculated that if you disappeared, your partner would probably do nothing. If the papers came to light they would say they were forgeries. Interesting picture,' the man reflected. 'Wrong, of course, but they couldn't possibly know you were setting them up to be murdered. They thought it was worth the risk to get rid of you. Blackmore used a middle man to hire the two heavies.'

Pilgrim reflected how accurate had been the barrister's assessment of the situation. He'd obviously revealed more of his hand than he'd realised. They were clever men, cleverer than he was, and if it had not been for Foster Rowles, he would certainly have been murdered by the two hired killers. 'What happened to them?' he enquired.

The man considered him coldly. 'They've taken up residence in Essex. At the bottom of a flooded quarry. So has the man Blackmore used as go-between.'

Pilgrim stared at him, shocked at his cold, matter-of-fact tone.

'We have to protect our interests.' The man leaned forward. 'Why did you go back to the hotel when you knew we were on to you?'

Pilgrim recalled the night the men had waylaid him and his return to the hotel in a state of shock and shaking terror. 'I'd nowhere else to go,' he said simply. It may have been his tone of voice, but the man seemed to accept it. 'Why didn't you pick me up there?' he enquired. 'You had the chance that night or the next morning.'

'Because by then we had realised the pattern,' the man told him. 'A dark-haired American woman had booked the room in which Blackmore was murdered. It all began to fit: you had an appointment to see them, then she murdered them. After our forensic people had been over the room we knew that the woman had reddish hair, was in her early thirties, and was probably English. We had an idea what she looked like, but we didn't know who she was. We needed you to lead us to her.'

Pilgrim was beginning to see it. Somehow it did all make some sort of mad sense. Susan's plan to use him as a decoy had been almost perfect. The only factor she hadn't foreseen was that they would come up against such ruthless men. 'So you followed me,' he stated flatly. Then he remembered that that morning, Thursday, he had been to see Susan. Why hadn't they come for them then?

The man answered the unasked question. 'You gave us the slip. Not many people do that, not twice in twelve hours,' he said coldly. 'You went to see Bronwyn-Taylor, didn't you?'

Pilgrim nodded.

'You changed your plans. We should have realised it. When you went back to the hotel you were a decoy. You thought you could shake my men off any time you wanted, so you decided to keep us pinned down watching you in Gretton while your partner planned to murder Sir Henry.'

Pilgrim said nothing.

'We were monitoring Dundonald's place. We picked up the call you made. We knew you were going to see him on the Monday morning.'

'So why didn't you grab us then?' enquired Pilgrim.

'For God's sake, you know why. You switched the plan. We expected you to frighten Dundonald with these papers and then Bronwyn-Taylor to turn up later to kill him. But you switched. She got to him first. We were following you, expecting her to come afterwards. You knew all the time she was going to be there first. You made fools out of us.' The man paused, his eyes hard. 'So we lost Dundonald. But you were just a bit too cocky. Your timing was off. Bronwyn-Taylor was in such a hurry to get away, she almost crashed into the vehicle we had following you. My men got the number. We had the police searching for that car for days. When we found your car abandoned close to Frimley- Kimpton's house, we guessed that you would be holed up somewhere in London. Then we had a piece of luck.' He flexed the muscles of his jaw for a moment. 'You should learn to be a better driver.'

'What do you mean?'

'We monitored a routine police report. You had been reported by some lorry driver for dangerous driving on the motorway. We questioned him, he remembered seeing your car again, going over Putney bridge. We had the police scouring the whole of West London for your car. So we found you.'

Pilgrim's mind went back to the morning and the ghastly scene of blood and splattered brains.

'Did you have to shoot her?' he asked quietly. 'Like that? Like some dog? You didn't give her a chance to surrender.'

'Would she have surrendered? I doubt it. She wanted to go down screaming defiance. What chance do you think she gave Blackmore and the others?'

'Maybe they deserved it,' said Pilgrim. 'They were thieves. And murderers. All of them. What chance did those poor bloody squaddies on Pinta Leone get, or Richard Thornbury, or George Stansgate for that matter.'

The man across the desk contemplated him, the thin face blank, the hands clasped easily together, resting on the desk. 'What on earth has that got to do with it?' he enquired. 'Bronwyn-Taylor was a killer, and a brutal killer at that. What's more, I'm pretty sure that she had been trained to do what she did. I think she was part of a plan to destroy most of this country's key people.'

Pilgrim was scarcely listening. He had picked up on something the man had said, or more accurately something he hadn't said, a connection that he hadn't made. He was beginning to see an angle.

'Why didn't you pick her up at Frimley-Kimpton's?' he asked. 'You could have laid a trap. You must have known she would go there.'

The man looked faintly puzzled. 'Why should we know that? We were expecting her, or you, at Lord Addingham's. We weren't monitoring Frimley-Kimpton's phone. He wasn't that important. A good candidate for a snivelling little blackmailer like you but not someone we could have expected your partner to go for first. But the others . . .' The man's voice trailed away, his eyes grew troubled and then hardened as he looked at Pilgrim. 'You have a lot to answer for, including the death of my men. So you had better start talking. How did you arrange that car smash?'

'I didn't arrange it, for Christ's sake. It was all their own fault.' Pilgrim heard the guard behind shift in his seat. He continued: 'Your blokes were trying to ram us, drive us off the road. They got careless. They couldn't see past our van. I drove off the road and they skidded into the lorry. We weren't responsible for that.'

'Who was driving?'

'I was.'

'What happened?'

Pilgrim described the nightmare ride, though he omitted to mention that Susan had achieved multiple orgasms all the way down the hill.

'So what happened after they crashed?'

'The car blew up, burst into flames. There couldn't have been much left afterwards.'

'There wasn't anything left?' Pilgrim heard the man sitting close behind him grunt. 'I mean before it blew up.'

Pilgrim thought for a few seconds before answering. 'We got out and went to the wreck to see if there was anything we could do. They were all dead. We went back to the van. The Volkswagen was in a mess, bashed about at the front and the back. Susan was worried about how she was going to drive it. Then the car burst into flames.'

'But you took the guns first?'

'What guns?'

'You took three automatic pistols belonging to the dead men in the car.'

'I don't know anything about any guns.'

This time Pilgrim didn't see the signal, he just felt the man's thick, hard fingers in his hair. He shouted as his head was jerked backwards, it felt as if the guard was about to rip his scalp clean off his skull. He tried to struggle but the man's other hand closed over his right ear. Slowly and deliberately he began to rip the top of it away from Pilgrim's head. He screamed with the pain, trying pathetically to wrench the hand away. Punctuating the agony he could hear, as if from a great distance, the precise, brittle voice from across the desk. 'If you continue to tell lies he will tear your ear right off your head . . . The gun in Bronwyn-Taylor's bag also had your fingerprints on it . . . smudged but there . . . Fire doesn't destroy everything . . . There should have been traces left of three guns . . . There were none . . . Where are the guns?'

Pilgrim could scarcely get his words out. The pain was thundering inside his head. 'All right, all right. I'll tell you,' he choked. The man behind let go. Pilgrim slumped forward in his seat, dropping his head to the right and with his hand pressing his damaged ear firmly against the side of his head. His face was screwed into a mask of agony. For a few seconds the room was quiet.

'Well, come on.'

Pilgrim raised his head. He was crying, great tears were rolling down his cheeks and dripping off his chin. He could feel his severed flesh, and when he took his hand away his fingers were covered in blood.

'Get on with it,' ordered the man.

'For God's sake, wait. Please, just a moment.' Pilgrim wept. 'Oh Christ, it hurts.'

'It'll hurt a bloody sight more if you don't get a move on.'

Pilgrim regarded his tormentor with abomination. How he hated the man, as thin and unfeeling as a stick, sitting so unperturbed, his bony fingers laced together elegantly above his desk. He wanted to hurt him, destroy him. Smash him, deny him what he wanted. Somewhere inside there was a small part of Pilgrim which was not consumed by the burning agony of his torture, a part which smouldered and crackled like dry ice, a small freezing element which coldly calculated the angles and the infinity of inappropriate answers.

'Well?'

'Susan saw that one of the bodies had a gun sticking out from under his jacket. So she asked me to get it for her.' Pilgrim's voice was flat and drained. He pressed his hand against his head to ease the agony, the blood from the ripped flesh seeping through his fingers.

'And?'

'She asked me to check if the others had guns.'

'So you took all three?'

Pilgrim nodded, his hand moving with his head.

'Did you take anything else?'

'No.' Pilgrim bunched his shoulder muscles, sending waves of pain into the side of his head, waiting for the blow that would mean he wasn't believed. None came.

'Where are the guns now?'

'I don't know, Susan had them.'

'She had one, where are the other two?'

'I don't know. I gave them to her.'

The man gave him a hard look. 'There's no trace of them in the flat. Where are they?'

Pilgrim was conscious of the guard close behind him. 'I don't know,' he gabbled in panic. 'I don't know.'

'You were her partner. You must know.'

Pilgrim took a deep breath. 'I wasn't her partner,' he said. 'I worked for her.'

The look on the man's face changed to puzzlement. 'What do you mean?'

'She's the one I was working for. I was working for her,' he repeated.

'Doing what?'

'Doing what you caught me doing.'

Again the man looked puzzled. Clearly, he was not hearing what he expected to hear. Pilgrim had managed to steal just a tiny bit of the initiative. 'She was using me to flush out Addingham and the others, to set them up, I suppose.'

'So you admit that you and she were in it together?'

'No, that's what I'm telling you. She gave me all the dirt so I could blackmail them. But she was using me as a kind of harbinger. I didn't know she was coming after to kill them.'

'Are you trying to tell me that you and she were not lovers?' the man said disbelievingly. 'And this outbreak of assassinations was not the result of your both working together?'

Pilgrim did his best to let out a hollow laugh. 'I was meant to be the last victim in the chain. If your men hadn't turned up, she was going to kill me after she'd killed Addingham.'

'You don't seriously expect me to believe that?'

'Think about it,' said Pilgrim. 'If you hadn't traced her car and found us when you did, and if I'd ended up dead alongside Addingham, how would you have been able to tie her in to the murders?'

'Simple, through you. You and she were having an affair. The connection would be obvious.'

'But we weren't,' said Pilgrim.

The man leaned forward slightly. 'You've already been warned about lying,' he said. 'Right now some of my people are conducting an autopsy on the body of your friend. You spent last night together in that flat. If you were lovers there is no way it will be hidden from my pathologist.'

Pilgrim closed his eyes against the vision of Susan's once lovely body lying torn open on a mortuary slab. 'I worked with her years ago on a newspaper,' he said tonelessly. 'Then a few months ago, she picked me up when I was down and out. She paid me to work for her.' Pilgrim thought of all the easily traced cheques Susan had paid him. 'That was all there was to it. I tried to get her to go to bed,' he said, 'but she didn't want to know.'

The man's eyes were narrowed in deep suspicion. 'What work were you doing for her?'

'All sorts of things but mainly she wanted me to do some research on a few people.'

'Who?'

Pilgrim paused before he answered. It was time to test his theory that there were some things the man across the desk didn't know. 'For a start, Sir Ashley Brighton and a man called Simon Woodberry. He's the man who wrote those,' he nodded to the papers on the desk. 'He was a kind of country squire in Gloucestershire.'

'I know who he was, for God's sake,' the man interrupted him. 'Why did she want you to research Brighton and Woodberry?'

'She didn't say, not then. She paid me and I found out as much as I could about them.'

'What did you find out? You didn't find anything out about this?' The man indicated the Woodberry papers on his desk.

For a moment Pilgrim thought there was a note of anxiety in his voice. 'No, I didn't know anything about those. Susan got hold of those papers after she murdered Woodberry.'

'What?'

Pilgrim had been right, there were things that the man didn't know, and those things made him anxious.

'After she murdered Woodberry she figured out where he had hidden the papers,' he continued.

'She murdered Woodberry?' The voice was incredulous, the long entwined fingers were gripping each other. 'Woodberry had an accident in Scotland.'

'She shot him with a hunting rifle.'

The man looked beyond Pilgrim to the guard.

'We found an Anschutz in the boot of the car,' came the deep voice from behind.

The man's eyes flicked back to Pilgrim. 'How do you know she'd murdered him?'

'She told me.'

The look of incredulity deepened. 'You seriously expect me to believe that Bronwyn-Taylor would risk everything to murder a county squire like Woodberry. Why? What would she expect to get out of that?'

'He was the only one she knew about for sure.'

The man looked blank. 'What do you mean?'

'She knew about Woodberry for certain and she suspected Brighton. She knew there had to be others but she didn't know who they were. Not until she found the papers.'

'What others?'

'The others who destroyed her father.'

The furrows on the brow deepened. 'What are you talking about?'

Pilgrim took a deep breath. 'You only know her as Susan Bronwyn-Taylor,' he said, 'but her real name, her maiden name, was Susan Stansgate. She was George Stansgate's daughter.'

The long entwined fingers broke apart. 'What?'

'Susan was George Stansgate's daughter.'

'I don't believe you.' The tall figure moved irritably in the seat.

'It's true,' said Pilgrim. 'She killed them all for revenge. Blackmore, Dundonald, Frimley-Kimpton – it was a vendetta. Maybe she even murdered Ashley Brighton, or at least helped him have his heart attack.'

The man was silent for some seconds, the fingers of his right hand drumming on the desk. 'But how did she know?' he asked, almost as if to himself.

'She had the papers,' Pilgrim said.

'Before that. You said she knew about Woodberry for certain. How?'

'Her father told her.'

'Her father was killed in a road accident soon after he left prison.'

'But he was out long enough to tell her what he suspected. He was a long time in prison. For something he didn't do. Plenty of time to think, to put things together. So when he got out he told Susan everything he suspected. She was only eleven. Impressionable. She didn't think anything about it then, but she remembered it all later on.'

'But her father couldn't have known for certain that Woodberry had anything to do with his imprisonment. He must have been even less sure about Brighton. Yet you're telling me that that bloody woman fanatically decided to kill both of them merely on the suspicions of her gross, stupid father?'

'He was her father and they framed him. To her it was justice. Anyway, it wasn't just on his suspicions. She was absolutely sure before she killed him that Woodberry was involved.'

'How?'

'She lived in America for a few years. While she was there she decided to go to Panama to trace Max Gonzales.'

'Gonzales left Panama in 1967.'

'She traced him all the same. She was good at tracking people. Don't forget, Gonzales and Portalier were the only people her father knew for certain had conspired against him. She caught up with Gonzales in Santa Cruz. He told her everything.'

'Everything? What do you mean everything? He hardly knew anything.'

The thin body beyond the desk was agitated. The man's eyes flickered continually between Pilgrim and his guard. It seemed almost as if he had become uncomfortable at Pilgrim's presence in his office. With what seemed an effort he fixed his eyes on Pilgrim. They had lost their needle-sharp glare, they seemed misted over, as if there was something in what he had been told which worried him.

'Gonzales knew it was Woodberry who had come to brief him in the first place. He'd checked.'

The man was silent for a few seconds, shaking his head slowly as if in regret. 'So, he told her about Woodberry and from there she went on to dig up these?' He nodded at the papers. 'And with your help she wipes out the Attorney General and the Governor of the Bank of England. God knows where she would have stopped if we hadn't caught up with her.' He paused. 'Where are the originals of these papers?'

'I don't know,' Pilgrim lied. 'I never saw any originals.'

'There's a lot you don't know, isn't there, Pilgrim?' The thin man's voice was sarcastic. 'You don't know where the originals are.' He jabbed his finger at the papers on the desk. 'You don't know where the guns are. For a man who knows so much irrelevant rubbish about this affair, you know unbelievably little about the really important elements.'

'How should I know about your bloody guns?' Pilgrim said angrily. 'I'm not into guns. It was Susan who knew all about guns, she learnt about them in America. Maybe she's hidden them. Or given them to someone.'

'America?' The man stared vacantly past Pilgrim, deep in thought. 'That's where she was trained, was it?' He turned his attention back to Pilgrim. 'Given them to someone,' he repeated. 'Who else knows about all this?'

Pilgrim shrugged. The pain on the right side of his head was coming in waves. 'I told you I was just the hired help, the poor bastard who has been stuck with all the blame. She wouldn't have told me if anybody else was involved.'

The man frowned at him. 'Why did you agree to help her?'

'Money,' said Pilgrim simply.

'How much did she pay you?'

'Not very much,' Pilgrim responded. 'When you are as broke as I am, not much is a lot.'

'So, she asked you to research Woodberry and Brighton. What then?'

'After that she asked me to research all the others.'

'Why?'

'She didn't tell me. She just paid me. That was good enough.'

'But you must have wondered why.'

'I did and then one day she came to the cottage in Gretton with these papers and that explained it all.'

'The originals?' The man leapt on it.

'No,' Pilgrim replied. 'Copies. She'd found them at Woodberry's home.'

'Did she tell you then that she'd shot him?'

'No, she spoke as if she had liked him. She called him uncle. He was the person who had introduced her stepfather to her mother.'

The man looked thoughtful. 'Go on,' he ordered.

'She told me that with the papers we could blackmail everyone. They would all pay to keep us quiet.'

'So you agreed?'

Pilgrim shrugged. 'I figured they would pay a lot of money not to be exposed.'

'You meant to double-cross her and keep the money?'

'No, she was too cute for that. She'd opened a Swiss bank account. I was to tell them to transfer their money into that.'

The man raised his eyebrows. 'So how did you intend to make any money?'

'I told them to transfer one hundred thousand pounds into the Swiss account and have another one hundred thousand pounds made out to Richard Thornbury as a banker's draft.'

The man said nothing.

'I went to see Blackmore and Addingham and I tried to see Brighton, but he was dead. Then Addingham's heavies got hold of me. After that I wanted to get out. It was too dangerous, it wasn't worth the money. I told Susan I wanted out on Thursday morning.'

'Having lost the men I had tailing you. If you told her you

wanted to get out of her little scheme, why did you go to see Dundonald?'

'After I got over the fright of those men attacking me, I thought about it. It seemed worth the chance. I still needed the money.'

'Yet even after you had seen what your friend had left of Dundonald you went to see Frimley-Kimpton.'

Pilgrim closed his eyes, the pain of his torn ear made thinking difficult. 'He was the last chance,' he said weakly. 'The newspapers said that Dundonald had shot himself. I didn't know Susan had shot him.'

'Why did you go to Frimley-Kimpton's with Bronwyn-Taylor?'

'I didn't. She was there already. She had just killed Frimley-Kimpton when I arrived. She forced me to go back to Fulham with her where she told me the whole story.'

There was silence in the room. 'You expect me to believe all this?' asked the man finally.

'It's the truth,' Pilgrim said.

'If she knew Woodberry so well that she could call him uncle, why should she ask you to research him? She knew enough about him already.'

Pilgrim had seen the question coming some time before. 'She told me afterwards that it was a test, just to see how good my research was. I checked up everything on him, his private phone number, life style, habits, friends, his clubs in London, all of that. She told me I'd done a good job.'

'If you were supposed to blackmail them,' the man persisted, 'why did Bronwyn-Taylor kill them before they paid you?'

'She thought Blackmore had already moved the money to Switzerland. She went to see Dundonald because I'd told her I didn't want any more part in her plan.'

'So, if you couldn't make them pay blackmail money, she was going to murder them?'

Pilgrim stared directly at the man. 'I didn't know she had

always intended to kill them. Not until yesterday. But I do know that once I'd got her in to see Lord Addingham, by posing as Richard Thornbury, and she'd killed him, my usefulness would have been at an end. She'd have killed me too.'

The man across the desk stared intently at him, the familiar piercing look back in his eyes. 'All right,' he said abruptly. 'That will do for now. I'm going to have everything you've told me checked and double-checked. I've a good idea that it's all a pack of lies and if it is, then I promise you, you will suffer. You'd better think about that tonight.'

Pilgrim felt the heavy hand of his guard pulling him to his feet. The pain of his injured ear was intense. 'Wait a minute,' he said loudly. 'You can't keep me here. I haven't done anything, for Christ's sake. I've told you the truth. You can't keep me locked up.'

The thin man looked up at him. 'Yes I can.' His voice was as cold and sharp as the arctic wind. 'I can do what I like with you, Pilgrim. I can hurt you, make you scream in agony, make you confess to whatever I want. I can destroy you. Remember that.'

His words made the skin on the back of Pilgrim's neck crawl. As the guard grabbed his arm to haul him away from the desk he caught sight of a chandelier hanging from a dirty, alabaster rose in the centre of the ceiling. On it, festooned in tiers, were hundreds of crystal drops. They were shaped like coffins.

He was taken, holding his bloodied head and stumbling, back to his cellar in silence. He turned as the guard was pushing him through the doorway. 'I'm hungry,' he said. 'I haven't eaten since breakfast.' The heavy door slammed shut in his face.

As the light from the barred skylights was fading, they brought him a mattress, a pillow and a couple of blankets. The light was too far gone for him to examine the bed clothes closely. They did not smell too clean, but he was past caring. He was grateful for somewhere to lie down to ease the pain in his head. The cellar was cold. He huddled on the mattress fully clothed and wrapped the blankets round himself. In the middle of the evening they brought him a plate of lukewarm fish and chips, some bread and a cup of hot tea. Pilgrim gobbled it down and afterwards felt better. Later the single fluorescent light went out and the cellar became as black as a tomb. Pilgrim took off his shoes and lay down beneath the blankets. The pain on the right side of his face had become a steady throb. He brought his hand up to within inches of his eyes; it was so dark he could see nothing. It was like being blind, he thought, or maybe dead.

Death was a spectre that had dogged him for days, ever since he had become involved in the Archbishop's Enterprise. In the last twenty-four hours the spectre had been close, waiting silently at his left shoulder, watching. He had become almost used to it, like a hunchback to his deformity. Much of his terror had gone, or at least subsided. There was still fear, tremors of it would ripple through his body from time to time like the aftermath of some fever, but it was no more than a frisson, momentarily distracting him from his preoccupation with the jigsaw of intrigue which filled his brain. He felt as he had felt earlier that day, that there were things he had heard which could give him answers, words that could tell him the truth, signals which might show him the way out. There were things, too, that Susan had said way back, centuries ago, before he had started on the mad escapade to blackmail the most powerful men in England. There was what the thin man had said, and what he hadn't said. If he could only put them together, they might make a pattern. But he didn't even know what they were. He knew that information of great significance had been conveyed to him, but he hadn't recognised it and it had disappeared into his subconscious.

He wished Susan had been there, she wouldn't have missed anything, she had always been quick to make connections. The tears pricked his eyes. Throughout his interrogation he had blamed Susan, made her responsible for everything. Yet he felt that she wouldn't have minded that. She would have understood. She had been a realist, she would have accepted that as she was dead and he wasn't, his only course of action was to survive. And if that meant blaming her, then he had to do it. Not that he really thought it was her fault that he was here. It had been her idea to start with and she had murdered those men, but he knew that it was as much his own greed and weakness that had got him where he was. It was almost as if from the start he had been destined to find himself in a cellar, hurt, tortured, and facing death.

He thought about his interrogation. The thin man had been shocked at the news that the woman his men had shot that morning was George Stansgate's daughter. Pilgrim wondered why that should disturb him so much and why he was so concerned about the Woodberry papers. His reaction to their existence was all wrong. Pilgrim stared into the blackness. The dark had no answers.

The throbbing in his head had subsided. He could feel his tense and aching muscles beginning to relax. His mind was turning in on itself as sleep closed in. He had survived the day and that, in his new-found philosophy, was sufficient. He'd been hurt but he'd had some victories. He had induced the man to tell him what he knew and had got him to accept his story. At least for the present. If he checked it out thoroughly he might find the holes in it and then . . . but that was tomorrow and sleep would not be denied by fears of another day.

Chapter Ten

He awoke to a grey morning. The dirty glass of the cellar windows was streaked with rain. Sunday was coming down as dull as the ache in Pilgrim's body. There was a large scab at the top of his ear which hurt to his touch. He hadn't shaved for two days, he felt filthy and he could smell himself.

About an hour later, one of the men brought him some bread and margarine and a cup of lukewarm tea. 'When are you going to let me out of here?' Pilgrim wailed.

The man said nothing as he locked the cellar door.

Pilgrim spent the morning lying on the mattress, his hands behind his head, staring at the ceiling. It was quiet, occasionally he heard the swish of tyres on the wet roads outside the warehouse, but beyond that the city was silent. In the middle of the morning he heard the sound of distant church bells and calculated it was near eleven o'clock. He remembered the Sundays he had spent as a child, trailing behind his mother in search of God, sitting in churches and chapels and meeting houses and prayer groups; the great deserts of dull and tedious time which were his Sundays, filled with insipid ritual and howling prejudice, and all manner of Gods except the one his mother sought to bring her comfort.

He practised some yoga, sitting cross-legged on the mattress breathing deeply, emptying his mind, concentrating on a white gull wheeling above the waves. It made him feel better but unlike the previous day his meditation did nothing to draw out any answers to the puzzles in his brain. The rain stopped and a band of watery sunlight trickled through the windows.

They came for him at about midday.

Without a word he and the guards retraced their steps up to the fourth floor and into the large panelled office. The thin man seated behind the desk was dressed exactly as he had been the previous day. His face showed no emotion as Pilgrim was pushed roughly into his chair. He heard the guard sit down behind him.

'I've had a busy night checking your story,' the man told him. 'It seems you were right, Bronwyn-Taylor was Stansgate's daughter.'

'I told you she was.' Pilgrim was defiant.

'We've checked up on Woodberry. Until we can compare the bullet which killed him with Bronwyn-Taylor's gun, we can't be sure but it's quite possible that he was murdered. We've had a report that a dark-haired woman was seen getting out of a Peugeot near Ashley Brighton's home on the day he died. We know Brighton had a bad heart. It would have been easy enough to frighten him to death.'

'Right,' said Pilgrim, 'now you've found out I was telling the truth, you can let me go.'

The man gave him a frosty smile. 'On the contrary. You've told us about another two murders to which you are an accessory. You supplied Bronwyn-Taylor with the information which enabled her to kill these men. You omitted to tell me that Gonzales was dead, murdered by your girl friend, and you also conveniently forgot about the briefcase you deposited at King's Cross. And I still need to know what role you played in all this.'

'I told you, I did some work for Susan. Then she used me as cover. She set me up. She would have killed me once she'd finished with me. Why don't you just let me go? You don't need me now.'

The man contemplated him for a few seconds, the silent,

Sunday light streaming through the tall windows behind him. Slowly, he shook his head. 'I'm not letting you go, Pilgrim. Not now. Maybe not ever. Certainly not until you've told me the truth.'

'I've told you the truth,' Pilgrim insisted.

'You little bastard. You wouldn't know the truth if it jumped up and bit you in the throat. Did you honestly believe that I was going to sit here and swallow that fairy tale you told me yesterday?'

'It's not a fairy tale.'

'Of course it is. I really ought to have you severely punished for wasting my time with all that nonsense about her merely employing you. You were lovers.'

Pilgrim said nothing. He knew that this was a time to keep silent.

'You had me fooled at first, there were no traces of love-making in her body from the night you spent in the flat. But since then we've been right through the flat and we've also been through the house in Elizabeth Street with a fine-tooth comb.'

Pilgrim looked surprised.

'The house is empty so we've had time to search thoroughly and do the job properly. Nobody would know we'd been there. We found flight tickets and a hotel reservation. One double room,' he emphasised, 'in her name and yours. The Swiss bank account is in both your names, you are co-signatory.'

Pilgrim stared at him, appalled at the meaning in the man's words.

'We found letters in the flat,' the man continued. 'Some go back years to when you first met. Letters from you to her and from her to you. She wrote letters to you from America but never posted them. They're full of pathetic rubbish about love and being together. The last one is dated a few days ago. Apart from some more sentimental drivel, it's clear she had no remorse about killing anyone, she was concerned with not getting caught and,' he leaned forward, 'with ensuring you weren't implicated. You and she were both partners and lovers.'

Pilgrim gazed woodenly at the man whose words were his sentence of death. Pilgrim's entire case, his hope of a way out, had been based on his belief that Susan had set him up. But everything she had told him had been true. She had genuinely planned for them to make a lot of money and to enjoy it together. She had, as she told him, planned that they go away for a while after it was all over. In her own way, she had loved him and now her love was going to kill him. The man's discoveries destroyed all Pilgrim's defences.

Again, he felt tears pricking behind his eyes. Not tears of self-pity, but tears of shame. He had mistrusted Susan and his attempts to escape had been based upon that mistrust. He had betrayed her. Again.

But instead of tears, he began to laugh. He couldn't stop. He held the aching side of his head as his body shook with uncontrollable chuckling. It was all hysterically funny. Only he, he thought, could get it so wrong, so badly, so often. Only he could have made such a terrible misjudgement about his lover and friend. It was hilarious. Whatever the thin man had in store for him, Pilgrim reckoned that he deserved it; anybody who got things as screwed up as he did, deserved everything they had coming. Pilgrim's mood had turned kamikaze.

The man waited for his laughter to subside. 'You're not in a position which normally gives rise to much hilarity,' he observed.

'Oh?' said Pilgrim and went off into another bout of insane chuckling.

The man became angry. 'If you waste any more of my time or if you continue to evade my questions or tell me lies, I shall order him,' he nodded at the guard seated close behind whom Pilgrim had forgotten, 'to tear that ear right off.'

The threat sobered Pilgrim immediately.

'That's better,' said the man. 'Yesterday's little fairy tale was a waste of my time. It was quite clever, I'll give you that. It was loose enough to fit all the facts. It could have been true only we both know it wasn't. Was it?'

Pilgrim shook his head. 'No.'

'We both know that you're not the innocent pawn you've tried to make out. Are you? You weren't working for Bronwyn-Taylor, were you? It was the other way round. She was working for you, wasn't she?'

Pilgrim said nothing, he was fascinated to hear the man's version of events.

'You see, Pilgrim, we know what you were after. There are in this world certain people who spend their time trawling for the disaffected, looking out for the impressionable, the idealistic, the gullible. And when they've found them, they recruit them. To become whatever they want them to become, traitors or terrorists or whatever. We've had our share of such people in this country, academics mainly, at Cambridge, but now and again we uncover such a procurer in some other gutter. Like you. You recruited Bronwyn-Taylor. You set her up to kill Dundonald, Blackmore and the others, but before you let her loose, you went to see them, to put the black on them. Only she was too eager, wasn't she? She couldn't wait. You wanted their money all right. But it was to fund some other activities of yours, wasn't it? Terrorism maybe, and high-level assassination. Whatever activities they are, Pilgrim, you are going to tell me about them and about where you get your orders.'

Pilgrim had the mad desire to start laughing again at his discovery that he wasn't the only person in that room who was capable of getting things completely wrong. He pretended a coughing fit to cover the gurgling he felt welling up inside him. 'You're crazy,' was all he could manage.

'Am I? I don't think so. It's you who are crazy if you expect me to believe that you went to see those men just to blackmail them for money. No one in their right mind would demand part payment for blackmail, some in Switzerland and some in England. No, you wanted money in Switzerland because from Switzerland money can be moved easily, can't it? To Russia or maybe somewhere else in Eastern Europe. Or to Libya or Iran or Eire. Or even America. It's one of those places, isn't it, Pilgrim? Of course, you also needed funds here in England to support your activities. So that's why you told them to divide the money. It was a clever plan, I'll give you that,' the man continued. 'Blackmail them and then murder them. All you needed was somebody like Bronwyn-Taylor. And once you had found her you went to great lengths to invent a story which would induce her to kill the most important people in this country.'

'Invent?' Pilgrim queried. 'I didn't invent any story.'

'Of course you did.' The man was insistent. He picked up the Woodberry papers from his desk. 'This is a complete fabrication.'

Pilgrim was startled. Even the man across the desk couldn't get it that wrong. 'No it's not,' he protested. 'That's the truth. All those things happened. I've seen the newspaper cuttings. The massacre on Pinta Leone, Thornbury going missing, his firm going bust. You can check. It all happened.'

'I know it happened. I know the actual events happened, but you wove this fairy tale around them.' He waved the papers above his head. 'You invented the story of the land fraud to fit the events. It's easy enough for someone like you. And then you induced Bronwyn-Taylor to kill the men in the Archbishop's Enterprise because you got her to believe they'd murdered her father.'

'But that's Addingham's writing. And Woodberry's. And there's all those receipts and things.' The man's insistence that the fraud was an invention, that it never happened, disturbed Pilgrim.

'Forgeries,' the man replied flatly. 'All of it is forged.'

'They're not forged, for Christ's sake,' Pilgrim retorted angrily. He heard the guard move ominously behind him; he sat further back in his seat and tried to calm himself. 'Compare their handwriting,' he said more slowly, 'you'll see. Those papers are genuine.'

'There's no way I can tell,' said the man. 'These are photocopies. I could compare if I had the originals, but they don't exist, do they? You created all these papers, copied them and then destroyed the originals.'

Pilgrim was cornered. The existence of the originals in Norfolk was his only remaining card. Maybe the man had been trying to get him to play it but he knew now wasn't the time. There was a long silence. The man opposite slowly and deliberately placed the wad of documents back on the desk. His baleful eyes flickered between Pilgrim and the silent guard.

'This story of revenge for crimes against her father is complete rubbish. These killings were political. Bronwyn-Taylor's father was a paranoid slob who believed that the world owed him a living and who went to prison for petty fraud. She was a neurotic, she had a nervous breakdown in America. A woman like her would believe anything. All it would need to set her off would be some little worm like you to fabricate a story like this. You put her up to it. She was just a puppet, it was you who was pulling her strings.'

'You've got it all wrong. I went to see Addingham and Blackmore about the story. Remember? They didn't deny it. You yourself said that they were both worried after I had been to see them. That proves it.'

'It proves nothing of the sort. Mud sticks. They were worried because accusations had been made, not because they were true. These were powerful men, with enemies. They have reputations to protect.'

'To the extent of trying to have me murdered?'

'Naturally. Reputations are hard won. They worked hard to get where they were. So did we. And then you and that bloody woman came along and destroyed it all.' The man's face was tense with pent-up fury.

'I didn't destroy it.' Pilgrim's voice was beginning to whine. 'Susan did it for revenge. It was justice.'

'It was political. There was nothing to revenge. You made it all up.'

'I didn't make it up.' Pilgrim couldn't understand why the man was so insistent that the story was false. 'It's all true. The fraud, the land deal on Pinta Leone, it all happened. Susan went to see Gonzales. She made him talk. Then she came to London to look for John Portalier.'

The man aross the desk shook his head. 'Portalier died of a heart attack in 1964.' There was a knock on the door. The thin man kept his eyes on Pilgrim's face. 'Come,' he barked.

The double doors behind Pilgrim were pushed open and a man strode into the room. He was carrying an envelope which he handed to the thin man who dismissed him with a sharp nod of his head. The messenger took one brief glance at Pilgrim before disappearing the way he had come. Pilgrim heard the double doors close firmly behind him as he vacantly watched the man read the contents of the envelope. His mind was elsewhere. Something in what the man had just told him, in the way he had said it, triggered something in his understanding. About Portalier. The way the man had told him about an event long past, well known, accepted, lived with.

The man looked up from his reading. His thin features had grown sharper, cold steel glinted in his malicious eyes. 'Who is your contact in Holland?'

'What?' Pilgrim wasn't listening. His head was full of jigsaw pieces falling into place.

'We traced the hotel you were staying at and we found the remains of a flight ticket to Amsterdam in your name. You flew there on Thursday. Whoever is controlling you does so out of Holland. Who is your contact?'

Pilgrim was still scarcely listening. 'I went for a day out,' he said off-handedly. 'I'm like Don Quixote. I've got the hots for windmills.'

The man's face reddened with fury. 'I'm tired of your games, Pilgrim, and I'm sick of your smart answers. We've wasted a whole day on you, listening to fairy stories, being sidetracked by your evasions. Now you are going to tell us the truth. All of it. Every last detail. We are going to do this the painful way. You are going to lose that ear.'

Pilgrim hadn't heard a word. The daylight which flooded through the tall windows behind the man had suddenly changed its character. Now, the light streaming across the river came all the way from Damascus. Pilgrim was staring above the man's head, his eyes fixed on the vision, his brain bathed in the cold clear illumination of understanding. He leaned forward in his chair just as the man motioned his guard.

'You know!' he cried out, rising to his feet. His voice was hoarse. 'You know!' The guard's heavy hand fell on his left shoulder. He dropped his body, slipped out of the grip and sprang to the edge of the desk. 'You've always known,' he screamed. 'You've known for years.' He heard his chair clatter as the guard kicked it to one side. Then a brawny forearm shot round his neck and a hand began to twist his head to one side. The man meant to break his neck. 'You don't fool me, Histon,' he shouted. 'You know it's all true.' The pressure on his neck was tremendous. At any second he knew it would crack. It was too late, all too late. He'd seen the truth too late.

The man suddenly let Pilgrim go. The release of pressure on his neck brought the blood rushing to his head. He staggered about on the carpet in front of the desk and almost dropped to his knees. The man who seconds before had been trying to twist his head off his spinal column now grabbed his arm and led him to his upturned chair. He righted it and dumped the dazed Pilgrim in it, then seated himself. They were back where they had started.

'How do you know my name?' The man's voice came to Pilgrim through a fog. He tried to focus his mind.

'How do you know my name?' the man repeated.

'I know a lot about you, Colonel Histon,' Pilgrim mumbled. There was silence for a few seconds.

'What exactly do you know?' The voice was inquisitive but the harshness had gone.

'I know this place is a warehouse behind Vauxhall Bridge and I know that Foster Rowles is just a front for your organisation.' Pilgrim saw the start of surprise in the man's eyes. 'And I know that you have always known about Addingham, Blackmore and the others. You knew about what they'd done almost from the start.'

'What makes you think that?' It was the first question that Histon had asked in two days which wasn't a demand.

'I don't think it, I know it,' Pilgrim retorted. 'You've known for years that John Portalier was dead.'

'Portalier's death is a matter of record,' Histon replied. 'He died from a heart attack in a hotel room in Bayswater. We have access to police records.'

'But he didn't die as John Portalier, did he? He wasn't using his real name. How would you know it was John Portalier? Unless you checked.'

'What makes you think he wasn't using his real name?' There was a hint of strain in Histon's voice.

Pilgrim ignored the question. 'You knew Max Gonzales left Panama in 1967. How would you know that? It took Susan weeks to track him down and she was good.' Something Susan had told him in the dingy flat in Fulham came back. 'One of your people went to see Gonzales. Promised him immunity if he told them what he knew. You've known ever since then, since 1967.'

Histon shook his head. 'Just another of your fairy tales,' he stated. His voice sounded calm but his body betrayed him. Pilgrim watched the long, lean frame shift nervously in the chair.

'How would you know Susan's father was fat and stupid and paranoid? You couldn't possible know that, not more than twenty years afterwards. And you knew that he died almost as soon as he got out of prison. You knew he'd been killed by a hit and run driver.' Pilgrim stopped abruptly. Another pure ray of Damascene light shone through the tall windows and lit up within his brain. 'How could you know that? You couldn't, not unless you killed him.' He paused for a moment. 'That's it,' he shouted. 'Of course. You murdered him. So he wouldn't talk. So he wouldn't find out who framed him.'

'Rubbish.' Histon's voice cracked above Pilgrim's like a whip. 'Bloody nonsense.' He smacked the surface of the oak desk with the palm of his hand. The noise made Pilgrim jump.

'It's not rubbish,' Pilgrim stated calmly. 'It's true. And I've got proof that it's true.' His voice began to rise. 'So don't give me any of your bullshit. Don't tell me you didn't know. You did.' His resentment was boiling up, anger at the pain and humiliation he had suffered and the need to revenge Susan was surging through him. The adrenaline was flowing once more, and with it the familiar feeling of a story coming together, when the pieces of the jigsaw were locking tight to become complete.

Pilgrim saw Histon shoot a look at the guard. Immediately he threw his arms over his head and crouched in his chair, waiting for the blow. He had said too much, gone too far, he'd discovered the truth and now they meant to kill him. He waited, the fear singing in his head, but no blow came. Slowly he swivelled in his seat and peered beneath his raised arm. One of the doors was closing silently. The guard had gone, the jailer had been dismissed. Immediately, Pilgrim realised why Histon had been so fidgety the day before, why he had tried to deny the truth of Woodberry's

521

papers. It was the presence of the guard who was hearing all that Pilgrim had to say that disturbed him. Whatever Histon knew, it was a secret that he wished to keep, even from his own people. Pilgrim turned back towards the desk as Histon addressed him.

'You say you've got proof. I doubt that. You couldn't prove any of what you've just said. It's guesswork.'

'I can prove it.' Pilgrim's voice was matter of fact. 'If I have to. But I don't have to, all I have to do is publish it. People would believe it.'

'I'd expect a hack reporter to say that,' Histon retorted. 'But you're forgetting one thing. You may think you've got proof, but to publish it you have to get out of here. And that isn't going to happen, Pilgrim. Not until I know what you know. Maybe then we'll let you go. Maybe.'

Pilgrim had shocked the man out of his complacency but in many ways his predicament was worse. He possessed dangerous secrets. Secrets known only to his captors, who were accessories to crimes long gone. Pilgrim needed time and he needed to know more of what his captors knew. 'How did you find out?' he asked.

Histon's eyes searched his face for a few seconds. 'They were greedy,' he said flatly. 'If they had been content to sell that land once, no one would ever have known. But Portalier told them about the oil and they couldn't resist it. They had to sell it back, double what they had made.' He paused. 'They sold it to an oil company called Miranda. Americans treat oil with respect. The president of Miranda smelled a rat. A worthless swamp in the Caribbean suddenly discovered to be brim full of oil, owned by a Liechtenstein trust: it didn't add up. The president had a contact in one of the US intelligence agencies whom he told about the land. The intelligence people sent one of their men to Liechtenstein to check out the trust. It turned out that the lawyer, Schellenberg, had a German working for him as a doorman, security guard, that kind of thing. The agent recognised him. The man was a Nazi war criminal, he'd been a sergeant in the SS. Nasty piece of work. He'd organised some of the worst civilian massacres in the Ukraine. The Americans decided they'd blackmail this fellow. They told him they'd tell the Russians where he was if he didn't let them in to photograph all the records. It took them more than a year to sift all they'd found; they found some pretty interesting financial deals.

'One of the things they found out was that an Englishman called Dundonald had been to see Schellenberg and had formed a trust using the names of past Archbishops of Canterbury. This was the trust that had bought and sold the land on Pinta Leone. Eventually the Americans told us about everything they had found, and we asked them to check out Gonzales. He was in a lot of trouble at the time. He was about to be arrested for pocketing aid project money from the World Bank. The Americans promised to get him out of Panama if he told them about all the deals he'd been involved in. He co-operated, and after a while they came back to us with the name of Woodberry. So we had three names, Woodberry, Dundonald, and of course Portalier. And we knew about the land. We checked the records of Stansgate's trial and the deals with the Bank of England and pretty soon we had a good idea of the size of the fraud. We also had a notion that Thornbury's disappearance wasn't an accident either. So we were anxious to know who the other archbishops really were.'

Pilgrim recalled something else Susan had told him. 'You traced them to Woodberry's club? The lunch on that Saturday. That's where you got the names.' He snorted softly. 'If they had never had that lunch,' he said almost to himself, 'no one would have ever known the whole story.'

'How did you know about that?' Histon was surprised.

'I've told you,' Pilgrim retorted. 'I know all about you.'

Histon studied him carefully and for some time the room was quiet. They were too far away from the river and from the main road to hear anything of the Sunday afternoon traffic and no sounds came from anywhere else in the building. For a time, Pilgrim stared back at Histon, then he switched his gaze to the light from the windows. It was no longer the light of his epiphany, it had changed, had lost its hard revealing coherence and had become diffused and gentle, mellow in the mood of an autumn Sunday. It made him think of the golden-red beech trees lining the Rutland hills; of the deep russet of Susan's hair, smelling sweetly, falling about her face in waves as she leaned over the scrubbed table in the kitchen at Gretton. Then, he understood. He knew the what of it and the when, and now he understood the why. But he was intrigued. 'What made you think of Woodberry's club.'

'Experience,' said Histon. 'Gentlemen's clubs are like gentlemen's universities, breeding grounds of treason and fraud. We merely worked our way through the records, first of Dundonald's club and then Woodberry's. Eventually we found it. The Archibishop's Enterprise with all the names.'

'So you knew it all in 1967?'

Histon nodded.

'You knew,' Pilgrim said accusingly, 'that those upper-class professional bastards had made millions out of a crooked land deal. You knew that they'd had those squaddies butchered on the island.'

'Actually,' Histon interrupted him, 'I didn't know that until I read Woodberry's notes. I should have seen it, made the connection, but I didn't.' He shook his head slightly as if in annoyance at himself.

'Would it have made any difference?' Pilgrim asked. 'You already knew enough to put them in prison ten times over. You knew about Thornbury, you knew they'd framed Stansgate, yet you did nothing. In fact you went out of your way to help cover it up. You murdered Stansgate to keep it quiet.'

Histon nodded in agreement. 'Of course,' he said mildly. 'As you say, Stansgate had time to think in prison. We couldn't take the risk that he would make trouble. Like Eastcote.'

'Eastcote?'

'Ah.' Histon jumped at the query in Pilgrim's voice. 'So you didn't know about Eastcote?'

Pilgrim shook his head dumbly.

'So you don't know everything about us, after all. I didn't think you did.' The hard edge had returned to Histon's voice. 'Eastcote was a troublemaker. Like Stansgate.' He paused. 'Like you. He wouldn't shut up about the money he had lost. Even after he had gone to Spain he kept on about it, whining that he had been robbed. So in the end he had an accident. In his car.'

Pilgrim felt the familiar shiver within. 'What kind of people are you? You murder the victims so the guilty can get off scot-free.'

'We're professionals,' Histon stated. He leaned forward on the desk and the bony fingers intertwined once more. He was back in control. 'We have a job to do and we do it.'

'What kind of job is it where you murder innocent people? Christ, compared to you, Susan was as harmless as a new-born kitten.'

The mention of Susan's name brought the fury back to Histon's face. 'We spent twenty years working on those men, developing them,' he seethed. 'She wiped it all out.' His words confirmed what Pilgrim knew.

'I always thought it was a coincidence,' he said, remembering Susan's words, 'that all of those men did so well. The money helped of course, but there had to be something else. You were behind them, fixing things.'

'Of course.'

'The world's gone raving mad,' Pilgrim said in despair. 'Murderers and thieves aren't put in prison, they're put in power. By the likes of you.'

'You really are quite naive. Those men had potential. They were bright, from the right kind of background.'

'I see. It's OK to be a murderer as long as you're upper class.'

Histon ignored the remark. 'They were clever. It was a brilliant scheme. And when things went a little wrong, they overcame the obstacles superbly. Getting martial law declared so they could see the deal through was a stroke of genius. Blackmore's idea probably.'

'Sure, it only cost the lives of a few poor squaddies.'

'Soldiers are there to ensure political stability, which is essential to the conduct of commerce. There was nothing different in their case. They were clever men, perfect for our purposes.'

'So you helped them get to the top?'

'Naturally. We eased their paths. Addingham, Blackmore and Dundonald were the real high flyers. We helped them along and quietly blocked off their rivals, eroded their credibility, a few hints, stories to the press, that kind of thing.'

'So you have dirt on the opposition too,' Pilgrim observed.

'Ashley Brighton had no aspirations to political office,' Histon continued, 'but we helped him become Lord Mayor, and his City connections were very powerful. He was influential behind the scenes. Frimley-Kimpton was the weakest of them. He was a liability in Parliament but we saw the possibilities if he moved into television. In his own way he was a highly influential political commentator. Woodberry was like Brighton, hidden power. Deputy Lord Lieutenant of the County. An influential committee member in the party.'

'You had it all worked out. They must have been very grateful for your help.'

Histon looked mildly surprised. 'They never knew. They never had any idea that someone had found out.'

Pilgrim contemplated the thin man opposite. 'You were waiting for the right moment. Once you had them in power you'd come along and say look, we know what you've done, so now you had better do as we say.'

'Not very subtle,' Histon observed, 'but basically that's how it works. You see,' he leaned forward, 'there are about sixty people in this country who hold all the power that's worth having; real power. There are a number of people in high places who if they take concerted action can make major changes. These people control our destinies, and three of them were Blackmore, Addingham and Dundonald – the Attorney General, the Lord Chief Justice and the Governor of the Bank of England. The others, well, they were influential too, quite useful in their way, but not really in the same league. We could, had we wanted to, have quietly persuaded all of them to make certain decisions or perhaps to change their minds on decisions they had already made. Nothing too dramatic, you understand, just slight changes in direction, subtle touches on the tiller which, combined with the obligations we could extract from other people, would move things in the way they ought to go.'

Pilgrim looked at the hands clasped together on the desk. They were the body of the spider, at the centre of a web that covered the entire country, that stretched into every part of life. Histon was the man who pulled the strings of the mighty and made them move to his will.

'Which way is that?' he enquired.

'The best way.'

'Who are you to say which is best? Who is anyone to say? It's not down to you to dictate what we want. You're not God. You're just some kind of secret policeman.'

Histon smiled frostily. 'That is the next best thing. Especially when he knows what I know. But we don't dictate, we merely persuade.'

'Who are you? Who is Foster Rowles? Are you security or what? Christ, you could be working for the Russians.'

Histon looked at him pityingly. 'Foster Rowles is an import export agency. That's it. Nothing else.'

'But you're covering for something else,' insisted Pilgrim. 'You're some kind of government agency. They call you Colonel. Unless you're a colonel in the KGB.'

Histon snorted. 'I was a colonel in the British Army, Special Forces. Now I run an import export operation. Whatever else I do doesn't exist. The operation that lies behind Foster Rowles doesn't exist. It isn't secret, it just isn't there. It goes far beyond anything someone like you could understand. There is no association with traditional allegiances here; no notions of King and Country. We have gone beyond all of that.'

Pilgrim didn't understand. 'What do you mean?'

'I mean,' Histon said deliberately, 'that the normal rules don't apply to us. This organisation has its own rules and its own ends. No one on the outside knows anything about us or what we do. Except you.' He looked directly at Pilgrim. 'You don't know very much but we all know what they say about a little knowledge. You are dangerous, Pilgrim. You've got close to us. That makes me think that you are trained. I'm not working for the Russians, Pilgrim, but I think you might be.'

'That's ridiculous.'

'Is it? Bronwyn-Taylor, Stansgate, whatever her name, was an assassin. Usually you can trace people like her back to about four or five sources, some of which use Holland as their centre of European operations. People like the Syrians, the Iranians, the North Koreans and most of the Eastern block, including Moscow. What you did is too low-key for the Arabs or the Koreans, which leaves the East Europeans. Moscow trains some of its people in America; Bronwyn-Taylor spent time in America. She had connections. I believe you were both working for the Russians.'

'That's rubbish,' Pilgrim said.

'Is it?' Histon replied evenly. 'I don't think so. You've

been trained somewhere. You were able to dodge my men when you wanted before you got them killed. Somehow you found out about the Archbishop's Enterprise, you got hold of the papers. You knew how vulnerable Bronwyn-Taylor was. Maybe you set her up in the first place, arranged things so she would go to America. Got her to marry into the establishment when she came back. What you did is the kind of cynical action we've come to expect from Moscow.'

'You're a great one to talk about what's cynical,' Pilgrim retorted. 'You could teach them a few things.'

'I like to think so,' Histon replied.

'Do you think Moscow would be interested if they knew everything? I mean if they had the originals of those papers?'

Histon's eyes narrowed. 'You mean they don't have the papers already?'

Pilgrim shrugged. 'Maybe. I don't know.'

Histon was quiet. 'Well, if the Russians had the papers and they decided to leak them,' he said finally, 'it would be embarrassing. For Addingham. And he would go to the wall, which would be a pity. But there are others. What you're forgetting is that these papers are now history. Everyone except Addingham is dead. Of course it's regrettable that we had such men in positions of influence but, well, as they're all dead, it doesn't make any difference. Does it?' Histon's tone was offhand.

'It makes a difference if Moscow got to know about your part in it and how you helped all of them get into power. And that you knew about the fraud in 1967.' Pilgrim watched the thin body across the desk twitch and the bony hands jerk apart. Histon's ascetic features took on a hunted look.

'How would Moscow know that? They don't know about this operation.'

'I know about it,' Pilgrim said. 'I know about Foster Rowles and I know who you are.'

'So now your masters in Moscow know.' Histon's voice was bleak.

'No.'

Histon frowned in puzzlement.

'In a way,' continued Pilgrim, 'I do work for Moscow, like I work for Washington and Bonn and Paris and London.'

'What do you mean?'

'I work for whoever pays me –'

'So who is paying you?' Histon interrupted.

'Whoever pays me the most,' Pilgrim continued, 'to find out what I know. You see, what I do goes far beyond anything someone like you could understand. I have no association with traditional allegiances, with politics, with the left or the right. I have no loyalties to King and Country. I have gone far beyond all that. I'm in it for the money.'

Histon scowled as he recognised the words. 'Are you trying to tell me that you are not working for someone? That you are not political?'

'I don't give a fuck about politics.'

'Do you mean to say that you are just a freelance agent, only interested in money?' Histon said it carefully, trying to define Pilgrim, to label him accurately.

Pilgrim nodded.

'And Bronwyn-Taylor?'

'She wasn't interested in politics either. She was only interested in being rich.'

Histon sat silently for a while, digesting what he had heard. 'How do you expect to get paid?' he asked. 'How is anyone going to get to know what you know while I'm holding you here?'

'You may hold me,' said Pilgrim, 'but you can't hold onto the message. That's out there. All of it. The fact that someone did a deal with Gonzales, the fact that you knew about the lunch at Woodberry's club. It's all documented. Along with the originals of those.' Pilgrim pointed to the papers on the desk.

530

'So you know where they are?' Histon accused.

Pilgrim nodded. 'Sure. They're safe. In Holland with my notes about your involvement in all of this. I wrote it all down. I knew about you, Colonel Histon, long before you knew about me.'

'Who else knows?'

'My contact in Holland.'

'Not Moscow?'

'Not yet. Moscow might get to know tomorrow. Or maybe Washington or one of the other places. That is, unless I stop it.'

'I see. If we don't let you go, the story will get out.'

'That's right. If I don't make a phone call tomorrow morning at ten o'clock, my contact in Holland will start the auction.'

'Auction?'

'If you don't let me go, my contact will start offering the information to the highest bidder.'

Histon let out a cackle of laughter. 'For God's sake, that's the oldest trick in the book. You don't expect me to believe it. You're bluffing. Anyway,' he continued, pointing a finger at Pilgrim, 'what you're forgetting is that there isn't a shred of proof to what you've written. If it did get out it might hurt but it couldn't be proved. Your story would be no more than a heap of baseless allegations written by a crooked journalist who,' he paused, 'had disappeared.'

'But my contact in Holland won't have disappeared. And there is proof, there's enough evidence to tie you and this organisation into everything that has happened.'

'Nonsense,' said Histon confidently. 'We don't leave evidence lying around.'

'You left evidence that you had checked up on the lunch at Woodberry's club,' Pilgrim replied. 'If I found out it was your organisation, other people could do the same.'

'We could always get rid of evidence like that.'

'That's an admission of guilt. You can imagine what the newspapers would make of that.'

'Newspapers?' Histon's voice was startled. 'What has it got to do with the newspapers?'

'Who the hell do you think will be bidding at the auction? You don't imagine we're only going to offer this story to the intelligence agencies? Not a chance. They are going to have to bid for it against the world's newspapers and television stations. You and I both know who will pay the most. Once the media gets this story you'll have teams of investigative reporters swarming over this place like ants over a heap of shit.'

'We would deny everything. We could put out a D-Notice to stop them publishing.' Histon's voice was hollow.

Pilgrim laughed weakly. 'The *New York Times*, *Pravda* or *Le Monde* would soon tell you where to stick your D-Notice. Anyway, you couldn't deny it, I've got too much on you.'

'You've got no more than guesswork.'

'I've got more than that. I've got clear evidence of your involvement. I've got you on your weakest point.'

'Which is?' Histon's voice was metallic.

'Whatever else this organisation may or may not be, it's a bureaucracy. That means paper, records, accounts. The car your men were driving. I've got its number. When they crashed I took not only their guns but also their wallets. Those two men – Eric O'Kelly, was it? And the other one, Bob Mair – they'll be on the payroll here. And those guns. They've got serial numbers. They've got to be registered to someone. I bet they're registered to this place.'

'So you did take those guns. Where are they now?'

'With all the other evidence.'

'Are you trying to tell me you smuggled guns out of the country?' Histon was contemptuous.

'Sure, I did. On the back seat of my car is a tool box. They went out in pieces. In that tool box. It was easy enough. No, I've got you, Histon. You bureaucrats are all the same, you hang yourselves with your own paper. In a country like this, it's impossible to have a secret organisation. "We don't exist," ' he mimicked Histon. 'What a lot of crap. Scores of little civil servants know about Foster Rowles. There's no way any organisation can be really secret, here or in Russia, or anywhere else for that matter. Someone has to sanction the money and then some little clerk pushes the paper. Who pays the rates for this dump?' Pilgrim swept his arm round the room. 'Some bureaucrat somewhere. Who pays you, Histon? Who processes your requisitions for staplers. Secret, my arse. Records, serial numbers, car registrations, that's the stuff of which you are made. The stuff that leaves a trail. Newspapers love it.'

'That's all circumstantial,' Histon replied. 'Even if they did prove that we exist, we would deny your story, say it wasn't true.'

Pilgrim looked at him and shook his head in disbelief. The movement caused him to wince from the pain of his torn ear.

'You really are a dumb bastard, aren't you? The media wouldn't care a crap about whether it's true or not. It's a great story. That's what counts. And you've left a mountain of evidence and a trail a mile wide. There are plenty of civil servants who would leak documents to the press. Especially if they can earn a few hundred pounds doing so.'

Histon looked as if he'd been insulted. 'They've all signed the Official Secrets Act.'

'Fuck your Official Secrets Act,' Pilgrim said vehemently. 'Why should anyone give a shit about that. There's no association with traditional allegiances here. No notions of King and Country. Remember? If you believe that, then I bet all your pen-pushing little clerks believe it too. If you break the rules, then why shouldn't they? You're ruined, Histon. Finished. But what's worse, once you're discovered, there'll be a major crisis of confidence. You and this organisation will have set this country back years.'

Histon's face, as bleak and rigid as a glacier, frowned at him. 'How is that?'

'Christ.' Pilgrim shifted his position in his chair. 'Don't you see? Dundonald and Blackmore and the others, they're not the only ones you had some dirt on. You've already said that there are others. How long do you think it will take the papers to figure that out? Then every single person in power, every leader or judge or politician will be suspect. What secrets have they got, what happened in their past, what shadowy organisation is pulling their strings? Are they being blackmailed by some foreign government? It will be anarchy. And it will be your fault.'

There was a long pause. 'So what do you want?' Histon asked quietly.

'I want what you want,' Pilgrim replied. 'I want to keep it all quiet. That means I want to get out of here. And that means I want you to pay me to keep quiet.'

Histon's face showed no trace of emotion. His eyes were focused needle-sharp on Pilgrim's face, seeking almost to pierce his brain and pick at the truth beneath his skull. Pilgrim stared silently back at him and as he did so there slid into his mind a mental picture of himself seated in a large room in an old country house somewhere in Burnham Beaches. He was on a training course, learning how to sell insurance. He and about a dozen others were being taught the steps of the sale. He could hear the voice of the man teaching them. 'There comes a time,' he was telling them, 'in any sale, when you must ask for the order. Once you've made the proposition then you close the sale. And after that you must shut up, for the first person who speaks after you've closed the sale loses. So keep your mouth shut, no matter how long it takes.' They had practised the technique on each other in that large, sunlight-dappled room; learned how to make a proposition, close the sale, and then wait out the long embarrassing minutes until one of them, buyer or seller, gave in and spoke. It was a good lesson and it had worked for him often.

Pilgrim knew that now was the time to practise the technique and this time it was his life that was in the balance. What he couldn't work out was whether he was the buyer or the seller. Was he buying his life or selling his silence? It didn't matter. It was the silence that mattered.

Histon was examining him, deciding if his story was true; whether it was better to pay him off or quietly to deposit his body at the bottom of a flooded quarry. Pilgrim felt an almost uncontrollable urge to press home his advantage. He bit his lip to keep quiet. Histon's eyes moved away from Pilgrim's face to stare vacantly at the desk as if he had lost interest. Pilgrim opened his mouth ready to say something, anything, that would recapture his interest. He stopped himself and looked up at the ceiling. His chair, after it had been kicked over by the guard, had been repositioned directly beneath the dusty chandelier. Pilgrim caught sight of the coffin-shaped droplets hanging still and dead above his head, the fading light from the windows gleaming dully among them.

Histon's voice came as a shock. 'You don't really think that we would pay you to keep quiet, do you? As you've already pointed out, we are an official organisation, we have a budget and we must account for it. This is a department of government. Do you honestly believe that Her Majesty's Government can be blackmailed?'

Pilgrim breathed a quiet sigh of relief. 'Shit. Anyone can blackmail a government. It happens all the time. Any poor benighted bastard can blackmail Her Majesty's Government. All he needs is something the government wants. Governments are easily blackmailed. They've got plenty to hide and lots of taxpayers' money to pay to keep things hidden.'

'How much do you want?' Histon's voice cut across him.

Pilgrim remembered Susan's advice. Don't be greedy, he

told himself. Greed had almost cost him his life; could even yet cost him his life. But he wanted enough to make all the pain and humiliation worthwhile, enough to make them pay for Susan, enough to stàrt again. 'I came down here,' he said slowly, 'expecting to get two hundred thousand pounds from each of five men.'

'That's a million pounds.'

Pilgrim sensed the shock in Histon's voice. 'Susan wiped all that out,' he continued, 'so I'll settle for a quarter of a million from you.'

'What?' Histon was appalled. 'You can't be serious. I don't have that kind of money in my budget.'

Pilgrim snorted. 'You probably spend more than that a year on toilet rolls.'

'I can't pay that,' Histon continued. 'It has to go through too many channels. Questions will be asked. I'll pay you fifty thousand pounds, that's as much as I'm allowed to authorise.'

Pilgrim guessed that it wasn't. Foster Rowles was an organisation like any other. Histon's authority would go higher than that. 'I'll settle for two hundred thousand,' he said.

'Too much. I'll pay you one hundred thousand. That's it. No more.'

Pilgrim sensed it was his final offer. 'When?'

'Just a minute. Before we discuss that, I want to know what I'm getting for my money.'

'Guaranteed silence. A once and for all payment of one hundred thousand pounds and I'll disappear. Completely.'

'I want more than that,' said Histon. 'I want the papers back. The originals.'

'Not a chance,' Pilgrim declared defiantly. 'They're my insurance. Once I've given those to you I could fall under a bus. No, I'm keeping them.'

'What guarantee do I have that you won't publish, tell all you know anyway?'

'Once you've paid me, I'm implicated. Where's the advantage in that? If everything came out into the open, I'd be on the run for the rest of my life. Waiting for someone, maybe you, to catch up with me.'

'That may be so but I want something, some proof that you have what you say you have.'

Pilgrim thought for a moment. 'I have to call Holland tomorrow morning. If I have the money in cash by then, I shall tell my contact in Amsterdam to leave copies of the papers and notes that I've written as well as one of the guns in a place where one of your men can pick them up. The originals of those,' he nodded at the Woodberry papers on the desk, 'and the other gun stays where it is.'

It was Histon's turn to contemplate. 'Very well,' he said finally, 'but in the meantime we shall keep your passport, just in case.'

'So when do I get my money?'

'Tomorrow morning. After the banks have opened.'

'Make it soon after they've opened. I have to call Holland, don't forget.'

'I never forget anything,' Histon told him quietly. He moved a bony finger to press a button at the edge of his desk; a few seconds later, Pilgrim heard the doors behind him open. Histon glanced at the guard, then jerked his head towards Pilgrim who felt a heavy hand fall on his shoulder.

'I want my car back and all my things,' he said to Histon. The guard hauled him roughly to his feet. 'Wait a minute,' he protested. 'There's no need for that. Tell him,' he ordered Histon, 'you're letting me go.'

Histon ignored him, his head was bent over his desk, his attention on the papers. The guard grabbed Pilgrim's arm and dragged him towards the door. 'What the hell is this?' Pilgrim shouted. 'I thought we'd done a deal.'

Outside, the other man was waiting; the two of them marched the protesting Pilgrim down three flights of stairs and along the stone corridor to his prison. They pushed him inside and locked the door. Pilgrim beat against it shouting obscene abuse at the retreating footsteps. After a short while he stopped; his kicks and blows had no effect upon the impenetrable wood and his voice had become hoarse. Histon had played with him, tricked him and now was calling his bluff. They would keep him locked up until they were sure that the story was not to be circulated and then . . .

Pilgrim peered into the gloom of the cellar. He could scarcely see the opposite wall and could only just make out the flattened shape of what had been his bed on the stone floor. He dragged the mattress and the blankets across the cellar and sat down, leaning his back against the door. He wished he had a cigarette. Better still, a pack of cigarettes and a bottle of whisky; the hazards they presented to his health seemed irrelevant when he knew that he would be dead, murdered, in less than forty-eight hours. He had come full circle. He had left the cellar earlier that day without hope and had now returned to it in the same condition. For a while he had thought that he had a chance, that he really had got Histon worried and willing to pay to keep him quiet. He couldn't see where he had gone wrong.

The intense darkness of the cellar crawled up the walls like a reptile. He looked towards the skylights; they too were black, there was no starlight to relieve the gloom, no serene glow from an uncaring moon. Only round the cellar door, at its edges, was there any indication that there was light somewhere in the world, and even then the narrow lines that picked out the door's place in the wall could be hardly called light, merely a paler shade of dark.

Pilgrim contemplated what was left of his future. In twenty-four hours they would be pretty sure that he had been lying, in forty-eight they would be certain. They wouldn't feed him. Why feed a man that you're going to murder? Two nights and two days in the cellar and then he would die hungry. He leaned back further against the door and waited, pulling the blankets up round him.

Chapter Eleven

They came for him about an hour later. Perhaps it was longer, Pilgrim had no way of judging the passage of time. Suddenly the edges of the door lit up, slivers of yellow as thin as razors sliced the darkness around him. He stumbled to his feet, dragging the mattress away from the door, as he heard a key rattle in the lock. The door opened and framed in the blinding light of the corridor was the ominous bulk of the guard who had tortured him.

'Come on,' the man ordered. Pilgrim stumbled out, his head bowed, his eyes screwed against the brightness. The guard took his arm and led him along the stone corridor and up the now familiar staircase. Instead of turning left into the vast emptiness of the warehouse, they turned right along another corridor at the far end of which was a heavy door. Close to the door, propped against the wall, was a rickety card table. Two men stood by the table. One of them Pilgrim recognised as a guard, the other was the long shape of Colonel Histon. It was the first time Pilgrim had seen him standing up. He was taller even than he had imagined, thin and spindly like a stick insect. Pilgrim and his guard reached the table.

'Check that everything of yours is here,' Histon ordered.

'What?' Pilgrim didn't understand. His brain had gone into a trance, he was wondering in a detached way how they intended to kill him.

'Is everything there?' Histon's voice was impatient.

Pilgrim looked at the objects on the table. They looked

familiar. The watch looked like his own, so did the wallet. Slowly, it dawned on him that everything on the table was his, the watch, wallet, pens, keys, things he had last seen almost thirty-six hours before.

'Check that all your money is there.'

Pilgrim opened the wallet, there were notes sticking out, tens, fives, it looked about right. He couldn't remember how much he had.

'Everything there?' Histon queried.

Pilgrim nodded dumbly.

One of the men handed Pilgrim a clipboard and a pen. 'Sign this.' He scrawled his name beneath the list of items on the table.

'Well, go on,' ordered Histon. 'Pick them up. They're yours.' Almost in slow motion, Pilgrim picked up the objects and stuffed them into the pockets of his jacket. He thought for a moment whether he should put his tie on, but his hands were too feeble. He put it into his pocket.

'Very well,' said Histon. 'This is the address of a safe house.' He handed Pilgrim a piece of paper. 'You are to drive there now and stay the night. Tomorrow morning, a man will come to your room with the sum we agreed. After that you will be free to leave, but please don't think you can double-cross us. We shall know where you are all the time and you'll notice that your passport isn't there.'

The truth finally seeped through the wadding in Pilgrim's brain: they were letting him go. He was getting out. The guard pushed open the heavy door. Outside, the night air was fresh and damp. Pilgrim stepped out into a dimly lit courtyard; his 1100 was parked in a far corner. Histon waved the guard back and walked with Pilgrim to the car.

'You'll find everything else is in the car. Do you know the way to the safe house?'

Pilgrim nodded. The paper he had been given showed an address in Eccleston Square, less than a mile from Susan's house in Elizabeth Street.

They reached the car. Pilgrim fumbled for his keys.

'It's open,' Histon told him. 'Now understand this. I think it's probably worth paying you off. You're a disgusting shit but I'm pretty sure you prefer money to anything else. I reckon you'll keep quiet. However, if so much as a whiff of this story gets out, then our contract is immediately terminated and I'll ensure that your life follows suit within hours. Do you understand me?'

Pilgrim nodded.

'Go on then, get out.'

'There's one other thing,' said Pilgrim. 'The letters you found, Susan's letters, in the flat. Can I have them?'

Histon looked down at him. 'You are a pathetic little bastard. No, you can't bloody well have them. They were full of sentimental drivel, no use to us. We burned them.'

Pilgrim was wounded by his words. 'You didn't have to do that,' he said. 'What have you done with Susan?'

'Done? We haven't done anything. She had a crash in the Peugeot late on Saturday night. The car caught fire. Nothing left of her, I'm afraid. They had to identify her through her teeth. Tragic. The family is most upset.'

Pilgrim was stunned at his callousness. 'Christ,' he muttered. 'I hope I never ever see you again.'

'Oh, you'll see me again, Pilgrim. My organisation will keep tabs on you for the rest of your life. You see, one day I might need you. You might be useful. In the meantime, you may continue your sordid existence. Just remember, there's no more money. This is a one-off payment. Don't come back for more.'

The tall man leaned forward and slapped Pilgrim hard on the wounded side of his face. Pilgrim let out a yelp and stepped back into the wing of the car as Histon turned on his heel and marched away. Pilgrim's face stung in the cold air. He watched Histon disappear towards the warehouse as hate worked into his heart like a flood of acid. 'One day,

Colonel Histon,' he whispered to himself, 'I'm going to watch you die.'

He climbed into the car. His anorak, suitcase and the tool box were on the back seat. After a few attempts he got the vehicle started. He was surprised, as he negotiated the car through the courtyard gates and into the dark empty street, that after all the traumas of the past thirty-six hours, he could still remember how to drive. The Sunday evening traffic was light and he drove at a snail's pace across Vauxhall Bridge. His cheek stung, his head hurt and his entire body was trembling. Slowly he drove into Eccleston Square and found the address he sought. It was a tall narrow town house which had been converted into a kind of hostel on the west side of the square.

A tough-looking man was seated in a small cubicle near the front door. Pilgrim was expected. He was handed a key before trudging up three flights of stairs with his suitcase. The room was like a cell, small with a mean and narrow bed, a cracked sink, an ancient mirror and a few old sticks of furniture. In one corner was a shower cubicle. Pilgrim dropped his case and anorak onto the bed and moved to the sink. The face that stared back at him from the mottled mirror was ghastly. Whole areas of his scalp were visible beneath his sparse and greasy hair which, matted with dirt, stood out from his head like spikes. A line of congealed blood ran down from the top of his right ear, following the line of his chin. Deeply lined black rings circled his eyes, making him look like a demented panda. Three days' growth of stubble and a face as white as a sheet completed the apparition. He looked what he was, a man newly back from the dead.

Slowly and painfully he took off his jacket and the rest of his clothes. He stepped into the shower and turned on the tap. The water was lukewarm but Pilgrim was grateful for it all the same. He stood for more than twenty minutes with his back resting against the plastic cubicle, letting the water cascade over him. After a while he soaped himself and it seemed that some of his pain flowed off his body with the streams of soapy water. Afterwards he wrapped a towel round himself and shaved. It was a long painful process. The side of his face below his damaged ear was tender and he could feel every drag of the razor. He brushed his hair and looked into the mirror. He looked better. He searched among his jumbled clothes in the suitcase and found the half-full bottle of whisky he had packed on Friday morning. It seemed a million years ago, yet the hotel in Ebury Street where he had stayed was no more than a few hundred yards round the corner, and Susan's home, or what had been Susan's home, was less than a mile away. She wasn't there now. She wasn't anywhere; she'd been completely eliminated. He felt sorry for her family, grieving, like he was, at their loss.

When he had started on Susan's plan, he had been a naive and pathetic blackmailer, a little fish who had swum into a big and malevolent pond and been trapped there. Now he knew the nature of the pond, the predatory laws by which it lived. Somehow he had managed to slip the net. Well, almost. Tomorrow would tell for sure. He was still in enemy territory, vulnerable and defenceless. Even so, it was a vast improvement on his former state and for now he was content to drink himself to sleep, grateful to be no longer incarcerated in a cellar behind Vauxhall station. He put on a crumpled shirt, for the small cell of a room was cold and the blankets on the narrow bed looked threadbare. He climbed between the clammy sheets and took a swig from the bottle. The whisky exploded in his empty stomach and suffused him with warmth. He snuggled further down and took another pull from the bottle before setting it by the side of the bed. The vapour reached his brain, he felt his cheeks burn and the right side of his face slowly turned numb.

His dreams were filled with moving shadows and the

dead ghastly face of Susan. He awoke suddenly. The room was dark and cold. He switched on the light and saw that it was almost five. His restless sleep had lasted almost eight hours. He felt hungry and as he sat up in bed, the need in his stomach sharpened his brain and quickened his senses. He'd slept enough. He wouldn't sleep again. What he needed now was to finish what he had started. He dressed as warmly as he could before rummaging in his suitcase for the exercise book he'd bought before flying to Holland.

He sat down at the small dressing table and, starting from the beginning, once more wrote everything down. Only this time he knew it all. What he had written before had described the events, recorded the facts, but then he had not been able to supply explanations or to make any connections. Now, he knew the strands which bound the incredible story together, he understood the formula which had triggered the chain reaction of explosive violence.

It was almost eight o'clock by the time he finished. The room had become filled with the hard brittle light of early day. He leaned back in his chair to survey his work and as he did so he noticed the pens on the dressing table. Ever since he had learned to write, Pilgrim had always assembled his writing tools neatly before he started. This time had been no exception. Now he noticed that he had acquired a new pen. It was an unremarkable pen, a cheap ballpoint, yet he knew it was not his. He tried it out on a piece of paper. It wrote well enough, but Pilgrim remained mystified. He didn't use ballpoints, his handwriting was only just readable when he wrote with a pencil or fountain pen.

There seemed to be something strange about the pen. Cautiously he unscrewed the top. Inside was a small silver perforated disc as thin as a stamp, with two thin wires leading down into the body of the pen. It was a listening device. Pilgrim dropped it as if it were a snake; it bounced off the edge of the table and fell to the floor. He stared at the tiny, treacherous, silvered droplet with repugnance.

They hadn't really let him go, all they had done was to play him out a little. They had him hooked by invisible electronic wires. The threat of the device sank into his brain. They would hear what he said to Sjef de Bok in Holland. They would learn the truth, discover how much of what he had told them was a sham. Then they would come for him. The pay-off wouldn't be a case full of money, it would be a one-way trip to a quarry in Essex.

'Bastards.' The word punctured the cold still air of the tiny room. Pilgrim stood up and raised his foot to stamp on the bug to smash it, pulverise it, scatter its evil intent into a silicone dust on the threadbare carpet. Something held him back. The bug was meant to trap him, designed to expose him from behind his façade. It was deadly, as deadly as a typhus louse, and he had carried it unknowingly upon his person like a rat carries the plague flea. Even so, he reasoned, as he lowered his foot slowly to the floor, it could be useful to him. For the electronic insect was infallible, it would faithfully record everything he said. And thereby he could turn it to his advantage, for if Histon and his men were not allowed to suspect that he had discovered their treachery, then they would believe, absolutely and without question, everything they heard. His could be the voice of God and the pen the cloud above the mountain. Carefully, he retrieved the pen and screwed its top back into place over the silver button. Then he searched everything he owned. Thoroughly. He found two more bugs, thin square wafers of silver metal smaller than his fingernail. One was sewn into the lining of the lapel of his anorak, the other stitched inside his navy knitted tie. He doubted if he would have noticed them if he had not been looking. He sat on the edge of the bed, his brain racing. Gradually a plan began to emerge, a sequence of events, a list of what to do, where to go, whom to see, what to say. He wrote it down. When he had finished, the paper looked like an inventory. He put approximate timings beside each of the items. If it all went according to plan, by the end of the day he could be rich and free. If it didn't, well, he chose not to think of that, the cellar in Vauxhall was too close. He had got this far, he had escaped the cellar once, he now had to concentrate on completing his freedom.

His plan energised him. He sprung up from the bed and almost collapsed as the blood rushed to his head. His body was tired and sore after the beatings of the past few days and he hadn't eaten for hours. He'd omitted to put breakfast on his list. He hadn't thought about food and anyway he knew he wouldn't have time to eat.

He shaved and showered. He looked better than he had done the night before, although his face was pale and pinched and the dark patches beneath his eyes remained. His right ear was red and inflamed; beneath his hair along his temple a tender scab had formed. He put on his navy blue suit, a blue shirt and his knitted tie. He looked presentable enough. He pulled on his anorak and clipped the ballpoint pen in the inside pocket of his jacket. He was wired for sound. He picked up his wallet from the dresser and clomped down the staircase. The hard-eyed man in the booth near the front door of the building watched him as he walked past.

'Just off to make a telephone call,' Pilgrim announced with a wan smile.

The man said nothing.

Eccleston Square was busy with traffic. Pilgrim contemplated his car which was parked on a yellow line. His plans did not include the car until later. He shrugged and turned towards Victoria station; whatever was to happen in the next few hours, a parking ticket would make no difference. He walked swiftly. It had occurred to him in his room that to eavesdrop on his conversation via the bugs, Histon's men would need to be reasonably close. He turned a few times to see if he could identify Histon's mobile listening post. On his third attempt, just as he reached the crest of Eccleston

Bridge, he spotted it. A dark blue Ford transit moving slowly about three hundred yards behind him. He had noticed it parked near his car in Eccleston Square. In fact, he suddenly recalled, he had seen a similar van parked near the cottage in Gretton. He was sure that the van was the enemy. Somehow he felt better, safer; he could see the opposition.

He reached the shops near the station. It was eight thirty, but many of them were already open. He found the shop he wanted and stepped inside to buy the first of the items on his list. From the diminishing supply of money in his wallet, he purchased a Polaroid camera and a box of film. He said as little as possible to the shop assistant, he merely grunted in monosyllables and nodded in the direction of the items he required. He had no wish to tell the listeners in the closely lurking van any more than was necessary. He left the shop and found a tobacconist where he spent a few moments locating the second item on his list. He asked for a packet of cigarettes and a box of matches.

'And a tin of that,' he said pointing to what he wanted. The assistant pushed the purchases across the counter and took his money. He found the third shop a few doors away. It sold umbrellas, cheap briefcases and clothes. He bought a navy blue tie and a cheap mock-leather briefcase into which he put his purchases. Outside, the morning light was hard and bright, a watery sun was trying unsuccessfully to warm the steel-grey sky.

He couldn't see the transit van but he knew it would be somewhere close. He was anxious to keep it that way; it was his turn to have them hooked and he was enjoying pulling them along in his wake. He walked quickly along Victoria Street before turning left into Palace Street and then right into Buckingham Gate. He crossed Queen's Gardens in front of the palace and, maintaining his brisk pace, marched eastwards along the Mall. At no time during his walk did he look back. He reached the Duke of York steps and trotted up them, past the memorial and into Waterloo Place. By turning off the Mall he had lost the van. He smiled to himself as he thought of the consternation of its occupants as they were forced to go with the flow of traffic towards Admiralty Arch. They would need to drive round in a large semi-circle before they could pick him up again. He stopped at the corner of Pall Mall and Waterloo Place, took off his anorak and bundled it into his newly purchased briefcase. He loitered on the corner until, out of the corner of his eye, he saw the van shoot round the corner from Cockspur Street. He waited a few seconds until he was sure they had seen him and then he walked towards the solid, four-square building on his right: the headquarters of the Institute of Directors.

It was just turned nine o'clock but already a number of dark-suited businessmen were in the institute's lobby. The uniformed commissionaire was busy at the reception counter. Pilgrim walked through the lobby, into the great entrance hall and past the magnificent central staircase which led to the conference rooms on the floor above. The building had once been a military club, the walls of its great rooms were bedecked with massive, gold-framed oil paintings of long dead generals and their battles. He crossed the hall and entered the library which was a large, rectangular room with long windows on its far side looking out into the gardens which bordered Carlton House Terrace. At one end, to Pilgrim's left, were the library assistants already at their desks; at the other end of the room were nests of tables with screens dividing them. Elsewhere, scattered about between the booklined shelves, were square tables inlaid with green leather, surrounded by solid mahogany chairs. Two men were already installed in the library, seated at separate tables, each reading a copy of the *Financial Times*.

Pilgrim turned to his right and chose a desk out of sight of the library assistants. He took everything out of his brief-case before carefully taking off his tie. He slipped the newly purchased tie beneath his shirt collar and quickly knotted it. In the absence of a mirror he had no idea if he had done a good job, but he didn't have time to go trotting off to the lavatory to check his appearance. Time was all-important. He took the perfidious pen from his pocket and laid it on the desk with his anorak and tie. He walked the length of the long library to the desk of an assistant.

'Hello,' he said affably.

The woman looked up. She frowned and Pilgrim concluded he hadn't done a very good job on the tie.

'I'm a member,' he lied easily. 'I'm doing some research. Do you think I could get some notes photocopied?'

'Do you have your membership card?' she asked him.

'I'm afraid not. I had a suitcase stolen yesterday, it was in there. You can check on me, though, my name is David Bronwyn-Taylor.'

The woman's face softened. 'I'm sorry to hear you've had your case stolen. I'll check your name.' She got up and walked to a filing cabinet. She returned a few moments later. 'How many copies would you like, Mr Bronwyn-Taylor?'

'Three.' Pilgrim pulled the manuscripts from his inside pocket and handed them over.

'I'll bring them to you if you wish.'

'No, that's all right,' Pilgrim responded quickly. 'I'll wait.' He watched her closely. She placed each sheet of paper face down on the platen without a glance at the contents. She handed him the papers. 'I would like to use a telephone. Can I have desk number four?'

The woman looked along the length of the quiet library. Apart from the two men, it remained empty. She nodded and took a key from her desk which she handed to him. He paid her for the photocopying and walked back to the desk where he had left his anorak. He divided the papers he carried into four separate sets, then with the key he unlocked a cupboard fixed to the top of the dividing screen between the desks, and took out a telephone which he plugged in below.

He retrieved from his jacket the notes he had written that morning. Written on it was Sjef de Bok's phone number in Amsterdam. Below that was a detailed script. He put the bugged pen in the top pocket of his jacket and arranged the tie and anorak so that the microphones would pick up everything he said. He was almost ready.

There was one more thing. He took a small tin he had purchased at the tobacconist, opened it and spread a quantity of snuff on the back of his hand. He sniffed it up long and hard, picked up the handset and began dialling Sjef's number. The irritation in his nostrils reacted by the time he was dialling the fifth digit; without warning he let out a tremendous sneeze followed immediately by three more. He did nothing to prevent or cover them but carried on dialling the numbers. He had almost finished when he started to cough, loud wracking coughs which, like the sneezing, covered any other sounds. He finished the sequence of numbers and as he produced another loud sneeze he pressed the phone's cradle to break the connection. He sniffed loudly to clear his head and drew his script closer to him. He waited a few seconds.

'It's me,' he said into the mouthpiece of the quietly buzzing phone. He paused, reading the question he'd written to put into the mouth of his phantom connection. 'Yes, I'm OK. No, it's all right. No. No. Listen, for Christ's sake. I haven't got long. I got picked up by Histon's men. They shot Susan. Yes. She's dead.' There was a slight pause. 'Yes, I know. It was Saturday. They held me for the weekend.' A pause. 'Never mind how, it doesn't matter. Listen, listen for God's sake.' He waited a second. 'OK, that's better. Look, hold onto all the papers.' Again he waited. 'I've done a deal with them. They let me go. They'll pay us if we don't send them.' He waited, silently reading the next words in the drama, waiting for his cue. 'I know that's what we said but you've heard from me and I'm OK. We can't do anything about Susan. Just keep the papers where they are. And the gun. They said they'll pay up this morning. So hold off.' A pause. 'No, don't do anything. Wait until tomorrow. If I don't phone you again by then, you'll know they've double-crossed us.' He waited another second. 'Oh, and tell the papers that Histon's men also killed three guys and dumped them in a flooded quarry in Essex. If I don't phone, that's where they'll put me. Tell the police to search.'

He waited for some seconds. 'No, just do as I say. I can't tell you the whole story, it'll take too long. Just do as I say, OK? Right, you'll hear from me, I hope.' He stopped for an instant and then, in an urgent voice, continued: 'Wait, Sjef, hang on, there's something else. If I don't call, tell the papers why.' A pause. 'Yes, why. You know, that Histon's people had known about the fraud for years. They kept it to themselves because they meant to blackmail Addingham and the others when the time was right. They actually helped them all to get to the top. So who else at the top is being blackmailed, eh? Think about that.' He waited.

He allowed a long pause, time for him to catch his breath. He was enjoying his performance. 'I know we can't prove it. But if I don't call you back you can also tell that to the newspapers. With all the other stuff you've got for them, they'll believe it. Wait for my call.' He allowed a final pause. 'Thanks, goodbye.'

Pilgrim replaced the handset and breathed a long but silent sigh of relief. He was sure that it had been a convincing performance. The bugs planted on him would not have picked up the fact there was no connection, that he had been speaking into thin air. For the listener, it would have seemed real.

He was sorry for Sjef de Bok. He had used him, made him a scapegoat. With the technology Foster Rowles had at its disposal, Histon would be able to screen out the cacophony of noise and identify the number he had dialled. The tape of the conversation would probably be sent to the special laboratory near Sandridge where they would analyse it and where they would probably also discover that Pilgrim had been talking into thin air. But it would take time; masking the sequence of numbers by sneezing and coughing had allowed Pilgrim a few more days' grace. When eventually the number was discovered, someone would pay Sjef a visit. Then, if the rest of Pilgrim's morning went according to plan, they would discover that he had tricked them. By then it would be too late. Maybe, he mused, Sjef would get into serious trouble, perhaps he too would disappear or maybe his body would be discovered floating in the canal. He knew some of the story and was holding one of the guns and that could be enough to induce Histon to dispose of him. Pilgrim shrugged. He would be sorry if that happened. Perversely, both Pilgrim and Colonel Histon were now on the same side: they both had a vested interest in ensuring that nothing about the Archbishop's Enterprise or the existence of Foster Rowles came out. Sjef had become unwittingly implicated and thereby represented a risk.

Pilgrim jerked himself out of his reverie. He had a lot to do. He took the pen from his top pocket and put it, along with the tie, into the pocket of his anorak which he carried over his arm as he walked past the shelves of books towards the library assistants. The library was now empty of visitors. The two men he had seen earlier reading the *Financial Times* had disappeared, driven out by his fit of sneezing.

'Can I hang this somewhere?' he quietly enquired of an assistant.

She nodded at a coat stand.

Pilgrim hung up his anorak and went in search of a telephone directory, a copy of *Who's Who* and a few directories which would distil the information he required for the next item on his list. It took him fifteen minutes to find what he wanted. He retreated back to the desk and the telephone.

He dialled the number of the London club which had once boasted Simon Woodberry as a member. He asked to be put through to the club secretary. When the man answered, Pilgrim in a haughty tone informed him that he was a programme editor with one of the independent television companies. He was making a programme, he said, on graphology, the science of studying character through handwriting. His chairman and a number of his directors were members of the club and they had suggested that he get examples of famous men's signatures from the club's archives.

The club secretary was hesitant. 'Well, I don't know.'

Pilgrim assumed the bitchy aggression of a media executive. 'For God's sake,' he said, 'my chairman . . .' he dropped the name assuredly, 'said you'd be delighted to help. So did . . .' the famous names fell easily from his lips. 'All it takes is a few quick snaps of some of your old records, you know, pages where famous men have signed. Look, old boy,' he continued, 'I've got one of my researchers on the way over to you now. He'll be there soon. All you need to do is to get one of your chappies to take him down to your archives, dig out a couple of your old registers. He's got a camera with him, it'll be snap snap and he'll be on his way. I promise it'll be no trouble. He won't be there for more than ten minutes. Bloody grateful if you'd help, old boy. Happy to give the club a mention in the credits if you like.'

The man at the other end was persuaded. He liked the idea of a discreet mention for the club in the programme credits.

'Jolly good,' said Pilgrim full of bonhomie, 'knew you'd be helpful. My man will be with you in about five minutes. His name is Pilgrim. Thanks, old boy. God bless.' He hung up and glanced at his watch. It was past nine thirty. He had to hurry. He disconnected the phone, locked it back in its cupboard, picked up the papers and photocopies from the desk and put them carefully into his briefcase. He retraced his steps and handed the assistant the key to the phone cupboard.

'I'll pay you for the phone call,' he told her. After he had settled the bill he said, 'I'm going to meet someone in the lounge but I'll be back.' The assistant nodded.

Pilgrim left the library and headed for the small telephone kiosk situated below the great staircase. Inside he took out the Polaroid camera from his briefcase, unpacked it, and loaded it with film. He left the kiosk but instead of making his way across the great hall he headed down a narrow corridor towards the kitchens where a couple of waiters were preparing morning coffee. One of them looked up as Pilgrim strode into the kitchens. 'Morning,' Pilgrim said cheerfully. 'Insurance assessors. I've got to take some pictures of the outside.' He indicated the camera which he'd slung round his neck. 'Where's the way out?' The waiter jerked his head in the direction of the exit. Pilgrim nodded his thanks, strode down a short flight of stairs and pushed open one of the double doors. He found himself in Warwick House Street which was hardly more than an alley leading into Cockspur Street where he hailed a cab. The driver pulled a face when he told him his destination; the club was less than 500 yards away. Pilgrim glanced along Waterloo Place as they swept past; the transit van was parked at a meter halfway along.

'My name's Pilgrim,' he told the commissionaire of the club, 'your secretary is expecting me. I've come to take a few pictures.'

The man took an age phoning through for the secretary who took a long time to make an appearance in the reception hall. 'So,' he said haughtily, 'you're the man from television, yes?'

Pilgrim agreed.

'What exactly is it you want?'

Pilgrim explained.

'We don't usually allow visitors to our archives,' the man told him coldly, 'let alone permit them to take photographs.'

Pilgrim let out a sigh of exasperation. 'I thought my producer had agreed it with you.'

The tall figure stared down at Pilgrim. 'Very well,' he said finally, 'as your chairman is a member, I suppose it will be all right. Follow me.'

He led Pilgrim down a narrow staircase to a cellar. Pilgrim felt himself shudder, he'd had enough of cellars. The man unlocked a heavy metal door which led into a large dusty room lined with the bound volumes of past admission books.

'Do you have any dates in mind?'

Pilgrim remembered the results of his research a few minutes before. 'Yes, 1850 to 1876, 1914,' he said, 'and can I see 1963 first.'

'Sixty-three?' the man queried.

'We would like some more recent signatures too,' Pilgrim explained. The man pulled a heavy volume off one of the shelves and placed it on the table. It was dated 1963. He turned to look for the other volumes as Pilgrim leafed through the book. He found the date written in fine copperplate at the top of the page. Saturday, 23rd November 1963. There were a few signatures below it and then, in large dominant handwriting, the name Simon Woodberry, next to which was written the Archbishop's Enterprise. All the signatures were there, Addingham, Dundonald, Portalier and the others. Pilgrim looked for the impression on the opposite page that Susan had mentioned. It was easily found; running his fingers over the paper he could feel where the imprint of the ball point had come through. He focused his camera on the page of signatures and snapped a picture. The flash startled the man searching the shelves. Pilgrim waited until the film developed then adjusted the aperture control of the camera, before taking four more shots.

The secretary returned to the table with the volumes Pilgrim had requested. 'Do you mind if I take a picture of you pointing to this page?' Pilgrim asked. The man looked surprised but did as he was asked. Pilgrim took another three snaps. 'I'm afraid I'm out of film,' he said apologetically. 'I'll have to go out and get some more.'

The man stared at him in disbelief. 'For God's sake,' he said, 'you people.'

Pilgrim followed him as they tramped up the stairs to the front entrance. 'I won't be long,' he promised as he ran down the broad steps of the entrance. He glanced at his watch, it was after ten.

Outside, he hailed a passing cab which dropped him at Admiralty Arch. He made his way back to the rear entrance of the institute of Directors. The doors were open. He ran up the stairs into the kitchen. 'Remember me,' he said to a waiter, 'insurance.' He waved the camera in front of the man who shrugged. 'He remembers me.' Pilgrim pointed to the waiter to whom he had spoken earlier. He hurried through the kitchens and into the library which was now quietly busy with groups of men talking in subdued voices across the scattered tables. A couple of men were seated by themselves reading newspapers. Pilgrim eyed them suspiciously; he had no way of telling if any were Histon's men sent in to see what he was up to. He retrieved his anorak and paid one of the library assistants for some large square envelopes. On his way back to the desks at the other end of the library he saw on one of the tables a tray littered with abandoned coffee cups and a plate of biscuits. Almost without stopping he lifted the plate and emptied all the biscuits into his anorak pocket.

Seated at a desk he took a couple of sheets of notepaper from a pad provided at the desk and wrote a note to Sjef de Bok. His instructions were clear. Enclosed with his note was a sealed envelope which he had signed along the seal. Sjef was to put the envelope with the other papers and the gun that Pilgrim had handed to him a few days previously. Under no circumstances was he to open the sealed envelope until he heard again from Pilgrim. Inside the envelope were a couple of the pictures he had taken minutes before and one set of photocopied notes. He sealed and addressed the whole package. He calculated that it would reach de Bok just before Histon.

It was the best Pilgrim could do. He was pretty sure that de Bok would follow his instructions and leave the envelope unopened. If he did open it, then almost certainly Histon would have him killed; if he broadcast the story, then Pilgrim's own life wouldn't be worth a damn. Histon, he knew, would make good on his promise to hunt him down if the story got out. His plan was full of danger; the envelope might get lost, be picked up by Customs, anything. But it was the best way he could think of telling Histon what information he had. Histon would realise that the information he found in Holland was exactly duplicated by the originals of the papers elsewhere. He would realise he had been tricked but by then it would be too late. Pilgrim glanced along the length of the library. No one appeared to be paying him the slightest attention.

He took another sheet of paper and wrote a note to Trixie Hayhoe asking her to hold the enclosed sealed envelope, which contained a copy of his notes, until he saw her. He addressed the outer envelope to the riding stables. He sent a set of the photocopied notes and more pictures to himself, care of Malcolm at the local pub, the Dutch Mill, and finally he addressed an envelope to himself at the cottage in which he put his original notes and the remaining pictures. He collected up his briefcase and anorak and walked out of the library. Again he left the building through the kitchens, with the camera slung round his neck; he was becoming a familiar sight. He scampered round Cockspur Street, dashed across Pall Mall and ran up Haymarket. He turned into Charles II Street and stopped, waiting to see if he was being followed. After a few minutes, he was certain that nobody was tailing him. He hurried along the length of the street and arrived at the corner of Lower Regent Street. From there he could see down Lower Regent Street to Waterloo Place. The transit van had gone. He dashed across to the post office where he sent the letter to Amsterdam via Swift Air; the rest of the letters he posted first class.

It was almost ten forty-five. He hurried out of the post office and hailed a cab. He flopped back in his seat and allowed himself to relax for the first time that morning. The first part of his agenda had gone better than he could have hoped. Apart from the papers en route to Holland, which ultimately Histon was meant to discover, Pilgrim calculated that there was a good chance that all the other copies of his notes would get through. By the time they arrived in Gretton, Pilgrim expected, if all went well, to be there himself, ready to possess them. After that, as soon as he felt it was safe, he would trace Susan's old school mistress, obtain the key to the deposit box and then somehow find a way of getting to the contents of the box. Once the papers he had written that morning were securely lodged, along with the other evidence in his own deposit box, then he would feel safe.

The cab dropped him at the corner of Eccleston Square and he hurried to the safe house. There was a different man sitting in the booth but he shared the same watchful eyes as the other man. Pilgrim nodded curtly and climbed the stairs.

As far as he could tell, nothing in his room had been disturbed. He sat on the edge of his bed and took out his list. There were only two items not crossed out and he could not attempt either until Histon arrived with the money. All he could do was wait and wonder darkly if Histon meant to double-cross him. To take his mind off his worries he wandered along the corridor to the lavatory where he tore into small pieces the script he had written for his one-sided conversation with Sjef. He flushed the scraps of paper down the pan. Back in his room he remembered the biscuits he had swiped. He took them one by one from his anorak pocket and washed them down with the last of the whisky. Afterwards, he packed his clothes into his case, making sure to wrap the Polaroid camera in a crumpled shirt. Then he returned to his original position on the bed.

It was eleven fifteen and still no sign of the money. He felt in his pocket to see if there were more biscuits. Apart from the tie and pen nestling treacherously there, he found the packet of cigarettes he had bought earlier. He lit one. It was the first cigarette he had bought for a long time. It didn't taste as good as the ones he had once bummed off Susan. He thought it strange that less than twelve hours earlier he had been yearning for a pack of cigarettes and a bottle of whisky. Now that he had both, neither tasted as good as he had imagined.

It was because he was excited, he told himself, anticipating victory. The previous night he had been waiting for the ultimate defeat and everything that he had expected to lose had seemed somehow better than it really was. Neither the way he felt now, nor the way he had felt then were normal, though when he came to think about it, Pilgrim found it hard to remember, ever, a time when he had felt normal. Nothing in his entire life had ever been balanced, he had always lived in extremes.

He heard a noise below. Someone was treading heavily up the narrow staircase. He stood up. His palms were clammy, his breath short and rapid. He watched the bedroom door, waiting for the person climbing the stairs to knock, wondering whether he would be carrying Histon's promised one hundred thousand, or orders to drag him back to the cellar in Vauxhall, en route to the quarry in Essex.

The knock never came. Instead the door burst open with a crash and a large man walked slowly into the room. It was Pilgrim's tormentor, his guard from the day before.

Pilgrim stepped back. The man saw him and moved further into the room. He stopped close to the edge of the bed. He was carrying a cheap tartan holdall. 'This is for you,' he snarled, lifting the bag.

Pilgrim edged closer. 'What is it?'

'It's a lot of money. That's what it is. One hundred thousand pounds.'

'Is it all there?' Pilgrim asked.

The man took a threatening step towards him and Pilgrim backed away. Then he emptied the bag onto the unmade bed. Tightly-bound bundles of ten and twenty pound notes spilled over the worn candlewick bedspread. 'The twenties are in bundles of fifty,' he said, 'and so are the tens. There are eighty bundles of twenties and forty bundles of tens.' He picked up a wad of notes and drew his thumb along its edge. 'Here.' He threw the bundle to Pilgrim who rifled the bundle with his clammy fingers. 'Right, you satisfied now?' The voice was filled with bitter sarcasm. He took another step towards Pilgrim who backed away. 'Sign this,' he ordered.

Pilgrim wrote Mickey Mouse with a flourish on the typed receipt. The man put it in his pocket without looking. He glared at Pilgrim who was backed up against the wall close to the window. 'I don't know how you got away with this,' he said. 'You were as good as dead, now all of a sudden we're paying you off. Well, let me tell you something, you little shit, this money buys you. Even if you have got friends who might talk if you disappear, if doesn't mean you're safe. We've got orders to keep our distance, but we'll be watching you all the same. I'll tell you something, we own you. That money means we bought you. You belong to us now. Sooner or later Histon will want something in return. You may think you've beaten us, you cocky little bastard, but you haven't. No one beats the system.' He glowered at Pilgrim for a few seconds, then turned on his heel and marched out of the room.

Cautiously Pilgrim followed him and stood at the top of the stairs watching him descend. 'Hey,' he called out.

The man stopped on the half-landing and looked up.

'I didn't beat the system, you stupid bastard. I just joined it.' He jerked two fingers at him.

The man made as if to ascend the stairs, paused, then smiled wolfishly at Pilgrim. 'I'll be seeing you,' he called and continued down the stairs.

Pilgrim returned to his room and closed the door. He was shaking. The spectacle of the heaped bundles of money on the untidy bed was like a mirage. He sat down amidst the wads, touching them, clutching them to him, scared that they might disappear. He counted it. It was all there. He owned one hundred thousand pounds. After a few minutes, he glanced at his watch. It was eleven forty-five. He had just over an hour before he had to make his next and final move.

He decided it was time to sever the invisible link between himself and Histon. He searched for the place in the collar of his anorak where the tiny bug had been inserted and carefully unpicked the threads which had sewn it into place. He extracted the tiny gleaming button and dropped it into the pocket of his anorak with the pen and tie. He checked the contents of his suitcase, closed it and then replaced all but thirty thousand pounds of the money in the tartan hold-all. The rest he stuffed into every available pocket. With a final glance he left the room and descended the stairs carrying the holdall, his suitcase and his new briefcase. The man in the booth by the front door watched him go. Outside, his car had attracted a parking ticket. Pilgrim tore it off the windscreen and dropped it into the gutter. After a few false starts the 1100 gurgled into life and Pilgrim drove into Warwick Way. He crossed the lights and parked on a yellow line at the far end of Rochester Row.

He got out of the car, taking the holdall with him, crossed Horseferry Road and walked into the noisy hubbub of the street market in Petty Cury. One of the market stalls sold ties. Pilgrim cautiously eased his knitted tie out of his pocket and laid it on the stall. Sooner or later someone would buy it. Pilgrim deposited the pen on another stall and left the final bug next to a street vendor's transistor which was blaring out heavy metal. He walked out of the market and found a bank.

'I've just sold my car for cash,' he told the woman behind the counter. 'I'd like to deposit this. I hate walking about with a lot of money.' He filled in a credit slip with the name and code of his bank in Uppingham and then pushed five thousand pounds across the counter. His bank manager was in for a shock. Within the next few days, Pilgrim's account would be credited with one hundred thousand pounds, all of it arriving in sums of five thousand from a variety of London banks. At least, he thought, it would wipe out his overdraft. The woman stamped his receipt and he was out.

He repeated the process at five other banks in the area before hurrying back to his car, the holdall banging against his leg as he trotted. The car had attracted another ticket. Pilgrim impatiently ripped it off the windscreen and threw it away. He was in a hurry. From what he remembered of Susan's research, he needed to be on the other side of the city within minutes. He drove to Parliament Square and then turned left along the Embankment. The lunchtime traffic was busy but he was able to make good time past Charing Cross and beneath Waterloo Bridge. He turned into Temple Place and parked on another yellow line in Arundel Street.

He took the holdall off the back seat, locked the car and walked through Maltravers Street towards the Inner Temple. He arrived outside Addingham's chambers a couple of minutes before one o'clcok. There was no sign of the official car. Every Monday morning when the courts were sitting, the Lord Chief Justice drove from his home to his chambers, arriving at about one o'clock. Pilgrim had no way of telling if Addingham had already arrived. If so, he would have more than an hour's wait before Addingham emerged from the chambers. Pilgrim put the precious hold-all down beside him and zipped up his anorak. The day was bright but a strong breeze swirled the leaves boisterously within the open spaces of the Middle Temple gardens.

Pilgrim stuck his hands in his pockets and prepared for the wait. The narrow terraces were busy with hurrying dark-suited figures; barristers and solicitors going about the business of the law like eager rats scurrying in and out of their traps.

At the end of the narrow street a large, dark, gleaming car purred into view and majestically turned into the narrow thoroughfare. Pilgrim straightened up and moved forward so that the occupant of the car's back seat might see him outside the entrance to the chambers. The car stopped. The security man in the front passenger seat leapt out and opened the car's rear door. The tall, gangling, slightly stooped figure of Addingham emerged. He saw Pilgrim immediately and stood still, staring over the security man's shoulder at the figure in the navy blue anorak. Pilgrim jerked his head, indicating that Addingham should come to him. The Lord Chief Justice remained where he was, eyes wide in surprise; the security man who was waiting for his master to move so that he might shut the car door sensed something was wrong. Seeing the intensity of Addingham's gaze he turned to stare suspiciously at Pilgrim. Addingham murmured something briefly to the man, then slowly and cautiously walked towards Pilgrim. The security man closed the car door, turned and leaned against it, his eyes locked on Pilgrim, his right hand ominously out of sight inside his jacket.

'What are you doing here?' demanded Addingham.

'Surprised, eh?' Pilgrim's voice was loud and vehement. 'You thought those two bastards you hired had got rid of me, didn't you? Well, they're dead and I'm still here.'

'For God's sake.' Addingham stepped closer to Pilgrim, partially to block the security man's view but mainly to make Pilgrim keep his voice down. 'What have you done? What did you do to Blackmore and Dundonald and the others?'

'They're dead,' Pilgrim said coldly.

'I know that. But why? There was no need to kill them.'

'You tried to kill me.'

'They would have paid you. We would all have paid you. You didn't give anyone a chance.'

'What chance did you give me? Or George Stansgate, or Richard Thornbury, or those poor sodding soldiers?' Pilgrim stared up into the thin face with the beaky nose and the bald freckled head. He noticed that Addingham was smacking his lips together and pulling a face, as if he had a vile taste in his mouth.

'Why have you come?' he asked. 'Do you intend to kill me now? Here, right in front of everyone?'

Pilgrim shook his head slowly. 'Not unless I have to.'

Addingham's eyes widened.

Pilgrim determined to press home his advantage. 'You know how the others died?' he asked pointedly.

'Of course. What I don't understand . . .' His voice trailed off. 'What I don't understand is how you've got away with it. The papers said Blackmore accidentally electrocuted himself and that Dundonald committed suicide. No one who knew him believes that. He wasn't the type. Now Frimley-Kimpton is dead. They say he had an accident in his garden. How have you got away with it?' He paused. 'Who are you?'

'I'm a man who gets away with things,' Pilgrim retorted. 'Just like you. You've managed to get away with what you did for twenty years. So will I.'

'What do you want?'

'Money. If you want to keep on getting away with it, for the next twenty years, then you'd better pay me.'

'And if I don't?'

'Then you'll have to take the consequences. Like the

others. They're all dead. In the end, what they did caught up with them. They didn't get away with it.'

'You mean I'll have an accident like the others?'

Pilgrim nodded. 'Probably.'

'How much do you want?'

'You owe me for those two blokes you set up to kill me. But I'm not greedy. I want two hundred and fifty thousand pounds, only fifty thousand more than last time.'

'That's a lot of money for one person to pay.'

'A lot less than you stole. Anyway, how much do you think your life is worth? No, it's not a lot. I'm letting you off lightly. But I want it quickly. I want it all paid into that account by Wednesday midday.' He handed Addingham the number of his bank account in Uppingham.

Addingham frowned at the piece of paper in his hand. 'This isn't a Swiss account.'

'No, that's mine,' said Pilgrim. 'It doesn't matter if you find out who I am, you're not going to do anything about it.'

'You're very confident.' Addingham was scathing.

'With friends like mine, I can afford to be. Just remember what happened to the others.'

'How do I know that you won't kill me anyway after I've paid you?'

'You don't. But you're the only one left. The rest are all dead. You're my golden goose.'

'So you'll be back for more?'

'Not if I can help it,' Pilgrim said with feeling. 'And certainly not for a few years. But if I do, you'll just have to pay. You can afford it. Anyway, the whole thing was your idea in the first place. It's only right you should be the one who ends up paying for it.'

Addingham was smacking his lips together noisily.

'Don't look so pissed off, my Lord Chief Justice,' Pilgrim told him. 'You're paying a fucking sight less than your friends.'

Addingham said nothing.

'Don't get any ideas about trying to trace me and having me quietly disposed of,' Pilgrim continued. 'I've still got the originals of the documents, and remember my friends.'

Pilgrim moved to one side, ready to walk away. The big security man was still leaning against the car, staring suspiciously at them.

'Don't forget,' he said quietly. 'Wednesday noon. That's your deadline. It's enough time to transfer the money.' He began to walk away.

'Wait,' Addingham's voice cracked out. Pilgrim stopped and swivelled round as the security man straightened up away from the car. 'Did you say they are all dead?'

Pilgrim nodded.

'What about John Portalier?'

'Portalier died twenty years ago,' Pilgrim told him, 'here, in London.' For an instant a look of grief passed across Addingham's face, a look that recalled another time in another hemisphere.

'How?'

'Heart attack. In fact,' Pilgrim paused, 'he was probably the only one to die naturally.' He took a step closer to Addingham. 'Except you, of course, if you make the payment by Wednesday noon.' He smiled grimly before marching briskly away. Addingham watched him, then slowly turned and walked towards his chambers.

Another, by now familiar, plastic pouch was attached to the windscreen of the car when Pilgrim arrived back in Arundel Street. He had spent almost two hours after leaving Addingham depositing the rest of his money in banks in the Strand and the Aldwych. He had also treated himself to his first hot meal in days. He ripped the parking ticket off the windscreen, dropped it in the gutter and threw the empty canvas bag into the rear seat of the 1100. He drove to the end of the street, out into the Aldwych, heading for Kingsway and the A1 north. He was going home.

The car purred through Highgate and Finchley. It moved

in tune with his mood, competent, powerful and assured. He had won but his success was tainted with the loss of Susan. He had become rich, but he had lost Susan in the process.

But at least, he reasoned, now he could shrug off the debt that had for years driven him down. Now he could educate his children. Now he would have no need to feel that he had failed them. He could divorce Patricia. He could be free.

The car moved easily through the light traffic in Mill Hill and out onto the dual carriageway going north. Pilgrim found a tape of Vivaldi's *Gloria* and with one hand inserted it into the cassette player next to him. He wound down his window and let the voices, high and jubilant, pass him and be sucked out into the rushing air.

On the motorway he began to make plans. He had one hundred thousand pounds already and would have another quarter of a million by Wednesday. He was sure Addingham would pay. He could make plans now because he was rich and his immediate plan was to become an awful lot richer. It had occurred to him driving past Hatfield that lying somewhere beneath the streets of Zurich was a fortune of more than four million pounds. Once it had belonged to John Portalier, but he had never claimed it. He had died too soon. All Pilgrim had to do was find the name and number of that account and the money would be his. It would be simple. He believed it would be easy because his veins were infused with euphoria and the wind, filled with mandolins, strummed past his ears into the reddening autumn sky.

The car purred along the carriageway, pulling the miles and the road as easily as silk beneath its wheels. It looked like a G registered clapped-out 1100, but on that day it rode like a Mercedes. Like its owner, it wasn't what it seemed. Pilgrim looked like a nondescript, middle-aged nothing, his hair thinning, his strength going, the feeling in his bones growing older by the day. But he wasn't what he appeared, not any more. He was a winner. He was a star; rich, fast,

powerful, light on his feet, quick in his mind. He was Jack
the lad. Once more.

The countryside to the right was changing, flattening
itself into Cambridgeshire and the Fens. The car flew the
tarmac. Pilgrim watched the lorries trundling up the long
sloped bridge crossing the road at Alconbury. Silhouetted
against the north-eastern sky, they looked like giant ants,
slow and loaded down by the bulks upon their backs; like
the men driving them, buried by the weight of trying to
survive. Heads down, unthinking, unknowing. Pilgrim
wasn't one of them. He was apart, separated from all that.
He had never been one of them, he told himself. He had
always been separate, different from the ordinary. Now the
money would show it, it would insulate and distance him
from what he believed he had never been.

Just before the turn westwards towards Uppingham and
Gretton, Pilgrim pulled into the car park of a roadside
restaurant. He had often called Susan from the pay phone
in the diner. He felt the stabbing pang of her loss. How he
wished that she could have been there to share his triumph.
She had never known him when he was rich and winning,
only when he was poor and pathetic. Despite the money, he
felt desolation at her loss. No matter how much money he
made, he was not sure that he would ever get over the
emptiness of her absence.

He got out of the car. To the west the sun had turned
itself into a great red ball dropping upon the horizon.
Already there were long wisps of pink cirrus pulled like
stretch marks high across the purpling sky. He felt the hint
of chill in the sharp breeze which flapped his anorak and
pricked the aching side of his face. Far to the north-east,
beyond the dark flat Fens, the arctic wind was gathering.
Winter was coming down.

More Compulsive Fiction from Headline:

PETER WATSON

CRUSADE

**'The most compelling thriller
of its kind to come my way since
THE DAY OF THE JACKAL'**

*Harold Harris **

Behind the scenes at the Vatican, the Pope offers
David Colwyn, chief executive of the international
auctioneering house of Hamilton's, a spectacular
deal. In an audacious and provocative scheme to raise
money for a crusade against poverty and injustice,
the Pope wants David to organise a series of worldwide
auctions to sell the fabled treasures of the Vatican:
Michelangelo's sculpture, Leonardo da Vinci's
painting, Giotto's altarpiece – all will go.

Despite protests, the Pope's plan proceeds and the
world watches as David, in the glare of publicity,
raises millions of pounds. But now powerful forces
range in fierce and treacherous opposition – and the
Pope's plans go disastrously wrong, perverted by
revolutionaries and international criminals. Soon a
furious battle of power politics rages, a battle that can
end only in a bloody and shocking climax...

"Crusade's real edge is that it could be next week's news."
Daily Mail

"Peter Watson's imaginative near-future thriller stands
out... classy entertainment."
The Evening Standard

"Non-stop action, an incredible vortex of
fights and frauds."
The Guardian

* original publisher of Frederick Forsyth

FICTION/THRILLER   0 7472 3143 5   £3.99

Headline books are available at your bookshop or newsagent, or can be ordered from the following address:

Headline Book Publishing PLC
Cash Sales Department
PO Box 11
Falmouth
Cornwall
TR10 9EN
England

UK customers please send cheque or postal order (no currency), allowing 60p for postage and packing for the first book, plus 25p for the second book and 15p for each additional book ordered up to a maximum charge of £1.90 in UK.

BFPO customers please allow 60p for postage and packing for the first book, plus 25p for the second book and 15p per copy for the next seven books, thereafter 9p per book.

Overseas and Eire customers please allow £1.25 for postage and packing for the first book, plus 75p for the second book and 28p for each subsequent book.